# The Jamesons, U.S. Marshals
## The Anthology

## Diane Benefiel

# PRAISE FOR USA TODAY BESTSELLING AUTHOR DIANE BENEFIEL

## *Solitary Man*

## NATIONAL READERS' CHOICE AWARD WINNING NOVEL

*"I am in love with this story. I devoured this book and didn't want it to end. The chemistry between the characters and the plot kept me wanting to read late into the night. This is my first read from Diane Benefiel but definitely not my last. I can't wait to read more from this amazing author. Thank you Diane Benefiel for getting me hooked on your books!"* ~ CJ's Book Corner

*"Ryder was exactly who Brenna needed in her life, and trust me when I say you will love him because yeah he really is that good of a guy. Solitary Man is my first book by this author and it will not be the last. I really think you all will enjoy this one as much as I did it is one I do recommend."* ~ I'm A Sweet And Sassy Book Whore

*"I really enjoyed this book and there were a few twists and turns that kept me completely involved in the story. This is the first time I have read this author and it definitely won't be my last!"* ~ Sassy Southern Book Blog

# PAYBACK MOUNTAIN SERIES

## *Dangerous Secrets*

*"I couldn't resist this compelling tale of a wrongly convicted man and the woman who never stopped loving him."* ~ Sue's Reviews

*"This is a fast-paced story, steamy and action-packed with likable characters. The story line is engaging and pulls the reader right in with detailed world building to make it feel like you are right there with them."* ~ Di Kecap

*"Benefiel has written a great first book in her new series. The suspense was good with plenty of action. The romance was well done with plenty of realistic conflict between the characters. I'm looking forward to the next in the series."* ~NancyJ

## *Honest Secrets*

*"Between the grand gestures and the little things, Shane is the ranch owner everyone wants for their own. His rough edges are balanced by his consideration for what other people need. The meet-cute with Emery sets the stage for some hot chemistry between them. Bad guys have plans for the small town where Emery is working, and where Shane's ranch is, creating all kinds of danger. Can't wait for book three."* ~MoKnows

*"Honest Secrets by Diane Benefiel is a good and enjoyable small mountain town cowboy romantic suspense read. The story has a great story line. The characters are great, wonderful, and they have great sizzling chemistry. This story is a very entertaining and interesting page turning read."* ~Kimberly

# THE JAMESONS U.S. MARSHALS SERIES

### Hidden Betrayal

*"As someone who never pre-orders ANYTHING, I put my order in a WEEK before it came out. Know why? Because I just didn't want to wait! Not to give away any spoilers but this is my favorite book from this author yet, in no small part because Mikayla is my favorite type of heroine. Right from the get-go, she's absolutely determined to meet everything on her terms. I loved the dialogue between her and Linc--with her saying, "I didn't stay back because *I* was handling it." Yes, he's a hottie with a protective streak, but she's certainly no little woman. It really WORKS. In the end, 10/10. Can't wait to pre-order the next one too!"* ~Amelia

*"An exciting, romantic read with a sexy hero and a determined heroine who is hell-bent on doing things her own way. The romance heats up as the plot thickens. Linc and Mikayla need to work together to survive, but along the way, the sparks start flying. You need to read this!"* ~danube eichinger

### Hidden Judgment

*"Don't buy this book if you want to get anything done!! I couldn't put it down! I laughed, I cried, I felt all the emotions that a brilliantly written romance novel brings. I am anxiously awaiting the third novel in the series!"* ~Sandy Morris

*"I couldn't put this book down. I thoroughly enjoyed the story line and the characters. Diane Benefiel does a great job bringing her characters to life, and weaves a compelling story. Looking forward to the next installment of this series!"* ~Becca E H

### *Hidden Loyalty*

*"5 EXPLOSIVE STARS!! This book was explosive and had me flipping pages. I love law enforcement and this one was perfect....Seth was hot and bossy, Bella kept him on his toes. This was my first book by this author and it will not be my last."* ~Rhonda

*"I really loved this book, and enjoyed reading the sparks fly out of control between these two characters who have both so clearly been suppressing their true feelings for one and other.*
*But beyond the romance Benefiel also addresses Bella's troubled past and creates a strong but nuanced heroine. The connection between these protagonists is instantaneous and will have readers anxiously awaiting the steam between the two when they finally get together. Loved this book!"* ~ Pri R

## HIGH SIERRAS SERIES

### *Flash Point*

*"Diane Benefiel takes us on a story filled with mystery, suspense, and action as we try to solve what is going on in the small town of Hangman's Loss. Flash Point is a story that will have you flipping the pages and wondering who is the behind the attacks against Hangman's newest resident and why."* ~ Sarah Reads

*"**Flash Point** really surprised me. It's not what I was expecting but I really enjoyed reading it. It's a fun easy read that captured me from the start."* ~ Coffee Chat

## *Dead Giveaway*

*"Diane has written yet another winner in her High Sierra series. Murder witness and 'person of interest' Gwen flees with her godson to Cameron's uncle Eli. Gwen and Eli have no use for one another but come together for Cameron's sake and to find the true murderer...and in the process find their way to one another. My evening with Gwen and Eli couldn't have been more delightful, and I look forward to the next installment of the High Sierras."* ~seniorphotog

*"I loved this second book in the High Sierras series. This is a story of two people who are attracted to each other, but reconnecting under the worst of circumstances. I discovered Ms. Benefiel's books and have loved the careful way she draws you in to the story with characters that make you feel as if you are reading about friends. I am really looking forward to the next High Sierras book, **Already Gone**."* ~paytonpuppy

## *Already Gone*

*"This series has only gotten better and better! Seriously, there's something that really speaks to my heart about Maddy and Logan, and Hangman's Loss FEELS like a small California town tucked away in the Sierras. They're such a power couple! I read this book in just a couple of days--totally sucked me in. It's that perfect blend of fun, sizzle, and suspense! I just want to live in Maddy's life forever but since I can't--I can't wait for the next book!"* ~Katharine Montgomery

*"A wonderful story about second chances. The minute you start reading, you will be instantly hooked. The author weaves a tale of drama and romance that keeps you enthralled and turning the pages.*

Maddie is feisty and Logan is her brooding and over protective suffering hero. The sparks fly every time they see each other. Eventually they give in and realize that they are perfect for each other and have always been. This is a great story right up to the last word." ~Simatsu

## Burnover in Rescued Anthology

"Sweet, Sexy stories featuring furbabies and helping to save lives, it's a win win for all." ~Kara's Books

"8 stories by 8 outstanding authors. In these stories, there is a tattoo artist, two firefighters, two sheriff deputies, a famous furniture maker, a veterinarian, and a country music singer, and I loved them all. Then add in that each story has a dog or puppy that is rescued, along with a story of love and romance, it is a winning combination." ~Susan D

## Deadly Purpose

"I loved everything about this book, and it made me want to check out the other books in the series! The immediate suspense drew me in, and the High Sierras setting was perfect, as was the mysterious stranger Meg finds in her cabin. This novel had a well-written, exciting, and descriptive narrative that kept me glued from start to finish. Without giving away spoilers, the author has crafted one exciting, romantic ride, full of twists and turns. I highly recommend this book and can't wait to see what the author comes up with next. ~Sebastian Moran

"This book took me by surprise. I didn't expect to get so caught up in this book that my whole day was spent captured in its pages. It has been a long time since I couldn't put a book down but *Deadly Purpose* did this to me. I loved every page. ~WildfireJane

## Clear Intent

"I'd been waiting on this one awhile!! I truly loved the story! I laughed, cried and got so frustrated I couldn't see straight! I'm now hoping there will be more from Hangman's Loss, I don't want to see this series end! Thank you for a very wonderful getaway!! I highly recommend this complete series!!!! Wow! Just Wow!!" ~Linda Helms

"I've looked forward to every book in this series and have enjoyed each one, loving the characters as it feels you walk with them through exciting, scary situations and sigh as relationships become beautiful. This was an exciting story with almost nonstop action and heart stopping dangers. All of my favorite people in Hangman's Loss are together to help Jack, Dory, Adrian and the town through crisis." ~JLocke

## Break Away

"Oh man did I love this book. It was well written and has a great storyline. It's emotional and has a nice amount of suspense. I really need to go back and read the first six books in the series. Now saying that, this book definitely reads as a standalone. I haven't read the first six books, but I never felt lost or like I am missing anything with this story. You will obviously have some small spoilers since the books are all connected. ~CrazyBookLover

*"Break Away is Diane Benefiel's seventh book in the High Sierra series and is definitely a second chance at romance. Zoey had a high school crush on Levi, and when he returns home after many years, she realises her feelings have not diminished. I'm a sucker for the sexy, broody bad boy vibe, and Levi has it in spades! But the storyline also has emotion, danger and a powerful attraction that is not only undeniable, but totally unavoidable too. These characters have great chemistry and the romantic suspense plot is well written and a real page-turner."* ~Arch_Angel

**Boroughs**
Publishing Group
www.BOROUGHSPUBLISHINGGROUP.com

THE JAMESONS - U.S. MARSHALS, THE ANTHOLOGY
HIDDEN BETRAY, HIDDEN JUDGMENT, HIDDEN LOYALTY

ISBN 978-1-957295-47-3

# HIDDEN BETRAYAL

# Chapter One

Gun gripped tight, back to the wall, Linc breathed slowly to settle himself. Shit. A leak. There had to be a leak within the Marshals Service. No other explanation fit. Bullets still slamming into the not-so-safe safe house were evidence enough. The witness he'd dragged out was cowering next to him. Adrenaline surging, Linc pulled out his cell and yelled, "We're under fire. Get me backup." He shoved the phone back in his pocket.

*Odds are by the time help arrived they'd all be dead.*

"What the fuck, man?" Rounds fired and his witness had lost the gangster swagger. "You marshals are supposed to protect my ass." Joey "the Mouse" Medrano huddled beside him in the shadowed hallway. Blood dripped from a cut over Joey's eye, adding a scarlet bloom to the teardrop etched onto his right cheek. Linc wiped the blood from his own forehead. Shots through the front windows had sent shattered glass flying.

"You're alive, aren't you?"

"That's the fuckin' cartel out there. Fuckin' trying to kill me, man." His voice, irritatingly high pitched—hence "the mouse"— quavered. Linc suspected the tattoos covering every available skin surface, including Joey's eyelids, were more an attempt to appear badass than proof.

"Don't know what happened, but we'll get you out of this." Linc listened intently. Where the hell was his partner? "Donny!"

Outside, tires squealed and a door slammed.

"They're fuckin' coming for me. You gotta fuckin' protect me."

He didn't have time to marvel at Joey's ability to use "fuck" at least once in every sentence. Linc yelled for his partner again. "Donny, you hit?"

"I'm fine." Donny's voice came from the other side of the wall in the kitchen. He sounded odd, like he had to force the words out. He spoke again, clearer this time. "I think we can get him out the back, through the gate. Take him out through the alley."

"I ain't goin' through the fuckin' alley. They'll know you'll fuckin' go that way."

"Shut up. Let me think." Footsteps rushing the front door decided for him. Grabbing Joey by the collar, Linc pulled the other man with him into the kitchen. And came to a skidding stop. "Shit, Donny. Lower your weapon before you shoot me."

His partner didn't lower his weapon. "Sorry, Linc."

The front door crashed against the wall.

"What the—"

Even as Linc raised his gun, a muzzle flashed with a sharp cracking sound. The instantaneous punch to his chest sent Linc reeling. A second flash and the world went dark.

***

"Wake up, Lincoln. Wake up, baby."

The warm caress on his forehead soothed, almost enough to lull him back into the gray.

"Oh no you don't. Stay with me this time."

"Mom?" He must have actually spoken, because the hand against his skin stilled. He blinked open his eyes to see his mother's face crumble. Shit.

"Good job, you made Mom cry."

His gaze traveled around the hospital room before resting on the tall woman standing on the other side of the bed. Despite the jibe, his sister's lowered brows over serious blue eyes and clenched jaw screamed worried. Couldn't mistake that. He would have tried for a snide comment but his throat felt like he'd swallowed rocks.

"Water."

His mother dabbed her eyes with a tissue and dipped her face to kiss his forehead before reaching for a plastic cup with a straw. "You bet, sweetie."

He swallowed the icy water with relief. His gaze sought out his sister's. "What happened?"

"Your double-crossing, snake-in-the-grass, backstabbing partner is what happened."

"Ellie, not now. Your brother needs to rest." Margaret Bollinger's voice held the same tone that had kept a teenaged Linc from straying too far out of line.

"Did he get Joey?" They needed the pathetic bastard to testify against the crime boss of the Zecena cartel. And the trial started in less than two months. But more than that, it had been Linc's job, his sworn duty, to protect the witness.

The hospital door swung open before Ellie could answer. Two men entered, completing the family. Linc's brother, Seth, and their stepfather, retired Chief Deputy US Marshal Archer Bollinger. Like Ellie, Seth wore his Marshals' badge hanging from a chain around his neck. His brother's face might have been carved from granite. Seth didn't do feelings. Arch Bollinger didn't give much more away, other than a decided air of tension. Seeing that Linc was awake, Arch crossed the room to put an arm around Mom's shoulders. "Glad you've decided to stay with the living, Lincoln."

"What the hell happened?" Linc's voice cracked like an old man's.

"What do you remember?" Seth's slate-gray eyes narrowed.

Wishing for a dose of his brother's cool focus, Linc tried to shake his head to clear the lingering fuzziness, but even that small motion resulted in a throbbing that made him wince. He found the button to raise the head of the bed so he was sort of sitting up, clenching his jaw at the pain in his chest that accompanied the movement. He rasped out the words. "Enough to know Donny shot me. I want to know what happened to my witness."

"Medrano's dead." Seth's clipped words fell like bricks.

"Shit. God damn, son of a bitch." He held Seth's gaze. "I lost a witness."

"This isn't on you, Linc." Anger whipped through his sister's voice. "Donny Bertola owns this one."

"I'm sworn to protect my witness. I told the little shit I'd get him out of there alive." The Marshals Service had never lost a witness who'd followed the rules. That made him the first. The weight of his failure settled over him like an iron blanket. "He's dead. That's on me."

Ellie looked ready to argue the point, but Seth cut in. "Chief Deputy Montrose said he'd be in tomorrow morning to take your statement. You up for it?"

"I will be." He'd been awake for a few measly minutes and Linc felt like he'd run a full marathon. Exhaustion with an added layer of abject failure dragged at him. His mother held up the straw and he took another sip of water, and then directed a question to his brother. "What happened with Donny?"

"He's on the run. We've got his laptop, phone records, bank records. The usual. Only thing we know for sure is they got to him."

A tiny nurse in polka dot scrubs and a cap of pewter hair whisked into the room. "Sorry, folks, it's time for the shift change. You all will need to step out." She assessed Linc with a shrewd gaze. "And it's time for Mr. Jameson's meds. You're welcome to come back in forty minutes or so."

Margaret kissed him again, squeezing his hand like she couldn't stop touching him. Linc was grateful when Arch gently urged her out the door. Ellie took his face in her hands and kissed his cheek. "You scared me."

"I scared myself."

"Don't do it again." She left, and Seth moved closer to the side of the bed.

"You're not going to kiss me too, are you?"

"You wish." Seth paused, then continued, voice deeper than usual. "We're tracking Donny, Linc. We'll get him."

# Chapter Two

Linc sat in the driver's seat of his Jeep Wrangler to wait out the storm, watching the rain come down in sheets. Listening to the drumming on the roof, he hoped like hell his tent would hold up against the deluge. He narrowed his eyes to peer at the campsite across the road from his and wondered how the Celtic goddess would deal with the inclement weather.

She'd driven in the day before in a Subaru Outback, then proceeded to amaze him. He had to admit he'd been entertained watching her unpack her vehicle and organize her site with the efficiency of an army quartermaster. Her tent went up with a minimum of fuss, looking roomy enough for a scout troop. Loaded plastic bins and an ice chest went in the bear-proof locker, then she'd spread a plastic tablecloth over the picnic table and secured it with metal clips. Wouldn't do to eat on bare wood. Dinner for him? Canned chili heated over his tiny backpacking stove. For the Celtic goddess? Something chopped, shredded, and sautéed over a Coleman camp stove that smelled truly amazing. And no doubt tasted a damned sight better than canned chili.

What had about killed him was the coffee. For his morning dose, he'd made do with freeze-dried granules spooned into water he'd been too impatient to let get hot enough. He wasn't even sure it really was coffee, the flavor more how he thought wood pulp steeped in motor oil might taste. The redheaded goddess brewed her coffee in some fancy-looking pot. The aroma drifting into his campsite had nearly sent him over to beg for a cup, only the knowledge he'd have to actually talk to another human being, even one as compelling as the Celtic goddess, stopping him.

The pounding on the roof eased, then tapered to the occasional drip from the trees. The woman's tent flap flipped open and she emerged under the little awning sheltering the front of her tent. He shifted uncomfortably as lust gave him a sneaky hit to the gut.

Resting back against the headrest, he decided watching her offered an eye-feast diversion that he would indulge. Long and lithe with an incredible mass of deep red hair, now covered by the hood of a parka, she looked the part of an Irish queen of old. He bet her eyes were green, a nice go-with for skin that appeared to be pale cream. He'd always been a sucker for green eyes. Right now, with brows lowered and abrupt movements, she looked pissed. He wished he was close enough to tell if she had freckles. She'd slathered herself with sunscreen early in the morning even though it had been cloudy, and now she was meticulously packing a medium-size daypack. He'd lay odds she consulted a checklist. Water, check. Trail map, check. Granola bars, check.

His ex would have never considered taking a hike, unless it was up the stairs at the mall, and then only because the escalator was broken. He closed his eyes and reminded himself Lana had been more fun and games than a soul connection. The acknowledgment left him feeling hollowed out. He'd been cheating himself, putting values important to him on hold for a good time. Four months with her and only now did he own up to the fact there'd been absolutely no depth to their relationship. A waste of time and effort.

He pushed back at the dragging mood. Sudden brightening had him opening his eyes. The sun broke through the rapidly thinning clouds, reflecting off water droplets shining on about every leaf and twig. His campsite neighbor, looking like a well-prepared and earnest Girl Scout, shouldered her pack and set off toward the river.

He sighed. Now even the Celtic goddess couldn't distract him from the clusterfuck that was his life.

Two weeks ago he'd checked himself out of the hospital against doctor's orders. The simple task of taking a Lyft to his apartment and he'd been nearly comatose with fatigue. But no matter that he could hardly get himself to the toilet. Anything was better than lying in that hospital bed. Then his mother had found out.

As soon as she realized her son wasn't where she'd left him, she'd swooped into his apartment and chewed his ass. The only way to placate her short of returning to the hospital, which not even she could make him do, was to agree to let her take care of him. He'd figured that was what she'd wanted all along, and ended up at her and Arch's place in the hills. It hadn't been so bad. His mom let him be for the most part, and Linc knew he had his stepfather to thank for that. And for the long conversations that held him off from his decision to turn in his badge.

Retired or not, Arch knew the job, and he knew burnout. His straightforward, cut-the-bullshit talks had swayed Linc, and he ended up asking for a leave of absence, length of time undetermined.

So here he sat, four days into a camping trip, trying to find the man he'd once been.

A light breeze scattered drops of water from the trees and the mid-afternoon sun reflected off the spectacular red rock cliffs surrounding the Lower Falls campground. Getting out of San Diego had been the right move, and he'd figured if he headed to Utah he could camp for a bit in what he considered the best part of the world. He'd thrown his gear in the Jeep and driven northeast for most of a day. When he'd spotted this campground, he'd decided it was as good a place as any, and pitched his tent.

Linc rubbed absently where the bullet had passed between two ribs. It ached less today than it had the day before, and he'd stopped taking any meds. That was damn good progress by his measure. Now if he could only shut down the memories. Donny's blank expression. The muzzle flash. The incredible pressure in his chest. Sinking into blackness.

Shaking his head, Linc got out of the Jeep. He grabbed the thick biography on the explorer George Mallory he'd been reading. A movement on the road caught his attention. A guy in a long-sleeved t-shirt and baggy jeans, looking out of place in his city clothes, crossed the road. He glanced around like he was afraid of being followed and took the same trail the goddess had taken. Linc frowned. He knew a banger when he saw one.

Where'd the guy come from? No one had driven into the campground in the past forty minutes. The guy wasn't from one of the campsites because Linc had checked them out. He opened the back door of the Jeep to retrieve his folding chair, then stopped. Now that the sun was out, he wanted a spot where he could prop his feet on a tree stump, read for a while, maybe close his eyes if he got tired. He didn't want to get involved in someone else's business. He frowned, staring at the trail where the guy had disappeared. Shit.

Linc shut the door with more force than necessary, leaving the chair inside.

\*\*\*

Mikayla took the trail at a swift pace, puffing a bit at the steady climb. The sign at the trailhead had arrows pointing the way to a waterfall two miles up the river. Red rock canyon walls, the rushing river below, pines and cottonwoods, all should serve to soothe, to help work off her mad. A mad that had stuck with her for three days. Being angry was a waste of energy, and made her feel guilty, but holding on to her anger in gorgeous Utah was plain stupid.

Why couldn't the people who loved her most—her mother, sister, and fiancé—why couldn't they respect that she was perfectly capable of making her own decisions? Having her judgment constantly undermined, questioned, and challenged plain sucked. And when she thought she was finding her own way, then wham-o, it turned out good old Mom had been manipulating behind the scenes all along. The accomplished puppet master pulling all the right strings.

For as long as Mikayla could remember, Martha O'Kane Bauman had tried to force her daughter into a mold so constraining, so stifling, so horrifyingly mind-numbing, Mikayla knew giving in was tantamount to pulling closed the bars to her own prison. She feared the relentless pressure to comply "for her own protection" would one day erode her resolve and she'd find herself locked securely behind the bars of a privileged life with no meaning.

This time she wouldn't budge, not one fraction of an inch. No matter how much she'd like to ease her mother's worries, she wouldn't live a life dictated by fear. She'd been fighting that war since age thirteen, and while she'd won a few battles, a truce had yet to be called.

Mikayla paused to catch her breath, tilting back her head to catch the breeze. The sun stood poised over the western ridge of the canyon, and once it went down, she'd be hiking in the dark. She sighed. The rain had forced a late start, and now the waterfall would have to wait for tomorrow. Looking at her muddy shoes, she thought the trail might be a little drier then as well. Adjusting the straps of her daypack, she turned around to retrace her steps.

Solitary camping trips were hardly on her mother's list of approved activities, and her objections had been constant and unrelenting. Worried phone calls, threats, and dire pronouncements hadn't budged Mikayla, even when heaped on by her mother *and* her fiancé. Ex-fiancé, she corrected.

The idea of getting away from *everyone,* from all the expectations, the guilt, the constant pressure, so she could just *be,* had been too seductive to ignore. She had the semester off from teaching, and if she was going to retain her sanity, she needed some alone time. The bonus: the trip got her out of the blast zone when her mother found out she'd broken off her engagement to Peter. Being two states away seemed prudent.

Twilight faded the colors from the canyon walls and Mikayla quickened her pace. The trail followed the swollen river. Where the day before the water had moved in calm swirls, it now roared down the canyon in a torrent, lapping at the edge of the path. The trail climbed until it wound through a dense copse of trees crowding the bank of the river, filtering the light.

She plodded along until, suddenly wary, she paused. Her heart thudded heavily. She wasn't sure what had changed, but she never took her safety for granted. The chill snaking along her spine brought her to full alert. She gauged the dim pathway. Crap. This was not the time to get the jitters. It wasn't like she was passing a dark alley in a bad neighborhood of Los Angeles. She was on a hiking trail in the middle of the wilderness. And besides, there was no other way back to the campground but through that shadowy darkness.

She pressed on, watchful, while her feet slipped a little in the mud. The setting sun cast deep shadows in the canyon, and she'd be lucky to be back at her campsite before complete darkness fell. A sound, a barely discernable clink of rock on rock, had her stopping to look over her shoulder, ears straining for any clue of who or what was near. Most likely, it was another hiker trying to get back before the trail became too dangerous to travel. She rubbed the goosebumps raising the flesh on her arms.

A sharp crack echoed from deep in the trees, eerily like a gunshot. She whirled, searching for the source. Nothing. She stood motionless, heart hammering, her hand resting against the solid presence of a tree. Could be a bear. She swallowed with a nervous gulp. A bear would want to be left alone. More likely it was a branch breaking, or some other non-large wild animal natural occurrence.

She waited, trying to slow the rapid beating of her heart. Tall tree trunks cast pillars of black along the path, not wide enough to hide a bear. But wide enough to hide a man.

Cursing her overactive imagination, she set out again. The incident the day before had her spooked. Replaying it, she still wasn't sure if she'd been overreacting.

On the highway heading east, she'd seen the same dark car every time she'd looked in the rearview mirror. Sometimes a few cars behind her, sometimes right on her tail. The same car that had followed her out of the parking lot of the little diner where she'd had breakfast. Stopping for gas, the black sedan had pulled up to a pump at the next island. The driver, a young Hispanic man with a baseball cap pulled low over his eyes, had gotten out and began pumping fuel. Mikayla paid inside, then lingered in the market, watching him through the window. At the time, she'd worried her mother's dire predictions that she'd end up murdered in her sleep by some crazed serial killer had triggered a bout of paranoia.

Giving herself a mental shake, Mikayla marched on toward her campsite. That guy had freaked her out, nothing more. The trail rose above the channel of the river and wound along a high bank among tall pines and an occasional jumble of boulders. Once past this part, the trail followed the river maybe another quarter mile and then she would cross the bridge to the other side and be back, safe, sound, and among other people at the campground.

Nearly through the thick grouping of trees, she shivered. She could *feel* something, *someone,* behind her. She quickened her steps. A hurried glance over her shoulder brought her to a stumbling halt. A man stood on the trail not fifteen feet behind her. Her heart slammed in her chest. It was him. The driver of the dark sedan. The man from the gas station.

The baseball cap was the same, and he wore a black t-shirt. A sickle-shaped scar shone through dark stubble on his chin.

He raised his hands as if to show he wasn't a threat. "Hey, lady. I just want to talk to you."

Like hell. She was physically fit, and she'd trained to defend herself. But Mikayla didn't question instinct, and instinct screamed *run.* Abandoning all pretense, she whipped around and broke into a mad dash.

Sprinting along the trail in the deepening twilight, she couldn't risk looking back. A single misstep meant slipping in the mud or hurtling down the embankment into the raging river. Footsteps thudded behind her, ominously close. What did he want? Definitely not conversation.

Lengthening her stride as much as she dared, she put everything she had into gaining distance from her pursuer. Trees thinned ahead.

It wasn't far to the bridge. She could make it, maybe if—a jerk at the shoulder straps of her pack had her reeling, a cry of alarm escaping her lips.

Mikayla twisted, off balance, arms impeded by the pack. "Let me go, you bastard." She gasped the words as she gave a sharp backward kick, connecting with his shin. He uttered a short grunt, then a blow to her head had stars exploding.

She reeled sideways and his sharp intake of breath made her think she'd caught him off guard. He lost his hold on her pack and she spun around. Forcing back the panic, she struggled to remember her training. Stay focused. Keep the attacker at a distance. Fight smart. Her instructor's words played like a mantra in her mind. Number one rule: escape. If escape wasn't possible, fight. She'd trained for this, exactly this. She could do it.

She faced her opponent, arms out, body set. He took a similar stance.

"You want my backpack?" She shucked the pack free and threw it at him. "Take it."

He caught the pack and threw it aside, launching himself at her in a fluid move. A swift jump to the side and she avoided the fist flying past her shoulder. He skidded in the slick mud and went to his knees.

"Fucking bitch."

Mikayla kicked out with her hiking boot, striking him in the ribs. His grunt of pain brought grim satisfaction. Moving on instinct, she whirled to run, then staggered as he whipped out a hand and snagged her ankle. She went down, flipping over to scramble backward when he crawled toward her. She managed to get to her feet and made three running steps on the trail before he caught her again, wiry arms grasping her from behind. Shit, shit, shit. Resisting the instinct to fight, she went limp. It worked. His grip loosened, and she swung her head back with hard force, gratified at the crunching sound.

Wrenching free, she backed away, uncomfortably aware of the steep drop behind her. The river sounded ferociously loud and she couldn't smother a scream as the earth shifted and began to crumble beneath her feet. In a desperate struggle for purchase, she grabbed a spindly tree trunk that tilted crazily toward the torrent of foaming water. Seething anger vied horribly with grinding fear. The bastard wouldn't win. She wouldn't let him win. Gaining a precarious balance at the edge of the embankment, she let go of the tree and faced her attacker.

His cap had come off to reveal black hair trimmed close to the scalp. He reached into the pocket of his baggy jeans and pulled out a folded knife. Her stomach dropped. Baring his teeth, he used them to pry it open. The wicked-looking blade glinted dully in the fading light. The odds now tipped heavily in his favor.

# Chapter Three

Linc took the trail at a jog, swearing ripely under his breath. What was he doing? He didn't even know the woman, and yet here he was tromping along a trail with the sun going down and the temperature falling along with it. He could count on one hand the number of people he would put himself out for, so what the hell was he doing looking out for the Celtic goddess? He supposed he could chalk it up to boredom. Too many weeks off the job while his body mended. Too much time spent in his own head, going over his partner's betrayal. Not to mention his father's betrayal.

Linc couldn't count Lana's breakup text as a betrayal. She simply hadn't meant enough. Not that she hadn't had cause: she hadn't known he'd been shot and when he hadn't answered the dozens of texts she'd sent during days he'd been too out of it to check his phone, she'd finally gotten pissed enough to tell him to go fuck himself. It hadn't been worth trying to explain.

Yeah, well, a guy in gangster threads walking through a campground in Utah set off alarm bells in Linc's head. The dude stuck out like a Hell's Angel at a dentist's convention. The thought of the Celtic goddess being tracked by the banger had Linc doing what he was trained to do.

He kept up the pace as the trail threaded up a slope through tall trees, the rain-swollen river a steady roar. A yell, a woman's voice sharp and frightened, had him surging forward until he was running full out around a curve in the trail. And skidded to an abrupt stop. The goddess stood, arms at the ready, heels dangerously close to the steep embankment over the river. Several feet in front of her and with his back to Linc, the man he'd seen earlier crouched, facing her. Only now he gripped a short-bladed tactical knife.

The sound of the river must have drowned out Linc's approach because the guy didn't turn or look over his shoulder. Not even with a flicker of an eyelid did the woman give away Linc's presence. The banger wiped his nose, leaving a dark smear on the back of his hand.

Giving himself a mental kick for not grabbing his Glock, Linc quickly assessed the situation. While the dude looked lean and barely matched the woman in height, his stance and the way he held the knife said *I do this for a living*. Linc would have to use the advantage of surprise. The attacker crouched and Linc didn't second-guess his instincts. He leapt forward, striking out with a booted foot, and caught the banger in the side of his neck. The blow sent him reeling toward the embankment and the woman scrambled aside.

The dude recovered his balance, knife still gripped firmly in his hand. He turned to Linc, a sneer on his face. "Fuck off, man. This ain't your fight."

"It is now." Linc circled toward the drop-off, trying to get between the attacker and the woman.

"I'm gonna cut you, asshole. Hurt you real bad." Even in the falling light Linc could see the sick smile. "Then I'll do the same to the *mamacita*, but I think I'll enjoy that one more." The words had barely left his mouth when he leapt forward, blade slashing.

Linc jumped back to keep his skin intact, then shifted, forcing the attacker to move away from the woman if he wanted to keep Linc in sight. A blur of motion had Linc stifling an oath. The woman launched herself. She landed on her attacker's back and wrapped an arm around his neck. Linc rushed forward even as the dude swung backward with the blade. She uttered a sharp cry but kept hold, using one arm to pull the other tight against the attacker's throat. Linc plowed a fist into the man's gut and with a sweeping motion, kicked the guy's feet out from under him. The woman jumped free and immediately began scrambling as the edge of the trail crumpled beneath her feet.

Linc caught the goddess's arm, the sharp drop only inches away. Quick as a feral cat, the attacker flipped and sprang to his feet.

Weapon still clenched in his hand, he lunged at the woman, the slashing blade coming way too close to her face.

She reeled back. Linc whipped out an arm and grabbed her around the waist when the embankment gave way.

He let out a surprised grunt when she struggled against him. "Stop that. Are you crazy?"

"Let me go, I've got this."

"You are crazy." Linc set her on her feet and pushed her behind him, reflexively catching a fist full of her parka when she tried to lunge past.

The attacker wasn't waiting for them to sort it out. He took a running leap toward them. Linc turned in a tight pivot. He landed a hard jab to the guy's kidneys, following with a mean kick to his forearm. The kick had the desired effect. The knife flew, briefly silhouetted against the twilight sky before it disappeared over the embankment.

Linc crouched low, arms spread to grapple, and the man took a similar stance. A stealthy movement drew Linc's attention. Son of a bitch. Crazy didn't even begin to describe her. While the attacker focused on Linc, she'd taken the opportunity to move through the shadows. The way she was going he thought she meant to circle a huge boulder and come up behind the guy. The movement also took her perilously close to the slippery edge of the riverbank.

"Stay the hell back," Linc hissed.

"*You* stay the hell back. I can take him." Celtic warrior was more apt than goddess. She sprang at her attacker, and Linc had to admire the smooth fluidity of her moves. Clearly, the woman had some training. But so had her attacker. Likely realizing that without the knife he'd lost any advantage, the man grabbed the woman when she lunged. When Linc leapt to her defense, the guy shoved her at him. Linc caught her in a rough embrace and they both went down on the muddy trail. His breath left in a whoosh as she landed solidly against his chest. The sound of running feet faded until they were drowned by the roar of the river.

He pushed himself to his feet, bringing the woman up with him. He grasped her shoulders to steady her. "You okay?"

"Yes."

"Then stay put. I'll come back for you." He paused. "I mean it. I'll catch him if I can but you're not to go after him."

She gave a curt nod, and he turned to run after the attacker, who'd already disappeared into the shadows cast by the dense wood.

\*\*\*

Mikayla leaned back against a boulder, heart beating frantically, the smooth stone under her hand still warm from the sun. Adrenaline hummed through her body so that even her fingertips tingled.

She felt amazing. Shaking all over, but amazing. This time she hadn't frozen in fear or cowered. She'd fought back, refusing to give her assailant the advantage. She'd been scared but not so scared that she hadn't been able to act. All those classes had paid off and she'd protected herself. It felt like a test. Even if the big guy with the Jeep from the campsite across from hers hadn't intervened, she wanted to believe she could have disarmed her attacker.

She drew in a wobbly breath, held it a moment, and then let it out in a whoosh. She repeated the process, trying to regain her equilibrium and make sense out of what had happened.

She leaned against the sturdy mass of rock. Water rushing below filled the air with a steady crashing thunder and the sky had faded to deep gray. Everything appeared normal, the way it was supposed to be. Except things weren't normal. Even now two men were on the trail, one who'd been intent on hurting her. The other, seemingly in the right place at the right time, had intervened and fought like a street brawler.

Forcing herself to move, she stooped to retrieve her backpack and winced in pain. Her head throbbed. She must have taken a hit to her ribs because she ached all along her left side. The pain in her shoulder was only now registering. Not a bruising pain, more a razor-sharp sting. Her attacker had swung back with that knife, and she now remembered the burn as the knife sliced into her shoulder. Crap. It couldn't be too bad because her arm still functioned, but she had no way to examine it. She drew in another calming breath. She might be unsteady, but she'd survived.

Unclenching shaky hands, she unzipped the front pocket of the backpack and found her small LED flashlight. She pressed the switch and the bright light offered comfort in the gathering gloom. Slinging the pack over her uninjured shoulder, she straightened, unsure what to do. Her rescuer had said to stay put, but she wanted nothing more than to get back to her campsite, down a couple of pain relievers, and burrow into her sleeping bag. That would have to wait. She had no doubt her savior could handle himself if he caught up with her attacker, but if the guy managed to get away, he could be a threat to some other woman. Either way, she needed to alert law enforcement.

The darkening sky decided for her. A misstep in the dark could send her tumbling into the water. Now more careful than ever, she followed the path around the edge of the bluff, heaving a sigh of relief when the track widened as it descended to the river. The wide plank bridge loomed ahead. She'd nearly reached the middle of the span when she once again heard heavy footfalls behind her. A tall form loped toward her. Height and broad shoulders gave him away: it was the man from the campsite across from hers, the man who'd fought for her.

He crossed the bridge, coming to a stop beside her. She didn't know how much he could see in the dim light, but his dark gaze traveled over her, seeming to take in every detail. "You didn't stay put."

"No."

He made an irritated noise. "You hurt?"

"More shocked than hurt. I don't know why he attacked me, what he was after."

He gave her another long look, then held out his hand. "I need the flashlight."

She held it out, hoping he wouldn't notice her shaking hand. He took the light and cast the beam over her face and neck. "Any blows to the head?"

"Yes."

"Look at me." He passed the light over one eye, then the other. "Any dizziness?" She shook her head. "Headache or nausea?"

"Headache, but no nausea. I don't have a concussion."

"You might. Could be your addled brain accounts for you not staying back and letting me handle it."

"Addled brain? I didn't stay back because *I* was handling it."

He touched her elbow. "Turn this way. I want to see where he got you with the knife."

Deciding to forgive the bossy tone, she turned toward him. He'd fought a man with a knife, a man who'd attacked her. She'd cut him some slack.

With the flashlight beam aimed at her shoulder, he let out a low whistle. "There's an inch-long slice in the parka and plenty of blood. How's the movement in your arm?"

"I'm fine. He nicked me but it doesn't feel deep."

"I'll take a better look at it when we get to the campground. See if you need stiches."

"I can do it."

He brought the light around to shine in her face once more. "And how would you manage looking at an injury on your shoulder blade?"

She shrugged, then winced at the twinge of pain. "Right." She cast a glance over his dark form. He was tall, really tall, with the tough build of a linebacker.

"What about you? Are you hurt?"

"No."

"Did you catch him?"

"No. There's a trail beyond the waterfall that goes to another campground. I think he went that way." Annoyance was clear in his tone.

She studied him in the flashlight's glow. As much as she'd wanted to take the attacker down herself, and absolutely *hated* having to rely on someone else for protection, the sensation of the embankment giving way under her feet was seared into her memory. This man had risked himself to catch her and pull her to safety. "Thank you. I think I could have disarmed him myself, but thanks."

The shadow of a smile crossed his features, softening the hard lines of his face. "You're welcome."

The sound of the river rushing under the bridge filled the night air. Through the trees the campground was visible. Campfires burned, orange flames reaching into the night sky.

"You're in the campsite across from me, aren't you?"

"Yeah." He hesitated, then stuck out a hand. "Linc Jameson."

She held out her own hand and found it engulfed in his. "Mikayla O'Kane."

He gave a short laugh as he released her. "I should have guessed something like that."

Puzzled, she frowned. "Why?"

"Never mind. I'll walk back with you. We need to alert the ranger."

# Chapter Four

Linc followed Mikayla across the bridge. He'd thought of her as a Celtic goddess, and she had a name to match. Wide eyes a deep forest-green were set off by smooth skin over high cheekbones. Irish warriors would have fought battles for her. He tried not to think of what her body looked like under that bulky parka. But he knew she had long legs, and her lengthy, purposeful stride had them at the campground in seconds, the sound of the river fading as they passed between campsites to the road.

The smell of wood smoke drifted on the breeze and a couple of kids darted by making whooping noises, beams from flashlights bobbing as they ran. Linc gestured to the huge motorhome with Wisconsin plates, hard to miss with strings of lights decorating the trees around it. A wooden sign on a post read "The Weingartners" in loopy script. Mikayla knocked on the door, then stepped back.

A voice called, "Be there in a minute."

Linc watched Mikayla. She stood with her arms folded tightly in front of her, hands gripping her elbows. She was shaking.

"It's normal, you know."

She didn't answer immediately, but finally asked, "What?"

"Shaking from adrenaline crash."

She hitched her shoulder in a jerky shrug and he could all but feel the tremors she was struggling to control. "I know. I'll be fine."

He had to hand it to her, she held it together when it counted. He didn't figure the questions he had to ask would make her feel any better, so he might as well get them over with.

"You know why anyone would want you dead?"

She turned toward him, eyes dark and depthless, face impossibly pale under the string of lights. She didn't dispute his conclusion. "No." She cleared her throat.

"Any threats against you?"

Before she could answer, the RV door rattled and a woman, probably late sixties and with bright silver hair, opened the door and stepped out onto the step. "Yes?"

"Mrs. Weingartner? My name is Mikayla O'Kane and I'm camping in site twenty-four."

"Oh yes. You have the blue Subaru."

"That's me. I want to report an incident."

A man Linc had seen driving around in an electric cart, tall and rail thin with a ball cap that declared "Old Guys Rule," stepped out to stand beside his wife.

Linc stood quietly while Mikayla related what had happened. The hosts listened intently, Mrs. Weingartner putting her hand over her mouth when Mikayla told how the attacker had pulled a knife. "I don't know why he wanted to hurt me."

"Oh, my dear, you must have been terrified." The older woman descended the steps to lay a hand on Mikayla's arm.

"I didn't really have time to think, I was trying to avoid that knife and keep from falling into the river." She glanced sideways at Linc. "I fought him, bloodied his nose. Then Mr. Jameson showed up and kicked the knife out of his hand, landed some solid blows. There was no way the guy could take on both of us and win. That's probably why he took off." She cast another look in his direction. "Mr. Jameson probably saved my life."

Crap. The Weingartners turned toward him, curiosity evident. Not that he regretted the impulse that had sent him after Mikayla, but he didn't want the attention. He'd rather fly below the radar, do his job, and leave it at that. And now he'd be drawn into the investigation. "Can you radio for a ranger, Mr. Weingartner?"

The man bobbed his head, and said, "Surely can," with an upper-Midwest twang. He reached through the door and returned with a radio in hand, then he put in the call for a ranger to contact him. After disconnecting, he said, "Better get a hold of Joe and Conrad. They're the hosts over at the Upper Falls campground. They'll keep an eye out for our perpetrator. There's a day-use parking lot up there, though, so it could be the assailant isn't a camper."

They listened to Weingartner relay information to the other hosts. He'd clicked off his radio when a buzzing emanated from his pocket. His cellular reception must be better than Linc's, because he answered the call. A few minutes later he thumbed off the phone and slipped it back into his pocket. "The ranger has to come up from Bryce so it'll take him an hour or so to get here, but he said he'd come tonight." He waved to some folded chairs leaning against their motorhome. "You folks want to make yourselves comfortable and wait here for him?"

Mikayla glanced at Linc before responding. "I'll wait at my site, if you don't mind. I need to change out of these muddy pants. I'll keep an eye out for the ranger." Linc had to hand it to her, she held up pretty damn well after what she'd been through. When she turned to walk down the dirt road to her campsite, he followed, the light from her flashlight guiding the way. Besides the fact that he had more questions, he couldn't bring himself to leave her alone, and there was that shoulder to attend to.

Her movements were sharp and jerky as she went to the bear-proof locker and pulled out a bin and set it on the picnic bench next to the Coleman stove, following that with a camp lantern. He watched her, hands in his pockets. She looked like a spring coiled under high tension, and that shoulder had to hurt like hell.

Laying her flashlight on the table so she could see, and with a box of matches in hand, she pressurized the lantern, then struck a match. The hand holding the match shook so violently it went out. She fumbled with another but dropped it in the dirt.

"Let me do it." He took the matches from her, struck one, and held it to the mantle while he adjusted the fuel. Within seconds a warm glow pushed back the darkness.

"Take off the parka. I want to a look at that cut."

She nodded slowly and stood to open the plastic bin. She pulled out a first-aid kit and set it on the table before shrugging out of the parka, moving cautiously while drawing her left arm out of the sleeve. He helped her pull it over her head.

Blood stained the shirt dark. "You'll need to lose the t-shirt, too."

"Not gonna happen." Her shaky tone weakened the bravado.

"Yeah, your blood's a real turn-on. I have to see if you need stiches, princess."

"Bite me." The words might have had greater impact if she weren't gripping her fingers together to control their trembling.

He motioned toward her tent. "Got a blanket in there?"

She shook her head. "Just a sleeping bag."

He stared at her a moment then reached for the back collar of the pullover sweater he was wearing and tugged it over his head. "Put this on."

Her dubious sideways glance had him rolling his eyes. She needed him, whether she admitted it or not.

"Look, with the zipper down, this will be big enough around the neck that I'll be able to see your shoulder. Your shirt is trashed, so I'll cut it away from the injury." It would help if she wasn't looking at him like he was a pervert. "I can bandage your shoulder and your princess modesty will be protected."

"Princess, my ass."

"We can take a look at that too, darling, but for starters let me see the shoulder." He held out the sweater and, moving gingerly, she put up her arms. He helped her on with it, her fingers fumbling against his when they both reached for the zipper. He grasped her hand. "Jesus, your hands are cold."

She didn't say anything and he turned her chin toward the light. "Hold still," he muttered when she would have pulled away.

"Look, I'm—"

"You feeling dizzy? Nauseous?" he interrupted.

"No. I told you I don't have a concussion."

Taking her hand, he turned it palm up, and lay a finger over the pulse point at her wrist. For as tall as she was, she had a slender wrist, her bones delicate beneath his touch. Her heart beat strong, maybe a bit fast. "It's not concussion I'm worried about."

"Are you a doctor?"

"No, but I know first aid and I'd think you were in shock except for that smart mouth of yours."

That mouth with its full, sexy lips snapped shut and he silently cursed himself. She'd been violently attacked, and the attitude was probably helping her to hold it together. He should back off. He turned his attention to her injury, easing the sweater off her shoulder. "Hold still while I cut the shirt."

She pulled her hair to the side and tilted her head to give him room. He had to force himself to concentrate, to ignore the arc of creamy skin spanning from ear to collarbone. She even smelled good. Damn it.

"Turn toward the light." His voice sounded gruff.

She shifted and he tugged the sweater a bit farther. "Doesn't look too bad." The cut was a shallow slice and hadn't penetrated through the layer of skin.

Mikayla ripped open a packet from the first aid kit, handing him a moist antiseptic wipe. She didn't utter a sound as he carefully cleaned the wound.

"You have butterfly bandages in there?"

She opened a box and handed him the strips. Her hands still shook, but less now. He pulled the edges of the wound together and applied the butterflies.

He reached into the bin and took out a small bottle of Bactine and removed the cap. "Hold still," he muttered, then sprayed the wound site. Next, he taped cotton gauze over the butterflies. "There," he said as he pressed on the last bandage. "That ought to do it."

"Thanks."

He pulled the sweater back over her shoulder, then tugged the zipper up under her throat. "You should take a couple of painkillers, but I think you're good to go."

She nodded jerkily and rose from the bench, arms again crossed defensively in front of her. He'd dealt with plenty of female victims of violence, and if those women had taught him anything, it was that they hated falling apart in front of strangers. "You feel like you need to let loose?"

Her gaze flew to his and he expected a pithy response, but she turned her back and bent to reach into the locker. A small pan rattled as she set it on the camp stove, followed by the clunk of a tomato soup can on the table. Eyes downcast, she kept her hands busy with the can opener. "I'm fine and thank you for your help. Is there anything you need, Mr. Jameson?" Her tone was decidedly formal.

"Linc." He didn't like feeling responsible for her. And the whole incident up on the trail bothered him to hell and back. He settled for the simplest reply. "I have a couple more questions."

She didn't say anything, shoulders stiff. The can opener clattered against the lid before she cinched it tight.

"You can ask your questions later. I'm going to have my dinner before the ranger gets here. Don't let me keep you."

If he'd had a hat, she'd be shoving it in his hand. He sucked at dealing with trauma victims. "Look, it's okay to be upset." Upset was such a weak word. "Cry if you want. Yell at me if it helps. Do whatever you need to do. Get it out and you'll get your balance back."

The busy hands stilled. She rose and, without saying a word, walked stiffly to the tent and undid the flap. She slipped inside and zipped it closed behind her.

Well, shit. Linc stared at the tent. Why hadn't he kept his mouth shut? He listened for sounds of crying. Nothing but the nighttime sounds of the campground. He crossed to his tent and quickly changed his jeans, then returned to sit at her picnic table. Heaving a sigh, he picked up the can opener.

Fifteen minutes later he figured he'd done as much as he could. A search of the locker confirmed what he'd already guessed, Mikayla O'Kane was an organized soul. All her supplies and utensils were neatly arranged in bins, making it easy to find a bowl and spoon. A few seconds to light the stove, and now the soup bubbled as it warmed. He hadn't heard a peep from inside the tent.

Linc dipped his head under the awning in front of her tent and purposefully kept his voice low. "Soup's hot." When that got no response, he returned to the table, setting the pan on a cutting board, the lid on to keep the contents warm. He put the bottle of Tylenol he'd found in her first-aid bin next to the soup and sat down to wait. Several minutes later the zipper rasped and Mikayla stepped out. She approached the table and he took a long look. She didn't meet his gaze, but her eyes didn't look red or puffy. Maybe she hadn't been crying.

She glanced up, gaze snagging his. "I told you I'm fine."

"Good. Eat while the soup is still warm."

"Why are you doing this?"

He shrugged. "Not sure." Her question bothered him because he really didn't know. Not getting in people's personal business was like a religion to him. Don't get involved and people were more likely to leave him alone. But the guy following her had triggered his cop instincts and he'd gone after her. And a damn good thing he had.

Heating soup for her hadn't been his only moment out of character. Sure, watching her had been a distraction, but if he was honest his reaction when he'd first seen her had been equally unusual. When she'd pulled in the previous afternoon and stepped out of the car, he'd felt an uncomfortable hitch, like something inside him had shifted. And he hadn't been able to keep his eyes off her as she'd set up her camp. He'd had the uneasy feeling that this woman marked a break from his previous life, a life that was currently a fucked-up mess and hardly in need of more complications.

Mikayla picked up her soup spoon, then paused. "You might as well have some."

Not the most welcoming of invitations, and he guessed she didn't want company any more than he did. But he simply couldn't bring himself to leave her alone. He got a bowl and spoon from the open bin and sat opposite her. Tomato soup had never been his favorite but tonight it tasted surprisingly good. He swallowed his last spoonful and pushed his bowl aside, resting his forearms against the table.

The glow of the lantern cast a circle of warm light around them, luring a moth to flutter against the glass.

She lifted her gaze to his. "You said you have questions for me."

"Yeah." He watched carefully to gauge her reaction. "I want to know why someone wants you dead."

# Chapter Five

Mikayla stared at Linc as she rubbed at her forehead where a dull throbbing made its presence known. He'd been wrong when he'd said she'd needed to let loose. What she'd needed was to get herself under control. The shock of the attack had crashed over her like a rogue wave at the beach, and she'd done what had worked since age thirteen when she'd hidden herself away in her bed, clutching a pillow to her with eyes tightly closed, pushing back on her emotions until the crisis passed. She never allowed herself to cry. This evening she'd pulled the sleeping bag over her head, curled into a miserable knot, and waited until the shaking stopped. As usual, the tight control left her with an aching head and bone-weary exhaustion. She owed Linc for fighting off her attacker, for tending to her, so she would answer his questions, but what she really wanted was to crawl back into her tent and sleep the clock around. She cleared her throat. "I have no idea."

"This doesn't feel random to me."

She narrowed her eyes. "You a cop or something?"

"Or something."

She frowned, watching a moth fluttering around the lantern. "I don't have enemies."

Sitting across from Linc within the small circle of light, his face shadowed, felt oddly intimate. He seemed at ease, but she had the sense there was a lot of pent-up energy in that big muscular body, like a heavyweight boxer waiting for the bell to ring.

"Think. Consider anyone who might want to hurt you, who has a beef."

"You mean besides the crazy guy with the knife?"

"I mean someone who would hire him to come after you."

"Hire him? Now you're the one who's acting crazy. No one would hire someone to hurt me. No one even knows where I am."

"No one?"

She shifted restlessly. "My mom and brother do, that's all. Give it a few days and my mom may want to disown me, but she doesn't want to hurt me."

"Disown you?"

She waved her hands. "Family issues that aren't relevant. My brother knows what campground I'm at, but he's the only one. Mom knows I'm somewhere in Utah."

"It's usually not that hard to figure out where people are. Have you used a credit card today?"

She shook her head. She'd paid cash when she'd put her engagement ring in the mail the day before.

He lifted a brow. "Did you have reservations for this campsite?"

"Yes, I made reservations. But no one wants to hurt me so the question is irrelevant."

Headlights shone through the trees and a truck stopped at the Weingartners' site.

"That'll be the ranger. I'll walk over there with you."

Mikayla nodded. As defensive as his questions made her feel, she was unreasonably glad for his company.

As they approached, the park ranger got out of his truck, leaving the headlights on. He set his Smokey Bear hat on his head and Mikayla saw the gun holstered at his side. He tipped his head toward the Weingartners when they stepped out of their motorhome. "Bob, Janice, good to see you." The ranger ushered them to stand in front of the truck where they could talk in the beam of the headlights.

Bob Weingartner waved toward Mikayla. "This here's Mikayla O'Kane, the young lady who was attacked up on the river trail. The fella is Linc Jameson, who helped beat the guy off."

The ranger turned to them. He looked to be in his early forties, with high cheekbones on a strong, round face. He held out his hand. "Alex Smallcanyon."

They shook, then he released his hand to shake Linc's. He tipped his head toward Mikayla. "Would you mind going over what happened for me?"

She related the incident, describing how she'd turned back when the sky had started to darken. How she'd felt someone watching her. Her heart tripped faster as she described the moment she'd turned to find the man behind her. Throughout, she was aware of Linc standing at her elbow, arms crossed in front of him. "Mr. Jameson kicked the knife out of his hand and it flew into the river. The guy pretty much gave up at that point and took off."

The ranger's dark gaze settled on Linc before moving back to Mikayla. Mrs. Weingartner uttered a quiet, "I'm so glad you're safe."

Mikayla cleared her throat. "I think the guy had been following me since yesterday."

"You didn't tell me that," Linc said abruptly.

"I didn't have a chance to."

Smallcanyon motioned for Mikayla to continue.

She cast a wary glance at Linc. "I kept seeing the same car in my rearview mirror. It was a black four-door sedan. He was behind me when I left the restaurant outside Las Vegas where I had breakfast, and when I stopped for gas in St. George, he stopped too."

"He followed you all the way to the campground?" The ranger had taken out a notepad and pen, and now paused his busy scribbling.

"Ah, no. I, um, disabled his car."

"You what?" Linc's words came out in a bark, and his gaze narrowed. She got the feeling that by nature Linc Jameson was an intense guy, and being the focus of that intensity was a bit unnerving. Exciting, but unnerving.

"I let the air out of one of his tires when he was in the bathroom. I thought I could shake him."

Linc flashed a grin, white teeth briefly visible. Mikayla caught her breath. Holy cow.

"Smart girl, but why didn't you call the police if he was following you?" Linc asked.

"I couldn't be sure, and since he had to deal with his tire and I got off the interstate pretty soon after that, I thought I'd taken care of it."

Smallcanyon spoke to Linc. "What were you doing on the trail at the same time she was attacked? That was a bit late to start off on a hike."

Linc gave Mikayla a long look before turning to the other man. "I saw the guy head for the trail shortly after Mikayla left. There were enough red flags about his appearance I decided to follow him."

The ranger nodded. "Okay, tell me what happened from your perspective."

"He must have been traveling fast because he'd flanked her and was already on her by the time I heard her yell. When I got there, Mikayla was facing him, her back to the river. She'd bloodied the guy's nose. He had a tactical knife and looked ready to jump her. We exchanged a few blows, I disarmed him, then pulled her away from the drop-off. That's when he took off."

Smallcanyon narrowed his gaze. "Can you give me a description?"

"Hispanic, five ten, one seventy, short beard, black and brown. Baggy blue jeans, long-sleeved black t-shirt, Dodgers ball cap, which he retrieved before he ran off."

The ranger gave a short laugh. "What agency you with?"

Blowing on her hands for warmth, Mikayla paused. Agency?

Linc reached for his wallet, opening it to show a badge with a star and ID. "Marshal's service."

"Deputy US Marshal Lincoln Jameson," Smallcanyon read.

She should have guessed. Quick thinking, skilled fighter, the big guy was a cop.

"Thanks, Marshal." Smallcanyon made a note in his pad. "You went after him?"

"Yeah. He had a jump on me and by the time I got through the trees, he was out of sight. He could have hidden somewhere. I looked around best I could given it was getting dark, but I was concerned about Mikayla so I started back."

Smallcanyon nodded and made another notation before looking up. "I stopped at the Upper Falls campground on my way here. The camp hosts hadn't noticed anything out of the ordinary, but they don't monitor the day-use parking area. The guy could have had a car there."

"That's likely. There's no car here that could be his. My guess? He was waiting for Mikayla to go off on her own so he could follow her. He could have hiked here from the other campground, or been dropped off." Linc lifted his chin at the ranger. "Any cases with the same MO recently?"

Smallcanyon shook his head. "Nothing. Things have been quiet since the summer season. There was a report of a guy having his phone stolen off him over in Zion, but that was weeks ago." His gaze settled on Mikayla. "If your attacker is the same guy who followed you yesterday, then you weren't a random target."

Linc nodded his agreement. "That's what I think."

"Wait a minute. You can't seriously believe this guy was after me personally. I mean, yes, I think he saw me at the diner and targeted me. So maybe he was looking for a woman traveling alone and I fit the bill. But he's not someone I know from California."

"That doesn't mean he doesn't know you."

Mikayla shivered. "That's crazy."

"Not crazy. I'll be back in a sec."

Linc walked away from the group. Alex Smallcanyon spoke quietly. "Mikayla, when did you first meet Jameson?"

She frowned. Did the ranger suspect Linc was involved? Linc might come off as a bit cocky, but that likely came from self-confidence. He seemed to think over a situation and then have unwavering conviction that his assessment was correct. However much that self-assurance might rankle, she could use a dose herself.

"I first met him when he disarmed a guy attacking me with a knife. As much as I'd like to say that I can protect myself, he most likely saved my life."

"Yes, ma'am. I'm just covering all my bases. You two are camping in sites across from each other. Who was here first?"

"He was."

"Had you spoken to him before the incident on the trail?"

"No."

"Has he said or done anything to make you think he knew your attacker?"

"No." Her responses were blunt, but Linc had literally jumped in to help her and for that she felt she owed him her loyalty. She might have been able to defend herself, but she also might have ended up in the river or lying bloody on the trail if Linc hadn't decided to follow the guy.

Linc returned to the group and she saw he'd pulled on a sweatshirt. He handed Mikayla a heavy jacket. "Here, put this on."

Donning the jacket over his sweater, the added layer immediately warmed her. Feeling self-conscious wearing Linc's clothing, she hoped the darkness hid the flush she felt creeping up her neck. The curse of fair skin. She wasn't used to someone looking out for her.

Smallcanyon put his hands in the pockets of his coat. "If the assailant's intention was to do you harm, Mikayla, and if he's not someone you know, he could be, as you say, someone looking for a vulnerable female." He shrugged. "It's also possible, as Mr. Jameson suggested, he's someone who knows you but of whom you are unaware. Regardless, he had criminal intent."

Mikayla stared at the ranger, a feeling of unreality settling on her. This couldn't be happening. The world might be full of crazy people, but *her* world wasn't.

He continued. "I've alerted rangers in all the nearby parks as well as local law enforcement. I'll send out a description of the assailant. Can I have cell phone numbers for both of you?"

Mikayla recited her cell number and saw Linc keying it into his phone. He gave Smallcanyon his number, then cocked his head at her. "Do you have your phone on you? I want you to put in my number."

She pulled her phone from her pocket and took his number, but felt compelled to point out the obvious. "I don't know what good this will do. Cell reception at the campground is super weak, and close to nonexistent anywhere else."

"It's better than nothing."

Alex Smallcanyon said his good-byes with a promise to be in touch if anything developed. The Weingartners returned to their motorhome.

Mikayla walked back to her campsite beside a silent Linc. Her mind raced with a confusing kaleidoscope of images from the day. The early rainstorm, the sun reflecting off the canyon walls as she hiked the trail, the frightening grip of the unknown assailant, the river racing fast and dangerous below. The big man speeding around the bend. Using fists and feet, he'd fought to protect her. Then there'd been that breathless moment when the ground was collapsing beneath her and he'd clamped his arms around her and pulled her against his body. She knew that had simply been part of the effort to keep her safe, likely instinctive on his part, but she couldn't deny in retrospect that moment when, for the first time in far too long, she'd felt a surge of awareness.

And when they'd returned to camp, he'd bandaged her wound and made her soup. Heady stuff, and she'd need to be careful not to be seduced by the romance of the big, strong hero-type swooping in and rescuing her. Mentally, she recited the mantra she lived by. *Take care of yourself, don't rely on others. Only you are responsible for your own happiness.*

They reached her campsite and she turned to him. He stood silent, broad shoulders blocking out a wide swath of the night sky, making him seem impossibly strong. Her hands burrowed into the deep pockets of his jacket. "I should have guessed you were in law enforcement."

"Why is that?"

She shrugged. "It explains a lot. The way you reacted on the trail, the questions you asked." She figured his watchful expression must be habitual.

"I have more questions, but they can wait until morning. I think we've both had enough."

She gave a brief nod and started to shrug out of the jacket. The night temperature had plummeted, but she felt warm under the layers of Linc's clothing.

He held up a hand. "Keep it on. I'll get my things back from you later." He gave a half salute and turned toward his camp.

Mikayla stepped into her tent to ready herself for bed. When packing for this trip, she hadn't expected the nights to be quite so cold, and wished now she'd packed an extra blanket and her heavy coat. Feeling a bit guilty, she crawled into her sleeping bag still wearing Linc's sweater with her flannel pants, and then she spread his jacket on top of her bedding.

She lay curled on her side, groaning as bruises made their presence known, more grateful than ever that she'd bought an inflatable air mattress for the trip. What happened on that trail would have kept her awake for long hours, but the security of knowing Linc lay in his own tent only a short distance across the road allowed her mind to rest enough for her to slip into sleep.

*** 

Mikayla blinked her eyes open to the light of daybreak. She shifted to her back, ignoring the discomfort in her shoulder. The river was a muted rumble in the early morning quiet, while closer the distinctive call of a blue jay sounded.

Sitting up, she unzipped the tent flap, cocking her head to see past the awning. The stars had faded from view and the canyon wall stood in dark silhouette against the pink and lavender of the dawn sky. Leaves rustled in the cottonwoods and Mikayla spied movement where the campground bordered the forest. A doe stepped tentatively into the clearing, pausing to nibble on a tuft of grass.

Mikayla slipped on her shearling boots and stepped outside, breathing the earth-scented air deep into her lungs. Not a cloud in sight, which meant the day would be beautiful and likely warm by mid-afternoon.

She glanced across the road to Linc's campsite. The tent flap was open, which made her wonder if he was still inside. She'd noticed him the previous day before the rain had started. Where other campers spent the day hiking or fishing, he'd hung around his campsite. How anyone could spend so much time sitting in a camp chair when there was so much to see and explore, she had no idea.

He'd taken himself off on a short walk in the late morning, then returned to spend the next hour pretty much motionless, sometimes reading, sometimes not, long legs sprawled before him as he sat, butt planted in a sling-bottom chair. There were times she thought he'd been sleeping in that chair, but somehow she knew he hadn't been because she'd felt his eyes on her.

Hard to tell behind those mirrored aviator shades, but if it were possible to feel someone's gaze like a physical touch, she'd felt Linc's. When the rain started, he'd shoved his chair into the back of his Jeep and hitched himself inside. That was the last she'd seen of him until he'd rounded the bend in the trail to rescue her.

After a quick trip to the restroom, she opened her bear-proof locker. She filled a pot with water and lit the stove before setting it on the burner. Opening an airtight container, she spooned coffee beans she'd ground at home into her double-walled French press. Once boiling, she poured the steaming water over the grounds, set the lid in place to let it brew, and got out a pan to make oatmeal. She took a moment to gaze at the sky now streaked orange by the rising sun. This was why she'd come. The serenity and beauty of early morning in the outdoors did more to soothe her soul than anything else in the world.

A rustling noise from Linc's campsite caught her attention as she pressed down on the plunger of the French press. Her hand wobbled and she nearly dumped the pot as he emerged from his tent.

Oh Lord. Trying not to ogle, she peered at him from the corner of her eye. He'd looked dark and dangerous the previous evening, all tousled hair and scruffy beard. But this morning the man had transformed into a gorgeous specimen, as in mouthwateringly gorgeous. Dark briefs, the kind that came down the leg a bit, covered a tight butt, and unless you counted the black hair on his head, he wore nothing else.

# Chapter Six

Mikayla liked a man with body hair, and Linc Jameson had his share. His long legs had a light covering, but his chest, now that was something. Hair spread across heavy pecs to arrow under the waistband of those briefs. He was big everywhere. Great shoulders, wide chest, cut abs. And, ahem...

He turned and her stomach jolted. On the right side of his ribcage, a bright pink scar stood in sharp contrast to the tanned skin and dark hair. She didn't think that injury could be anything but a gunshot wound. Linc had been shot, and recently. Shock, dismay, and an unexpected a stab of fear for him swarmed through her. He stooped to reach inside the tent, then stood, pulling a dark shirt over his head. Mikayla forced herself to return to her task.

Stirring oats into boiling water, she looked up when she heard the back door of the Jeep open. A little sigh of disappointment escaped when she saw he'd donned a pair of blue jeans. He caught her looking. Grabbing something from the back of his Jeep, he trudged toward her.

"Hey." He held a large stainless steel mug.

"Hi."

"How's the shoulder?"

"Sore."

"It will be for a few days. Take the Tylenol." His gaze traveled to the French press. "Any way I can get a cup of that? I'll pay you the Starbucks rate."

She gave him a considering look. "No."

"No? You're killing me here, Mikayla. I haven't had a decent cup of coffee in days."

"How do you know I make decent coffee?"

"Smelled it."

She held out her hand, and without hesitation he handed over the mug. She tipped the French press and filled his mug to the brim, the dark, rich aroma scenting the air.

He sipped, blew on it and sipped again. "God, this is about perfect." His gaze snagged hers. "I thought you said 'no.'"

"The no was for the Starbucks rate."

"Thanks." He raised his mug in salute and moved closer to peer into the pan as she adjusted the flame.

"You making breakfast?"

"Oatmeal." His doubtful expression made her laugh.

"Oatmeal? You ever make pancakes?"

"Yes, but this morning it's oatmeal."

"Oh."

He sounded so disappointed, she laughed. "Don't you like oatmeal?"

Her breath caught in her throat as his gaze locked on her face. She'd thought his eyes were green, like hers, but now she saw they were hazel, the iris glowing gold around the center and light green at the outer rim. Her heart thudded heavily as he raised a forefinger to brush it lightly across the rise of her cheekbone. "You should have freckles."

"Well, I don't." Of course her voice would come out in a croak.

He moved closer and Mikayla held her breath. He reached behind her to switch off the burner on the stove. "I think your oatmeal is done."

She turned to find he'd saved the pan from boiling over. A lock of hair fell to shield her face, and she was grateful for a break from his intense scrutiny. *Careful*, she told herself. It would be too easy to fall for the magnetic pull of Lincoln Jameson. The man had rescued her from danger and she wasn't immune to his inherent charisma. Given the circumstances, her attraction to him was understandable, but would likely fade away. She stirred brown sugar and raisins into the oatmeal, all the while aware of his fixed attention. She cleared her throat. "Do you want some?"

"No, thanks. Can't say oatmeal appeals." She was aware of his continued regard as she spooned the hot cereal into a bowl. "You good to talk when you're done with breakfast?"

She nodded silently.

"I'll be back in fifteen." He raised his mug in salute. "Thanks again." He returned to his camp and she took a seat at the table.

Being near Linc Jameson wasn't for the fainthearted. She spooned up a mouthful of oatmeal and watched him walk toward the showers with a towel hanging around his neck and a mesh bag in one hand, coffee mug in the other. The fact that he'd dominated her thoughts the entire morning should be a warning. She couldn't be attracted to him. She *wouldn't* be attracted to him.

She could excuse herself for nearly drooling when he'd stepped out of his tent in his underwear, because, hey, he wore those briefs *really* well. But her heart jumping into her throat when he'd touched her cheek moments before was completely unacceptable.

Whatever emotions she'd felt for him since the attack were the product of relief and gratitude. His sheer size, his powerful presence, his no-holds-barred willingness to fight on her behalf most likely had triggered an instinctive response. Something biologically driven that compelled a woman to find a strong protector attractive. That made sense, and now that she knew her response was science-based, she could more easily dismiss it.

Ignoring an attraction to Linc Jameson was a matter of self-preservation. She simply couldn't handle making another poor choice in men. She'd just broken up with her fiancé, for goodness sake. The profound sense of liberation she'd felt when she'd passed that small box, duly insured, to the clerk was all the proof she'd needed that she'd made the right decision.

Taking a sip of coffee, she remembered her brother telling her Peter reminded him of a glossy photo of a pinup girl, pretty to look at but totally lacking in depth. Peter might be perfect for some other woman, some woman who never wanted to make her own decisions, but not for Mikayla. She should never have accepted his marriage proposal.

Now wasn't the time to get fluttery feelings over someone else. A small voice in the back of her head reminded her she'd never had fluttery feelings over Peter. Regardless, she refused to be a cliché, the woman who falls for the guy who saved her life. Despite questionable judgment about Peter, she was an intelligent, competent, even-keeled kind of person. She had a doctorate in modern American history, and considered herself a levelheaded woman.

Ignoring her reaction to Linc was a matter of reason triumphing over emotion.

He returned from the showers, damp hair curling at his neck, and wearing a deep maroon Henley with the sleeves pushed to his elbows and faded Levi's. He rummaged in the back of his Jeep before crossing to her campsite. He placed a bright red apple on the table in front of her and sat across from her, white teeth biting into his own apple.

"An apple?"

"Yeah, payment for the coffee."

"Ah, okay." She narrowed her eyes. "And what's my payment to you for disarming the guy yesterday? For saving my life?"

He flashed a fast, wicked smile. "I'll hold that back for later."

Mikayla drew in a quick breath. That smile was lethal.

"Besides, you didn't seem too pleased that I'd interfered yesterday."

She set her empty bowl aside and picked up the apple. She bit in and chewed, swallowing before responding. "It's not that I wasn't pleased you were there." She shrugged, not sure how to explain. "I like to deal with my own problems. Sure, I was scared, but also supremely pissed. Who the hell was he to attack me like that? To hurt me? I guess I wanted a chance to prove I could protect myself."

"Understandable." His gaze traveled over her features, and Mikayla got the feeling he was a man who would notice the small details, like if a woman wore a new pair of earrings or styled her hair differently. "Look, you know I'm with the Marshals Service. Investigation is part of what I do, so I want to get back to those questions. See if I can get a handle on what that guy was after."

She finished chewing a bite of apple. "Are you here for work?"

His expression closed. "No, but I still have questions. Take me through it again. But this time, start from when you left home. You're from California?"

"Yes, Los Angeles."

"What made you take this trip by yourself? And why here?"

"Here because I'd heard southern Utah is spectacular, and by myself because I needed to get away from things."

She didn't mention Peter, didn't want to talk about him, mostly because she felt embarrassed she'd ever considered marrying him. Having known Linc Jameson less than twenty-four hours, she already understood he was the extreme opposite of Peter by almost every measure: where Peter was charming, gregarious, and in his element with a crowd, Linc appeared to be more reserved and watchful. Maybe the vigilance, the way he seemed to be constantly assessing his surroundings, was a law enforcement thing. And while she would consider both men attractive, Peter possessed a suave, urban polish quite different from Linc's powerful build and untamed looks. Linc exuded a rugged maleness that pulled at her on an elemental level.

He raised his brows and waited. "'Get away from things'? Want to explain?"

"Let's say I've had a lot of family pressure, and taking myself on a vacation made more sense than committing felony assault."

His eyes turned speculative and she thought for a minute he'd press the issue. "Is there anyone, and I mean anyone, at home, work, social group, who might want to harm you?"

"Most of my family is frequently unhappy with me, but so far they've held off on murder."

He raised dark brows.

"Look, that sounds pathetic. I know." She heaved a sigh. "My mom and sister simply have different ideas about what I should be doing. You know, where I should live, the type of career I should have. Even the kind of car I drive. Basically, they believe I make poor decisions on every damn thing in my life. This trip was supposed to give me some distance so I can figure out what it is *I* want, not what everyone else wants for me."

"You have a husband?" When she shook her head, he reached across the table and picked up her left hand, holding it up between them. His thumb moved across her ring finger, his hand warming her chilled fingers. "You've got a pale line here where you've recently taken off a ring. You skip out on a husband?"

"No, I haven't skipped out on a husband."

He waited, attention unwavering.

"Okay, okay. Damn it." She looked away. "I broke up with my boyfriend."

His thumb brushing her ring finger again brought her gaze back to his. "Boyfriend?"

"Fine, fiancé. I broke up with my fiancé."

She didn't know how to interpret the glint in his eye. "And how did the fiancé react?"

She hitched a shoulder. "The usual. Peter hears what he wants to hear and pays no attention to the rest. He refused to accept it was over."

"Was he angry?"

She tugged her hand free and jammed it into her pocket. And realized she still wore Linc's sweater. Great. She was like the cheerleader wearing the quarterback's letterman jacket. She set the core of the apple in her bowl and stood. "I'll get your jacket. There's probably blood on the sweater. I'll wash it before I give it back."

He held up a hand. "I'm not worried about the sweater. You said the fiancé wouldn't accept that you broke up with him, but you sound like it's a done deal."

She hesitated, then sat again. He certainly knew how to stick to a subject. "Right. Well, here's the thing. Peter doesn't know we're officially broken up."

"How's that?"

"I tried to break up with him. Twice. He simply refused to acknowledge what I was saying. I felt like he wanted to pat my head and say, 'there, there,' like I was a recalcitrant child. He'd slip around the conversation, and by the time we were done, I was frustrated and angry, and still engaged."

She felt the steam rising out of the top of her head all over again. "So yesterday on my way here, I stopped at a post office and put the ring in the mail to send back to him. A big, fat diamond solitaire. I never liked it. Diamonds are so cold." She closed her eyes and willed the irritation to subside. She hadn't meant to give away so much. "Anyway, that has nothing to do with the guy on the trail yesterday."

"The guy on the trail wasn't local. He was from the city."

"How do you know that?"

"How he dressed."

"Because he wasn't wearing Patagonia or REI? Every hiker doesn't wear the same thing, you know."

He gave a short laugh. "I do know. But even without traditional outdoor gear this guy wasn't dressed for hiking or camping. He had city written all over him. I'd say street thug, likely a cartel member. You notice the tattoo on the back of his left hand?"

"No. I was too busy staying away from that knife."

"I didn't get a good look either, but I'd put money down that I've seen it before. There's a cartel in Mexico that cuts off the tattooed hands of this group when they can catch them."

"You've got to be kidding. Aren't we a little outside cartel territory?"

"Exactly. Which is why I'm wondering who would send a cartel thug after you."

Before she could respond, a white and green National Park truck pulled to a stop next to Linc's Jeep, and Alex Smallcanyon stepped out. He nodded in their direction. "'Mornin'."

They greeted the ranger, and Mikayla asked, "Mr. Smallcanyon, can I make you some coffee?"

"It's Alex, and if it's no trouble, that would be great."

Mikayla rose from the bench to put water on the stove. She rinsed out the coffeepot before adding scoops of ground coffee.

Alex walked over to watch her work. "I haven't used a press before. Are you happy with it?"

"I think it's the best thing if you don't have electricity. It works for me."

"You have anything to report?" Linc's voice sounded abrupt, and she glanced over Alex's shoulder and caught Linc's lowered brows.

Alex laughed, dark eyes tracking from her to Linc. "Actually, yeah. Last night local sheriff's deputies spotted a car with California plates stuck in the mud over near Concord. That's about twenty-five miles from here. There'd been some flooding and the fool drove right through it." He nodded toward Linc. "He matched your description. We caught a lucky break."

"I want to question him."

Alex smiled thinly. "Might have a little jurisdictional squabble over that one. He didn't give up peaceably and punched the arresting officer, so the county boys want to hold on to him for now. Sheriff's a real hard-ass. He wants you both to ID him in a lineup before he'll even consider turning him over to the Department of Justice for federal charges."

\*\*\*

Linc stepped ahead of Mikayla and held open the door of a squat sheriff's office painted institutional beige. Despite his impatience to get going, she'd kept him waiting at the campground until she'd had her shower. They'd driven in his Jeep to the small town of Concord, and throughout the journey Mikayla found herself watching him— the way he handled the vehicle, his big hands on the gear shift, his narrowed gaze moving from road to mirror.

They stepped inside and, after introducing themselves, the deputy manning the front desk had them wait in the lobby.

Mikayla pulled her phone from her back pocket and sat on an upholstered bench. The phone had dinged about a dozen times once they'd gotten close to town and within service range, streaming a backlog of text messages. She thumbed through them as Linc leaned against a wall and tapped on his phone.

She could feel tension building in the back of her neck as she read the texts. Most of the messages were from her mother and had been sent on the day she'd driven to Utah, trying to get her to change her mind about the trip. The final one had been the classic I-refuse-to-talk-to-you-until-you-see-reason effort at control.

Mikayla slumped in her seat. She hated the guilt trip, the manipulation, the sheer drama hurled at her from a distance of several hundred miles. She'd gone on her camping trip to get away from the toxic atmosphere created by her mother, sister, and fiancé. Odd, though, there were no messages from Peter. The ring would be delivered sometime today. She'd bet there'd be messages then.

Refusing to get sucked in again, she began hitting the delete button. She deleted all texts except one from Monday evening that said, **"You get to Utah okay?"**

Her brother wasn't one to waste words. She tapped out a response. **"Yes. This is the smartest thing I've done in a long time."**

He'd be satisfied that she was alive, and she'd wait to relate the rest. Telling big brother about the assault on the trail didn't bear thinking about. One peep and he'd be at her campsite by nightfall.

Heavy footsteps drew near and Mikayla looked up. A beefy older man in a flannel shirt, a silver star pinned to his pocket and a sidearm on his hip, approached. Mikayla bet he binge-watched John Wayne movies on his evenings off. He gave Linc a flinty-eyed stare.

"I'm Sheriff Otis Bland." He didn't offer to shake hands.

"Deputy US Marshal Lincoln Jameson." He nodded to Mikayla. "This is Mikayla O'Kane." Mikayla got to her feet. She noticed the sheriff straightening as if trying to look taller. If she had to guess, she'd put Linc's height at 6'4", maybe a bit more. The sheriff wasn't going to top Linc unless he got a stool.

"Can't say I like feds poking their noses into local business." Bland said the word "feds" with a sneer.

Linc kept his expression neutral. "I think our boy in there may be involved in criminal activities in California, and the assault on Ms. O'Kane happened in a national park. Seems like straightforward federal jurisdiction to me."

"Our boy, as you say, coldcocked one of my deputies. Knocked a tooth loose. I'm going to hold on to him until we can sort out the local charges." Bland held up a hand before Linc could reply. "But we'll get to all that after a lineup. Make sure he's really your boy." He nodded at Mikayla. "Ma'am. Sorry about the trouble you had. You can come with me." He turned abruptly and left them to follow him down a long corridor, stopping at a closed door. He looked pointedly at Linc. "I'll need you to wait out here, Marshal."

Mikayla caught Linc's frown behind the sheriff's back as the older man ushered her through the door. She glanced around the darkened room. A woman with a bulging briefcase and a man in a business suit sat in hard plastic chairs. Bland introduced them as lawyers, one representing the accused and the other a county prosecutor, then explained the procedures for the lineup.

The room held a one-way mirror and on the other side stood five men, each with a number on the wall above their heads, and all with roughly the same height, build, and coloring. She looked for the tattoo but wondered from the way the men were standing whether they'd been instructed to hide their left hands.

Mikayla studied each man in turn, carefully examining their features. Her assailant had worn a long-sleeved t-shirt and the hat pulled low over his brow had made most of his features indistinguishable. But the hat had come off during the fight, and she'd seen his face. She closed her eyes to better bring up a mental image. Opening them again, she peered intently through the mirror. Three she could dismiss immediately. They weren't the guy. Some unseen person directed the men to turn to give her a right profile, and then a left. Once they faced her again, she leaned forward. Of the two she thought were possibilities, both were clean-shaven, but one man had a curved scar on his chin.

"Number three."

The woman with the briefcase stepped forward. "Are you positive, Ms. O'Kane?"

Mikayla wondered if there'd been two men with scars if it would have been as straightforward. "Pretty sure. The guy who attacked me had a scar on his chin, like number three."

Sheriff Bland thanked her, and then it was Linc's turn. He was in the room less than two minutes before he returned to the hall. She could hear the muted voices of the others through the closed door.

"That was quick."

"Doesn't take long when you know what you're looking for. I identified the same guy you did. Bland gave me his name." He took her elbow and they walked back down the hall. "Look, I want to interview him, but first we need to talk."

He eyed closed doors until they came to one marked "Storeroom" and, after a quick look inside, pulled Mikayla into a room crowded with boxes and supplies stacked on metal shelves. Linc flipped a switch and a fluorescent light flickered on.

"What are you doing? We shouldn't be in here."

"Why not? It's a storeroom, and I want to talk to you without Sheriff Deadeye out there looking at me like I'm planning to rob the stagecoach."

She laughed at his apt description and felt some of her tension seep away. "He did take a dislike to you. But I think he's more like Yosemite Sam, all bluff and bluster."

Linc's eyes sharpened, and her smile faded when his attention dropped to her mouth. The burn of his gaze lit a fire low in her belly. Silence stretched as the air between them crackled.

She had the irrational desire to kiss him just to see how hot the fire would flash.

# Chapter Seven

Linc cleared his throat and took a step back. Mikayla wondered if he felt the spark between them or if it was only her. From the first moment she'd seen him, she'd been battling attraction and it wouldn't be fair if it was all one-sided.

"Tell me about the fiancé."

Her mind blanked. "Fiancé?" It was taking her a few minutes to get all the synapses in her brain firing again.

"Yours?" he deadpanned. The hint of humor around his eyes told her he knew where her mind had wandered. Damn.

"Right, mine. Peter. Why do you want to know about him? He's got nothing to do with this."

"Quit trying to protect him. If he's not involved, that'll be apparent soon enough. The man who assaulted you is Hector Lopez, a low-level hustler from LA. I want to know what puts a kid from LA with a rap sheet going back to middle school on the same trail as you four hundred miles away. He targeted you, Mikayla."

"You don't know that. He may have followed me, and I don't like the possibility that he might be a psychopath or had sexual assault on his mind, but it's likely one of those things. The idea that someone I know would try to hurt me is preposterous." She knew the words were coming too fast, but it was all so insane. No one had reason to target her.

"I want to know about the fiancé. If he's as innocent as you claim, then I can clear him and move on. His name is Peter? Last name?"

"He's not my fiancé anymore."

"You said he doesn't know that. And ex-boyfriends are the most likely suspects. Last name?"

"Wellington. Peter Wellington the third."

He raised his brows.

"I know. Pretentious."

"What does he do? How did you meet?"

"He's in real estate."

Linc waited expectantly, and Mikayla heaved a sigh. "Okay, okay. He does commercial real estate, and he's getting into property development. I met him at an event a friend catered. She'd asked me to help. I was on appetizers."

"On appetizers?"

"Yeah. You know, walking around with a platter of mini pot stickers or stuffed mushrooms with toothpicks in them."

"Right. The hot chick with a short skirt, passing out the eats." The gold in his eyes glowed warm.

"Hot chick aside, yes. This guy had imbibed a little too much Dom Perignon. He patted my butt and made a sloppy pass. He was sure I wasn't serious when I told him I wouldn't run into the bathroom with him so we could have a quickie. Peter came to my rescue. Actually, I was about to kick the guy in the balls when Peter stepped in, so he actually came to the butt patter's rescue."

"Go on."

"Peter has a way. When he chooses to use it, he has this incredible charm. He not only convinced the guy he shouldn't have his hand on my butt, but kept the situation from getting ugly. And believe me, it was heading toward ugly. Within ten minutes they were buddies and planning a round of golf for Sunday afternoon. And after another ten minutes the guy had been sent on his way and Peter had asked me out."

"You didn't know him before that?"

"No."

"Why did you dump him?"

She really hated talking about her failures. "Linc, don't you think you should see if they're ready for you to interview Lopez?"

"He's not going anywhere. Why, Mikayla?"

"You're really persistent, you know that, right? It's a bit annoying." He said nothing and she held up her hands in surrender. It shouldn't matter that she'd end up sounding like a spineless wimp. "All right. Fine. First off, I never said yes."

"Yes to what?"

"To marrying him."

"Then how did you end up with his ring on your finger?"

"He assumed I'd say yes. Peter's good at that, assuming things will simply go the way he wants them to. And they usually do."

"Sounds like a charmer."

"That's exactly what he is. Anyway, he had the proposal all planned out. We were on a cruise around Newport Harbor on New Year's Eve with three other couples we hung out with a lot. Honestly, he made it so romantic. The twinkling lights on the boat, flutes of Cristal, and he'd requested the band play a special song. He said it was our song. I didn't even know we had a song."

She shrugged. "Then the clock strikes midnight, there's fireworks going off over the water, and Peter is on one knee in front of all these people. He's holding up this huge diamond solitaire and asking me to marry him. I stood there speechless, in shock. I know I didn't say anything. I couldn't say anything. Our friends are taking pictures, and the next thing I know, I've got a ring on my finger and Peter is swinging me around, saying I've made him the happiest man in the world."

"But you didn't want to marry him."

"I didn't *not* want to marry him, if you know what I mean."

"No, can't say that I do."

Linc wasn't going to make this any easier so she might as well make a full confession. Then he'd know how spineless she'd been. "Peter's a good guy. I kept it secret from my family for a while, but when they found out, my mom, my sister, they were over the moon. Everyone was saying how we were this perfect couple. I know this sounds weak and shallow, but I wanted to believe it so I went along with it. Peter is handsome, fun, and charming. I didn't love him, but I thought I could, if I gave it some time."

"But you couldn't."

"No. I tried. Don't get me wrong. We had a good time together. Peter is attentive. He never forgets to send flowers, and he tells me he calls just to hear my voice." She shrugged. "I tried to talk to my mom about my misgivings, and my sister. I thought Mom's head would explode. She'd had such a tough time when my dad died. There were money problems and she never felt safe, and here I had this rich guy over the moon for me. But he likes modern furniture and resort vacations." She didn't know why, but those two things had been the clinchers.

Linc's lips quirked in a slight smile. "You mean like furniture with lots of glass and chrome and trips to luxury hotels in Cancun."

"Exactly. It all seemed so soulless. I know that sounds harsh, and there's absolutely nothing wrong with a resort vacation every now and then, but there's everything wrong with modern furniture. He likes his world all clean and sanitized. Then he put a bid on a house for us without consulting me. He said it was a surprise."

"A lot of women would be happy to trade places with you."

"I doubt it. I think most women would resent having their lives managed for them since they have the brains to figure out what they want for themselves. I know I got damn tired of being told what is best for me."

She looked at her hands. Anything was better than looking at Linc. "The consensus was almost one hundred percent that Peter was so amazing I'd be crazy not to be in love with him. So, I tried. At first it was fun to have someone to go out with, to talk to. I listened to all his plans. He talked about the development project he was working on. But then I realized we always talked about him. He didn't want to know my plans, what I wanted. I was supposed to fit myself into his life and give up any aspirations I had of my own. He wanted me to quit my job once we were married."

"What do you do?"

"I teach American history at a private university in Los Angeles."

"You're a brain? Cool."

"I enjoy teaching. But regardless, I should have told him straight out that I didn't want to marry him."

Linc was quiet for so long she finally raised her gaze to find him studying her with a slight frown. "I think you gave it a shot and had the guts to dig in your heels when you wanted to change the status quo. You said the consensus was almost one hundred percent in favor of the guy. Who was the holdout?"

He listened, and Mikayla had to admit there was a definite allure to a man who really paid attention. It was so different from Peter, who always complimented her hair or clothing, but would have been bewildered if asked to identify her favorite author or what classes she was teaching. "My brother. We've always been a team. We're alike in so many ways. But he never liked Peter."

"Why?"

"He says Peter is all flash and show, but no substance." She shrugged. "It took me a while to see it, but I finally realized he was right."

"You said you tried to break it off and Peter wouldn't let you."

"He'd always turn it around to make it seem that I was being silly, that I didn't really know what I wanted."

"Then you got out of town and mailed him the ring so he couldn't convince you not to break up with him."

"Not exactly."

"Then what exactly?"

"I went to his house the night before I left on my trip. I absolutely was going to break up, and wasn't going to let him talk me out of it. And no matter what, I'd leave the ring." She remembered driving up the winding road toward the house on the bluffs over the ocean, and the fog bank rolling in from the sea slowly overtaking her until all she could see was the ten feet in front of her lit by the headlights.

When she had reached her destination, it had looked like every light in Peter's house was burning, shining through windows to reflect off the fog. She'd parked beside Peter's Mercedes and an unfamiliar Audi sports car. "I hadn't told him I was coming over. I knew he was home, and I'd decided catching him by surprise might be to my advantage. But when I got there, he had company."

"Another woman?"

"No. I went around the side to the kitchen door. We always went in the house that way. I used my key. That's when I heard him yelling at someone. They were in his office. I walked down the hall a little bit and saw their reflections in a mirror. There were two guys, one was arguing with Peter, but cool, not raising his voice. That guy had a lot of swagger in the way he spoke, like he was enjoying himself. The other man didn't say a word. Peter referred to the guy who was talking as Paco."

Linc's expression turned grim, eyes going flat. "You're sure he said Paco."

"I'm sure. That's a nickname for Francisco, right?"

"Yeah. What did Paco say?"

"That he was running out of patience."

"What did he look like?"

She frowned in concentration, trying to remember. "Short. I'd guess five-five or six. Heavy, with a really thick neck. Short black hair combed back from his forehead."

"Did you notice any tattoos or birthmarks?"

"No, but like I said, I only saw their reflections in the mirror, and a side view at that. He had a sport coat on so I couldn't see his arms."

"What were they arguing about?"

"Something about the development Peter has been gathering investors for. It sounded like he had gotten money from Paco as part of the deal and was supposed to use that to leverage more investors, but hadn't. Paco wanted to know what happened to the money. Peter said he'd get the investors that he needed in a few more days. He didn't want Paco to pull out of the deal. He said they'd all make money if he'd give Peter a chance. The argument was getting really intense, and I didn't want to interrupt. Peter is always pretty controlled, and honestly, it was kind of scary hearing him losing it."

"Did he sound scared, like he was being threatened?"

Mikayla replayed the conversation in her head, trying to recall the tone. "I couldn't see Peter because he was around the corner where his desk is. But he sounded more like how he gets when he's thwarted. He likes things to go his way, and when they don't, he can get belligerent. Angry." She paused. "He has this image of himself that he's smart, that he always knows what to do. He thinks people should accept what he does, the decisions he makes, without question, because questioning him means you don't trust him, that you doubt his abilities."

"And Paco was questioning his abilities, so Peter was pissed."

"Exactly."

"Did they see you?"

She shook her head. "I don't think so. Paco and the other guy had their backs to the doorway facing Peter, who was out of sight. I don't think they could see me."

"The guy with Paco, can you describe him?"

She shrugged. "Dark hair, cut short. Maybe a little taller than average. I couldn't see his eyes. He was a little heavy, but not overweight like Paco. I don't think he was Hispanic."

"Which could describe a good portion of the male population. Any identifying marks?"

She shook her head.

"Did you notice if Paco or the other man were carrying weapons?"

She looked at him in surprise, then shook her head again. "Like I said, Paco was wearing a sport coat, and the other guy had on a leather jacket. They didn't have anything in their hands, but if they had holsters, I wouldn't have been able to see them."

"Okay, so you heard them arguing. Then what?"

"I left and drove home. I'd already packed my car and was ready to go on my trip. I left before dawn the next morning. Two days ago I mailed Peter the ring, with his house key and a note."

Linc stared at the floor, hand on his hip, brows lowered in what she was starting to recognize as his thinking look.

"This can't have anything to do with Hector Lopez. Just because I broke up with Peter doesn't mean he'd try to kill me. I'm not even sure he loved me. I'm presentable and able to make small talk at social events."

Linc's eyes came up at that. No longer flat, the gold around the irises glowed in sharp contrast to the green. "You're selling yourself short if you believe that."

She fought the warmth creeping up her neck. "Ah, it's not that I lack self-confidence, but Peter wasn't looking for any depth to our relationship. But anyway," she went on hastily, "like I said, that guy who attacked me has nothing to do with Peter."

***

Linc stood silent for a long moment. A fist to the gut wouldn't have surprised him more than Mikayla naming Paco as the man arguing with her ex. If Paco was who Linc thought he was, she'd all but walked in on a confrontation between the ex and the head of the Zecena cartel in Southern California. Seems like dear old Peter was involved with the organization, which was the focus of the Marshals' investigation. If he had to guess, Peter was laundering cartel money through real estate transactions. Talk about a clusterfuck.

Mikayla looked worried, a small furrow dipping between her eyebrows, those pretty green eyes clouded.

"I don't like the feeling of this. I'm going to check it out." He motioned toward the door. "Let's go. Bland will have Lopez ready for questioning."

They exited the closet and walked down the hall. Mikayla turned to him. Those eyes of hers were sure a distraction. "I want to hear you question the guy."

"No. We'll find someplace where you can be comfortable for a half hour while I'm with him."

"I should hear what he has to say. There will be one of those two-way mirrors, right? He won't even know I'm there. If he was targeting me, like you said, he may say something that makes sense to me, but you may not catch."

Linc didn't like it. Instinct drove him to keep Mikayla as far as possible from the guy who'd attacked her, who'd come at her with a knife, for Christ sake. But she was right. She might pick up on something he would miss. He stopped her with a hand to her arm outside a door marked Observation Room. "Look, I don't like it, but you could be right. But I'll have to get it past Sheriff Deadeye first."

"That's fine." She smiled up at him and Linc saw a dimple in her right cheek he'd never noticed before.

He wished to god she wasn't so damned appealing. She looked as fresh and pretty as the daffodils that grew in his mother's garden in spring, completely separate from the ugliness that came with the people he dealt with every day. He had an uneasy feeling that what had happened to Mikayla out on that trail was the tip of a very dirty iceberg. And if Paco was who Linc thought he was, the underside of the iceberg was as nasty as it gets.

First things first. When she would have turned to the door of the observation room, he reached for her again, his fingers closing over the smooth skin of her forearm. "Wait. You need to know something. Questioning a suspect isn't like going to Sunday school. The cop wants to know something and generally, the person being interviewed wants to keep something hidden. That means there's conflict right from the start."

"Do you want me to join you and play the good cop, Lincoln, so you can be the bad cop? I've watched enough police shows. I think I could do it." The dimple winked again.

"Funny. All I'm saying is that interrogations can get ugly."
"Duly noted and warned."

# Chapter Eight

Linc entered the interrogation room carrying two bottles of water. The defense lawyer sat next to Lopez, a yellow legal pad in front of her. She held out a hand to shake. "I'm Stacy Browning, Marshal. I represent Mr. Lopez."

Lopez had an attorney in a higher tax bracket than a public defender. Interesting. He shook her hand. Hector Lopez sat slouched in his chair, his disinterested pose contradicted by the tension in his body. He looked coiled tight and ready to spring, the sneer on his face an indication of the sullen bad attitude of a career criminal. The kid was all of twenty-two years old.

Linc sat in the straight-backed chair opposite Lopez, staring the younger man in the eye for a long-drawn-out minute. Lopez broke the stare and looked at his hands.

Linc handed Lopez and the attorney each a water bottle. He'd found it was always a good idea to start friendly. Lopez reached for the bottle with his left hand and Linc got a good look at the tattoo. The triangular head of a rattlesnake, jaws opened wide and fangs prominent, covered the back of his hand. The letter Z was interwoven with the diamond pattern on the head of the snake. He might as well have a neon sign over his head blinking Zecena.

"Look, Hector, let's not waste your time or mine. Both your victim and I identified you as the guy on the trail with the knife yesterday."

Lopez didn't raise his head. Instead, he studiously picked at the skin next to his thumbnail.

"My client denies being on any trail yesterday afternoon, Marshal."

Linc spared her a glance. "I'm sure he does, but the fact remains that he was there." He focused on Lopez. "We know you were hired to attack Ms. O'Kane."

The young man brought his thumb to his mouth to use his teeth to chew the skin.

Linc didn't take his eyes off him. "Interesting tattoo you have on the back of your hand, Hector." Lopez paused, sucking where his thumb had begun to bleed. His gaze flitted to Linc's, then away again. "That's the Zecena brand. You run with the cartel, Hector?"

"Mr. Lopez is not affiliated with any crime organization. Many young people have tattoos, Marshal. That's hardly unique."

"I'd say his is unique." Linc continued to watch Lopez as he began chewing on the nail of his index finger. "Paco know you failed, Hector? That you didn't kill the woman?"

Lopez's head jerked up, sitting straighter, and he drew in a quick breath. The attorney laid a hand on his arm. He slumped in his seat, but the look of panic was undeniable. Linc turned his attention to the lawyer. "Who hired you, Ms. Browning?"

"I'm not obligated to tell you that."

The interrogation continued in the same vein with Linc asking and Lopez silent as the attorney deflected. It didn't matter. It would have pissed Linc off if it hadn't been for the flash of fear in Lopez's eyes when he'd taken the chance and mentioned Paco. That reaction confirmed that Peter the ex was the connection.

Linc studied the kid. Money could buy loyalty, but in this case, fear appeared to be the motivator keeping his mouth shut. Having gotten all he would, Linc concluded the interview.

He entered the observation room where Mikayla sat, still gazing through the glass at Lopez. The sheriff stood, posture erect, in the back of the room. He hadn't wanted to let Linc conduct the interrogation, but since the attack had happened in federal jurisdiction, the sheriff hadn't had much leverage. Not getting anything out of the kid irked Linc more when he saw the sheriff's smirk.

Linc motioned to Mikayla and she preceded him from the room. He tortured himself by inhaling as she passed in front of him. He shouldn't notice things about her. Didn't want to notice things about her. Things like dimples and the clean fragrance of her shampoo.

Shit. She was getting to him.

Once in the hall she turned to face him and when that green gaze locked on his, he had to brace himself. Like in the storeroom, he had the uncomfortable feeling he was foundering, sinking with water closing in over his head. Experiencing such a heightened response to any woman was new and distracting. He didn't like it.

"What's next?"

Linc started walking, his hand on her elbow. "Lopez will be formally charged and bail set. You'll have to give a statement and attend the trial, whenever that is. I'll have to testify as well."

"Unless he pleads guilty."

"Yeah, unless he pleads guilty."

She nodded. "Okay."

They passed a breakroom. Linc reached for his wallet and pulled out a couple of bills. "You want coffee? I want coffee. Would you buy us some while I make a quick call?"

Mikayla gave him a quizzical look but took the bills. Once she was out of earshot he called his brother, whose voice came over the line, terse and harried. Terse was par for the course with Seth Jameson. Harried? Not so much.

"Where the fuck are you?"

"Utah, what's going on?"

"Hang on a sec." Linc could hear a door slamming shut before his brother came back on the line. "Okay, I can talk now."

"You're in your office and you can't talk with the door open?"

"Not anymore. I've got a new deputy who's a pain in the ass."

Linc laughed at the exasperation in Seth's voice. It took a lot to get under his brother's skin. In fact, he couldn't remember the last time anyone had. "What's he done? Or is it a she?"

"She. Definitely a she. And she never gives me a moment's peace. I should have her reassigned."

"Is she a rookie? If she's that bad, she'll wash out."

"Yeah, she's a rookie, and she's damn good at her job. But she's still a constant source of tension headaches. Can we talk about something else, like why Mom's riding my ass because you haven't called her?"

"Ah, shit. Sorry. But listen, I'm involved in something here I need your help with. Tell Mom I'm fine and I'll call her when I get a minute."

"What do you need?" No one could cut through the bullshit as well as Seth.

"You at your computer?"

"Yeah."

"Look up this name. Peter Wellington. The third, if that matters. See if he's got a history." Linc could hear faint tapping on a keyboard as his brother put the name into the system. He paced the hall, then frowned when he glanced through the window into the breakroom where Mikayla was filling paper cups with coffee. Leaning back against the counter, a heavyset deputy was having a great time, chatting and smiling at her like a dumbass. Didn't Bland run a tighter ship than this?

Seth's voice came across the line. "What's your interest in Wellington, Linc?"

"I'll explain later, tell me what you've got."

"A dead guy."

"What?" He lowered his voice. "Wellington's dead?"

"Housekeeper found him with a bullet to the brain when she arrived for work."

"Burglary gone bad? Suicide?"

"No, homicide. From the look of it he knew his killer."

"When was this?"

"Housekeeper got there at eight o'clock Monday morning. The coroner puts time of death between nine and ten-thirty Sunday night."

"Fuck." Linc rubbed the back of his neck, his eyes never leaving Mikayla. She'd capped the cups and stood holding them while the deputy yakked away.

"There's not much here, but if you give me an hour, I'll see what I can dig up. The only note in the file is that there's a suspected tie to the Zecena cartel."

"Son of a bitch. I had a feeling."

"Okay, like I said, give me that hour." Seth paused. "You back on the job?"

He knew Seth was asking about more than his physical recovery. Mikayla walked into the hall and handed him a cup. He was back on the job as long as it took to keep her safe. "Looks like. I'll call you back later." He disconnected and slipped the phone in his pocket.

"Girlfriend?"

"No." Damn. He'd have to tell her. He paused as a thought struck and felt his blood turn to ice. Mikayla would be a suspect. She'd already admitted to being at Wellington's house at the approximate time of death. She'd tried to break up with him and he hadn't let her. Love and money, the two strongest motives for murder.

He considered the possibility she might have killed her ex, then rejected it. His sister might be the one with the famously reliable gut instincts, but in this case Linc knew his were dead on. Mikayla could no more have killed Peter Wellington than Linc could have.

When the thought occurred that his gut had failed him before, and that he hadn't suspected his partner's betrayal or had any clue that his father was a traitor, he pushed it firmly back. He'd begun to realize that with Donny he'd ignored what he should have attended to. There had been things about his partner that were off, that had stuck him as incongruent at the time, but he'd dismissed them out of loyalty. Or perhaps his irritation with his partner's ongoing drama.

Whatever it was, Linc had left Donny to sort out his own issues and had nearly gotten killed as a result.

His father, though, had been a master at deceit and had caught everyone unaware.

But Mikayla? He wasn't wrong about her. Now it was even more imperative to tie Lopez and the attack the previous day to the cartel. If Wellington had ties to the Zecena, it was likely his killers did too. The quicker that was established as fact, the quicker Mikayla could be cleared.

He looked around the dingy hall. The antiseptic odor only added to the bleakness. Not here. He couldn't tell her Wellington was dead in this place. He took a sip of coffee and found it surprisingly good. Making a quick decision, he took Mikayla's hand and hurried her through the hall and out the glass doors to the parking lot.

She tugged at the hold. "Wait, Linc. Don't I need to give my statement?"

"Yeah, we'll take care of that later." He unlocked the Jeep and put his cup in the holder. Once they were both belted in, he reversed the vehicle out of the space and drove onto West Main Street.

"Where are we going?"

"Not sure."

Concord wasn't all that big and he needed to find someplace they could talk without being overheard. He saw a sign and took a quick turn to the right, then whipped the Jeep into a tight U-turn to stop at the curb of a city park. There were a few moms with strollers and kids on the swings, but the rest of the park was deserted. Rounding the hood, he found Mikayla hadn't moved so he opened her door.

She sat in the seat. That furrow forming again between her brows. "What's going on?"

"We need to talk. Come with me." When she didn't move, he added, "Please."

She got out of the vehicle slowly, and they walked through the grass to a park bench where Mikayla sat, expression troubled. "You're starting to make me nervous."

God, he hated death notifications. They were the worst part of his job, and this one made him sick to his stomach. He sat next to her and took her hand, rubbing a thumb over her knuckles. He was stalling. He cleared his throat and began. "I was on the phone with my brother. He's also a US Marshal, chief deputy of the LA office. I had him look up Wellington, see if he has a criminal history."

Her hand clenched in his. "Geez, Linc. I told you—"

"Mikayla, Peter Wellington is dead."

He didn't think he'd ever before seen a person's face actually leach of all color. Already fair, the blood drained from her cheeks, leaving her skin ashen. That reaction alone would have convinced him if he'd had any doubt of her innocence.

"That's not true. Peter is alive."

"It is true. I'm sorry."

She surged to her feet, pulling her hand free, arms crossing defensively in front of her. "No, I saw him three days ago. He's not dead. Your brother got it wrong."

He checked the urge to pull her close. The impulse caught him off guard. All he knew was that he'd gotten way past the "don't get personally involved" mantra that was drilled into the head of any law enforcement officer.

"I don't know why you're telling me this when you don't have proof."

"I'm sorry," he repeated. "There's not much chance it's a mistake."

She tightened her arms as if she could somehow cage in her emotions. A muscle twitched in her jaw and her eyes looked dry and hot. "How did this person you *think* is Peter die?"

Telling himself he was all kinds of an idiot, he gave in to the need and cupped her shoulders, holding firm when she stiffened at his touch. "He was shot. A housekeeper found him Monday morning." He didn't think it was possible for her to lose any more color, but now even her lips looked bloodless.

"Oh god." She let him draw her close and dipped her head forward and laid it against his chest. He wrapped his arms around her, resting his cheek on top of her head.

"Peter's alive, I know he is. Someone got it wrong."

The words were muffled against his shirt. And he was doubly an idiot to feel a stab of jealousy over a dead man. Of course she was devastated. Even if she'd broken up with him, she'd been engaged to the guy. Most assuredly had sex with him. Linc's brain shied away from that one. He rubbed a hand slowly up and down her back. "I got you, Mikayla. Hold on to me for a minute."

She finally unclenched her arms and he pulled her closer when she wrapped them around his waist. He couldn't help noticing how perfectly she fit with her head nestled under his chin. "You're positive it's him?"

"Yes."

She stood in his embrace for several long minutes, until finally loosening her hold and tilting up her face. The furrow was back between her eyebrows. "You had my fiancé investigated?"

"Ex," he corrected automatically.

"Why? I told you he didn't have anything to do with the attack."

"He might have had something to do with it. In fact, now I'm thinking it's likely."

"You're being mean. I don't know why you don't like Peter, but that's no reason to have him investigated." Anger brought a touch of color back to her cheeks.

"He was the obvious person to look at when I realized Lopez was working for someone, and probably someone from LA."

Green eyes glittered, but there were no tears. Reluctantly, he loosened his hold and she stepped back. He wondered if she missed the contact as much as he did.

"You said you saw him the night before you left. What day was that?"

"Sunday, a little before nine." She cleared her throat. "Is he really dead?"

"Yes." He knew how this worked. Unless a person actually witnessed a death, all sorts of scenarios suddenly became plausible. There'd been a mistake. Someone had misidentified the body. The loved one would appear any minute now and clear up all the confusion.

She seemed to draw further into herself, her arms again locked in front of her, a protective shield against the pain. "When was he killed?" Her voice quavered on the last word.

"That night. The coroner said between nine and ten-thirty."

Whatever color had returned to her cheeks disappeared, leaving her looking so pale he thought she might need to sit with her head between her knees to keep her from fainting.

"I'm a suspect, aren't I? The police will think I did it once they know I was there."

"You'll be questioned."

"Do you think I did it? That I shot him?"

He shook his head slowly. "No."

"Those men." She drew a deep breath. "Those men he was arguing with. They must have killed him." He nodded, and she stared at him with a heartbreaking expression. "If I'd gone in there, into Peter's office and let them know I was there, they might have left. But I didn't, and now Peter's dead."

"Sweetheart, if you'd done that you'd be dead, too."

When she raised troubled eyes to his, he knew she had made the connection. "You believe the killers sent Lopez after me."

"I want you to think carefully. Could either of those men have seen you?"

"I don't think so."

"But you saw them."

"Yes. I'd started down the hall when I heard the argument coming from Peter's office. There's a big mirror on the far wall of the room so even though the men were around the corner, I could see them in the mirror." She sat on the park bench and drew her knees up, wrapping her arms around them, pulling into herself. "I listened for a few minutes, thinking I would go in when there was a pause in the conversation. But then I realized Peter wouldn't want me seeing him losing control like that. It was so out of character. Plus, the argument scared me. I wouldn't be able to give Peter his ring back in front of strangers anyway. So I turned around and went back out the kitchen door. I left Peter there to die."

"There was nothing you could have done. If you'd stayed, you'd be dead, too." He paused. "Think about it. Leaving saved your life."

Haunted eyes rose to meet his and he realized she'd reached the other obvious conclusion.

"I'm the only witness then."

"Yeah, you are. And somehow they knew you were there, because they sent that little shit sitting in the sheriff's office after you."

She frowned. "He doesn't seem particularly good at his job."

"No, which makes me think he's someone new and they were testing him. Or he was expendable. He failed and my bet is he knows he's in trouble. They probably figured if Lopez blew it, you'd come back to LA and they could hit you where they've got resources and where it's easy to keep tabs on you."

"How'd they know where I am? I don't see how they could have gotten my credit card number to track me. I hadn't even told Peter where I was going. I mean, I told him I would be camping in Utah, but not what campground, or even what part of the state."

"Did you and Peter have tracking apps on your phones?"

Her eyes darkened and stood in sharp contrast to the pinched pallor of her skin. "Of course, that's how they found me." She fumbled her phone out of her pocket. After tapping through several screens she shoved it into her pack. "I deleted the app and powered off my phone so I can't be tracked. Anymore, at least."

Linc studied her face, then came to an abrupt conclusion. Mikayla was scared and shaken to the core. She needed to regroup. "Let's go get some lunch. We can come back tomorrow to give your statement. Sheriff Deadeye can wait."

# Chapter Nine

Mikayla stared at the menu, not seeing the words. Dead. Peter was dead. It didn't feel real. Maybe, despite Linc's conviction that he had the facts, there'd been a mistake. There must be more than one Peter Wellington in the world. In fact, she'd bet in a city the size of Los Angeles there'd be multiple Peter Wellingtons. She peered out the window next to the table. Linc had stepped outside to take a phone call. She spotted him with his phone to his ear, standing on a little strip of grass. He wore a shirt tucked into jeans belted low at his lean waist. His eyes were hidden behind the mirrored sunglasses. She didn't think it was an accident that he stood where he could monitor anyone who walked through the entrance.

Mikayla felt like her world had spiraled out of control and nothing was how it should be. The attack the day before had seemed random, completely out of the blue, but now it appeared to be connected to the men who'd been at Peter's house. And Peter – beautiful, charming, unfailingly optimistic Peter – was dead. Someone she'd laughed with, had been frustrated with, and had made love with had been killed by a stranger who'd pulled the trigger on a gun and killed him. And overlaying everything that had happened over the past twenty-four hours was the disquieting appearance of Lincoln Jameson. If she was honest, she could attribute a good portion of her confusion and emotional upheaval to his presence.

She'd felt attracted to a few men over the years but had always managed to keep them from getting too close. The sad truth was that despite their engagement, she'd kept Peter at an emotional distance. It had been easy because he hadn't wanted to look below the surface either, which probably explained a lot. She'd gone along with marrying him because he didn't make her feel too much. Even if she hadn't really understood her motives, at least she'd finally realized that their marriage would never last if there wasn't more to it than friendship and affection.

But Linc was different. He had a way of getting to her that didn't allow her to keep things at a superficial level. Attentive, caring, he made her feel like she actually meant something to him. He probably acted that way with everyone. Part of his job description. No way would she let him know that her response to him scared her. She reacted to him on an elemental level that made her feel vulnerable, like her emotions were laid bare.

Still on the phone, Linc stared at her through the window, expression grim. Why did she have the feeling he knew what she was thinking? He spoke a few more words, then stuck the phone in his pocket and strode to the door. It felt like she had to brace herself for the force of his presence when he neared the table. She set down the menu as he slid into the booth to sit opposite her, his gaze traveling over her features.

"You okay?"

She nodded jerkily. "I've been thinking, there's got to be more than one Peter Wellington in Los Angeles. Your brother could have found some other Peter Wellington who was murdered." The words tumbled out and she could see Linc's expression change, his eyes soften. There was compassion behind the tough exterior. He probably knew she was grasping at anything that would change reality and didn't want to quash her hopes.

"How many Peter Wellingtons live on Sea Cliff Drive off the Pacific Coast Highway?" He reached for her hand, tightening his grip when she would have pulled away. "He's dead, Mikayla."

She bore down on the terrible ball of misery that threatened to break loose. She pulled her hand from his grasp and crossed her arms in front of her. What she really needed was a quiet place where she could be alone and find her control. Breaking down in front of Linc, in front of anyone, was never an option.

"Anything look good on the menu? Some soup and a cup of tea and you might feel steadier."

Comfort foods. She wondered if Linc tended to everyone. She had the feeling he didn't, but for whatever reason was making an exception for her. She gave him a brief nod. "That sounds fine."

They didn't talk during the meal, and she thought Linc was giving her space. She pushed the half-finished bowl of potato-corn chowder back and watched him demolish the last of a thick pastrami sandwich. His phone buzzed. Linc looked at the screen and let it go to voicemail. At her raised eyebrow he gave a half-smile. "Sheriff Deadeye. He won't be happy we took off."

He nodded to the waitress when she came around to refill his coffee mug and leaned back in his seat. "I spoke to my brother again. He talked to a contact in the LAPD." He gave her an assessing look. "Were you aware Wellington had security cameras in and around his home?" At her nod, he continued. "The system has been accessed and all data for the day Wellington was killed was erased." He paused. "Do you know how to access Wellington's security system?"

"No. I knew he had one, and Peter told me the alarm passcode to disarm it, but I've never gotten into the system."

"Those men must have examined the video before they erased it, and that's how they know you were there. It wouldn't take much digging to find out who you are." He studied her features. "Mikayla, do you know anything about Wellington being connected to a Mexican drug cartel?"

"Drug cartel? No way." She shook her head emphatically. "He couldn't be."

"It's looking like he might have been laundering money for the cartel through commercial real estate deals."

"I can't believe this. First you tell me Peter's dead, and now that he was involved with a drug cartel. That Peter was a criminal."

"Sorry, but yes. Think carefully. Had he ever said or done anything to make you think he was involved in illegal activities of any sort?"

"No." She rubbed at her forehead, trying to ease a dull ache that signaled the start of a tension headache. If she'd been told Peter wanted to give up his Mercedes and go on a spiritual pilgrimage to Tibet, she couldn't have been any more surprised. She lowered her hand and locked her gaze on Linc's. "The cartel sent Lopez after me." The words came out slowly, each carefully enunciated as the full reality of her situation dawned. "Those men he was arguing with were with the cartel. It's not run-of-the-mill bad guys who are after me, but a Mexican cartel. They know I saw them there Sunday night." She fisted her hands to hide their trembling.

"That's my bet. My brother is starting the ball rolling on getting you into WITSEC."

"You have got to be kidding."

"WITSEC is the Witness Security Program run by the Marshals Service."

"I know what WITSEC is. I don't want to do that. Go arrest that Paco guy and his minion and there won't be any reason to put me in witness protection."

"Look, you're scared and you want this whole thing to go away. I get that. But it won't go away and I need to keep you safe until the cartel can be dealt with." He glanced around and pitched his voice low. "Paco Zecena is in charge of the cartel's Southern California operations. The FBI and the Marshals Service have been working to build a case against him for the past year. Zecena is slick. He's been careful to keep his hands clean, let others do the dirty work. But if he's the same Paco you saw at Wellington's house, and I think he is, then he's finally made a mistake."

"His mistake being leaving a witness alive."

"Yeah. You're the only person who can link Zecena directly to murder. And if we can prove Wellington was laundering money for the cartel, then we've got a case not just for murder, but one that can bring down the California Zecena operation."

"Good, so if you can do that you won't need me to assume a new identity or give up my job."

"You can be under witness protection without changing your name. We'll keep you in a safe house until you give your testimony."

"What about after? How do you know whether the threat will be gone? These guys are only one part of the cartel, right?"

"True, so we reassess at that point."

Mikayla felt her head spinning. What had happened to her life? Three days ago she was a college professor and was engaged to a charming man. Now that man was dead and she was being told she'd need to give up her life so she wouldn't end up dead. Like Peter. "What about my family? I won't be able to see them?"

"If we consider them in danger, they can be put into WITSEC as well. We'll work it out." Her expression must have given away what she was feeling because he reached out to take her hand again, this time holding firmly. "You've had a lot to absorb, Mikayla. Don't try to figure it all out at once. My primary goal is keeping you safe. To do that, I need to know everything you know. I want you to go over again what you saw Sunday night." He glanced around the mostly empty restaurant. "We're good to talk here. You okay?" He rubbed his thumb over her knuckles then released her hand.

At her slow nod, he continued. "Take me through that evening again, but this time think back to any additional details you remember. Tell me anything that was different or seemed off, no matter how insignificant you think it is."

When she sat numbly, he prompted her. "You said you drove to Peter's house Sunday evening. You hadn't called him and he wasn't expecting you?"

"No."

"Had you talked to him that day?"

"Kind of. We'd texted that morning."

"About what?"

"Nothing really, it was just chitchat. He asked when I was leaving on my trip, said he wished I wasn't going so far away. I knew he didn't want me to go. In Peter's world, women don't go on trips without their men. Who would carry their bags? And women certainly don't do anything as uncivilized as camping, much less go camping alone. He and my mother were relentless in trying to get me to change my mind."

"What about when you got to his house. Think details."

"There was a strange car parked in the driveway next to Peter's Mercedes. An Audi sports car that still had paper dealer plates so it must have been new. And it was unusual for Peter not to have parked his car in the garage."

"Do you remember what dealership the Audi was from?"

Mikayla tilted her head back in thought. "No, but I remember the logo on the license frame was in italics lettering and the color scheme was red letters on a yellow background. That's probably not much help."

"It might be." He made a rolling motion with his hand. "Walking up to the house, in the house, did anything else strike you as odd or different?"

She shook her head. "Not until I heard them yelling at each other." He continued to grill her, asking follow-up questions to his follow-up questions, until Mikayla finally held up her hands in surrender. "Linc, there's nothing else I can tell you."

He picked up his coffee mug and sipped, hazel eyes studying her over the rim. "Bottom line, Mikayla, those two men know you can place them at the scene of Peter's murder. They sent Lopez to kill you, and they'll try again. And not with a novice this time. We need to keep you safe, and the Marshals Service is developing a plan to do that. Until then, you stay glued to me."

\*\*\*

When they left Concord, dark clouds building in the western sky shifted the colors of the landscape to monochrome. Gray sky, granite mountains, black trees. Mikayla sat silently in the passenger seat, arms folded against her stomach. Her tension was obvious, but she was holding it together.

Linc pulled his cell from his pocket, glancing from the road and back as he tapped the screen until he found the number he was looking for. He needed to touch base with the sheriff. The guy may be an ass, but as local law enforcement, Linc had to work with him. Bland picked up, and Linc shared his theory about Lopez's connection to the cartel. He also let the sheriff know he and Mikayla wouldn't be back in. Bland blustered about needing a statement from Mikayla. Linc held the phone away from his ear at the stream of profanities when he told the sheriff that he would take her statement and send it to him. It took every ounce of his short supply of diplomacy not to tell Bland to pull his head out of his ass. Finishing the call, Linc handed his phone to Mikayla. "Plug this in for me."

She performed the task silently. Linc cast a glance at her and couldn't help his growing concern. Knife attack, ex murdered, either one would shake up the steadiest of individuals. She'd gotten past the initial shock of learning of the ex's death, and they'd talked at the diner, but now she'd withdrawn behind a wall of reserve that worried him.

A gust of wind buffeted the Jeep and Linc tightened his grip on the steering wheel. They drove out of the valley that sheltered the town of Concord, the highway taking them deeper into the mountains. Lightning forked across the sky and the leading edge of a rainstorm formed a dark wall heading their direction.

Miles later they finally crossed the bridge over the river where water rushed in a wild torrent. They took the turnoff to the campground just as the clouds let loose with a deluge. There were only a few other campers and the empty sites made the place look deserted. He wondered if the others had heard the forecast and taken off to avoid the inclement weather. He parked the Jeep at his site and sat back in his seat. "Might as well sit tight until the rain stops."

Mikayla nodded her agreement, looking silently out into the rain.

"You okay?"

"Yep, doing fine."

He turned to study her profile. Last night after the attack she hadn't reacted like he'd expected her to. No crying or hysterics for Mikayla O'Kane then, and there weren't any now.

Everyone needed to yell or cry at some point. Punching something was his go-to, if for nothing else than to vent some of the emotion. But she looked like she had her feelings locked tight.

Before the news about the ex there'd been a spark, an irresistible vitality about her he found incredibly appealing. Now that spark was gone. He had the urge to gather her up in his arms to comfort her, to hold her until she understood she was safe, that he wouldn't let anything happen to her. Christ, he had it bad.

Same as the day before, the rain pounded on the roof of the Jeep, but this time he felt more content with the Celtic goddess in the car with him. She stared out the window as the storm raged across the sky. Lightning streaked in an arc followed almost immediately by booming thunder that echoed down the canyon. As a nature show this one was spectacular, but he sure wasn't looking forward to crawling into his tent to spend the night in the mud. Once the storm passed, they might be more comfortable if they packed up and drove until they found a motel. And he'd feel safer with Mikayla under lock and key in a room he could defend.

"How were you shot?"

He looked over, startled. The furrow was back between her brows and she was staring at him with fierce concentration. How had she known? Then he remembered. That morning he'd come out of his tent without a shirt. Or pants.

After he'd all but grilled her over the past twenty-four hours, this was the first personal question she'd asked. She was probably looking for a distraction. He didn't want to talk about getting shot, but he thought he owed her something.

"My partner. He shot me."

"By accident?"

"No, he was definitely trying to kill me."

The furrow deepened. "That's really, really horrible."

"And yet that's an understatement. But I'm alive. The nurses kept saying I was lucky."

"Getting shot isn't lucky."

"That's what I told them. But I guess surviving is."

She nodded. After a long moment, she spoke again. "Why did he shoot you?"

"I'm still working that out." But after his conversation with Seth, he had more information. "My brother gave me an update. There was a woman involved, and Donny was always stupid about women."

"He shot you over a woman?"

"Not like you mean. The woman was apparently the catalyst and managed to lure him into a deal with some bad actors. He had gambling debts and they paid them. But that put Donny into a different kind of debt, a debt he thought he could pay by killing a witness we were protecting. Kill me and he could get away clean."

"But he didn't kill you."

"No, but only due to good timing from the Marshals Service."

"How bad was it?"

"Bad enough."

She studied him quietly. "I'll bet you're supposed to be taking it easy. Recuperating. And instead you ended up in a fight against a guy armed with a knife."

In the half-light of the storm, her eyes looked impossibly dark. He looked away before he did something stupid, something like pulling her into his arms. Finding out if kissing her would be as good as he thought it would be.

"Linc." His name said in that husky tone made him think she also felt the attraction.

"I'm recovered. Don't worry about me."

He couldn't deny that something had shifted. That somehow in twenty-four short hours she'd come uncomfortably close to becoming the focus of his world. Even arresting Donny had retreated in importance behind the need to protect the woman sitting next to him.

When she'd first arrived at the campground, she'd captivated him on all sorts of levels. The Celtic goddess looks were a hook, no doubt about that. Then he'd found the competence with which she'd set up her camp somehow sexy. Go figure on that one. But there had been something more elemental that had snagged his attention, and had sent him out on that trail looking for her when his gut told him she could be in trouble. He reminded himself she'd had a shitty day, and didn't need him adding to the upset, but he couldn't ignore the attraction, even if he couldn't act on it.

"Right now, my primary goal is keeping you safe." And he wouldn't compromise that goal by letting his emotions tangle him up.

She was quiet for a long moment, staring out the window. When she finally spoke, her voice gave nothing away. "The rain is letting up."

Like a faucet turning off, the rain stopped. A gusty wind scattered droplets of water from the tree branches and even as he watched, clouds scuttled across the sky to reveal patches of blue.

"Was your partner caught? Was he arrested?"

It was like that moment that had passed between them had never existed. He tried to convince himself it was for the best. "No. He's on the run."

"I can't see you not going after him."

"Got that right, but my boss said he'd kick my ass if I didn't give myself time to recuperate." He shrugged. "Got some thinking to do so I came out here to do it."

"And ended up neck deep in my mess."

He sighed, deciding she had the right to the information. "Our messes are connected. The witness I was protecting? He was in WITSEC because the Zecena cartel was after him."

"You're kidding."

"Not kidding. Your friend Paco? Joey was there when Paco Zecena ordered a rival tortured. When he ordered certain body parts men are very sensitive about carved up."

"Okay, that's disturbing. What about the other guy at Peter's house that night?"

"Haven't identified him, but likely one of his lieutenants."

They should get out of the Jeep before they lost all the daylight, but he sat there beside her, looking out through windows beginning to fog up. He gave himself a mental shake. "Look, if I'm right, this campground is the last location the cartel can tie you to. I want to pack up our gear and get out of here. We'll find a motel where we can spend the night and get an early start first thing in the morning. We'll head to the Marshals office in Salt Lake City. I'd feel safer if you were under Marshals' protection, and keeping you out of Southern California seems prudent right now."

He wondered what it said about his awareness of her that he sensed her opposition before she spoke.

"I don't want to go to Salt Lake City. What about Peter? His parents are dead. He only had a brother who lives in New Jersey and they weren't close. Who's going to make the arrangements to bury him? And my family is in California. They might have heard about Peter's death and they'll be worried about me." She clenched her fists tightly in her lap. "God, my mom. I hadn't even thought about what Peter being murdered will do to her. She's got...issues. This will be upsetting to her."

He'd reached for her hands, enfolding them in his, and found her fingers chilled. "Mikayla, your safety is more important than dealing with Wellington's burial arrangements. And your mother won't want you to risk going back to California if you could be in danger. You can call her using my cell when we get someplace where there's service and let her know you're safe." He brought her hands to his mouth, blowing softly to warm them. He paused when he realized what he was doing, his lips resting on her knuckles, his eyes looking straight into hers. Awareness zinged between them.

She hitched a breath. "Linc, I can't—"

"—do this. I know." He held onto her hands a moment longer before brushing a kiss over her knuckles and releasing her.

# Chapter Ten

Her hands were erogenous zones. Erogenous zones she'd only now discovered because they were only sensitive to one man's touch. Lincoln Jameson. The tingling sensations zipped all the way up her arms, bringing a tide of warmth with them. She no longer felt cold, that was for sure. Her cheeks felt flushed, and with the liquid warmth low in her belly she thought she'd better get out of the Jeep and away from him before she leaned over the center console to see how his lips would feel against hers. If the reaction to him brushing her knuckles with those lips was any indication, most likely she'd end up in an orgasmic puddle on the seat.

With a jerky motion she pulled open the door latch, breathing damp air deep into her lungs to help cool herself. The whir of a motor caught her attention and she saw Bob Weingartner pulling his electric golf cart to the side of the road. "Hey there, Mikayla."

The sun was beginning its descent over the western wall of the canyon, lighting up the remaining clouds in brilliant vermillion. Linc came around the Jeep to join her as the older man approached and dipped his head as a hello.

"Bob."

"Marshal. Hope you two are good to stay another night. Had a rockslide out on the highway about twenty minutes ago that blocked all lanes."

Linc shoved his hands in his pockets and rocked back on his heels. "Must have happened after we passed through. Any idea when it'll be cleared?"

"County crew is coming out, but it may be a while before they get here. This here's not the only place the storm caused some trouble, but I expect it'll be clear by morning. As it's the only road in or out, we're all staying put tonight."

Mikayla glanced at Linc then nodded to Mr. Weingartner. "We're fine, Bob. Thanks for the news."

They stood in silence as he drove off in his cart, making his rounds to the other remaining campers. Mikayla wondered what Linc was thinking. Whether that moment in the Jeep had affected him as much as it had her.

Odd that after only a day with him she felt connected to Linc in a way she never had with Peter. She and Peter had been engaged for nine months and they'd never had a conversation that got to who they really were. And that had been okay with her. She wondered if that was one of the things that had attracted Peter. While he hadn't pressed for any great understanding of her, she hadn't looked for that in him either. If she had, perhaps she would have known he was involved in something criminal.

With Linc she felt laid bare, as if he intuitively looked below the surface to really *see* her. There was something seductive about that intrinsic awareness. But reading people, assessing them, was probably part of his marshal training and there was nothing personal about it.

Then she remembered those warm lips on her fingers. She'd bet her last dollar that wasn't a technique found in the Marshals' handbook. She gave herself an internal shake. Being careful was second nature to her, and being careful meant she couldn't allow herself to tumble into an emotional entanglement when she'd just gotten herself out of one.

Regardless, the practicalities of camping demanded attention. Ignoring any feelings of awkwardness, she turned to Linc. "Look, I overpacked on food if you want to eat together."

"I'm going to owe you more than apples."

"Ha. You've been pulled into my mess, remember? You wouldn't have had to go into Concord today if you hadn't come to my rescue. I think the balance of debt is in your favor."

"You are not responsible for any of this. You don't owe me a thing."

She shrugged and moved toward the bear locker. Opening the latch, she swung open the door. Linc followed and at her direction pulled out the heavy ice chest to set on the end of the bench at the picnic table. While she set up the camp stove, he took a sponge and wiped rainwater off the plastic tablecloth and the benches, and set the lantern on the table. "What are you cooking?"

"Pasta with sliced sausage and vegetables. Sound good?"

"Sounds amazing, and a hell of a lot better than the freeze-dried mac and cheese packets I packed."

They worked side by side chopping mushrooms, zucchini, and onions. Mikayla tried not to let the intimacy of working together to prepare a meal affect her. Not that it was easy to ignore a guy with such an imposing physical presence. Or that she felt safe with him.

She'd prepared to protect herself by taking self-defense classes and keeping fit, and thought she'd passed the test when Lopez had attacked her. But a Mexican drug cartel brought the threat to a whole new level. Taking precautions to protect herself from someone breaking into her home in the middle of the night was a hell of a lot different from keeping safe from a highly organized, incredibly vicious, criminal organization.

Lincoln Jameson had the training and the disposition to handle that. And she hadn't missed that after Bob Weingartner had left, Linc had opened the rear door of the Jeep and a few minutes later was threading his belt through a holster, the black butt of a gun visible. He didn't make a big deal about it, but Marshal Jameson wasn't leaving their safety to chance.

Once the vegetables and sausage were sizzling and the pasta cooking, Linc went over to his campsite. Minutes later he returned, hands full. He set two bottles of beer on the table and a couple of candy bars next to them. Mikayla glanced at the bounty. "You brought Snickers? God bless you."

He flashed that lethal smile and Mikayla forced back a moan of appreciation. Having that smile directed at her felt like striking gold, a rare but heady experience. Reminding herself why she shouldn't dive in with Linc to see where things went, she turned back to the stove.

While Linc lit the lantern, she drained the pasta and drizzled on herbed olive oil. Giving Linc a heftier portion, she loaded their plates. Picking up a small grater, she topped the steaming meal with Romano cheese. Linc used the bottle opener on the beer and they sat across from each other at the picnic table.

"I like your way of camping better than mine."

"Camping doesn't have to mean freeze-dried food or sleeping on the ground."

"I guess not, though my brother would say that's not camping then."

"He'd be wrong." She paused. "Tell me about your family."

He hesitated, tapping a finger on the side of his bottle, and she wondered if he'd respond. But he did, his voice a low rumble. "We're solid. Seth's older than me by three years, and Ellie is younger by two. My stepdad is a stand-up guy. He flat out adores my mom and he's been a good dad to us. Mom, she's the center of it all. She keeps us grounded. Not counting her, we're all with the Marshals Service."

"All of you? Your stepdad, sister, and brother? You're all marshals?"

"Yeah."

"How did that happen?"

He was quiet for a long moment, took a sip of beer, and then spoke. "Influence of our stepdad. Arch Bollinger was in the Marshals Service and got assigned to my biological father's case. He'd gotten into some illegal shit and disappeared. The marshals have been tracking him ever since. Arch is as steady as they come and turned out to be a damn good role model for three shell-shocked kids."

"He fell for your mother while on the case?"

"Like a dozen loads of bricks. Even my highly stupid fourteen-year-old self could tell that he had it bad for her. Mom didn't pay attention. Dad's betrayal cut deep, but she wasn't as blindsided by what my dad had done as us kids were. She'd had suspicions he was up to something. I learned that later. But after what Dad did, she never wanted to be with anyone ever again. Didn't think she could trust a man."

"Your stepdad must have been persistent to end up married to her."

"The guy doesn't know the meaning of no. Arch would show up on a Sunday afternoon on some pretense about the case and end up playing football with us kids, or help one of us on whatever homework project we were working on. He'd stick around until he got himself invited to Sunday dinner. Then he started calling a couple of evenings a week, then every evening. He'd talk to whoever answered, ask about school or whatever sport we were playing at the time. But he'd always manage to end up talking to Mom. Sometimes for only a minute, but I could tell, we all could tell, Mom started looking forward to those calls. Took long enough, but eventually he wore her down and now they've been married over a dozen years."

"That's sweet. It's quite a testament to him that you and your siblings all joined the Marshals Service."

Plate cleared, Linc handed her a Snickers bar and unwrapped his own. "Yeah. There's also the issue with my dad. Marshals hunt fugitives and Dad is a fugitive. Any one of us would love to nail his ass."

"You're looking for him?" She bit in, savoring the chocolate and peanuts.

"His case is cold, but when we can, each one of us digs into whatever might give us a lead. We'll get him eventually." His gaze rested on her. "Thanks for the amazing meal, Mikayla."

"Quick and easy, but you're welcome."

She rose and filled a pan with water, setting it on the stove to heat for washing dishes. The storm had passed and most of the clouds had cleared away. The western sky glowed lavender against the encroaching night.

Linc found the basin and shot in a squirt of dish soap, and when she picked up a sponge, he took it from her, handing her a towel instead. "I'll wash."

"You don't have to do that."

"You fed me so the least I can do is help with the cleanup. You can dry."

She watched him scrub the pan, his sleeves pushed up past his elbows, muscles rippling along strong forearms dusted with black hair. The glow of the lantern showed his profile, the high forehead, the ridge of his nose, dark brows lowered as he concentrated on his task. The memory of his lips, warm against her knuckles, had her sucking in a careful breath. She wondered if she was the only one feeling off balance.

"Mikayla—"

Afraid he was reading her mind, she kept her head bent as she dried their plates.

"—you're still in danger, even if there is a rockslide."

Her breath left in a whoosh. Okay, right. She was in danger. "Ah, Bob said no one could get in or out. Seems like a bit of a reprieve."

He dunked the utensils in the sudsy water. "True, but someone could have come in before the slide, or hiked from Upper Falls like Lopez did. Zecena knows you're at this campground and that Lopez failed. He's going to try again, and this time he won't mess around sending a punk like Lopez."

"Well, that's wonderful news."

"I don't want you to be scared, I want you to be alert. There are two new campers in here tonight. I really can't see Zecena going to the trouble to send people disguised as campers, but it's possible."

"Okay, I'll keep an eye out."

"You'll do more than that. Remember I said you aren't leaving my side until I can get you into a safe house?"

"I don't want to go to a safe house."

He held up a damp hand. "We'll get to that later. But it's the not leaving my side part I'm talking about now. Your tent is big enough for both of us to sleep in."

"Excuse me?" After all those sexy thoughts about him, her reaction was knee-jerk. Warmth spread up her cheeks. "You're taking this whole thing too far. I'm not sleeping with you."

His gaze charged, an instant blaze of fire, but his tone remained neutral. "I'm not suggesting we share a sleeping bag. What I am saying is the best way for me to keep an eye on you is to be in that tent with you."

"I *don't* need you to keep an eye on me. I can keep an eye on myself. I've been doing it for a long time now."

"Don't make a big deal out of this. If it makes you any happier, I can say I don't need to keep an eye on you as much as keep an eye out for people who have their eye on you."

"That's semantics, and no."

"Christ almighty, Mikayla. Be logical. You're a witness against a really dangerous player in a Mexican cartel. They eat little girls like you for breakfast."

"I am logical and I'm not a little girl. And I refuse to live my life ruled by fear. Been there, done that."

He rinsed the last of the dishes and dried his hands. He faced her, hands on hips, brows lowered in a scowl. His movements looked carefully controlled, like he was using the moment to grab hold of his patience. Then she saw the flare in his eyes. Or maybe not.

"How about I take you into protective custody? I can do it, you know."

She set her jaw. "You can try."

He took a step toward her, leaning forward until they were nose to nose. "You don't think I could do that, sweetheart? You think because you've got attitude, you can push me back and I won't do my job?"

"I'm not your job."

"You are now. Even if you weren't mixed up with Paco Zecena, I'd still be looking out for you."

She fought the warmth his words brought. "I don't need your big, bad self looking out for me."

He reached out and took her chin between his thumb and fingers, angling her face up until her lips were nearly lined up with his.

"What are you going to do, big guy? Gonna take a shot at me?"

When his hot gaze settled on her mouth, she realized she'd made a tactical error. He raised his eyes, the want and the hunger laid bare.

Oh god, oh god, oh god. She wanted that, the heat, the desire that pulsed off him. She wanted him to beat aside all the barriers and kiss her so she would know what he felt like. How he tasted. Know if his lips, his tongue, were as fiery as her rebellious imagination suggested they would be.

He let go and took a decisive step back, arms crossing over his chest. The message came through loud and clear. He wasn't going there.

If it wouldn't be so obvious, she'd get something to fan her cheeks, which she knew were flushed. It was time to rectify the tactical error. "Look, I appreciate what you're doing for me but you're operating under some false assumptions here."

"Like what?"

"Like that I want Marshals' protection. Like I'm willing to go to Salt Lake City and into a safe house."

"What the hell are you talking about? You want to stay alive, don't you?"

"Sure. But I refuse to live my life under someone else's control. Like I said, I've done that before and I won't do it again."

"Care to explain?"

"No. It doesn't matter. I won't live my life closed off because I'm afraid, because someone tells me it'll be safer for me. Fear can become a cage."

He scrubbed his hands over his face, and the fatigue she could see in the gesture reminded her he was still recovering from being shot. "Look, we'll have to deal with the rest as it comes. But tonight I'm either sleeping in that tent with the promise that I'll be a good boy, or I sit all night in a chair right outside your doorway. Either way, I'm not letting anyone near you."

"Linc, you don't have to do this. You're supposed to be recovering from being shot, not guarding me."

"Do you think my job is all there is to this?" His voice was laced with exasperation.

"No, I know there's a connection to your partner who betrayed you, and that makes it personal."

"*You* make it personal, Mikayla. You may not want to hear it, but we've got more going on between us than your safety." With a frown pulling the lines of his face, he looked every inch the tired, frustrated male. "What's it going to be?"

His declaration set off a quivering reaction low in her belly that she had to force herself to ignore. She hated being maneuvered, but she had no doubt he'd do what he promised and spend the night parked outside her tent if she didn't agree. "Okay, fine. You can sleep in the tent. But if you snore, I'm kicking you out."

He turned and strode toward his campsite, she assumed to get his sleeping bag.

It was going to be a long night.

***

Linc lay on his back, listening to Mikayla's even breathing, the night so dark it made no difference if his eyes were open or shut. He hadn't anticipated the precise logistics of sleeping in her tent, and now understood at least some of her reluctance. The full-size air mattress took up most of the floor space, and what was left was occupied by a couple duffel bags of clothing. But while the setup might be fine for a woman sleeping alone, for two adults on the taller side it had its limitations. If he lay on his back, his feet hung off the end and his shoulders were wide enough it didn't leave Mikayla much room. And he liked sleeping on his back. She was a side sleeper and if he lay on his side facing her, they were nose to nose. Which meant nearly lips to lips. Not a good idea. So they'd started off back to back, each cocooned in their own sleeping bag, and neither one of them with enough space.

Two adults' body heat made the tent too warm. He wasn't used to sleeping in anything more than briefs, yet he'd pulled on a t-shirt and flannel pants. For her.

He'd fallen into an exhausted sleep only to wake a few minutes ago to find himself on his back, his sleeping bag and the blanket he'd brought over to cover them pushed to his waist.

Mikayla shifted and he felt her burrow closer. She'd pushed down her own bag enough that her arms were free and she lay curled into him, hair smelling like orange blossoms. Her hand rested on his chest and he covered it with his own. He hadn't planned to end up snuggled together like this, but he couldn't deny a feeling of coming home like he'd never known.

All he needed to do was ignore his body's hungry reaction. Telling himself that shifting away would only wake her, that she needed her sleep, he eased his arm around her shoulders and, pulling her closer, drifted back to sleep.

# Chapter Eleven

Linc sat in the camp chair, legs stretched in front of him and his head tilted back so he could view the last of the stars. The time was maybe half past five in the morning and the eastern sky held only the faintest hint of dawn. He'd awoken with Mikayla entwined in his arms, his face buried in her hair, and a morning erection that had left him aching. Forcing himself to let her go and crawl out of his sleeping bag had seemed prudent, if highly unsatisfying.

Desire had subsided to a level he could function with and now it was like a toothache, always there but in the background. While not a cure, a cup of coffee might make him feel at least somewhat human, but he knew fumbling around with the gear would wake Mikayla.

He gazed at the stars, collar pulled up, his hands deep in his pockets, and mulled over the realization that the discontent, the restlessness that had plagued him for...god, he didn't know how long, but certainly from before he'd been shot...had disappeared. That Mikayla appeared to be the catalyst for that peace should have been alarming, but in the calm of the morning it wasn't. He felt a renewed purpose. Finding Donny, destroying the cartel, was important, but not as vital as building a relationship with Mikayla.

A rustling from inside the tent followed by the zipper on the flap let him know she was up and around. She emerged wearing a hooded sweatshirt, the thin stretchy pants she'd slept in, and shearling boots on her feet.

She stepped out from under the awning into the early morning darkness, tilting her head back as he had. He looked up again. The vast expanse of the moonless sky stretched overhead. The Milky

Way, invisible at home because of city lights, glowed in a misty swath stretching into the universe.

"The stars are beautiful."

"Yeah. This is what people who never get out of the city can't understand." He kept his voice low because the predawn darkness seemed to call for quiet.

"And it's what keeps us coming back."

He couldn't shake the feeling of affinity, that they *got* each other.

She tugged the zipper of her sweatshirt higher and hunched her shoulders.

"Where's your coat?"

"At home in my closet."

"You're so organized, I'm surprised you didn't pack something warmer."

He caught her shrug in the faint light. "I didn't expect it to get so cold."

He got to his feet and crossed to the tent, reaching inside to grab the blanket. He stopped in front of her and wrapped the wool around her shoulders. "Sit down and get warm, I'll make the coffee."

***

Day broke with the sun rising in a cloudless sky. Birds chattered, swooping and chirping in the chill morning air. A jay perched on the wire handle of the lantern, tilted its head at Linc, then flew off with a noisy squawk. Mikayla had walked to the showers and Linc set about straightening the campsite in anticipation of packing up and leaving. He put the lantern in a plastic bin, snapping the lid in place. In the tent, he rolled his sleeping bag and folded the blanket before stowing both in the Jeep, then began the process of dismantling his own tent.

Mikayla had been quiet through breakfast. Sad, he thought. Probably missing the asshole boyfriend. She'd made pancakes. He knew they were for him as she'd hardly eaten any, and the leftovers lay stacked on a paper plate, covered with foil.

He'd help her pack her gear, get them ready to head out. He felt antsy. He wanted to get on the road, far away from any place where Zecena knew to look for her. He hadn't been kidding about her staying close to his side, and with two vehicles, even if she followed him to Salt Lake City in her Subaru, that wasn't close enough by a long shot. He hoped she'd see the sense in his plan for her car, but he had a feeling he was in for some serious resistance.

The sound of a vehicle broke the quiet and Linc watched a dark pickup turn from the highway into the campground. That meant the road was clear for traffic to get through. They'd be able to leave, but Zecena's crew could also get in.

Mikayla trudged up from the showers. The black leggings she wore tucked into boots made her legs look a mile long. She'd done something to her hair. Instead of the curly mass, she'd twisted it into a pretty braid that left a few curls loose to frame her face. He was starting to get that he liked her looks no matter what she was wearing or how her hair was done.

"Let me take a look at your shoulder."

"It's fine."

"I need to check, make sure there's no infection."

She gave him a look that was difficult to decipher but turned around. Holding the front across her breasts, she hitched up the back of her loose-knit top. He helped ease it up far enough to reveal the wound. He tried to ignore the smooth expanse of skin across her back, the column of her spine, and that she wasn't wearing a bra.

As if reading his mind, she said, "My bra strap was making it sore."

"Right." While she held up her top, he examined the injury. She'd taken off the gauze bandage and while the butterflies were peeling a little around the edges, they still held, and the wound looked healthily pink.

"I'll check it again this evening, but it looks good for now." He let her shirt drop and stepped back. She picked up the French press and poured the last of the coffee into her mug. Linc glanced up when he saw the pickup he'd spotted earlier rounding the bend in the road and come to a stop next to Mikayla's Subaru. The muscles in his shoulders tightened and he moved in front of her.

First thing that morning he'd belted on his Glock .40 caliber, and tucked an extra clip in his back pocket. Securing his marshal's star to his belt had felt as normal as tying his shoelaces. He hadn't really expected trouble to simply drive up and park, but he wasn't taking any chances. He put a hand on Mikayla's arm to keep her behind him as a tall form stepped out of the truck.

"Stay back."

She shifted to look around his shoulder.

"Damn it, Mikayla, let me—"

She surged past him. "Brady!"

He tried to grab her but she was fast. She ran toward the man, leaping forward to launch herself at him. The guy opened his arms to catch her, wrapping her in a tight embrace.

A friend. Not a threat. Irritation rippled through Linc. He'd awoken with her in his arms, and that following an intense couple of days together. All in all, he was feeling more than a little proprietary. Linc moved forward when the guy held on for too long before releasing her.

She kept her hands on his shoulders, a big grin bringing out her dimple. "What are you doing here?"

"Aren't you glad to see me?"

"Yes, always." Her smile dimmed. "But not if you're checking up on me. What's going on? Why are you here?"

Linc moved to stand squarely in the guy's line of sight and had the pleasure of seeing him narrow his eyes.

"Who the hell are you?"

Linc smiled at the tone. "I could ask the same of you, pal." The guy was tall with a rangy build. Linc shifted his gaze from the man to Mikayla, then back again. Now that he got a good look, he could see a resemblance. Hair of the same shade somewhere between dark red and brown, and the same slightly almond-shaped eyes, though Mikayla's were a deeper, darker green.

"Brady, this is Lincoln Jameson. He's camping in the site across the road from me. Linc, this is my brother, Brady O'Kane."

Her brother. Linc felt some of his tension ease. A brother was good. A potential ally, one more person to help protect Mikayla. He was wearing an unzipped navy blue jacket with a familiar patch on the shoulder and "O'Kane" stitched on the front. Linc stuck out his hand, and after a moment's hesitation, Brady offered his and the men shook.

"Brady, what's going on?"

"Look, Mike, we need to talk."

"What is it?" She grabbed her brother's arm. "Is it Mom? Or Penny? Is everyone okay?"

"The family is fine."

Linc saw it then. Brady had come to give his sister bad news, and he'd bet his marshal's badge he knew what it was. In the excitement of seeing her brother, Mikayla seemed to have forgotten about Wellington. He saw her face fall the instant realization dawned.

"I already know about Peter."

Brady ran a hand through his hair. "Shit. Sorry, sis. I told people not to contact you. I didn't want you to find out in a text."

"You drove all the way up here to tell me in person?"

"Yeah."

Mikayla went up on her tiptoes and kissed his cheek. "Thank you. I didn't hear it through a text. Linc told me." Brady's gaze cut to him, and Linc saw it snag at the badge on his belt.

"That's a marshal's star. You're a US Marshal?" He turned to his sister. "You're camping with a marshal?"

"We're not camping together, or at least hadn't been. We were camping in the same campground and Linc kind of got drawn into a mess. My mess."

Brady studied Linc. "You'd better explain what's going on."

"Don't go getting all big brother on me, Brady. *I'll* tell you what's going on."

He flicked a glance at his sister. "First, your fiancé was murdered so you're going to have to deal with me being concerned. And second, if *you* tell me what's going on, you'll try to make whatever it is seem less important so I don't worry about you." He jerked a thumb toward Linc. "He won't bullshit me."

"You can be supremely annoying, you know that?"

"But you love me anyway."

"Lucky for you."

Linc watched the byplay, and since it wasn't so different from what he experienced with his siblings, he understood they'd gotten to the stage where they could talk. "You want coffee?" At Brady's nod, he filled a pot with water and set it on the stove.

"Did you drive through the night?" Mikayla stacked the leftover pancakes in a pan on the stove, put the foil over them, and turned it on low.

"No. I stayed in a motel in St. George, then headed out around four this morning. I wanted to get here early since I didn't know how long you were staying at this campground. I didn't want to miss you and have to chase you all over the state."

Mikayla rummaged in the plastic bin and withdrew the syrup while Linc spooned coffee into the French press.

Linc nodded to indicate the patch. "You're with Cal Fire?"

"Yeah. Stationed in Julian."

"He's a captain. We're so proud." Mikayla batted her eyelashes at her brother as she set a plate of warmed pancakes on the table.

"Cut it out." He grabbed a fork and sat. "Thanks, Mike."

Swallowing a mouthful of syrupy pancake, he directed his attention to Linc. "What's a US Marshal doing with my sister?"

"Linc's not *with* me. I told you that." She sat in a camp chair and propped her feet on the bench.

"Then how come there's only one tent and he knows his way around your things?"

"That's none of your business."

"It is my business. *You're* my business, so tell me straight."

"Brady O'Kane, I swear I'll smother you in your sleep if you keep this up."

Linc brought the coffeepot and three mugs to the table. "Your sister was attacked by a guy with a knife, and there's reason to believe he was sent by the men who murdered Peter Wellington."

Brady jerked his head around to stare at his sister. Mikayla leaned her head against the back of her chair and closed her eyes. "Now you've done it."

"Were you hurt?"

"Some bruises. A nick on the back of my shoulder with the knife. I bloodied his nose."

"Jesus, Mike."

Linc sat at the table while the brother demolished the leftover pancakes. As Brady ate, Linc related the events of the past two days, from the attack on the trail, to the visit to the sheriff's office, and finally what he'd learned from Seth about Wellington. Brady's attention didn't waver for a second.

"So the bastard who attacked her has been arrested."

"He's in custody, and bail has been set at one hundred thousand dollars. But I don't think Lopez is too anxious to get out since he failed at his job. He might be safer in jail."

Brady narrowed his eyes. "His job was to kill my sister?"

"That's what I'm thinking. Mikayla is a material witness who can place a member of the Zecena cartel at Wellington's home shortly before his murder."

"What the fuck?"

Mikayla drew her knees up, wrapping her arms around her legs, and buried her face. Her voice sounded muffled when she spoke. "I didn't see him get killed. But I was at his house before he was killed, and I saw the two men Linc thinks did it. I'm a witness."

"And the guy who attacked her was sent by them?"

Linc nodded. "That's my guess." He eyed Mikayla and the feeling that she was his returned with force. He needed to remind himself that days before, she'd been engaged to be married to another man.

"And what was a US Marshal doing on a hiking trail at exactly the time my sister was attacked? Not that I'm complaining."

"Your sister was handling herself pretty well, but a knife changes the odds a bit."

Mikayla lifted her head. "If you hadn't done that flying kick thing, I was going to get him to lunge at me and try to use his momentum to push him into the river."

"Jesus, you don't think he might have taken you with him? Or taken a slice out of you on the way? You should have run." The memory of Mikayla tangling with Lopez still made Linc's blood run cold.

Brady gaze tracked between Linc and Mikayla before repeating his question. "And why were you on the trail?"

"I'm on leave. Supposed to be recovering from an injury. I saw Mikayla head out for a hike, and then Lopez taking the same trail ten minutes later. He looked suspicious, out of place."

"I see. You were watching her, got concerned when this guy took the same trail, and followed him to make sure she was okay?"

Shit, it made it sound like he was interested in more than her safety. Which he was, but still. "Yeah, pretty much."

Brady stared at him, eyes narrowed. Then he grunted, seeming to come to some conclusion. "Good." He rose to put the paper plate from his breakfast in the garbage bag. "What's the plan?"

"The Marshals Service wants to place Mikayla in witness protection, at least until Paco Zecena is arrested and brought to trial."

"Who is Paco Zecena?"

"He's boss of the Southern California arm of the Zecena cartel, and brother of *El Jefe* in Mexico. Zecena's MO is to let others do the dirty work, so the most likely scenario is that the guy your sister saw with him that night killed Wellington on Zecena's orders. But he was there and that's huge. For years the marshals and the FBI have been trying to get something we can pin on Paco Zecena. This is the best break we've had."

"And you're fucked if you think you can use my sister to get that asshole."

"We're not using her. We'll protect her and make sure justice is done. She was there that night and can place Zecena at Wellington's house minutes before his murder. With her testimony, we'll nail this bastard."

"Son of a bitch." Brady muttered the oath under his breath. "You're saying witness protection would keep her safe until this Zecena character is behind bars."

"That's the idea."

"I don't want to go into witness protection. I have a job, among other things. I don't want to put my life on hold for months." Mikayla's jaw took on a stubborn set.

"Or longer."

"I can't be imprisoned in a house, doing nothing, for 'longer.' No way. I'm not going through that again."

"If that's what needs to be done to keep you safe, Mike, that's what you'll do." Brady addressed Linc. "What does this mean for my sister?"

"It's not happening, Brady. Linc is delusional."

Linc ignored the comment but wondered what she'd meant by "going through that again." He answered Brady. "It means she gets protection from the Marshals Service with a minimum of two deputies, twenty-four hours a day, at a safe house."

Brady drummed his fingers on his knees and Linc figured he knew what Brady was thinking. If it had been Ellie, Linc wouldn't be trusting that some stranger could protect her as well as he could.

Mikayla slumped back in her chair, letting her feet drop. She'd been through a rough couple of days. She'd recovered some of the color in her cheeks, but her eyes held the hollowed-out look of someone dealing with trauma. Despite that, he was pretty sure she wasn't going down without a fight.

Sure enough, she held up her hand like a traffic cop to stop the conversation. "Look, as much as I appreciate two alpha men trying to figure out how best to protect me, I have a say in what happens to me."

"Not if it means you're unreasonable about it."

"You know what you can do with reasonable, don't you, Brady?" She smiled sweetly at her brother.

Linc had to hand it to the guy, Brady jumped in with both feet. Better he got his balls busted because no matter what she said, Linc would make sure Mikayla was under marshals' protection.

"How about you chill and realize you don't always get your way." When she opened her mouth with what Linc was sure to be a pithy comeback, Brady held up his hand. "I can always play my trump card, little sister."

She narrowed her eyes. "You wouldn't dare."

"Don't test me."

They stared at each other for a loaded moment. Mikayla finally leaned back in her seat, apparently resigned. "You fight dirty."

"I'll do whatever it takes to keep you safe." Apparently satisfied he had her acquiescence, Brady nodded at Linc. "Let's hear what the marshal has to say."

Linc had to guess that Mikayla was feeling confined, but at the moment it couldn't be helped. "It's too dangerous for Mikayla back in California. Makes it too easy for the cartel. I want her to come with me to Salt Lake City. There's a Marshals district office there and we'll find her a safe place until I can locate Zecena."

# Chapter Twelve

Mikayla gazed out the window at the incredible scenery. Fragmented red rock formations flew by, accented by the vibrant grays and greens of spruce and juniper trees. A pair of hawks circled high above in a sky of the deepest cerulean blue. If she didn't have her teaching job in California, she'd absolutely consider moving to Utah.

She drummed her fingers on her knee. The morning hadn't gone quite like she'd hoped.

Linc had insisted she ride with him to Salt Lake City. Their argument rang in her ears, her contending she could safely follow in her car, her brother and Linc "informing" her their way was best. With the two men double-teaming her, she hadn't stood a chance.

Before they left the campgrounds, Ranger Smallcanyon had come by and Linc had used his radio to contact the sheriff. The upshot: two deputies would come to the campsite and one would drive her car to a county storage yard.

So now here she was, heading north through Utah with Marshal Jameson. And talk about déjà vu. She was thirteen again when everyone worried about her and curtailed her freedom with iron bars of love and fear. At least that was the case when it came to Brady. With Linc, she wasn't entirely sure of his motivation. Duty, certainly, but he'd acknowledged there was *something* between them. So maybe she wasn't the only one experiencing those charged moments of attraction.

Regardless, the result was the same. She would be put in a safe house and have people hovering around her to keep her secure. Her career? Her independence? According to her brother, not as important as her safety. She wasn't stupid, and she was far from reckless. But what kind of life was she going to have even if Paco and his henchmen got locked up? It wasn't as if the cartels would dry up and go away.

Brady had agreed to the "plan" because he'd clicked with Linc. They were alike in many ways, men who shouldered responsibility easily and met problems head on. Added to that, both had a protective streak a mile wide. And despite having met like ten minutes ago, they were twins who spoke their own language, both instinctively understanding and accepting the other's opinion. Mikayla knew Brady would never have left her to return to California if he didn't trust Linc to keep her safe.

Linc's phone rang out a few bars of David Bowie's "Space Oddity." He put it to his ear, keeping one hand on the steering wheel.

"El." Even if the customized ringtone wasn't enough of an indication that the caller was someone close to him, the warm tone of his voice made it clear. El. Ellie. Linc's sister, another US Marshal.

Mikayla watched his expression turn from keen to flat. "The cell reception is spotty out here so tell me what you've found straight out." He listened for several long minutes. "Have you told Arch and Seth? Mom?" After a beat of silence, he said, "Okay, let me think on it. Seth's going to want to put together a team and go after him, and I want in on it. But we need more information before we move. We can't afford to rush it and make a mistake."

He listened for a few more minutes, then finished the call, putting the phone in a cup holder. His knuckles whitened as he gripped the steering wheel.

"Bad news?"

He was quiet for so long she thought he was going to let the words drop between them like foundation blocks for a wall. Then he sighed and scrubbed his face with one hand. "That was my sister. She got a lead on a case."

"A fairly personal case, I take it."

"Yeah."

He drove and the miles flew by outside the window. Finally, it seemed like he made a conscious effort to loosen his hold on the steering wheel. "My sister says she has a lead on where our father is."

"Your father? That's big, isn't it?"

"You could say that."

"That means you'll be going after him?"

His gaze cut to hers. "Not until I know you're safe and Zecena is behind bars."

They drove in silence and Mikayla could feel the tension radiating off him. They came to a crossroads where two highways intersected and Linc pulled the Jeep up to a service station. He pumped gas and Mikayla cleaned the windshield before heading to the restroom. She returned to the Jeep and Linc came out of the market. He handed her a cup with a lid. She took a sip, and found he'd added the sweetener she liked.

They were on the road before Linc spoke again. "What happened to you that made your family so protective of you?"

She cast him a startled gaze. "Brady has always been protective."

"Maybe, but something happened to you."

She shrugged, gazing intently out the window. They passed through a small town, not much more than a scattering of houses with battered pickups in dirt driveways and weatherworn fences penning cattle and horses. A boy chased a chicken in a front yard under a tall pine tree.

"Mikayla."

"It doesn't have anything to do with this."

"I think it does."

"That was over and done with years ago. Not relevant."

"Whatever happened then colors how you act now."

"Are we talking about me, or you?" The only indication he'd heard her was the whitening of his knuckles again on the steering wheel. She let her head fall back on the headrest. He was right, but she hated thinking that that one single event continued to have such an effect on her life. And knew she was lying to herself and Linc if she denied it. "Someone broke into our house when we were kids."

He turned to look at her, eyes hidden behind the mirrored aviator shades. "Were you hurt?"

"Terrified, but not physically hurt. Brady thinks he should have known it was going to happen and should have taken steps to prevent it. He blames himself."

He returned his gaze to the road ahead, but she could feel his heightened attention.

"Tell me what happened."

She'd had enough therapy that the memories no longer paralyzed her, but that didn't mean she liked talking about it. That one night had marked a turning point in her life. Her childhood ending as abruptly as if it had been hacked in two with a rusty blade.

Mikayla closed her eyes and once again the still-vivid images played across her consciousness.

*The night dark with heavy clouds, the sound of thunder in the distance, then the quiet hushing sound of summer rain. Waking to the sudden realization that someone was in her bedroom, then the terror of hands groping under her summer-light nightgown. Kicking, screaming, then biting down hard on the rough hand that clamped over her mouth.*

She could sense Linc waiting, not pushing, but somehow insistent nonetheless. Something about him made her want to explain. His patience, the way he had of really listening. He could sort through the extraneous to get to the heart of what was important.

She opened her eyes to look out the window rather than at the man sitting beside her. "It happened when I was thirteen. I was attacked in my bed in the middle of the night."

"Sexually assaulted?"

"Attempted. I woke up with him in my room, his hands on me. I fought and screamed. My dad charged in with Brady." Saying what happened next was the hard part and she was quiet, trying to gather her thoughts. A turnout appeared in the road up ahead and Linc eased the vehicle over and pulled to a stop. He turned off the engine and, after taking off his sunglasses, shifted in his seat to face her. He didn't say a word, simply waiting for her to continue.

"They fought. My dad and the guy. His name was Greg Saunders. He was naked, and high on drugs. He was twenty-two and lived next door. I didn't know him, had never spoken to him. But apparently he'd been watching me. Brady'd had words with him one time after he caught the guy watching me with binoculars when I was swimming in the pool."

She took a deep breath. "Saunders and Dad fought. Brady grabbed my softball bat, but he couldn't get a clear hit. Next thing I know Dad lost his balance and fell backward through the window. My bedroom was on the second story and had these big windows. Dad fell right through and took Saunders with him."

She leaned back in her seat, staring blankly out the window. "My dad was killed. They said he hit his head. Saunders landed on some patio furniture and broke his back. He's a paraplegic and still in prison."

"Christ. Jesus Christ, Mikayla. I'm sorry." Linc's warm hand closed over hers. She shouldn't have been surprised. Every time he thought something upset her, he took her hand. She wondered if that was Marshal Training 101. Lesson one on how to comfort a female witness: hold her hand.

For some reason, it worked for her. She cleared her throat and resisted the temptation to lace her fingers with his and hold on tight. "Ever since that night, Brady has felt he has to look out for me. He was only seventeen, but he's the one who's held our family together."

"So he drives hundreds of miles to tell you your ex is dead."

"Yeah."

"Any other siblings?"

"My sister. She was away at college at the time. Penny's the oldest and always did exactly what my parents wanted. She was the obedient, no-trouble child, and now she's married to the steadiest man you can imagine and seems perfectly content. It's a comfort to my mother not to have to worry about her."

"How did she deal? Your mom."

Mikayla stared at her hand resting in Linc's, his thumb rubbing over her knuckles. "Mom has issues. Mental health issues. She was likely neurotic before, but that night magnified the condition. Her response was to circle the wagons, to keep us locked up behind dead bolts and alarm systems. We moved to a gated, patrolled community. She married again and my step-father treats her like a porcelain doll."

"She was Brady's trump card, right? You don't want to worry her, but he'd tell her if that's what it took to get you to cooperate."

She didn't know why his perceptiveness surprised her. "Yeah. The jerk."

"I'd do the same if it was my sister." He raised a hand to stop what would be a hot response. "All I'm saying is that I get your brother. Does your mom feel safe now?"

"Maybe physically. Plus, having a man in the house helps. But it doesn't take much to shake that faith. And with Brady being in the fire department, there's always the potential that something could happen to him."

"What about with you?"

"The way I live is difficult for Mom." She hitched her shoulder and gazed at the wide vista spreading across a valley. Huge rolls of hay dotted the fields and a red barn stood out as a splash of color in the distance.

"Saunders had gotten into my room that night because I'd left one of my windows open. I loved sleeping with the night air coming in. For five years after Dad died, Mom kept me pretty much caged in. Everything I did made her afraid. I couldn't go out with friends, to the beach, or hiking in the mountains because she was sure something would happen and I would die.

"Getting my driver's license about sent her into a coma. The one thing she did allow me to do was take nearly every self-defense class known to man. I finally escaped when I went to college. Brady joining the fire department was a big deal, too. When he told Mom and she freaked, he calmly explained that this was what he was doing, that he'd be as safe as he could be, and he'd call daily to let her know he was okay. And he does. I think she boxes worry for Brady into a corner of her mind and doesn't allow herself to think about it. But she also trusts Brady. He's always cool and levelheaded. She doesn't trust me. I left the window open."

"That's tough on a kid. How did you survive?"

"By taking a page from Brady's playbook. After I graduated with my BA, Mom wanted me to move home, find a guy, get married. The richer the guy the better, because if he was rich, I too could live in a gated community where there's zero crime. But I wanted to pursue my PhD so I applied to grad school on the other side of the country."

"To get away from her?"

"That's not the only reason, but yeah. I had to breathe."

"Where'd you end up?"

"Columbia University. I loved living in New York, but Mom was a wreck and began obsessing over crime statistics. It helped when she met Arthur, who became my stepfather. He's a good guy and understands that I need to live my life separate from my mother. He's skilled at distracting her. But since I've moved back to California, she's made it her life's work to find me a wealthy husband."

She gave a self-deprecating laugh. "It's funny looking back on it now. A bonus with Peter had been that he was someone my mother would approve of, and I'd found him myself. I kept our relationship quiet at first because I knew she would be over the top about how perfect he was for me, and honestly, I didn't want to deal with all the fuss. Then I found out that, with his collusion, she'd actually arranged for him to be at the event where I was helping my friend."

Linc studied their joined hands. "Let's stretch our legs." He released her fingers, and after grabbing his phone, opened the door of the Jeep.

They stepped out into the brisk breeze, and Mikayla pulled up the zipper of her jacket. She walked to the guardrail. The recent storm had brought a dusting of snow to mountain peaks far in the distance. Closer, brown and white cattle grazed quietly in a scene she thought hadn't changed much in a hundred years. The chill in the air had her burying her hands deep in her pockets.

Linc came to stand beside her. "Do you love the outdoors because it gets you out of the cage your mother put you in after you were attacked?"

She turned to look at him, and found the directness of his gaze disconcerting, that and his ability to understand her. "You're pretty insightful."

"Goes with the job. And I'd guess your opposition to WITSEC is the same. You don't want to be confined."

She shrugged, the wind tugging her hair out of its braid. His dark hair ruffled in the breeze, and the black stubble on his chin only added to the tough-guy look. She had the nearly uncontrollable urge to walk into his arms to see if they'd wrap around her.

"Look, Mikayla, I—"

His phone pinged. That one little sound and the world came crashing back. They were no longer two people alone in the vastness of the open plain. He sighed and pulled the phone out of his pocket, stared at the message, his expression turning blank.

"Anything wrong?"

He tapped the screen, then shoved the phone in his pocket. "Nothing. Let's go."

"Linc."

"Come on, Mikayla. I need to get you someplace safe."

"And then what? You'll leave?"

"Once you're safe I can go after Zecena."

"And your partner."

He was rounding the hood of the Jeep and he checked his movement. "What makes you say that?"

She frowned. "Because he tried to kill you. I think you must be monumentally pissed and want to find him. And then there's the issue with your father. You've got a lot on your plate."

"Yeah."

"Stashing me in a safe house frees you up."

"It's not like that."

"It's exactly like that. Once I'm out of the way, you can get back to work."

She opened the vehicle door and slid into the seat. She didn't know what had her temper simmering under the surface. What had he been about to say? Was she hoping for some sort of declaration that she meant more to him than finding a killer?

Getting close to people probably happened any time he was on a protection detail. She'd bet he'd been on dozens of cases where his job was to safeguard someone in danger. Getting close was bound to happen. Put people together for an extended period and bonds formed. Add to that her and Linc's intense first encounter. He'd fought for her and likely saved her life. That certainly jumped the level of connection up a few notches. Barriers had broken down more quickly than might normally be the case.

She couldn't allow herself to read any more into their relationship.

They bumped over the verge and back onto the smooth highway, Linc shifting through the gears with controlled precision. His shades were back on, hiding his eyes. Whatever had been in that text, he wasn't sharing.

Mikayla resumed her study of the wide panorama of mountain, valley, and sky, her mind racing ahead to how she was going to keep herself out of witness protection.

# Chapter Thirteen

**"Looking for me?"**

Three words in a text and Linc was thrown back to the muzzle flash of Donny's gun, and the incredible pressure of the bullet ripping through his chest.

No caller ID, only a phone number with an area code Linc didn't recognize. Probably a burner phone tossed two ticks after the text was sent. Linc knew it was Donny as sure as he knew his own reflection.

Donny's betrayal had cut deep. There had always been something about their relationship that had bothered him. He'd thought they'd been friends, but every now and then there'd been a look in Donny's eyes, edgy and calculating, as if he wasn't fully there, totally on the job. Now Linc knew he should have looked deeper, not accepted Donny's loyalty as a given. That was on him.

After the shooting, Donny had run, and Linc had learned that idiot Joey Medrano had breached security and contacted someone in the Zecena organization. The Marshals Service had never lost a witness who had followed the rules, and Joey Medrano hadn't followed the rules. Linc wasn't going to wear the mark of being of the first marshal to lose a witness who'd done everything right.

Driving with one hand on the steering wheel, he wondered how Donny planned to stay alive. If the marshals found him, and damn, they were looking, he could flip to save his skin and testify against the cartel. Paco Zecena knew this, and sure as shit had his own men out hunting Donny.

Linc wondered if the woman who'd lured Donny in, who'd introduced him to the cartel as a way to pay his gambling debts, had bothered to stick around after he'd done the job. Linc guessed not. Donny had shit poor luck with women.

But that text. Donny was baiting him. It might make Linc wish he could break the guy's face, but it was also the first clue they'd gotten.

Had taunting Linc been Donny's only motivation? Why else would he have contacted him? Donny wasn't stupid. Contact was asking for attention. It meant leaving a trace with the potential of locating him. Why the hell would Donny take that risk?

Linc pressed on the gas pedal as the highway leveled out to cross an expanse of open range. He glanced at Mikayla and felt the now-familiar pull of an attraction that was amping up into something a lot deeper.

The sunlight slanting through the window highlighted the red in her hair, giving her a fiery aura, but he didn't miss the shadows under her eyes. His job was to keep her safe, and he'd do that. And that required him to keep a lid on the attraction. Getting personally involved meant lost objectivity. He'd get her safely stashed and go after Zecena.

And she was right that he wanted to go after Donny.

When the job was done, he'd come back for Mikayla.

For the first time ever, and to his surprise, he found himself contemplating forever with a woman.

\*\*\*

Mikayla blinked open her eyes to find that while she'd slept they'd entered what she assumed was Salt Lake City. Linc had parked in a near-empty lot next to a restaurant. A fortress-like, multistory structure stood across the street. An older building with classic architecture nearby shared the same city block. She turned her head to find Linc tapping on his phone, dark hair falling across his forehead. Why this one man appealed to her on so many levels, she didn't know. He lifted his eyes and their gazes locked for a long-drawn-out minute.

She cleared her throat. "Where are we?"

"Federal courthouse in Salt Lake City. The Marshals office is in the new courthouse." He indicated the building with a nod of his head.

A feeling of dread fell over her like an oppressive cloak. They were going through with it. Linc would see that she was placed in witness protection. She'd be locked in a prison until Paco Zecena was apprehended and put on trial.

Even then, she might still be in danger. She didn't think it was beyond the realm of possibility for Zecena to retaliate against her from inside a federal penitentiary. And if he wasn't convicted, the threat was even more dire. She pushed back on the urge to jump out of the vehicle and run as fast and far as she could.

Linc opened his door and got out. Mikayla moved more slowly. She stepped out into the chilly afternoon, shutting the door of the Jeep and leaning back against it, arms folded. "I don't want to do this, Linc. If I go in there, my life won't be my own."

He crossed the pavement to stand in front of her, brows lowered in a frown. "You don't want to go into WITSEC. I get that. But it's the only way. I want you safe."

She didn't move, instead tilting back her head and staring into the deep blue sky. Running to the store for milk, going for a sunrise walk, the little freedoms normal people never had to think about wouldn't be allowed. She was supposed to teach a class on Cold War America next semester. "I don't want to do it."

"WITSEC is the safest option." Frustration tinged his voice. "You'll be someplace safe until you can testify."

"Paco Zecena isn't even in custody. You might never catch him. I don't want to put my life on hold forever."

"At least you'll have a life, Mikayla. Don't underestimate these guys. Zecena is one of the cartel's top operators. His brother is the cartel chief in Mexico, and they'll throw everything they have into protecting him. You think you'll be safe but you never will. If you testify against Zecena, then he's out of commission. And we'll bring down his organization with him. This is our chance to cripple the Zecena cartel. But we need you alive to do that."

"You can't use me as a tool to get at the cartel."

"Damn it. I'm not using you as a tool." He paced away from her, then back again. "Do you think that's all we've had these past few days?"

"I don't really know."

His eyes blazed. "We have more than that. You know we do."

"I don't know anything of the sort. You're all about the job." She didn't know why she was goading him.

"My first priority is protecting you."

"I can take care of myself."

"Christ, Mikayla." He reached out and gripped her shoulders, the movement of his thumbs brushing along her neck in direct opposition to the hard expression on his face. "These guys aren't amateurs. They use torture and murder to settle disputes."

"I don't want to be put in a cage."

He yanked her to him. She thought he would shake her, but instead long fingers slid into her hair to cradle her head. Frustration, anger, heat, all flashed in his eyes. She gripped his arms as he held her like that for a long moment. As she felt the hot flames of desire racing along skin already sensitized to his touch, he dipped his head.

Firm lips seared across hers and Mikayla felt the burn like a flash-fire. His taste, his smell, the *feel* of him, overstimulated her senses. Desire flared, more intense than she'd ever felt. His fingers stroked her scalp, as warm lips parted hers.

His tongue swept past her lips to tangle with hers, charging a jolt of pure pleasure through her body. Gripping the waistband of his jeans, she pulled him closer, rising on tiptoes to meet the kiss. The knotted emotions of the past few days surged through her, exploding in a hot fireball of longing. He broke the kiss to brush his lips across her jaw and then back to the corner of her mouth, before easing back to create a few scant inches between them.

Their gazes met and held. "That wasn't supposed to happen."

"It doesn't change anything, Linc." She forced the words past the tumult of emotions.

"It sure as hell does. I'm not exactly sure what, but you mean something to me."

"That doesn't give you the right to dictate what I do."

"Mikayla, you're going into WITSEC if I have to strap you into a straitjacket to do it."

She wondered if he realized that his hands were still on her face, a thumb stroking along her cheekbone, even as he threatened her. It was hard to resist his conviction that he knew what was best, that she would be safe and everything would turn out fine if she simply followed his rules.

Confusion seemed to be the mental state of the day. He may have kissed her out of frustration, but her own reaction had been revealing. And alarming. He had turned her world upside down with that kiss, brought out raw and edgy emotions she'd never experienced before.

He bent his head forward, eyes hot and urgent as he dropped his hands from her face to entwine his fingers with hers. "Trust me, Mikayla." Slowly, he released her, the warmth that had lit his eyes now banked behind a wall of determination. "They're waiting for us. Let's go."

With a sigh of utter dejection, she walked with him toward the doors at the front of the fortress-like building. The Marshals Service would put her in witness protection, but it might as well be prison. The cartel could be after her, and objectively she knew WITSEC was for her own safety, but she couldn't help feeling like steel doors were locking behind her.

Linc showed his badge and credentials to the armed security guard, who waved them past without having to go through the screening process. They walked down a short hall, then Linc ushered her into the elevator with a hand at her back. He moved it to her shoulder as the car rose and she wondered if he was worried she would bolt.

They stepped off the elevator and through glass doors marked US Marshals Office, District of Utah. A couple of men stood talking in the lobby. The taller of the two, a man with a rangy build wearing a marshal's badge on his belt like Linc, stopped speaking when he saw them. Nodding to the other man, he said, "I'll catch up with you later, Jess."

Linc strode up to him. They shook hands, and the rangy marshal gripped him on the shoulder.

"Glad you came," Linc said.

"Never even a question about that."

Linc turned to Mikayla and beckoned her forward. "Mikayla, this is my brother, Seth. Seth, this is Mikayla O'Kane."

Seth Jameson held out his hand and Mikayla saw the familial resemblance. Both men were well over six foot, though Linc's body type was more muscular while Seth's was long and lean. She shook the hand he held out.

"I'm sorry about the loss of your fiancé, Ms. O'Kane."

"Ex-fiancé," Linc growled.

Seth glanced at his brother before turning back to her. "We're assembling a team to ensure your safety, Ms. O'Kane, if you'll come with me."

"Finally, you're here." A woman with enviably long legs approached, her step quick. She too wore a marshal's star, hers hanging around her neck on a lanyard. She stopped in front of Linc and placed her hands on her hips, frowning as she studied him.

"I'm fine." Linc sounded defensive.

"You're supposed to be recovering, not getting into knife fights."

"I've recovered."

She reached out and plucked at his shirt like she intended to tug it up and have a look at the bullet wound for herself.

He batted her hand away. "Knock it off."

"I want to see how you're healing. That way I can give Mom a full report when she calls. And she will call."

"You are not pulling up my shirt in the middle of the office. I'll call Mom and let her know I'm fine."

Ellie, Mikayla thought as she watched the exchange with interest. The woman, blonde hair held back in a tortoiseshell clip and with serious blue eyes, studied her brother for a long moment. Apparently deciding he was indeed fine, she rose up to kiss his cheek and he enfolded her in a brief hug. "Glad you're here, big guy." Ellie turned her attention to Mikayla, gaze frankly assessing. "I'm Ellie Jameson." She presented a smart, no-nonsense image, from the cut of her jacket to the clean, almost makeup-free face. This woman worked in a male-dominated field and looked like she could more than hold her own.

Mikayla shook her hand. "I'm Mikayla O'Kane."

The siblings were clear winners of the genetic lottery. While the men shared the same dark hair, Ellie looked to be a natural blonde, but their faces revealed common parentage. High cheekbones, wide foreheads, and the set of their eyes were similar. And while at five foot nine, Mikayla had never thought herself lacking in stature, next to these three she felt positively petite.

"We'd better get the meeting started." Seth motioned to the open door of a glass-walled room. Inside, a dark-haired woman sat at a conference table, working intently on a laptop while a balding man with a slight paunch read the screen over her shoulder. They were probably deciding what safe house to stash her in, Mikayla thought glumly.

She glanced around. The ladies' room was down the hall. And past it was a green EXIT sign over a door labeled with the symbol for stairs. "Excuse me, please."

# Chapter Fourteen

Five minutes later Mikayla leaned against the counter in the restroom, a heated internal debate spinning through her head. Should she do it? She could be down those stairs and out of the building in seconds. The temptation to make a break for it, to simply disappear, was almost overwhelming. Linc would be after her in a split second, but it might be worth a try. God knew if she walked into that conference room her life would no longer be her own.

She tapped her fist against her forehead. She couldn't do that to Linc. He'd asked her to trust him. And beyond Linc was Brady, who would track her down himself, then lock her in a safe house. Then there was Peter. She'd been engaged to the man and she owed it to him to do her part to bring his killer to justice. Disappearing to evade the prison bars of witness protection was like a shiny mirage, oh so seductive, but in the end a fantasy.

The bathroom door swung open and Ellie walked in. She put her hands on her hips, and Mikayla felt herself being thoroughly studied before the woman moved to lean against the counter next to Mikayla. "Have you decided whether to make a run for it?"

"Did Linc send you in here to get me?"

"He hasn't taken his eyes off the door since you came in. He's getting impatient and is ready to come in himself. I convinced him to let me."

"Is he always this intense?"

The corner of her mouth lifted, the first hint of warmth. "He's a born rescuer. Make that a woman in distress and he's a goner. He'll pull out all the stops to keep her safe."

Mikayla studied Linc's sister. She likely wasn't aware she was sounding a warning not to take Linc's attention personally. But her description of Linc in the role of champion hit a note of truth. The little bubble of hope that there really was something beyond the initial attraction, that the kiss had meant something besides a release of frustration, deflated like a day-old balloon.

Mikayla straightened to pace the length of the room. "I can take care of myself. Linc's been great, but he doesn't need to look after me."

"He won't see it that way." Ellie paused. "Have you decided?"

Mikayla stopped pacing. "I wasn't going to run out on him," she mumbled.

"I think he's in the trust but verify stage of your relationship."

Heat crept into her cheeks. "We're not in a relationship."

Ellie offered a full smile. "Seeing as how I merely meant your marshal/witness relationship and you assumed I meant a personal relationship, I get the idea that there *is* a personal relationship."

"A minute ago you suggested I shouldn't read anything into Linc's attention. That he'd have helped any woman in my situation."

"Absolutely. But that doesn't mean there's not something more when it comes to you."

"Right. Regardless, this conversation is pointless. There isn't anything between Linc and me."

"Hmm, I could argue that I know chemistry when I see it, but we don't have time to debate. You ready to go out there again? Because I give my brother less than a minute and he'll be coming through that door himself."

Mikayla nodded. She pulled open the door to find Linc on the other side, leaning against the wall. The scowl cleared from his face when he saw her. He glanced over her shoulder at Ellie. "Thanks, El."

"I wasn't going to run."

"But you were thinking about it." He nodded toward the door to the stairs. "Escape hatch is a little too close for comfort." His hand returned to her back, a light touch guiding her to the conference room where Seth stood talking to the older man. A half-dozen bottles of water were arranged on a sideboard.

Both men looked up when they entered. The older man had a pleasantly lined face. He nodded at Mikayla and motioned to a chair. "Ms. O'Kane, have a seat here. I'm Chief Deputy Rob Sanford. Can I get you anything? Coffee? Tea? Water?"

"Water would be great."

"Here you go." He passed her a bottle.

They all took their seats, Linc at her right, the others around the conference table. The woman with the laptop continued busily tapping away.

Sanford addressed the group. "Okay, folks, let's get started. So we all know what's what, let me lay out the players." He pointed at Seth. "That's Chief Deputy Marshal Seth Jameson, head of the Los Angeles Marshals' office. To his left is Deputy Marshal Eleanor Jameson, and then Deputy Marshal Lincoln Jameson, both of the Southern District of California." He motioned to his right. "And this here's Deputy Marshal Gabriela Robles." The woman at the laptop lifted a hand to wave before refocusing on the computer screen.

"Now, Ms. O'Kane, we need to go over the events of the evening of October second. I know you've been through all this before, but we'd all like to hear it from the horse's mouth, so to speak. Can you walk us through it?"

She nodded. Once again she described the events of the night she went to Peter's house, how she'd heard the raised voices, then crept toward the office and saw the two men reflected in the mirror. "That's all what I told Linc. I don't remember anything more."

Seth spoke, his gaze direct. "Can you tell us what they were arguing about?"

She knew there was a point to having her go over and over what she'd witnessed, but she wished she was back at the campground with nothing more important to do than decide which trail she wanted to hike. But she concentrated, trying to remember the actual words and not only the loud voices.

"They were arguing about money. I didn't hear the entire conversation, but what I heard was about money. From what I could tell, Paco had given Peter a large sum. Peter was gathering investors who had apparently made deposits into specific bank accounts. The man you think is Zecena was angry because the number of investors, or the amount they had invested, wasn't enough. Peter is a—" She cleared her throat. "Peter *was* a commercial real estate broker."

Linc shifted closer, his shoulder brushing hers. The movement was subtle, but it reminded her she wasn't alone.

Seth continued his line of questioning. "Had Peter talked about anything big happening for him in the days leading up to that Sunday? Was he particularly nervous? Distracted?"

"Yes, he had talked about a big deal he was putting together. He said it had to do with a mixed-use development downtown. He bragged that he was working with someone big, and this was a turning point in his career. He'd made the comment that there would be no more small potatoes. That he was finally in the big time. But honestly, Peter always talked like that. It's not an admirable trait, but he liked people to think he was important, so he was always boasting about big shots who depended on him. About how the rich and powerful came to him because they knew he could deliver."

"Sounds like a prince," Linc muttered.

Mikayla shrugged. "I know Peter dealt with a lot of insecurities. The talk was his way of compensating."

"Can you give us any details? The names of the investors? The financial institutions they were using?" Mikayla guessed Seth was in his mid-thirties, and in this short time she was getting an idea why he'd already made Chief Deputy. The man exuded a self-possessed leadership that suggested a certain strength of character. She felt she could trust him implicitly.

She considered his question. "I'm sorry, but I don't recall anything like that." She looked at her hands. "It doesn't say much about me to admit that I tuned him out. He liked to talk and sometimes went on and on about people I didn't know. It was one of the things that made me realize I had to break our engagement. It wasn't fair to him that I wasn't interested in what he had to say. I couldn't marry a man I was beginning to find boring."

"Ms. O'Kane." She turned to face Sanford. He rested his chin on steepled fingers. "Have you ever fired a gun?"

Linc sat up abruptly. "Where the hell are you going with that, Sanford?"

"Easy, Deputy Jameson." Sanford leaned back in his chair.

"With so many Marshal Jamesons here you might as well use our first names," Ellie said sharply.

Sanford smiled thinly. His gaze tracked from Mikayla to Linc, then back again. "Have you, Ms. O'Kane? Have you ever fired a gun?"

Linc edged closer to her, body tense.

"Yes, I have."

"When was the last time you fired a gun?"

"It's been years. I'm not sure exactly."

"Wellington was killed with a 9mm semiautomatic. Do you own such a weapon?"

"No."

Sanford picked up a pen and began turning it over and over in his fingers. "You said you had previously attempted to break your engagement to Peter Wellington. That he'd refused to accept that your relationship was over. In fact, you had gone to his home that Sunday evening to give him back his ring. Do I have it right?"

"Yes."

Mikayla glanced around the table at the others. While Linc appeared coiled tight, fingers drumming on the table, Seth locked a cool, assessing gaze on Sanford while Ellie watched him through narrowed eyes. Even Deputy Robles paused in her typing to look at her boss.

Ignoring them, Sanford continued his line of inquiry. "And yet, Ms. O'Kane, you say you left that night without speaking to your fiancé."

"That's true."

"Why didn't you wait for him? You must have been familiar with his home. It seems you could have hung out somewhere until he was free and not wasted a trip."

Mikayla pulled in a steadying breath, exhaled, then repeated the process. When she spoke, she forced her voice to remain even. Sanford wasn't going to fluster her. "I was scared. They were arguing loudly, angrily. I'd never seen Peter that furious. He wouldn't have wanted me to see him like that. And I didn't know those men. So I left."

"If you thought those men were a threat, why not call nine-one-one? Why leave your fiancé alone with men who you say scared you?"

"Back off, Sanford." Mikayla wasn't sure Linc wasn't about to leap across the table and throttle the man.

The chief leaned forward, looking pointedly at Linc. "Lincoln, I spoke with your boss less than an hour ago. Your presence at this meeting is a privilege because of your intervention in the knife attack on Ms. O'Kane. Understand that you haven't been cleared to return to active duty since you were shot, and yet you are acting like this is your case. Get in my way? I'll send your ass back to San Diego and let your chief deal with you." He glanced at Mikayla, then back again to Linc. "And a personal relationship between you and Ms. O'Kane will get you booted back home just as quick."

Under the table, Mikayla nudged Linc with her knee. The thought of having to cope without him made her feel panicky. He'd been her rock, a source of strength she could draw on to do what needed to be done.

After a quick glance at Linc, she spoke. "I understand you are doing your job, Chief Sanford. But honestly? I wouldn't be here if it wasn't for Linc. That said, I'll answer whatever questions you have if that will help us move on."

Linc stayed quiet, and after a moment Sanford nodded. "Sorry to sound like a hard-ass." He raised his hands in a placating gesture.

"But the questions have to be asked. If we don't look at the obvious conflict between you and Peter Wellington, we're not doing our jobs. All we've got is your statement that a man called Paco was at Peter Wellington's home, approximately one hour before he was murdered. Security camera footage was deleted for the time in question. It's more than likely a man's fiancée would have some knowledge of his security system." He turned his attention to the others gathered around the table, gesturing toward Mikayla. "If she testifies at Zecena's trial, the defense will tear her apart, and rightly so. If we don't have anything stronger than her say-so, we haven't got shit."

***

Sanford was right. They had to look at this from all angles, but that sure as hell didn't make it sit right that he was painting Mikayla as a suspect. Linc caught a look from his brother. The slight shake of his head meant back off. His jaw was starting to ache from being clenched to keep his mouth shut. He trusted Seth but that didn't mean he liked the way this was going.

Sanders continued his questioning. "Ms. O'Kane, where did you go after you left Wellington's house that evening?"

"I went home."

"Did you stop anywhere? The grocery store? Starbucks?"

"I stopped for gas. I wanted to fill the tank before leaving on my trip in the morning."

"Can you give me the location of the gas station?"

She told Sanders and a flood of relief had Linc relaxing. She was holding it together. And, better yet, nearly every gas station had video surveillance, and the timestamp would place Mikayla well away from Wellington's house at the time of the murder.

"Good. We'll get the camera footage from that station and that should clear you." Sanford seemed genuinely relieved.

Seth rose to his feet. He'd folded the sleeves of his dark gray shirt back to the elbows and loosened his tie. He opened a folder and leaned over the table, laying out a series of photos in front of Mikayla. "Ms. O'Kane, we'd like to confirm that the man you saw at Wellington's house is Paco Zecena."

Mikayla studied the pictures, her attention returning several times to an image of a middle-aged man with thick jowls, dark hair slicked back from a high forehead. She tapped the photo. "This is the man I saw in the room with Peter. The man Peter referred to as Paco."

Linc leaned forward and picked up the photo, holding it up for everyone to see. "This is Paco Zecena, leader of the Southern California branch of the Zecena cartel."

Seth nodded. "Zecena is known to be involved in extortion, drugs and weapons smuggling, money laundering, human trafficking, aggravated assault, and murder. He's slippery, always careful to be somewhere else, to have an alibi when bad things happen."

He pulled out another group of photos, arranging them in front of Mikayla. All were Latino, a couple with tattoos on their necks, one with a scar across a cheekbone.

"Do any of these men look familiar, Ms. O'Kane?"

She shook her head.

"Mikayla." She looked up at Seth. "Think about that evening when you saw those men talking to Wellington. You identified Zecena. What about the other man? Was there any detail about their appearance that would help you to identify him?" He pointed to the photos. "These are known members of the Zecena organization. Any look familiar?"

"No. None of these men were at Peter's house."

He nodded, then gathered the photos before taking his seat across the table from her.

"Shit." Everyone seated at the table looked at Linc. He gazed with focused intensity on Mikayla, a feeling of unreality settling over him. He spoke abruptly. "Describe the other man with Zecena."

"I told you what he looked like."

"Close your eyes, Mikayla. Bring up a mental image."

Leaning back in her seat, she closed her eyes. A slight frown lowered auburn brows on her forehead. She shook her head and raised her eyelids. "He was pretty unremarkable. I didn't really notice him that much. Zecena seemed to suck the attention to himself. He has a presence."

"But you did see him."

"Only in the mirror, but yes. He was tall. Not as tall as you, but probably six foot. He was heavy, had a paunch starting. He had black hair cut short. I couldn't see his eyes."

"Any identifying characteristics? Birthmarks, moles, scars, tattoos, anything you can remember."

She took a sip from her water bottle. "It's hard to be sure because I was scared. I don't think I noticed as much as I might otherwise have picked up on. I did see a large, flat mole here." She pointed to her right temple. "I saw it in the mirror. If his hair was any longer, it would have been hidden."

He stared as the pieces settled into place. Ellie opened her mouth to speak, but Linc stopped her with a look. "Wait." He reached for his phone and tapped on the photos app. He swiped through until he found the one he was looking for and held it up for Mikayla.

She bent forward to scrutinize it. "He's a marshal? The guy with Paco Zecena was a federal officer?"

He turned the phone to show the image to the others. He remembered when that photo was taken. He and Donny, outfitted in bulletproof vests and jackets emblazoned with the USMS insignia, had led an early-morning raid looking for a fugitive. The photo clearly showed the mole on the right side of his partner's face. He turned to Mikayla. "You ID'd Donny Bertola."

"The fucker." This came from Seth, while Ellie looked at the photo with such hatred he thought she'd shred the man with her bare hands if they ever came face-to-face again.

Sanford spoke, voice calm. "Ms. O'Kane, I'm sure Linc briefed you on WITSEC. I think that's the best option for you currently. In addition to your testimony against Zecena and your attacker, Hector Lopez, identifying Bertola helps tremendously in putting the whole picture together. Your testimony is crucial and when you're in WITSEC, we can keep you safe." He motioned across the table and Robles looked up from the computer screen. "Gabs, brief us on what you've arranged."

"Sure. Ms. O'Kane, you'll be placed in a safe house close to Salt Lake, but outside of town. On Seth Jameson's recommendation, I chose a house in a semirural area so you'll have more freedom to get outdoors. Two marshals will be with you at all times to ensure your safety."

Mikayla's shoulders sagged and she slumped back in her seat as she nodded slowly.

# Chapter Fifteen

Mikayla dumped her duffel bag on the neatly made queen-size bed and took a moment to survey the room's furnishings. The dresser, nightstand, and framed prints on the wall all looked like they'd been recently purchased from IKEA. She thought of her painstakingly restored four-poster bed at home, and the beautiful Southwestern rug she'd found to match the sand-colored paint she'd chosen for her walls. The crown molding she'd had installed and painted herself. She shook off the mood. She had no idea how long she'd be staying here, but she had to make the best of it. Unpacking took only a few minutes. She hadn't brought more than a few changes of clothing on her camping trip so there wasn't much to unpack.

She peered into the drawers in the small, attached bathroom, thankful to see the supply of toiletries. Returning to the bedroom, she sat on a low bench in front of a wide window. Everything looked comfortable and welcoming. The decision had been made and she refused to let loose with any of the complaints she wanted to make. This wasn't home, but bright side, she'd get a taste of living in Utah.

The rumble of voices downstairs told her the marshals were figuring out their plan, what they would do to keep her safe. Linc's voice was easily identifiable, his low tone reassuring. He planned to spend the first night in the safe house, to help her get settled, he'd said. But he was getting antsy and she knew he wanted to be off hunting for Zecena and Bertola.

She descended the stairs and followed the voices to the kitchen at the back of the house. A group of men and women stood talking, some of whom she recognized from the meeting at the Marshals' office.

Linc broke off when he saw her and beckoned her to follow him. He led the way out the kitchen door and onto a wide deck. A small table and cushioned chairs in one corner would provide a pretty place to have a meal if the weather stayed nice. Late afternoon sunlight filtered through leafy trees ringing the yard. She turned to find Linc studying her with a frown. The gun at his hip and the badge on his belt served as clear reminders that he was on the job.

"You going to be okay?"

"Of course. Don't worry about me, Linc."

"Easier said than done."

She didn't know what to say to that. Simple attraction was one thing, but she hadn't been able to get that kiss outside the courthouse out of her mind. He'd laid bare emotions she didn't know how to deal with. She'd only known him a few days and yet he'd drawn more out of her than Peter ever had. Peter had been safe because he hadn't made her feel. Love—there, she'd allowed herself to think the word—came with all sorts of risks, and it worried her that it wouldn't take much for her feelings to tip over the edge into love. She'd had enough therapy to understand that losing her father had made her afraid to care deeply for someone.

He reached out to grasp her hand. "Mikayla, something's come up."

Energy seemed to vibrate off him. He had the focused intensity of a warrior going into battle.

"What?"

"Intel came in that the top tier of the Zecena organization is meeting in San Diego tomorrow. Word is Paco Zecena will be there, as will two of his brothers from Tijuana. Not *El Jefe*, but top lieutenants of the organization."

"You're going after him."

He nodded.

"How? I mean, you're not on active duty."

Linc sighed. "I haven't been medically cleared, but I was able to speak to my boss and I'm on provisional duty pending final medical clearance."

"Well, don't get hurt again."

His lips twitched. "Worried about me, sweetheart?"

She wanted to tell him the truth. That she was scared something would happen to him. Instead she shrugged. "I'm sure you know what you're doing."

"Such a vote of confidence." He focused and she knew he was back to business. "We've got enough to arrest Paco. If we can get charges on them here in the states, we'll prosecute. But if not, the Mexican government can deal with them."

"This is unusual, right? For the leaders of the cartel to be meeting, and for the marshals to know about it."

"Yeah. Ellie has a source inside the cartel. I don't trust the bastard, but this seems solid. They'll be armed and have guards. We've got to be prepared so this goes the way we want it to, without anyone getting hurt."

"Do you have to be there?" She didn't want to act needy, to ask him to stay with her.

The gold in his hazel eyes glowed brighter. "Sweetheart, I know I said I'd stay here tonight, and I'd rather not leave you. But the house is secure. You'll have two marshals with you at all times." He stuck a hand in his pocket and came out with his keys. He took her hand and set them in her palm. "Here are the keys to the Jeep. Keep them on you so if something happens, you can get yourself out of here." He frowned. "But only if things go sideways."

"Geez, Linc. Do you think I'd run out on them? I'm not an idiot."

"No, you're not an idiot. But you also don't want to be here."

"I'll play nice, I promise."

"Can you promise me something else?"

"What?"

"That when this is over, when Zecena is in prison and the threat is gone, that you'll give me a chance."

Mikayla's heart stumbled. "A chance?"

"Yeah, a chance to see if we have something together."

"Linc, I'm not good at relationships."

"I'm not good at relationships either. Or haven't been. I think I could be better at it with you."

Usually, he was so confident, so self-assured, she hadn't expected uncertainty from him. Going with the impulse, she moved closer. Gripping his belt, she pulled him to her as she leaned in on tiptoes, raising her face to brush a kiss across his lips. She'd meant to keep it light, a brief touching of lips, but his hands locked on her hips and brought her body full against his. His mouth opened and the kiss turned from casual to hot in a heartbeat.

"Break it up, kids. We've got work to do."

Mikayla tried to jerk back, but Linc took his time ending the kiss. He was still holding her close when he spoke. "Get lost, Seth."

"The car's leaving in five minutes. You want to be on that plane to California, you need to wrap up things here." The screen door slapped shut.

"Shit. Sorry, sweetheart. I have to go."

Mikayla nodded. She swallowed, the gravity of what he was heading into making her quake inside. "Be careful, Linc."

He brought up a hand to brush a finger across her cheek. "Always."

*** 

Mikayla spent the next hour familiarizing herself with her new living situation. Marshal Gabriela Robles, the deputy on the computer at the meeting earlier in the day, had been assigned to guard her, as well as Marshal David Tran. Both were busy on laptops set up on the kitchen table. Mikayla took boxes of Chinese takeout from the fridge.

"Do you guys want me to heat up enough for you?"

David looked up, round glasses giving him a quizzical look. "Sounds good. You need help?"

"No, I've got it." Making use of the microwave, she heated the cartons then set them on the table. The kitchen came stocked with stone-colored place settings and flatware, and she gathered up enough for three people and brought them to the table.

Her phone pinged with an incoming text. She'd been given a different cell phone with restrictions on who she could contact. She glanced at the message and let out a perplexed laugh. Linc had sent her possibly the most sappily cute photo of a kitten she'd ever seen. It even had a pink bow on its head.

She texted back: **"A kitten? Why?"**

**"Did you smile?"**

**"Yeah...point?"**

**"Just that."**

Well, hmm. Linc surprised her again. She sat at the table and passed cartons of fried rice, mushroom chicken, and chop suey to Dave and Gabriela. The marshals chatted, including her in their conversation, but throughout the meal her thoughts kept returning to Linc's message.

Once dinner was over and the kitchen straightened, she headed upstairs. A long soak in the tub did a lot to ease the surface tension, but she couldn't get out of her mind the danger Linc faced confronting Paco Zecena and his crew.

Back in the bedroom, after running a brush through her wet hair, she picked up her phone. Another text from Linc. Two chimpanzees touching lips.

**"Chimps kissing? Why?"**

**"Made me think of you?"**

She didn't know if she should be insulted. **"Are you flirting with me?"**

**"Maybe."**

**"You're on the plane with nothing to do, right?"**

"Maybe... Flirt back and save me from boredom."

Mikayla imagined Linc sitting in his seat on the plane, smiling as he texted. She searched Google, inserted an image, and hit send.

"A puffer fish??? Prickly and toxic. This is you flirting?"

"They're cute."

"Not as cute as you."

She groaned. "That's your best line?"

"No. How's this? I'd share a tent with you anytime."

"We each kept to our own side of the air mattress. Not very sexy."

"Did not."

"What?"

"You didn't stay on your side."

"Did so."

"Nope. When I woke up you were wrapped around me. Very sexy."

"Was not!!!"

"Yep. Not complaining."

Mikayla could feel heat rise in her cheeks. She'd slept dreamlessly and woken well rested. She certainly had no recollection of being wrapped around Linc. Now she wished she'd gotten up earlier.

"You're blushing."

"You don't know that."

"You are. I can tell." The text was accompanied by a blushing emoticon.

"Shut up."

"I'll have to. Getting ready to land."

"Okay."

She stared at the now-quiet phone for several long seconds, giving a little jump when it pinged as another text came in.

"Aren't you going to say it?"

"Say what?"

"What you said before I left."

"Be careful?"

"Yeah, that."

"Okay. Be careful." She hesitated, then tapped again. "I like you better in one piece."

"That's promising. Something to hold on to."

\*\*\*

Linc sat in the back of the police van, listening to the other officers talking quietly. Ellie was seated next to him, calm, at ease. His sister wasn't one for drumming her fingers or fidgeting. Any nervousness would be strapped down and controlled. Besides his brother, there was no officer he'd rather have covering his back during an operation. Seth was in charge, and the team included agents from the FBI, plus local law enforcement who had been deputized by the Marshals Service. They all wore body armor vests, and jackets identifying them as either FBI or US Marshals.

The van sat parked outside a palatial Spanish-style home perched on two acres atop a hill and surrounded by a six-foot stone wall. The Zecenas had the advantage of the high ground, but they also had limited getaway options.

The officers on surveillance had reported three large black SUVs with heavily tinted windows entering the compound an hour previous. Linc figured unless Zecena was an idiot, and he didn't think he was, Paco and his *compadres* had to know they were surrounded and were prepared to defend themselves.

Linc knew his job, had gone over the plan with the team, and was reasonably confident of the outcome. Nothing could be planned a hundred percent, so there was always a certain amount of improvising. They probably had ten minutes before they moved.

He let his mind wander to his text exchange with Mikayla. The Celtic goddess had him hooked, and honestly? He was good with that. Once they had Zecena, she'd likely be moved to a secure location in California. The trial would be in the state and having her close made sense. He'd be able to see her.

Ellie bumped his knee. "You're smiling."

"So?"

"So you've got it bad."

"I don't know what you're talking about." Admitting his feelings to himself was one thing. Admitting them to his sister wasn't going to happen.

She smirked. "Lincoln's got a girlfriend," she said in the singsong voice she'd used in her annoying tween years when tormenting her older brothers seemed to be Ellie's primary function in life.

He ignored her.

She bumped his knee again. "I like her, by the way. She's got brains, and she definitely has guts."

He really didn't want to have this conversation, but that didn't stop Ellie.

"Your type has tended more toward women who look like Victoria's Secret models. Which of course doesn't mean they couldn't be smart as well as beautiful, but I never saw the smart side."

"Mikayla has a doctorate in American history." As usual, Ellie could get him to say things he had no intention of saying.

She nearly chortled with glee. "Yep. You were thinking of her." She smiled smugly.

He leaned back in his seat, letting his head rest on the inside wall of the van. "I miss her already."

Ellie's mouth formed a perfect O, her eyes widening. "Oh my god, Linc. You're in love with her."

"What? Don't get ahead of yourself."

"You are. Does she know?"

He opened his mouth to deny it, but the words wouldn't form. Instead, he said, "I've only known her a few days."

"I don't think that has anything to do with it." Ellie leaned over and planted a kiss on his cheek. "Congratulations, big guy. My money's on you. And I won't tell her all your secrets until later so she doesn't get scared off. Things like how you used to run naked through the house, or when you refused to take a shower because you said you were conducting an experiment on bacteria in your armpits. She won't hear those things from me."

"Gee, thanks. Besides, I get a pass on the naked thing because I was only seven, and Seth convinced me that my superhero identity was Naked Boy. And I had a cape so I wasn't completely naked."

He enjoyed the sound of his sister's muted laughter, then Seth's voice came through his earpiece. When the countdown was over, Linc unlatched the back door to the van. His squad was assembled outside, and he addressed the officers. "We're ready to roll. Get in position, remember your training, and don't do anything stupid."

# Chapter Sixteen

In the chilly half-light of early dawn, they arranged themselves near the back wall of the compound, weapons at the ready. Luckily the area was semirural, and there were no houses close enough to worry about nosy neighbors or collateral damage.

The sound of the San Diego PD armored SWAT vehicle idling in place at the front gate was audible as a low rumble. Barely detectible was the high-pitched whine Linc knew came from a drone flying over the compound to get a bird's-eye view. When the signal came, Team One at the front would flatten the gate and rush the house. Linc's Team Two included Ellie, two FBI agents, and two local LEOs from San Diego PD. Every one of them trained marksmen. In addition to their service pistols, each was armed with AR-15 rifles. He eyed the team members and was satisfied with what he saw. All the weapons in the world wouldn't help them without mental readiness. Their job was to clear the perimeter and trap cartel members and their security between the two law enforcement teams. Linc didn't need the drone to confirm the Zecenas would be heavily armed, making a firefight inevitable.

Linc listened to the communication through his earpiece. The signal came, followed almost instantaneously by the crash of the front gate. With Linc in the lead, each team member slung their rifles to their backs, scaled the wall, and dropped to the other side. Gunfire erupted as they moved in pairs through trees and shrubs. Linc took point, with Ellie behind him.

The house came into view. Two men dressed in black were using a low wall around a patio as cover as they fired toward the front.

Linc motioned to Ellie, and at her nod she took position behind the wide trunk of a eucalyptus tree. Once Ellie found her spot, he motioned to indicate which was his target. They both pulled up their rifles and sighted. Linc gave the low command and they fired. Gunfire cracked through the air, and the men behind the low wall collapsed to the concrete patio.

Linc and Ellie moved forward as two others from their team got into position. He radioed they were ready and got the go-ahead. The drone had spotted an armed individual in the room closest to the patio. He motioned to the San Diego cop holding a heavy launcher who braced himself, sighted, and squeezed the trigger. The flash-bang grenade crashed through the sliding door, shattering the plate glass. The concussion from the blast blew out other windows in the room. Officers ran forward, verified it was safe to enter, then an officer used his baton to break off the remaining shards of glass and the rest of the team swarmed the house.

Relieved the flash-bang hadn't started a fire, Linc scanned the room as the team fanned out. A man lay on the floor, a rifle next to him. Ellie kicked the rifle away and knelt with a knee in his back. She pinned his arm when he tried to reach for a .45 in his waistband, retrieved the weapon, and handed it to Linc. He took the gun, unloaded the clip and the bullet in the chamber, and stuck them in the cargo pocket of his pants. Ellie cuffed the man and left him face down on the floor.

The crash of the front door reverberated through the house as Team One entered the building. They would search the second floor while Linc took Team Two downstairs. The house was built into the contours of the hillside, and when they descended the stairs, they found the bottom floor set up for entertainment with French doors opening onto another deck. His ears pricked at the wump-wump sound of an approaching helicopter.

He pressed a button on his radio. "Seth, chopper incoming."

"I hear it. I'll check it out."

Linc's team fanned out. Where was Paco Zecena and his *hermanos* from Mexico? The black SUVs were still parked in the front of the house. The few guards had been dealt with, but there had to be more. Linc studied the house, taking in every detail, anything that could provide a clue as to where the Zecenas had gotten to. He was almost ready to pull his team out when he noticed something. A wet leaf lay on the floor in front of a row of floor-to-ceiling cabinets. He glanced outside the patio doors. The high dew point meant a lot of condensation on the grass. If someone had come in from outside, they could have tracked in a wet leaf. The question was, where had they gone?

The sound of the helicopter grew louder.

He pulled open a cabinet door to reveal an organizer full of CDs. Another door showed a stereo system, complete with an old-school record player. He pulled open the third door. Bingo. A hidden door had been built into the side of the hill. After alerting his team, Linc tried the knob. Locked. He stepped back, then hit the door with a forceful kick.

Linc and his team followed a long hallway. Daylight shone ahead, and they reached an outside door in time to see the chopper landing, sending debris blowing into the sky.

Several men in dark business suits were running toward the chopper even as it landed. "Shit. They're making a getaway," Linc spoke through the radio to Seth. "I can take out the pilot before he gets airborne. Am I clear to take the shot?"

Seth's voice was clipped. "Affirmative, but keep him alive if you can."

Linc ran for the door and onto the lawn. Squinting against the rotor wash, he swung his rifle into position, bracing it on a stone fence. The runners of the helicopter touched the ground and four men swarmed to get onboard. He had a clear shot at the pilot's knee through the glass door of the chopper, and Linc went with that. He may not be able to use the knee, but he wouldn't be dead. Sighting his target, he held his breath and squeezed the trigger. The pilot spun in his seat.

Sporadic gunfire erupted. Linc held his position until he was sure no one would try to take command and fly the helicopter. The injured pilot maneuvered the controls and the rotors began to slow. Team One fanned out from protected positions to surround the helicopter.

After a few tense minutes, the men on board exited with their hands in the air. Linc made sure he was the one to nab Paco Zecena and couldn't help a stab of satisfaction when he snapped the cuffs in place. They'd gotten the bastard. He recited the Miranda warning by rote. Holding him by the elbow, Linc nudged Zecena in the direction of the waiting vehicle that would transport him to a holding cell. "Let's go."

An FBI agent approached. "Team Two leader?"

"That's me."

"The building is secure. Team One leader wants you to wait here for him."

Linc nodded to the man. "Thanks."

Zecena narrowed his gaze at him. "You're making a mistake to arrest me, *hombre*." Zecena's voice was gravelly, the smell of cigarette smoke on his clothing.

"Don't think so."

"The pretty *señorita* with the long red-brown hair, auburn I think you call it. She wasn't so hard to find."

Linc spun Zecena around and pushed him against a tree. "What the hell are you talking about?"

"What do you think I'm talking about? A pretty woman with *casteño* hair. You think she's safe in that little house?"

Linc grabbed the collar of Zecena's shirt and twisted it around the thick neck. "Tell me what you know."

"*Cuidado, hombre.* I got a problem with a Jameson. That would be you, Marshal. You got in the way of an associate. An associate sent to do a job. The lady won't testify against me. That's being taken care of as we speak."

Linc felt the blood in his veins turn to ice and buzzing sounded in his ears. He shoved his forearm under Zecena's jaw and had the satisfaction of seeing the man's eyes bulge and his face begin turning purple. "Anything happens to that woman and I'll tear your heart out and feed it to you, you bastard."

"Utah is far from here, *hombre*," Zecena squeezed out roughly. "What are you going to do about it?"

Linc shoved harder and had Zecena gasping for air.

"That's enough, Linc." Seth grabbed him by the shoulder and shoved back.

"He threatened...*her*."

Zecena wheezed, then laughed. "He's got a thing for the pretty *señorita*, who will be dead within the day." All levity left his face as he focused on Linc. "You may take me into custody, *hombre*, but I'll be out again in a matter of hours. And you will be looking over your shoulder because I will be coming for you."

Zecena reeled back when Linc broke free from Seth's hold. This time Ellie, with the help of an FBI agent, pulled him back. Seth thrust his face into Linc's. "Back off," he snarled. "You're not jeopardizing this arrest by beating a cuffed man. Use your head."

The buzzing in his brain quieted and Linc sucked in a steadying breath.

Seth didn't move. "You under control?"

Linc shoved his brother back. "Yeah."

"Good. Then get on your phone and call into the local office and tell him what Zecena said. He'll check in with his marshals."

As Ellie took Zecena to the waiting vehicle, Linc pulled out his phone, hesitated, then swiped through screens. He wouldn't rest easy until her heard directly from Mikayla. The phone rang on her end, then the mechanical voice of the default voicemail gave him the option to leave a message. "Mikayla, call me as soon as you get this." Shit. Double-fucking shit.

He tapped out Sanford's direct number. He didn't care that it was still early on a Saturday morning.

"This better be damned good."

"Call your deputies at the safe house."

"What the hell?"

"Call them. Zecena knows where Mikayla is, said she'll be dead before the day is done."

"Okay, okay. Let me grab my other phone."

Linc waited, patience stretched to the limit, mind filled with images of all that could go wrong. Mikayla was seven hundred miles away. Linc swore viciously, pacing, the phone plastered to his ear.

Sanford came back on the line. "Robles picked up, said everything is fine. Untwist your panties, Jameson. Zecena's messing with you. I'll assign a couple more marshals to guard your girl. She'll be fine."

Linc reported the conversation to Seth and Ellie. He paced, trying to determine how Zecena had known of Linc's involvement in the case. He stopped, head bent in thought as he considered what seemed like the obvious conclusion. Hector Lopez. Linc had identified himself when he'd questioned Mikayla's attacker. There were a dozen different ways Lopez could get information out of the jail. Hector was the source.

Linc's phone vibrated in his hand. Caller ID said "Mikayla." He swiped a finger across the screen and held it to his ear.

"Mikayla."

"Linc, you're safe." Hearing her voice loosened everything that was coiled tight inside him. Her obvious relief made it even sweeter. "I got your message to call. I was in the shower. How did it go? Did you get Zecena?"

"Yeah, we got him." Her voice washed over him, making him wish she was here beside him so he could touch her.

"Anything wrong?"

"Not sure. Zecena threatened you. He knows you're in a safe house in Utah. He might know more than that."

"How could he?"

"I don't know. He could have been bluffing that he knows exactly where you are, but I don't like it." His mind spun with the possibilities. "I want you to stay away from windows, don't let yourself be visible to anyone outside. Don't go outside."

"Okay."

"Sanford is going to send more marshals to add to your detail."

"Then I'll be safe, Linc. Don't worry."

"I'll stop worrying when I'm with you."

There was a long pause. "Listen, Linc, I—"

Seth signaled for him to join the team. "Damn, I can't talk now. I've got to go. Keep your phone with you at all times. I'll call later to check on you."

"Okay."

He couldn't bring himself to disconnect. He said in a low voice, "I don't want anything to happen to you, Mikayla." Lame-ass words when he wanted to say so much more.

"I know. I'll talk to you later."

The connection ended and Linc shoved the phone in his pocket, frustration simmering. Why couldn't he have told her straight out that he cared about her? That maybe, just maybe, care had gone up a couple of notches and was teetering toward something more.

"Everything good?"

Linc faced Seth. "No, everything is not good. Can you call your office and have them get me on the earliest flight to Salt Lake City?"

"Sanford said he'd send additional marshals, Linc, and he will. They'll keep Mikayla safe." He held up both hands in a placating gesture when Linc scowled. "But I'll get you on a flight."

The vans transporting the cartel members rolled away in a motorcade sandwiched between official vehicles. Seth pulled his phone out and motioned Linc over. He shoved the phone in his pocket and grabbed his brother's elbow. "Let's go. You're booked on a flight leaving in thirty-five minutes. You can bypass security and they'll hold the plane if they have to." His brother's steadiness helped calm his nerves. "This flight only had a seat for you. Ellie and I will be coming right behind you on the next available flight."

"Thanks, brother."

"We got your back."

"Yeah, I know."

Within minutes Linc was seated in a police car next to the San Diego cop who'd launched the flash-bang, racing toward the airport with lights flashing and siren screaming, while a sense of foreboding ate at his gut.

***

Mikayla skimmed through the titles on the bookshelf. She needed something to occupy her time or she'd go stir crazy. Thrillers, mysteries, romance—which somehow got her to wondering about the logistics of WITSEC setting up a safe house. Part of their job must be to keep their witnesses safe *and* sane, so supplying reading material was a smart move. She paused, the sound of car tires crunching gravel coming from the front of the house. Clutching the romance she'd chosen, she slipped into a bedroom that would have a front-facing view, approaching the second-story window from an angle.

A large sedan was parked behind Linc's Jeep, and a man got out to approach the porch. She couldn't see his face, or whether he was armed. Maybe he was one of the marshals Linc said Sanford was sending. The man stepped onto the porch and disappeared from view. She crept along a wall of the second-floor landing near the banister as a knock sounded at the front door. As unobtrusively as possible, Mikayla peered down the stairs. Marshal Tran, dressed in chinos and button-down shirt, his sidearm in a shoulder holster, opened the door. The newcomer stood outside the entryway, a marshal's star on his belt, a pistol in its holster strapped to his belt. Tran stepped back to let the new marshal in.

Mikayla frowned. He was maybe six feet tall, dark hair parted on the side, a beard covering most of his face. A sudden chill crept like icy fingers down her spine.

He spoke to Tran in a low voice and she strained to make out the words. She heard "location's compromised" and "need to relocate."

Tran's response was clearer. "Sanford has to follow protocol, just like everyone else. I'll call him to verify so you sit tight, Deputy."

An expression crossed the new man's face that was hard to read. Possibly anger. Or maybe irritation at having his directive questioned. He looked toward the kitchen and when he turned in profile to scan the living room, Mikayla saw the mole and knew for certain. She ducked back, paused to take a shaky breath to steady herself, then ran lightly into the room where she'd slept.

That profile was indelibly etched into her consciousness. That man had stood quietly by the night Paco Zecena had argued with Peter. If he hadn't committed the murder himself, he was an accomplice to murder. He'd shot Linc. Now Donny Bertola had come for her. Fighting fear that wanted to freeze her into paralysis, she forced herself to take the valuable seconds to send a hasty text to Tran and Robles. With shaking hands, she tapped: **"Imposter! Get out!"**

That was all she had time for. They would have to defend themselves. As quickly as she could and with her heartbeat thundering in her ears, she shoved her feet into her shoes, yanked on a sweatshirt, and a coat over that. Her cell went in her jeans pocket and her wallet into an inner pocket of her coat. She grabbed the keys Linc had left her, then pushed open the bedroom window to eased out onto the roof, a cold wind chilling her face.

A muffled yell sounded from inside and Mikayla's stomach sank. She should have called 9-1-1. She would as soon as she had a second, but her first priority was getting to safety. Ears straining for any sound that would indicate what was happening inside the house, she crept across the dark shingles of the roof.

She scrambled around to the front side of the house. She'd seen a trellis with a climbing vine attached to a post. Without giving herself time to talk herself out of it, she lay on her belly and scooted over the edge of the roof until she could gain a toehold. The biting wind tugged at her hair and she wished she'd had a chance to braid it. She reached the ground, then darted across the lawn toward Linc's Jeep, just as the front door burst open.

"Stop right there."

She kept going, skidding around the end of the vehicle. She reached the door handle on the driver's side and jerked to a stop. Bertola stood squarely in front of her, arms raised in a shooting stance, the ugly muzzle of his gun pointed at her head.

# Chapter Seventeen

"Easy does it. Put your hands up and no sudden moves."

She raised her hands slowly over her head. This couldn't be the end. She looked into the dark eyes of the man holding the gun, eyes that gleamed with suppressed emotion. He reminded her of shallow water where an alligator lurked, calm on the surface but deadly underneath. He smiled, showing small, widely spaced teeth. Would he shoot her dead right here, or did he plan to take her someplace and kill her?

"Well now, Ms. O'Kane. Do you remember me?"

"You're Donny Bertola."

"Got that right. You didn't bother to introduce yourself that night at your fiancé's home. If you had, it would have saved me some trouble." There was something about the man that seemed off. She didn't know what she thought a killer might look like, but there was too much excitement in this man's eyes, like he'd discovered something that thrilled him. He nodded to the nondescript sedan parked on the road. "Get in, we're going for a little ride."

"What did you do to Robles and Tran? Are they hurt?"

"Aw, that's sweet of you to worry about them. But they're okay. Embarrassed, humiliated probably, because they lost a witness. Might lose their jobs, but it's a sucky job."

Delay. She had to delay, stall him, keep him talking, so the marshals Linc said were coming would get there. Mikayla had a feeling that if she got in that car, her odds of surviving dropped significantly. Her mind scrambled for some way of stalling him. "How could you do this? How could you turn on your own people?"

He gave an unpleasant laugh. "Easier than I thought it would be, and they were never my people. Like I said, it's a sucky job. New job's not much better, but I can take a little more leeway with it." He pointed toward the sedan with the muzzle of his gun. "Move it."

"What do you want with me?"

The smile turned feral. "No more discussion. Get in the car."

Mikayla moved, but slowly. There were no houses nearby. No nosy neighbors to get suspicious and call 9-1-1 about a man with a gun. She wished desperately she'd taken a second to make that call herself.

"Move it, Ms. O'Kane. You see, if I were following my boss's orders, you'd be dead by now. But he's an asshole so I don't mind making my own rules. But that only goes so far. If you make this more difficult than it's worth, I'll simply follow orders and dump your body. You want to live a little longer? You'll cooperate."

He moved ahead of her and opened the front passenger door. Transferring the pistol to his left hand, he reached behind his waist and brought out a pair of handcuffs and held them out to her. "Cuff yourself."

She stared at the cuffs, mind racing for an alternative. She really, really didn't want to be restrained.

"Put them on. You can keep your hands in front, but I want them tight." The gun pointed at her robbed her of any options. Moving mechanically, she did as she was told. Clicking the handcuffs around her wrists felt like he was pulling closed the bars of a cage.

Bertola reached out and grabbed her right hand, fingers cold against her skin, and cinched the metal even tighter around her wrists. He reached into his front pocket and pulled out a phone, then tapped the screen and held it up to snap a picture.

"Now give me your cell."

Her stomach fell, leaving a hollow feeling of helplessness. The tiny sliver of hope that he wouldn't think to take her phone shriveled and died. She managed to reach around to her rear pocket with her cuffed hands and retrieved the phone. He took it from her and held the button until it was completely powered off, then slipped it into his coat pocket. She didn't know until that moment how much hope was contained in that miniscule electronic device. The locator app Linc had downloaded wouldn't do her any good now.

"Get in."

With no other option, she slid into the seat. He slammed the door shut and rounded the hood. Even with her hands cuffed, she was able to snap the seatbelt in place. He got in the car, turned the key, and the engine roared to life. Within seconds they were speeding down the road.

He'd said Tran and Robles weren't dead—she hadn't heard gunshots—but they had to be injured, and she didn't think he'd have left them in any position to help her. They had to hold on until the other marshals arrived.

The car flew along the highway. Mikayla forced herself to push back on the fear gnawing at the edge of her mind. Fear paralyzed and gave the enemy the edge. She couldn't sit around and wait to be rescued. If she was going to survive, she had to be smarter than her captor. She steadied her breathing and focused on her environment, watchful for anything that might be a means of escape. They were on a busy highway so she read the signs, and noted they were driving east toward the mountains. The scenery zipped past and Bertola weaved around other drivers, constantly accelerating and then braking. Where was the highway patrol? She tried to think how she could get a message to Linc. But he was in California. He would come. He would search for her.

But in the meantime, she had to rely in herself.

The thought that Linc would look for her helped block some of the fear. Her heart warmed a little at the memory of those silly texts. He'd claimed she'd slept in his arms that night in the tent. What would have happened if she'd woken when he had, had been conscious of snuggling up against all that hard muscle? But she'd slept soundly, better than she had in weeks, probably because he made her feel safe. In his arms, she'd been free from the fears that dogged her.

She cast a considering glance at Bertola. Because of Linc, she knew more about the man than he might realize. Maybe she could use that to her advantage. He knew she could place him at Peter's house, but maybe he didn't realize she knew Linc, or that Donny had been Linc's partner.

"It won't matter, you know." Maybe if she could get him talking, he'd give up some information, something that could give her an edge.

"What won't matter, Mikayla? I like that name. Pretty name for a pretty girl."

Her stomach gave an uneasy roll at the comment. "If you kill me, it won't matter that I can't testify at Zecena's trial. I already identified Paco Zecena as being present at Peter's house before he was killed. They'll be able to use that in the trial. Kidnapping me isn't going to make a difference in that. Zecena will still go to prison."

"There's this little thing about the defense being able to question a witness, so any statement you've made has limited use if you're dead."

"Then why haven't you killed me? Why bother to take me with you?"

"Because you have some use to me alive. But don't worry, the end will be the same." He took his eyes off the road to glance in her direction. "Nice Jeep you had there."

Her skin chilled. "Jeep? It's not mine." Her stomach sank. He must have recognized the Jeep as Linc's.

"Do you like driving it?"

"I've never driven it. It belongs to a marshal."

"Boyfriend?" He acted like he wasn't that interested, until he snaked out a hand and grabbed her chin, jerking her face toward him even as he swerved around a slow-moving van. "Answer me," he barked, spittle coming out of his mouth.

She recoiled, pulling her chin away. "Not my boyfriend. One of the marshals was flying to California and left it in case I needed it."

"You're lying."

She glanced uneasily at his profile and decided saying nothing was safest. Her spirits sank. She looked out the window, studying her surroundings as he lapsed into silence. The safe house had been east of Salt Lake City, and they'd continued in that direction through several towns and were climbing in altitude as they drove into the mountains. The sky had turned a dull, sullen gray.

With a glance in his rearview mirror, Donny pulled over into a turnout at the side of the highway. Taking out his phone, he tapped out a message. His attention was diverted, so Mikayla cocked her head to see the screen. The message he was sending contained the picture he'd taken of her, wrists in handcuffs.

"God, I wish I could see his expression when he gets this. That would be *priceless*." His voice revealed barely contained excitement. He sat for a moment, fingers drumming on the steering wheel, knee bouncing. Then he slammed his fists repeatedly against the wheel in a frenzy of violence. "Fuck! Fuck! Fuck! Okay, okay." The repeated words seemed to calm him. He gripped the steering wheel. "Okay, this will have to do. It'll be worth it to see him beg, then to shoot him dead. Finish the job." He glanced at Mikayla before putting the car in drive and stomping on the accelerator so they skidded back onto the highway. The car surged ahead, hugging the tight mountain curves, tires squealing. She gripped the door hold as best she could with cuffed hands to keep from sliding in the seat.

Bertola continued his monologue. "He'll beg. He'll beg for me to let you go. I'll let him think I will, then when he thinks he's got you, I'll shoot you. He should witness that. Make him realize how absolutely powerless he is. But we need to make finding you a challenge. Not too difficult, though. Make him think he's got a chance to rescue you. Fucking white knight, that's what he thinks he is. So goddamn idealistic. Thinks he's better than me. I hate his fucking guts."

"Who are you talking about?"

"Your boyfriend, of course. Lincoln fucking Jameson." He looked at Mikayla's expression and laughed so hard he let the car drift to the side of the road, tires spinning as he jerked it back onto the highway. Mikayla's heart dropped and she clutched at the door handle when the car came perilously close to the guardrail that didn't look sturdy enough to keep them from tumbling down the steep drop-off.

"Want to guess how I know he's your boyfriend?" When she didn't say anything, he goaded her. "Come on, Mikayla. Ask me, how do you know Linc's my boyfriend?"

"Okay, how do you know Linc's my boyfriend? Which he's not."

"God, you're a piss-poor liar, but I'll tell you anyway. See, I called Otis Bland, sheriff of Podunk, Utah. He's almost as big an asshole as dear old Lincoln. Told him I was Linc's supervisor, and he couldn't wait to give me an earful. Linc never had much finesse, and he managed to tick the guy off royal. He was pretty eager to tell me that you and Linc had come in and a blind man could see something was going on between the two of you. Then you disappeared into a supply room, and he thought you must have been locking lips in there. Said Linc didn't have a professional demeanor. I told him I'd write him up, but I'll do better than that. This time I'll go for a head shot."

Cold crept around her heart. Donny's motivation had become clear. Sure, he wanted to get rid of the only witness who could place both him and Paco Zecena at Peter's murder, but more than that, he wanted to make Linc suffer. Whatever Linc had thought his relationship with his partner had been, Donny Bertola had never been his friend.

She glanced at him and he took his gaze off the road to look at her, then broke into his overloud laughter, like he was losing it completely.

\*\*\*

Linc strode across the airport concourse, frustration in every step. The sparse news he'd gotten had told him something had happened at the safe house and he had no idea whether Mikayla had been harmed. A call to her phone had gone straight to voicemail. The Wi-Fi on the plane had been abysmally weak and he'd only been able to receive the single text message from Sanford saying there had been a breach. A fucking breach. Where had he heard that before?

He passed through the wide doors into the cool, late afternoon of a cloudy day. A black SUV, red and blue lights flashing, was parked in the passenger pick-up area. When Linc walked out of the terminal, a tall man with bright red hair flashed his marshal's badge and credentials. "Marshal Jameson?" At Linc's nod, he continued. "I'm Marshal Royce Beltran. Chief Sanford sent me to pick you up."

"Fill me in while you drive."

The crawl through the congestion surrounding the airport had Linc's patience stretching to a near breaking point. Beltran described what had happened. Someone had breached the safe house, gotten the drop on two US Marshals, and walked out with the witness they were supposed to protect. "We're still piecing it together. Tran and Robles were both knocked senseless and are at the hospital."

"What happened to the witness? Where's Mikayla O'Kane?"

"She's unaccounted for."

"What the hell do you mean she's unaccounted for?" Fear, anger, frustration welled up until Linc felt like his emotions were choking him. He wanted to lash out, punch something. He forced the temper back. He had to use his head. How could this have gone so badly wrong? He'd promised Mikayla she would be safe, he'd left her in the care of others, and now she was "unaccounted for."

"She sent Robles and Tran a text to get out. The window to her bedroom was open, along with an indication she got off the roof by climbing a trellis."

"Is my Jeep still parked at the curb?" Please god, let her have driven off in it.

"Yes."

"Son of a bitch." He swore under his breath.

Linc pulled out his phone. He ignored the text message, instead flipping to the screen with the locator app. He activated the search for Mikayla, waiting impatiently for the little wheel to stop spinning. Location not available. Shit. She could be out of range of a cell tower. Or the app could have been disabled.

"Where are we going?"

"Marshals' office downtown. Sanford wants to brief everyone and give out assignments. Finding Ms. O'Kane is top priority."

"Damn well better be," Linc growled. He went back to the text message. It was from Ellie. She and Seth were booked on a flight and would be in Salt Lake City within a couple of hours.

***

Linc stood at the back of the conference room, too wound up to sit. He set down the coffee cup he'd been sipping from. He was already wired and didn't want his thinking addled by too much caffeine.

He'd tried to locate Mikayla using the app a half dozen times, but the "location not available" message kept coming up, making him want to heave his phone through the window. The bastard who'd taken her had probably trashed her phone. Linc tried to put a lid on the frustration and rage. Losing control wouldn't help him find Mikayla. As much as he wanted to commandeer a vehicle and go search for her himself, he knew there was better chance at success if he was part of a team.

A half dozen marshals sat in attendance while Sanford briefed them. His voice was grim. "Finding Ms. O'Kane is our priority. We're looking for an imposter, folks. This bastard posed as a marshal to gain access to the safe house and get the drop on Marshals Robles and Tran. Tran has yet to regain consciousness. Robles has a concussion but was able to give us a limited description."

Linc's phone vibrated with an incoming text. Number unknown, he thumbed it open, tapped the text icon, then stared at the image that made the blood freeze in his veins. Mikayla stared at him, green eyes sparking defiance, wrists shackled in handcuffs held in front of her. No message. Only that image to let him know that his heart had been taken.

"Fuck."

Sanford raised a brow. "Marshal Jameson?"

Son of a bitch. God damn it. Linc stood stock-still as all the pieces came together like a tightly packed Tetris screen.

"Stay with me for a minute. What's the description?" he interrupted. At Sanford's blank look, Linc spat out, "Robles's description of the imposter. What's he look like?"

Sanford frowned. "White male, mid-thirties. About six foot. Dark hair." He paused, eyes sharpening. "You think it's Bertola."

"I'll bet my pension it's Bertola."

Linc tapped on the photos icon to pull up the one he'd shown at the meeting the day before. He tapped again before speaking. "I'm sending you the photo. Send it to Robles, ask if he's the guy."

Sanford retrieved his phone and adjusted his reading glasses. A moment later he muttered, "Got it." He tapped a few times. "I sent it to her. Might take her a few minutes to get back to us."

Linc handed his phone to Sanford, his throat so tight he could barely speak. "This came in a minute ago."

Sanford's head snapped up and his lips thinned to nonexistent.

He glanced at the rest of the marshals. "We have confirmation Mikayla O'Kane is a hostage."

The room erupted with curses. "This doesn't change the plan, people. We suspected as much. Now we know." Sanford handed Linc's phone to the marshal working on a laptop. "Get this distributed everywhere." The marshal took the phone, tapped for a moment, then handed it back to Linc.

Voices came from the hall outside the conference room and Ellie walked in, followed by Seth and a female marshal Linc didn't recognize. He felt the tension inside him ease a fraction, and for the first time in hours felt a flicker of hope. He didn't have anything against Sanford, he was a good leader, but hands down, Seth was the best there was, and Ellie brought her own special mojo.

Seth beckoned the unknown woman forward. "Linc, this is my rookie, Deputy Marshal Isabella Nikolaev."

Linc shook the woman's hand. Tall and willowy, she had long black hair plastered in a tight bun at the back of her neck and startling blue eyes. She gave him a wide smile. "It's Bella, and pleased to meet you." The words held the whisper of an accent.

Sanford approached, phone in hand. His gaze zeroed in on Linc. "Robles confirmed Bertola's our guy."

Linc strapped down on the rage bubbling inside him. He'd see Mikayla safe, then he'd take grim satisfaction in pulling the trigger and shooting his former partner between the eyes.

Linc showed Seth the photo of Mikayla in handcuffs.

"What the hell? That fucker has Mikayla." Seth rarely let loose, but his iron control had been shaken.

"Yeah." Linc shook his head. "He still has his marshal's star and creds and used them to get into the safe house."

"How would Bertola know your connection to Mikayla?"

Linc looked at his brother. "The only way I can figure is that Hector Lopez must have gotten word to Zecena, identifying me as the marshal with Mikayla. We know Donny's working for Zecena, and Zecena knows I'm on the case." His mind reeled. "I hope to God Donny hasn't figured out—" He broke off when Sanford moved forward and everyone in the room went quiet.

"Figured out what? No holding back now," the chief deputy said.

"That Mikayla and I are involved. It'll make things that much worse for her." He'd get busted for that later, but he didn't give a damn. Hell, Sanford had already called Mikayla Linc's girl.

"Why is that?" the marshal at the laptop asked.

Ellie answered. "Donny has always been jealous of Linc."

"Not always. Only about women."

"Always, Linc." Ellie turned to Sanford. "Linc is smarter and he's a better marshal. Women respond to him. Donny is a screw-up, as well as an idiot around women. I ran into him at a bar once." She glanced at her brother. "I told you about it, but you blew me off." She continued, "Donny was pretty lit, and sloppy with it. He couldn't stop blabbing. Kept making comments about Linc. He acted like it was all in fun, but it was clear he resented Linc. Said he lived a charmed life. He thought my brothers and I get special privileges because our stepdad is Arch Bollinger."

Sanford's brows went up and someone in the room whistled. "Your stepdad is Archer Bollinger?"

Ellie rolled her eyes. "Yep, he is."

"Don't you start," Linc muttered.

"The man's a legend."

"He's our stepdad," she stated.

Seth brought them back on task. "Our original theory that Bertola was a liability to the cartel wasn't correct. Instead of running *from* them, he ran *for* them. If Mikayla testifies, Bertola and Zecena are looking at the death penalty. Zecena's goal is to kill Mikayla so she can't testify. No doubt, that's Bertola's ultimate goal as well." Seth glanced at Linc. "Sorry, but that's the bottom line."

"I know." Linc rubbed the center of his chest.

"Our advantage is Bertola's relationship to Linc," Seth continued. "My brother knows him, knows his moves, how he acts in a clutch situation. We need to use Donny's resentment against him. He already screwed up by sending the picture of Mikayla. He wants to fuck with Linc. But Bertola tipped his hand. No one else would bother taunting Linc."

Seth eyed the assembled marshals. "My bet is Bertola wants to finish the job he failed at a few months ago. He wants to take Linc out. From what Ellie said, resentment has been building beneath the surface for years, and it's got to eat at him that he failed to kill him the first time around."

Linc nodded. "Ellie's right. Donny's made this personal. He wants to finish what he started when he shot me. Finishing it means killing me, and using Mikayla to get at me feeds into the narrative."

Another marshal came in and handed Sanford a folded slip of paper. Linc took a second to pull out his phone to try again with the locator app.

"Then we'll use that to our advantage." Seth addressed Sanford. "Can you track the location of the phone used to send Linc the photo of Mikayla?"

Sanford waved the paper. "Says here it was a burner phone, so no."

"I got her."

All eyes went to Linc. He held up his phone so Sanford could see the map. "Where's this?"

Sanford brought the reading glasses from the top of his head to perch on the end of his nose. "Mountains east of here. Cell coverage is spotty up there, so I'm surprised you got anything."

Linc shook his head. "I'm not surprised. Donny had her phone off until he was ready for me to know her location. He picked someplace with cell coverage because he wants me to come for her.

"He's laying a trap."

# Chapter Eighteen

Mikayla locked the bathroom door, sat on the toilet seat, and let her head rest in her hands. She needed a minute to breathe. She'd survived this far, but the thought of spending the night in the little cabin with Donny terrified her. He was planning something, and she figured he intended to hurt her. His motivation certainly went beyond removing her as a witness. He'd targeted her because of her relationship with Linc.

She stood and went to the sink and ran the icy water over her hands. Her reflection in the mirror showed fear and exhaustion evident in her drawn appearance. She dried her hands, then pulled the zipper on her coat to her chin as she gave careful scrutiny to the small, cramped bathroom. The only window was tiny, too small for escape. Even if she could squeeze through, the sky was darkening and the temperature falling, so fleeing on foot would likely mean frostbite and hypothermia.

If somehow she could wait out Donny, stay alert until he fell asleep, maybe she could steal the car keys. The likelihood that she'd be able to get the keys from him was remote, but it was the only plan she could think of.

Rubbing at the pressure marks on her wrists, she stepped out into the main room of the small cabin. She'd convinced Donny to take off the cuffs so she could use the toilet. Maybe he'd forget about them. He'd gone outside and Mikayla cast an assessing gaze around the cabin. Neat and tidy, the place was furnished in bear décor. Carved bears climbed a lampstand, embroidered cubs smiled from throw pillows, and even the area rug had a big bear surrounded by paw prints woven into the fabric. Why didn't the owners have a telephone? They probably wanted their little cabin to be a refuge, but damn, she'd give anything for a phone. She pulled open a drawer on an end table and found a box of dominos and a couple decks of playing cards with bears (no surprise there) on the backs.

She wondered who owned the place. After driving into the mountains for what seemed like hours, Donny had finally slowed when icy rain started pelting the windshield. They'd continued to climb in altitude and the precipitation had turned to snow. They'd come to a mountain community and he'd pulled out his phone. Mikayla thought he was checking for cell coverage. Then he'd begun driving up and down dirt roads, slowing to study structures before finally stopping at this one.

There were only a couple of cabins nearby, no lights shone from the windows, and porches and driveways were covered in undisturbed snow. He'd picked the lock and made himself at home, and even turned on the water to the house so she could use the bathroom. The bear-loving owners, whoever they were, had no idea a killer was hiding out in their little slice of mountain heaven.

Donny pushed open the door, arms laden with several logs. Mikayla went to shut the door behind him, glancing with worry at the driving snow. The wind had risen, blowing the snow nearly sideways. The likelihood of rescue was becoming more and more doubtful. Her head spun, and she realized she hadn't eaten all day. Her constant state of anxiety probably didn't help either. She shook off the dizziness. She had to keep her wits about her and watch for any opportunity to escape.

Donny dumped the logs onto the stone hearth and straightened. "Oh yeah. Can't forget the plan." He reached into his coat pocket and retrieved her phone. He tapped the screen and frowned as he waited for it to power on. "What's your passcode?"

She hesitated and his gaze snapped up to hers. "Don't fuck with me, Mikayla. Tell me your code."

She told him and he thumbed in the numbers. After tapping on the screen, he barked out a laugh. "That's beautiful, absolutely beautiful. Linc Jameson is the only person on your location app." He walked over to her and shoved the screen in her face. "You want to tell me again that he's not your boyfriend?"

She didn't say anything. She could see the spark of rage in his eyes. His hand whipped up and seized her by the back of the neck. "Don't ever lie to me again." He shook her. "You hear me?"

Mikayla gripped his wrist. "I hear you."

He released her, his mood shifting, and in a split second he was grinning again, making her think of a gargoyle's grotesquely contorted face. "God, this is working out even better than I imagined. The fucking white knight will charge up here, half-cocked as usual, ready to rescue the damsel." He wagged his brows at Mikayla. "But we'll be ready for him, sweet thing. You and me, we're a team now."

Donny stacked large logs onto the fireplace grate and opened the box of extra-long matches sitting on the mantel. He struck one and held it to a log where it fizzled before going out. He tried it two more times before throwing the lighted match into the fireplace where it flared and died. "Damned logs won't light."

He caught her watching him. "You do it. Get the logs to light or we're going to freeze. I've got stuff to do outside."

He pushed through the front door, leaving her staring after him. She did a quick scan of the cabin to see if there was anything she could use as a weapon. The only things were heavy wrought-iron fireplace tools. Something to keep in mind, but they wouldn't be much use against a gun.

She glanced in the kitchen and noticed a back door. Maybe she shouldn't dismiss a simple escape. Sure, it was snowing and running into the woods was risky, but there had been other cabins farther away. Down the road there'd been one with lighted windows. Or she could find another deserted cabin and take shelter there until morning. She had to do something before he handcuffed her again.

With her ears attuned to any sound of Donny returning, she crossed to the kitchen and pulled back a bear-print curtain to look out the window. She stumbled backwards, nearly knocking over a chair when she spied Donny standing on the other side of the glass. His back was to her, and he seemed to be staring into the woods behind the house. Her stomach sank at the big rifle, what she thought must be some sort of assault weapon, gripped in his hand.

With a hand over her rapidly beating heart, she leaned against the refrigerator. Maybe if she was more useful to her captor with her hands free, he'd leave off the cuffs. She opened cupboard doors and took a quick survey of the contents. The shelves contained several varieties of canned soup, chili, sliced peaches, blue boxes of mac and cheese, and mixes of various sorts. She'd figure out something to make for dinner. Powdered milk and a quart of vegetable oil made baking something a possibility. She opened the refrigerator. There were supplies that wouldn't go bad, like butter and condiments, but that was about it.

Feeling the cold seep in from under the doorsill, she rummaged around the kitchen, looking for something she could use as tinder for a fire. Spying paper bags wedged between a cabinet and the fridge, she grabbed those and returned to the fireplace. A metal box held kindling, so she used a poker to shift the logs so she could lay kindling on the grate. She wadded the paper bags and stuffed them beneath the grate, arranged the logs over the kindling, and struck another match. Within seconds, orange flames curled around the logs and a warm glow pushed back the chill.

Rising, she peeked out the front window. Donny was bent over the open trunk of the car, pulling out a bag loaded with something bulky. He brought it to the porch, where he set it down, and returned to the car. He wore the big rifle strapped across his back. And that was in addition to the pistol at his hip.

Donny's plan had been to lure Linc to a remote location to kill him. Using her as bait was the icing on the cake. But, as far as she could tell, he didn't have the supplies to remain here for any length of time so he must believe this would end quickly.

She sat on the hearth, her back to the warming fire, and tried to keep her rising panic at bay.

***

Conversation in the conference room rose and fell around him. Planning was crucial to success. Patient, meticulous planning, but Linc battled to clamp a lid on his festering impatience. He could be halfway up those mountains by now, that much closer to ending Donny Bertola.

Mikayla was Linc's, and the bastard had kidnapped her. Smart, capable, strong Mikayla who somehow had broken through his defenses and settled in his heart. Even though she'd hated going into WITSEC, she'd trusted him that it would work out in the end. And he'd let her down.

Linc knew if he lost her, he'd lose himself too. She believed in him, and made him see the man he wanted to be. He wanted to pursue a life with her. She was the only woman who'd ever made him think in terms of commitment and forever. And that fucker Bertola was using her to lure him in.

The discussion between Seth and Sanford grew heated, or as heated as anything ever got with Seth. Seth never raised his voice. He always kept his temper lashed down. The temper was there, but Seth's control was legendary.

"No, we don't wait for morning. I don't give a damn if there is a storm. That's to our advantage because Bertola will think that we'll wait for the storm to clear, wait until it's light. We're going in tonight."

Sanford ran his hands over his mostly nonexistent hair and shook his head. "Fine, but I want it on record that I advised waiting until morning. You're taking lead on this, Jameson, and it'll be your ass if you all get shot to hell."

"That works for me. I want a small team that I know. That means me, Linc, Ellie, and Nikolaev."

"Be sure about this, Jameson. You're going into terrain you're unfamiliar with, a mother of a storm is about to dump a few feet of snow, and you're up against someone who trained as a marshal and knows your moves."

"I'm sure."

Ellie stood and pointed to the screen of the laptop she'd been working on. "According to the GPS on Linc's app, Mikayla's phone is at a cabin near a small town in the mountains called Pine Cove."

Seth turned to her. "Good. I want you to find a satellite image of the cabin and what's around it. Let me know when you've got it."

Within a half hour, which Linc knew was damn good time no matter if it felt like an eternity, they were on the road in a big SUV. Seated in the passenger side, Ellie navigated using GPS, guiding them into the mountains. Linc was in back with Bella, who sat with a kind of contained quiet that didn't give away what she was thinking.

Before setting out, he'd checked the locator app one last time. Mikayla hadn't moved, or at least her phone was still in the same location. Powering off his phone felt like cutting his tie to her, but he didn't want Donny using the app in reverse to track Linc.

According to the satellite image, a heavily wooded area edged along the back of the property, and there was an outbuilding in the back separate from the cabin that could provide some cover.

Linc touched the window and found it icy. They were climbing in elevation, and a driving snow was pelting the windshield, the wipers swiping back and forth.

Ellie checked the GPS. "Five miles until our turnoff."

Next to him, Bella checked her Remington 700 with its scope, then pulled on black gloves. Her competent, practiced movements told him this wasn't her first rodeo.

"The access road is coming up on the right, Seth," Ellie directed.

Seth nodded. "Nikolaev, go over the plan one more time to make sure we have all the details."

"Yes, sir. We will take US Forest Service access road fourteen N ten for approximately two miles. We'll stop in a wooded area behind the cabin, which should allow us to approach undetected. Chief Deputy Jameson will reconnoiter the outbuilding as a potential site from which to set up surveillance as well as maintain cover during a firefight. Ellie will find a suitable place in the perimeter of the woods from which she can provide cover fire.

"I will take a position at the front of the building with the understanding that if the opportunity to take out Bertola presents itself, Chief Deputy Seth Jameson needs to approve the kill shot. Linc will use the cover of darkness to approach the cabin to determine where Ms. O'Kane is being held. Ms. O'Kane's situation will determine how we proceed."

"Precise," Seth commented as he steered the Suburban onto the access road.

Linc caught the expression on Bella's face. Interesting. Her recitation had been disciplined and dispassionate, but the look she shot his brother was anything but.

They turned off the highway and bumped along a road until Ellie directed Seth to pull over. The snow had let up, and the wind with it. Linc saw the outside temperature on the dash read 27°.

They exited the vehicle and took a moment to tighten the straps on their Kevlar vests and grab their weapons. The others went through their radio check. Linc was going in dark. He tugged his beanie over his ears and pulled on gloves designed to provide both warmth and dexterity. Seth and Ellie were armed with AR15s in addition to their handguns. Linc had his Glock at his hip and another in a holster strapped to his thigh. He added one extra clip of ammo and figured he was set. Each team member had tactical flashlights with filters to diffuse the light and make them less likely to be detected.

They set out through the woods toward the cabin.

With the clouds blocking any celestial light, the dark was near absolute. They moved through the woods using the flashlights sparingly. Linc spotted the cabin in a clearing ahead. The two windows to the back were dark. A faint glow came from the front, which wasn't visible. Following the plan, Seth and Linc moved to the left toward the outbuilding, Bella stayed within the trees to circle the cabin and get into position in the front.

Ellie slogged through the brush. Linc knew she would look for a tree that could offer some protection as well as a vantage point from which to cover the far side of the cabin. Feeling a cold touch on his cheek, he looked up to see the ghostly white of snowflakes gently wafting from the low clouds.

Linc followed Seth to the side of the shed not visible from the cabin. It had only one point of access, a rolling garage-type door. A recently cut lock lay in pieces on the ground. Seth crouched at a corner that offered him a view of the back door, Linc directly behind him. He pulled out his earpiece and held it away from his ear. Linc tilted his head to listen.

Bella spoke in a quiet voice. "Male subject approximately six feet tall has exited cabin through front door. Picking up something, looks like metal boxes, and is taking them inside."

Seth spoke into the mic. "Can you see anything through the front windows?"

"Curtains on the windows limit visibility, but I detect movement of two individuals inside. Flickering light suggests a fire, and smoke from the chimney indicates the fire is contained to the fireplace. The only other source of light appears to be a lamp on a table. When the door opened, I had verification of a woman inside."

"Description?"

"Taller than average, slender, long, dark-colored hair."

Mikayla. Linc had to take a steadying breath. She was alive.

Until that moment, the possibility that Donny had killed her but kept her phone to lure Linc to his location had been a constant, unspoken worry.

"Okay, we're good to go." Seth turned to look at Linc. "You ready?"

"Yeah."

"Be careful." At Seth's go-ahead gesture, Linc sprinted across the open space. Once at the cabin and with his back to the wall near the kitchen door, he glanced at Seth and caught the shake of his head. No one visible. Linc eased forward and took a quick peek inside. Kitchen empty, but evidence of a meal. Pot on the stove, empty cans, two bowls next to the sink.

Linc could hear the sound of a door shutting. Moments later what sounded like furniture being dragged across the floor came from the other side of the wall.

\*\*\*

Mikayla frowned at the whiff of an oily smell as Donny lugged a couple of gallon containers into the cabin. "What's that?"

"Found some kerosene in the shed. Might be fun to rig up a little explosion for your boyfriend when he arrives."

After his earlier outburst, she didn't bother to correct his assumption that she and Linc had something going. Maybe they did. She was more worried about what Donny intended to do with the kerosene.

She crossed her arms in front of her for warmth. The fire had died and with no more wood to feed it, would soon go out. She'd offered to get logs from wherever he'd gotten them, but he'd told her to shut up. She hadn't pressed her luck. She'd heated soup and baked a small tray of cornbread made from a mix she'd found in the cupboard. So far, he hadn't put the cuffs back on.

"And he'll arrive, all right." Donny picked up his monologue without missing a beat. "Fuckin' Linc Jameson thinks he's a hero. Not this time. This time he'll try his white knight routine and I'll laugh my ass off. Laugh all the way to Mexico and you two will be dead as the idiots the Jamesons are named after. Then everyone will see him for the shithead he is."

"Come here." He motioned her to the kitchen, pointing to a freestanding cabinet. "Push that in front of the door to block it."

Seeing no alternative, she did as he'd directed. When she returned to the living room, Donny had moved a small table next to the hearth and pushed a sofa so it faced the door and the window that looked out the front of the cabin. Through the window, something was barely visible in the faint light coming from the cabin. Mikayla moved closer and peered through the glass into the darkness outside. It took a moment before she realized she was seeing gently falling snowflakes.

"Son of a bitch, it's cold in here. Why'd you let the fire go out?"

"We need more wood. I can get some if you want."

His bark of laughter startled her. "You're like him, you know? Always underestimating me. You should have seen his face when I shot him. So goddamned *ironic*. Always acted so superior, so *ethical*, like his shit didn't stink. But I rushed it and the frigging bastard didn't die."

Mikayla let him spew his hate without commenting. She sat in a chair with overstuffed cushions, hands jammed deep in her coat pockets for warmth, wondering if Donny was right and Linc would come before the night was through.

"I know exactly what he'll do. By now he knows where you are, and that's only because I want him to so he'll come charging up here to rescue you. I know how the Marshals Service works. They'll want to wait for morning, especially since there's a storm. But Linc won't wait. He's so fucking predictable. He'll think he can overpower me or outsmart me. He'll come because he wants to be a hero, but I'll nail him, and this time I'll make sure the shot goes through his heart. Knowing the Jamesons, he'll have his brother and sister with him. They think they're goddamn Marshals Service royalty. Won't matter, though. They can die with him. I'll be ready and I'll destroy the fucking bastards."

He blew on his hands for warmth. "I'll get the wood." He paused, hands still at his lips. "What's that?"

"What?"

"That noise."

"I didn't—"

"Shut up. I need to hear." He stood motionless, head cocked as he listened.

Mikayla heard it this time. A faint scraping sound coming from outside. Her heart thumped heavily. If it was Linc, Donny was ready for him and he was walking into a trap. But he had to know that.

"Sounds like it's on the porch." He rushed to where she sat and grabbed her arm to yank her to her feet. He slapped the cuffs on one wrist, forced her to the floor, then looped the other cuff through the leg of the sturdy coffee table before fastening the second cuff. Without the key, the only way to get free of the table was to break it into pieces.

With his rifle still hanging behind his back from a strap across his shoulder, Donny drew his pistol and waved it in front of her face. "Now shut up. Not a word or I'll blow a hole in your brains and be done with it."

He crossed the room to stand beside the window. After a quick glance through the glass, he went to the door, eased it open, and slipped into the night.

Mikayla stared out the window. If Linc was out there, she needed to warn him. It didn't matter if Donny followed through with his threat. He was going to kill her anyway, but if she could save Linc, the risk was worth it.

The crosspiece connecting the legs of the coffee table kept her from lifting the leg and sliding the cuffs free, but she thought it was the weakest piece of the table. She maneuvered to set her feet on the opposite leg, grasped the crosspiece, and pulled with all her might. It gave a fraction of an inch, but before she could try again, something solid banged against the outside wall of the cabin, followed by the sounds of scuffling feet.

The door flew open to bang against the wall. Linc stumbled through, Donny following close behind, hand cinched around Linc's elbow and his gun snugged firmly behind Linc's ear.

# Chapter Nineteen

Blood dripped from a gash on the side of Linc's forehead. His gaze locked on Mikayla's before sweeping over her. He zeroed in on the handcuffs and his expression hardened.

Her heart thundered in her chest and a ringing started in her ears. She wanted nothing more than to run to him and feel those strong arms wrap around her. His rescue plan must have gone horribly wrong. He'd put himself in danger to rescue her, and now Donny would get what he wanted—a second chance to kill Linc.

Donny pushed Linc farther into the room and slammed the door shut before twisting the lock. "What did I tell you? He wanted to be a fuckin' hero and he blew it."

Holding the gun with one hand trained on Linc, he fished the handcuff key out of his pocket. He held it up by a short leather strip and bent to push it into Mikayla's hand. "Unlock those. No sudden moves or your boyfriend gets it."

She moved slowly, deliberately fumbling with the key to give herself time to think. The only thing she could do was pay attention and be ready to act if an opportunity presented itself. She unlocked one cuff, then the other.

"Get a move on. I want you to cuff him, hands behind his back. Pull his gloves off first so you can cinch them tight. And don't try anything. I could end you both in seconds, and don't think I won't do a better job on the shithead than I did last time."

She moved behind Linc and pulled back his hands, then tugged off his gloves. In a subtle move, he slid his fingers between hers and squeezed firmly. The touch made her chest ache. With him near, she felt stronger. She tipped her head to rest her forehead on his back while she cuffed his wrist, wishing she could absorb his strength.

She focused on her task, and on trying to find a way out of their situation.

Donny had captured Linc, but there had to be a way to work together to get free. Maybe Linc had a plan, but she couldn't be sure. She needed to do what she could. And she still had the key in her hand.

She chanced a quick glance at Donny, then tilted her head again to perform her task. His eyes were focused on Linc, a disconcerting look of glee in his expression. Getting the upper hand on Linc mattered. Maybe she could use that. She wrapped the metal bracelets around Linc's wrists, then, holding her breath, heart pounding, took the risk. She slid the key into his palm before moving away from him.

A diversion. She needed to create a diversion. "Donny, why don't I get some wood for the fire?" She moved to the door, raised her hand to the knob.

"Get the hell away from that door." He grabbed her by the elbow and shoved her back toward Linc, then moved to the side of the window and pulled back the thin curtain to look out. "You're not going out there. This asshole didn't come alone."

He turned back to Linc, a sneer on his face. "Your brother and sister out there, shithead? Did fucking Seth and the oh-so-hot Ellie come with you? Not like you aren't arrogant enough to come by yourself, but the Jamesons usually travel in a pack." He moved back across the room, thrusting his face up into Linc's. "Admit it, asshole. They're out there trying to figure how to get you out of the clusterfuck you've created." He gave Linc a hard shove, and when that didn't move him, shoved again.

Linc held himself with his feet planted wide. With a steady voice, he said, "A half dozen marshals have this cabin surrounded. Unless you walk out of here with your hands in the air, you'll be dead before this is over."

Donny lashed out and backhanded Linc across the mouth, snapping his head back. Mikayla couldn't smother a cry of alarm.

"God, that was a long time coming." Donny snickered as blood welled, bright red, at the corner of Linc's mouth. "I'm not walking out of here with my hands up, dumbass. Don't forget I know how the marshals work. Somebody's out there, other marshals, local LEOs, doesn't matter. You brought backup to cover your ass. But you fucked up and now I have two hostages."

Donny moved behind Linc and Mikayla held her breath. He cinched the cuffs even tighter, then set about disarming Linc. He pulled on the Velcro straps holding the guns with their holsters secured to Linc's hip and thigh, and transferred them to his own body, strapping them on in the same manner Linc had worn them. He patted Linc's pockets and retrieved a clip. Next, he pulled the straps on Linc's bulletproof vest and transferred it to his own body, pressing the Velcro to make the fit snug.

"Well, now, this worked out fine. I'm better armed and wearing body armor. Thanks, buddy." He kept away from the windows, his lips turning in a smirk as he glanced around the room. "Now let's see how we're going to do this."

Mikayla had the unsettling feeling he was eyeing potential sites to commit murder.

"What are you doing, Donny? It's not too late, you can still walk away."

Donny's loud laugh grated on her nerves. "That's what I should do, right? Let you two go. The almighty Lincoln Jameson thinks I should walk away. You are so full of shit, Linc."

"You know they'll go for the death penalty if you kill me or Mikayla. Juries hate when witnesses or law enforcement are murdered. Walk out and you're only on the hook for Joey Medrano. You know surrendering without a fight will give you leverage for a lower sentence."

"They're not going to catch me, you smug bastard. I'm going to walk out of here and go wherever the hell I want to go. You'll be my shields when I want to get to the car. I'll take one or both of you to ensure a clean getaway. But we're going to have a little fun first, a little payback."

Donny pushed Linc toward a chair near the now-cold fireplace, then again, harder, when Linc didn't move. Linc stumbled against Mikayla and she grabbed his wrists to steady him.

"Into that chair. We'll chat like old times. Only now it won't be about how great the fucking Jamesons are. You're going to listen while I list all the ways you're an asshole. Then I'll have the enjoyment of hurting your girlfriend while you watch. But don't think I'm like Paco Zecena. Now that bastard is sick. The enjoyment I'll get is watching you suffer. The asshole who failed at being a hero."

Mikayla swallowed convulsively as her stomach heaved. She stood uncertainly, mind working feverishly. She caught Linc's gaze. He flicked his eyes toward the window, a subtle twitch. She followed his glance. The curtains were slightly open. She looked at Linc again, unsure what he wanted.

"Son of a bitch!" Donny's outburst had Mikayla jumping, heart in her throat. "Where's the key? Where's the fucking key for the cuffs?" He grabbed her by the arm, swinging her around to face him.

She stuck out her hand, palm up. "Here."

He snatched it up, giving her a suspicious look, and thrust it into his pocket, then grabbed her arm, propelling her to the chair by the table a few feet from Linc.

She didn't know how he could have unlocked the cuffs, but then why had he passed the key back to her if he hadn't used it? He must have managed somehow and was biding his time while letting Donny think he was still restrained.

While she searched for some way to distract Donny, Linc kept up his efforts at verbal persuasion. "If you won't walk away, then let Mikayla go. You've got me. I'm the one you wanted to kill. You don't need her."

"Don't tell me what I need. She's not going anywhere. You think this is all about you, asshole? There's a little problem with your girl here. She saw me and she saw Zecena at that prick Wellington's house. The Zecenas want her dead. If I want to stay in that organization, then dead is what she's going to be."

"Why'd you get involved with them? You were one of us, Donny."

"I was never one of you." Donny's face flushed red with anger. "I'm done talking. We need to get this done." He raised the hand holding the gun and pointed it at Mikayla.

Her field of vision narrowed until all she could see was the muzzle of the gun pointed at her like a deadly black eye. Adrenaline spiked and she reacted on instinct. She dove to the side, tipping over the seat in the same instant a sharp crack of gunfire sounded. A small hole appeared in the front window as Donny spun around, the gun flying from his hand and landing on the floor near the fireplace.

Linc all but flew from his seat, handcuff swinging from one wrist, arms outstretched as he launched himself to tackle Donny, who kicked and rolled, gaining his knees as he scrambled for the gun. Linc leapt onto Donny's back. With controlled violence, Linc heaved him onto his stomach with a knee to his back.

"You're breaking my ribs," Donny gasped. "I can't breathe."

"Yeah, and I'm worried about that."

Mikayla wasn't even aware she was standing. She moved to add her weight on Donny, but Linc barked, "Stay back." He wrenched Donny's hands behind his back, then reached into his former partner's pocket and retrieved the key. Donny made choking sounds as Linc transferred the handcuffs to his prisoner's wrists.

Pounding steps sounded on the porch and the door crashed open. Seth flew in, followed by Ellie and another female marshal, all of them wearing tactical gear, big guns held ready. Mikayla scrambled out of the way. Once they saw Donny on the floor, they lowered their weapons.

Seth retrieved Donny's gun and passed it to the second female marshal. "Let's see where he's hit." Seth crouched next to Donny. Linc rolled him over and he continued to gasp for breath.

"There." Seth pointed to what looked like a metal tab embedded in the vest. The armor had done its job and stopped the bullet. Donny clutched at his arm, mouth moving as he tried to suck in air.

"Got the wind knocked out of him, but he'll live. More's the pity." Linc's voice sounded distracted as he surged to his feet. He wiped the blood from his lip with the back of a hand, his gaze tracking across the room until zeroing in on Mikayla. He ignored something Seth said and strode toward her. When he reached her, he didn't stop moving, backing her against the wall, big hands cradling her head, tilting up her face. Mikayla could almost feel the burn on her skin from the intensity of his gaze. The blood on his forehead made him look like a battle-tested warrior.

"Did he hurt you?"

Emotions swelled, rising in her throat to nearly choke her, and she struggled to push them back. The events of the past few minutes had flashed past in a blur of sight and sound, and now she was having trouble accepting that the danger had passed.

Thumbs brushed her cheeks. "Mikayla?"

Unable to speak, she gave her head a quick shake. She wanted to burrow into him and feel his arms close around her, to be encircled by his strength. He loosened one hand, grazing his fingers across her temple to brush hair away from her eyes.

"Anywhere, Mikayla? Did he hurt you? Assault you?"

She drew in a shaky breath. "No, no. I'm okay."

He pinned her with his gaze, heat from his body warming her.

"Really, I'm okay. You're here. I thought he was going to kill you. I was terrified, but now I'm not. You're here." The words tumbled out of her mouth.

He didn't let her go, his hazel eyes storm clouds of emotion.

Seth's voice cut across the room. "Ellie, radio Sanford, give him the sit rep. Nikolaev, secure Bertola's weapon. Linc, I need you here. I want the vest off to see if the bastard's really hurt."

Linc hesitated, his hands still on her face. Mikayla felt like an unrelenting sea was threatening to batter her against sharp rocks. He watched her carefully even as he stepped back. She forced herself to focus on the scene around her to gain some control.

He joined his brother and knelt beside Donny, who seemed to have finally managed to catch his breath. Seth pulled on the Velcro straps of the body armor and removed the vest. "He's damned lucky the vest stopped that round. Going to hurt like a bitch, though." He pulled up Donny's shirt to reveal an area on his ribs sporting an angry red bruise. Seth and Linc each grabbed an arm and despite Donny's cries of pain, hoisted him to sit in the chair by the fireplace.

The female marshal approached Mikayla. "I'm Deputy US Marshal Bella Nikolaev." She pronounced her name with an exotic inflection. "I'm glad you are safe, Ms. O'Kane."

"It's Mikayla, and thank you." She tried to speak normally even though she felt like a single touch would shatter her. She hated feeling fragile. "I'm glad no one was killed. Even him."

"Nikolaev, see if there's ice or frozen peas in the freezer to put on Bertola's bruises." Seth's tone was brusque.

"Yes, sir."

Seth nodded to the door where snowflakes drifted lazily in the circle of light cast from the cabin. "Let's see if we can get that door to shut and keep whatever warmth there is inside."

The doorframe had splintered and the handleset broke when the door had been kicked in, but it still hung on its hinges and Linc and Ellie were able to prop it closed. Once it was secured, Seth turned and surveyed the group, his gaze snagging on his brother. "You need to clean that cut on your head."

Donny uttered a protracted groan. "I need to go to the hospital. This is blunt force trauma. I've got internal injuries."

Linc speared Donny with a murderous look, fists clenched. "You shot me in the chest, you fucking shithead. You've got a bruise. Hard to be worried."

"I am hurt. I think you broke my ribs." Donny's voice rose to a whine.

Linc unclenched his fists, shaking his head. "I'm done with you."
He glanced at his brother. "I'll get some wood to get a fire going."

Seth shook his head. "Head wound first."

Mikayla stepped forward. "I'll look in the bathroom for a first
aid kit." At Seth's nod, she crossed to the bathroom. She stepped
inside and flipped on the light, and once out of sight of the group,
lowered the lid to the toilet and sat abruptly. She brought up her legs
and wrapped shaky arms around them, tilting her head until her
forehead rested on her knees, then squeezed her eyes shut.

She took a deep breath, letting it out slowly even as it hitched. A
minute, she needed a minute to get herself under control. The image
of Linc with Donny's gun held to his head flashed in her mind. Once
again she could hear the crack of the rifle and found herself reliving
that moment of terror when she hadn't known if he'd been hit. The
fear and anxiety that had been her constant companions all day were
eroding the bulwarks she'd so carefully erected around her emotions.

A tremor shook her body. No matter how tightly she held herself
the trembling didn't ease. She began to shake so violently she feared
she would break apart, simply splinter into hundreds of jagged
pieces. The bathroom door shut and she jerked her head up, and had
only a second to take in Linc's presence before he bent and scooped
her into his arms. He turned to sit on the toilet lid, settling her on his
lap with his arms wrapped securely around her. He didn't say a
word. He tucked her against his chest and held on tight.

Her breath hitched and she shook her head back and forth in
jerky movements. "Go away. I told you I'm fine."

"I'm not going anywhere."

"No, no, no. I don't cry. I never cry. You need to go." Despite
her protest, she made no effort to move from his arms.

"It's okay, sweetheart. I got you. You're safe. You can cry if you
want. I got you," he murmured, his voice a low rumble in the ear she
had pressed against his chest. She tried to take in a deep breath, but it
heaved out, hitching and ragged. Despite squeezing her eyes shut she
felt Linc's shirt grow damp under her cheek.

"That's it, baby. Cry it out."

She had never allowed herself to cry since the night her father had been killed. But there on Linc's lap, his arms a fortress, she felt the knot she'd kept pulled tight for so many years begin to unravel, one thread at a time. Gulping sobs broke loose, shaking her with their intensity.

Linc's lips moved in her hair, murmuring words she couldn't make out, comforting all the same. He freed one arm to tear off some toilet paper. He wiped her eyes and nose and made her feel like she was ten years old, which only made her cry big, heaving sobs she thought would tear her in half.

He kept hold of her, cradling her, one big hand stroking her back. He continued to speak in his low, rumbly voice that touched something deep inside. She felt those bindings she had used to keep control of her emotions being wound together again to form another kind of bond, one she was afraid was attached directly to Linc.

The sobs and tears wound down. She took a tissue from him and blew her nose. She felt raw, drained, and vulnerable. And no doubt looked a mess. She shifted to get up and Linc held on a moment longer, dipping his head to brush firm lips across hers. And with that simple gesture, the mood between them sparked into something more than comfort.

She scrambled to her feet and turned her back to him. At the sink, she splashed water on her face and used a towel to pat it dry, then opened the medicine cabinet. She took a long minute staring blindly at the contents. The barriers that protected her from heartache and loss had crumbled, and she needed time to shore up the foundations. If she allowed the intense emotion Linc pulled from her to grow, she was opening herself up to greater pain than she had ever endured. She stiffened when firm hands settled on her shoulders.

"I'm okay." She grabbed the boxes of bandages and gauze and turned to face him. And quickly realized she'd made a strategic mistake.

The tiny bathroom left little room to maneuver, especially for two people who never shopped in petite. Linc held his ground, resting his hands on the sink on either side of her hips.

"Sit, Linc. I'll clean that scrape."

He didn't move, instead narrowing hazel eyes. "Don't shut me out."

"I don't know what you're talking about."

"You know exactly what I'm talking about. You're pulling back because you're scared."

"I'm not scared."

"You are."

"Am not."

His eyes reflected the quick flare of amusement at her juvenile response. "You lost your father horrifically, and it hurt you. You've kept your heart safe so you don't get hurt again."

"I was engaged to be married only a week ago, Linc, so obviously I was willing to risk my heart." Even as she said the words she knew she was lying, and from his patient look, he knew it, too.

"Don't close me out, sweetheart."

The look on his face was so compelling, so honest, she heaved a broken sigh. "I'll try not to." At the moment, that was all she could give him.

He studied her, then nodded. "Good enough for now."

# Chapter Twenty

Linc talked with Ellie, but his gaze tracked Mikayla as she and Bella worked on putting together a meal. They sat at the table in the dining area to the left of the living room, providing an unobstructed view. Ellie nodded toward the now-silent Donny. "Glad he finally shut up."

"Yeah, me too."

Donny'd refused to use the bag of frozen corn on his swelling ribs, complaining it was too cold. They'd given him over-the-counter painkillers, and he'd complained they weren't strong enough. He'd protested vociferously when they'd bound his arms and legs to the chair but had finally wound down and now sat sullenly gazing at the burning logs in the fireplace. Linc wondered if, for all the years they'd worked together, he'd simply ignored the fact that his partner was a huge pain in the ass.

He rose, crossing to the kitchen window to gaze out at the snow swirling from a dark sky. "Still coming down."

Mikayla opened the door of the small oven, and Linc grabbed the oven mitts. "I'll get that." He reached in and pulled out the dish bubbling with scalloped potatoes, setting it on a hot pad on the table. Ellie brought utensils and plates, while Bella opened a can of sliced peaches. Seth stood looking out of the front window, phone to his ear. Linc had wadded up a scrap of paper and wedged it into the bullet hole in the glass to help keep in the heat.

"Hey, you gonna give me any of that?" Donny had perked up.

"You'll get yours when we're done."

They sat, ignoring Donny's swearing.

"Looks pretty good for coming from a box," Ellie commented as she spooned potatoes onto the plates.

Bella beamed her a smile. "We found ham in the freezer. There's some cooked with the potatoes."

Linc pulled another chair to the table and motioned for Mikayla to sit next to him. He took a loaded plate from Ellie and set it in front of her. He raised a brow when Seth sat across from him, laying his phone on the table next to his plate. "What did Sanford say?"

"He agrees we bring him off the mountain tonight. He's called the county and they're sending up a plow. Once it gets here, we'll follow it down. I checked the Ford Donny drove and it's got enough fuel."

He pointed to Linc. "You and Mikayla will drive the Ford. Ellie, Nikolaev, and I will transport Bertola in the Suburban." His gaze took in the others seated at the table. "We all need to stay alert."

Mikayla frowned. "I thought you arrested Paco Zecena along with the top guys from Mexico. How can we still be in danger?"

"We did arrest them, and the marshals in San Diego and Los Angeles conducted a sweep on the entire cartel. It's looking like we've decimated their operations in California, and it's a step to crippling their organization in Mexico as well." His eyes were a calm gray. "That doesn't mean *El Jefe* in Mexico still can't send someone to take out the witness who can place his brother at the scene of a murder."

"Then I'll never be safe."

Linc laid a hand over the one she'd fisted on her thigh.

"Yeah, you're still in danger. But the Mexican government is conducting coordinated raids, and they're closing in on the Zecena compound in Sinaloa. If they get *El Jefe*, the organization is done."

\*\*\*

Mikayla sat on the couch, swiping through the messages on her phone. Linc had retrieved it from Donny's pocket, and now she had limited battery life and texts from a worried mother to deal with. She heaved a heartfelt sigh. Martha had sent the first text of the day at about ten in the morning, and the messages had gotten increasingly peeved when Mikayla hadn't responded. Around one in the afternoon, the tone had switched to angry, and then a little before five, alarm had crept into the pleading accusations. Contrast that with the single message from Brady, which was, as usual, blunt and to the point. She was to call their mother and reassure her, then call Brady and tell him what was really going on.

She glanced around the room. Donny slouched in the chair, eyes half closed. She had the uneasy feeling something was going on in his head, and he wasn't as defeated as he looked. Claiming that the chore calmed her, Bella was singing softly in what sounded like Russian as she washed the dishes, while the Jameson siblings were huddled around the table, talking in quiet tones.

She gave some thought to the text to her mother, wording it carefully so she wasn't lying, but didn't reveal the serious nature of what had happened. Then she opened her favorites list and tapped on her brother's name.

He picked up on the first ring. "You okay?"

"Yeah. Scary day, but I'm fine."

"What the hell happened?"

She gave him a quick rundown on the events of the day, glancing up when she felt the couch give as Linc sat beside her.

"Really, Brady, I'm fine. Once it gets here, we'll follow a snowplow down the mountain and should be back in Salt Lake City before dawn. Then we'll get a chance to sleep."

"I don't like it, Mike. With all that protection, you shouldn't have been kidnapped."

She found herself reassuring her brother. "Linc is here, and three other marshals. They've got lots of guns."

Linc motioned to her. "Let me talk to him."

Mikayla raised a brow, then shrugged. Brady would probably feel better hearing it from Linc. "I'm passing the phone to Linc so you men can get your testosterone in order." She handed off the phone, then leaned back on the couch, feeling the exhaustion creeping up on her.

She glanced at the clock on the mantel, little bear hands pointing straight up. Midnight. She closed her eyes, letting herself drift, the voices in the room flowing quietly around her.

Mikayla didn't think she'd slept, but when she blinked her eyes open, she found herself tucked against Linc's shoulder. She tipped back her head and saw he had also nodded off. Dark stubble along his jaw highlighted the beauty of his long eyelashes resting on his cheekbones. She winced at the bandage on his forehead.

She reached up and ran a finger lightly along his hairline at the edge of the bandage. He could so easily have been killed. At any point, Donny could have simply pulled the trigger and that would have been it. Like her father, gone trying to protect her.

Linc reached up and gripped her hand, his eyes focused on her, a wealth of meaning in that look. Without breaking his gaze, he brought up her hand and kissed her palm, then shifted to bite lightly at the pulse point of her wrist.

She stifled a groan as heat rose from low in her belly. His lips moved back to her palm, his stubble brushing against her skin. When he sucked the tip of her pinkie into his mouth, sliding his tongue over it, she thought she could melt into a hot puddle of lust. "God, Linc," she whispered.

He paused, then removed the finger from his mouth. He leaned down to murmur into her ear. "I want to use my mouth all over you, sweetheart."

She reached up to grip the back of his neck and pulled his lips to hers, opening her mouth in a kiss that edged toward desperate. He responded in kind, tugging her onto his lap, sliding his tongue against hers.

"Hate to break up the party, kids, but the snowplow's here."

Linc took his time, ending the kiss with a little nibble on her bottom lip before lifting his head. "You always had shitty timing, Eleanor."

"I consider that my sisterly job."

When Mikayla thought her wobbly legs would support her, she set her feet on the floor and stood. Linc rose behind her, and when she shifted and brushed against him, she felt gratified by the evidence of his arousal.

While Linc and Seth freed Donny and took him to use the bathroom, Mikayla glanced around the room. It wasn't in the neat and tidy condition it had been in when she and Donny had arrived that afternoon. She turned to Ellie. "Shouldn't we straighten up the place? It doesn't seem right to leave this mess for the owner to discover."

Ellie shook her head. "We need to go. The Marshals Service will contact the owner, and pay for a crew to come up here to clean the place and do any repairs. They'll pay the owners compensation to make it right."

The sound of feet stomping on the porch made Mikayla's heart jump, but when the door opened and she saw it was Bella, she sighed with relief. Bella stood on the mat inside the door, snow melting from her boots, the smile on her face suggesting she liked nothing better than tromping through the snow at night. "The snowplow is on the highway, and I moved the SUV to the front of the cabin. We are ready to go." Mikayla was beginning to think Bella was the most naturally cheerful person she'd ever met. Even the most mundane tasks seemed to delight her.

Seth left Linc with Donny, who now had his hands cuffed behind him, and strode toward Bella, hand outstretched. "Keys."

The light in Bella's eyes drained away, and her expression turned serious. "I will drive. People from California don't know how to drive in the snow."

Seth looked like he would argue, then gave a curt nod and turned to Ellie. "You're riding shotgun. I'll be in the back with the prisoner." He tipped his head to Linc. "I want you and Mikayla in front of us in the Ford. Make sure one of you has the Salt Lake Marshals' office in your phones so you can get us there."

Within minutes, Mikayla was once again in the front seat of Donny's car, securing the seat belt in place, but this time she was thrilled to be in the vehicle. The snow had stopped, and the moon glowed behind thinning clouds. Linc turned over the engine, adjusted the seat and heat controls, and drove along the dirt road covered in slushy snow. She glanced over her shoulder and saw the headlights of the big SUV behind them. They came to the highway, and Linc flicked his high beams. The snowplow engine rumbled into gear and the heavy truck pushed ahead of them, the blade pushing snow to the side of the road. The plow moved faster than she'd anticipated and they began the descent down the mountain through the dark night.

She eyed Linc. "You tired?"

His eyes flicked from the road to her, then back again. "Yeah. You?"

"Yes, but I think I'm getting my second wind. Do you want me to talk to you, help keep you awake?"

"Hell yeah."

"Okay." She paused for a minute, then asked, "How did you and your siblings get your names?"

He snorted out a laugh. "Not what I thought you'd ask. We're named after famous historical figures my parents admired who had character traits worthy of naming their children for." He shrugged. "You can probably guess who I'm named for."

"I'm assuming Abraham Lincoln, certainly an admirable man. Is Ellie after Eleanor Roosevelt?"

"Yeah. My father had read a biography on Lincoln before I was born, so the name was on his mind. Mom told me once she admired Mrs. Roosevelt's resilience in the face of a husband who neglected her emotional needs. Which I think says a lot about their marriage."

"Hmm, and Seth?"

"Ever hear of Deadwood?"

"Oh, of course. Marshal Seth Bullock, lawman in the wild days of South Dakota. That's fitting."

"Says the history prof. Bet you're a killer playing Jeopardy."

"Depends on the category. I don't do well with pop-culture-type questions or sports."

"You don't like sports?"

"Ambivalent."

He shook his head like he was gravely disappointed.

"I take it you're a fan."

"I'll play and watch about anything with a ball." He tapped his fingers on the steering wheel. "Even baseball? Surely you like baseball. It's un-American not to like baseball."

"Baseball is like watching paint dry, slow and boring."

"Have you ever been to a game?"

"Brady played Little League for many years, and I went to almost all his games. Paint drying."

"What about a major league game? It's like magic, your first look at the field, being part of the crowd, singing 'Take Me Out to the Ballgame' during the seventh inning stretch. I'll take you to a Padres game, you'll see."

It was the first time he'd mentioned that there might be even something as simple as a baseball game to share in her uncertain future. Maybe she'd even like a baseball game if she was with Linc.

They lapsed into silence as he drove along the winding mountain road. They had dropped enough in elevation that there was less and less snow on the road. The plow eventually pulled over, and they sped past with a honk of the horn. Linc's navigation app said they still had over a half hour until they got to Salt Lake City.

Staring out the window with the dark shadows of trees flying by, she asked, "How did Donny get the drop on you outside?"

"He didn't get the drop on me."

"Linc, he caught you and brought you into the cabin with the gun pointed at your head."

"That was the plan. I let him grab me."

"You're kidding."

"Not kidding."

She stared at him, incredulous. "You let him catch you? Are you crazy?"

"Not crazy, either. I needed to get in the cabin, see where you were, make sure you were safe before we took him out."

She leaned back against the headrest. "Linc, he could have shot you dead at any point."

"Could have. I was counting on the fact that Donny would want to get in my face, lord it over me that he was in charge before he shot me again."

"So you gambled with your life that he wouldn't shoot you on sight."

He reached out a gloved hand and enfolded hers. "I was right, and he didn't, so no point getting upset. You were awesome, by the way."

"Yeah, awesome."

His eyes gleamed in the glow from the dashboard. "You kept your cool, got me the key to the handcuffs. That was a huge bonus. You kept it together when it counted." He raised a brow. "Cut yourself some slack, Mikayla."

Once again she felt like her shaky defenses were crumbling. Maybe exhaustion was adding to her emotional instability.

"What's wrong, sweetheart?"

She shrugged. "You're pretty cavalier about the risk you took."

He pulled her hand up and pressed his lips to her knuckles, and her fingers tightened convulsively around his. "We both got through this relatively unscathed. That was the goal, and that's what happened. There's no point in thinking about what ifs."

"Right."

"Mikayla."

She glanced over to find him frowning, eyes on the road, fingers tapping on the steering wheel. "What?"

He didn't speak for a long minute. "I've got feelings for you. Strong feelings." He shot her a quick glance, and his words, plus the hot look in his eyes, had her heart doing a slow somersault in her chest. "I want to know that I'm not the only one. That you've felt it too. I don't want to make an idiot of myself."

"Linc, I..." She stumbled over the words. The risk of opening herself to him, exposing those raw emotions, made her feel uneasy. Vulnerable. Exposed. She'd laid so much open to him already there would be nothing left if she told him she thought she was tumbling down a slippery slope toward love. She didn't know if when she reached the bottom she'd land in his arms or broken in emotional pieces on the rocks.

But then he looked over and they locked gazes and for one heart-stopping moment, she saw a flash of vulnerability.

"I have feelings, too. Strong feelings." The words came out in a rush.

"For me."

That brought out a laugh. "Of course, for you."

"Good." He kissed her fingers again, then let them go.

The lights of the city were getting closer as they made the final descent out of the mountains. Mikayla tapped on the navigation app and studied the map. "The highway takes us straight into downtown, then you'll have to take the exit."

"Why don't you tell me what else is worrying you."

She gave a startled laugh. "After what's gone on today, you have to ask?"

"Are you still worried about the cartel?"

"Of course. Do you really think the Zecenas will leave me alone?"

"I think it's likely. My guess is the organization will bring their people back to Mexico until things calm down on this side of the border. And as much as the Zecenas protect family, Paco messed up badly, and *El Jefe* will be pissed."

"Then I won't need to go into witness protection."

"That's not decided yet."

She nodded slowly. "Regardless, I need to get my car before going back to California. Maybe someone from the Salt Lake City Marshals' office can give me a ride to Concord."

He turned his head toward her. They had entered the city and streetlights cast bands of light, enough she could make out his frown. "*Someone* from the Marshals' office? Don't you mean me, Mikayla?"

"I thought you'd have to get to California."

"I'm going with you. Or I'll hire someone to pick up your car and transport it to California. Either way, I'm not letting you out of my sight."

# Chapter Twenty-One

By the time the five of them entered the hotel lobby, Mikayla was convinced only sheer grit and determination were keeping her upright. They'd checked in at the Marshals' office and turned Donny over for booking. Sanford had arranged the hotel, and the clerk checking them in assured them the rooms had been stocked with sleepwear and toiletries, including toothbrushes.

As they moved toward the elevators, Linc held her back with a hand to her arm.

"What?"

"Look, I don't want you by yourself. I don't think the Zecenas will send someone after you, but I'm not taking any chances."

Lines of fatigue fanned out from his tired eyes, making Mikayla remember that if Linc hadn't been drawn into her mess, he would still be on sick leave, recovering from a serious gunshot wound. "I'm fine, Linc. It's late. You said you thought the Zecenas are done in the US, at least for the moment. I don't think we have anything to worry about, and we all need to get some sleep."

He was shaking his head before she'd finished speaking. "No, I won't leave you unprotected. We all have our own rooms, but they all have two beds. You and I can share a room."

With the heat between her and Linc, even as exhausted as she was, she didn't think they'd be sleeping in separate beds. And sex with Linc was too important, too fraught with meaning, for her to make that choice lightly. She wanted to sleep with him, but on her own terms.

"No. We aren't sharing a room."

His expression gave nothing away. They reached the elevator where the others had stopped. He turned to his sister. "El, you're sharing a room with Mikayla."

His sister raised a brow, then glanced at Mikayla. "Okay." She looked like she was going to say something more, but the elevator chimed.

Linc leaned against the back wall of the elevator, arms crossed over his chest. He was probably irritated, but since her only goal was to crawl into bed and sleep the clock around, she figured she'd deal with Linc in the morning.

They stepped out on the fifth floor. Ellie stopped at a door on the right. Linc nudged his brother, had a short conversation, and they exchanged room keys. Bella and Seth disappeared into their rooms, and when Mikayla would have followed Ellie into theirs, Linc stopped her with a hand on her shoulder. "She'll be in in a minute, El." Ellie gave him a knowing smirk as she shut the door.

He took Mikayla's hands in his, interlacing their fingers, and pulled her close. "Those feelings, they go pretty deep."

"We haven't known each other long, Linc."

"Doesn't seem to make a difference. Does it matter to you?"

The intensity of his gaze forced her to answer honestly. She shook her head.

He pulled her closer, releasing her hands so he could bring his up to trace a finger along her jaw. He leaned forward, closing his eyes the moment before his lips met hers. She leaned forward, hands going behind his neck to pull him to her as his touch sent fiery heat leaping through her veins. He bit her lower lip, and when she opened her mouth, his tongue slid against hers, hot and sensuous. He threaded his fingers through her hair, cradling her head, and gentled the kiss, using his tongue to soothe. He eased back, tilting his forehead against hers. When she opened her mouth to speak, he gave his head a quick shake.

"Give me a minute, Mikayla." He inhaled deeply, his breath feathering across her face as he let out a controlled exhale. When he opened his eyes, she saw the banked desire. "What were you going to say?"

"Nothing," she murmured, glad she'd had the moment to reconsider asking him to take her to his room.

His eyes flared with sudden awareness, letting her know he'd guessed what she'd been thinking. With an abrupt movement, he knocked on her hotel room door, and when Ellie opened, he all but shoved Mikayla through.

*** 

Linc sat in the booth in the crowded diner across from the hotel, waiting for everyone to arrive. The smells of frying bacon and strong coffee reminded him of Sunday mornings when he was a kid. Maybe he'd get his mom to have everyone over for breakfast once the case was tied up. Give his family some time to be together without the stress of the job, and meet Mikayla.

His mom would make a fuss about him bringing someone, but she'd like Mikayla. The thought nearly snuck by him. He'd decided to take a woman home to meet his mother and stepfather. He'd never considered a long-term relationship before, let alone a forever relationship, but that was exactly what he wanted with Mikayla. Forever.

Rubbing the heel of his palm over his heart, he spied her coming toward him ahead of the others, weaving between tables with her long-legged stride. Curves in all the right places, deep red hair, and those green eyes that made him go weak at the knees. In a word, perfect. He rose, and when she approached the table, he slipped an arm around her waist and pulled her into a kiss. Her hand clutched at his shirt and he felt more than heard her hum of pleasure.

"Hey, break it up, kids."

Linc took his time releasing Mikayla, smiling when he whispered, "Good morning."

She looked a little dazed. "Good morning back."

"Think we can sit?"

He shifted to glance at his brother. Bella and Ellie were behind him. "Oh, you're here." He tugged on Mikayla's hand to bring her into the booth next to him. Seth sat, and Bella scooted in next to him to make room for Ellie. Linc wondered if he was the only one who noticed that Seth was careful not to touch Bella.

Within seconds their waitress, her hair bright orange and frizzy and with a pair of blinged-out cheaters on the end of her nose, appeared armed with a coffeepot and a stack of menus she passed around. "You folks want coffee?"

"Like oxygen, and keep it coming," Ellie said, nudging her mug closer to the pot. The woman filled mugs around the table, though Seth put his hand over Bella's. "She'll want tea."

Linc caught the look when Bella glanced at Seth, surprise in her eyes.

The waitress paused. "That all right with you, sugar?"

"Yes, please. Green tea, if you have it."

"I'll bring you the little basket that has our selection, and you can pick what you want."

"Thank you."

"Be back to take your orders in a quick minute, folks," the waitress said before leaving them.

Linc didn't bother looking at the menu. Taking a sip from his steaming mug, he raised a brow at his brother. "Talk to Sanford this morning?"

"Yeah. Donny complained enough about the bruise on his ribs that they took him to the hospital last night. Doc gave him some painkillers, and said he'll be fine. But since he kidnapped Mikayla and assaulted federal marshals in Utah, he'll be held here for formal charges before being taken to California to deal with the charges there."

"He's a popular guy."

"Most likely you and Mikayla will have to give testimony in both trials, so there will be a lot of back and forth."

The waitress returned to set the little pot of hot water and basket of teabags in front of Bella, then pulled out her tablet. She made her way around the table. Mikayla ordered oatmeal and fruit salad. When it was his turn, Linc went with heart attack on a plate: eggs over easy, bacon, and hash browns. When the waitress had bustled off, Ellie skewered him with a look. "Mom told me not to bother you, but you've got to call her, Linc."

"Jesus, you're right. I was going to this morning, but I thought it was too early with the time difference."

"Your mother is worried because you were injured?" Bella asked.

"Yeah. I'm fine but she's been holding on pretty tight since I was shot."

"It is natural. You should call your mother."

"I will."

Linc raised a brow at Mikayla. "Did you call your mother?"

"Yes. She gets up early so I called from the hotel. Like your mother, she won't be completely happy until she sees for herself that I'm safe."

The food arrived and they all dug in. Linc noticed Ellie giving Seth the eye as she worked her way through a stack of pancakes. Linc pushed his plate back and leaned into the seat, sipping his coffee.

Watching his sister, he waited. She didn't disappoint. Ellie leaned forward, resting her elbows on the table.

Seth's hand stilled with a bite of omelet halfway to his mouth. "What?"

"Spill."

"Spill what?"

"Whatever is bugging you."

Seth didn't even try to deny it. Ellie had the ability to read people, a skill that was annoying when they'd been kids, but served her well in the Marshals Service. Linc was glad she wasn't turning her superpowers on him.

Seth chewed, swallowed, then spoke. "Richard Jameson is in Texas."

Carefully, Linc set his coffee on the table. "How do you know that?" Mikayla shifted in her seat, and under the table her hand gripped his.

"We had a lead, the one Ellie called you about a few days ago. Turns out to have been a good one." Seth drummed his fingers on the table, a rare sign of agitation. "There's a compound west of the Louisiana border that's off grid. They have their own electricity, wells, grow a lot of their own food. Locals say they're armed to the teeth. There's evidence he's there, or at least has been there in the past few months."

"What's the evidence?"

"They've been pretty much in a constant state of warfare with the local LEOs ever since they tried to serve a warrant and got shot at for their trouble. The group in the compound are trying to claim sovereignty, say they're seceding from the US in order to live like real Americans. Best I can tell, that means they want to shoot any weapon they can get their hands on and blow shit up."

"What are they blowing up?"

"Federal courthouse, most recently. Went after a judge who didn't buy their argument that they're the true defenders of the Constitution."

"And Dad's role?"

"Not sure, but the Marshals Service ran an image they got on the court's security video through facial recognition and came up with a match to fugitive Richard Jameson and another person linked to the Texas compound."

"Have you told Mom?" Ellie asked before Linc could.

"Arch told her. Marshals are going after Richard."

"I want in on it," Linc said.

"We all want in on it. I'll make that happen."

∗∗∗

Linc drove while Mikayla reclined in the passenger seat, the Foo Fighters playing from a satellite radio channel. The day was beautiful and unseasonably warm, and they'd shucked their jackets. They could have been any couple heading out of town on a short trip. But they weren't a couple. They were something, but she wasn't exactly sure what.

The return trip to southern Utah should have felt a lot less stressful than the drive north had been, but Linc seemed as watchful and alert as ever, his gaze shifting from the rearview mirror to the road ahead, then back again.

She tried to force herself to relax. The Marshals Service had put both Donny Bertola and Paco Zecena behind bars. The Zecena cartel had been decimated. Maybe the trauma of the past few days was catching up to her, but she still felt on edge.

"You okay?"

"Sure. I'm fine."

"How come," Linc shot her a glance, "I get the feeling that you say you're fine whether you are or not. It's your go-to answer."

There wasn't much she could say to that because he was right. But it wasn't only worry about the continuing threat from the cartel that had her keyed up. It was Linc. She found herself hyperaware of him. How he looked, smelled, spoke. The way he had of always being watchful, not only of their surroundings, but of her, like he took in every detail of her movements and her mood.

No doubt, with him she felt safe, but there were so many times when she'd glance at him and her breath would hitch, because those green-gold eyes would be watching her with that steady look. He was…attentive, in the extreme. And having never experienced a man so focused on her before, especially anywhere near this degree, she found the ever-increasing spiral of sexual tension…distracting. Unsettling. Add to that the uncertainty of their situation, and she felt keyed up all the time. She didn't know if Linc was thinking long term. She didn't know if *she* was thinking long term. They'd shared some truly stupendous kisses, but other than the throwaway comment about going to a baseball game, they'd made no plans.

Linc had admitted that his feelings ran deep. But what did that mean?

She watched him out of the corner of her eye. He wore a waffle-knit Henley with the sleeves pushed up to his elbows, the tendons in his forearms rippling as he shifted gears. Even those small movements had her fantasizing about him. His hand working the gearshift made her think about his hands working her body. His wide palms, strong, agile fingers soothing, stroking, flexing. The imagery had heat burning in her belly and warmth starting up from her neck.

"Looks like everyone in the county is in town this weekend."

"What?"

He glanced at her and his eyebrows shot up. Wide eyed, she jerked her attention to look out the windshield. It said something about how distracted she'd been that she hadn't realized they had arrived in Concord and were following a long line of pickups, some pulling horse trailers, onto Main Street. A banner strung from light posts proclaimed the weekend as "Concord Cowboy Days."

"Sweetheart, if we didn't have to get to the sheriff's office before they close for the day, we'd do something about what's on your mind." The drawl in his voice sent tingles up her spine.

"Never mind, just drive."

He gave a lazy chuckle that did nothing to cool the blood burning in her veins. She forced herself to focus on the scenery, the people, anything at all to distract her. By the time Linc put the Jeep in park outside the familiar beige building, she felt like she had found some measure of control.

He held open the door to the sheriff's headquarters and she preceded him into the reception area. The on-duty deputy looked up, a smile breaking across his round face.

"Well, hey there. Came back to visit, did you?"

It took her a second to place him as the deputy she'd spent a few minutes chatting with while preparing coffee. Only days before, it felt like weeks.

"I didn't introduce myself last time, Ms. O'Kane. I'm Deputy Jorgensen. Nice to see you again." He nodded at Linc before turning his attention back to Mikayla.

She smiled at his contagious cheerfulness. "Hi. We're here to pick up my car. Sheriff Bland let me store it in the county yard."

"Sure, I know all about that. Sheriff's not in right now, but I can help you out. Follow me back and we'll get the keys and then I'll walk you over to the lot where it's parked."

Linc's warm hand settled against the small of her back as she moved to follow the deputy. She looked up in question, but Linc kept his gaze straight ahead. Deputy Jorgensen kept up one-sided chatter as they moved through the office.

"I pulled the short straw, so I'm the only one in the office today. Don't even have a prisoner to watch over since Lopez made bail. All the other deputies are part of the law enforcement presence for Cowboy Days. Brings a lot of folks to town. Not that there's much trouble, unless you count the drunk and disorderlies that always crop up about the time the bars are closing. But that's to be expected, I guess."

He pulled keys from his pocket and opened a file drawer, retrieved a set of keys and handed them to Mikayla, then scribbled a notation on the bag they'd been stored in.

"You planning to stay in town tonight?"

Mikayla glanced at Linc. "That was our plan."

"Well, unless you had the foresight to get motel reservations, good luck with that. Every place for ten miles around is booked up. There's a dance later, biggest social event of the year. Folks like to get together before winter kicks in. C'mon, we'll go out through the back door."

They exited the building and followed the deputy across the parking lot to a chain-link fence, where he pushed a button that had the gate rolling open. Seeing her Subaru parked inside the gate made Mikayla feel like maybe she was getting her life back.

"Now, you drive on out, and I'll shut the gate behind you."

"Thank you, Deputy. I appreciate your help."

The deputy glanced at Linc, then back at Mikayla. "You both are welcome to come to the dance. It's over at the rodeo grounds. I guarantee you'll have a good time."

Mikayla smiled. "Thanks for the invitation."

Linc held up a hand before Jorgensen could move away. "When did Lopez get out?"

"Yesterday. Buddy of mine took it in the face when the little shit, pardon my French, ma'am, got himself arrested. Wasn't sorry to see him go."

"You know his whereabouts?"

"Said he was heading back to California until the trial. Got his car out of impound and took off."

"Know who paid his bail and the impound fees?"

Jorgensen shrugged. "Not off the top of my head. I can find out if you like."

Linc nodded while pulling his phone from his pocket. "Yeah, I would."

They exchanged numbers. Mikayla unlocked the Subaru and got behind the wheel as Linc slid into the passenger seat. She drove through the gate with a wave to the deputy, then rounded the building to pull up next to the Jeep.

Instead of getting out, Linc leaned back in his seat, fingers tapping on his knee.

"What's up?"

"You want to go to a dance?"

"Are you serious?"

"Yep."

"Lincoln Jameson, I did not expect that from you."

"Why? I like to have a good time." He reached out a finger to tuck a strand of hair behind her ear. "What do you say we spend a little time together where we don't have to worry that you're in danger. Get to know each other better." He paused, his gaze direct. "I want to go dancing with you."

Mikayla heart thudded in her chest. "That sounds fun, but I'm going to be a girl and say I don't have anything to wear to a dance."

"I don't think a dance at the rodeo grounds has the same dress code as a club in LA. Wear jeans, nobody will care."

"I've been clubbing exactly one time in my life, and never again. But okay, I'll make something work. But what about where we'll stay tonight?"

"Let me take care of that. There's a grocery store a few blocks from here. Follow me there. What you're wearing is fine, but if you want to change or wash up or whatever, you can do that in their restroom while I pick up a few supplies."

In the grocery store restroom, she used the little makeup she'd brought to apply eyeshadow and mascara. With her mood lighter than it had been in weeks, she pulled on a clean tank top, tucking it into her jeans, then donned a light shirt, leaving several buttons undone. She studied herself in the mirror. Not clubbing sexy, but that wasn't her look anyway. She guessed her look would be considered more nature girl, and that seemed to work fine for Linc.

She hadn't been this excited about going out with someone in a long time. Maybe forever.

# Chapter Twenty-Two

How odd to have been engaged to Peter without ever experiencing the thrill of anticipation. Being afraid to risk her heart had nearly resulted in exactly what Mikayla had tried so hard to avoid—a cage.

Her mother had wanted to physically put her behind bars of security to keep her safe. But Mikayla had done more damage to herself than any amount of overprotection her family had imposed. By locking up her emotions to avoid the anguish of losing someone she cherished, she had missed out on life. And love.

Peter had been safe. Linc was a risk. Mikayla put a hand to her quivering belly. She was in love with him. And wasn't that a moment of self-revelation. She was in love with Linc Jameson, and she wasn't entirely sure she could handle it.

A text from Linc told her to meet him at their cars when she was done. She dragged a brush through her hair and, with one last look at herself in the mirror, hitched her backpack over her shoulder and exited the restroom.

Crossing the parking lot, she saw Linc standing at the back of his Jeep with the rear door swung open. He'd shucked the Henley, and with his back to her, she had a perfect view of wide, muscular shoulders and a taut waist before he shook out a dark green button-down shirt and put it on. He turned and caught sight of her, his gaze steady on hers as he slowly fastened the buttons. "Hey."

"Hey yourself."

His eyes warmed, and when she stopped in front of him, he leaned forward to brush his lips to hers. "You okay?"

"Yeah."

He must have caught something in her expression, because his brows lowered, and he spoke softly. "You worried about the Zecenas?"

She shook her head. "No, more like first-date jitters."

He smiled. "Me too."

"Really?" He nodded. "That makes me feel better."

*** 

Linc took Mikayla's hand as they approached the long wooden building at the rodeo grounds. Country music poured out of wide doors opened to the cool night. Barbecue wafted from the commercial-size charcoal grill operated by a beefy man sporting a spectacular handlebar mustache. People streamed by, many wearing plaid shirts, jeans, and cowboy boots.

Linc draped an arm around her shoulder and pulled her close to his side as the crowd gathered at the door. He tipped his head toward her ear. "While I was waiting for you, I called around. Jorgensen was right, there are no motel rooms available anywhere."

"What are we going to do?"

"I went ahead and made reservations at the Lower Falls campground. They only had a few sites available. That okay?"

"Uh-huh, but we'll be putting up our tents in the dark."

His smile flashed. "I was a Boy Scout, not a problem."

They stood waiting for the crowd to move through the door. Mikayla looked over her shoulder. She was feeling jittery again, like when she'd been hiking on the trail and felt someone watching her.

"Anything wrong?"

She started to shake her head, then a couple several feet behind her moved apart and a chill snaked up her spine. "Linc."

He whirled around and pushed her behind him all in one move. "What?"

The crowd had shifted back and she moved to the side, trying again to see if she was imagining the face obscured by the bill of a ball cap. "Nothing, I guess."

He pulled her a few steps away from the crowd, eyes scanning. "Something spooked you."

"I'm not sure what it was. Let's go in."

Mikayla shook off the uncomfortable feeling as they walked through the doors to the sound of Dierks Bentley's "5-1-5-0" blasting from the speakers. The cover band played on a raised stage and already people were dancing on the wide-planked wooden floor.

"Damn."

"What?"

"I forgot my cowboy hat."

Mikayla smiled. Indeed, nearly every man wore a cowboy hat, and many of the women, too. "Not just your cowboy hat. These guys have rodeo buckles. I don't think I can dance with a guy who isn't wearing a rodeo buckle. And Wrangler jeans. Gotta have Wrangler jeans."

"Is that right? Can't dance with a guy wearing Levi's?"

"Well, you do have a marshal's star in your back pocket. That's pretty sexy."

His smile turned a little bit wicked. "You think?"

"Well, maybe a lot sexy. But it's not the same as a rodeo buckle."

"Let's see if I can convince you that my buckle is as big as any man's here." She laughed as he tugged her onto the dance floor. Linc looked damn fine in snug jeans that molded his strong thighs, and a body without an ounce of fat. By far, the best-looking man on the dance floor.

He swung her into the dance, twirling her out, then bringing her back up against his swaying body. The beat grew stronger, matching the rising tempo of her heartbeat. More couples crowded the floor, and Linc pulled her closer.

The band transitioned to the next song, the crowd cheering at the opening riff of "Sweet Home Alabama." People moved into rows for line dancing.

"Can you do this?"

A ruddy-faced man in a white shirt and black cowboy hat moved forward. "If she don't know how to do this, son, I'd be happy to teach her."

"I know it." Mikayla took Linc's hand and pulled him next to her in the line, and Black Hat eased in on her other side. Linc matched her moves, and as the music pumped louder his hands were at her waist for the slide. Mikayla had never had a better time. The floor reverberated as everyone stomped in unison, and when she spun from Linc, Black Hat caught her and spun her back.

Mikayla hadn't known how much she'd needed an evening like this. The crowd was friendly, the music great, and Linc's sexy moves were welcome eye candy.

A woman with flowing black hair and high-heeled cowboy boots took the mic and had couples pairing up as she sang a throaty rendition of Shania Twain's "Dance With the One That Brought You."

Mikayla rested one hand at Linc's waist while he clasped her other in his and swept her into a two-step. She matched him step for step, clapping when the song ended and the woman on stage bowed to the crowd.

The lead male vocalist, dressed in a plaid shirt with the sleeves ripped off, took the mic again and the mood changed, the tempo slowing, when he crooned out a country ballad.

"Oh yeah. Gotta love the slow songs." Linc drew her into him, his hips moving in a lazy slide against hers. He rested his cheek against her temple, his lips brushing her fingers held clasped in his.

"I wouldn't have guessed you could dance to country music."

"You kidding? Country is the best music to dance to. Mom's from Oklahoma and she taught all of us to two-step and line dance." She felt more than heard his words, the vibration of his voice rumbling against the palm she had flattened against his chest. "And I learned early on that girls like guys who can dance."

"Of course you did."

"Where'd you learn to dance?"

"I taught myself. Mom would never let me go anywhere, so I watched music videos and practiced dancing."

He pulled her even closer. "Sounds lonely."

She shrugged, suddenly self-conscious. "It's what I knew."

"And when you were in college?"

"Of all things to find in New York City, a country music bar was near my apartment. Groups of us went there a lot."

"No boyfriends?"

"None that mattered."

He held her closer, arms secure around her as the music reverberated through the air. She could have stayed like that forever, wrapped in Linc's arms, swaying to the music. She turned her face into his neck and breathed in his warm male scent.

Before she could check the impulse, she pressed an open-mouthed kiss to his heated skin. A rumbling growl emanated from low in his throat. He shifted, releasing her to spear long fingers into her hair, tilting up her chin with his thumbs. His kiss consumed her. Hot lips, smooth tongue, hips moving against hers in unrestrained sensuality, all twined together to build an aching need.

The music faded, and Linc slowly ended the kiss. Dancers moved around them to exit the floor when the band called a break, but Linc kept them there, still cupping her face, the gold of his eyes burning into hers. His voice was husky when he spoke. "Those feelings we were talking about, Mikayla, haven't gone away."

She nodded.

"Fact is, they're getting deeper."

Her heart thudded heavily. Loving him meant she would never be whole again unless he was with her. The thought terrified her. Linc had a dangerous profession, and he certainly wasn't a man who could turn away from someone in need even if it put him in danger.

She was living proof of that. If the worst happened to him, she didn't think she'd survive.

She stepped back and he dropped his hands. "That scares me."

"You and me both, sweetheart." Breaking the tension, he tilted his head toward the far side of the room where everyone was crowded around small tables jammed with beer bottles and plates piled with barbecue. "Ready for dinner?"

\*\*\*

Mikayla should have been tired. Around midnight, she drove behind Linc into the campground, energy thrumming through her. Dancing with him had been foreplay. She hadn't had a whole lot of sexual experience, but she knew where this was going.

Making love with Linc, getting that close, put her heart at risk. And she knew him well enough to believe he wanted everything: her body and her heart.

Just for tonight, she'd put all her fears and worries aside and let herself experience all of him without overthinking.

She followed the Jeep along the dirt road until finally turning into a vacant site. She swung her Subaru around to back in and make it easier to get her gear from the car. Another vehicle turned into the campground, driving slowly, headlights slicing through the night. She shivered. The temperature had plummeted, and the stars arcing overhead looked like glittering ice crystals.

The Jeep's headlights illuminated the campsite, and when she opened the rear hatch, Linc moved out of the shadows to her side. He pulled out the nylon bag holding her tent, then handed her the folded tarp. "Lay out the tarp in the level area and I'll help you set up your tent, then I'll do mine."

Huh? Those slow dances were proof of where they were heading tonight. She eyed him as he unfolded her tent. He was trying to work quietly, probably so he wouldn't disturb campers sleeping in neighboring sites, but she saw the way a muscle in his cheek twitched, and his body seemed coiled with pent-up energy. And he was trying to avoid touching her.

He pulled the corners of the tent taut and pushed in the stakes with sheer muscle. Reminding herself her job wasn't to watch the hot guy, she put together the shock-corded tent poles. Sliding a pole through the loops at the top of the tent, she bent to anchor the corner. Backing up, she bumped into Linc. Her butt landed against his crotch and he gulped in a breath before setting her away from him.

She held in a smirk. "Sorry, did I hurt you?"

He gave a pained laugh. "Not hurt, no."

She took a testing step toward him. He made a move back.

"What's wrong? You're jumpy."

"Nothing's wrong. I'm fine."

She eased forward slowly. "Is this like me when I say I'm fine, but I'm really not?"

"Jesus, no. Well, maybe. I don't know." She inched forward again and he narrowed his eyes. She thought he was going to hold his ground, but he put up his hands and heaved out an exasperated breath. "Look, I'm trying to be good here."

With a little thrill of triumph, she stepped forward again. He sidestepped and edged around her to the back of the Subaru. She followed, and when he turned, he held the bulky air mattress in front of him like a shield.

"Maybe I don't want you to be good."

He froze, dark gaze scanning her features. "You sure about that?"

"Pretty much."

"Pretty much? You need to be all the way sure, Mikayla. If you're not ready, we'll get your tent set up and zip you up in it. We might have to add a padlock, but I'll leave you alone."

And he'd do that. She grasped his hands where they were clutching the mattress and leaned across it to press her lips to his. "I'm sure, Linc. I want to be with you. You don't have to be so careful with me."

His breath came out in a hiss. "I do have to be careful with you. You've been through so damn much." He tossed the air mattress back into the car, then turned and reached for her, pulling her close. He ran his hands down her arms to grasp her wrists. "This past week has been hell. That fucker attacked you with a knife, my batshit partner kidnapped you, and your ex was murdered. You need to process, so I'm trying to give you space. We've got something good between us, and I won't jeopardize it by rushing you."

She raised a hand to lay her fingers against his lips. "I'm fine, and I mean it this time. You're right that I need to process. But you left something out. This week I met you, and as difficult as everything else has been, you're what's kept me together."

"Thanks, but you're wrong. You're strong. You'd have gotten through this without me."

She shook her head. "I am strong. But since the first moment I met you, you've had my back. Knowing you were there has made me stronger."

His eyes seemed to glow. "I love you, Mikayla."

Her heart stumbled. "What?"

"It's you. You're the one I've been waiting for."

Her breath hitched and she fought for breath. It felt like flower buds tightly closed inside her had suddenly burst into bloom, dazzling and overwhelming. "Wait. Just wait a second. You love me? I—"

He laid a finger across her lips. "Don't say anything yet. It's too soon after Wellington died. I want you to be sure."

"I don't know if I can ever give you that back, Linc. I think there's something broken inside me."

"There's not. You're beautiful. There's nothing broken about you. We'll work this through. If you want to wait to make love, we can wait. Whatever is right for you."

"God, Linc. You're too good for me."

"I'm not. If I'm good for you it's because we're good together. You make me feel more honest emotions than anyone ever has. I'm ready to see where that takes us."

Her heart swelled until she felt if she didn't offer it a release valve it would burst open. She launched herself at him. He caught her against his rock-solid chest, arms enfolding, hands supporting her when she wrapped her legs around his waist. Their lips met, tongues tangling in a kiss brought to flash point by the week of simmering attraction. He pulled her tighter and a groan escaped from low in her throat when the hard ridge of his erection pressed against her.

Until the restraints had been lifted, she hadn't known how much she needed this deep dive into this burning need, or how it would intensify exponentially. Before she lost all brainpower, she put her hands in his hair and gently pulled. He broke the kiss to move his lips to the curve of her neck. She tightened her grip. "Linc."

"Hmm?" He'd nipped her earlobe, then pulled it between his lips and began gently sucking.

"Listen to me." The words lost impact when everything inside her was melting at his touch.

He released her for a brief second. "Busy here."

And he was. His attention was so complete he made her feel like the center of the universe. "You're good at this." He pressed his lips against the sensitive skin below her ear and sent tingles racing through her body.

"Linc."

"I'm listening."

"I don't think you are."

"I heard that sexy moan."

"I couldn't help that."

He pulled back, and his mouth turned up in a grin that had her grabbing his face and pulling his lips back to hers.

"What, sweetheart?" The words vibrated against her lips.

"Never mind." She squashed the little voice in the back of her head telling her that there would be no turning back. She'd been so careful with her emotions for so long, she knew she could be making a mistake. But she couldn't muster the willpower to force herself to back away, to slow down.

Still holding her firmly, he breathed deep and pulled back. "You're sure about this?"

"Yes."

"Let's finish setting up. Quick."

# Chapter Twenty-Three

The tent was up in ten minutes. Mikayla was willing to forego the air mattress, but Linc insisted. He dragged out the pump and while he worked it, she zipped together their sleeping bags, and laid the extra blanket over them for extra warmth.

She walked quickly to the bathroom. Once away from the campsite and the Jeep's headlights, she pulled out her phone to use its flashlight. Bugs circled the fixture in the restroom and she hurriedly finished her business, trying not to get lost in the feeling of anticipation. She was reaching for the stall door when the overhead light went out. Letting out a startled yelp, she pulled her phone from her pocket, fingers fumbling to find the flashlight function.

The scrape of a shoe against concrete sounded outside the bathroom door. She froze, hand hovering over the dead bolt. She was in a single-stall, unisex bathroom, and she'd turned the dead bolt when she'd entered. It was well after midnight, and anyone in the campground could be up for a bathroom break. But what if it was more than that? And why had the lights gone out?

The past week had given her enough scary moments that she wasn't taking a chance. She'd text Linc and have him walk over. She checked her phone for service. One bar.

"Mikayla? You in there?"

"Linc?" She turned the lock and pulled open the door. There he stood, solid and real, the light from her phone hitting him in his broad chest. "The lights went out. It scared me."

"I saw that from the campsite so I came over." He pointed the beam of his flashlight into the shadows on either side of the structure. "We'll let the Weingartners know there's a problem in the morning." He held out a hand, palm up. "C'mon, sweetheart."

They walked back to the campsite. With the Jeep's headlights off, the darkness was near complete. They reached the tent and Linc switched off his flashlight. Tall pines looked like dark sentinels against the wash of the Milky Way.

Her nerves were jumbled, but he took care of her. He cupped her face, then leaned down to kiss her in a long-drawn-out mating of lips. She felt her anxiety melt away. She went up on her tiptoes, and at his urging, wrapped her legs around his waist.

He shouldered open the flap and carried her into the tent, and once inside eased her back on the bedding. He lay over her, hips cradled intimately against hers as he traced his tongue along her lower lip, moving along her jaw when she let out a breathy groan.

"I think that sexy moan of yours has become my all-time favorite sound," he whispered in her ear.

He shifted his weight to one side and slipped his hand under her shirt. Warm fingers moved with tantalizing slowness, and her whimper of impatience brought out a throaty chuckle. She brought up a hand and rapped her knuckles against his chin.

He grunted and she stifled a laugh. "Sorry. I can't see a thing in here."

He shifted again and turned on the flashlight. "Hang on a minute, sweetheart." Rising to his knees, he zipped the tent flap closed and whipped off his sweater. Mikayla scooted back to open the sleeping bag. She shucked her jacket, and when her hands moved to her shirt buttons, he stopped her. "Why don't you let me do that?"

She paused and he switched off the flashlight. A moment later he slid into the sleeping bag. He must have taken a moment to remove his shirt because her fingers skimmed along warm skin and into the mat of hair across his chest.

Without sight to communicate intent, every touch became magnified. Linc's strong fingers traced along her ribs, his thumb brushing on the underside of her bra, then ever so slowly slipping beneath the cup. He paused, anticipation building, making her breath catch in her throat.

He rose to his knees and pulled her up against him. Her shirt buttons were small and his fingers big, but he worked them with unerring accuracy and within a minute he was tugging the shirt off her shoulders. It caught at her elbows, trapping her hands. In the darkness, she couldn't see him move, but she felt warm lips glide along her collarbone, then slowly over the rise of her breast. When she would have freed her arms, he said, "Uh-uh."

A touch nudged her bra and tank straps off her shoulder. The scratch of his stubble was the only warning she had before he nuzzled aside the cup of her bra and his warm tongue lapped at her nipple. Heat raced through her, and she thought she'd go off like a firecracker.

He reached behind her and unhooked her bra. There was the rasp of his beard again, this time he captured her nipple fully in his mouth, drawing it in and sucking hard. She felt the pull deep in her core. Her head dropped forward and she nuzzled into the thick hair at the back of his head and breathed deep. He smelled of shampoo and hot male.

When he shifted to her right breast, she renewed her efforts and finally pulled off her shirt. Now free, she skimmed her hands down taut muscles and over his ribs to find his belt buckle.

He sucked in a breath when she worked it free and released the first button of his jeans. His lips left her breast to press hot kisses over her collarbone and her neck. She angled her chin to give him more room even as she undid the buttons at his fly. Reaching in, she rubbed her fingers along his length, his erection jerking in her hand, straining against the material of his briefs.

When she would have reached under the elastic waistband, he caught her hands and brought them up to his mouth to press his lips against her knuckles. "Hang on, darlin'. Let me get a condom."

"I'm on the pill, and disease free."

"Thank the lord. Same here."

Linc sat back to remove his jeans, then stilled her hands when she would have unbuttoned hers. He laid her back against the pillows. She felt the mattress dip as he shifted over her. They weren't touching, but she sensed his big body above hers. Then his lips found hers, his mouth hot and wet. He clasped her hands in his as he moved his lips along her neck to her breasts, then farther down her belly. He released her hands to unfasten her jeans, and when she reached to touch him, he growled low in his throat. "No. I get you first."

With her heart hammering in her throat, he used his teeth to tug aside the waistband of her pants, then pressed a kiss low on her hipbone. He tugged down her jeans, pulling them free, then returned to nuzzle her through her cotton panties. The fleeting wish she'd worn sexier underwear evaporated when Linc slipped a finger under the elastic. Warm fingers followed a long and silky route that had her climbing close to the point of eruption.

With a ripping sound, he removed the barrier of her panties. His lips and tongue traced along her thigh, his fingers touching and sliding until she writhed with the growing tension.

"Oh my god, Linc." Everything inside her coiled tighter and tighter, her breath coming in hot, gasping pants.

"That's it, darlin'. Come for me."

When his mouth found her core and long fingers slid inside her, she exploded with a keening moan. She could swear she saw stars rocketing over their heads.

He kept up the pressure even as she spiraled downward, his mouth insistent, hands working her. She reached for him. "Let me, let me." She grasped him even as he moved between her legs, nudging her thighs apart. She guided him home, his lips joining hers as he pushed at her entrance.

He thrust forward with a throaty groan, burying himself deep. He held himself there, and she wrapped her legs around him, lifting her hips to pull him in deeper. His mouth claimed hers and she felt his desperation as he pulled out to thrust again. Her fingers clawed into his back as the tightness coiled once more in a delicious mounting pressure. He drove forward, and she felt his control slipping. The deep moan against her lips was all she needed to send her over the edge a second time. She convulsed around him as he came with a subdued roar, reveling in the feel of him buried in her body.

He lay against her, his face buried in her neck, and his breath coming in hot pants against her skin. When she thought she could move, she rubbed her hand from his buttocks to his spine, then back again. He shifted and she groaned as she felt the movement deep inside. "Let's stay like this."

She felt his lips move against her neck as he smiled. "For at least a day."

"Maybe a week."

"Okay, if you insist, a week."

Still joined, they spoke softly, words of love drifting into the night until his erection stretched her. "You don't need more recovery time?"

"Apparently not." He moved, pumping slow, allowing the pleasure to build. His lips moved to her nipple, tugging, licking, sucking, all the while continuing to thrust, withdraw, then thrust again. "I want you with me." His voice sounded ragged around the edges.

"I don't think I can."

"You can."

He rose up on one elbow without breaking his rhythm, reaching between them, and making her moan.

"That's it, baby. Again."

When he squeezed gently, she spiraled skyward in an explosion of sensation. He pushed her knees up, braced his arms on either side of her shoulders, and thrust forcefully to his completion. He collapsed on top of her, his body a welcome weight.

There were no words. She'd had sex before, but this was more. Now she truly knew what it meant to make love. To express your feelings with your body. She hadn't spoken the words, but her body had betrayed her.

She loved him and was afraid he knew it.

***

Linc shifted to his side, reaching out a hand. Nothing. He opened his eyes. She was gone. The muted light inside the tent made him think the sun hadn't been up long. He sat, running his fingers through his hair. Making love to Mikayla had rocked his world. Any hesitation he'd had as to whether she was the one had vanished. Their connection had been absolute, his mind and body so attuned to hers he'd felt like they were a single unit. He'd heard people say that in wedding vows and thought it was hyperbole, part of the sappiness of being in love. Now he knew better.

Mikayla was his in every sense of the word: his soulmate, his friend, and now his lover. And now he knew she felt the same. Whether she was ready to admit her feelings was a different matter.

Her feelings for him frightened her. He knew that. The trauma of losing her father had scarred her, made her instinctively draw in to protect herself. He'd gotten past that barrier when they'd made love, and now he had to find her before she could try to rebuild that wall.

He rose and grabbed his jeans, wondering how long she'd been up. He checked the time on his phone. Almost six, and there was a text from Seth to call him. He stepped outside, frowning when he didn't immediately see her. The whine of an electric motor had him looking over. Bob Weingartner drove by in his golf cart, and Linc waved him over.

"Hey there, Marshal. Beautiful morning."

"Yeah. You see Mikayla?"

"Lose track of your girlfriend?"

"Not exactly. She's an early riser."

"Shoulda left you a note. Notes help keep the peace in a relationship." Weingartner nodded as he delivered his nugget of sage marital wisdom.

"Well, did you?"

"Yup, saw her on the way to the showers with a towel and a bag." Why the old guy hadn't said that straight up, Linc didn't know, but some of his tension eased.

"Okay. Thanks."

With a cheery wave, Bob drove off.

Linc pulled out his phone again. Two bars. He phoned his brother, who should already be back in California, pacing as he waited for him to pick up. He wanted to break camp, get all their gear stowed, and as soon as Mikayla returned, hit the road. But before everything else, he needed to make sure they were good. See her, touch her, be sure her leaving without waking him only meant she was being considerate.

When they'd made love, he'd felt attuned to her in a way he'd never experienced with anyone before. Maybe that's why he could feel her trying to hold back, to keep a part of herself separate. That worried him.

Seth finally picked up. "Where the hell are you?"

"At the campground. There was no place to stay in town."

"You need to get to California as soon as possible. Chief Deputy Montrose wants to question Mikayla, and he's got a safe house ready for her."

"WITSEC again? She's not going to like that."

"She'll be safe until we get all the loose ends tied off."

"For how long?"

"Probably until she testifies against Zecena."

Linc rubbed a hand over his face. "Shit, okay."

"Hit the road, Linc. Things are happening and you both need to be here."

"Got it." He disconnected the call, slipping his phone into his pocket. He'd take down the tent, and then—

He stopped short. She stood at the edge of the campsite, back ramrod straight, hands on her hips. If there was any doubt she was pissed, he only needed to look in her eyes to see the blazing anger.

"I'm not going into WITSEC again." Her furious tone made the words sound like slashing blades cutting through the air.

His hands went up in a bid for peace. "Look, sweetheart—"

"Don't 'sweetheart' me. I will not be going back into WITSEC."

She tossed her bag onto the table and advanced toward him, a sleek panther stalking its prey. His heart jerked in his chest. She was everything. Passionate, brainy, and gorgeous. And everything he was sought to shield her, protect her, keep her safe until they were past the danger and able to begin their life together.

First things first. "WITSEC is safest until Zecena's trial is over."

"Safe? Like in Salt Lake City? I was *kidnapped* while in WITSEC, remember?"

She had a point. "That was an anomaly. You'll be safer in WITSEC than on your own."

"You were shot protecting a guy in WITSEC, right? And wasn't the witness killed?"

Something must have shown in his expression, because she sucked in a breath. "I'm sorry. That was a low blow. You're not responsible for what Donny did."

Anger over that still gnawed at him, but at least he'd put aside the guilt. Linc had done his job, his partner had not. "Listen, we can discuss what will happen later. We need to get on the road."

"No, *you* need to get on the road. *I* don't need to go anywhere."

Linc took a breath hoping for a dose of calm. They wouldn't get anywhere if he let his temper go. "I'm not leaving you here."

"What's wrong, Marshal? Afraid your witness won't be ready to testify in your big case?"

He narrowed his eyes. "You know there's more to us than that. I love you, Mikayla. I was being honest when I told you that last night. You're it for me."

He reached for her hand, but she evaded him, clasping her hands behind her back. His temper ticked up another notch. "Want to know something, sweetheart? I think you're afraid of me loving you. You deny it because you're scared. You're afraid to love me because the people you love either die, or they let you down. I'm going to do my damned best not to die, and I won't let you down. You'll have to trust me on that. And you want to know what else? I don't hear you saying you don't love me."

She backed away from his outreached hand. "I may care for you, but we can't be together long-term. You act like it's so simple to trust that I won't be scared something could happen to you like it happened to my dad. You were shot by your partner and you almost died. Next time it might not be almost." She whirled away, stalking down the road at a furious pace.

Damn it. Instinct urged him to go after her, make her see reason. But experience had taught him reason was a matter of perspective.

His gaze followed her retreating form as she strode through the campground.

# Chapter Twenty-Four

Mikayla walked at a furious pace, trying to burn off the mad and convince herself not to be angry that Linc didn't understand. He wanted to protect her, but the idea that *another* safe house awaited her in California was madness.

She slowed her pace. Okay, she acknowledged that most of her agitation came from her feelings for Linc. Waking in his arms had felt so amazingly natural. She'd imagined doing that for the rest of her days. Even in sleep, he'd held her protectively, big hands keeping her close, and when she'd shifted away from him, he'd tightened his hold.

She'd gotten up early because she knew if she'd stayed they would have made love again, tightening their bond even more. Their connection had been so absolute, so overwhelmingly perfect, if she had any hope of remaining whole, she had to get away.

He said he loved her, but love could be its own prison. As devastated as she'd been by her father's death, her mother's absolute desolation had been more destructive. Loving her husband with such utter devotion had devastated her, and had nearly destroyed their family. If Mikayla didn't protect herself, she could love Linc just as completely, leaving herself open and vulnerable.

Which made her a coward.

She continued her circuit of the sparsely populated campground, letting the muted roar of the river and the sun shining in the bright blue sky cool her agitation. As angry as it made her that Linc had been arranging for her to once again go into WITSEC, she'd have to do it. If she could help put Paco Zecena behind bars, then she'd be safe, and so would any number of people who were victims of the cartel.

But what was she going to do about Linc? She'd go back to California and testify, but she'd have to put the brakes on their relationship. She couldn't be with him and survive with her heart intact.

Her decision should have made her feel more settled. Instead, dread washed through her. Linc would be hurt, but better now. The memory of his utter sincerity when he'd told her he loved her made her wonder if she was too late.

She rounded a curve in the road, passing an old Ford van with Nevada plates. A quick movement from behind the vehicle caught her attention. Mikayla let out a startled yelp even as a dark figure leapt toward her. She recognized Hector Lopez in the fraction of a second before he grabbed her around her neck. With the advantage of surprise he pulled her around the vehicle, away from view from the road.

Blood pounded in her ears and Mikayla tried to beat back the burst of panic. She couldn't run so she had to fight. With his arm around her neck, she spotted the open sliding door of the van. If he got her inside, she'd be at his mercy. She struck him in the gut with her elbow, and when his grip loosened a fraction, she ducked her chin into the inside of his arm. Pushing with both hands on the elbow joint, she pivoted. The maneuver worked, breaking his hold. She spun, managing to break free and face her attacker. A sneer twisted Lopez's lips.

"You won't get away from me this time, bitch."

She stared in disbelief as, once again, he pulled a knife from his pocket, yanking the blade open.

Was this really happening?

Lopez lunged, and Mikayla scrambled back, frantic to avoid the lethal blade. A thud of running feet came at them and Lopez jerked toward the sound. Like an avenging angel, Linc launched himself at Hector in a flying tackle. The knife blade glinted in the bright morning sun. The two men rolled in the dirt in a tangle of limbs. Both fought viciously, but Lopez was no match for Linc's sheer size and ferocity. He rammed the heel of his palm into Lopez's throat, then used an elbow for a solid jab to the solar plexus.

Lopez wheezed, struggling to breathe, giving Linc the opportunity to heave him onto his stomach, face in the dirt. With a knee jammed in his back, Linc wrenched Lopez's arm behind his back, forcing him to loosen his grip on the blade fisted in his hand. Linc grabbed the knife and folded the blade before sliding it into his back pocket. He pulled out his keys and held them in an outstretched hand.

"My handcuffs are in the Jeep in the glove box. Go get them."

She'd been okay until she saw a deep red stain seeping through his shirt on his left side. "Linc, you're bleeding."

"It's not bad. Go, now."

She took the keys and ran back to their campsite. She spotted Janice Weingartner in the golf cart and flagged her down, and asked her to radio for a ranger.

Mikayla's hands trembled as she fumbled with Linc's keys. She got the door open and found the handcuffs. She took a precious few moments to grab the first aid kit from her bin before running back to where Linc held Hector Lopez immobilized. Blood had saturated the side of Linc's shirt and seeped into his jeans.

The golf cart whizzed up to the campsite, Janice at the wheel, Bob riding shotgun, arriving at the same time as Mikayla. She handed the cuffs to Linc. He cinched them around Hector's wrists, then rose slowly to his feet.

Bob stepped forward, pulling his bottom lip in contemplation. "This here the same fella that caused the trouble before?"

"Yeah," Linc said, strain evident in his voice.

"Losing a lot of blood there, son. I'll keep an eye on our assailant if you want to get that injury looked at."

"Okay."

"Sit down." Mikayla took Linc's arm to lead him to the picnic bench.

The look he shot her set her back on her heels. She'd seen him in a lot of different moods, but she'd never seen him truly angry.

And that anger was directed at her.

He moved carefully, sagging onto the bench, face ashen. Mikayla fumbled open the first aid kit, donning nitrile gloves and tearing open the gauze packaging. She pulled up his bloody shirt and bit back an oath. Blood oozed from the wound beneath his rib cage. Despite his claim to the contrary, this was serious. She pressed a thick pad to the injury.

She turned to Mrs. Weingartner. "Janice, he needs to get to a hospital. Call for a helicopter."

"God damn it. I don't want to go to the hospital." Linc's words slurred together.

"No cell reception here. I'll radio it in."

"You're going, Linc. Don't argue."

He didn't respond and she glanced up. Eyes glassy, lines on his face set in a ferocious frown, he looked like all his energy was focused on not losing consciousness.

The static-y exchange from Janice's radio confirmed a medevac chopper would be dispatched. Mikayla added another thick pad of gauze to the soaked one. The amount of blood he'd lost frightened her. She felt her range of vision narrowing so all she could see was Linc. Damn him, he'd thrown himself into danger to protect her.

Her father had done the same thing and ended up dying.

Linc's breathing was shallow. "Christ, it hurts."

"I know, I know." She tamped down the threatening tears. "Linc, you're going to be okay. You have to be."

Janice Weingartner spoke at her elbow. "Anything I can do, hon? Chopper is on its way."

Mikayla shook her head. "I don't know what else we can do but try to stop the bleeding." She added more gauze, keeping constant pressure on the wound.

Time slowed. Linc closed his eyes, and Mikayla had never felt so helpless. All she could do was keep pressing on the wound and hope and pray the helicopter would arrive soon.

And that another man she loved wouldn't die protecting her.

After what seemed like hours but was probably less than one, the whump-whump of an approaching helicopter reverberated through the air. The minutes that followed were a kaleidoscope of sounds and images. The chopper set down in a clearing at the far side of the campground. A crew rushed to the scene carrying a basket-like stretcher and tote bags. They swarmed around Linc, and Mikayla was gently but firmly pushed aside.

With speed and efficiency, an EMT applied a pressure bandage and Linc was moved to the stretcher. Mikayla put a hand on the arm of the woman who appeared to be in charge. "I want to go with him."

The woman regarded her with warm brown eyes. "Sorry, no room for passengers. We're taking him to Memorial Hospital in Cedar City. They've got an excellent team there." She must have seen something in Mikayla's face because her expression softened. "We'll take good care of him."

Within minutes the chopper was airborne and Mikayla watched it lift into the sky, her heart hollow.

***

Linc felt the familiar tightness as a blood pressure cuff inflated around his arm, then seconds later deflated. He recognized the sounds—the beeps and clicks of monitors, the muffled tread of crepe-soled shoes. He blinked open his eyes. Instead of palm trees swaying in a breeze, the window showed shadowed mountains in the distance. Judging from the light, the sun had set but it wasn't quite dark.

Damn. Back where he'd started: wounded and in the hospital. He turned his head, gaze searching, then settling on the form curled in the padded chair next to his bed. Mikayla slept with her cheek resting on an open palm, long legs curled under her. Dark smudges under her eyes stood out against her pale skin.

The door swished open and a middle-aged man entered, wearing a white lab coat and a stethoscope around his neck. "Hello, Mr. Jameson. I am Doctor Koroma." His accent suggested West Africa. "How are you feeling?"

Linc could sense Mikayla stirring beside him. "Been better."

"Ah, but you are alive and awake, so that means you will survive."

"Give me the rundown, Doc. Any permanent damage?"

"Nothing permanent. The blade penetrated into the abdominal cavity but missed vital structures. You are lucky."

Linc grimaced. There was that word again.

The doctor continued. "You received a transfusion to offset the blood loss. We sutured the wound. You have led a violent life, Mr. Jameson, to have a scar from a gunshot as well as a knife."

"Yeah." He glanced at Mikayla but she didn't meet his gaze. "When can I get out of here?"

"We'd like to keep you in our fine hospital at least twelve more hours, maybe a whole day. Make sure there is no infection. You are being treated with antibiotics as a precaution."

"Thanks."

The doctor left, and Mikayla sat up, hair tumbling loose from a messy knot. The shadows under her eyes looked more pronounced.

"Where am I?" he asked.

"Cedar City, Utah. It's about a hundred and fifty miles from Concord."

"You drove here?"

She nodded. "I drove your Jeep because it had more gas than my car."

"Okay." Something else was going on. She was looking at him, but not *really* looking at him. "There a problem, Mikayla?"

She leaned back, eyes drifting shut. "I'm fine, Linc."

"We're past that. Tell me what's really going on."

Her eyelids lifted. The anguish in her expression shredded his heart. "You almost died."

He frowned. "Doc didn't say I almost died. I was stabbed, sure. But they patched me up and I'll be out of here soon."

"Hector Lopez stabbed you because you were protecting me. God, Linc. You lost so much blood."

He softened his tone. "But I didn't die."

"You were angry with me."

"What?"

"After you handcuffed Lopez. If you hadn't been bleeding to death, I think you would have been yelling at me."

Flashes of memory returned. Watching Mikayla stalking off, then disappearing around a van. His spike of fear when she hadn't appeared on the other side of the vehicle: Lopez holding her with his arm around her neck.

"Yeah, I was pissed. You ran off when it wasn't safe. That fucker Lopez had you again."

She firmed her chin. "Linc, I—"

The door swung open and Seth and Ellie entered the room, cutting off the discussion. Linc endured their questions and his sister's chiding. At Ellie's insistence, he called their mother to reassure her, only a promise to follow doctor's orders keeping her from jumping on the next plane to Utah.

He frowned when Mikayla quietly slipped out of the room.

"Marshals have Lopez in custody. He's already flipped." Seth's comment distracted him. "He and Donny are spilling their guts."

"No shit?"

"Nope. This is it, Linc. Lopez is willing to testify against the Zecenas. Even better, his orders to kill Mikayla came straight from Paco. Add that to Donny's statement that Zecena ordered him to kill Wellington, and the Zecena cartel's US operations are done. Paco will be in federal prison for the rest of his life."

Linc's eyes strayed to the door. He shifted, trying to ease the pain in his side. "That's good. Really good. And Mikayla won't have to go into WITSEC."

"No, your girlfriend will be happy."

He glanced at his sister, her attention focused on her phone, thumbs flying as she tapped out a message. She slid it in her pocket, her expression serious.

"What?"

"Mikayla texted. She's getting a ride back to the campground with a ranger named Smallcanyon."

"What the hell?"

"She said Smallcanyon had been in to see you when you were still out of it and since she'd left her car at the campground, she couldn't miss the opportunity to get a ride back for it."

Linc felt like he'd been sucker punched, and it hurt a lot more than being stabbed. "Something's going on with her. Tell her to come back and talk to me."

Ellie raised a brow with a look that told him she didn't like being the go-between.

"I'd do it myself but I've been stabbed."

That got her. "Jesus, Linc." She tapped out the message, and a moment later her phone vibrated. Ellie scanned the message, expression sober. "She says she left your keys in the drawer of the stand beside your bed." Ellie walked over and opened the drawer, holding up the keys for Linc to see. "She's already on the road with Smallcanyon."

"Fuck." Linc pushed himself up to a sitting position.

"Where the fuck do you think you're going?" Seth growled.

"To get her."

"No way in hell."

"You're not going to stop me."

"I will." Ellie stepped forward. "You promised Mom you'd follow doctor's orders. You don't? I'll call and let her deal with you."

"Damn it, Ellie."

"You're in no condition to go tearing across the state. It may not be what you want to hear, big guy, but if Mikayla wanted to be here, she'd be here."

# Chapter Twenty-Five

Mikayla pulled into the driveway of her town house. The two weeks she'd been gone felt like a lifetime. She pushed open the front door to a space that offered no welcome. A layer of dust had settled on the surfaces, and the air felt closed in and stuffy.

She disarmed the alarm and opened a few windows, letting in the cool evening air. If she'd felt absolutely safe, she would have opened the sliding door to the patio, but until the whole cartel issue was settled, she'd keep to the side of caution. Maybe she'd get a dog. A dog would be another layer of security and would help make where she lived feel more like a home.

With a sigh, she set down her purse, then forced herself to return to her car. Several trips later she'd brought in most of her bags, as well as the plastic bins. Dirty laundry got sorted into piles to be washed in the morning, and perishable food moved to the refrigerator. Other than the ice chest, there was no urgency. She could have cleared out the car in the morning, but right now she needed to keep busy so she'd stop thinking about Linc.

Alex Smallcanyon had offered her an unwitting escape hatch, and like a coward she'd taken it, leaving Linc at the hospital without saying good-bye. She'd expected her phone to blow up with texts and calls. That it hadn't served her right.

Earlier that morning while driving west through the Nevada desert, it occurred to her that perhaps the reason Linc hadn't contacted her was because there'd been some complication. What if he'd developed an infection? Or the wound had reopened? Those thoughts had her speeding at eighty miles per hour to the next town where she could get cell service.

After a painfully long wait, the nurse at the Cedar City hospital came on the line only to tell her she wasn't free to share a patient's information. That left her only option to text Ellie, who assured her that Linc was doing well, and would be released before noon. Ellie had finished the message with a blunt order to call him.

Chewing her lip, Mikayla had done that, only to have the call go through to voicemail.

So that was that. Maybe he'd accepted the wisdom of putting the brakes on their relationship.

She'd have to face him at some point. She was sure the Marshals Service would want to interview her, and depending on how the cases went, both she and Linc would likely testify at the trials of Donny Bertola, Hector Lopez, and Paco Zecena.

She wouldn't be able to avoid Linc forever, but a little distance might allow her to figure out what she wanted. Well, she knew she wanted Linc, but she feared she couldn't keep herself whole if she was in a relationship with him.

After changing into a tank top and lightweight cotton pants to sleep in, she found herself pacing back and forth across her bedroom, cell phone in hand. The urge to call him again, just to make sure he was okay, was so strong her finger was hovering over his name on her favorites list before good sense prevailed. If she wanted to break up with him, not that they were formally together, then she shouldn't call him. That wasn't fair.

She threw herself face down on her bed, head resting on folded arms. She had never felt so alone. Even when her mother had kept her closed in and isolated, she hadn't felt this craving to be with someone—a particular someone, in this case.

She must have fallen asleep. A loud rapping at her front door startled her awake. She sat up and glanced at the clock on her nightstand. Almost ten o'clock. Heart racing, she stepped out onto the landing. Had the Zecena cartel found her? The knock sounded again.

"Mikayla, it's me."

"Linc." Her breath hitched. In seconds she was down the stairs, hands fumbling over the lock and dead bolt. She pulled open the door. He stood in the glow of the porch light, solid and real, and her heart turned over. She gripped the doorknob to keep from hurling herself into his arms.

"Can I come in?"

She nodded mutely and stepped back.

He followed her into the living room, filling the space with his presence. He looked good, not like a guy who had been stabbed only a day earlier.

"Why aren't you in the hospital?"

"Doctor cleared me to check out."

"Are you in pain?"

He shrugged. "Sore, but I can deal."

She nodded, and the silence stretched between them. "Can I get you anything to drink? To eat?"

"No." He watched her with that innate stillness she recognized he used whenever he puzzled over a problem.

"Did you drive all the way here today?" When he nodded, she asked, "How did you find where I live?"

He gave her a look, and she found herself nervously rubbing her hands together. "Oh, right. You're a marshal." Desperate for some way to break the tension, she sidestepped him to enter the kitchen. "Do you want tea? I want tea. I have herbal tea with no caffeine, if you like, so it won't keep you awake." She grabbed the kettle and began filling it with water.

"I don't want herbal tea."

"I have black tea, too. Earl Grey. Do you like Earl Grey?" She bit her lip to stem the flow of inane comments. She set the kettle on the stove and turned on the burner.

She turned around to find he'd come up behind her. He'd moved closer. Heat shot through her, and she could feel the flush searing her cheeks. "What do you want?"

"You."

Her heart stuttered. "Linc."

"Mikayla."

Longing mixed with heat made her want to lean into him and hold on tight.

"Why didn't you tell me you were leaving with Smallcanyon?"

She folded her arms across her chest. "Because I'm a coward. I can't do this. I can't do us, and I didn't want to tell you."

"Why do you think you can't do us?"

The stubble covering his chin reminded her what it felt like when he'd kissed his way all over her body. The desire to touch him made her fingers itchy. The corner of his mouth lifted.

"Sweetheart?"

She raised her gaze and found his eyes warm. He tugged her hand loose, bringing it to his face. As if he'd read her mind, he rubbed the tips of her fingers along his jaw, the texture of his beard bristly. "*We* can do this, together. You feel it. I know you do. Whenever I'm around you, I know I can handle anything. You're what centers me, what grounds me." He paused once more, voice deepening. "I love you."

She fought to keep the tears at bay, to push back on the emotions as she always did. But, like at the cabin, something about him broke past her barriers. Tears clogged her throat. "No." Her throat felt ragged. "I can't love you. It will kill me."

He swept a thumb across her cheek, wiping away tears. "Too late. You already love me."

She shook her head vigorously. "You could have died trying to save me. Three times. Donny could have killed you in that cabin. And Hector nearly did kill you."

She gave a mighty sniffle, then reached past Linc for a paper towel. She pressed it into her eyes.

Finally, she drew in a deep breath, the paper towel clenched in her fist. The kettle whistled and Linc reached over to shut off the flame. He turned back to her, his big hands framing her face.

"Sweetheart." His expression had her gulping air. "There are no guarantees. Your father died protecting you. I know that has made you guard your heart extra tight. My dad left me, but in a different way. There are risks with my profession, but honestly? Most of the time, my job is pretty mundane."

"It doesn't seem mundane."

He grinned. "You caught me at a busy time."

She set aside the crumpled towel, raising a hand to his chest when he leaned forward. If he kissed her, she was sunk.

"I'm a coward, I know that. But I don't think I'd survive if anything happened to you."

"That's bullshit about you being a coward. But more importantly, why wouldn't you survive if anything happened to me?"

She stared at him, heart hammering, knowing what he was asking.

"I need the words too, Mikayla. Once I know for sure, we can take care of anything that comes our way."

She sighed, unable to deny the truth. Since he'd walked in the door, her house had lost the feeling of emptiness. He was her home, her heart.

Looking into his eyes, she pushed back on the fear so she could free herself for something better. She placed her hands on either side of his face. Taking a steadying breath, she said, "I love you, Lincoln Jameson. I am completely, totally, helplessly in love with you."

Light filled his eyes, and he leaned forward to capture her lips with his. Heat and emotions swelled, sweeping them together in a maelstrom of sensation. His tongue slid into her mouth, hot and potent.

Where moments before her hands had been pushing him back, now she gripped his shirt to pull him closer. The kiss spun out, and he took his time, like he was savoring a feast.

Finally freeing her lips, he shifted to nibble on the soft skin on the underside of her jaw, hands caressing her side, thumbs rubbing against her breasts. She breathed in his warm scent, shifting to run her lips along the column of his throat. When she reached the strong muscle above his collarbone, she bit softly, and when he groaned, she stroked the sensitive spot with her tongue.

He pulled her tight against him, his hard length nestled firm against her belly. Warm, open-mouthed kisses to the sensitive skin beneath her ear had her turning her head to give him better access.

"Is there a bed around here someplace?"

She shivered. "Uh-huh." Her brain was so addled she could hardly form a coherent thought.

He hitched her up and she tightened her legs around his waist.

His sharply sucked-in breath made her remember his injury. "Sorry. Sorry. I forgot."

He dropped her on the counter and tipped his head onto her shoulder as he breathed through the pain. "I'm fine, it only hurts when I pick up my girl."

She rubbed his back. "You sure you're up for this?"

Humor replaced the pain in his eyes. "In more ways than one."

She scooted off the counter, rubbing against him until her toes touched the floor. She gripped his hand. "Follow me. All you'll have to do is sit back and enjoy yourself."

"Yeah?"

"Yeah."

*** 

Forty minutes later, satiated and lying on his back with Mikayla snuggled against his uninjured side, Linc didn't think he'd ever felt more content. He ran his fingers lightly up and down the smooth skin of her naked back, then brushed back a curl of auburn hair from her cheek.

Her hand lazily raked through his chest hair, staying away from the bandaged wound. Her brows lowered slightly, and he rubbed the furrow between them with the pad of his thumb. "What's going on in that head of yours?"

Her shoulder hitched in a shrug. "WITSEC. I know I'll have to do it. I only hope the trial is over quickly."

"You won't need to go into WITSEC."

She lifted her head abruptly, eyes wide. "Really?"

"Yeah, really. Both Hector and Donny are taking a plea bargain. In exchange for lighter sentences, they'll give up whatever they have about the cartel in general, and Paco Zecena in particular."

"Sheesh, there really is no honor among thieves."

"None whatsoever."

"I thought the marshals were concerned there might be other cartel members, loyal cartel members, who would try to get to me before I can testify."

He traced a finger down the side of her face, suddenly nervous. "While remote at this point, it's still a possibility. But I, ah, convinced them you'd be safe. With me."

"With you? What do you mean with you?"

"I mean, you'd be safe if you moved in with me. Or I moved in with you."

"So basically WITSEC, but in my own home, or yours. And with my own personal marshal?"

"Kind of, but not exactly."

"How not exactly?"

"Hang on a second." Before he lost his nerve, he got out of bed to fish the small box out of his jeans pocket, then pulled on the jeans because damned if he was going to do this buck naked.

"Look, I know we haven't talked about this, and it might be too soon." He stood looking at her. She'd rolled onto her back, auburn hair a tumble around her head, eyes a deep dark green. His breath backed up in his throat.

This was what he wanted. *She* was what he wanted. He wasn't going to stumble around about it.

"Marry me."

She jerked upright, bringing the sheet up to cover her breasts. "Linc."

If she was going to look at him like he'd proposed hijacking a plane and flying to Cuba, he might as well go all in. He opened the box, stared at the contents for a long moment, then handed it to her. "Here."

Donny pulling a gun on him hadn't scared him this much.

Her mouth formed a perfect O as she studied the ring.

"You said you didn't like diamonds, so I thought you might like an emerald. This one matches your eyes. But if you don't like it, we can take it back. To Las Vegas. I stopped on my way here, figured if any city would have a jewelry store open on a Sunday, it would be Vegas."

His gut clenched into a tight knot when she handed the box back to him. He stared at the box in his hand.

"Right. So that's a no."

Could he have fucked it up any worse? He should have been patient. Taken her out to a fancy dinner, given her some romance. If the dead fiancé had been able to put together a proposal on a harbor cruise on New Year's Eve, Linc should have at least attempted to do something special. Something to show how much he loved her. Instead, he'd acted like an idiot, practically throwing the box at her.

"Yes."

He jerked his head up. Sitting on the edge of the bed with the sheet wrapped around her, she held out her left hand.

"Yes?"

"My answer is yes, Linc. I will marry you." She fluttered her fingers. "You have to put the ring on my finger."

His heart felt like it would burst out of his chest, and he couldn't help what he was sure was a stupid grin from splitting his face.

The ring felt warm in his hand as he slipped it onto the fourth finger of her left hand. When it slid home, he lifted his gaze to find her blinking rapidly against tearing eyes. Dropping to one knee in front of her, he lifted her palm to his lips, closing his eyes when she tilted her head over his, encircling his neck with her other hand.

After a long moment, he lifted his head, his gaze seeking hers. "I did it all wrong. I love you, and I should have proposed in a way that shows how much I love you."

She laid a finger across his lips. "You were perfect, Linc. The ring is perfect. You're what I want."

He vowed then and there to show her every day how much he loved her.

They lay back on the pillows, nose to nose. He brought her ring finger up to his lips and kissed her knuckle above the emerald.

He pulled her closer, and when she snuggled into his arms, for the first time ever, he felt like he had found his home.

# HIDDEN JUDGMENT

# Chapter One

Ellie strode from the restroom to the bank of elevators then jabbed her finger on the up button. She didn't usually pay much attention to her appearance, but she'd slipped into the bathroom to check her makeup. That morning she'd been compelled to put on her game face, which meant brushing on mascara and applying lipstick she normally didn't wear. Neither had been smudged, and her hair had stayed back in its tortoiseshell clip. Her marshal's star hung securely from the lanyard around her neck, and her Glock was safe in its shoulder holster. If she was honest, she'd also made the stop to take a breath and force herself to relax. Whatever happened in this meeting, she would rein in her hair-trigger reaction, and listen before forming an opinion.

She tapped her foot. Waiting sucked, and only served to make her more nervous. She caught herself before she could chew off her lipstick. *I can do this.* Two other people joined her at the elevator bank, looking up at the progress of each car: a balding man who needed to cut back on the carbs, and a petite Asian woman with stiletto heels. Both, like her, wore professional attire.

The elevator binged and they entered the car. Ellie chose her floor, then waited through stops on lower floors before getting to hers. She'd tried to get information about this meeting, but all she'd been able to learn was that it involved protection for a federal judge. Samuel Creed.

Everyone knew about Judge Creed. Four months ago, a defendant had somehow smuggled a knife into his courtroom and the video of him all but flying over the bench to help take down the guy had been played and replayed on social media and news programs around the world. He'd refused interviews and downplayed his role, but that had only sharpened curiosity about him. It didn't hurt that there was *something* about him—his looks, his presence, his steely gray eyes—that made everyone sit up and pay attention.

For over a decade, she'd been able to tuck memories of the man into a corner of her brain labeled "best forgotten." Hard to do now with social media being what it was.

After his superhero maneuver, other aspects of his judicial career began gaining attention, like the unconventional sentences and statements from the bench that had led one fan to create a blog titled "Creed's Law," which had garnered tens of thousands of followers.

At thirty-seven, Samuel Creed was the youngest federal judge in the country, and there was that forceful *something* about him that had memes speculating about what lay hidden under the judge's black robes. Not that she paid any attention except in her capacity as a US Marshal, whose responsibilities included the protection of federal judges.

She was counting on him not remembering her.

She exited the elevator, went through the frosted glass doors stenciled with "US Marshals Service, District of Oregon," waved to the receptionist, and walked briskly to the door of the conference room. Another steadying breath and she opened the door.

The whole team was present. Seth, her eldest brother, was Chief Deputy in charge of the unorthodox group assembled to locate their father, fugitive Richard Jameson, as well as other members of his right-wing extremist group.

Seth stood at the counter with the coffeepot that filled the air with its life-giving aroma, sipping from a cup while her other brother Linc poured coffee into a travel mug. They'd both shed their suit jackets, and wore their holsters under their shoulders and marshal's stars on their belts. When Linc saw her, he raised a brow and held up the pot, and at her nod filled another cup. Rounding out the team was Marshal Isabella Nikolaev.

There'd been some major pushback from the higher-ups in Marshals Service when the three offspring of Richard Jameson had been assigned to hunt him down. But Seth had argued their case and used every ounce of influence he had, and finally, the brass approved.

Which didn't explain the presence of the man standing with his back to her, gazing out the window. He stood separate and alone. Outside was a dazzling example of perfect Portland fall weather, but she wondered if Sam Creed even saw the view. He hadn't turned when she'd come into the room, and she was glad for the momentary reprieve.

Taking the steaming cup from Linc, she sat next to Bella. Ellie and the other female marshal had become fast friends. They needed to stick together to make their voices heard over the two men on the team who thought they were right about every damn thing.

"Let's get started," Seth spoke with firm authority.

Creed turned and Ellie braced herself. His gaze rested briefly on her before moving on to the others.

*So far so good.*

Seth sat at the head of the conference table. "Let's get the introductions over with." He indicated the man who sat to his left. "This is Judge Samuel Creed of the US District Court in Pendleton." Seth gave the team members' names.

Ellie watched Sam's face carefully when Seth said her name. Nothing changed in the judge's expression. No flash of recognition, no confusion over trying to place her. Relief brought a slight easing of her tension. Apparently, thirteen years was long enough to erase any memory of her.

"Here's the background," Seth continued. "Judge Creed is the recipient of anonymous threats with a commonality that says they're from the same or similar sender. We believe the threats are linked to right-wing militias active in eastern Oregon. Our investigation has turned up evidence connecting some of those groups with the larger American Freedom Confederation we've been after."

"What do they want?" Linc asked.

"Primarily, someone freed from prison who we suspect is affiliated with their organization. They've included general warnings against US government facilities, then more specific threats against the judge for decisions he's made that they consider attacks on Second Amendment rights. They claim the country would be better off without traitors who refuse to defend the Constitution, and the judge has been warned to watch his back. You know, typical shit." Seth sipped his coffee before continuing. "We've offered a protection detail, which His Honor turned down."

Ellie glanced at Sam, whose gaze remained fixed on Seth.

"He's made a somewhat irregular proposition to deal with the threats." Seth tipped his head to Sam. "Judge, you want to explain?"

Sam nodded at Seth before running his gaze over the group. "Thank you for agreeing to this meeting." He spoke in a low, clear voice Ellie thought likely helped him maintain control of his courtroom. "Protection is reactionary. It won't find whoever's threatening me. My plan is to lure in those involved, open myself to action on their part, and hopefully trap the bastards before they can harm me or anyone else."

Seth commented, "The Marshals Service sees value in this plan, but is unwilling to leave him undefended, so Judge Creed's girlfriend is moving in with him. That will be you, Ellie."

Ellie could almost hear the click as Sam's gaze locked on her. Panic had her sitting up straight. "Ah, I'd make a terrible girlfriend. Bella's a much better choice."

Ellie shifted when Bella's heel came down on Ellie's toe. *Way to throw a friend under the bus.* Moving her foot out of range, she continued, "I'd like to follow up on the leads I've uncovered on the AFC."

Seth never gave much away, but over thirty years of knowing her brother allowed her to read the slightly raised brow to mean *What the hell, Ellie?* as clearly as if he'd said the words out loud.

His voice held cool authority. "Sam and I discussed the options, and we agreed you're the best choice to act as the girlfriend, in part because you both attended University of Oregon at roughly the same time so it's plausible you could have met there. Bonus, you have a law degree, so you come from the same background."

Damn. Seth was right. No way out of this without giving herself away. Ellie forced a nod of agreement. "Okay. What about the rest of the team?"

"Bella, Linc, and I will relocate to Pendleton for as long as you're providing the judge's protection. In addition to adding to the judge's security, we'll continue working on our ongoing investigation of the anti-government movement in eastern Oregon and Idaho. We think the threats against Sam are connected."

"Four marshals in Pendleton, Oregon?" Bella's brow furrowed over her exotic eyes. "Something else must have happened to justify that level of protection."

"Correct. You want to tell the team what you found on your car, Sam?"

A flash of some emotion crossed his expression, but his tone remained dispassionate. "C-four attached to an inside wheel well of my vehicle."

Linc leaned forward in his seat. "No shit? How'd you find it?"

Sam shrugged. "This was two weeks ago. I was parked on dirt. It'd rained, and I noticed fresh boot prints around my car. There were indications someone had knelt by the rear passenger tire. I took a look and saw a brick of plastic explosive, complete with a detonator, attached with duct tape."

His voice had deepened, become richer in the years since he'd been in law school. Ellie ignored the shiver snaking down her spine. Focus was the word of the day. "Where was your car parked? Were there any witnesses?"

"I was parked along the River Parkway. The chief deputy can better answer your question about witnesses."

"The investigation is ongoing, but as of now we have no witnesses," Seth affirmed. "The C-four had a motion-activated detonator. We're looking into possible sources for the bomb materials, but it appears likely the C-four is from a batch stolen from a military base near Portland. Part of our investigation is determining whether there was inside help at the base."

Someone attempting to blow up a federal judge was serious business and added a layer of urgency and danger to the job of protecting Judge Creed. "What are the details of my cover?"

"We're keeping it simple. You and Sam were long-distance boyfriend and girlfriend, and decided to take your relationship up a notch. You've come to Oregon to live together. You'll use the name Rachel Sinclair. Cover documents are being made. You're a lawyer and have been working for a firm in San Diego. Your plan is to spend your time studying for the Oregon bar exam."

"And what will you be doing while I'm moving in with my boyfriend?"

"We've procured a short-term rental, a residence not far from the judge's house. Linc will be the marshal assigned to the courthouse, and since a marshal's job is to protect federal judges, that won't be remarkable. To keep anyone from being tipped off by the large number of marshals assigned, Bella and I will pose as lawyers representing a client. Our cover will allow us access to the courthouse and keep our investigation under wraps."

Bella set down the mug she'd been sipping from, the string from the teabag trailing over the side. "Why keep our mission to protect Judge Creed secret? As federal marshals, it shouldn't be so unusual to see us at the courthouse."

"True," Seth replied. "But we're going to maintain cover so we don't tip off the court staff about what's going on. We can't assume the threat is only from the outside."

"You think the messages could be a misdirection," Ellie surmised.

"Actually, I don't think they are, but we can't ignore the possibility."

"Wouldn't locals, court staff included, already know about the threats to the judge? People tend to pay attention when a bomb is found attached to a judge's car." This question came from Linc.

Seth shook his head. "You'd think, but Sam did us a favor. Instead of calling local law enforcement, he called ATF to deal with the bomb. They defused it and the locals are none the wiser."

"Except for the bomber, who must have wondered why his toy didn't work," Ellie pointed out.

Seth nodded. "We control what we can control. Here's our immediate plan. Bella, Linc, and I will travel separate from you and the judge so no one sees us together and connects us." Seth turned to the judge. "Sam, you flew here?" At Sam's nod, Seth said, "We'll arrange a rental car so you and Ellie can drive back to Pendleton."

A woman wearing a marshal's star came in and passed an envelope to Seth. He opened it and tipped out the contents. "Here's your new identity, Ellie. You're now Rachel Sinclair, so give me everything for Eleanor Jameson. You can keep your weapon, but don't wear it."

Ellie transferred her new identity into her wallet and couldn't help feeling that she was being stripped bare as she handed over her badge and ID.

"I need to go back to the hotel to pack."

Sam spoke directly to Ellie for the first time. "Did you drive here today?"

She shook her head. "I took a rideshare."

He nodded. "We'll pick up the rental and stop at the hotel to get your things, then we'll get on the road."

They had a good, sensible plan, but she couldn't help feeling she needed a little alone time to fortify her defenses before she and Sam Creed were thrown together as lovers.

## Chapter Two

Ellie stared out the window of the rental sedan as they drove through the outskirts of Portland, Mount Hood looking austere and imposing in the distance. Kind of like Judge Creed. They hadn't spoken much since leaving the Marshals Office. He'd been distant and preoccupied, except for the couple times when she'd caught his hawk-like gaze on her, making her feel like a novice defense lawyer arguing her first case before the bench. In fact, the whole situation made her uncomfortable. She resented feeling like she had as a young undergrad, dazzled by the attention of the hot law student. She reminded herself she wasn't that naïve sophomore any longer. She could handle herself with Judge Creed.

It didn't help that Sam had grown into his looks. As a law student he'd been thin to the point of gawkiness. Thirteen years and he'd filled out some, though he was still lean. The hair he wore combed back from his forehead now had threads of silver that matched the slate gray of his eyes. Combined with the slashing cheekbones, he had the look of a seasoned warrior.

She stifled a sigh. Their shared history made the current situation a messy business. That history was like a block wall between them that only she could see. Which made it her problem to deal with. She and Sam had had sex, that was all. Despite the distance of time, she remembered that night in crisp detail.

From the moment she'd arrived at the party, she'd been aware of the longhaired law student with the fast grin. He'd caught her attention on campus before then, and she'd even made a point of going by the coffee shop where she'd once seen him on the off chance he'd be there. She'd been thrilled when a friend had introduced them.

They'd ended up talking, flirting back and forth, and drinking more than they should. He'd been cool and sexy, and so much more mature than the other guys at the party. They'd gone up the back stairs to his bedroom.

Later, he'd asked her to go out with him, and promised to call to set up a date. She'd never heard from him again. The man sitting beside her gave no indication he remembered any of that. She'd never completely forgiven or forgotten him, and when he'd appeared on the news with his takedown heroics, the memories had planted themselves once again firmly in her psyche, a distraction she worked hard to ignore.

Acting as his fake girlfriend was *not* the way to get past the stupidest of college mistakes.

He put on the turn signal and glanced over his shoulder before changing lanes, his mirrored sunglasses hiding his eyes. "We should fill in our story." His voice rolled over her like warm chocolate, smooth and sensuous.

Judge Creed and warm chocolate did not belong in the same thought. "Right."

He'd pulled off his tie and unbuttoned the top button on his shirt, turning back his sleeves to above his elbows. His suit jacket lay across the backseat. A few locks of thick black hair had fallen over his forehead, softening his rather severe image. The intelligence and intense personality that had drawn her all those years ago hadn't abated. Okay, that was an understatement. The added maturity pegged the needle on the hot meter all the way over to the bonfire zone.

"We should keep it simple, like your brother suggested. When I was in law school, you would have been an undergrad. Let's say we met at a party, then again years later at a conference, and have kept in touch since."

Ellie didn't allow anything in her demeanor to give away that what he'd described was exactly how they had met. "Fine. Where was the conference?"

"You've been to Las Vegas?" At her nod, he said, "I attended a conference there last year. Let's say we met there, hooked up, and kept in touch."

"Wow, super romantic. If you plan on telling people this story, you better inject some emotion."

The corner of his mouth lifted a fraction. "I'll assure anyone who asks that you're the love of my life."

Only sheer force of will kept her gaze steady on his. "Let's not go overboard, Creed. But there's a problem. Rachel Sinclair is a smart, confident, modern woman, and she wouldn't be willing to take all the risk in this relationship. She's given up a position at her firm—where she was on track to make partner, by the way—to move to the wilderness to see if it'll work out with her judge boyfriend. I think she'd want more of a commitment than that."

"You want me to ask you to marry me?"

Ellie couldn't hold back the laugh. He didn't give much away, but the flash of panic on his face was gratifying.

"Take it easy. I don't think the bent knee thing would suit you. But yeah. Rachel Sinclair is in love, but not stupid kind of love. I'll talk with Seth and get him to approve the purchase of an engagement ring."

Another long look, then he said, "I'll take care of it."

She shrugged. "Fine, you talk to him."

He drummed long, squared-off fingers on the steering wheel. "Pendleton is not the wilderness."

"I'm from Southern California where wilderness is a prized commodity, so my observation is no insult. Regardless, I looked at a map. Pendleton is a remote outpost in the wilderness."

He opened his mouth like he would argue the point, but shook his head and said, "Give me a rundown of what I need to know about you."

She so didn't want to do this. Any of it. She didn't want to have a cozy chat with Sam Creed on a long drive to his home in Pendleton. She didn't want to pretend she was engaged to him. She didn't want to share her life story. All of it made her feel vulnerable, which she simply needed to get over.

"Right. I'm thirty-two. I was born and raised in San Diego where my mom and stepfather still live. For the most part, my brothers and I had a typical suburban childhood. I attended college at the University of Oregon, then law school at Hastings."

He waited a beat. "That's all you've got? There's not more to Eleanor Jameson?"

"I'm telling you about Rachel Sinclair. Granted, I'm keeping close to my own story, but all you need to know are the basics."

"We want this to work, don't we? If people are going to believe we have a soul connection, you'll have to go deeper, get past the superficial. Tell me more about Eleanor Jameson."

It took all her self-control not to lean away from him with arms folded over her chest in a defensive posture. "Like what?"

"Like why Oregon for college?"

The question was the same a much younger Sam Creed had asked her sophomore self. She kept her tone level. "University of Oregon offered me a full ride with a sports scholarship."

"What sport?"

She lifted a brow. "What do you think?"

"Since you're all leg and have to be nearly six feet tall, I'd guess basketball."

"You'd guess right. And I'm five eleven, damn it."

"Damn it?"

"Another inch and I could make Linc stop calling me Shorty. There's respect in my family if you hit six feet."

"Ah, understood. So you played basketball for the Ducks. Major?"

"History. You?"

"History as well, but at Cal."

"You went to Berkeley?"

He nodded. "But I only played intramural basketball."

She narrowed her gaze. "You'd have had to pay out-of-state tuition, which would have made Berkeley expensive in addition to the cost of living in the Bay area. Either your family is wealthy, you have a boatload of student debt, or you earned a scholarship."

He gave a wry laugh. "My family was not wealthy. I got an academic scholarship along with some debt."

"Then you went to University of Oregon for law school."

"Right."

The questions went back and forth. He told her he'd clerked for a federal judge, but she'd had to pry out of him that the judge had been on the Ninth Circuit Court of Appeals and was now a Supreme Court justice. Obviously, a prestigious appointment he wanted to downplay.

After his clerkship, he'd been with the US Attorney's office while teaching classes at the University of Oregon. Then had come the federal bench appointment. Ellie knew his was an amazing upward trajectory. But while he answered her questions about his career, he was reticent about his personal life. Sam hadn't revealed much about himself that couldn't be learned in a quick web search.

"Were you raised in Pendleton?"

"Thereabouts."

"What's that supposed to mean? Either you were or you weren't."

He shrugged. "My dad owned a ranch about thirty miles south of Pendleton until he died. That's where I grew up."

"Was it a real ranch with cows and horses, or a hobby ranch with a nine-hole golf course?"

"Rock Creek is a real ranch with cattle, not cows." Something shifted in his expression. "My brother is running it now."

"You have a brother? Sisters?"

"No."

"Do you have a girlfriend who'll wonder why you're suddenly engaged and not to her?"

"No girlfriend. How about you? Any ghosts from the past who'll show up to beat me bloody for grabbing you from under their noses?"

He was the only ghost from her past. "Nope. No guy for me."

He fell silent, and Ellie turned to look out the window, glad for the reprieve. She tamped down the ember of resentment that had flared to life. It was stupid. She *knew* it was stupid to let that one night affect her so hard. They'd had a hookup. Not a big deal in and of itself, but his careless and soon forgotten promise to contact her after had been a blow to her confidence. What she thought would be the beginning of something had turned into a one-night stand she'd never intended. Add that to her father's abandonment: no wonder she was distrustful of relationships.

They arrived at the Pendleton airport where they were to turn in the rental car and pick up Sam's vehicle. After parking, they approached the airport's double glass doors when an older woman stopped suddenly in front of Ellie. She stepped back and found herself against Sam's solid chest. His warmth radiated in the cool afternoon and she found the sudden closeness uncomfortable.

"Excuse me, sorry for being so scattered." The woman gave a flustered laugh. "My son and daughter-in-law are arriving with my new grandson and I'm so excited to see him that I completely forgot my phone in the car."

"A new grandson is exciting. Congratulations." Ellie pasted a smile on her face as she struggled to ignore the blazing heat where her body connected with Sam's. Layers of clothing didn't seem to have any effect on the intensity generated by their proximity.

She filed that knowledge away for future use: physical distance must be maintained if equilibrium is desired when dealing with Sam Creed.

They were crossing to the car rental kiosk when Sam caught her hand in his. She glanced at him in surprise and he kept a firm hold when she tried to tug free. "I think we need to establish some boundaries, pal."

"We'll establish boundaries later. Go with it," he muttered.

"Sammy, my man. How's it going?" A short, florid-faced man zoomed toward them like a heat-seeking missile, his voice booming in greeting. He slapped Sam on the shoulder and Ellie wanted to kick the guy when his gaze traveled over her, making a prolonged stop at her breasts before rising to her face. She felt the sudden need to take a shower.

Sam pulled her closer to his side.

"Didn't know you were out of town. Where you been?" While his tone was overly jovial and on the surface he appeared affable, Ellie detected calculation in his eyes.

"Finster." If he noticed Sam hadn't answered his question, he didn't acknowledge the fact.

"Who's your gorgeous friend, Sammy?"

"Gordon Finster, Rachel Sinclair." Sam's introduction was abrupt to the point of rudeness.

Ellie nodded her head. "Mr. Finster."

"Call me Gordy, sweetheart, everyone does." His gaze headed south once more. Once past her breasts, he seemed to focus on their clasped hands. "Here I am, gone for a couple days and it looks like things happen."

"Looks like," Sam agreed as he nudged Ellie so they could move around the unpleasant man.

"See you at work on Monday, then," Gordon spoke to their backs as they resumed walking.

It wasn't until they'd picked up Sam's vehicle and were on their way to his home that Ellie felt they could talk without the danger of being overheard. "Tell me about Gordon Finster."

"Besides being an obnoxious asshole, he's case administrator for the federal court in Pendleton." Sam glanced at her, then back at the road as he steered his Land Cruiser onto the highway on ramp. "He's also under investigation for sexual harassment after two female clerks made complaints against him."

"Are you involved in the investigation?"

"Peripherally. Gordon is looking for allies, hence the bro act. You'd think he wouldn't leer at my girlfriend, but he's an idiot as well as an asshole."

"Any motive for him to send you threatening messages?"

Sam shrugged. "I supported the complainants, plus my interview didn't go well for him and maybe he got wind of that, but I don't think he has the balls to retaliate. I also don't think he knows shit about C-four."

Ellie considered his response as she took in the landscape of rolling hills and farmland as they drove from the airport. She was a little surprised at Sam's vehicle choice. The Land Cruiser had to be at least twenty years old and appeared well cared for. If she'd given it any thought, she'd have pegged him as driving a cool Audi or BMW.

A semi ahead of them forced them to slow. She watched Sam step on the clutch and shift the manual transmission into a lower gear. She'd always wanted to learn how to drive a stick. Linc had promised to teach her, but after one lesson he'd banned her from ever touching his Jeep again, claiming she'd likely stripped the gears in his transmission.

She couldn't really blame him after the horrible grinding sound it'd made. She eyed Sam. Maybe he'd teach her. Not that he was exactly approachable, but maybe he'd be friendlier once they were more comfortable with each other.

Ellie had been on plenty of witness protection assignments that sometimes had involved working closely with interesting men. While the number of female marshals was larger than it'd ever been, the Marshals Service was still dominated by men who tended to be take-charge, I'm-the-coolest, alpha-male kind of guys. But she'd *never* had trouble separating personal feelings from her job.

She was starting to wonder if that would become a problem with Sam. Maybe she should have shared their previous connection with Seth. But she already knew how that conversation would've gone. He and Linc would've turned all protective big brother and pummeled Sam to a pulp, which wouldn't bode well for their careers.

She'd had a hookup with Sam, and in college that had been normal for so many young women, though not normal for her. She'd never engaged in casual sex before or after that event. But then, at the time, she hadn't thought what had happened with Sam had been casual. She'd thought he'd shared that instant connection.

She'd given him her phone number but hadn't gotten his, and when he'd failed to contact her, she'd been hurt. It had taken a stern talk from a girlfriend to discourage her from going to Sam's house and asking him what was up.

After their one-night stand, she'd avoided the campus coffee shop. In the end, she'd had to chalk it up to a lesson learned. Being with him now, she couldn't help thinking about it. But that was her problem. She was ninety-nine percent certain that if she asked him why he'd never called her, he'd have no recollection of that evening, which had been so significant to her.

# Chapter Three

Ellie tried to appreciate the scenery, but the reality of living with Sam was drawing ever closer. She needed to put a lid on her emotions before they got her in trouble.

How exactly she and Sam would figure out their living arrangements had yet to be determined. As much as she could, she'd rely on the normal procedures for witness protection. Out in public they had be a couple, but in his home she was a marshal protecting a judge. She'd be friendly but professional, remain clear-headed and logical, and she'd get through this assignment. Pulls of attraction would have to be ignored.

They crossed a bridge, and the river below swirled with deep currents.

"That's the Umatilla River."

"It's beautiful."

"You ever kayaked?"

"Sure, down in Baja and in the Sierras. I kayaked in Morro Bay once."

"I've got a couple of kayaks. We could take them out." She caught his speculative look and her heart gave a heavy thud. "All in the interest of doing couples activities, of course."

"Of course."

Being engaged to Sam was going to be tougher than she'd anticipated.

He slowed the Cruiser as he drove through an old, established neighborhood with houses on large lots separated by wooded areas. He turned into a driveway that ran along one edge of a sloping lawn bordered on the far side by groupings of tall pines before circling to the back of the house.

The house was a surprisingly appealing two-story colonial with clapboard siding painted a weathered gray with white trim. A wide porch framed a door painted deep red that matched the shutters on the dormer windows on the upper story. Sam clicked a device on his visor and the door on the detached garage rolled up.

Two kayaks hung suspended from overhead beams and he parked beneath them. Along one wall was a rack doubling as a stand for skis as well as fishing poles. He appeared to enjoy his outdoor activities.

Ellie stepped out of the garage and did a slow survey of the property, stuffing her hands deep in her coat pockets against the cool temperature. An area around the back door of the house was enclosed with a wire fence, but the rest of the property was open. While the garage matched the house, it appeared to be a more recent construction.

Behind it the land sloped up a hillside dotted with shrubs, rounded granite boulders, and clumps of tall trees. A short border wall of moss-covered rocks delineated the property and the weathered look of it made her think it had been around for most of the past century. She loved the rustic atmosphere that gave the property a homey appeal.

Nice as it was, she wasn't moving into Sam Creed's home for the environment. Rock walls, trees, boulders—all were nice for a person living a comfortable life without enemies. But that wasn't the case here, and the yard offered too much cover for someone interested in hanging out with a rifle and scope and taking shots at Judge Creed.

She tipped back her head to take in the gorgeous early-November leaves of red, yellow, and orange on a huge tree that spread wide branches over the lawn near the enclosed pen.

"This is the most beautiful tree I've ever seen. What is it?" The not-so-keep-it-professional words were out of her mouth before she could think to hold them back.

Sam stood at the back of the SUV. She glanced over when she felt him staring at her and caught an expression that made her think she'd surprised him. Then he was opening the rear door and pulling out her luggage. "Oregon white oak. Pretty common around here."

Right. *Pull it in, Ellie.* Most Southern California trees never wore fall colors like Sam's Oregon white oak. She didn't need to make a fool of herself about it. Good thing she hadn't gushed about the rock wall or he'd think she was really a nut. She fully intended to get a closer look at that wall, but later without Sam's unsettling presence.

Sam took the larger of her two suitcases, and Ellie didn't bother objecting. It was exactly what her brothers would do regardless that she was perfectly capable of managing her own luggage. She grabbed the remaining suitcase and they went through the gate to the fenced area. Wild barking echoed from inside.

"What kind of security do you have for your house?" She eyed the eaves and spied cameras and security lights at both rear corners.

He pulled a ring of keys from his pocket. "Besides the dogs, I had an alarm system installed when I moved in." He pointed. "The security lights are motion-activated."

"Are there cameras throughout the property or only around the house?"

"Around the house."

"Who does the system alert when there's been a breach?"

"There's no alert for the outside cameras—they only record. With the alarm system, I get a text if there's a breach, and the local police are notified. We good to go in or do you want to search the house first?"

"Doing my job, Creed. We'll want to put cameras up that slope." She indicated the hill at the back of the house.

He didn't say anything, and carried her suitcase as he climbed the steps and pushed open the door. Ellie followed him into a mudroom lined with hooks holding hats, jackets, and dog leashes, and a bench with shoe bins beneath it. There was a scrambling clatter of nails on the wood floor followed by a firm command to "sit." A matching pair of tri-colored beagles quivered with their butts planted on a mat that ran the length of the mudroom's hardwood floor. Sam deactivated the house alarm.

"Oh, you have beagles." Ellie's heart melted.

As far as she was concerned, beagles were the most adorable of all dogs, and she'd promised herself she'd adopt one once her job wasn't constantly taking her away from home.

Setting her suitcase onto the bench, she went down to her knees and offered a hand for the dogs to sniff. "Hey, guys. Aren't you gorgeous?" She turned her face up to Sam. "What are their names?"

"Tony and Cleo."

Tony and Cleo took hearing their names as a sign they were free to move. They rushed her with wagging tails, sniffing noisily at her feet as she stroked sleek coats.

"Let me guess, Marc Antony and Cleopatra. Am I right?"

"You win the cookie." Sam indicated hooks. "You can hang your coat here. I'll show you the house, then we'll take your suitcases up."

"Okay."

After coaxing the dogs outside, Sam took her from room to room, his tone not unwelcoming, but not exactly hospitable. He was doing his duty as her host, all without revealing much of what he was thinking.

She didn't want to be curious about Sam Creed, but being in his house only made her wonder about him more.

If she'd had to guess the type of home he'd live in, she'd have thought a low-maintenance town house with a minimum of fuss and clutter. But as with his vehicle, the opposite of that guess couldn't have been more extreme.

His home was richly decorated with solid furniture, and colors and textures that combined to make it inviting. The house's décor made up for his lack of welcome.

The history nerd in her loved the antique pieces, especially because they weren't confined to a specific period. The desk in his office looked like it dated from the antebellum era, while the drop leaf table in the living room with its gorgeous slag glass lamp looked late Victorian. The mix gave the home a comfortable, settled feel, one she could see herself happily living in.

Making mental notes of points of entry, as well as views from various windows, helped her to store the insights Sam's home gave into his personality. But the fat gray and white cat who lay curled at one end of a couch and the finely crocheted doilies under some of the knickknacks seemed so incongruous they made her frown.

Sam did not look like a fat cat or doily kind of guy. She reached out to stroke the cat, which stretched under her hand, extending needle-like claws.

"Her name is Gumbie."

Ellie couldn't hold back a laugh. "Someone's read their T. S. Eliot." She straightened and caught the considering look. "What?"

"Nothing."

She gave Gumbie a final rub. "How long have you lived here?"

"Year and a half."

"What did you do, buy out an antiques store to furnish it?"

"I inherited the house fully furnished from my aunt, and it came with the dogs and cat. She was a middle school English teacher, hence the animals' literary names. I haven't changed much of anything." He turned to the stairs. "I'll show you your room."

She wondered if he hadn't changed anything out of sentimentality or lack of interest. If she had to guess, the latter seemed more likely.

The upstairs landing led to a long hallway with doors on either side. He pointed to a door directly across the landing. "That opens to the back stairway that goes to the kitchen." At the end of the hall, he indicated a room on the left that faced the front of the house. "That's my room."

The open door revealed a room with a sloped ceiling and west-facing dormer windows that showed the sun setting through the trees and cast the room in a half-light. A wide bed with four posters of what looked like polished mahogany was covered with a gorgeous quilt in a traditional wedding ring pattern. The colors of deep burgundy and cream were a beautiful contrast to the golden wood floor and the painted white walls.

"Oh wow, I love your bed." She felt him check his movement, and her gaze flew to his. His expression remained unchanged, except for the minute lift of the corner of his mouth. "Don't get any ideas, Creed. I appreciate antiques, and you've got some beautiful pieces."

"Then you'll like your room." He motioned across the hall.

Ellie stepped through the door and all thoughts of focusing simply on her job fled. "Oh my god. Is that a pewter bed frame?" She brushed past him to run her fingers over the burnished metal. The head- and footboards had a classic curved design and she guessed it had to be over a hundred years old. "And look at the quilt. Oh, I love the colors. This is a broken star pattern. Did your aunt make the quilts?"

She looked up. His expression had lost that distant look and her heart gave an uncomfortable thud in her chest. "You keep looking at me like I'm a weirdo."

Sam shook his head. "Not a weirdo, and yes, my aunt made the quilts. I'll bring up your suitcases."

He moved down the hall and she let out a careful breath, trying to find her mental balance. The man stirred her up, and she had no idea how he felt about her. Not that it mattered. She was here to protect him and that was it. No way was she opening herself to hurt like she'd experienced from his disinterest when she was young and foolish. She was neither now, and she reminded herself that she avoided the love 'em and leave 'em types like snakes in the grass.

Sam brought in her suitcase and smaller tote and deposited them at the foot of the bed. "We'll have to share the bathroom next door, unless you'd rather use the three-quarter bath downstairs. Put what you want in whichever you choose. I'll leave you to settle in." He pulled her bedroom door closed behind him.

Ellie sat on the edge of the bed, fingering the classically patterned quilt. She needed to build up her defenses because whatever had drawn her to a much younger Sam Creed was still there, waiting for those moments when all she could think about was that he was the most intriguing man she'd ever known.

He wasn't the most handsome, and he certainly wasn't the most charming, but he was hands-down the most *compelling*.

Maybe she should try viewing him as she did her brothers. They were both great guys, and women certainly found them attractive, but to her they were simply her brothers, sometimes dorks, sometimes annoying, but always decent humans.

The temperature in the house was on the cool side so she changed into leggings and a warm sweater that fell below her hips, and dug out the fleece-lined boots she was glad she'd ordered online when their assignment had sent the team away from sunny Southern California. She paused at the top of the stairs when her phone chimed with an incoming text.

Bella: *How's it going with Judge Hottie?*

Ellie rolled her eyes and texted back: *Really?*

Bella sent a meme that had Ellie choking back a laugh. It showed Sam in black judge's robes with a sexy scowl. The caption read "Spank me, please."

Bella: *Definitely. So?*

Ellie: *Fine, so far. We're figuring it out. He's working under the assumption that I'm a little deranged. I like his house. He has BEAGLES!*

Bella knew Ellie was obsessed with beagles, and had even taken her to a beagle rescue farm on her last birthday. Ellie had been able to play with beagle puppies to her heart's delight.

Bella: *Don't let them sleep in your bed. It's a bad precedent.*

Ellie: *I don't think their daddy would allow that, it seems a bit warm and cuddly for him. I get frostbite if I get within five feet of him.*

Bella: *Harsh. We'll be at Judge Hottie's house as soon as your brother gets over himself and lets me navigate.*

Ellie didn't have to ask which brother Bella was referring to. If Sam gave Ellie frostbite, Seth and Bella shared a deep freeze as frigid as a Siberian winter.

Ellie texted a thumbs up.

Tucking her phone under the waistband of her leggings and telling herself she was a coward for being nervous, she made her way downstairs.

She passed through the living room where a gas fire burned in the fireplace. The room felt so cozy she could easily spend the evening curled on the couch with a good book. Sam must've started the fire. Maybe she'd been too quick to judge the judge when she'd been texting Bella.

Framed photos on a shelf caught her attention. One showed a young Sam standing with an older woman with a self-conscious smile who had her hand on his shoulder. The image appeared to have been taken in front of this house. His aunt?

Ellie made her way to the kitchen to find Sam standing at the sink peeling sweet potatoes. He too had changed and wore a dark gray Henley with the sleeves pushed to his elbows and loose-fitting athletic pants. The hair that had earlier been combed back now fell over his forehead, softening his appearance. Damn. He was way too appealing.

"Bella texted. The team's on their way here. We weren't that far ahead of them, but I'm glad they're arriving under cover of night. We can't be seen with them. We're not supposed to know them."

He nodded. "Agreed." He set the potatoes on a cutting board. "They probably hit rush hour traffic. Lots of people who work in Portland live in the country." He toweled off his hands. "Tell Bella I'll feed you all. You a picky eater?"

"No. Especially if I don't have to cook what I'm eating."

She texted Bella about dinner.

"You don't cook?"

"I cook, but I don't particularly enjoy figuring out meals."

"How are you with prep work?"

"Excellent. What can I help with?" They were having a normal conversation. Normal was good. Normal would keep the one-sided erotic thoughts at bay.

# Chapter Four

Sam pulled a knife from a drawer and set it next to the sweet potatoes. "Cut these in one-inch chunks."

She did as directed, chopping the sweet potatoes, then the onions he handed her, and finally brussels sprouts, all while listening to the local NPR station playing through a Bluetooth speaker.

Every moment they worked quietly together she was uncomfortably aware of him. How he looked, how he moved, and when he reached in front of her for the pepper grinder, how he smelled of what made her think of the outdoors on a crisp fall day.

He lined a baking pan with foil and arranged the veggies on the tray, his movements competent. He drizzled them with olive oil, then sprinkled herbs and sea salt. He took filleted chicken breasts from the bag where they'd been marinating and arranged them in another pan, then put both chicken and veggies in the oven. A bottle of wine sat uncorked on the counter.

"You want a glass?"

"Hmm?"

"Wine, Eleanor. Would you like a glass of wine?"

*Head in the game, Ellie. Head in the game.* "That would be nice. Do you mind if I make a pot of coffee? My brothers will want some."

"Sure." He opened a cupboard over the coffee \maker and pulled down a canister. When she was filling the carafe with water, she said, "Do you have copies of the threats you received? I'd like to see them."

"I emailed them to Seth. He didn't share them with you?"

"No. I only know what was said at the meeting today. I haven't seen the actual emails."

"Right." He poured wine for them and set her glass on the counter where she was standing. "I'll get them."

Once the coffeemaker was glugging away, she took her wine to a table recessed in a corner nook of the kitchen. A cozy spot with windows in both walls showing the back and side yard of the house and the driveway, she imagined a pancake breakfast here would be fabulous.

A formal dining area lay between the living room and the kitchen. With the local newspaper folded next to her, she guessed that this more casual space was where Sam ate his meals.

He returned with a sheaf of papers and set them in front of her. He'd printed the emails and gave them to her in chronological order. All of them had been sent to Sam's official email address at the courthouse. The sender's email handle was "Freedom Defender." The first message, dated mid-September, was short and to the point.

*Traitor Judge, prepare your own defense. Come for our guns and we come for you. Heed the warning. Those who violate our rights die. Protect the real America. Free Frank Bannister.*

The next email, also from Freedom Defender, had been sent a week later.

*Judge Asshole, want to see your world burn? The sword of righteousness will destroy the symbols of tyranny. The defenders of America will prevail.*

Five days later, a third email was sent.

*We know where you live. We know what you drive. We know where you shop. Read the Constitution, traitor. Free Frank Bannister.*

She flipped through the pages. The emails had come nearly every week and the messages were along the same theme. A couple contained lengthier diatribes against restrictions on the Second Amendment, while most were brief and increasingly threatening. She glanced up to find Sam leaning against the counter, arms crossed over his chest, serious gray gaze on her.

"Who's Frank Bannister?"

"Member of a Constitutional militia group based east of here. ATF arrested him on weapons violations after he was pulled over and found to have a half dozen semiautomatic weapons and a couple of grenade launchers in his possession. They'd been stolen from a military base. I presided over his conviction and sentencing earlier this year. He's incarcerated at the federal penitentiary in Lompoc, California."

The dogs made a racket outside and Sam gave a half smile. "Early warning system." He tapped on an iPad and opened an app before handing it to her. "Here's what my security cameras show."

The cameras provided a wide angle, and the images they captured remarkably clear. Linc drove a large SUV that pulled up in front of the garage.

Setting down the iPad, she followed Sam through the mudroom to the back door. The beagles were at the fence, barking and howling. Ellie stood at the steps while Sam went to open the gate. Linc, Seth, and Bella approached the house. Bella had her huge purse slung over her shoulder and her arms crossed in front of her. Seth wore what as a teenager Ellie had dubbed his butt face, meaning completely expressionless, a look that meant he wanted to hide what he was thinking. Linc gave Ellie an eyeroll that she easily interpreted to mean that Seth and Bella had been in their usual prickly standoff, likely for the entire drive. It made Ellie feel a little better about travelling alone with Sam.

A few moments later, the kitchen was full of people and animals. Even the cat ventured in to investigate the commotion.

Seth gave Ellie a portable gun safe so she could safely store her weapon. She ran upstairs with it, and when she came down, Sam was offering beverages. As she expected, both Seth and Linc opted for coffee.

Sam took down mugs and Ellie began filling them. She felt more than saw her brother behind her back. Linc loomed over her shoulder in a way he knew she found annoying. Some things never changed.

He spoke in a low voice. "How are the new digs? Creed treating you right?"

She poured coffee and handed him the mug. "Back off, big brother." She leveled a look. "I can take care of myself."

"I know you can, but I'm still your brother."

"Then give me some respect." There was nothing new in this argument. Seth approached and she handed him a full mug. "At least you could be like Seth and not verbalize the big brother crap."

"Doesn't mean I don't think it," Seth muttered as he walked by.

She made a shooing motion. "You're crowding me."

Her brothers moved away as Sam approached. "What about Bella?"

Bella had left the room after being directed to the bathroom. "She'll want tea. Point me in the direction of a tea kettle and I'll put it on."

He shook his head even as he was reaching over her into an overhead cupboard. Before she could move out of his way, he'd brought down a little red kettle.

"I'll rinse it out and put the water on." He pointed to another cabinet. "Look in there for teabags."

She rummaged around and found a box in the back. She hoped tea didn't go bad. With the kettle on a cooktop burner, Sam found another mug. He nodded to Seth. "Why don't you all go in the living room. We'll eat in about half an hour."

The aroma of baking chicken vied with the stronger smell of full-bodied coffee. While the others trooped out of the kitchen, Ellie stayed behind, sipping her wine while waiting for the water in the kettle to boil. The slightly smaller of the beagles sat next to Sam, staring longingly into his face.

"Is that Tony or Cleo?"

"Cleo. Besides being a girl, she has more brown than black on her coat. She's reminding me it's time for their dinner."

"Show me what they're fed and I'll do it."

*** 

Sam studied the people sitting around his living room. He was always interested in family dynamics, maybe because growing up in his own family had been so atypical, and watching his father had been key to survival. As a judge, he paid attention to the defendants in his courtroom—if they fidgeted, how they talked to their lawyers, whether they acknowledged any friends or family among the spectators. The habit often gained him valuable insight into their character.

While he figured any of the Jameson siblings could easily take on the group leader job, they seemed satisfied leaving that role to Seth.

The four-member team appeared tight, the Jamesons tighter still, and while he detected tension between Bella and Seth, they appeared able to work around it. Bella sat next to Linc, who currently had his eyes glued to his phone, a grin on his face as he tapped out a message. Seth sat in the recliner, and instead of opting for the second single seat, Sam sat on the loveseat next to Ellie. He caught her surprised look. Too bad. If they were going to pull this thing off, she'd have to get used to being close to him.

He hadn't been kidding when he'd said she was all leg. She was wearing some sort of tights that showed off those long, toned legs perfectly. When they'd talked on the drive, he'd had a moment of déjà vu. That bugged him, because he generally had an excellent memory for names and faces. They'd barely scratched the surface of learning about each other. At some point she'd say something that would jog his memory and he'd figure out where they'd met before.

When the emailed threats had started coming in, he'd contacted the US Marshals Service and spoken to Chief Deputy Seth Jameson. Seth had started the investigation and wanted to assign a two-deputy security detail. Before that could happen, Sam had discovered the C-4 attached to his car. There'd been enough explosive power that if that bomb had detonated, he'd have been dead, and anyone in a thirty-yard radius would have been as well.

He'd been so pissed he'd come up with the plan to leave himself open and flush out whoever was targeting him. Seth hadn't liked the idea so the compromise was Sam's "fiancée" would be an undercover marshal. He didn't want a babysitter, but he acknowledged his safety was compromised.

Of all people to play the part he had to get a woman who wound him up. That reality had to do with more than her looks. Ellie made observations and asked questions that revealed an inquisitive mind, and he knew for damn sure that if he'd met her under different circumstances he'd have asked her out.

The plan was for them to live in the same house, sleep across the hall from each other, and, in public, behave like an engaged couple. That instant punch-in-the-gut attraction he'd felt when he'd first laid eyes on her? He'd have to ignore that. Hell, he hadn't even had to lay eyes on her. His back had been turned when she'd walked into the conference room, but he'd felt the air suddenly charge like a lightning storm was imminent. and had turned to find she'd been the cause.

He wondered if she felt the connection, and if that was why she seemed to be trying to rein in what he guessed was her naturally open behavior when she was around him. Maybe she wanted to maintain a professional distance between them. She appeared comfortable in his home, willing to help out, and at least with her brothers and Bella, had a ready smile or laugh. She only held back around him.

Ellie reached out her booted foot and nudged Linc. "You texting Mikayla heart emojis, lover boy?"

"Maybe."

"How's she doing with you being gone?"

"Looking forward to our assignment being done, but she gets that being away from home is part of my job."

"Well, tell her smoochie-smoochie bye-bye. We've got work to do."

"My wife misses me. What can I say?" He was still smiling when he stuffed the phone into the front pocket of his jeans. He jerked his chin toward the papers his sister held. "What do you have there?"

"These are the threats emailed to Sam." She handed the sheaf of papers to Linc, then turned to Seth. "Judge Creed filled me in on his connection with Frank Bannister. What else do we know?"

"Bannister was raised in a small town east of here. His father was suspected in the bombing of a BLM office in eastern Oregon three years ago. While ATF was looking into that, the elder Bannister and another son blew themselves up in their barn in what appears to be an accident. Our guess is they were constructing a bomb and likely would have targeted some other federal facility. That was a little over two years ago. We found they were members of an anti-government group calling themselves 'SecAm,' short for Second Amendment, that appears supported by the American Freedom Confederation."

"Any similarities to the bomb found on Sam's car?" Linc asked.

Seth shook his head. "Not that we've been able to verify other than it's the same type of explosive. When the Bannister father and son blew themselves to hell, they also destroyed physical evidence that might have connected the two devices, so right now we've got nothing."

Ellie arranged a cushion so she could lean against it. "I'm calling Freedom Defender FD, and he feels like a guy to me. I'm sticking with that unless I learn differently. Any ideas who FD is or where his emails are coming from?"

"No. The emails were sent from a public library in a small town east of here. We requested and received video surveillance footage, but the only cameras are on the outside of the building and weren't helpful. We're focusing on known associates of Bannister, but FD could simply be an admirer and not know Bannister personally."

"Are Bannister's visitors and mail being monitored, and has anyone else received emails from FD?" The questions came from Bella. She spoke with a hint of an accent. Given the surname Nikolaev, Sam guessed if not Russian, then something close to it.

Seth nodded. "There are no reports of other judges or federal officials receiving communications from Freedom Defender. All contact with Bannister is being scrutinized. Our investigation has focused on members of SecAm. Their primary ideology is that the US government is illegitimate because it isn't upholding the Constitution, in particular by allowing restrictions on gun ownership. While their primary goal is what they consider defense of the Second Amendment, there is an underpinning of white supremacism, and some members espouse neo-Nazi bullshit. They believe in a version of Social Darwinism, arguing that Americans of northern European descent are naturally superior, and their job is to defend the country from the invasion by people of 'inferior' races." Seth turned to Sam. "Anything you can add to that?"

Sam nodded. "SecAm has held or participated in rallies in various locations in the northwest. Videos have surfaced definitively credited to them showing bonfires where people give the Nazi salute as books and brown-skinned dolls are thrown onto the flames. There's a case coming up on my docket involving four members of SecAm accused of kidnapping three migrant workers from Guatemala. The arrest records state the workers were taken from a farm in Oregon to a cabin across the state line in Idaho where they were beaten and held. One of the three hostages, the only woman, escaped and notified authorities."

"Fucking bastards," Linc muttered. He turned to Seth. "Have you interviewed these four about SecAm?"

Seth nodded. "We tried, but they sat mute next to their lawyers." He shrugged when Linc scowled. "We have their records, which go back a few years, and we've been trying to make connections to other members through their former cellmates or known associates. The group is careful and insular. Nailing these four is the first break we've had, but SecAm is cagey. They haven't gone back to that farm or anywhere near that area. We're keeping a close watch on a few places where there are clusters of migrant workers, but I'm sure they're not going to repeat that mistake."

Ellie turned to Sam. "How can you be impartial when you're being threatened by that group?" She scrunched her brows. "I'd want to kick their asses."

"There's nothing to indicate these four had anything to do with the emails or the explosive strapped to my Cruiser. In and of itself, group affiliation, no matter how distasteful the group, is a liberty protected by the Fourteenth Amendment. They're entitled to a fair trial based on the evidence that's presented. Besides, most of what we've talked about is circumstantial. You've inferred that the bomb is connected to the person sending the emails, and that the person sending the emails is connected to cases I've tried, or to the SecAm group. You went to law school, you know you'd need a hell of a lot more hard evidence if you want to draw a solid line between your suppositions."

"I'd still want to kick their circumstantial asses."

Sam smothered a smile as Bella and Linc both laughed.

"But seriously," Ellie persisted, "couldn't they claim that you're biased because of the threats?"

"Their lawyers might try to have me recused, and the case might be given to a different judge, but so far that hasn't happened. We'll have to see how it plays out."

A timer chimed and Ellie rose when Sam did and followed him into the kitchen. "What can I do?"

He pointed. "Get plates from that cabinet. Dining room table is bigger so we'll eat in there. Utensils are in the drawer by the dishwasher."

Sam opened the oven and used a fork to test the food, then took the trays out to set on the cooktop to cool. Ellie gathered plates, stacked them with knives and forks, and took them to the table.

When she returned, he handed her cutting boards. "Put these on the table and I'll bring out the food."

"You're serving dinner in what you cooked the food in? Your aunt must have had serving dishes."

"What's wrong with serving in the pans?"

"Nothing, if you're eating by yourself. You're not, and nice tableware makes a difference."

"And a lot more dirty dishes. Let's keep it simple."

"Nope." She began opening cupboard doors. "Don't worry about cleanup, we'll make Linc and Seth do it. I love doing that. Here we are." She reached to an upper shelf, her sweater hitching up to give him a view of an enticingly cupped ass. She brought down a platter and oval-shaped bowl he wasn't even sure he knew he owned.

She examined the blue and white pattern, then turned over the bowl to look at the mark on the bottom. "Ooh, made in England. I love English pottery."

She set the serving pieces now laden with the chicken and veggies on the table, and Sam had to admit the table looked nice using the old dishes. They took their seats, Linc again busy texting.

"Pardon my brother, Sam," Ellie told him. "Linc's been married only six weeks and is still in the stupid-love stage of being a newlywed."

Linc looked up with a wry grin and pocketed his phone.

"I think it's sweet," Bella commented. "Mikayla is lucky Linc is so devoted to her."

Sam caught the heated glance Seth shot Bella. From what he could see, the two marshals seemed to avoid speaking directly to each other, but there were little things that gave away what he was beginning to suspect was a keen attraction they both appeared to be fighting.

It didn't go unnoticed that Seth had nudged his brother aside so he could sit next to Bella, or that when their hands brushed, they both froze before jerking back. He caught a look of amusement pass between Ellie and Linc after they also witnessed the exchange.

Sitting beside him, Ellie turned to Sam. "Tomorrow's Saturday. What do you usually do on weekends?"

"It varies." He nudged the platter of chicken toward her. "I catch up on reading for upcoming cases, and I get outside, try to do something physical. Take the dogs out, spend time with friends." He paused to sip wine. "Be ready for questions when I introduce you. People will wonder how I've suddenly acquired a fiancée." He reached into his pocket. "Here."

He set a jeweler's box on the table between them.

"What's that?" She eyed the box with suspicion.

"Engagement ring. You said you wanted one."

"That was quick." She looked at the box like it was going to bite her. "Did a previous girlfriend return it?"

With a sigh of frustration he opened it himself. "Give me your hand." He held out his, palm up.

"I'll put it on."

"Eleanor, give me your hand."

"Don't be bossy. Besides, it won't fit."

He waited until she laid her hand in his with a huff of breath.

He slipped the ring onto her finger and their gazes locked like puzzle pieces fitting perfectly together. Looking away was impossible, her deep blue gaze pulling him in.

"Aw, that's sweet." The comment broke the tension. Across the table Bella held her phone up in front of her. "Let me know if you want the pictures to post. It would make your cover story more believable."

Ellie tugged on her hand and Sam realized he still held it gripped in his. He loosened his hold as Seth raised his brows.

"You two are acting engaged?"

Ellie gave a definitive nod, as Bella said, "It's an excellent idea. Rachel Sinclair wouldn't move in with her boyfriend unless she had a commitment."

"Exactly," Ellie stated. She held her hand up to the light. "Classic ring, Creed, and bonus that it fits. Either you or your previous girlfriend had excellent taste."

Sam figured it was time to change the subject. "Where exactly are you all staying?"

# Chapter Five

Ellie's eyes popped open and she groaned. Nope, sleep would not be returning. She pushed back the quilt and swung her legs out of bed. No matter how late she stayed up the night before, when five a.m. rolled around, she was awake and there was no getting back to sleep. She pulled on her shearling boots, and after a quick trip to the bathroom, crept down the back stairs, trying to make as little noise as possible. She thought of returning to her room to get her phone to use as a flashlight, but a dim light from the kitchen allowed her to see the outline of the steps.

She'd made it to the bottom tread when a dark shadow moved toward her. She had a split second to think how stupid she'd been to leave her gun in her room before a light blazed on and she let out a wheezy breath. "Jesus Christ, Sam. Are you trying to scare a year off my life?"

"Why didn't you turn on the light instead of creeping down the stairs in the dark?"

"Because I thought you were sleeping and I didn't want to wake you."

"My bedroom door is closed. How would the light have woken me?"

"I don't know. I was trying to be considerate. Next time I won't be."

Now that she no longer felt like her life was in danger, her brain was catching up with what she was seeing, which was Sam with tousled hair, low-slung flannel pants, and no shirt. She wondered fleetingly how someone with such a full head of thick dark hair could be hairless on his chest.

She bit her tongue before she could ask if he waxed.

Of one thing she was certain: she could now tell the many women who'd panted over social media posts speculating about what Judge Creed had hidden under his robes that they wouldn't be disappointed if they ever scored a peek. Ripped, cut, however you wanted to describe the muscular perfection, this guy had it.

She cleared her throat. "Aren't you cold? Shouldn't you put on a shirt or something to cover all that," she waved her hand up and down the length of his body as her gaze traveled over him, "um, skin?" She gripped her hands together before she gave in to the urge to trace her fingers over the fascinating ridges of muscle from his chest to abdomen.

He cocked his head and the corner of his mouth turned up. He was standing far too close and she could feel heat radiating off him. His gaze traveled over her. "I could say the same about you. That's a lot of leg you've got there, marshal."

He had a point. While her top was a waffle-knit thermal, her sleeping shorts barely covered her butt, and with her feet in the clunky boots, she probably looked more like a surfer chick than a federal marshal. She gave the shorts a quick tug down in what she hoped was a casual move. "I didn't pack thinking I'd be going on a sleepover."

"It might be contrary to my own interests, but I could offer you sleep pants to borrow."

"Ah, no. I'm good." He didn't reveal his thoughts much, but there was no doubt the gleam in his eyes indicated appreciation. That plus the implied compliment was making her more than a little jittery.

"What are you doing up so early?" His voice was early-morning rough and for some reason made her salivate.

She swallowed. "Curse of a morning person. I can't sleep past five. I was going to make coffee."

"Already made."

If she hadn't been so focused on the male specimen in front of her, she would've smelled the rich aroma of coffee. "Right. What about you? You an early riser, too?" Did she sound as overly chipper to him as she did to herself?

He nodded. "You better change into exercise gear."

"Why? It's five a.m. No one needs to exercise at five a.m. I'm having coffee."

"You're my bodyguard. I run every morning. How can you protect me if you don't go running with me?"

"I'm not your bodyguard. I'm a Deputy US Marshal assigned to protect a judge, and every morning, really? Don't you have a treadmill or elliptical machine? You could stay inside and exercise. That would be much safer than running around your neighborhood."

"I'm leaving in ten minutes. That should be enough time to inhale a cup of coffee and change into workout gear."

"You're mean."

There was that upturned corner of his mouth again, and she thought a mere glimpse of it was like holding a winning lottery ticket. That she was starting to think her life wouldn't be complete until she saw him give a full-throated, all-in laugh alarmed her more than a little.

He moved past her to climb the stairs, taking his body heat with him.

*\*\**

Sam wasn't kidding about ten minutes. He was waiting when she descended the stairs wearing her black running pants, a long-sleeved athletic top in neon green, and her favorite running shoes. She'd pulled her hair back in a ponytail and wore a wide band around her head that went over her ears to keep them warm.

She stood with gloved hands on her hips as he went through a series of high knees and heel kicks.

"You should warm up. Warm your muscles, loosen the joints."

"The sun's not even up."

"Your point?"

Seeing no alternative, she groaned only a little bit as she did a few heel kicks and leg swings.

"Did you get coffee?"

She shot him a dirty look. "A measly half cup."

"Then you're good to go."

"You're all heart, Creed." She did a few more halfhearted leg swings then followed him to the front door. "Don't you take the dogs?"

"No. There are two of them and they're a pain in the ass when you're running. Cleo gives me about two miles before she decides she's gone far enough and wants to be carried, and Tony tries to follow every damn scent he comes across. They're in their pen in the backyard. They're fine."

She followed him out the front door, which he locked, and then set off at an easy lope down the driveway and onto the street. Ellie followed a few paces behind. His shirt and pants had reflector panels, and he wore blinking red lights around his biceps and carried a flashlight. All good for warning drivers that he was on the road, but also a beacon to someone with nefarious intent.

She matched his pace, her gaze constantly scanning the area around them for potential threats. Tall trees bordered the street in front of his house for about fifty yards, then opened to reveal a farm-style home set back from the street.

Farther on, more houses sat on smaller lots. Other than a dog barking in the distance, the only sound was the slapping of their feet on the pavement and their breathing. Well, Ellie's breathing. Sam wasn't breathing heavily at all.

Overhead, an incredible blaze of stars swept across the sky, the payoff for getting out the door so early. In the east, a thin layer of pink had begun to push against the darkness. Reminding herself to focus on her job and pay attention to their surroundings, she caught up to Sam, matching his warm-up pace as they jogged side by side.

"How far do you usually run?"

"Five or six miles. I'm not training for anything, so I only run to maintain."

"Do you go at the same time every day, and run the same route?"

"Unless the weather is really bad, I run daily about this time, and I generally run the same route along the river."

"Then you need to vary your routine, break up the pattern."

"Right. Today we'll run through town. We'll go by the address of the rental house so you can see where your team is staying, and I can point out the courthouse."

Despite her complaining, Ellie found herself enjoying the run. She'd gotten into the habit of using a gym and realized that she missed being outdoors as the sun rose and the world was still quiet. Following Sam's gesture, she caught the quick movement of an animal as it disappeared into the brush.

"What was that?"

"Wild turkey. We have a few around here."

They turned onto another street where the houses sat on small lots and the road sloped downward. They ran through pools of light cast by the occasional streetlamp. The sound of an engine starting some distance away broke the peace. Through a gap between two houses she saw the headlights of a large vehicle on a parallel street as it pulled a U-turn in the middle of the block.

"That's where your brothers and Bella are staying." Sam pointed to a small house with the SUV Linc had driven parked under a carport. "It's been a short-term rental for about a year."

Given that the residence was not far from Sam's house, Ellie thought it a good choice. They reached the bottom of the street where lights illuminated the wide expanse of a bridge over the Umatilla River.

While she would have liked to take a minute to look at the river, Sam continued across. On the other side, businesses started to edge out residences, and within a few blocks they were in the downtown area. The rising sun, still hidden behind the mountains to the east, had turned the sky lavender and the underside of the puffy clouds glowed golden. They passed a church with a domed steeple, and Sam indicated a three-story building with a brick façade. "There's the courthouse."

"Oh, I love the architecture. It's beautiful. That's what a courthouse should look like."

"Agreed."

Ellie was puffing, but she refused to ask Mr. Fitness to slow down. He maintained the pace as they turned back toward the river. The bridge had a pedestrian walkway bordered by a short concrete guardrail, but with no traffic they ran side by side on the narrow road.

She was going to suggest they stop and view the swirling waters below when a vehicle with high beams appeared coming the opposite direction, fog lights glowing amber. Since the sun had now risen over the horizon, the lights were overkill. Sam moved ahead so they were single file. They were less than halfway across the bridge when the vehicle started over the span. The engine revved and the car picked up speed. She didn't second-guess the instinct that had her racing forward to grab Sam's arm. She saw now that it was a truck, its engine roaring, high beams blinding as it approached, crossing the center dividing line and barreling straight at them.

"Over the guardrail!"

The shout was barely past her lips when Sam grabbed her arm and they both vaulted over the concrete rail. Without slowing, the truck careened over the pavement where they'd been running only moments before, scraping the barrier in front of them before it sped away.

Ellie whipped out her phone, concentrating on controlling her breathing as she called nine-one-one. In clipped tones, she gave the description of the truck, an older model Dodge Ram, dark gray with a white shell over the bed, aftermarket fog lights in front, the driver a heavyset male whose ethnicity or race she hadn't been able to determine.

She tucked the phone back in her pocket and looked at Sam, who appeared amazingly calm for having just avoided being flattened like roadkill. "The dispatcher said to stay here and she'd send over a patrol car."

"I'd rather the patrol car be out looking for that truck." His gaze blazed over her, and she realized he wasn't as unaffected as she'd assumed. "Those are pretty good reflexes, Marshal Jameson. Thanks." He reached for her hand again.

A patrol car approached with its light bar flashing red and blue, but no siren. Ellie tried to pull her hand free but Sam wasn't letting go. She scowled at him.

"You'll have to control that 'fuck off' look whenever I touch you. Engaged couples surviving a near-death experience would likely hold on to each other." The recollection that she was playing the part of his fiancée came rushing back. She'd been in marshal mode, and had forgotten she was undercover.

With her hand still in his, they stepped back over the concrete guardrail and onto the roadway. "And that report to the dispatcher," he muttered. "It sounded like how a cop would speak."

*So noted, Your Honor.*

The officer, a tall Hispanic woman with stripes on the sleeve of her coat, stepped out of the cruiser and settled a wide-brimmed campaign hat securely on her head. She nodded in their direction. "Judge Creed."

"Barb. This is Rachel Sinclair, my fiancée. Rachel, this is Officer Barbara Herrera."

Ellie nodded at the other woman.

"Fiancée?" The comment was directed at Sam, and the officer didn't bother hiding her surprise. "I didn't know you were getting married. Congratulations."

"Thanks, it's a new development."

She nodded, then got down to business. "Tell me what happened."

When Ellie would have opened her mouth, Sam tightened his grip on her fingers. "Dodge Ram came straight at us," he said. "Would have hit us if we hadn't jumped over the barrier."

"Is there any chance the driver might have drifted over the center divider line, that maybe he was distracted or DUI?"

"He may have been DUI, but he wasn't drifting. It felt intentional. He was accelerating and steering straight at us." Sam pointed at the dark scrape on the guardrail. "He left some paint there so you're looking for a vehicle with some front driver-side damage."

"I'll add that to the description we got over the radio. Did you recognize the vehicle?"

When Sam shook his head, she asked, "How about the driver, did you get a look at him?"

"No."

Officer Herrera turned her attention to Ellie. "Same questions, Ms. Sinclair. Did you recognize the vehicle?"

"No. I've only been in town since yesterday, so I wouldn't have. I did get a glimpse of the driver through the side window as he sped away. I think medium height, and maybe heavy, though that impression might have been due to him wearing a bulky coat."

The officer continued to ask questions, making notes in a little booklet. After a few minutes, she tucked the booklet into the cargo pocket on her pants. "There's a BOLO out for the vehicle. Judge Creed, you want me to give you two a ride back to your place?"

"No, but thanks, Barb."

"Okay. Be careful." With a half salute, Officer Herrera returned to her cruiser.

*** 

Sam listened as Ellie spoke on her phone, filling Seth in on what had happened. They were walking back to his house, and turned onto Sam's street as she disconnected. He caught her hand.

"Geez, you sure like holding hands, Creed."

"Get with the program, Eleanor," he muttered.

Earlier, when she'd called her brother, she'd put her gloves in her pocket. Now, he rubbed his thumb over her finger where the engagement ring should have been.

Two women, both bundled in brightly colored parkas, came down a driveway to the street being led by equally bundled dogs on leashes. He and Ellie were about to get their first real test.

"Hey there, Sam." Yvonne wore a yellow parka and had tightly coiled gray hair peeking from under a matching beanie. Her skin was a shade lighter than that of her ebony-skinned friend, Francie. Yvonne waved as her dachshund in a matching yellow sweater strutted on the end of his leash. Francie's color choice was red and her small poodle looked like he was dressed for a party in his red sweater and black bowtie.

Sam nodded. "Morning, Yvonne, Francie."

Francie eyed his and Ellie's joined hands. "Who's your friend?"

"This is my fiancée, Rachel Sinclair." He wasn't surprised at his neighbors' matching shocked expressions. He turned to Ellie. "This is Yvonne Jackson and Francie Hogan. In addition to being neighbors, Yvonne works at the post office and Francie is the city's librarian."

Ellie dipped her chin. "Nice to meet you both."

Francie's eyebrows had disappeared under her beanie. She ignored her poodle tugging on the leash. "Well, aren't you a sly one, Sam Creed. We never even knew you were seeing someone."

"It's been a long-distance relationship. Rachel is moving here from California."

Francie finally let the little dog pull her to a bush where he lifted his leg.

"Well, isn't that something." Yvonne smiled as she spoke. "Welcome to Pendleton, Rachel."

"Thank you. You have a beautiful community."

"That we do. We're proud of what we have here."

Neighborly pleasantries over, the women and dogs continued their walk on the other side of the street. Sam could all but feel their speculative looks. He and Ellie reached his driveway and he stopped, tugging her closer so he could speak in a quiet voice. "Listen, we need to make our cover story work."

He brought her hand to his lips, gaze riveted on hers. She went stock-still, and he had the thought that the flush on her cheeks wasn't all from the cold. He found flustering her didn't bother him one bit.

She licked her lips. "Okay."

"Part of that is you wearing your ring. Where is it?"

"It's your ring, and I left it on my nightstand. I don't want to lose it."

"You won't lose it. You need to wear it. People will notice if you don't have an engagement ring."

"Right."

"And the least engaged couples do is hold hands." He leaned forward. "Unless we're in the house, we act the part, and that means keeping up the pretense so that anyone looking gets the message. You can't act like I'm about to assault you every time I take your hand."

"You're right." She seemed to make a herculean effort to recover herself. "But honestly? I'm operating on that measly half cup of coffee, and we were almost run down by a crazy person."

"Excuses, marshal. Get in the game."

His skin prickled as Yvonne and Francie walked past.

"Go with it," he muttered, not for the first time. He dipped his head and pressed his lips to hers. A brief kiss that lasted no more than a heartbeat, but sent a jolt through his body that struck all the way to the soles of his feet.

He pulled back, the raw heat on her face hard to miss. "What the hell, Creed?" Her voice was pitched low, and any observer might have thought she was vowing everlasting love.

"My name is Sam, and it's all part of the cover." The impulse for the kiss, he told himself, had at least started out that way. The problem was he was finding too many things about Eleanor Jameson that appealed to him.

Like the fact that she was nearly as tall as he was, and with only a slight duck of his head they were matched lip to lip. Like the suspicion in those deep blue eyes that was incredibly sexy. Like her quick brain, which kept him on his toes.

He leaned forward, his breath frosting the air between them. "Those two women have lived in Pendleton their entire lives, and between them they know everyone in town. You can bet that within the hour news that Judge Creed has a fiancée will be spreading like wildfire. Seeing us kissing makes it more believable. It'll go a long way to countering anything that comes from your marshal-like nine-one-one call."

Her gaze dropped to his lips. "Fine, then. Let's make it a good one."

She gripped the front of his shirt and yanked him down, all but fusing her lips with his. This time he expected the jolt, but not the explosion of heat that seared his blood. He wouldn't be surprised if steam was billowing from the top of his head into the chilly morning air.

She pressed that long, lithe body against his, and it took all his willpower to keep from pulling her hips into his where all the heat in his body was pooling.

Judges were supposed to maintain a certain level of decorum when in public, and it was a hard-fought contest to keep control when her mouth was avid on his, their tongues mating in a way that promised incineration if they ever ended up in bed.

She eased her grip and broke the kiss, but not before giving his bottom lip a nip that had a groan rumbling from low in his throat. "They gone?"

"Ah…" He was supposed to be able to think?

"Yvonne and Francie and their dogs. Are they gone?" Her expression was entirely too smug.

"Jesus." He rubbed a hand over his face. "Yeah, long gone."

Her smirk turned into a laugh. "This was all for show, right?"

"Yeah, for show. Let's get inside."

He had the uncomfortable feeling their situation had just gotten a lot more complicated.

# Chapter Six

Ellie sat on the couch, the gas fire in the fireplace making the room warm and homey. Since their morning run, clouds had blown in and the temperature had dropped. A glance out the window showed a blustery wind stripping trees of their fall foliage. She guessed there'd be rain within the hour.

Gumbie stretched her paws out in front of her, yawning in the way only cats could manage, then settled again on the back of the couch. Ellie glanced at the door to Sam's office, ajar by about half a foot. Wide enough for her to hear him over the past hour, on the phone, tapping on a keyboard, or shuffling papers.

Thank god he'd disappeared into his office after his shower and breakfast. She needed to be alone to gather her thoughts without him distracting her. What had she been thinking to kiss him like that? Sure, she'd been curious, and he wore his maleness like a banner, but they had a history she shouldn't forget.

She'd gotten over him pretending to be interested in her when all he'd really wanted was a hookup. That didn't mean she trusted him now. The man who'd acted like that as a young law student wasn't likely to have changed who he was at heart.

So she'd been caught up in the moment and kissed him. It didn't mean anything other than proof that whatever pheromones he possessed worked extra well on her. She'd take it as a cautionary lesson not to get too invested in the role of fiancée. She settled back against the cushions with her computer on her lap.

A search found plenty of newspaper articles on Frank Bannister, as well as his father, and the groups they were affiliated with. She read through those, then dug deeper, using her security clearance to find more detailed information in government databases.

It didn't surprise her at all to find her father's name came up in conjunction with some of the same groups as the Bannisters dabbled in. Richard Jameson was linked to not only the American Freedom Confederation, but also to SecAm.

Next, she scoured social media platforms, following threads down the rabbit holes of right-wing conspiracy theories. There was an entire world of craziness once you dug beneath the surface of groups who self-identified as patriot militias.

Some simply wanted a platform to spout off their anti-government, often racist, warped worldviews. She figured they'd always been present to a degree in American society, but the Internet had given them an avenue to crawl out from under the rocks that had hidden them to reach like-minded people.

Others held ideologies that had evolved to the point where they'd become radicalized and fit the definition of domestic terrorists. Her father matched that profile, which made finding him more urgent before he caused greater destruction and pain than he'd already done.

She opened her secure memo app to note the names and handles of those posting manifestos, delving into databases of known right-wing domestic terrorists, and found numerous references to the bombing of a federal courthouse in east Texas attributed to Richard Jameson. Not for the first time did she wonder what had turned her father down that path.

Shaking off the mood that always accompanied evidence of her father's betrayal, she continued working, noting her observations and research in files she saved on secure servers.

A flash caught her attention and had her glancing out the window. The sky had darkened to a half-light and another bolt of lightning gave a strobe-like burst, followed by a crack of thunder echoing through the valley. The muffled patter of rain sounded against the roof as it began to pelt from the sky. Ellie set her laptop aside and rose to her feet to stand at the front-facing window and watch the show through the semi-sheer curtains.

Treetops swayed, leaves caught a gust of wind and skittered across the road, and the darkened sky let loose with a deluge. Maybe it was because Southern California got so little real weather that she found the storm exciting. Lighting forked across the sky, and the thunder rolled through her. There was a click of nails on the hardwood floor and Cleo came to stand beside her, whimpering.

"It's okay, baby. You're safe inside." Ellie reached down to soothe the scared dog.

Movement outside had her looking out the window again. A battered pickup turned onto the driveway, its headlights slicing the gloom. She watched until it passed out of sight as it drove around the house.

With Cleo following close on her heels, Ellie crossed the room, stopping to rap her knuckles on the doorframe of Sam's office. She pushed open the door. He sat at his desk, his hair fell across his forehead and retro horn-rimmed glasses were perched on his nose.

She'd always been a sucker for the sexy nerd. Hot and brainy did it for her. If they were really engaged, she could see herself moving across the room to slide onto his lap, then taking off those glasses to see if she could distract him.

Sam looked up from the papers in front of him at the same time as a chime sounded from his phone. He ignored the phone as his gaze snagged hers.

She tried to will away the heat coming up her neck and cleared her throat. "We've got company."

He looked away to retrieve his phone and she let out her breath with a faint whistle. Fantasies like climbing onto his lap were going to get her in trouble. She should remember if that scenario ever played out, he'd likely finish it off by dumping her.

He tapped the screen, then threw it down on the desk. "Damn. I'll be right back."

When he would have brushed past her, she caught his arm. "Hold it, Creed. Tell me who it is."

"My brother. I'll get rid of him."

"You have to introduce us."

"Not today."

"Now who's not playing the part of the fiancé? And why wouldn't you introduce me to your brother?"

"Because he's got nothing to do with this, and I don't want to lie to him."

"A little while ago you were claiming that the women we met this morning would tell everyone in town we're engaged. Plus, I'm *living* here. The first person you should have told about our engagement is your brother."

He sighed. "It's not like that." He held up a hand when she opened her mouth. "But you're right."

"Of course I'm right."

The corner of his mouth twitched. "Come meet my brother."

While Sam moved to the kitchen, Ellie slipped up the stairs and grabbed the engagement ring off her nightstand. She returned to the kitchen as Sam ushered in a dark-haired man from the mudroom. Cleo and Tony pranced around, sniffing the visitor's shoes and pants as he bent to scratch heads.

"Drew, I want you to meet someone." He beckoned her and Ellie stepped forward into the curve of his arm.

Sam's brother was not what she expected. Physically, the differences weren't so great. Both men were tall, but while Sam had a rangy build that spoke of sinewy strength, Drew looked thin to the point of gauntness. Sam was clean-shaven, his hair long on top while neatly trimmed on the sides. Drew grew his lank and unkempt hair past his collar, a black baseball hat with yellow stitching that read *Cattlemen's Association* on his head. She wondered if this was the brother Sam had mentioned on the drive, the one who ran the ranch where Sam had been raised.

"This is Rachel. I've asked her to marry me, and she's accepted."

Drew's eyebrows rose in unison. "No shit, you're getting married?"

"Yeah. The long-distance thing wasn't working for either of us. We were ready to get married, so I proposed."

Ellie gave an internal grimace. Sam explained their engagement with all the romance of a practical and advantageous business merger.

Drew didn't appear surprised to learn that his brother had been involved in a long-distance thing. If she ever popped a surprise engagement on her brothers, she couldn't see their reaction being anywhere near subdued. Explosive was more like it. If she'd been seeing someone long distance and hadn't told them, they'd be all up in her business about it, grilling her like she was a murder suspect.

Drew's pale blue gaze traveled over her. His expression looked puzzled, which she could understand, but what she didn't understand was the flash of anger.

Sam offered coffee, and Drew nodded, gaze still on Ellie. She was usually good at reading people, but none of his reactions were what she'd consider typical of a man meeting his brother's fiancée for the first time.

"You pregnant?"

"Drew." Sam's tone slapped out a warning.

"Ah, no," Ellie said. "We didn't get engaged because I'm pregnant."

He grunted, then turned to his brother. "We've got trouble again out at the ranch."

Sam opened a cupboard and retrieved three mugs before turning to face Drew. "What trouble?"

"Damn fucking wolf killed a bull calf. Pete won't go after it."

"Why do you think it was a wolf? Wolves are rare around here."

"Animal was gutted, chewed to shit. What else could it have been? Damn environmental liberation bastards brought the wolves back when we'd gotten rid of them a hundred years ago. They want to drive ranchers out so wolves and grizzlies can have the land to themselves." He took the coffee Sam poured for him. "Good thing we've got our guns. You've got to talk to Pete, get him to track it down."

"Pete doesn't do anything he doesn't want to do."

"He'll listen to you."

"Could be he doesn't think it's a wolf."

"I'm telling you, it was a wolf. You track nearly as good as Pete. You could go after it."

Sam passed Ellie a steaming mug. There was an odd dynamic between Sam and Drew she found puzzling. Drew clearly deferred to his brother, but she sensed that he felt Sam owed him. She wondered for what.

Sam sipped his coffee. "That why you drove into town, to tell me about a dead bull calf?"

Drew shrugged. "Shouldn't need a reason to visit my brother." He glanced at Ellie. "Wouldn't know you were engaged if I hadn't. Not like you called to tell me."

"Phone goes both ways, brother."

Drew slid his gaze to Ellie before giving Sam a long look. "She know about us?"

Sam paused, mug halfway to his mouth.

Drew gave a wheezy laugh before turning to Ellie. "Make sure he tells you about our screwed-up family before you walk down the aisle, sweet thing, because you'll likely want to hightail it in the other direction."

"Everybody's family is screwed up in one way or another. Whatever it is won't change how I feel about Sam." She looked at Drew over the rim of her own mug, her gaze cool. "And 'sweet thing' doesn't work for me. You can call me Rachel."

Drew gave a bark of laughter. "Now I know what Sam sees in you." He finished his coffee and turned to his brother. "You coming to the ranch?"

"I'll call Pete. If he says it's a wolf, I'll make the appropriate call."

"Then you'll go hunting with me."

Sam shook his head. "I'm not hunting wolf. They're needed to balance the ecosystem."

"That's bullshit."

"No, that's science."

\*\*\*

Drew left and the muted ticking of a wall clock could be heard in the quiet of the kitchen. Tony sighed as he lay down on a large, flat cushion in one corner of the floor. Next to him, Cleo lay with her nose on her paws, big brown eyes following the movements of the humans in the room.

"What do I need to know about your family?"

Sam remained standing at the sink, staring out the window. When he finally spoke, she thought he sounded tired. "Drew's last name is Martin. His mother married my father when Drew was four."

"So he's your stepbrother. How old were you when they got married?"

"Ten." He finally turned to face her. "Drew was this skinny little kid. He'd never say boo, but followed me around like a damn shadow."

"What happened to your mother?"

"Died." He looked down. "I was eight. We weren't earning enough with the ranch so she worked in town as a waitress. She was coming home from a late shift and got hit head on by a pickup. Drunk driver crossed the double yellow."

"Jesus, Sam. I'm so sorry." Her own father had disappeared from her life when she was about that age so she understood some of what Sam was feeling. She wondered if Richard Jameson choosing to abandon his family made it better or worse.

"It was a long time ago."

"What about your dad?"

He shrugged. "Joss Creed was a tough man. His way of dealing with grief was to take it out on his son. My aunt, Mom's sister, found out he was beating the shit out of me and called the authorities. I was placed with her for a while, but eventually ended up back at the ranch."

"You were just a boy."

"It doesn't feel like I was just a boy. But I'd learned things were better if I could stay out of my dad's way. Anything I could do to get away from the house and him, I did. Went hunting for days on end, hiked all over the mountains, worked the ranch. Spent most of my time with the foreman's family. Then Dad married Jane, Drew's mom. After that, things got better."

"Did your dad mistreat Drew?"

"He ignored Drew, for the most part. I guess that's its own form of mistreatment." He shrugged. "He was strict, and certainly not a loving father, but he didn't beat him. I don't know that Jane ever loved Dad, but marrying him got her out of a bad situation and she seemed content with that. She took care of us, made the house a home."

Sam arranged the mugs in the dishwasher. When he didn't continue his narrative, she said, "That doesn't explain Drew's comment about your family being screwed up. It seems like your family came together."

"Sounds pretty screwed up to me."

There was more there, she was sure of it, but his tone said that avenue was closed. She made a mental note to look into Drew Martin's background. "What was your aunt like?"

"How is she relevant to the investigation?"

His question was a good reminder that her interest shouldn't be personal.

"The more I know, the better I can fit together the pieces of the puzzle. Plus, we could be in a social situation where someone would expect that I know something about you."

"Right." He shut the dishwasher and leaned back against the counter, arms crossed over his chest. "Her name was Nan Beauchamp. She was my mom's older sister. They were close. They'd been raised on the reservation until their dad died, then my grandmother moved them to town."

"You're Native American?"

"Part, from her side. Nan was engaged to her high school sweetheart. He proposed before being shipped off to Vietnam. He was killed in the Battle of Khe Sanh a week after getting off the troop transport. She never married or had kids of her own, but she made a good life for herself. I told you she taught English, and she loved to learn. I owe her for where I am today."

Ellie wasn't so sure about that. Even all those years ago, she'd recognized in Sam an inner drive and intensity that she was confident would have taken him as far as he wanted, even without support from his aunt.

Sam caught her gaze. "What about you? Won't I need to know something about Ellie Jameson for social situations?"

"Rachel Sinclair."

"I want to know about Ellie Jameson. It's got to be hard on a kid when her dad abandons her family and eventually becomes a fugitive."

"How'd you know about that?"

He gave her a look. "Really? Three siblings, all with the Marshals Service, and all on the same team assigned to investigate extremist groups in Oregon? You don't think I'd do a little investigating of my own?"

"I guess you would." She could talk about the crimes her father had committed, about his activities with right-wing terrorist groups, but she was never comfortable opening up about how her father's abandonment had affected her family. "I don't want to talk about him."

"Ellie—"

The dogs sprung to their feet to scramble across the floor a moment before a knock sounded at the front door. Ellie heaved a mental sigh of relief for the reprieve.

"Who do you know that uses the front door?"

"There's a few people."

"Let me check it out."

He raised a brow. "You putting yourself between me and danger, Eleanor?"

"That *is* my job."

"The hell with that." He strode to the front of the house, and when he would have reached for the doorknob, she stopped him with a hand on his arm.

"Hold on a minute. We need to have a serious discussion about our roles, Creed, but for now, at least slow down enough to look through the peephole."

"Fine." He put his eye up to the hole, and a moment later yanked open the door.

The man standing in the other side had jet-black hair pulled back in a ponytail and facial features that looked carved from granite. He also had a baby on his shoulder and dark brows pulled into a frown as he glared at Sam.

What looked like a daypack hung from one shoulder, a capped baby bottle sat in a side pouch. "What the hell, man?"

His gaze shifted to focus on Ellie and he brushed past Sam to step inside.

## Chapter Seven

"You must be Rachel. I'm Ben Montoya." Ben shifted the baby so he could hold out a hand. Ellie shook it cautiously.

"Nice to meet you."

"This is my daughter, Georgie." He turned so she could see the tiny face with infant-blue eyes open to the world. "I hear you've gotten engaged to my best friend." He gave Sam a hard look. "And I didn't even know you existed."

"Ah, yes."

Sam shut the door. "Come in and I'll explain."

Ben settled on the couch, laying the baby on his lap. A little foot in a pink and green striped sock stuck out from under a fluffy blanket.

Ellie caught an enigmatic look from Sam before he said, "We're not engaged."

"Sam!"

He turned to her. "Ben isn't threatening me."

"We don't know who's threatening you, and if you tell one person, you can't control where it goes. He tells his wife, she tells her sister, who then tells a coworker, and it spreads."

"That would be husband," Ben cut in.

"What?"

"I have a husband," he stated. "Not that it matters given your concerns. Are you law enforcement?"

"Ben, this is Deputy US Marshal Eleanor Jameson. Using the name Rachel Sinclair, she's posing as my fiancée while the threats against me are investigated."

Ellie threw up her hands. "Great, just great. Why don't you write me a list of all the people you think aren't threats and we'll gather them all together at the same time to tell them our engagement is fake?"

"Ben is the only person I told about the emails. He's the one who urged me to contact the Marshals Service."

"Which, being a federal judge, you should have done immediately."

"I planned to contact the marshals, but I talked to Ben first. A few things had happened out at the ranch and I wanted Ben's take on whether he thought they were related to the threats."

Ellie had to restrain herself from pulling her hair out by the roots. "You mean things happening at the ranch that you failed to mention before now?"

"Yeah. Ben and I grew up together at Rock Creek. His father is the foreman, Pete Montoya. Drew mentioned him."

"You talked to Drew?" The baby made little squeaky noises while she sucked on a pacifier and Ben stroked her cheek with a long finger. "Did he complain that Dad hasn't grabbed a rifle and gone wolf hunting?"

"Yeah. Was it wolf?"

"No. Dad thinks human, but Drew's not buying it. He's already posted shit online blaming environmentalists and insisting defending gun rights is the only thing that will keep us safe from marauding carnivores."

"Hang on, Creed. Can we get back to the point at hand?" Ellie tried to keep the anger out of her voice. "You've jeopardized our mission, and since this is the first I've heard about events at your ranch, it's apparent you haven't been forthcoming. Me posing as your fiancée to provide protection and doing the investigation this way was your idea, and the team agreed because it had merit. But if you can't maintain our cover story and aren't willing to bring the Marshals Service all the way in, you should have told us up front and we could have done this differently."

"I haven't jeopardized our cover story. Ben's a vault. He won't tell anyone."

His assertion only irritated her more, but while her words might have been biting, she worked to keep her tone even so as not to disturb the baby. "You should have told us about the ranch at the beginning, and giving away our cover to even one person is irresponsible." She glanced at Ben. "No offense, but that's how it is." She pulled her phone from her pocket. "I need to call Seth and let him know."

With the phone to her ear listening to it ring, she watched Sam reach down to scoop up the little girl. Ben rose to his feet and headed to the kitchen with the baby bottle.

Seth picked up, and Ellie explained the situation. A few minutes later, she tucked her phone back in her pocket.

"Your brother pissed?" Sam held the baby with ease. Judge Hottie holding a baby should look incongruous, but he looked perfectly natural and at ease.

Georgie stretched out a little hand. Ellie couldn't resist and held out a finger for the tiny girl to grip. Ellie matched Sam's quiet tone. "Not as pissed as I am. He seems to trust your judgment, but says to get a promise from Ben that he won't tell anyone, including his husband." She frowned. "Tell me what's going on at your ranch."

"Five weeks ago someone started a brushfire. It scorched a couple acres but would have been a hell of a lot worse if the guys hadn't jumped on it. There's been some vandalism. Rocks through windows on a couple trucks, and some fences pulled down. Drew wants to hire armed militia. A dead calf raises the stakes."

The baby cooed and Ellie smiled. "Hey there, sweet pea." She glanced up to find Sam looking at her with his usual hard-to-read expression, and realized they were standing close enough that she could see silver glints in his dark gray eyes.

Ben returned, shaking the bottle, and Ellie took a quick step back. He took Georgie and settled back on the couch, where the baby immediately latched onto the bottle.

"How'd you hear about my engagement?" Sam sat in the recliner.

"Went to the grocery store for formula and ran into two different people who asked me what I thought of your fiancée. If you'd wanted me to put on a good show, you should have given me a heads-up. As it is, I told them I had yet to meet your intended but meant to soon. So here I am."

Figuring she had to make do with the cards she'd been dealt, Ellie decided to pick Ben's brain. "What's your take on the threats Sam's been receiving? Do you have any thoughts on who might have sent them?"

"Not specifically, but I can guess. I'm sure you know Eastern Oregon has been plagued by right-wing, anti-government groups. Many of their members think owning a gun is the basis of all political freedom. They've built their entire identity around the use and ownership of firearms. Sam has handed down a few decisions that they perceive as restricting their Second Amendment rights. Some of them are batshit enough to go after a federal judge. That's where I'd start looking."

"We have been. Any other ideas?"

He looked thoughtful. "There are also people who harbor resentment against Indians, particularly Indians who have done well for themselves. Sam is Umatilla. My people are Nez Percé. Sam's a federal judge. I'm a doctor. Some folks don't like when people like us don't stay where they think we belong."

"How has that resentment manifested itself?"

"Comments." Sam shrugged. "I've been called 'chief,' been told to go back to the rez, had my impartiality doubted. It's infrequent, but it happens. More people than I can count are dumbfounded that I don't practice tribal law, like that's the only choice for native lawyers."

"Me, I've had my credentials questioned. Comments like 'I didn't know Indians went to med school.' Shit like that."

Sam's phone rang and he crossed to his office to answer it. Georgie was making good progress with her bottle. "How old is Georgie?"

"Six weeks. She was two days old when Justin and I got her. It's been a crash course on being dads. Thank god for our parents." He gave Ellie a look that made her understand she was being assessed. "This goes against Sam's core makeup, you know."

Ellie raised her brows. "What does?"

"You two posing as an engaged couple. Intellectually, he gets it, but Sam's the most honest person I know. He has a basic, bone-deep integrity that's unshakable, and lying will weird him out."

"Having a fake fiancée was his idea. The Marshals Service wanted to provide a security detail. Sam's plan was to try to draw out whoever is making threats against him."

"It might work, but that doesn't mean it'll be easy for him. I don't think he planned on telling me the truth about you, but when I showed up at the door, he couldn't lie."

Sam came back into the room. "That was Officer Herrera. They found the truck that nearly ran us down. It had been abandoned on a dirt road out near the quarry."

"Abandoned? Who's it registered to?"

"The woman who reported it stolen last night."

"They recover any prints?"

"They're still processing the vehicle, but the steering wheel was clean so whoever was driving this morning wiped it down or was wearing gloves."

"Damn."

Ben put Georgie to his shoulder and gently patted her back, despite the fire that leapt in his eyes. "What the hell do you mean you were nearly run over?"

"Hey, can I burp her?"

"Sure." Ben handed Ellie a cloth. "Put this on your shoulder." He shifted his daughter over.

Ellie settled her and sniffed the dark little head. "She smells so sweet."

She looked up to find Sam's gaze on hers, the corner of his mouth lifting in his not-quite-a-smile smile. He reached out to run a hand over the baby's head, the back of his hand brushing Ellie's cheek.

"Sorry to interrupt the moment, but the being-almost-run-over thing? I'd like an explanation."

"Right." Sam recounted the incident, bringing back for Ellie the vivid memory of the roar of the engine and the blinding high beams as the truck barreled straight at them. "Good thing we were where we were. The guardrail offered good protection."

"You're positive it was intentional?"

"Given what else is going on and the fact that the truck was reported stolen? Yeah, I do."

"If the driver is known to you, he took a risk of being identified."

Ellie patted Georgie's back. "The sun wasn't all the way up and he had his high beams on, surely to intentionally blind us. Maybe he counted on that minimizing the risk."

"You two be careful." Ben stowed the empty bottle in the daypack. "I need to get going. Georgie naps about this time, and hopefully Justin will have put together the baby swing."

Sam shook his head. "Used to be you and Justin would be planning your next rock-climbing goal. Times sure have changed."

"For the better, brother. Still love rock climbing, but nothing beats being a dad."

*** 

Sam ran along the dirt road on the outskirts of town, Ellie keeping pace, their footfalls beating a steady rhythm. To vary his routine, they'd delayed the morning run by forty-five minutes and chosen a route he rarely followed. He hated having to change his life because of some assholes. But one of the reasons he'd opted for this type of operation was because he wanted those assholes caught. It wasn't good enough to simply keep himself safe. If the investigation could produce enough evidence, they might be able to imprison individuals who posed a fundamental threat to law and order, and hopefully cripple their organization and its ability to radicalize. That made the risk to himself worth it.

The best thing to come out of the situation for him personally was the woman running at his side. Eleanor Jameson presented an intriguing package, one that hit about all the marks for him. She might be frustrated with her struggle to keep things professional, to rein in her emotions as she tried to remain analytical, but he found that tension fascinating.

Case in point? That kiss yesterday morning.

She'd gone with the impulse, and maybe it had started as a show for his neighbors, but her lips had landed on his and she'd taken him under until all he could think about was having more. The conflict was that she was a professional doing her job, and he respected that. Plus, she had two brothers who would likely beat him to a pulp if he made a move in that direction. Not that that would stop him if that's where he wanted to go, but it was a consideration.

The sun rising over the eastern mountains colored the thin layers of clouds pink and gold. They passed a house with smoke wafting from its chimney and the smell of wood smoke tinged the crisp air.

Wide fields already harvested of their wheat flanked one side of the road, the other dotted with pastures for grazing cattle and horses. He liked Pendleton's small-town vibe, with the added bonus of being surrounded by the charm of farms and pockets of land left wild. Ellie seemed to appreciate it, but that might be more because it was different from San Diego, but not as a place where she'd like to settle.

And why was his mind going there?

"You talked to Ben's father last evening." Her breath came in frosty puffs of vapor. She caught his look. "The office door wasn't all the way closed. Besides, it's my job to be nosy."

"I wasn't thinking you were nosy. My life's an open book."

She made a "pfft" sound.

"You don't think I've been open?"

"Honestly? I think you've been open about what you deem valid areas for our investigation, but the rest you hold back. I get that. It's human nature, but not helpful in allowing my team to get the full picture."

She had a point.

"Pete says someone killed the calf. Sheriff said no other ranchers have reported problems like we've had."

"Did he take pictures?"

They crested a hill, their strides getting longer as they took the downhill slope toward town.

"No. I asked, but Pete doesn't even own a cell phone. Reception is crap out there so he and Drew carry walkie-talkies, and they don't carry cameras."

"How many people work on the ranch?"

"Pete and Drew, plus a guy who comes in when needed."

"I'll talk to the team, but we may need to go out there."

"That's where I thought you were heading. I have a full schedule this week so it's not likely to be before next weekend."

"What's wrong with today?"

He glanced at her. Things were moving a little faster than he'd anticipated, but he could adjust. "Nothing."

They transitioned to a cool-down pace as they took the last half-mile uphill to his street.

They returned to the house and Ellie's phone chimed as they stepped inside. She read the text, then said, "Linc says to come by their place. He's cooking breakfast, and Seth wants to go over the plan for tomorrow."

That worked for him. The less time he spent alone with Ellie, the less opportunity he had to do something stupid, like following up on that kiss.

# Chapter Eight

Forty minutes later, after they took a circuitous route to the rental, they parked behind the house and went up a small stoop to knock on the back door. Bella opened the door dressed in the type of professional attire women often wore in his courtroom. She grabbed Ellie's arm and pulled her inside. "Good, you're here. Your brother is giving orders like he's the last tsar of Russia. He should remember how things ended for that autocrat."

Seth came up behind her. "I wasn't giving orders. I only made a simple suggestion."

Sam followed Ellie into the house.

Bella's expression remained frigid enough that he was surprised Seth wasn't suffering from frostbite. "It's a suggestion that I change how I dress while I'm at work? That I adopt a hairstyle that is not professional? I have read the US Marshals rules and regulations. I am dressed appropriately for my profession."

Seth rubbed a hand over his face. "I merely suggested that since we're hanging out here this morning, you might be more comfortable wearing something, you know, looser. And 'letting your hair down' is an American idiom meaning to relax, but since your hair is in a bun as tight as your—"

"Time out. C'mon, clueless brother." Ellie caught Seth's arm, giving him a sunny smile as she asked, "What's for breakfast?"

Sam's sympathy was with Seth, but he thought it wise to keep his mouth shut. He closed the door behind them and followed the others across a small living room that opened to the kitchen, the spaces separated by an island lined with stools.

Linc stood at the stove using a fork to lift bacon from a pan onto paper towels laid out on a plate. "Hey there. Everything's keeping warm in the oven. Get it on the table and we're ready to eat. There's coffee, tea, and OJ so get your own drinks."

Since breakfast for Sam usually ran to coffee and cold cereal or toast, he appreciated the bounty before him as he took his seat, placing his steaming mug of coffee next to his plate. Bacon, eggs, hash browns, toast, and sliced melon all looked pretty damn good. Ellie sat across from him. He guessed it wasn't by accident that she placed herself between Seth and Bella.

"This looks great, Linc."

"I am master of the breakfast." He grinned at his sister. "You're on cleanup detail."

Ellie nodded as if she expected no less. "Any new developments since yesterday?"

Seth shook his head. "Nothing new." He pointed to Sam. "We've got a team installing security cameras around your property. We'll cover the front down to the street and the slope behind your house. The company that's doing the installation will be there Tuesday morning. Next, the Marshals Service has taken possession of the stolen truck that was recovered yesterday. We're also looking for footage from any traffic or commercial surveillance cameras that might show the movement of the truck before and after the driver tried to hit you. Hopefully we'll get a hit from that."

Ellie frowned. "When we were starting out on our run yesterday, we were about a block from Sam's house when a big truck started its engine the next street over. I could see it between the houses as it turned around. Did you see it?" Her gaze turned to Sam and he was struck again by the intense blue of her eyes. Something flickered, an impression of those eyes from somewhere in his past. He frowned to bring the image to mind but the memory was gone. He shook his head. "I didn't notice anything."

"I just remembered that. It was on that street one block farther down the hill from the first street we turned onto. Do you usually run that way?"

"Yeah. The trailhead for the river path I usually take is off that road. Did it look like the truck that tried to hit us?"

"It was the same general size. Since that's your usual route, the driver could have been waiting for you."

"At their own homes, people don't usually park in a way that they'll have to turn around, and that's early for folks to be up and around." Linc gestured with a crispy piece of bacon. "Maybe it was someone waiting for you. Would they have been able to see you on the street you were on?"

"There were streetlights, plus Sam has visibility arm bands that have blinking red lights. They're distinctive. If the driver had been waiting and noticed him a street over, he would have had time to adjust his plans."

"Perhaps there are homes on that street that have cameras."

Sam nodded at Bella's comment. "It's possible, though home security cameras are not that common in Pendleton. My current situation aside, there's not a lot of crime here."

"We'll look into it." Seth added ketchup to his hash browns.

Sam forked up excellent scrambled eggs cooked with peppers. "Explain something to me. The point of my plan is to draw out whoever has been threatening me. If that's the case, why aren't I running the same route, at the same time I normally do?"

"And then what?" Ellie asked. "Give him another chance to run you over?"

"We could be armed. The rest of your team could be in vehicles at a couple different places along the route, ready to catch the guy. It seems a reasonable way to draw out the perpetrator."

Ellie was already shaking her head. "I think it's too dangerous. We were lucky we could jump over the guardrail yesterday morning. Next time, there may not be anyplace to jump. I'm all for luring out our perpetrator, but I'd like it to be a situation where we have more control."

"Let's hold that idea back for now." Seth spread jam on a piece of toast. "It appears they already know you're varying your routine, so it may be too late anyway." He nodded to Sam. "Tell us about your relationship with Gordon Finster."

"I've known him for several years. He's case administrator at the courthouse. Our relationship is professional."

"The statements from the women who filed complaints against him indicate that you guided them through the process."

"True."

"Finster likely knows what you did."

"If he does, his behavior toward me hasn't changed. He's been acting like his usual sycophantic self, though it's possible he's putting on an act." He leveled his gaze at Seth. "You think he's behind the threats?"

"There's no evidence of that currently. We're looking for motivation. What's your opinion of his competence?"

Sam shrugged. "He's sloppy, doesn't pay attention to details, and gets by because staff has saved his ass more than once. Anyplace else, he'd have been fired. Because we're a court servicing a large geographical area, but we're in a small community with a low population, I think there's a fear we wouldn't be able to replace him if he was fired."

"Did you witness any instances of the harassment he's been charged with?"

"No. He's careful not to pull shit in front of the judges, but I'd heard rumors so I asked around. Both complaints were made by members of the custodial staff. One confided in me, introduced me to her friend who had a similar experience with Gordon, and they both asked for my help. I walked them through the grievance process."

"Are you aware that Gordon Finster has a side business buying and selling firearms?"

Sam set down his fork. "You're shitting me."

Seth shook his head. "That's what put him on our radar. He attends gun shows and is active in a couple of pro-Second

Amendment organizations. Nothing real extreme. Has he ever talked with you about his political views?"

"No. I avoid conversations with him."

"Do you see him socially?"

"We run into each other occasionally, like Ellie and I did at the airport Friday, but that's about it. I know he's divorced and has a teenage son. I think the kid recently graduated from high school."

"I can corroborate Sam's assessment of Finster's attitude," Ellie cut in. "At the airport, their encounter seemed like the high school loser trying to ingratiate himself with the star quarterback. There's definitely a power dynamic at play."

"I'll be at the courthouse tomorrow," Linc said, "as a marshal providing the usual court security. I'll find Finster and work up a conversation with him, bring up guns, make him think I'm a fellow traveler. Could be he'll volunteer some information."

Seth nodded. "That's solid."

"I think Sam and I should drive out to his ranch this afternoon. Someone killed a calf."

That announcement resulted in a series of questions and required that Sam reiterate what he'd told Ellie about his family issues. It frustrated the hell out of him because he didn't think it had anything to do with the threats emailed to him, or the explosive taped to his vehicle. "I think you all are getting off on the wrong track. You're better off spending your time investigating right-wing militias."

"You don't want your family involved. I understand that." Bella spoke softly, which brought the conversation ping-ponging around the table to a stop. He'd noticed that before. She tended to listen quietly and not interject much when the Jameson siblings got going, but when she did speak, her words carried weight. "But," she continued, "that doesn't mean we can ignore the possibility that what's happened at your ranch is related to the threats against you."

Seth nodded. "We need a marshal there to ask questions, so visiting the ranch today is a good plan."

"What about tomorrow? Linc will tackle Finster, but what will the rest of us be doing?" Ellie asked.

"I think Ellie should drop Sam off at work because he wouldn't want to leave her without a car," Seth said.

"They should meet for lunch someplace where a lot of people eat. We want the newly engaged couple to draw attention and perhaps push FD into acting."

"Thanks, Bella. That's an excellent idea." Ellie's wide smile had Sam checking his movement, his fork halfway to his mouth.

"Why the hell does that make you so happy?" Linc asked.

"Because Sam's Land Cruiser is a stick shift and he'll have to teach me to drive it since my *brother*," she shot Linc a dirty look, "won't teach me."

"Oh, shit. Sorry, Sam."

"Wait, what am I in for?"

"She about stripped the gears on my Jeep transmission." Linc's face took on a pained expression.

"That wasn't my fault. You weren't teaching me right, and only gave me one chance before banning me forever from the driver's seat."

"Got that right."

"Learning to drive stick aside, dropping Sam off at work's not a bad idea," Seth broke in. "And when she's not with him, El can keep following the leads online she's been working on. Linc will show up tomorrow as the new marshal assigned to court security. He'll conduct sweeps of the courtroom and Sam's chambers and be present during court proceedings."

"What will you and Bella be doing?" Ellie asked.

"We've adapted our role to the current situation. We're posing as the lawyers for the complainants against Gordon Finster. We've already cleared it with the agency handling the complaint. That will give us the cover we need to question courthouse staff."

\*\*\*

After they said their good-byes, Ellie followed Sam to his Land Cruiser. "I should drive."

"Ah, maybe later."

"No time like the present. C'mon, Creed. Driving to the ranch will be good practice, which I'll need if I'm driving on my own tomorrow." She patted the hood of the car. "It'll be fun."

He snorted. "Like getting a tooth pulled is fun."

"You're exaggerating.

"I'm terrified."

"You are not. It would have been no big deal if Linc hadn't been a baby about his Jeep."

"The Land Cruiser was my first car. I worked my ass off to buy it."

"Which means it has to be well over twenty years old, so it's about time to get a new transmission anyway." She laughed at his expression. "You actually went pale. I'm kidding. Really, don't worry. I'm a good driver. It's the shifting part I need practice on. C'mon, be a sport." She held out her hand, palm up.

He fished the keys from his pocket with obvious reluctance, then drew them away when she reached for them. "You have to promise to listen to me, and to be gentle."

"Of course." She reached out and rolled her eyes when he pulled the keys back again.

"And you have to step all the way down on the clutch before you shift or the tranny won't disengage. That's what causes the grinding."

"Yeah, yeah." She snagged the keys before he could make any more conditions and crossed to the driver's door. "Lighten up, Creed. Where's your sense of adventure?"

He was still grumbling when they were both belted in. "Look, step on the brake with one foot, and the clutch with the other, then you can start the engine."

"Yes, Dad."

"I'm not joking, Eleanor. You need to take this seriously or you'll damage my car."

"I am taking it seriously. You're worse than Linc, and that's saying something."

That brought more grumbling, and he kept an eagle eye on her as she did as directed, then turned the key in the ignition.

"Okay, look." She thought he was sounding a little panicked. "Every standard transmission has a different feel. Put the clutch in and move the selector to get a sense of where the gears are."

She did as directed. She struggled with finding reverse and he put his hand over hers, wide palm covering her knuckles. Ignoring the shot of hormones she got whenever he touched her was becoming routine, and she didn't like it.

He let go of her hand. "Now you're in reverse. Do you understand the mechanics of what the clutch does?" At her nod, he continued. "Ease out the clutch until you feel it start to engage, then give it some gas."

She followed his instructions and stalled the engine. She cast a glance at the house. "If Linc comes out to laugh at me, I'm going to flip him off. You might want to cover your eyes."

"I'll flip him off for you. Don't worry about your brother. Focus. You want me to turn it around so you don't have to start out in reverse?"

"No, I'll do it."

It took two more tries before she succeeded in getting the vehicle to move in the direction she wanted. She backed out of the driveway.

"Clutch in when you come to a stop."

She managed to stop without stalling and accomplish a rough shift into first. The shift to second was smoother, and into third, smoother still. "Ha, look at that. I'm doing fine." She glanced at Sam. "You can let go of the armrest now. I think your fingernails have left grooves in the upholstery."

"Just drive, Eleanor."

He really was a patient teacher. The scariest moment was when she came to a stop sign on an incline and a car pulled up behind her. He talked her through it and after only one stall, she got the Cruiser moving again. She was feeling quite accomplished by the time they reached the highway that took them south.

The day was spectacular with the sun shining brightly in a deep blue sky. The highway wound through small towns scattered through rolling hills dotted with cattle, and wide-open stretches of grassland that made her feel glad not every inch of land had been developed. "Are those deer?" She pointed to brown and white animals grazing in an area of scrub brush along the highway.

"Pronghorn antelope. We usually don't see them this close to the highway."

"Antelope, really? That's awesome." Something must have spooked the animals because in a split second they were a blur racing across the land. "Wow, they're fast."

"Outrunning predators is how they survive." Sam pointed to a highway sign. "Our turn is coming up."

She slowed the Land Cruiser, downshifting easily into third to take a curve. She was getting the hang of the standard transmission.

Following Sam's directions on a road that had them traveling due west, about fifteen minutes after leaving the highway she saw a sign for Rock Creek Ranch and turned onto a gravel road.

# Chapter Nine

"Park beside that truck next to the barn."

She did as directed. A tall man with long white hair strode out of the barn, a pair of dogs running ahead of him. With their identical features, Ellie could see what Ben would look like in thirty years.

Sam and Ellie got out of the SUV, the dogs busily sniffing their legs and shoes. The man caught Sam in a one-armed hug before turning to face Ellie, sharp brows lowered over black eyes giving him the look of a hawk on the hunt. Sam's face was tight as he introduced her as Rachel Sinclair. She remembered Ben's words and understood that lying to Pete Montoya cost Sam.

"If you meant to see your brother, you've wasted your time. He's off somewhere."

"I came to see you. Wanted you to meet Rachel."

Pete stared at her hard, then gave a quick nod. "You ride, girl?"

"Not recently. I took lessons when I was a teenager." She wondered if she was being tested.

"Come see my mare."

Ellie glanced at Sam, then they followed Pete into the barn. He led the way past a row of stalls, most empty, until they got to the last and largest one. A sorrel horse with a white star on her face stuck her head over the door and gave a soft whickering sound in welcome.

"Oh, she's beautiful." Ellie stroked the mare's neck, and a glance inside the stable had her commenting, "And very, very pregnant."

The door was on rails and Sam slid it back to step inside. A thick layer of straw covered the floor. He ran his hands over the mare's side, talking softly. "Hey there, Minnie. How's it going, girl?"

The mare responded by nibbling on his sleeve. "She's due any day now, isn't she?" he asked Pete.

"I'm guessing tonight or tomorrow. She's not in labor, though she's been restless for the last hour or so." Pete held Minnie's head and gazed into her velvety brown eyes. "I don't see pain yet."

Ellie could only have sympathy for the pretty mare and what she would endure to have her baby. Sam stepped out of the stall, sliding the door shut. He leaned back against the half wall, arms crossed over his chest. "You going to tell me what's going on?"

Pete gave a dry laugh. "What the hell you think is going on? We got someone who's got a bug up their ass about Rock Creek and is making their displeasure known."

"In a serious way."

"God damn serious when they start a fire. Even more serious when they butcher a calf."

"It wasn't wolf."

"It wasn't wolf," Pete agreed. "Had its neck slit, then was cut open. Guts strewn all over the place. His poor mama was crying her heart out." He glanced at Ellie. "Sorry, miss. But that's the way it is."

"Don't worry about me," Ellie told him. "I'm sorry to hear you lost a calf in that manner. It has to hurt."

"It does. Damn shame. Whoever would do a thing like that is sick."

"Guts strewn about will attract other animals," Sam said.

Ellie could read behind the disgust on Sam's face to see that killing the calf hurt him.

"Probably that was the idea." Pete spread his hands in front of him. "Coyotes got to it, made it harder to tell that it was killed by human hand. But the sheriff saw it for what it was."

"Drew's convinced it was wolf." A look passed between the two men that made Ellie think there was more about Drew that they were holding back on.

Pete shook his head. "It wasn't."

\*\*\*

The Gator bumped along the road back to the barn, Sam steering the utility vehicle around ruts. The ranch roads needed grading before winter hit. He glanced at the woman sitting beside him. Ellie had listened attentively as he'd driven around the property. She'd asked good questions that showed she was giving thought to the operation. He couldn't help finding satisfaction in sharing with her something that was important to him. That thought alone should give him pause, but he found he didn't give a damn. He liked her, and if he was honest, he'd given her a tour of the ranch because he wanted her to see where he came from. There was nothing to be gained from her seeing the land except an understanding of him.

He parked the Gator under the shed overhang. They went in search of Pete and found him in a small office in the barn, sitting at a desk piled with papers weighted down with a horseshoe. He looked up when they walked in.

"We're heading out." Sam paused. "Never thought I'd say it, but be careful. You're alone here until Drew gets back, and who knows when that will be. Whoever killed that calf might not be done messing with us."

Pete nodded to a gun cabinet on the far wall. "Figure I can still hit what I'm aiming at, if it comes to that. And god knows Drew likes his guns." His face took on a scowl. "I put that damn ad in the paper like you told me to. A guy's coming in tomorrow morning for a trial period. Likely won't know a pitchfork from a shovel."

"Don't make him pass on the job because you're a hardass."

"If he can't handle a hardass, he shouldn't take the job." He raised a weathered hand to stop a comeback. "But if he can work, I'll hire him. I'll keep my word."

"Make sure he knows what's going on so he can keep an eye out for anything unusual."

Pete nodded. "When Minnie goes into labor, they'll be more folks here. Ron Harder's daughters want to be here when she delivers. Told them I'd give them a call when the time comes. They'll liven up the place."

"They're kids, you sure they won't get in the way?"

Pete smiled, and the resemblance to Ben was stronger. "Lot you know. Those girls are thirteen and sixteen. The older one's bent on being a big animal vet and wants the experience, and the younger one's not about to be left out of anything her sister does. Ron hardly lets those girls out of his sight, so he'll be here, too."

"Thirteen and sixteen? When the hell did that happen?" Sam turned to Ellie. "The Harders are neighbors to the south."

Pete rose and walked with them out of the barn.

"Kids grow up and there's not a damn thing you can do about it. I got me a granddaughter now, and pretty soon she'll be big enough for her grandpa to take her out on a horse." He gave Sam a long look. "Don't worry about me."

\*\*\*

"You're still worried about him."

"Yeah, of course I am. Pete's closer to seventy than sixty, but he won't slow down. It took both Ben and me leaning on him heavy before he agreed to hire another hand."

"I get why you're worried, but there's a serenity to that man that makes me think he's contented with his life. Makes me a little envious."

Sam glanced at her in question as she waited at a stoplight on the outskirts of Pendleton.

"You discontented with your life, Ellie?"

She shrugged and he caught her pensive expression. "Not really, but I've been thinking about the future a lot lately. I'm not sure the Marshals Service will be a lifelong career for me." She blew out a gusty breath. "Whew. I've never said that out loud before, much less told anyone that I've even thought it."

"Why not?"

"My singular goal since he left has been to find my father and bring him to justice for what he's done. We're getting closer, and it's made me wonder, what then? What will my goal be after Richard Jameson is behind bars?"

"There are plenty of fugitives who need to be brought to justice."

"True." She steered onto Sam's street, her expression still thoughtful.

They pulled in front of the garage. Sam gripped her arm when she went to open the car door.

"Hang on."

"What?" She went instantly alert.

"Someone's been here." He pointed to an area under the white oak where deep grooves gouged the sod, and dirt and grass had been churned into a muddy mess. Sam pulled his phone from his pocket.

"It looks like someone drove a vehicle and spun their wheels. Did you get a security alert?"

"Only the house alarm gives an alert, but I can access the camera recordings on my phone."

When the app opened, he held his phone so she could see the screen. The image was remarkably clear. An older model dark gray truck had turned onto the driveway from the street, then sped around the house to the back where it spun around a couple of times on the lawn under the tree. It sat idling for a moment, dark tinted windows making it impossible to see the driver. Then, with tires throwing up sprays of dirt, the vehicle spun in another tight circle before speeding back up the driveway.

Ellie frowned. "Do you recognize the vehicle?"

"No. But about everyone around here has a truck. It's not one I recognize, though. It has plastic covers over the license plates so they can't be read."

"This seems juvenile, like something a kid would do."

Sam considered her comment. "Yeah. An immature dumbass. How would they have known we weren't home? I park in the garage, so unless they saw us leave, they risked me coming out with my shotgun."

"Judge Creed has a shotgun?"

"Judge Creed protects what's his within the limits of the law."

What'd been a nice grassy area shaded by the big tree was now a gaping wound in the land with tree roots laid bare and mud sprayed in all directions. His aunt had spent hours tending that yard and it ate at him to see it laid waste.

They stepped out of the Land Cruiser. Ellie had her phone out, taking pictures of the muddy mess. The dogs barked from inside.

Sam touched her elbow. "I want to take a look around before we go in the house."

She nodded, walking with him around the garage, and up the back slope along a narrow path. "Anything look different?"

"Someone's been through here since it rained yesterday."

A bunch of grass and wet leaves may not look suspicious to her, but Pete had taught him to know when someone had tromped around his property. They reached the top of the hill and the posts that formed the boundary of his property, then followed the stone wall back down the slope. He pointed to a couple of clearly marked footprints.

"When's the last time you were up here?"

"Not sure. A couple of weeks at least."

"Do you have a gardener or neighbor who might come this way?"

He shook his head.

"Okay. Let's see if anything's been disturbed around the house. You should file a police report, and I'll call Seth to let the team know."

\*\*\*

Ellie sat on the couch with her laptop, legs curled under her. Cleo and Tony lay on a rug in front of the fireplace, and Gumbie purred as she stretched. The cat had decided that the cushion next to Ellie was her current favorite spot. Ellie scratched under Gumbie's chin, making her purr louder. Sam sat in the recliner reading something on his iPad. They were one big happy family. It bugged her that she couldn't lock Sam away in a corner of her brain and focus on her work.

Seth had sent her a bulletin on a bank robbery that had occurred in southern Idaho the previous week. He'd also sent information that their father had been identified on surveillance footage at a gas station in the same town the day before the bank robbery. The three bank robbers wore bulky coats, and parking lot cameras showed them with ski masks on as they'd emerged from their vehicle, which, she noted, was not the same one Richard Jameson had filled up at the gas station.

The three had robbed the bank and returned to their vehicle with their haul, speeding away before police arrived. The robbers had to've spent the night somewhere and Ellie made a mental note to check short-term rentals. Investigators usually checked motels, but sometimes neglected other housing options.

Significant as the developments were, all the while she was reading through the email and viewing the attachments, she was cognizant of Sam in a way that was truly annoying. He breathed and she felt the air move, he tapped his fingers on the armrest and it sounded like a snare drum, he rubbed his hand over his chin and she could hear the rasp of the whiskers.

He was driving her crazy.

Maybe she should jump him, they'd have wild jungle sex, and he'd be purged from her system.

She tried watching him out of the corner of her eye without turning her head. Keen intelligence, integrity, and that long, lean body – yeah, her type of guy.

"You keep looking at me like that and there'll be trouble."

"Maybe I want trouble." She slapped a hand over her mouth.

He set aside his iPad and when she looked at him directly, his smoldering eyes told her he wasn't unaffected by whatever was simmering between them, but he was doing a better job of reining in any crazy impulses.

"I wouldn't mind some of that trouble myself, but I'm not scratching that itch for you, Eleanor. We get together, I want it to be for the right reasons, not because it's convenient."

"Jesus, there's irony for you."

"What's the hell's that supposed to mean?"

She could tell him what had happened all those years ago, expose the wall between them, but she didn't want to risk the complications. "Nothing. It means nothing." She stood up. "I'm going to bed."

***

The next morning she steered into the parking lot near the federal courthouse, Sam sitting in the passenger seat.

"I'll meet you at the diner at noon. You can park here and walk, it's a half block down that street." He pointed. "You okay to drive without me?"

"I'm fine. I didn't stall it once this morning. I've got this."

He cocked his head. "You should come in and see my chambers. That seems like an engaged couple kind of thing."

Her heart gave an extra-hard thud that she hid behind nonchalance. "Sure."

They walked to the courthouse hand in hand, and she realized she was getting used to the physical connection. They entered the building through a side entrance that led to a long, narrow hall lined with closed doors on either side.

A woman with glasses perched on top of a wild mass of salt-and-pepper hair gave a wide smile when she saw them. "Sam Creed, the rumors are true then."

"Liz, this is my fiancée, Rachel Sinclair. Rachel, this is Liz Potenciano, also a judge in this court."

"Nice to meet you, Liz." Ellie shook the other woman's hand.

"I'm pleased to meet *you*. I never thought I'd see this guy settle down. He's a sly one. No one even knew he had a girlfriend." Her phone chimed. "I've got to run, but I'll expect an invitation to the wedding."

Sam looked resigned as he took Ellie down another hallway. Ellie hoped his friends would forgive him when they "broke up." He stopped at a door with a nameplate that read "The Honorable Samuel D. Creed."

"What's the 'D' stand for?"

"David. My parents went for the conventional."

"It's a strong name."

"When I was a boy I wanted a name like Running Bear or White Eagle in the worst way."

"Who wouldn't?" she asked with a smile.

He unlocked the door and pushed it open. "Here are my chambers."

Ellie stepped into a paneled room with dark wood floors upon which sat a huge deep maroon rug with blue and white scrollwork throughout. In the right corner of the sizeable room was a large dark wood desk with a computer monitor on the left side, and an old-fashioned blotter with maroon edging in the middle of the desk. The chair behind the massive desk was a high-back executive chair in dark leather with brass studding around the edges. Behind the chair was a dark wood credenza, and several tall wood filing cabinets lined the wall opposite the desk.

"What, no bookcases full of law books?"

"That's what the Internet and my law clerk are for."

"How iconoclastic of you. When I was in law school, it seemed like a judge wasn't serious unless he had a wall of law books behind his desk."

"And I bet not one of those books was ever opened."

She approached the door on the opposite wall. "Do you mind?"

"Go ahead, but you're a US Marshal, you've seen dozens of courtrooms."

"But not yours." She stepped through the door and took in the space. The high wood-paneled judge's bench with the courtroom deputy clerk's lower attached desk dominated the room. In front of a half wall were two long tables for the defense and US attorneys, each with three chairs. Behind the half wall was a center aisle with seven rows of seats for the gallery on each side, and to the left of the bench was the jury box. In front of the bench was the court reporter's chair, and beside it was the judge's personal clerk's desk.

She liked courtrooms with their traditions and ceremony. They were emblematic of the rule of law that was the bedrock of a democratic society.

She returned to Sam's chambers and spied his black robe hanging from a hook. "You know, you're popular on social media."

"Huh?"

"Social media. You're popular."

"I don't know what you're talking about. I avoid social media like leprosy."

"It doesn't avoid you. The video of you taking down that guy with a knife went viral with over a million views. Women thought you were hot."

His expression held horror that could not be faked. "You're making that up."

She couldn't stifle her giggle. She pulled out her phone. "I'm not making it up. I can't believe people haven't shown you." She tapped out a search, then held up her screen. "Look."

First she showed the video of his heroics, then she shared a meme of a woman licking her lips and leering at an image of Sam, sexy in his judge's robes, the thought bubble over her head suggesting that she knew who she wanted delivering her punishment.

"What the hell?" Red stained his cheeks.

"Want to see others?"

"There are others? How do I take them down?"

"You don't. That's the price you pay for being a hot federal judge."

"You think this is funny," he said, accusation vibrating in his tone.

They stepped out of his chambers and she couldn't help laying her hands on the lapels of his suit jacket. She knew she shouldn't be enjoying his discomfort quite so much. "Maybe a little bit. No more heroic leaps over your bench and you'll fade into obscurity."

He was still scowling when she gave in to impulse and leaned forward to brush her lips against his. The warmth in his eyes turned flat when a loud "woohoo" echoing down the hall had them both turning their heads.

Gordon Finster flashed his toothy smile, wagging a finger like he'd caught them doing something naughty. Sam obviously thought she'd spied Finster and that her kiss had been for show. Better than the truth, Ellie assured herself.

"Christ, that man can't get a clue," Sam muttered.

"Let's give him something to gossip about." She went up on tiptoes for a kiss that was more than a simple brush of lips. Tension eased like a deep sigh. This was what she'd been missing since the last time they'd kissed, that rush of feeling from the top of her head to that hot curl of lust in her belly. It made her want to forget about being a marshal on the job and find a quiet place where they could explore that flare of heat that ignited whenever they touched.

"You're playing with fire, Ellie," he murmured against her lips. Then he was opening his mouth and his tongue swept across hers and she wasn't thinking at all.

# Chapter Ten

Ellie parked the Land Cruiser on the driveway behind Sam's house. She eyed the mess left by the truck and found herself angry all over again. Someone had willfully violated the pretty and peaceful setting Sam and his aunt had created. Ellie was fairly certain that whoever had spun out their vehicle under the tree didn't have the same agenda as the person or persons threatening Sam. Tearing up a lawn didn't have the same impact as plastic explosives strapped to a judge's car.

With the bag of groceries in her hand, she dug out the house key Sam had given her. The wind had picked up to blow icy fingers down her collar, and the dome of the sky gleamed a hard and brittle blue. A honking sound above had her tipping back her head to witness a long V of geese flying overhead. She watched until they disappeared. While she loved San Diego with its diversity and quirky vibe, the wildness in this part of Oregon held an equally strong appeal.

Cleo and Tony rushed her with tails wagging as she went through their enclosure to the back door. They looked dapper in the plaid coats she and Sam had put on them that morning. Once inside, she disengaged the alarm, set the bag on the counter, and began putting away the milk, produce, and bread she'd bought.

Feeling unsettled, she filled the coffeemaker with water, measured out ground coffee, and set the machine to do its thing. Forty minutes after that sublime kiss she was still riding the high. She'd been an idiot going with impulse rather than control. Again. But she was done beating herself up about it.

Whatever had attracted her to Sam thirteen years ago still resonated. She liked his quick brain, the occasional flash of humor when he wasn't being so controlled, and while she didn't think him conventionally handsome, what he had did it for her in spades.

This whole fake engagement thing had definite disadvantages. Two healthy unattached adults, a lot of time spent together, and a few fake kisses to make it look good could turn into a recipe for disaster.

On an impulse, she returned to the mudroom for her coat, grabbed the dogs' leashes, and after snapping them on their collars, took them out the back door, through the gate, and out of the pen. With Cleo and Tony nosing and sniffing everywhere, she wandered Sam's property. She didn't find any fresh footprints on the slope but followed the rock wall past the posts marking his property line to the top of the ridge where a view of the valley spread out before her. The hill dropped steeply to a road below, and beyond that a stand of trees lined the swirling dark waters of the river.

Returning down the hill, she and the dogs circled to the front of the house. The deep red leaves of a Japanese maple gave a splash of color at the front corner of the house. Bright orange mums flowered next to the steps to the porch and Ellie made a mental note to bring some of the blooms inside. She couldn't imagine they would survive much longer given the cool temperatures.

She returned to the house, and after taking off the dogs' jackets, she opened a bag of treats. "Okay, babies, sit." They both went down on their haunches, quivering, staring fixedly at the little bone-shaped biscuits in her hand. They each took the treats politely, carrying them to their bed to enjoy.

Ellie poured herself coffee and made her way to the front room with her steaming mug to where she'd left her laptop on the coffee table. The dogs followed her, lying on the area rug beside the couch. Her phone chimed with a text from Linc.

**L:** *Met case admin Finster. He's an ass. He found out I'm assigned to Creed's court and about fell over himself to tell me he found the judge in a lip lock with hot fiancée. (I'll omit crude comment about fiancée, but what the hell, El?) Immediate* *impression – he's not our guy. Whatever he's thinking comes out his mouth. Still bears investigation, but don't think he has the self-control to plan anything beyond his next meal.*

As usual, Linc was able to cut through the bullshit and get right to the core. She ignored his reference to the kiss when she replied.

E: *Tend to agree. Finster's a cheap thrill kind of guy. Can't see him planning for a long game. Talk guns with him?*

L: *No. Will work it into conversation later.*

E: *Thx for update.*

While it was possible that there was more going on in Finster's head than they gave him credit for, and he did have connections with the gun rights community, she agreed with Linc that they needed to keep looking for the source of the threats against Sam. Computer humming, she searched for information on Drew Martin. Figuring Drew was short for Andrew, she went to work.

Sam may have been convinced his brother wasn't part of any plot, but Ellie wasn't so certain. She searched one database, then others without much luck. His name was fairly common, and she tried different search parameters to narrow the field.

It would help to know his middle name. That came up on census data, and with that information she was finally able to make some progress.

Drew hadn't served in the military and didn't turn up in any federal criminal databases. She dug deeper, even doing newspaper searches, until bingo, she found an incident from five months previous. A woman had filed a complaint that an intoxicated Andrew Martin had showed up at her home and threatened her. The woman claimed that the reported incident hadn't been the first time since she'd ended a romantic relationship with him that he'd come to her home uninvited. She'd obtained a restraining order. The reporter had mentioned that Andrew Martin was the stepbrother of Judge Samuel D. Creed. Drew's lawyer had managed to get the charges reduced to trespassing and Drew had been sentenced to thirty days in jail, less time served.

Ellie wondered if she could get a copy of the police report. She'd get Seth on that. Sam must know about his brother's brush with the law and had made a decision not to tell her about it. He'd been insistent that his brother wasn't involved with the threats, but Ellie thought Sam was being willfully blind. Family loyalty could cloud the judgment of the most rational and clear-thinking individuals.

Sunlight glinted off glass through the front window. Ellie rose to her feet to watch a truck turn onto the driveway. Speak of the devil. Barking wildly, the dogs rushed to the back door, nails clicking on the wood floor. Ellie shut the top of her laptop, then dashed up the stairs to grab her Glock from the gun safe. Down the back stairs, she slipped into the kitchen and stashed the gun in a drawer under neatly folded kitchen towels.

She opened the door to find Drew standing in the driveway, staring at the destruction under the white oak. Today he was hatless and wore a Sherpa-lined denim jacket open in front. He also wore a gun in a holster on his belt.

He glanced over as she crossed the dogs' enclosure to the wire fence, the beagles running ahead of her. "What happened here?"

"Someone with a pickup drove back here and spun donuts in the mud when Sam and I were out yesterday."

"Well, shit. Who'd do that?"

"Don't know." She pointed to the camera at the corner of the house. "Camera caught the truck, but we weren't able to make out the license plate or the driver."

He narrowed his eyes. "When did Sam put cameras in?"

She shrugged. "I didn't think to ask him."

He scanned the eaves, then the garage, before turning to face her. "You asking me in, future sister-in-law?"

She eyed the gun at his waist and gauged how to play the part. "I don't know, future brother-in-law. Seems weird that you showed up here when you know Sam would be in court, and with a gun on your belt."

"Oregon is an open-carry state, so it's legal."

"That may be, but my concern remains the same. Why did you come, Drew?"

Something flashed across his expression she couldn't decipher. "I thought you should know what you're getting into by marrying Sam. I don't think he's told you the truth, or at least the whole truth, about how fucked up our family is."

"And somehow you're concerned about me and want to correct that omission."

He hitched a shoulder in the jacket that hung loosely on his shoulders. "Sam gets every damn thing laid at his feet. He should at least be honest before he gets you, too."

She studied him. If she'd truly been Sam's fiancée, she'd tell Drew to get lost. But she was a marshal charged with protecting Sam, and his brother might have information that would benefit her team's investigation. "I'll invite you in, but the gun makes me uncomfortable. I'd like you to leave it in your truck."

"It's my right to carry a gun."

"Not on someone else's property, it's not."

He narrowed his gaze. "You a lawyer, too?"

"As a matter of fact, I am."

He looked at the house, then at her, and appeared to weigh his options. Whatever he wanted to tell her must have won out, because with a muttered oath he went to his truck and locked the gun inside.

"Thank you." Ellie held open the gate for Drew to pass through.

Once indoors, Drew paced the kitchen floor. He stopped at the window, stared out at the yard with a frown on his face, then paced again. The dogs sat on their cushion, eyes tracking the visitor.

"Would you like coffee?"

"Yeah." She moved to prepare it, and he said, "You know I'd never been in this house until my brother inherited it."

"No, I didn't know that."

"Sam's aunt thought he walked on water. She tolerated me, acted nice enough, but I wasn't kin so she didn't see me as part of her family. Had to have native blood for that. Left this place to Sam, and not a penny to me."

She handed him the mug.

"Got nothing to say to that, sister?"

"I've moved up from future sister-in-law to sister? That's quick. And no, I have nothing to say about that. Obviously, I never met Nan Beauchamp, and have no insight into her decision."

"You're a cool one, aren't you? No wonder Sam fell for you." When she didn't respond, he continued. "My mom married Sam's dad when I was a little kid. Sam tell you we aren't real brothers?"

"He refers to you as his brother, but did acknowledge that you're step-siblings."

"Mom worked like a slave for Joss Creed. Cooked for him, kept the house clean, even trucked feed to the cattle and mucked stalls if she had to. When I was old enough, I worked my tail off, too. Learned a lot, but got my ass whipped more times than I can count. Worked on that ranch more than Sam did. Sam didn't like the old man's discipline style so he'd take off every chance he got. He and Ben would go fishing, hiking, rock-climbing, whatever they wanted to do. Or he'd come here and stay with his aunt. Leave me behind."

Ellie wasn't even sure Drew remembered she was in the room. Once again he stood at the kitchen sink, sipping coffee as he stared out the window, seemingly lost in the past. Then he turned to face her and he was totally in the present, anger flaring hot behind pale eyes. "The old man let me call him Dad, said I was his son, and I stayed on at the ranch even after my mom died. He acted like I meant something. Then last year the fucker up and dies and he doesn't leave me shit. Left the ranch a hundred percent to Sam, because I don't have his blood coursing through my veins."

He pointed a finger at her, emphatic in his air jabs. "But you know what really burns? My holier-than-thou brother, the man who sits in judgment over others, didn't make it right. He didn't tell that lawyer to add my name to the deed. So now I'm working my ass off again, for nothing."

He set the mug on the counter with a snap. "That's what I got to say to you, sister. You should know who it is you're marrying. May seem to you that bagging a judge gives you a nice, secure future, but he'll screw you over like he does everyone else. Like he did me."

Once again, Drew began prowling the room, then jabbed a finger toward the window. "Must have pissed someone off big time to have them coming on his property to destroy shit. His line of work, he pisses off folks regular. He sends honest, hardworking men, men who are true patriots, to prison every day. No one should have that much power and privilege. You should consider that before you marry him." Drew's shoulders slumped and his anger seemed to have run its course. "You've been warned. That's all I got to say."

He slammed out the backdoor, and through the window she watched him tramp across the yard to his truck.

Ellie picked up her phone, and when Seth answered, she said, "We have a suspect."

*** 

Sam scanned the crowded diner and spotted Ellie sitting in a booth toward the back. His heart gave an unexpected lurch, and he rubbed the heel of his hand over his chest to ease the discomfort. He made his way across the floor, weaving between occupied tables. A few people said hello as he passed, or waved to acknowledge him, but he didn't stop.

Ellie looked up from the menu she'd been studying as he dropped onto the bench across from her. The smile she flashed him had to be for effect, but he couldn't ignore how it transformed her face. He leaned forward, cupped his hand behind her neck, and caught her lips with his, reining back the desire to take it deeper. Anyone looking would see Judge Creed greeting his fiancée.

He couldn't help the satisfaction at her flustered expression when he released her. She cleared her throat. "Sam."

"Eleanor. How was your morning?"

"Interesting. How was yours?" The mundane words belied the charged physical greeting he thought neither of them was ready to acknowledge.

"Routine, other than lots of congratulations on our engagement. Want to tell me about your interesting morning?" The group at the table nearest them left so there was little chance their conversation would be overheard as long as they spoke in quiet voices.

"Your brother came by this morning, guess he wanted to welcome me to the family."

He kept his expression relaxed even though a muscle jumped in his jaw. He was saved from having to respond by the arrival of the short, round woman holding a steaming coffeepot who rubbed a hand on his shoulder.

"Hey there, Judy."

Judy wasn't an inch over five feet and wore her bright red hair tied back in a frizzy poof behind her head. She carried menus tucked under her arm and had a pocketed apron tied around her waist that bulged with pens and straws, and wore more eye shadow than anyone he'd ever met. And she was hands-down one of his favorite people.

He rose from his seat to give her a hug. When he stepped back, she asked in her raspy voice, "How you doing, boy?"

"Better now that I've seen you. I want you to meet someone." He turned. "This is my fiancée, Rachel." Guilt gnawed another hole in his conscience as he considered how many people he was lying to.

"Wondering when you'd introduce me to your girl. Got wind of your engagement yesterday when Barb Herrera came in." She frowned. "You never told me you had a girlfriend, and now you've got yourself a fiancée."

Ellie stood, extending her hand. "Hello, Judy. It's nice to meet Sam's friends."

Judy shook her hand. "You're a tall one, aren't you? We'll be fine as long as you treat my boy right."

"I intend to."

"Good. Now you two sit and tell me what you want for lunch."

They gave their order, and Judy left after filling their mugs with coffee.

Sam bent forward, speaking softly. "Drew give you any trouble? He knew I'd be at work."

Ellie mimicked his posture and kept her voice pitched below the chatter around them. "Not really. He had a gun on his belt when he arrived. I met him outside and said I didn't feel comfortable with him coming in the house armed. He didn't like it but he left it in his truck." She gave Sam a considering look. "He didn't have a gun when he came by on Saturday."

"Because he knows better than to try that with me. I'm glad you called him on it." He picked up Ellie's hand and rubbed his thumb over her engagement ring, then brought it to his lips. He bit back a laugh at the scowl on her face. "Isn't this what an engaged guy would do when he meets his fiancée for lunch? He'd want to let her know he missed her. You should be smiling at me with little hearts in your eyes." He knew good and well that if they hadn't been in a dining room full of people, she'd bust his chops. "I'm new at this, so you'll have to tell me if I'm wrong."

"How should I know? I've never been engaged before." She tugged her hand and he let go. "But it feels over the top to me."

Sparring with her gave his mood a boost, and that after the heart-jolt when he'd spotted her. He felt a little like when he'd slid down an ice chute while hiking, unable to get traction. With effort, he reordered his thoughts. "What did Drew say?"

She tucked her hands under the table. "His basic implication was that you're a greedy bastard for inheriting the house from your aunt and the ranch from your dad when he didn't get a penny. He thinks you're privileged and that he's been treated like he's not part of the family."

The reminder of Drew's animosity had Sam's mood plummeting. He flattened his hands on the table when what he really wanted to do was hunt his brother down and give him a good kick in the ass.

"He shouldn't have dumped that shit on you. What he didn't tell you is that Dad did make provisions for him. It's not a lot because Dad's money was tied up in the ranch and he was cash poor, and Drew won't get that money until he turns thirty-five. Joss Creed was a strict son of a bitch and didn't suffer fools gladly. He didn't think Drew had the maturity to handle the ranch or a chunk of cash. I tend to agree. I told Drew I plan to give him a share of the ranch, but he's resentful that I haven't done it on his timetable."

"Are you waiting until he's older?"

He leaned back against his seat. "That was my original plan, but I don't know anymore. I'm not sure age will make a difference. Some people never become responsible adults. He had a girlfriend who kept pushing him to come to me for money, fed him a line that he deserved more, that I should put him on the deed to the ranch immediately. They confronted me, and I told them there was no way in hell that was happening. Guess she decided to cut her losses when it was apparent Drew wasn't coming into quick cash. She broke things off with him, so there's another thing he blames me for."

"He left out a lot when he came to set me straight about your family."

Sam gave a disgusted sigh. "Of course he did. Drew also had a run-in with the law that makes me question his judgment even more. He tell you about that?"

"No, but I've been looking into his background." She held up a hand when Sam's eyes narrowed. "Doing my job. His case popped up."

"Then you'll understand why I'm in a wait-and-see mode with his inheritance. I'll see how he deals with his issues, drinking being one of them, before I give him anything."

Ellie sipped her coffee, blue eyes steady on his over the rim of her mug. "That's a crappy position to be in, isn't it?"

"Yep. Drew resents me, and I don't see that changing."

"You're doing what's best, Sam, even if Drew doesn't understand it."

Sam felt a knot of tension in his gut loosen. He wasn't used to confiding in anyone about his issues with his brother. Ben knew, and Pete, but somehow telling Ellie lessened the burden, made him think how it could be between them if they were truly engaged. Which they weren't. He needed to keep reminding himself of that fact.

"He doesn't. But he has a roof over his head and work when he cares to do it; he just needs to get his shit together."

Their order arrived with extra avocado heaped on Ellie's cobb salad, and a huge slab of corn bread on the plate beside his turkey chili.

Judy put a hand on his shoulder and nodded to Ellie. "Sam tell you he used to sit at this very booth and do his homework when he was a boy?"

Ellie smiled. "No, he didn't tell me that."

"When I stayed with my aunt, I'd come here after school until she could pick me up. My mom had worked here, and Judy was one of her best friends."

"So you're family," Ellie said to Judy.

"You bet I am." Judy sniffed, squeezed his shoulder, and pulled a handkerchief from her pocket to wipe her eyes as she walked away.

Sam shook his head at Ellie's distressed expression. "That was the perfect thing to say to her. She's never quite gotten over my mom's death. Mom had been covering a shift for Judy the night she was killed."

"Oh jeez. What a burden to carry."

"Yeah." He motioned to the plate in front of her. "Eat up, or Judy will be back to find out why you're picking at the food."

As always, the chili was excellent, and Ellie dug into her salad. He'd been on dates with women who acted afraid to enjoy their food. He was glad to see Ellie wasn't like that.

She speared a slice of avocado, brows lowering over her eyes in a way that made him think she was carefully choosing her words. Keeping her voice low, she said, "Sam, you need to consider that Drew could be behind the threats against you. He carries a gun and is aggressive in defending it as his right. That suggests affinity with pro-gun rights ideology espoused by FD."

"It's not a crime to support the Second Amendment."

"As long as that support isn't extreme. He made a comment that every day you send hardworking men to prison, called them 'true patriots.' That suggests anti-government beliefs that may come down on the wrong side of the law."

Sam set his butter knife against the plate with the corn bread. "It's not him. I've considered it, but it's not him."

"Is that an emotional assumption, or a logical one based on evidence?"

"Drew's my brother. Despite the current issues between us, he would never do anything to hurt me, and certainly wouldn't have taped a brick of C-four in the wheel well of my car."

Her expression was troubled, and he knew as clearly as if she'd said it out loud that she wasn't convinced of his brother's loyalty.

"What happened to Drew's mother?"

He sighed in relief at the change in subject. "She passed away when he was a teenager."

"Your family has had it rough."

"Yeah." He cut a piece of corn bread and slathered on butter, offering it to her. "He took it hard."

"Who wouldn't?" She took the corn bread, and when she bit into it, closed her eyes with a hum of appreciation. "Wow, that's good."

He moved the corn bread between them. "Have as much as you want."

"Thanks. I could make a meal of the corn bread alone."

"Tell me about your mother."

The quick flash of her eyes told him he'd surprised her. "Margaret Bollinger is the best mom in the world. She was a rock when my dad abandoned us."

"How old were you when he left?"

"Twelve."

"Vulnerable age for a girl."

"Yeah. Things hadn't been right before that. Dad would take off for these long weekends without us, so it felt like there was buildup to him leaving. He worked for the military as a civilian. We found out he'd been stealing weapons and explosives and selling most of it on the black market. Mom was shocked, and she was hopping mad, but maybe not as much as you'd think because she had an inkling something was up. But no matter what she felt, she kept it together for her kids. Made us all go to family therapy."

"That help?"

"I think so. My brothers were hurt and angry. I guess we all were. Seth tended to bottle things inside. Still does. I was more emotional and prone to rants, and Linc was somewhere in between. The therapist was good and we worked through it as best we could."

"How's your mom now?"

"Awesome. She married the marshal in charge of Dad's case. He's the best thing that could have happened to her."

"Betrayal like that from a family member is hard to overcome. Some people never do."

She wondered if he was talking about her family or his. "Arch Bollinger, that's my stepdad, he doesn't know the meaning of the word 'quit.' He told me that when he met my mom for the first time, his heart did this hard flip in his chest, and he thought 'there she is.' He said he'd been waiting for her his entire life. At first Mom brushed him aside, refused to go out with him. He'd step back, take a breath, and try again."

Sam frowned. "I know that name. Chief Deputy Archer Bollinger."

"You've met him?"

"Yeah, I've met him. He oversaw the Marshals Office assigned to the Ninth Circuit when I was clerking. He's a good guy."

"Yes, he is."

"And now you and your brothers are all marshals, and on the team to locate your father."

"We're getting closer. We'll find him and bring him to justice."

"I have no doubt." Sam pushed the empty chili bowl aside, thanking Judy when she warmed his coffee and cleared his dishes. He waited until she was out of earshot to speak. "You okay to be at home alone this afternoon?"

Ellie gave him that grin that warmed her eyes, the one that made him wish for an instant that the engagement wasn't fake.

"Who's the marshal here? I think I can handle your brother if he decides to show up again. Or anyone else, for that matter."

"We don't know what they're planning. Whoever made that threat may have moved onto plan B since running me over with a truck didn't work out."

"I'll be on the lookout. Don't worry about me."

"I don't think that's possible."

She gave him a sharp look as Judy slid the check across the table to Sam as she passed. Ellie held out her hand. "I'll pay. We can put it on my expense account."

"I got it." She scowled, and he said, "I pay when I take my fiancée to lunch, Eleanor. Deal with it."

# Chapter Eleven

Ellie drove through the largest intersection in town and headed toward Sam's house. If something didn't break soon, she'd go crazy, as in running-down-the-street-naked crazy. She and Sam had settled into a rhythm and it'd been working for ten days. But she felt like she was a spring being wound tighter and tighter, and it was only a matter of time before she exploded. God knew where she'd end up when she finally sprung free.

There hadn't been any more disturbances at the house. No unexplained footprints, no trucks spinning out under the oak tree. Sam had hired a lawn crew to clean up the mess in the backyard and they'd evened out the soil and replaced sections of sod.

She and Sam went on outings together, took the dogs for walks and held hands for the neighbors, and even attended a social function where they'd acted the part of besotted lovers. Then they returned to the house where the barriers went up and they were roommates. Roommates whose mutual attraction was so palpable, it hung in the air.

Which resulted in her being on the brink of crazy.

Being around Sam meant being in a constant state of unrelenting lust.

Her perpetually aroused state wouldn't be so bad if she had an inkling that Sam reciprocated her feelings, but after the first weekend, the austere Judge Creed had returned. Now, he pretty much ignored her when they were home.

He no longer sat in the front room with her in the evenings, instead closing himself in his office until well after she'd gone upstairs. They still ran together in the mornings, taking a different route every day, but even then conversation was kept to a minimum.

She put on her blinker and glanced in her side mirror and saw the same work van that had followed her out of the grocery store parking lot was still behind her. The van turned left before the bridge. Could be nothing, but she recorded a voice memo on her phone noting the make, model, and time she thought its driver might have started to surveil her.

Once home, she brought the dogs in, set the alarm to "at home," and got to work on her laptop. Late in the afternoon, she tapped on the meeting app to join the team for a conference call.

Seth started with a general overview of their current status, then each team member gave an update of what they'd learned.

"I've interviewed more of the female staff about sexual harassment at the courthouse," Bella reported, her tone even and devoid of emotion. "The issue seems confined to Gordon Finster. An additional woman has sought to join the other complainants against him. Their case appears solid.

"Finster followed a pattern of staying late into the evening beyond his normal hours when the women were often working alone. He would use the opportunity to take advantage of them sexually. All the women feel indebted to Judge Creed, and believe his support provided them credibility and gave them the courage to make their cases. They are grateful to him."

Ellie made a conscious effort not to roll her eyes at the overly professional tone her friend adopted, particularly when she was around Seth, which was most of the time. Bella could be warm and fun, and interesting, but put her near authority and she projected all the emotion of a robot.

Ellie got Bella's reserve, and couldn't blame her given what she'd been through in her life, but Ellie couldn't seem to convince her that being a good marshal didn't mean she had to follow all rules and protocols to the letter. For Bella, rules brought security, though Ellie thought being constantly vigilant and afraid of making a mistake must be exhausting.

"I talked with other staff," Seth stated. "Not one claimed to be friends with Finster, and most find him obnoxious. He doesn't have much of a filter. He's the kind of guy who walks up to people and starts talking to them, but it's not a conversation. He simply disgorges whatever is on his mind, then moves on. He spewed out the details of his divorce, which apparently got nasty. Sympathy was with his kid for being the bone both parents were fighting over. The only topic he holds back on is his side business selling guns. Few people knew about that."

"Any rumors of someone on staff having a beef with Sam?" Ellie asked.

"No. He's well-liked and respected. I got the impression one of the women has a crush on him."

"Any talk of love interests?" Linc asked. "We haven't looked at Sam's romantic background. The threatening emails don't scream spurned lover, but could be there's an angry ex with an imagination messing with him. You'd have to be really pissed to duct tape C-four to your ex's car, but it's been done. He mention anyone to you, El?"

"No. He must have bought this engagement ring for someone, but he hasn't been exactly forthcoming."

Linc looked thoughtful. "I think a woman would be more personal, but a dude might go for explosives. El reported a visit from a close friend who is gay. Could be Creed is too."

"He's not," Ellie said, shaking her head.

"Have you asked him, or whether he has any angry exes?" Linc was sitting back in his chair, brow raised in a look of inquiry that for some reason always annoyed her.

"I haven't asked, but he's not gay."

She should have been more careful because Linc pounced. "And how do you know he's not gay?"

"Shut up, Linc. I know, okay?"

"Do you have anything for us today, Ellie?"

Grateful for Seth's rescue, Ellie mentioned the vehicle she thought had followed her. "Right now, I'd give it a fifty percent chance that it wasn't random and was following me."

"Anything more on Drew Martin?"

"Sam won't talk about him. My feeling is that Drew is angry and resentful because he hasn't made any economic advances in his life. He was counting on inheriting part of the ranch, and Sam is in the way of that. Losing his mother, not inheriting property he felt he deserved, and feeling overshadowed by his successful older brother are all adding up for him. The right-wing groups he identifies with reinforce this idea of injustice."

"Your analysis is on point," Seth said. "Joining a militia group would give him a sense of empowerment."

Ellie nodded. "The feeling that he never fully belonged to the Creed family has led to a nasty mix of anger and bitterness. One appeal of extremist groups is they make you feel like you've found your true home. They feed the anger and resentment to pull in the disaffected. If Drew found a place where he feels wanted within the right-wing militia movement, that could be our connection."

"Agreed," Seth said.

They concluded their meeting, and Ellie sat in the quiet house watching through the window as the last glow of daylight faded. A glance at her phone to check the time brought a frown. Every day, Sam was home from work shortly after five, and it was already six. She began to text him, then hesitated. Their engagement was fake and checking up on him felt too much like what a girlfriend would do. Which was stupid. She was a marshal, and her job was to protect her fiancé.

She tapped out a text, keeping it to a simple *You good?* before hitting send.

It took him a couple minutes, but his reply of *Fine, home soon* worked.

She went to the kitchen with Cleo and Tony following close behind. Getting the hint, she filled their dishes with kibble, then began gathering the ingredients for dinner that she'd purchased that morning at the grocery store.

Twenty minutes later she had a pot gently simmering on the stove. She was reaching for a wineglass when Tony and Cleo both sat up, ears perked. Her first thought was that Sam was home. Finally. But she hadn't heard the Land Cruiser or seen headlights of the vehicle driving to the back. The security lights on either end of the garage illuminated the area vacant of vehicles, so unless Sam had somehow already parked in the garage without her noticing, it wasn't him who had alerted the dogs.

Opting for caution, she ran up the back stairs and retrieved her Glock from the gun safe, tucking it into the back waistband of her jeans. Gumbie lay curled up and asleep on Ellie's bed so she shut the door rather than worrying about the cat getting out while she was looking for possible bad guys. She returned to the kitchen using the back stairs.

In the mudroom, she turned on the lights and opened the back door. The beagles bulleted out, barking furiously as they raced to the back fence. Movement, more of a shifting shadow at the side of the house than anything else, caught her attention. She dashed back inside, leaving the dogs out, flipping off lights as she went through the house so no one could see in.

From the side window of the library, she watched a dark figure leap from the rock wall to blend into the darkness under the low branches of a trio of trees.

Ellie stood still, waiting. After several minutes, she reached for the phone in her back pocket. The shadow moved, quick and furtive. Then the window exploded with a crash and she reeled back as shards of glass flew past her.

She dove for cover behind a couch and a thud sounded as something landed on the floor. Even with her eyelids squeezed shut and instinctively pressing her hands over her ears, she could detect the flash of light and explosive crack of sound.

The siren for the house alarm went off, sounding oddly muted. Ellie grabbed her Glock and rose cautiously to her feet. A quick look showed no fire. Slamming shut the door to the room, she ran for the front door, gun in hand.

The yard was empty, and the porch light on the neighbor's house came on. She tucked her gun back into the waistband of her jeans. Headlights gleamed through the trees as a vehicle raced up the street, barely slowing to take the turn into the driveway.

Sam's Land Cruiser skidded to a stop at the walkway and he jumped out of the car and raced toward her. The expression on his face as he ran his hands over her arms and shoulders had the breath backing up in her lungs.

Over the past week she'd decided he was indifferent to her, but now she realized he was a consummate actor. Silver glinted in his eyes as his wide palms reached up to frame her face as his thumbs brushed her cheeks.

"You okay? What the hell happened?"

His voice sounded like it was coming from deep in a well. She shook her head, trying to clear it, not sure if the feeling of disorientation was from the flashbang or the raw fear emanating from Sam.

"I think I'm fine, but I can't hear very well."

"Were you attacked?"

"No. Someone was outside by the wall. They threw a flashbang into the house. I ran outside but they were already gone."

"You could have been seriously hurt."

His grip tightened as his eyes blazed. This was the first time she'd seen Sam truly angry.

"But I wasn't."

"What room was it?"

"The library."

He nodded. Despite sounding muffled, she could hear the dogs in the back howling at the approaching sirens of three police cars, one arriving right after the other. They parked on the street, the fire truck following them coming up the driveway. The sirens were silenced, leaving circling blue and red lights slicing through the night.

As police officers approached, Sam took off his coat to drape around Ellie's shoulders. She sighed when he pulled her against his side, and she absorbed his heat like he was her own personal campfire.

"Be better if they didn't wonder why you're carrying."

Oh. Right. Sam's coat would hide her gun. At least he was thinking sensibly, while she'd been getting all warm and fuzzy feelings because of his apparent concern.

An officer, older than the others and with an extra stripe on the sleeve of his coat, asked them to follow him away from the house.

"Judge Creed." He nodded to Sam. "Are we looking for an intruder?"

"No. Whoever threw the device through the window took off. It sounds like it was a flashbang."

The officer relayed the information over his radio. "You in the house when all the fun started?"

Sam shook his head. "I was about two blocks from home when my phone alerted that the house alarm had gone off. Rachel was standing in front when I arrived."

The officer turned to Ellie. "Miss. I'm Officer Hickman. Had a bit of excitement, haven't you?" Officer Hickman was probably close to retirement age and had a pleasantly lined face and a comfortable paunch around his middle.

Ellie nodded. "Yes."

"Can you hear me all right? Flashbangs can cause temporary deafness."

"My ears are ringing, but I can hear you."

"Good, good. Are you hurt?"

She shook her head. "I'm okay."

"Our EMT is on another call, but someone with the fire crew will get you checked out. We can call an ambulance if you think you need a ride to the hospital."

"No ambulance."

Hickman nodded. "We'll get down to business, then." He licked a thumb to flip pages in a small notebook. "Let me get your name and whatnot."

While Ellie gave him the name Rachel Sinclair and other requested information, Sam released his hold on her and stepped away. The chilly breeze had her wrapping his coat more securely around her.

Officer Hickman finished writing her details. "Okay then, why don't you tell me what happened?"

"I was in the kitchen making dinner. Oh," she turned to find Sam on his phone. "I left soup cooking on the stove."

Hickman nodded toward the firefighters filing into the house. "They'll take care of that. Don't worry."

"All right." Ellie took a deep breath, then recounted how the dogs had alerted her, and when she'd let them outside, she'd seen someone by the rock wall. Skipping over how she'd run upstairs for her gun, she described the shattering glass, followed by the flash of light and loud noise.

Hickman nodded. "That's a flashbang. Good thing your instinct was to cover your ears as much as you did. Can you describe the person you saw?"

"My impression is male, medium height, average weight. He was wearing dark clothing, I think with a beanie low over his forehead and the hood on his sweatshirt pulled over that. I don't think that helps much."

"Everything helps," he assured her.

A firefighter came out of the house and approached them.

"What's the verdict, Lieutenant?" Hickman asked.

"There was no fire or scorching." The lieutenant looked at Ellie and Sam, who had returned to her side. "You folks are fortunate about that. Blew out some windows, and you've got a few broken knickknacks, but the damage is contained to that room."

"I left soup cooking on the stove. Did you turn it off?" Ellie asked.

"Yes, ma'am." He turned to Sam. "You have any plywood? We can board up the windows so you can secure your house until you get the glass replaced."

Sam dug keys out of his pocket, singling out one before handing it to the firefighter. "I appreciate it. The key is to the garage door, and there's plywood against the west wall. I want to stay with Rachel."

Ellie recognized a tall figure walking up from the street. Linc wore his marshal's star on his belt and no doubt his weapon in a shoulder holster under his leather jacket.

He nodded at Sam. "Judge Creed."

Sam introduced Linc as the US Marshal assigned to his court. Ellie found it more than a little weird to "meet" her brother as if they were strangers.

"Judge Creed called me to report the incident here at his house. I'll need to examine the scene."

Ellie waited for Hickman to put up the customary jurisdictional squabble, but the guy proved affable and waved Linc toward the house.

Once Hickman was done with his questions, he tucked his notebook into his pocket. "Guess you'll want to take a look at the damage. I'd like to have a look-see at your camera footage." He nodded to a camera under the eaves. "The deputy marshal will likely have the same request."

Hickman walked with them into the house now blazing with light. Linc came from the damaged room and met them inside the foyer, holding up two plastic bags so they could see the contents. "This one's your basic garden-variety rock." He held up the other bag. "This, however, is a military-grade flashbang device, which can cause a lot of property damage as well as physical harm that includes permanent hearing loss. Miss Sinclair will want to be checked out medically. The rock was thrown first to break the window, and then the flashbang was lobbed in."

Hickman was called outside, and the second they were alone, Linc's gaze drilled into Ellie's. "You good, El?"

"Yeah."

Sam bent at the waist and glared. "What the hell? Why didn't you tell me you were hurt?" Anger snapped through his words and he tugged her closer to a lamp.

"Sam, stop. I'm fine."

He held up his hand stained with drying blood. "Then where the fuck did this come from?"

# Chapter Twelve

"Oh." She didn't know why until that moment she'd been unaware of any discomfort, but now a stinging sensation behind her left ear made itself known. In fact, there was stinging in several places. She held up her hand where her knuckles oozed blood. "I didn't realize. I had my hands over my ears. Seems like it was a good thing."

In a controlled movement, Sam held up her hair from her neck. "You're bleeding here, too. This is from flying glass. Damn it. We need to get you to the hospital."

"No, we don't," she insisted.

Linc walked to the door. "I'm going to find a first aid kit."

They were alone when Ellie took her gun from the waistband of her jeans. With the safety already set, she slipped it into the drawer of a drop-leaf table. She straightened and found herself pulled into a kiss that threatened to blister her with its heat before Sam released her.

"Sam, what—"

Hickman came in the open door, carrying a red plastic box.

"Oh. Good cover," she murmured.

"Look who I found." Hickman indicated the man following behind him. "Dr. Montoya just happened to be wandering around out front."

"Sam is a good friend. He left a message saying Rachel had a possible concussion, so here I am," Ben explained.

Sam exhaled sharply. "Thanks for coming. I wasn't sure you got my voicemail."

"I did. And your texts, so here I am." He turned to Ellie. "Let's take a look at you."

She followed Ben into the kitchen where she shed Sam's coat and sat in the chair Ben had pulled under the light. She glanced at the stove. The firefighter had not only turned off the burner under the pot of tortilla soup, he'd also found a lid for it. The sound of a power drill came from the library and Ellie thought the Pendleton Fire Department was awesome.

Sam washed his hands at the sink, and Ben followed suit, then donned gloves before scooting a chair to sit in front of her.

"First thing we'll check for are signs of a concussion. Did you lose consciousness or experience nausea?"

"No."

"How about blurry vision or feeling sluggish or groggy?"

"No again."

He looked in her eyes with a light, then took the ear device from the medical kit and checked both ears. "Eyes and ears look fine, but there can be damage I can't see. How's your hearing?"

"Seems normal now. The ringing has stopped."

"Good. I'm on duty in the ER at the hospital tomorrow. Come by and I'll get you in with someone for a more thorough check, including running a couple of tests." He gathered gloves, gauze pads, and various packets from the kit. "These cuts are shallow but will be sore for a couple days." He kept his voice quiet, explaining what he was doing, and launching into stories about Georgie. "That girl has us figured out. She won't fall asleep unless we're rocking her. Justin and I agree we can't get her accustomed to that, but then we're so exhausted that we end up rocking her to sleep anyway."

As a distraction, Ben's tactic worked. Ellie found herself paying more attention to his story than having her injuries tended to. "You have an excellent bedside manner, Dr. Montoya," she commented.

"You bet I do. Works better than tranquilizers to keep my patients calm." He cleaned the cut on the back of her left hand and the one on her neck behind her ear where he applied butterfly strips. Sam did a good impression of a worried fiancée, resolutely staying by her side with his arms crossed over his chest and a scowl on his face.

Ben tipped his head toward Sam. "This guy, however, could get a clue. If he looked at the defendants or lawyers in his courtroom with that face, he'd have them all asking that he recuse himself because of bias."

Ellie eyed Sam. "Women must like that look. Have you seen the social media posts about him? There are women who fantasize about whether he's wearing anything under his robes."

Ben gave a bark of laughter as Sam's frown deepened.

"Cut it out. You're blowing it out of proportion."

"Some of those posts have thousands of likes," she said. "But since Sam is kind of cute when he's not glowering, I get it."

He gave a disgusted sigh and dropped into the chair beside her. "Are we done messing with me?"

"Yep, all done," Ben affirmed, gaze travelling over Ellie. "Any cuts we missed?"

"Maybe on my back. I didn't notice at the time, but it hurts now."

"Adrenaline masks a lot of pain."

Ellie winced when Ben lifted her shirt that had dried to a cut on her lower back while Sam swore ripely under his breath.

"Little more blood on this one, but it still didn't get through the epidermis. Doesn't need stitches. Between the glass and the blood, your shirt's trashed." Ben cleaned the wound, applied butterflies, and taped a bandage in place. "You'll want to keep these dry." He produced a lollipop from the medical kit and handed it to her. "Your reward for being the perfect patient."

"Cool. I don't know when I last had a lollipop, and it's cherry, my favorite." She unwrapped the treat and stuck it in her mouth. She spoke around the candy. "Thanks for tending my wounds, Ben. I'm sorry Sam pulled you away from home, but not sorry to avoid a visit to the ER tonight, which is where I think he would have dragged me."

Chilled, Ellie rubbed her arms. Any warmth in the house had disappeared with the constant stream of people in and out the front door.

"Damn straight, I would have," Sam muttered. He disappeared up the back stairs as Officer Hickman stepped into the kitchen.

"Looks like Dr. Montoya got you patched up, Ms. Sinclair."

"Yes, he did an excellent job."

Sam returned with a charcoal gray sweatshirt that he helped pull over her head. It was too big, but she was glad for the enfolding warmth.

Hickman addressed Sam. "Officers are talking to your neighbors to see if anyone heard or saw anything. The marshal fellow says you've got someone sending you nasty emails, and you had that incident in your backyard a couple weeks ago. We'll be beefing up patrols in your neighborhood. Got a sec to show us the recording from your security cameras?"

Hickman took a seat at the table on Sam's on his other side as he accessed the footage on his iPad and brought up the recordings from different camera angles. Ellie moved closer to look over his shoulder. He tapped the camera that showed the south side of the house, then scrolled to before the time the alert had come on his phone. It'd been dark, and with no lights on that side of the house, the video showed only a shadowy image crouching under the trees. Then the figure straightened to heave an object at the house.

"He's throwing the rock through the window," Hickman said. "Ah, and there's the money shot."

The figure had run forward to heave the flashbang device through the broken window, and for a brief second his hooded face had turned to the camera.

"Not much of a money shot." Ellie drew in a sharp breath when she shifted and the injury on her back made its presence known. She caught Sam's frown. "About all you can tell is he's male and looks young."

"And that he's left-handed," Sam said.

"Good observation," Hickman noted. "And that's more than we had before. Judge Creed, can you send that to me? Here's my email." He handed Sam a business card and rose to his feet. "We're about done here. Our firefighting brothers and sisters are about to leave. Don't be bashful about calling us back if you have more trouble or think of anything that might be helpful in tracking down this yahoo."

Hickman left and Linc came back in. Sam went into the living room to speak to him, so Ellie let the dogs in, giving them both a good rub before retrieving their bowls to feed them. She turned the burner back on under the soup and was leaning against the counter when Sam returned.

Once again, he gave her that all-encompassing look that made her think he was assessing every nuance of her appearance. He picked up her hand with the bandaged knuckles, rubbing his thumb lightly over the white tape. When he released her, she recognized the remote, controlled look as the same one he'd possessed at the Marshals Office in Portland. That had been less than two weeks ago, but somehow her life had changed fundamentally since then.

He opened a cupboard and set a bottle of pain reliever on the counter. "Take two."

"I will after dinner."

"Don't wait and let the pain set in."

"It's not that bad, Sam. A few small cuts, that's all."

Her comment seemed to light a fuse. "Fuck that. A flashbang all but blew up in your face, and you're damned lucky if you come out of this with no hearing loss. You've been cut by flying glass, and you've lost blood. You were hurt because you're my fiancée."

"Fake fiancée."

His gaze flashed, and she suddenly realized that the remote look wasn't due to lack of emotion but was a means to mask that he was feeling too much. "The guy who hurt you sees you as my fiancée, so the distinction is irrelevant."

"Okay." She cleared her throat, not sure how to deal with him in this kind of mood. Add in that he was doing a good impression of truly caring about her, and heat began coursing through her from her cheeks to low in her belly, dispelling any chill she might have felt earlier. "Um, the soup shouldn't take too long to heat if you're hungry."

He stepped back and filled a glass with water, and then shook two tablets from the pain medication bottle. He handed her both.

"Thanks, Dad."

"Take them, Eleanor."

She rolled her eyes but swallowed the pills.

"There enough soup for your team?"

"Why? Are they coming over?"

"I've called a meeting."

"Oh, good idea. We should make sure everyone is working with the same information, such as it is." She lifted the lid on the pot to find the tortilla soup beginning to simmer. "I'll text Seth. He and Bella can pick up tacos or something to go with the soup. This won't stretch to five people."

Linc came in while Ellie was finishing her message to Seth. She dug up a cheese grater and a block of Monterey Jack cheese and handed them to her brother.

Sam set bowls on the counter and Ellie opened a bag of tortilla chips. About thirty minutes later the dogs alerted them that someone was at the back door. Sam let in Seth and Bella who carried bags of tacos and a six-pack of beer.

When she entered the kitchen, Bella wrapped Ellie in a hug. "Are you okay, friend?"

She returned the embrace. "I'm fine. Sam is more upset about all this than I am."

"Of course he is. A man wants to protect his fiancée, even if she's a temporary fiancée."

Bella released her and Ellie felt Seth behind her. She turned and he took a long minute to study her appearance before opening his arms. Ellie stepped into the embrace to rest her head on his shoulder and felt some of the tension drain from her body.

Her eldest brother had always been her rock, had always looked out for her, and had always understood her. He pressed a kiss to her temple before letting her go.

"I'm fine, Seth."

"You will be." He stepped back and addressed the group. "Let's take a breather. We need a minute to be glad we're all here and that the injuries Ellie sustained are minimal. Talk about the investigation can wait until after we've eaten."

Ellie caught the unguarded expression on Bella's face as she watched Seth, and not for the first time wished her friend wasn't so determined to keep her feelings for Seth to herself. Ellie had broached the subject once and the pain on Bella's face had forced her to back off.

Ellie ladled soup into bowls while Linc sprinkled on the shredded cheese, then took the bowls to the table. She found a big basket in a cupboard and filled it with tortilla chips. Tacos were distributed, beer passed out, and everyone sat around the table to dig in.

Conversation flowed, tacos and soup were consumed with compliments to the chef, and with Cleo settled at her feet under the table, Ellie finally let herself relax.

The man sitting beside her, however, emanated tension.

Sam's participation in the conversation was minimal, she'd caught him more than once drumming his fingers on the side of his beer bottle, and a glance at his face showed a muscle twitching in his jaw. Having someone attack your home had to elicit a range of emotions. She'd cut him some slack. This type of thing happened in her world, not his.

When everyone had finished eating, Ellie rose to gather dishes to take into the kitchen. Sam followed her carrying empty beer bottles.

"Ellie."

Bent over the dishwasher, she glanced up at the serious tone.

"I don't want to blindside you."

She straightened and braced herself. That could only mean bad news. "What are you talking about?"

"I called your team over because I'm asking Seth to reassign you. I no longer want to act like we're a couple."

"You can't do that."

"I can and I will. I'm sorry, but this isn't working out."

She jerked back as if he'd slapped her, and she wouldn't have been any less surprised if he had. "What about my assignment isn't working out? My job is to protect you while I keep my eyes open to find who's threatening you and I've been doing that."

He held himself stiffly, eyes hooded and his expression once again austere. "I'll explain myself to all of you together. I wanted to give you the courtesy of telling you before then."

"You know what you can do with your courtesy."

"Ellie." Seth stood in the open doorway.

"What? Did you know about this?"

"No, but I'm not surprised."

"Why? What do you know?"

"Let's hear what Sam has to say before we parse it out."

Furious, she stalked past her brother. She joined Linc on the loveseat, crossing her arms over her chest.

"What's going on?" Linc asked.

Seth came in to sit beside Bella, and Sam crossed to the cold fireplace, standing with his back to the room.

"I have no idea. Ask Judge Creed."

Sam turned to face them, dark brows lowered. "I want to change our arrangement. Presenting Ellie as my fiancée while we try to draw out the person threatening me isn't working."

"What the hell?" This came from Linc. "It is working. You've successfully established your cover. The two incidents here at the house are escalation."

"Escalation? I found enough C-four on my car to blow me to kingdom come weeks ago. How is making a mess in my yard and a flashbang an escalation?"

"Because we're dealing with two different people," Linc stated.

Sam frowned. "Explain."

"That's the conclusion we've come to. The emailed threats and the C-four are separate from the mess in your yard, which we think is connected to the flashbang."

"You're sure about this?"

Linc nodded. "While you were in here getting El bandaged up, I conferenced with Seth and Bella. Our conclusion is the only explanation that makes sense. The emails and the C-four? Those are cold and unemotional. The truck destroying your lawn, and then a guy breaking a window and lobbing in a flashbang device? That's in your face, and it's personal. The first person probably doesn't have a direct connection to you, the second likely does."

Sam shook his head. "Okay, fine. We're looking for two people. That doesn't change my decision."

Ellie put a hand on her stomach to quiet the jumping nerves. She hoped the feeling was contained to today's incident, and that it had nothing to do with memories of when a younger Sam Creed had also disappeared from her life.

She controlled her voice to keep her tone level. "I don't get it. As Linc said, we've established ourselves as a happily engaged couple to your family, neighbors, and the people at the courthouse. What's changed?"

"You were hurt," Bella observed.

Ellie rubbed her thumb between her brows, suddenly glad Sam had insisted she take the pain meds. Without them the headache she was sporting would be worse. "So? I'm not badly hurt."

"You could have been." Sam's quiet voice had her turning to stare at him.

"Is that what this is about, that I was hurt?"

"We didn't think through the risk you'd be taking. You were hurt because someone wants to get at me. What if they decide that the best way to do that is through you? I don't want you to be a target."

"You may not have thought it through, but the team has. I was aware of the risk when I took this assignment. I'm a Deputy US Marshal. I'm trained for exactly this type of situation. Have some respect. You can't pull me off the job because you don't want me hurt. It's not appropriate, and you don't have that authority."

"It's not a matter of respect, and, like it or not, you need my cooperation for our fake relationship to work."

"It's all about respect. If Linc had been assigned to protect you and was hurt, would you want him pulled off the job?"

"That's ridiculous and not the point."

"It's exactly the point. You feel guilty because I got a few scratches. You may not notice it, but I'm constantly monitoring your situation. You need a person close to you to be on guard. You're a federal judge and it's my job as a US Marshal to protect you. If you take me out or choose not to cooperate, you leave yourself wide open and vulnerable. Is that what you want?"

"If that's the only alternative, then yes."

She threw up her hands in frustration. "You're not only ridiculous, you're irrational."

Seth held up a warning hand to Ellie. "Sam, let's talk. Outside."

Ellie surged to her feet. "No way. You two aren't working it out between you. I have a right to defend my job. I haven't done a damned thing wrong."

Seth shook his head. "I'm talking with him alone."

She knew when Seth got his I'm-the-boss look. Even an edict from heaven wouldn't budge him.

"Don't you dare sell me out, Seth Jameson."

# Chapter Thirteen

Seth and Sam went through the kitchen and mudroom, and out the back door, taking Cleo and Tony with them.

Ellie's anger vibrated through her body, looking for an outlet. She eyed Linc poking at his phone. He was probably texting Mikayla.

"Don't even think about it." He hadn't even looked at her.

"Too late." She kicked his foot from where it was resting on his knee.

"Is this you being a mature adult, Eleanor? You know it never ends well when you pick a fight with me."

"I can take you. I've done it before."

"You've never taken me." He held up his hand when she opened her mouth. "And the time when I had mono doesn't count, because I had *mono*."

She always hated it when Linc was right. But she didn't really want to fight with him when fighting with Sam would be so much more satisfying.

She wheeled around to stare out the window. Maybe she could sneak outside and spy on them. A glance at Bella had her checking the impulse.

"You're sitting there grinning like the damned Cheshire cat. I'd think you would be on my side about this."

"I am on your side. Sam should treat you as a professional, even if his personal feelings get in the way. You can trust Seth. He won't pull you from your assignment." She shrugged. "But still, I understand why Sam wants you off the case. I think it's sweet."

Before Ellie could ask Bella to explain, the back door opened and the dogs rushed in ahead of the two men, neither gave much away by their expressions.

Seth tipped his head to her. "Sam's agreed that we keep the situation as it is. The local PD will increase patrols in this area, and we'll check in with each other regularly. You're to take precautions to remain safe."

She nodded, relief flooding through her, Sam's blank expression telling her clearly the conversation hadn't gone the way he'd wanted.

\*\*\*

Sam crossed the hall from the bathroom to his bedroom. He glanced at Ellie's closed door. Maybe she was still awake. He owed her an explanation for trying to get her assignment pulled, not that he was willing to go there. And he wasn't apologizing, either. Which led to the question of why he was standing outside her door with his fist raised to knock. Seth had figured out Sam's issue and that was bad enough. He lowered his hand. What he really wanted was to talk to her, make sure she was okay, get her to dial back on being pissed at him.

A thud sounded from the first floor. Sam's first instinct was to grab his shotgun and confront any new danger. But Ellie had called him out on respect for her job as a marshal, and she'd been right to do that. He knocked softly, then opened her door and flipped on the light. Her bed was empty.

He crept down the stairs, keeping to the outer edge of the treads to avoid the ones that squeaked. The dogs weren't barking, a good sign. But given everything that had happened, noises in the night made him more than a little cautious.

He cut through the living room. Light shone around the library door, which stood slightly ajar. He pushed it open. Ellie stood with her back to him, using a broom to sweep glass into a pile.

"Don't do that."

She ignored him in keeping with what she'd been doing for most of the evening since her team had left.

He brought a hand down on her shoulder. In a single, smooth movement she dropped the broom and whipped around with her elbow aiming for his face. He lurched back and she missed giving him a broken nose by a scant inch. Her eyes widened and she pulled wireless earbuds from her ears.

"Good way to find yourself flattened, Creed."

"What are you doing in here?"

She looked at the broom and back at him. "Sweeping?"

He tensed his jaw and felt his molars grinding. "You don't need to. I have a lady who cleans for me. I'll call her in the morning and she'll take care of it."

The room looked like a tornado had spun through it and had him clenching his jaw against the surge of anger. That Ellie had been through that tornado only magnified the anger.

Her hair was piled in a messy bun. She still wore his sweatshirt, which hung below her hips, and fatigue lined her eyes. Not for the first time did he wish things were different between them, that he had the right to pull her into his arms and simply hold her.

Seth had done that, and Sam had found himself jealous of the close bond between the siblings.

"So now she won't have to sweep up this glass."

"Neither should you. You should be in bed."

"What's with you acting like I'm a child who needs to be told to go to bed or to take her medicine?"

"Christ, Ellie. I don't think you're a child."

"Okay, then a woman who can't make her own decisions or do her job."

He pinched the bridge of his nose and wished he'd ignored the thud and gone to bed. "Let's focus on what's going on right now. Why are you cleaning in here instead of getting some sleep?"

"Because there's glass all over the floor. Because I'm too wound up to sleep and needed something to do. Why don't you go away and leave me alone?"

He should do exactly that, but he was an idiot. He bent to retrieve the broom, but she grabbed it before he could and held it out of reach. "Oh no you don't. I'm going to sweep and finish the podcast I was listening to."

"Why do you have to be so difficult?"

"Difficult? I'm being difficult? You bastard." The snarled words hung in the air as she tossed the broom back on the floor and stepped toward him, eyes blazing like blue lightning.

Okay, wrong thing to say. Again.

"You question my competence, my ability to do my job, and now you want to pat me on the head and tell me to go to bed? You act like a condescending chauvinist, and I'm the one being difficult?"

His own temper spiked. "I never questioned your ability to do your job. That was your assumption."

She waited a beat. "That's all you've got? No explanation, nothing other than to say I'm making assumptions and you expect me to walk away from my assignment because you've got a burr up your butt about it? That's the way you work, Creed, not me. I don't walk away from people. And I don't lie to them."

He narrowed his eyes. "What's that supposed to mean? When have I lied or walked away from you?"

She stepped back and he could see shutters slamming down over her eyes. "Never mind."

He caught her arm and pulled her toward him. "Tell me."

"Why? It's not like we've ever been honest with each other."

He stared at her as a shadow of memory surfaced. "We met before."

She pulled free of his hold. "Forget it, Creed. I'm done here. You can deal with the glass."

He didn't let go. "Tell me, Eleanor."

She rounded on him and hissed the words. "Get your hand off me, or you're going to find yourself on the floor."

She had moves, he was sure of it, but he didn't think she'd be able to take him down. Still, he released her and backed up a step. "Okay, I've let go. But I'd still like an explanation. Where did we meet before?"

She moved farther away from him like space would be enough of a barrier between them. Whatever was going on in her head played out on her face as a war of indecision. "Fine, I'll tell you." She crossed her arms across her stomach. "We met thirteen years ago at U of O, at a party at your place."

He shook his head. "At my place? We didn't have many parties."

"You had at least one. My friend talked me into going. I was a sophomore and you were a law student. You and I talked, got a little tipsy. Flirted."

The memory slammed into him. The music, the smart, funny girl, the instant connection, then... "Shit."

"Yeah, shit. After, you asked for my number, said you knew a great place to get Thai food. Made a big deal that you'd call. But I never heard from you again." She puffed out a breath. "Let's just say my first and last hookup was a good lesson for me."

"There was more going on than that."

"It doesn't matter anymore. You got what you wanted that evening, and I learned a lot."

She turned and walked out of the room.

***

After a night of tossing and turning, Ellie dragged herself out of bed to tug on her workout clothes. She'd do her job if it killed her. She descended the back stairs to the kitchen to find Sam leaning against the counter, not in exercise gear, but sipping from a steaming mug, his hair mussed like he'd rolled out of bed five minutes ago.

"I'm ready to go." Cleo sniffed her shoes and gave her a doggie grin while wagging her tail. Ellie crouched down to pet her. Tony remained on his cushion, nose on his paws. She gave Sam a side look and found him watching her.

Telling Sam of their shared past had been a mistake, mostly because he'd hurt her all those years ago, and that made her feel vulnerable now. Vulnerability was one of her least favorite emotions.

"I can see that. But you're not going running until you've had a doctor clear you."

"I really don't like you making decisions for me."

"I'm not making decisions for you. You've already been hurt because of me. I don't want to make it any worse."

"I wasn't hurt because of you. I was hurt because a horrible person threw a rock and a flashbang into the house."

Denial was written clearly on his face, but he shrugged. "I want to explain why I didn't call you."

"Really? After thirteen years, now you want to explain? You could have called me. You didn't. No big deal. Can we leave it?"

"No."

She rubbed a fist on her forehead, then held up a hand. This was too much before she was caffeinated. "Right, whatever. But not one more word until I've consumed at least a quarter cup of coffee. No, make that half."

He poured coffee into a mug and handed it to her, then set the dog dishes on the counter to feed them. Ellie wrapped her hands around her mug, closed her eyes and breathed in the coffee. It took almost a full ten minutes before she felt like her belly had warmed and the synapses were firing in her brain.

Sam leaned against the counter, arms crossed over his chest, gaze on her.

"You may speak."

"The morning after we met at that party, I got a call that Jane, Drew's mom, was back in the hospital. She'd been diagnosed with ovarian cancer two months before, but the disease had already spread to her liver and lungs. Surgery and radiation hadn't helped. She died that week."

"Oh, Sam, that's horrible. No wonder you didn't call back."

Back then, she'd imagined he'd been in a car crash and suffered from amnesia, or had lost her number and searched but been unable to find her. Eventually, she'd stopped fooling herself and accepted that he simply hadn't felt the connection, and acting interested had been all about getting in her pants.

To learn that his family had been in crisis gave her an entirely different perspective.

"I took almost a month's leave from law school to help at home. Drew was a wreck, and Dad wasn't much better. His way of coping was to work from sunup to sundown and make everyone else do the same. When I got back to the university, I was buried in work trying to make up for lost time, and I still drove home every weekend." His gaze held hers. "I'm sorry."

"Wow, that's a lot. I'm glad you told me. It stung at the time, but I moved on."

He held her gaze. "Another confession. I've got feelings for you."

"Huh?" She couldn't have heard him right. She bobbled her mug and set it on the counter before she dropped it.

"You heard me. You walked into that room at the Marshals Office and I felt like I'd taken a hit to the gut. Nothing that's happened since has diminished that sensation. These feelings have been totally unexpected and, honestly, unwanted. They've complicated things. I'm having a hard time negotiating that on top of you being assigned to protect me. The deal breaker was you getting hurt in the process."

She tapped a fist over her heart to get it beating again, and when it did, Ellie was sure Sam could hear it thudding heavily in her chest.

He gave a self-deprecating laugh. "I've shocked you. That's something at least." He checked the clock on the wall. "I need to shower and get going. I have a breakfast meeting with another judge this morning. Can you call your team if you need a ride anywhere?"

"Ah, sure."

"Good. I'll be out of here in twenty minutes."

She stared at his back as he climbed the stairs.

That was it? *I've got feelings for you. Not only that, but those feelings are annoying and they complicate things. And, by the way, I've got a breakfast meeting so find your own ride.*

He hadn't asked if those pesky feelings of his were reciprocated, and he didn't seem to care how she felt about any of what he'd told her.

She stabbed her fingers through her hair to hold on to her head so that when it exploded, she could keep the pieces together.

Pipes clanked as the water was turned on upstairs. Learning that he'd had a damn good reason not to call her all those years ago might ease the lingering resentment she'd held on to, but it also made one of the reasons she'd fought against her own feelings no longer valid. Talk about complicated.

She refilled her mug and forced herself to slow her coffee intake and try to settle herself. Why hadn't he kept that little tidbit to himself so she could go on thinking he was a jerk who'd tried to get her pulled from her assignment? He'd still wanted her reassigned, but his confession lowered him on the jerk scale.

Damn him. He had to go ahead and admit to *feelings* like she'd know what to do about them.

She stomped up the stairs, bringing her mug with her. She'd gained the landing when Sam opened the bathroom door and stepped out. With his black hair combed back from his forehead, he wore nothing but a low-slung pair of flannel pants that showcased the V-shaped muscles cradling ripped abs. That his body wound her up didn't help her situation one bit. She'd had enough.

"What the hell, Sam?"

"What the hell what?"

"You 'shared' you've got feelings for me, which, by the way, you're not happy about. You don't ask what I think about that, or if I have any feelings of my own. And now you're happy to walk around half naked?"

"I'm walking from the bathroom to my bedroom where I plan to get dressed. The important parts are covered." He narrowed his eyes. "But tell me about those feelings you have for me."

His step toward her could only be described as predatory.

A warning signal echoed in her brain and nerves were making her jittery. "Never mind. I've changed my mind. I don't want to tell you."

"Oh no you don't. You started it."

He reached out to take her mug and set it on the little Duncan Phyfe table against the wall. He checked her instinctive step back by catching her hands in his.

"What are you doing?"

"What do you think I'm doing? I'm keeping you from running away so you can tell me about those feelings you mentioned."

"I wasn't running. Implementing a little self-preservation."

"You can trust me, Ellie. I hurt you before, but not with intent, and I'm sorry about that."

"It doesn't matter," she muttered.

"It does." She couldn't look away from the intensity of his gaze. "What are your feelings for me?"

It took her a long time to respond, and she felt like her heart was lodged in her throat. If he could be honest about his emotions, so could she. She took a breath and pushed back against the anxiety that had panic tickling in the back of her throat.

"It's hard for me to admit, Sam, but I like you a lot, and I'm really worried that 'like' could turn into something more."

He nodded. "I get that, because it's the same for me. All I can see is you."

Her breath hitched. "Jesus. I don't know if I'm ready for this."

He flashed a wicked grin that had her sucking in a breath. Those little corner lifts of his mouth had whetted her appetite, and his full smile was worth the wait. "I'm not sure I'm ready, either. Only way to figure it out is to move forward."

Amusement vanished, and his gray eyes took on a smoky color as he closed the space between them. She was sure there were a dozen reasons why they shouldn't be standing this close together, but she couldn't think of one. He dipped his head and murmured against her lips, "No one's watching, Eleanor. This one's for us."

Their fingers entwined and his lips caught hers in a kiss that brought an instant wave of warmth, and a spike to her blood pressure. His mouth on hers, their breaths mingling, and the feeling that she could spend the next several hours happily doing this made her yearn for more. His tongue swept into her mouth and he tasted of mint toothpaste.

He released her hands to grip her hips and bring her snug against him, heat to heat. Ever since that first morning when she'd seen him shirtless, she'd wanted her hands on him. Now she gave in to the desire and laid her palms flat against his chest, and when she stroked, she felt the strong beat of his heart beneath her fingers.

At least she wasn't the only one affected. He speared his fingers through her hair, and when they brushed against the bandage behind her ear, he broke the kiss to lay his lips lightly over it. "It kills me that you were hurt." The soft words were barely audible.

He moved his mouth along the column of her throat and nudged her chin up to allow him better access. She shivered as her nervous system went on overload. She decided his kisses provided a better morning pickup than the strongest coffee.

She took her turn nuzzling his neck where warm skin smelled of soap from his shower. Trailing down, her tongue explored the hollow between his collarbone and neck, and his breath grew heavier.

They were locked against each other center to center, and it was hard to miss his arousal. She rubbed against his erection and murmured, "How badly do you want to go to your breakfast meeting?"

He groaned deep in his throat and she had to lock her knees to keep them holding her up. There were reasons she and Sam shouldn't do what they were thinking about doing, but she put a block on that part of her brain. Then with one last open-mouth kiss, he gripped her shoulders and took a step back.

She couldn't miss the regret on his face.

"I guess the answer to that is pretty badly." She tried to make her tone light, but it came out sounding hesitant.

He rested his forehead against hers and seemed to struggle to control his breathing until, with a sigh, he straightened. "It's not that simple, Ellie. You already think I don't value you as a marshal because you're female. I'm not reinforcing that belief by taking advantage of you living in my home."

"Is it taking advantage if I want it, too?"

"Right now, yes."

# Chapter Fourteen

Despite feeling unsettled, Ellie spent a productive morning. Cleo and Tony kept her company while she finished the final report for an investigation she'd concluded the previous month. Next, she began whittling down a long list of emails, enjoying one from Mikayla with a picture of the mop-haired Labradoodle she and Linc had adopted. A call from Seth provided her another avenue to investigate their father's recent movements so she spent an hour delving into online forums frequented by right-wing militia types, digging deeper when she found reference to both Judge Creed and Frank Bannister.

Her phone buzzing broke her concentration. A glance at the caller ID had her smiling. She swiped the screen to answer the phone. "Sam."

"Ellie." His low voice reverberated in her ear and all the emotions of that morning came crashing back. Tension crackled through the connection. "Can you make a doctor's appointment at one?"

She'd forgotten about the directive Ben had issued the night before. "I don't need to go to the doctor. I don't even have a headache."

"Good, then the doctor will clear you with no problem. She's a friend of Ben's and, as a favor to him, is giving up half of her lunch hour to see you."

"Way to put on the pressure, Judge Creed. I'll call Seth and see if he can give me a ride."

"I'm going with you. I'm done with court, and I cleared my calendar for the rest of the day. I'll be home at noon."

"You know, I can't figure out if you're playing the concerned fiancée role really well, or if you like managing people."

"Let's keep it simple. This is me caring about you, but tangled up with it is that you got hurt because of me."

"You've got to let that go. It wasn't your fault."

"You being cleared by the doctor will help."

"Fine." A question had been niggling at her, so she voiced it. "Tell me, how did Seth convince you not to break up with me, I mean, convince you to keep up the fiancée pretense?"

"I'm not going there."

"Why? Is it a secret?"

"Leave it, Eleanor. I'll see you around noon."

\*\*\*

Hours later, after an all-clear from Ben's friend, Eleanor sat beside Sam in the Land Cruiser. They'd turned onto the street that led over the river and then home. She shifted to look at him. "Take me to where you were parked when you found the C-four on your car."

He gave her a considering gaze, nodded, and drove to a dead-end road where a couple of cars were parked. He pulled off the pavement and parked the Land Cruiser in a dirt area.

"This is it."

She looked around at what appeared to be an informal parking area. There were no neighboring homes or businesses, and no trees or brush to provide cover for someone attaching explosives to a vehicle. "What day of the week was that?"

"Sunday. I found the explosive when I returned from my run, which was before seven a.m."

"Did you habitually run here weekend mornings?"

"Not always, but frequently."

"Who would be familiar with your routine?"

"Anyone who paid attention." He opened the door. "Let's walk."

They took a worn path, the sound of the river reaching her before she saw it. They came to a paved walkway, and a sign said "River Parkway." It followed the Umatilla as it rushed over boulders, then slowed to form swirling eddies and dark pools. Deciduous trees along the banks showed bright fall colors and the autumn sun reflected off the water.

Ellie took a deep breath as the breeze carried the damp smell of the river. She zipped her jacket and tugged her beanie to cover her ears. The temperature didn't feel like it had warmed above fifty, and a stiff breeze chilled her cheeks. Despite that, she enjoyed the weather. "This is really nice. Cold, but nice."

"Yeah."

His distracted tone had her studying him. She didn't bother fighting the pull of attraction. Faded blue jeans encased his long legs, and he had his hands buried deep in the pockets of his forest green wool coat. His brows were drawn low over smokey gray eyes, and a muscle worked in his jaw. What she had to tell him wasn't going to improve his mood.

"Sam, we're looking at Drew for the threats against you."

He stopped to face her. "We've talked about this. It's not him."

"Why do you think that?"

Emotion crossed his face, then was blanked out. "Drew's writing skills are poor. He struggled all through school with a learning disability. That's not reflected in those emails."

"He could be working with someone. In fact, it's likely there's a conspiracy. We've found evidence that links him with SecAm." She hesitated, then went on. "There was a video posted showing a group of heavily armed people, many with illegal weapons, standing around a bonfire. They'd read pages from books, mostly by liberal historians or politicians, then throw the books into the fire while giving the Nazi salute. Drew was one of the participants."

His scowl deepened the lines on either side of his mouth. "I'll ask him about it, but he didn't send the emails."

"Please don't talk to him yet. We don't want to tip our hand. I'm only telling you because he's your brother."

"What do you mean, tip your hand? What are you doing?"

"We're conducting an investigation. There's no doubt Drew is connected to the militia, but whether he has threatened you is unclear. If he is innocent, as you claim, the best way to prove that is to let us do our job so we can find the true culprit."

He ran a hand through his hair, then gave a curt nod.

"You going to tell me how Seth talked you into keeping up the fiancée pretense?" She asked the question to try to lighten the mood, but Sam gave a frustrated sigh.

"The bastard blackmailed me."

"How'd he do that?"

"By being more perceptive than I gave him credit for. He figured out that my concern was for your safety and inferred that I may be developing a thing for you."

He'd said as much that morning, but that didn't stop her heart from doing a slow somersault in her chest at his admission.

"Oh."

"Yeah, oh. The blackmail was sneaky. He said if you got pulled from your current job that you'd go back to your original assignment, which had been to send you undercover to infiltrate a militia group."

"That's hardly blackmail. That had been the plan before I was assigned to be your girlfriend. I was getting friendly with a biker dude who's a member of SecAm. He has an online dating profile and we'd been flirting back and forth."

"You're my fiancée, not my girlfriend, and I didn't like that plan."

She nodded slowly, frowning. "Sometimes my job involves undercover work."

"It's fucking dangerous."

"It can be, but we mitigate the risk as best we can. Regardless, I think Seth was jerking your chain. We'd already decided not to go forward with that plan. There's too much risk that we could cross paths with Richard Jameson. That would have been dangerous and would've jeopardized our entire mission."

He grunted.

They returned to the car and, by unspoken agreement, checked for explosives. Satisfied there were no bombs, they got in and he started the car and pulled onto the street. He glanced at his watch, then said, "Dalia, the woman who cleans my house, is coming in to clean the library. What do you say we get some takeout for an early dinner? There's a Mediterranean place that has good falafel. We can pick up enough for her, too."

"Sounds good."

They arrived home thirty minutes later, passing an aged Honda SUV on the driveway to park in the garage. They walked into the kitchen carrying loaded bags with the dogs trailing behind them. Ellie wasn't sure what she expected Sam's cleaning lady to look like, maybe someone sturdy and middle-aged, but certainly not the petite twenty-something with a fall of black hair and gorgeous dark eyes that met them with a smile.

"Hi, Sam. Good timing, I just finished." She spotted Ellie and her smile widened. "You must be Rachel. I missed you last week. I'm Dalia. Ben told me about your engagement. Congratulations to both of you."

Since it appeared that Ben had kept their secret, Ellie said, "Thank you, it's nice to meet you."

Sam held out a bag. "This is for you and the boys."

"You didn't need to do that."

"You made time in your schedule to come out here today, so you earned it."

Dalia took the bag and opened it. "Since you got them gyros, it's hard to say no. Thanks."

Sam's tone changed. "You doing okay?"

Dalia raised shadowed eyes, her smile dimming. "I'm fine. I saw the lawyer you recommended and she's starting the divorce proceedings."

"It's the right thing to do."

"It is. But Rudy is the boys' father, and that makes it hard. But I have to move ahead." She glanced at Ellie. "I apologize for talking about something you wouldn't know about. Sam sentenced my husband to prison and we've been friends ever since."

"That had to be…unusual," Ellie half stuttered.

"For other judges, maybe, but not for Judge Creed. Sam does a lot behind the scenes for people who need help."

He glanced at Ellie. "Dalia is a member of my tribe."

"Did you know each other before the trial?" she asked.

"Not really. I knew who she was, but that was about it."

"But now we're friends." She held up the bag. "Thanks for this. My boys will enjoy their dinner. I'll be in as usual on Thursday. Nice to meet you, Rachel."

Dalia retrieved her belongings from the mudroom and left through the back door.

"I feel like there's an entire episode of *Law and Order* there."

Sam gave his half smile. "Good observation. Rudy was involved in drug trafficking, then upped the stakes when he tried smuggling guns into Canada. Dalia and the boys are better off without him."

"You're looking out for her."

He shrugged. "She's Umatilla."

"You're a good man, Sam Creed."

\*\*\*

Sam stood at the kitchen window, staring into the gathering darkness beyond the glass. The previous week, a crew had replaced his cameras and installed new ones with infrared as well as recording capability. Every member of the US Marshal team had access to the app and helped monitor his property, and still they hadn't been able to identify the guy who'd thrown the flashbang into his house. The cameras made him feel hemmed in, like his life wasn't his own, but until they caught the person threatening him, both he and Ellie were safer.

Gumbie rubbed against his leg and he reached down to pick up the cat and scratch her head.

He wanted to go for a run or to the gym in town and work out. He needed to do something to ease the restlessness plaguing him. But if he went out he could count on Ellie coming with him, and since he attributed more than half of his restlessness to his insane attraction to her, that wouldn't solve his problem.

He also suffered from frustration on top of the restlessness, and that had to do with his brother. When he'd left the courthouse the night before, Sam had walked to the parking lot to find Drew waiting for him, leaning against the Land Cruiser, his behavior the usual mix of insolence and bitterness.

*"I need a loan, Sam."*

That same stab of anger and frustration that almost choked him whenever he and Drew talked felt like a red-hot knife in his gut.

*"What are we talking about, a few hundred or a few thousand?"*

His brother's pale blue eyes had burned with resentment. *"I shouldn't even have to ask. You're holding on to money Dad left for me."*

*"You know the terms of the will. Dad worked his ass off for that money, and he didn't want you to waste it. He wanted you to use it for something that would help you get ahead."*

*"What, like going to college like my big brother? Is that what he wanted?"*

*"You could go to community college to learn business management so you could take over the ranch."*

*"You're forgetting one little fact."* Drew's face had twisted into a sneer. *"You inherited the ranch, not me. I worked like a slave for years on that place, fucking gave my life to it. In the end the old man didn't see me as his true son. You got the ranch and I got shit."*

*"If you gave any indication that you could manage the ranch, I'd deed you half right now. I've told you that."*

*"I don't want your fucking charity."*

*"You just asked me for a fucking loan."* Sam had forced himself to reel in the anger. Yelling at Drew would hardly solve their problems.

*"You won't give me what's rightfully mine? Fine. But I want a loan against that money. You owe me that much."*

*"No, I don't. I'm not giving you anything."*

They'd had variations on that conversation a dozen times and it always ended the same. Last evening had been no different. Drew had stormed off, anger evident in his stomping feet and the slammed door of his truck. He'd sped up the street, the truck fishtailing until he gained control.

Sam had the fleeting thought that he should give Drew the money and be done with it. He'd spend it on whatever it was he'd wanted the loan for, but unless Sam also gave him a share of the ranch, Drew would be back to repeat the same scenario once the cash was gone. Despite Sam's issues with Joss Creed, he knew his dad left his estate the way he had because in his own way he'd loved Drew and wanted what was best for him.

The click of the dogs' toenails on the wood floor had him looking over his shoulder. Cleo and Tony came in the room ahead of Ellie. He swallowed convulsively, then had to rap his fist on his chest as he coughed.

Endless legs were covered by second-skin leggings and fed the constant fantasy of her wrapping those legs around his hips. Naked. They'd both have to be naked for that.

An extra sledgehammer of lust hit him when he took in the white tank top folded up to expose a creamy stretch of skin covering her firm abdominal muscles. The top also showcased toned arms and shoulders, and her deliciously rounded breasts he itched to get his hands on.

All the edginess of living with her coalesced into a powerful desire he could barely control. He grabbed for the counter to keep from acting on his impulses.

"Hey, can you replace the bandages? They got wet in the shower." Ellie's voice was muffled as she craned her neck to look over her shoulder. "I got the one on my hand but can't see to do the ones behind my ear and my back."

"Jesus Christ, Ellie. Why didn't you ask for help? The doctor today told you to keep the bandages dry. Ben told you to keep them dry. You should have listened." Anger was a much safer emotion than lust.

"Desire for a shower surpassed concern over wet bandages."

She turned and pulled the long fall of blonde hair over her shoulder to give him a clear look at the wound behind her ear. That she also exposed the long column of her neck provided yet one more distraction. She smelled like her soap, fresh and faintly citrusy. He raised hands that weren't entirely steady to peel off the wet bandage behind her ear.

"The butterfly strips are holding, so I'm leaving those." He pressed a square of gauze over the strips and applied tape. It took all his willpower not to bury his nose in the warm skin at the nape of her neck and breathe her in.

He motioned her across the room, flipped on the light over the table, and sat in one of the chairs. "Stand in front of me and I'll take care of the cut on your back."

Some of what he was feeling must have been communicated to her because for one hot second their gazes clashed and the temperature in the room spiked. She moved to stand between his knees with her back to him while he peeled off the wet bandage.

He cleared his throat. "Color is healthy, looks like it's healing."

"That's good." Her breathy tone didn't do anything to cool him off.

His hands spanned her waist as he pressed tape around the clean gauze. The wound was covered, the bandage secure, and yet his hands stayed on the warm skin, his thumbs rubbing slowly. She looked over her shoulder and this time when their gazes clashed, neither looked away. Slowly, she turned under his hands and, without breaking eye contact, straddled him to sit on his lap.

He closed his eyes as all the blood drained from his head to pool in his groin.

Her breath was warm against his ear when she whispered, "This is a time-out. I'm declaring myself officially off duty."

# Chapter Fifteen

Any hold he had on sanity was slipping away. He opened his eyes to stare into the depthless blue of hers. "There are reasons."

"They don't count during a time-out." She nipped his earlobe and his control snapped with an audible crack.

Her lips hovered over his, and he used his hands on her back to push her closer.

Their lips met with an intensity that told him this time neither of them was holding back. Blood heating to boil, he took what she offered in that kiss. Lust, like, love—whatever had been building between them flared with every touch, every murmured word, every sigh. He pulled on her top, mindful of the injury to her back, reluctantly releasing her lips so he could tug the shirt over her head. Her hand fisted in his hair when he used his nose to push aside the cup of her bra.

"God, you're beautiful." His words were spoken with a hushed reverence as he buried his face in her breasts. He cupped one, then the other, nuzzling with his nose until pressing his lips to the deep valley between them. She threw her head back when he used the flat of his tongue to circle an areola, then her nipple. Her ribs quaked at her sharp intake of breath when he pulled the peak deep into his mouth.

She ground against his erection even as she tugged on the hem of his shirt. He let go of her breast and yanked his shirt over his head, the motion bringing him harder against her. With her heat pressed to his, he swore he could feel warm dampness through the layers of their clothing.

He bit back an oath and rose to his feet, bringing her with him. He wasn't making love with her on a kitchen chair. Deeming the beds upstairs too far away, he headed out of the kitchen. She wrapped her legs around his hips, not naked as in his fantasy, but good enough for now. Once again, her hands were in his hair and she was sliding her fingers through, using the pressure to bring his head up.

With her lips against his, she murmured, "You have the sexiest hair."

"Glad you like it." He boosted her higher, his hands cupping her ass. "Got some weight to you."

"Watch it, buster." She sank her teeth into his neck.

His swore at the jab of pain. "You watch it. I don't do vampires. And I like weight on a woman. Almost as much as I like long legs." He walked them into the shadowy living room, the only light coming from the open door of the kitchen. "Besides, at nearly six foot, you could hardly not have some weight to you."

"You're forgiven," she murmured, running her tongue over what he was sure would be a bite mark. At the moment, he couldn't draw the will to care how that would look on a judge.

He sat on the couch with her still straddling him, and she shimmied down until she was kneeling on the floor between his legs, her hands on the waistband of his workout pants. She rolled down the waistband with an expectant look, like she was unwrapping a birthday present. His erection sprang free and her eyes flashed hungrily.

"Yeah, baby," she murmured.

He'd hardly caught his breath before she'd taken him in her warm, wet mouth, and the incredible surge of pleasure had his eyes rolling straight back in his head. "Oh god."

She worked him with her mouth while her hands cupped and kneaded. He felt like he was charging full tilt to the edge of a cliff. That wonderful mouth of hers continued to tease him until his grip on sanity went slippery.

He reached to pull her up before he plummeted over the edge.

"My turn." He nudged her onto his lap, and with an arm around her waist, shifted so she lay beneath him, pulling a cushion under her head. He rose to shuck his pants, then hers and the sexy little scrap of material that passed for underwear.

He settled between her open legs and took in the glory that was Ellie. She reached for him and he held her off. "Hold still, woman."

"Don't want to hold still. I want you."

"You'll have me. But I get you first."

He started with her toes, nibbling along the arch of her foot, and when she twitched, he grinned. "You're ticklish."

"God, you have a great smile. And to my everlasting shame, yes, I'm ticklish."

He moved to her ankle. "I like ticklish. I'm beginning to think I like everything about you."

"Ticklish is a weakness when one has brothers." Her voice had gone throaty as he slid his tongue along the strong line of her shin and dipped into the hollow at the back of her knees. "Jesus, Creed, you'll bring me to orgasm just licking my knees."

"There's a thought."

While he continued his journey with his mouth, he used his fingers to stroke into the wetness of her, finding what made her moan. He followed his fingers with his lips and tongue.

She clutched his hair tight enough to make him worry that she would leave him with bald patches. He brought her to the brink, heard her breath catch in her throat, then, using tongue and hand, sent her surging over that cliff with a long, keening wail.

He battled back the nearly overwhelming urge to bury himself in her, slowing down to hold her while she came down from the euphoria.

She gave a shivering sigh then reached for him. "Come on, come on. I want you. Now."

Her words fueled his desperation, had it clawing at his throat. He was poised above her when he reared back. "Fuck, fuck, fuck."

"Don't say it, do it."

"I don't have a condom. I mean I do, but not on me. Can you stay like this and I'll be back in thirty seconds? Or twenty, I can make it upstairs and back in twenty seconds."

"You disease free?"

"Yes. You?"

"Yes, and on the pill. You're not going anywhere, big boy."

"Thank god."

She gripped his buttocks and he thrust forward, driving deep. Buried fully, he held himself still, the perfection of the moment coursing through him, etching itself in his mind. She tilted her pelvis and urged him on.

Hands on her breasts, he caught her mouth with his, and they began to move together, slowly at first, then building. The urge was there to let loose and drive blindly into her, but he wanted her with him.

"Again, baby. Again," he coaxed with a whisper in her ear.

He continued to thrust harder, deeper, with more intensity, urging her on, pushing her. Her breath gulped in, then shuddered out, and when once again she was flying apart, he let himself go with her, freefalling over the cliff and not even caring if he crashed.

They lay together, limbs tangled, neither moving. Sam decided breathing was necessary and turned her with him until they lay face-to-face on their sides. She snuggled into him and he wrapped his arms around her to pull her closer. He tugged the throw from the back of the couch to cover them both.

"Much better this time." Her lips moved against his neck as she spoke.

The reminder that this wasn't their first time together had him reaching out an arm to turn on the lamp.

"Why'd you do that?"

"To see you." He brushed hair back from her face. "I was an asshole."

"You were a young hottie and I didn't have anything by way of comparison. Not a good recipe for the perfect sexual encounter."

"You were a virgin?"

She nodded.

"Shit. Did I know that?"

"No. It was a long time ago, and in retrospect, not that big a deal. I shouldn't have said anything."

"Don't let me off so easily. It was a big deal, and I was a self-centered asshole."

She huffed out a breath. "Look, it wasn't for lack of trying on your part. But I was inexperienced, and nervous, and couldn't get there. You were sweet, talked to me. You suggested we could sneak out of the party and walk to a nearby coffee shop."

"But we didn't go to the coffee shop."

"No, I was there with a friend who was more than a little drunk. I didn't want to leave her."

Everything inside him froze, the pleasure from the orgasm evaporating. "You said earlier that you'd been drinking that night."

"I had." Even with the light blocked by the back of the couch, she must have read his expression. "Wait, Sam. Don't go there. I wasn't drunk, and was completely able to give consent."

His shook his head. "I'm sorry. I should have called you."

"I understand why you didn't. It's not an issue anymore."

She made a move to get up and he clicked off the light. "Curtains are open. Let's not give the neighbors a show."

***

Ellie plugged in her phone and crawled into bed. Alone. They'd had phenomenal sex, and things had been good between them after, even including the honest discussion about their first time together. But now the ramifications of what they'd done were beginning to prick her conscience.

Checking in with her team made her feel extra guilty. If Seth knew she and Sam had been together, Seth would yank her from the investigation without a qualm. And rightly so. She'd crossed a line by engaging in a physical relationship with the man it was her job to protect.

Calling a timeout didn't change reality.

Earlier in the evening, still feeling unsettled, she'd sat on one end of the couch with her feet tucked beneath her, absently scanning the news on her iPad. Sam had joined her with his laptop, the horn-rimmed glasses he'd put on to read fanning a hot ember of lust in her belly.

She'd turned blindly to an article on whether the Federal Reserve would raise the prime interest rate and forced herself to read. Dry economic forecasts didn't do a thing to redirect her brain because when she'd looked up again his hair had fallen over his forehead, and she'd had to clench her hands into fists to resist the temptation of running her fingers through that lush thickness.

Determinedly, she'd ducked her head and found another article, this one on Oregon state politics, which was a bit more interesting. Minutes later, she'd glanced up to catch Sam's gaze on her, his expression difficult to interpret. She'd lifted a brow in question, and he'd shaken his head and turned back to his computer. His posture had gone from relaxed to tense, brows low over his eyes, fingers on his keyboard clicking as he typed. Then he'd risen and, taking his laptop, disappeared into his office. Then she'd gone upstairs.

She flopped back on her pillow. She wouldn't analyze his every mood. If he had regrets or some other problem with their relationship, such as it was, well, he wasn't the only one. What concerned her more was the hunch that he wasn't being entirely forthcoming about the case.

A rumble of conversation had her frowning. She sat up, head cocked, trying to locate the sound, and realized Sam's voice was carrying through the heater ducts. While the words were unintelligible, the angry tone was evident. She slipped out of bed and opened the door, not making a sound in her stocking feet. She paused at the top of the stairs, then crept down until she reached the bottom step.

Light spilled from the partially open door of Sam's office. He stood facing the darkened window with the phone to his ear, shoulders rigid. Eavesdropping on Sam's conversation felt wrong, but the chance that he might reveal information he'd kept from the investigation overrode her conscience. She moved silently across the floor.

Fury snapped through his voice. "That's bullshit, you know it is. I told you I'm not giving you anything. If you come near her, if she breaks so much as a fingernail because of you, I'll rip you apart. Leave her out of it." He paused, obviously working to measure his tone. "Stop messing with me. You're making a huge mistake. I'll meet you again tomorrow and we'll talk."

She froze in the shadows when he crossed the room to close the door with a firm click. The expression on his face had been one of cold rage. The rumble of his voice followed her as she retreated up the stairs to her room.

Back in bed, she considered what she'd heard. What had he meant by "stop messing with me?" Had he been referring to the email threats? When he'd said to "leave her out of it," had he been referring to Ellie?

Had a threat been directed at her?

*** 

The next morning Ellie rose early, changed into her running gear, and went down the back stairs to the kitchen. A light was burning over the sink. Cleo rose from her cushion, stretching before approaching Ellie, tail wagging. She reached down to rub the dog's head, then picked up the note left on the counter next to the coffee maker.

*Something came up and I had to leave early. Dogs are fed. Talk to you later. Sam*

She stared at the note, her certainty there was something going on with Sam...something he wasn't sharing with her was becoming more than a hunch. What would lead him to betray the trust they'd built? The only answer that seemed to fit was his brother.

Despite their differences, Sam loved Drew and was worried about him. Sam's words from the previous night echoed through her head. Had he been talking to his brother? If so, then he'd lied to her when he'd insisted that Drew couldn't be behind the threats against him.

The light on the coffeemaker was still on, so Ellie poured coffee into a mug, considering her course of action as she sipped the steaming brew. What was Sam willing to sacrifice for the sake of his brother? The sad fact was that nothing in her interactions with Drew, nor what she'd observed between the brothers, made her think Drew shared that family loyalty. Sam had to realize that. God knew she understood what it felt like to be betrayed by someone you loved.

Feeling antsy and already dressed for a run with her holstered gun under her jacket, she retrieved her phone and key and let herself out of the house as the sun was rising. After sending a text to Seth informing him of her intended route, she set out at a steady lope, staying watchful even as an internal debate ping-ponged inside her head.

If she wanted to know what Sam was holding back, she could search his bedroom and office for clues. As a Deputy US Marshal working an investigation that was within her purview. But as a woman in a personal relationship with Sam Creed, searching his personal possessions would be a huge violation of trust.

Which was exactly why there were rules prohibiting that kind of relationship.

Grateful that she'd worn gloves because it was *cold,* she took the same route into town she and Sam had taken their first morning, keeping a wary eye out for anything unusual. Crossing the bridge over the river, a flash of white caught her attention. She paused to look over the swirling tributary.

A beautiful egret waded along the shore with stately elegance, poking its head in the water at studied intervals. She watched the bird until it took flight, then Ellie resumed her run into town.

She passed the parking lot to the courthouse, scanning for but not seeing Sam's Land Cruiser, nor was it at the diner. Transitioning to a cooldown pace, she puffed back up the hill to Sam's house and around the driveway to the back. She opened the back door and let the dogs in ahead of her.

She showered, ate breakfast, texted with Linc, all the while conscious of the time. Once she was sure Sam would be in court, she opened the door to his office. Telling her guilty conscience to shut up, she stepped inside. Desk drawers, filing cabinets, papers stacked on his desk—any of those places might reveal something that would tell her what Sam was hiding.

She sat in the high-backed leather chair behind his desk, running her hands over the smooth armrests, tipping it back with her feet. After ten minutes of procrastinating, she realized she couldn't go any farther. Searching Sam's things was wrong.

Finally, in a decision that made her a good human but not a solid Deputy US Marshal, she rose from the chair and walked out of the room.

# Chapter Sixteen

Ellie trudged the few blocks to Sam's house after taking the double long way around from what she thought of as Marshal Central where she'd met with Seth and Bella. Linc hadn't been there as he was on courthouse duty and had a lunch engagement scheduled with Gordon Finster. She, Seth, and Bella had reviewed the evidence they had in Sam's case, including what Ellie had heard Sam saying over the phone. She'd been ready for the order to search Sam's private possessions, but her brother had surprised her. He'd agreed that cooperation and trust between her and Sam was critical for the mission, and whatever she might find by searching his things wasn't worth sacrificing his faith in her if he found out. Which sounded good, except that Sam didn't have faith in her. If he did, he wouldn't be keeping secrets.

The Land Cruiser rumbled down the driveway as she was digging out her key to unlock the back door. She stood on the stoop to wait for Sam as he parked and secured the garage. The dogs greeted him at the gate with their snuffling woofs.

He came up the walkway and stopped in front of her. He looked tired. The grooves on either side of his mouth had deepened, his hair looked like he'd distractedly run his hands through it, and lines she hadn't noticed before bracketed his eyes. She wondered if he'd actually slept the night before. He carried his suit coat and briefcase and had loosened his tie, the top button on his dark blue dress shirt unbuttoned. She checked the impulse to brush the hair from his forehead, instead turning to push open the door.

They stepped into the house where he disarmed the alarm and she walked ahead of him into the kitchen. She lifted the lid on the slow cooker, the smell of chicken and herbs wafting up with a cloud of steam.

"You made dinner? I thought you didn't like to cook." He came up beside her and bent his head to peer into the pot.

"Cooking may not be my passion, but we have to eat." She worked to keep her tone light. "Thanks to this Crock Pot I found in the back of the cupboard we're having rosemary chicken with red potatoes. The only thing left to prepare is the asparagus."

"That sounds perfect." His mood seemed to lift and his eyes warmed, and they focused on her lips and for a brief moment he swayed toward her like he might kiss her, then checked himself. The air between them crackled, and she couldn't blame the warmth stealing up her cheeks on the steaming pot.

He backed up a step. "I'll get changed and be back down in a minute."

Ellie put her hand to her stomach to calm the nerves. She filled the dog dishes, her movements mechanical. Sam was nothing if not potent. One hot look and he had her all wound up.

He returned to the kitchen. While Sam in a suit had a certain appeal, she liked him in faded jeans and the red and black plaid shirt he wore open over a black t-shirt. His five o'clock shadow made him a little rough around the edges, a look that suited him. Or maybe it suited her.

"Want me to do the asparagus?"

"Sure."

Leaving the slow cooker on warm, she took a seat at the table, determined to act normal. She flipped through the newspaper, scanning several articles, then noticed Sam had rolled the sleeves of the plaid shirt above his elbows. She'd never thought about it before but somehow rolling sleeves above the elbows was unbelievably appealing, while below the elbows they were just rolled sleeves. Maybe it was because he had good arms, the corded muscles flexing as he used a knife.

Watching him deal with the asparagus struck her as all kinds of sexy. Where she would have steamed the spears, added a little salt, and called it good, he tossed them with olive oil, used a micro-grater to shred parmesan, sprinkled sea salt and pepper, then arranged them on a baking tray. After sliding the tray into the oven, he washed the dishes he'd used, then worked the cork out of a bottle of Chardonnay.

He brought her a glass and sat across from her. "Are we good?"

She sipped her wine, and then placed the glass carefully on the table. There were things they needed to discuss, but not until after dinner. But that wasn't what he was asking about. "Sure, we're good."

"Regrets about last night?"

She stared into the straw-colored wine. "Last night I said I was off duty, but I still crossed a line between my professional and personal life. I could get fired for that." She frowned. "But at the moment it felt worth it, so no, I have no regrets." She raised her gaze. "You?"

"Your job brought you into my house. I don't like feeling like I took advantage of you."

"Did I act like I was being taken advantage of?"

Gray eyes glinted silver. "No."

"Okay, then let's settle the ethical issues here and now. We both wanted what happened, neither of us was under duress, and we're both unattached, healthy adults."

"I can live with that." A timer chimed. "That's the asparagus."

They worked together to get dinner on the table. Maybe the air had been cleared somewhat, but she couldn't help wondering whether a repeat performance was off the table. Neither of them had mentioned it, but she'd bet Sam was thinking about it as she was.

Ellie gathered plates and utensils, he brought the food, and in minutes they were taking their seats. Sam had dimmed the kitchen lights, giving the room a cozy feel, and she wondered if she was the only one affected by the intimacy of sharing a meal at the small table. By unspoken agreement, they delayed talking about the investigation.

She found Sam easy to talk to. They shared an interest in history and discovered they'd both read the same biography on Eleanor Roosevelt.

"She should have left Franklin when she found out about his affair with Lucy Mercer." Ellie gestured with her fork to emphasize her point. "She should have demanded a divorce and published the love letters she'd found so everyone could see him for the dirty dog he was."

"Easy to say when you're not living under the social constraints of the early 1900s. People then tended to be more scandal averse, and divorce held a social stigma, which is why Franklin's mother pushed him to reject that option. She had political aspirations for her son."

"All true, but I hate that he treated Eleanor so badly, though she certainly came into her own during his presidency." She sampled the baked asparagus. "Mmm, this is really good."

"The entire meal is really good. Thank you."

"You're welcome. You know, I'm named after her."

"You're named after Eleanor Roosevelt?"

"Yeah, my brothers and I were all named for famous historical figures."

"Linc is short for Lincoln?" At her nod he said, "Then that one's not hard to figure out. What about Seth? The only historical Seth I can think of is Seth Bullock of Deadwood. He was a US Marshal, too, wasn't he?"

"That's the guy."

"Did Seth become a marshal to fulfill his historic destiny?"

"No, becoming a marshal was more our stepfather's influence. Being marshals gave us a legal way to pursue Richard Jameson and bring him to justice."

"And when he's behind bars, what then?"

"You think we'll get him?"

"I have no doubt."

His confidence pleased her. "When he's behind bars we'll have removed a threat to our government, and on some level made him pay for his betrayal. I want my mom and Arch to be at the trial."

"And when that's over, what will you do?"

She considered her answer as she carefully sliced her chicken. She knew how her brothers would respond. They would go on being US Marshals, pursuing fugitives, protecting witnesses, and guarding federal judges. They'd never even talked about it because the assumption was that they were marshals. It's what they did.

"I'm thinking about that."

He brows shot up. "As in you're thinking you might not continue your career as a marshal?"

"Let's say I'm considering my options."

"Like what?"

She chewed thoughtfully, swallowing before answering. "I went to law school, so I could take the bar."

"Why? Was bringing your father to justice the only reason you became a marshal?"

He watched her with the intense focus she found so stimulating. As Bella had said, Sam paid attention, and when he looked at you, he made you think you were the only person who mattered to him.

"Bringing Richard Jameson to justice was a big motivating factor, and I've enjoyed the work, but there are things I'd like to have in my life that being a marshal makes more difficult."

"Like what?"

"Like a home that's more than an apartment that I spend less than half my time in."

He nodded. "Understandable. What else?"

Get married, have a couple kids. But there were limits to what she was willing to reveal to him, so she went with what was easy. "A beagle."

"You're kidding."

"Not kidding. I've wanted a beagle since forever. But I'm always getting on a plane and flying somewhere, sometimes for weeks at a time. It wouldn't be fair to the dog if I'm away from home all the time."

He tipped his head to the two dogs sharing a cushion in the corner. "You could always come back here. I've got plenty of beagles, and Cleo follows you around like she's already yours."

A throwaway comment, or was he serious? This was the first time the possibility of seeing each other after the end of her assignment had been broached. But coming back to visit the dogs wasn't quite the same as coming back to see Sam.

She kept her tone nonchalant. "Sure, I'd love to see Cleo and Tony."

Sam pushed his plate aside and sat back in his chair. Ellie did the same, fiddling with the engagement ring on her left hand. He reached out and took her hand, holding it up where the emerald-cut diamond glittered as it caught the light. He brushed a thumb over her knuckles. "Looks good on you."

"Guess we're lucky it fits. Tell me about the previous fiancée, unless the subject is painful."

"Why do you assume there was a previous fiancée?"

"This is an engagement ring, Creed, you happened to have lying around? If it's a sore subject, you don't have to talk about it."

He shrugged. "There was no fiancée. The ring was my aunt's."

"Really? From the young man who died in Vietnam?" She stared at the ring with a new regard, rubbing a finger over its surface, then started working it off her finger. "This is special, Sam. You shouldn't have given it to me."

He took her hand and pushed the ring back in place. "Wear it. My aunt would have liked you. She wore the ring on special occasions, and she'd have been fine with you wearing it now."

She fisted her hand. "Okay, I'll be careful with it."

They took the dishes from the table to the counter. Sam filled the dishwasher while Ellie found containers for the leftover food, then ran hot water in the basin for the hand washing.

The connection with Sam had intensified throughout the meal. They were in a situation that demanded they spend a lot of time together. Add the undeniable attraction that had led to the shared intimacy the night before, and heated tension was bound to keep building. She felt like it was swelling beneath the surface, and that neither of them was as in control of their emotions as they'd like.

They went through their evening routines. Ellie felt they were tiptoeing around the pull. Last night had proven how good they could be together, but going there again was complicated. From her corner of the couch she watched him staring at the screen on his laptop, earbuds in his ears. His lips turned down in a frown, and he drummed his fingers on the arm of the chair.

When he looked up, she caught a look of raw emotion before it was blocked. She motioned to his ears and he pulled out the earbuds, setting his laptop on an end table.

"What happened this morning? Where did you go?"

A simple question, but the filters dropped over his eyes. "Personal issue, sorry." His tone made the boundary clear.

"There's no personal right now." She frowned as a thought occurred, one she didn't care to examine too closely. "If you're more comfortable talking with Seth or Linc, then do it, but you can't hold back with us."

Heat kindled in his gaze. "You think I left here this morning to meet a woman? After last night?"

"How would I know? You're not exactly Mr. Talkative. The night the flashbang was thrown in the house, you were late then, too."

"I'm not seeing anyone in the manner you're thinking."

When she didn't respond, he swore and ran a hand through his hair. "I'm trying to figure something out. I'll tell you when I can."

"That's not how this works, Sam. You have to be honest. Seth made that clear when we decided on this course of action."

"I'll tell you when I can," he repeated.

She couldn't keep the edge out of her tone. "You made a decision to bring us in when you reported the threatening emails to the Marshals Service. That was the right thing to do, because you're a federal judge, and, like it or not, a threat against you is a threat against our system of justice. You don't get to hold back when the information you have isn't convenient to share."

"Convenience has nothing to do with it. I told you it's personal."

"Personal because it's about Drew?"

"Leave him out of it."

"Leave him out of it when I think he's involved?" She shook her head. "I heard you last night."

"Heard what?"

"I heard you on the phone. Your voice carried through the vent to my room. I came downstairs. You were in your office and sounded angry. Was it Drew?"

"Back off, Ellie." His sharp tone told her he was at the edge of his patience.

"I won't back off. This is my job."

His gaze narrowed, eyes turning a flat gray. "How far will you go for your job, Eleanor? You listened in on what was obviously a private conversation, so you crossed that line. Was it your job to get close to me to get more information?"

Everything inside her froze. "What exactly do you mean?"

"I'm talking about you and me last night. Maybe it wasn't as spontaneous as I'd assumed. Maybe the marshals assigning you to be my girlfriend was more calculating than I gave you credit for."

"Calculating in what way?" But the hollow pit in her stomach told her she already knew what he was going to say.

"Did you tell Seth that you and I had been together when we were both at University of Oregon?"

She sat up, closing the cover of her iPad with careful, precise movements. "Let me get this straight. You think Seth and I manipulated you using an encounter you didn't even remember."

"Did you?"

"No. I was too embarrassed to admit to my brother what an idiot I'd been thirteen years ago. But let's get to the more important assumption, the one that I'd use sex as part of my job. You know, fake orgasms, get you off, all to gather information. That's what you're saying?"

"I didn't say the orgasms were fake. Nothing wrong with enjoying your job."

Her hands were shaking as she rose to her feet. "You may be an asshole, but I'm not a whore."

He scrubbed a hand over his face, the rasp of his beard drowning out the ticking clock. "I didn't say you were a whore."

"Really? Because that's what I heard. Except that instead of money, I get paid with information. So if my motivation was information, which I didn't get by the way, what was yours? Another sexual conquest like thirteen years ago?"

"Don't blow this out of proportion."

"You suggested I prostituted myself for the Marshals Service and I'm blowing this out of proportion?" Her voice rose despite trying to stay calm. "I think you said exactly what you meant. I'll talk to Seth about getting reassigned because we obviously can't work together."

The look of relief that flashed across his face was gone so quickly she might have imagined it.

"That might be best."

Hurt cut through her with a lancing pain. She forced herself to think past it. "Is that what this conversation has been about, you want me thrown off the case?" Realization dawned. "You bastard." She picked up a cushion and hurled it at him. "We're back to that, are we? You want me reassigned because you think I might get hurt."

He caught the cushion and tossed it back on the couch. "Cut it out."

"Well, fuck you. You have no respect for my ability to do my job. You want to tuck me someplace safe while others put themselves in danger to protect you."

"I would hardly have gone along with the fake engagement if I didn't think it was a good idea, but it hasn't worked out."

"Maybe I'm assuming you actually care about me when in reality you're worried I'll figure out what's going on with Drew. My bet is that you didn't know he was involved when this first started. Now that you do, you want to stop the investigation. I take it back. I'm not going anywhere. If your plan was to get rid of me so you can cover for your brother, I'm not cooperating. You're stuck with me."

***

The next morning, Ellie stood outside Sam's closed office door. Whatever had been developing between them was dead. Maybe he did care about her, but he was obstructing her ability to do her job.

They hadn't gone on their morning run, and she'd stayed in her room, watching through her bedroom window until he'd left for work. By now he was safely in court, so she put aside whatever misgivings she might have had and turned the knob. He'd locked it.

No matter, Arch Bollinger had taught his stepchildren how to pick locks using whatever tools were at hand. She went up the stairs to her room and returned a minute later with a bobby pin. Seconds later, she had the door open.

She started with the antique rolltop desk set against one wall and determined it was used for things related to the house: manuals for kitchen appliances and electronics, sample books for countertop material and flooring that suggested Sam planned to update the kitchen, and even an architectural drawing of the house dated nearly a hundred years before.

Tucked next to it she found an envelope with a school-project valentine printed in a child's careful hand to "Auntie Nan" and signed "Your nephew, Sam." In the center of the red construction-paper heart was a small school photo of a serious, dark-haired boy. Oh geez. Was there anything that could pull harder at her heartstrings than that lonely little boy who had lost his mother? She returned the valentine to the envelope and tried to put a lid on the emotions the card had pulled up.

She moved and sat in the high-backed leather chair in front of the wide desk Sam regularly used and shut down her apprehension about going through his personal things.

She started with the desk drawers first, pulling each open to examine their contents. The top left drawer was stacked with receipts, mostly from online retailers, while the middle one held bills. The deep bottom drawer held a couple of squeeze-type grip strengtheners.

She picked one up and worked it a few times before replacing it to continue her search. An organizer in the top right-hand drawer held paper clips, Post-its, pens and pencils. How could someone only have boring pale yellow Post-its, plain metal paper clips, and yellow wooden pencils? She wondered what that said about Sam's personality.

It wasn't until she got to the bottom right drawer that she found hanging files, one with a tab that read "Rock Creek Estate." Inside Joss Creed's will, the deed to the ranch, and correspondence with a lawyer were all neatly organized, Sam having written notes on the boring yellow Post-its with his precise script. She leafed through the documents, gaining a clearer picture of the difficult position Sam's father had left him in, and why Drew was so resentful.

She pulled out the last file in the drawer. Inside was an unlabeled manila folder containing a stack of papers. One glance told her these were copies of the threatening emails. She read through them again, reviewing the now familiar messages from the self-described Freedom Defender.

The last sheet contained the most recent email. She frowned as she read. This email had been sent two days ago, and Sam hadn't shared it with her or the team.

Like the others, FD claimed to be preserving the Second Amendment. After the usual diatribe against Judge Creed, accusing him of being part of a conspiracy to subvert the Constitution, the last line read: *Enjoy the time you have left with your girlfriend. When she dies, her blood will be on your hands. We'll keep you alive long enough to witness her death, then you'll follow her to hell.*

"Talk about overly dramatic," Ellie muttered to herself. She took out her phone and snapped a photo of the email and sent it to the rest of the team.

\*\*\*

The next morning, Ellie steered the Land Cruiser toward the grocery store, reviewing how everything had evolved over the past twenty-four hours. She bit back a sigh. The best way to describe her and Sam's current relationship was as a deep freeze with brief flashes of heat. After work he'd shut himself in his office, and an hour later she'd received an email from him. He'd forwarded the threat she'd found in his drawer to herself and the others.

Good thing, because now the team could talk openly about it in his presence without giving away that she'd snooped through his desk.

Seth had called. She and Sam had driven around for fifteen minutes to throw off anyone watching them before going to Marshal Central for a late evening meeting. Sam had hammered on about the threat to Ellie, but Seth had refused to change her assignment. She was becoming more and more discouraged with the lack of progress. Bella's questioning looks told Ellie that the tension between her and Sam hadn't gone unnoticed.

The friendship they'd seemed to be developing before their argument was a memory. Now they ignored each other. Or at least he ignored her. Her dilemma was that while she was putting on a good act, she couldn't help being hyperaware of everything about him.

His scent triggered a response if he walked too close to her, an aroma she labeled *Hot guy on a crisp fall day*. Maybe she should shorten it to *Sam*. When his hair fell over his forehead, she had to leave the room before she jumped him.

There was that moment in the courthouse parking lot earlier that morning. Sam had driven, so she'd stepped out of the Land Cruiser to switch seats. They were standing behind the vehicle when a pair of women had walked toward them. Sam's expression had turned speculative, then he'd leaned forward to cup the back of her neck and lowered his mouth to hers. The momentary touch of lips had been like flash lightning, scorching in its brief intensity.

He'd stepped back and released her to jam his hands in his pockets, expression unreadable. A moment later she was watching his back as he strode toward the courthouse.

She pulled up in front of the grocery store, her mind on trying to figure out something for dinner. The brooding sky and icy temperature matched her mood perfectly. Sam, who did aloof really well even as he was handing her an umbrella, had informed her of an impending storm. The clouds stacked up in the western sky and the biting wind made her grateful she'd opted for her padded down coat.

With her purse slung over her shoulder, she pulled up her hood, bent her head against a strong gust, and trudged toward the glass doors of the store. A van pulled to a stop, blocking her way, the passenger door opening as she stepped sideways to go around it. It wasn't the man who got out of the vehicle who caught her attention, but the pale face under the dark beanie of the driver. Frowning, she opened her mouth to speak. A movement in her peripheral vision was her only warning before a blow to her head had the world spinning into darkness.

# Chapter Seventeen

Ellie's head throbbed. She blinked open her eyes and bit back a groan as she tried to sort out her surroundings. The surface under her cheek vibrated, her clue that she was in the back of a moving vehicle. Her heart pounded heavily. Shit. This was bad.

Voices, loud and angry, carried from the front. Sharp pain radiating from her forehead muddled the words so she couldn't make them out. The smell of cigarette smoke permeated the air. She rolled to her side, fighting back a wave of nausea, and became aware that her hands were uncomfortably secured behind her. She pulled at the restraints and heard a metallic clink. Handcuffs.

A desperate thought had her awkwardly bending her arms and in that split second, her situation kicked up from bad to grim. Her holster was there, but the gun was gone. No doubt, if they'd found her gun, they'd found her phone.

Hoping desperately for a break, she cast around frantically for her purse but didn't see it. Then she remembered shoving her phone into a pocket of her coat. She couldn't get her hands to her front to check for that, but she didn't feel the weight of it. Something wet trickled along her eyebrow and she guessed it was blood. Gritting her teeth, she pushed herself up so she could lean against the sidewall.

Clearly, she'd been kidnapped, which meant whoever had taken her was trying to get to Sam. Linc was at the courthouse today, as were Seth and Bella. They would keep Sam safe.

She was in some sort of work van with a low, flat floor and two bucket seats in the front. Two men in heavy coats and beanies were taking turns snarling at each other. There were no windows in the back, only what looked like a couple of toolboxes and gray plastic bins with lids. A packing blanket wrapped around something bulky lay on the opposite side of the van.

"What the fuck was she doing with a gun?" Ellie jerked as she tuned into the conversation. Then she remembered that brief glimpse of the driver. His voice was pitched high with worry. Drew Martin glanced at the man in the passenger seat, then returned his attention to the road. For Sam's sake she wished her suspicions about his brother had proven unwarranted.

"This is an open carry state, half the people in this county are armed." The man in the passenger seat was heavier than Drew and appeared more relaxed as he sipped from a to-go cup, a cigarette dangling from his fingers.

"I'm telling you, there's something off there. She wouldn't let me come in the house with a gun. Said it made her *uncomfortable.* Why would she say that if she's one of us?"

"I'm not saying she's one of us, dickwad. I'm saying it doesn't prove anything. Creed could have given her the gun to carry for protection because we're threatening him."

"I don't think so. Maybe she's FBI or something."

"Does she look FBI?"

"How the fuck should I know what FBI looks like? Isn't that the point when they go undercover, that you don't know who they are? We need to get rid of her before they come after us. I kept telling you guys taking her is a mistake."

Her stomach knotted when she thought of what he meant by getting rid of her. And who were "you guys"?

"We stick with the plan. We grabbed her to get leverage over Creed. We want him to overturn Bannister's conviction, and we don't want the government taking our guns. If Big Dog wants us to get rid of her, then that's what we do, but not until then."

"We shouldn't have done this. You don't know my brother. You think he's all civilized, but I've seen him lose his shit. Thought he was going to kill a guy once who'd punched Ben for being a fag."

"We'll deal with Creed." The passenger looked over his shoulder, a wide smile splitting his round face. "Well, well, look who's awake. Hello, sweetheart." He frowned and pointed at his head. "Man, that looks painful. Sorry I hit you so hard. Had a job to do, that's all. How you feeling? Got a headache?"

She ignored his questions. "Who are you?"

"You can call me Sarge, everyone does."

"Why are you doing this? Where are you taking me?"

"We're taking you someplace safe, and we're going to hold on to you for a bit. You don't have anything to worry about."

"Shit, shit, shit!" Drew swerved and Ellie braced to keep from being rolled around.

"What the hell's wrong with you? I should never have let you drive."

"Cops are behind us with their lights on." Panic edged Drew's voice, and between the seats she could see his hands, knuckles white, gripping the steering wheel.

A thin, piercing wail sounded over the whine of the engine.

"Don't freak out. They can't be after us."

"Someone must have seen us grab her in the parking lot."

"No way. The van blocked the view from the store. There was no one in the parking lot when we grabbed her, and we had her in the car in less than thirty seconds. No one saw us. Pull over nice and easy like every other idiot out here and we'll be fine."

"The signal turned red. Should we run it? We get pulled over with her in the back and we're done for."

"Fuck no, we don't run it. You're such a dumbass."

Drew stomped on the brakes and Ellie tumbled to her side. The sirens drew closer.

"What the fuck, man? Are you *trying* to get their attention?" Drew wasn't the only one losing his cool.

The sirens passed, the sound fading, taking Ellie's brief hope with it.

"Holy shit, I nearly pissed myself."

Sarge made a sound of disgust. "If you'd listened to me in the first place, you'd save yourself a shitload of grief. Now get going before someone calls the cops to report a reckless driver." He turned in his seat. "How we doing back there?"

Ellie remained slumped on the floor, her shoulders aching from her hands being pulled behind her back. She squeezed her eyes shut. "Not good. My head hurts and I get motion sickness. I feel like throwing up." It didn't take much effort to put a tremor in her voice. "Why have you kidnapped me?"

"We're not planning to hurt you." She didn't believe that for a second. Maybe Sarge didn't realize she'd overheard him and Drew talking about "getting rid" of her.

Drew slowed the vehicle.

"What the fuck are you doing?" From the temper in his voice, Sarge was at the end of his patience.

"She throws up she'll stink up the whole van. I'm stopping. We got to look for a bag or something."

Ellie could feel the vehicle turning. She moaned and gulped in a breath. With the headache and being in the back of the van, her claim of nausea wasn't entirely a fabrication.

"Get back on the damn road. Who cares if she pukes all over herself? We've got to get her stashed before we're pulled over for real."

"She pukes, I puke. Happens every time."

"God, you're an idiot."

The van stopped and Drew threw it into park.

"Could you have picked a worse place to stop? Circle around to the back of the store, dickwad. There'll be dumpsters there and we'll find something for her to spew into so your delicate sensibilities aren't upset."

"Stop calling me that." The van rumbled to life again.

"What, dickwad? You are a dickwad, so that's what you're called."

"Everyone in the militia chooses a code name. Big Dog's is Big Dog. Mine's Lobo. That's what you're supposed to call me."

Sarge barked out a laugh lacking in amusement. "You got to earn your name, dickwad. I earned mine in the Marine Corps. Big Dog's earned his because he's big and he's the top dog. So far all you've earned is dickwad."

The van stopped and Ellie made a retching sound. She lay curled on her side, eyes closed.

"Shit, she's gonna hurl." Drew shoved open the driver's door.

"Jesus Christ on a crutch." Sarge opened his own door, and a second later, the rear doors of the van flew open. "Get out, girl."

Ellie opened her eyes and gave him a suffering look. "I don't feel good." Behind Sarge's silhouetted figure, the sky looked heavy with gray and sullen clouds.

He flicked away a lit cigarette. "We aren't taking you to a garden party so I don't really care if you don't feel good. You need to puke or not?"

"I think so, but I can't sit up with my hands behind my back."

"Well, I'm sure as hell not taking those cuffs off." He tugged her feet to draw her to the opening before grabbing her elbow and pulling her to a sitting position. "Get your feet under you and stand up."

Drew stuck his head around the open door. Ellie stood, bent over at the waist, and made herself dry heave, then breathed heavily through her nostrils.

"You faking it, sweet thing?" Sarge jerked her upright.

"I'm trying *not* to throw up." She groaned and pulled free to sit on the back bumper of the van. She looked at Drew. "Why are you doing this? Why are you trying to hurt Sam?"

Drew's face contorted. "He brought this on himself. He tell you I asked him for a loan against my inheritance, money that's rightfully mine to begin with? He told me to fuck off."

"Sam wouldn't have said that to you."

"Maybe not using those exact words, but the intent was the same. He thinks because he's a big-ass judge he can treat his own brother like shit. Us snatching you will get his attention. Then we'll have ourselves a conversation and he can give me some goddamn respect."

Sarge shoved Drew aside. "You're full of shit. This isn't some petty personal vendetta. We're doing this for the cause. Creed needs to be taught he can't fuck with the Constitution."

Ellie groaned and her legs shook. "Oh god. I have to find a bathroom."

"You have to pee?" Drew sounded nervous.

"I think I have diarrhea."

He reached into the front pocket of his jeans.

"What the hell are you doing?" Incredulity laced Sarge's words.

Drew pulled a ring of keys from his pocket. He fished through them, then held up a small handcuff key. "We can't take her to the bathroom in handcuffs. It'll draw too much attention. We've got to get her to a toilet or she'll shit her pants. I could use the john myself."

"Oh my god, could you be any more stupid? We're not taking her anywhere with blood dripping down her face." Sarge held out his hand. "Give me the goddam keys."

Ellie moaned. Sarge snatched the keys from Drew, then scooped her legs up and pushed her into the back of the van and slammed the doors. Through the closed doors she could hear Sarge telling Drew that if he didn't want to get left behind, he'd get in the van. The driver's door was thrown open and Sarge got behind the wheel, jamming the key into the ignition.

Drew took the passenger seat, slamming his door shut. "I've got to use the john, asshole, didn't I tell you that? And you didn't get a bag for her to puke in."

"She's faking it. We've got to do our job or there'll be hell to pay."

Sarge was more astute than she'd given him credit for. They set out again, turning onto what she thought must be the highway as the first drops of rain spattered against the windshield. She guessed they were traveling south but couldn't be entirely sure.

The rain began falling heavier, the drumming sound loud on the roof. There seemed to be fewer stops at intersections, so she guessed they were heading out of town. Eventually they turned, and then turned again. With the mental map she was trying to keep in her head, she thought they might be in the general area of Rock Creek Ranch. A strong wind was blowing the rain in sheets that the wipers struggled to keep up with. A particularly strong gust sent the van swerving.

"Stay on the road, asshole. We go down the embankment and we'll need a winch to pull us out." Drew's tone turned sullen. "I should be driving."

"I am staying on the road," Sarge growled. His earlier affability had evaporated.

Maybe twenty minutes later, with the rain beating harder, Drew swore. "There's flooding up ahead. You crossing that? We get stuck in the mud, we'll need to get towed out."

"We're going to my house, aren't we? I know what I'm doing. That dip in the road floods a couple times every winter. This van's got all-wheel drive. We won't get stuck."

"If that water's deep enough, unless you're driving a tank, we'll be stuck."

"We won't get stuck." Sarge sounded like he was pushing his words through gritted teeth.

Ellie scooted to the opposite side of the van to lean against the packing blanket. As much as she could with her cuffed hands, she felt along the blanket. Her suspicions were confirmed when her fingers closed around what was probably the barrel of a long gun. She scooted down until she could trace the hard cylinder, then the one next to it. When she sat back again, she was sure she was leaning against at least three rifles, most likely assault-type, rolled in the blanket.

The throbbing pain where she'd been hit on her forehead made her grimace and she had to force herself to think around it. *Focus, Ellie.* She wouldn't let fear paralyze her.

Drawing on her training, she tried to clear her mind and formulate a plan. The engine strained as they steadily climbed in elevation. Through the rain-spattered windscreen, she could make out the tips of pine trees silhouetted against the cloudy sky. They must be in the mountains. Paying attention to details could mean the difference between survival and death. She didn't intend to end up dead.

The road transitioned to an unpaved surface and they bumped along, gravel hitting the underside of the van. After about ten minutes, the road leveled out. Sarge steered around a bend, then applied the brakes, putting the van in park.

"Your place is a dump, as usual."

Sarge swung out an arm and backhanded Drew. A second later, Sarge had a gun out, eyes narrowed as he sighted down the barrel at Drew.

# Chapter Eighteen

"Watch what you say, dickwad, because it wouldn't take much to pull this trigger and blow your brains out. The only thing that's holding me back right now is that I'd have a mess to clean up." The expression on his face said Sarge was dead serious. A dog barked outside the van.

"All right! Fuck it. I didn't mean anything."

"You insulted me." Sarge's voice carried over the rain hammering on the roof. He eased back, though continuing to point his gun at Drew. He threw a glance over his shoulder. "Don't worry about this, sweetheart. We're not going to hurt you. This loser needs a reminder of who's in charge and what good manners are." His attention returned to Drew. "Come on, dickwad. We've got to get her settled."

He holstered his weapon and opened the driver's door, animosity evident on Drew's face as he watched Sarge. Sam wasn't the only one to have earned his brother's hatred.

Sarge opened the back of the van and Ellie scooted forward. A large mixed-breed dog sniffed Drew's jeans, then Ellie's. Sarge grabbed Ellie's arm to help her stand, using his knee to push the muddy dog aside. "Out of the way, Rex."

Ellie gazed around, trying to absorb details. They were in a valley between low hills with higher mountains rising behind them. The driveway led past the house to a barn with a sagging roof. She didn't see any sign of close neighbors. Rain pelted down, immediately soaking her and sending a rivulet of icy water under the collar of her coat.

Sarge pulled up her hood over her hair, and Ellie made a point of thanking him. She would exploit any division between her captors she could, even appearing to want to get on Sarge's good side.

He led them toward the house, and she surreptitiously studied Drew. His tight expression and clenched fists indicated seething anger. She wondered if Sarge had pushed him too far.

She stumbled over uneven bricks in the walkway. The area in front of the house couldn't really be called a yard. Weeds grew unchecked around used tires and broken-down machinery, and a large propane tank sat on a concrete pad.

Curls of peeling paint flaked from the window trim and eaves of the house, and the bottom third of the stucco walls looked damp. Ellie detected a faint skunky smell.

The dog followed them into the house, leaving a trail of muddy paw prints as he collapsed onto the carpet in front of a fireplace in need of having its ashes cleaned out. The cramped living room smelled of stale cigarette smoke.

One wall sported a mounted deer head, and a rack over the fireplace held two hunting rifles. An AR-15 leaned against one corner. On a desk shoved in a corner an old-style, bulky computer monitor sat next to a CPU that blinked a red light like a warning.

On the far side of the room a dining table was weighted down with stacks of papers, empty soda bottles, and a couple of overflowing ashtrays. Beyond the table was a sliding glass door that revealed a narrow patio with a rusting barbecue and a muddy backyard. In the middle of the yard was a blackened area that held charred chunks of wood, the remnants of a fire. She wondered if Sarge's backyard had been used for the book-burning bonfire.

He pushed her forward with a hand in the middle of her back. They passed by a wide doorway to the kitchen where a Nazi flag was held on the refrigerator with a magnet like one would keep their child's artwork. She glimpsed a backdoor through the kitchen, which meant there were at least three points of entry to the house.

Sarge stripped off his coat and threw it over the back of a chair and she spotted her gun tucked in the back waistband of his baggy jeans, another in a holster at his hip. With Drew trailing behind them, Sarge took her down a hallway where he opened a door and flipped a switch to light a narrow set of stairs that descended into darkness.

Ellie's stomach churned, the feeling that she was being led into a dungeon doing nothing to ease her apprehension. She hated feeling powerless and at the mercy of these two men. Nothing they had done suggested that they intended sexual assault, but they'd hit her hard enough for her to lose consciousness, and she didn't doubt they would hurt her again if they wanted. She had to come up with a plan to protect herself.

Sarge flipped on more lights at the bottom of the stairs to reveal a minimally furnished basement room. In one corner, a twin-size bed was neatly made, covered with a thick comforter. A table with a couple of folding chairs had been arranged next to a mini-refrigerator and counter with a small sink. A microwave that had to be twenty years old sat on top of the fridge, and a TV and VCR of possibly even older vintage were perched precariously on a small, wheeled cabinet.

"Here we are, sweetheart. Home sweet home, for the time being, anyway." He took out his phone and snapped a picture of her. "I'll be sending that to your boyfriend. Can't use you for leverage if he doesn't know we have you." He dug the keys out of his pocket, and whistling a jaunty tune, proceeded to unlock the handcuffs.

Ellie moved her arms, biting back a groan when pain shot from her shoulders down her arms. She rubbed her wrists as she looked around the room.

Sarge opened the cabinet doors under the sink. Cup O'Noodles, Cheez-Its, and a box of instant oatmeal packets were among the food items on the shelf next to stacked paper plates and napkins. Ellie had a flashback to her college dorm room.

"See? You won't starve. And there's even the VCR for entertainment. It's old school, but it works. TV's not attached to the cable, but there are movies you can choose from in the TV stand." Sarge seemed proud of the furnishings. He waved a hand at a closed door. "The bathroom's in there."

"I want to go home."

His eyes flashed. "Show some respect. We haven't violated you. We haven't harmed you other than that little bump on your head. We won't kill you unless there's no alternative. I've set up a nice place for you to stay where you'll be comfortable. Show some appreciation."

The offhand mention of killing her sent ice straight to her bones. "You *kidnapped* me and are holding me against my will, and I'm expected to show appreciation?" Ellie knew she was walking a fine line.

Sarge seemed to have certain standards for his personal behavior, not that those standards met societal norms. His casually violent treatment of Drew demonstrated how quickly his temper could flare. She would take care, but if she wanted to develop a viable escape plan, getting Sarge to talk might reveal information that could help her.

Still wearing her coat, she crossed her arms against the chill. "This does look comfortable, but I'm scared and confused, and want to go home. I don't understand why you brought me here. When are you going to let me go?"

"I'll tell you." Drew's face twisted in a sneer. "We brought you here to give my privileged brother the message that he can't mess with me and he can't mess with our movement. He hides behind the law to keep for himself what's rightfully mine. He thinks because he's a fucking judge he gets to decide who should be protected by the Constitution and who shouldn't. He's letting illegals overrun our country while throwing good people like Frank Bannister in prison for exercising their rights. The Second Amendment lays it out that we got a right to our guns. No judge can take that away." The words came from his mouth with a spray of spit.

"Shut up, dickwad. She doesn't need to know any of that."

"I can say what I want to say. She should know what kind of man she's engaged to."

"You're more of an idiot than I gave you credit for. Just shut up."

Drew's face flushed angry red. He reached for his holster, fumbled a moment, then raised his arm, gun in hand, and aimed at Sarge. With much cleaner movement, Sarge palmed his own pistol and mirrored Drew's stance. The sudden silence was broken only by the faint thudding of the rain.

"Well, well. Looks like we got ourselves a Mexican standoff." Sarge's sardonic tone indicated a decided lack of concern.

"You think you're so cool. I'm fucking tired of how you treat me, asshole." Drew's gun shook like a fall leaf in a stiff wind.

Ellie stepped toward the stairs, moving slowly.

"Interesting, since I'm fucking tired of you whining like an overgrown toddler. Go ahead and shoot. You're shaking so much I think I can put a hole between your eyes before you could steady yourself enough to pull the trigger. Want to try out that hypothesis, *dickwad*?"

Ellie could see the rage on Drew's face, the desire to pull the trigger as Sarge goaded him. As much as she wanted to bring in both men to face justice, shooting one another would take care of her immediate problem.

Seconds stretched until finally Drew lowered his gun. "I hate your fucking guts."

"You can hate me all you want, but we got a job to do." Sarge turned his own weapon toward Ellie. She froze with her foot on the bottom tread "You don't want to do that, sweetheart, because I won't have any problem shooting you if I have to. You asked when you'll be released. That'll depend on how much Judge Creed wants your freedom." Sarge motioned Drew to the door. The loathing on Drew's face made her determined to use his anger if she had a chance.

"You sure she can't get out of this place?" Drew asked.

"Not unless she's a freaking ghost. There's only one door and it's got a deadbolt. She's not getting out of here."

Drew climbed the stairs without a backward glance.

Sarge gestured to the room. "Make yourself at home. You may be here for a few days."

He turned to the stairs, and Ellie said, "Wait. Can't you give me my purse? I have Tylenol in there, and a hairbrush."

"Should I give you your Glock back, too? Nice try, sweetheart." Sarge shook his head. "Everything you need is here."

The deadbolt slid into place, locking the door to her prison. The quiet intensified, the only sound the faint hush of air through the vents.

With her arms locked over her stomach, Ellie turned slowly to scan the room. The desire to curl up on the bed and bury her head under the blankets nearly overwhelmed her. She was being held prisoner, her head ached relentlessly, and she could feel panic creeping over her skin like the plague.

She absolutely believed Sarge when he'd said he would have no problem shooting her. Practicing a breathing technique to calm herself, she tried to recall her training and what could help her in her current situation.

First things first. She made a beeline to the door Sarge had indicated. The bathroom appeared recently converted. The space was cramped, containing a toilet, a sink and vanity with a postage-stamp-size counter, and a shower stall so narrow she thought she'd likely bruise her elbows if she actually used it. There were still stickers on the glass door of the shower and the mirror over the sink. After using the toilet, she washed her hands, leaning forward to examine her reflection. "Jesus, I look like I'm made up for a Halloween party."

With the tap running to get hot water, she pulled open the drawers of the vanity, searching for a washcloth to clean the dried blood from her face. A top drawer contained a multi-pack of toothbrushes, the tube of toothpaste next to it promising to make her breath minty fresh. The next drawer held a hairbrush and comb, both new. She found a first aid kit and set it on the counter. It wasn't until she reached the bottom drawer that she allowed a tight smile. A metal towel bar and the attachments to fix it to the wall lay inside, along with a long screwdriver. She took out the screwdriver and slid it under the waistband of her jeans and lay the towel rod on the counter. They would be of no use against a gun but might prove worth having in hand-to-hand. She'd take what she could get.

Not finding a washcloth, she dampened the corner of a hand towel and scrubbed the blood. When she rinsed the cloth, red-stained water swirled into the drain. Lifting her hair, she examined the injury high on her forehead, close to the hairline. She hoped it was one of those cases that looked worse than it actually was, because it looked pretty bad.

At the crest of a raised lump, a deep half-inch semicircle cut into her skin, the surrounding area puffy and purple caused by a pipe or the muzzle of Sarge's gun. It probably needed stitches, but that wasn't happening.

She found antibacterial ointment in the first aid kit and swabbed it on, then used Band-Aids as best she could to cover the wound.

Once she was done tending to the wound, she went to the kitchen area and examined the contents of the cupboard. She was right about the food being like college all over again. A jumbo container of cheese balls in neon orange was nestled next to a tray of Oreos and little packets of soft cheese and crackers, but there was nothing that resembled what she considered real food.

She wandered through the room and determined Sarge had been telling the truth. Other than the door with the locked deadbolt (she'd tested it), there was no other way out of the basement.

Finding pain reliever in the cabinet, she downed a couple capsules. Lying on the bed, she pulled the comforter around her shoulders and closed her eyes. Worry churned in her stomach, but for the moment, she was safe.

She only meant to lie on the bed until her headache eased, but it was several hours before she stirred again. When she woke, the time on the VCR told her it was late afternoon. She rose, and keeping the comforter around her shoulders, opened the kitchenette cupboards again.

Cup O'Noodles, she decided. With the Styrofoam cup filled with water and heating in the microwave, she studied her surroundings more carefully. She didn't doubt that Sarge had hidden surveillance cameras. He might have seen her taking the screwdriver and towel rod from the bathroom. Cameras were tiny these days and easily camouflaged. If they were here, searching would tip them off that she knew about such things, and she wanted them to continue to think she was frightened and helpless.

Ellie sat at the small table and used a plastic fork to eat the noodles. The ceiling above made creaking noises as someone walked about on the first floor—or several someones because it sounded like too much creaking for only Sarge and Drew.

There was a rumble of voices, the slamming of a door, and even faint barking that made her think Rex was outside. She refused to give in to the temptation and lay her head on her arms and have a good cry. Deputy US Marshals didn't cry. While her situation was bad, it wasn't dire.

If Sarge had sent that photo to Sam, he was now aware she'd been kidnapped, and regardless of the current problems between them, he'd be worried about her and would notify the team. Her brothers and Bella were no doubt looking for her. She gave a fleeting thought that they might be able to track her phone but guessed her captors had taken out the sim card. Assuring herself that things could be much worse helped, but didn't do much to dispel the feeling that she was on her own without the tools she needed to get herself out of this place.

The soup's warmth radiated from her stomach and made her feel infinitesimally better. She munched on Cheez-Its, washing them down with water, and guessed she'd probably surpassed the recommended sodium consumption for an entire month. More creaking came from above, then voices, followed by thumping on the stairs. She sat up straight as the deadbolt slid back and the door to the stairs was thrust open.

Ellie's heart gave a hard lurch when Sam stumbled into the room, shoved from behind. She let go of the comforter and surged to her feet. The door slammed shut behind him, the deadbolt sliding home. He no longer wore the suit and tie he'd had on when she'd left him at the courthouse. He was dressed in denim jeans and a dark coat over a sweatshirt, shoulders and hair wet from the rain.

She rushed around the table. His face was a battered mess. His left eye was swollen so badly she wondered if he could see from it, and mottled bruising shadowed his jaw. He moved toward her, relief, rage, and something she couldn't identify sweeping across his face as he opened his arms, clutching her to him.

"You okay?" The words were a harsh whisper in her ear.

She nodded. "What happened? How'd they get you?"

"I went looking for them."

# Chapter Nineteen

Sam's arms remained tight around Ellie. She was alive. The terror he'd been living with the past several hours eased a fraction. They stood locked together until she huffed out a breath and loosened the grip she had on the back of his shirt. Now that he'd found her, he didn't want to let her go.

She pushed against his chest and forced him to loosen his grip.

"You okay?" he asked. "How did you get captured?"

She raised a hand to cover his mouth and shook her head, then pulled his shoulder down and put her lips to his ear. "There may be hidden video or listening devices."

He nodded. Before she could move away, he lifted the hair from her forehead to reveal the white bandage. She pulled against his hold.

"How bad is it?"

"It probably needed stitches." She shrugged. "I did the best I could with a first aid kit I found."

Fury welled, nearly choking him, a familiar pattern for the day. "And the pain?" He could see it in her eyes.

"It's better than it was. I took some ibuprofen a couple hours ago."

"They'll pay for this." He kept his tone low so only she could hear.

She backed out of his hold. "We should put a cold compress on your eye. How'd that happen?"

"I didn't come without a fight."

He followed her into the bathroom. Sam turned on the taps and the ceiling fan. The noise should drown out their voices if there were any listening devices. He stood on the toilet to examine the vent, then hopped down to search the rest of the bathroom. "We're clean in here."

Ellie leaned against a wall, still wearing her coat.

She nodded, then picked up a towel and moistened it before wringing out the excess water and carefully folding it into a pad.

His left eye had swelled shut and ached like he'd been hit with a hammer, which wasn't far off the truth since Big Dog's fist had felt like one. But it was the injury to Ellie's face that had him wanting to slam a fist through the wall. He closed his eyes and drew in a deep breath. Anger wouldn't help them to escape, and escape was the goal.

Ellie was avoiding looking at him, and he was reminded of the angry words spoken the night before. He'd make things right with her once they were free.

"Sit." She motioned to the closed lid of the toilet. He sat, and when she lay the compress on his eye, he groaned. The coolness felt good and eased the ache, but it was more than that. He'd found her, and, at least for the moment, she was safe. The fear that had lodged like a ball of ice in his belly melted at her touch.

His set his hands on her hips as she stood in front of him, his hand brushing over something under her coat. Lifting the hem and frowned. "What's that?"

She pulled a long screwdriver from under the waistband of her jeans. "I found it in a drawer, along with a metal towel rod. The rod is under the blanket on the bed, I'm carrying this just in case."

"Smart woman."

"Not smart enough to avoid getting caught. Who brought you here?"

"A guy they call Big Dog."

"Did you see Drew upstairs?"

He gave a curt nod. The betrayal cut deep. He'd been deluding himself about his brother. "Yeah, and another guy I don't know."

"That's Sarge. This is his house."

"Okay." He repeated his earlier question. "How'd they get you?"

"I was in the parking lot of the grocery store. A van stopped in front of me and a guy got out. I didn't think anything about it. I don't even remember him hitting me on the head, but the next thing I knew I was waking up in the back of a work van with blood running down my face."

The mental image of Ellie helpless and alone had his gut clenching. "You were knocked unconscious? Do you have headache or nausea?"

She ran water over the pad to cool it, then lay it again over his swollen eye. "Yes to all of that."

Her eyes appeared flat, the spark that always lit her face missing. He wasn't sure if it was due to their current predicament or the screwed-up state of their relationship. Maybe it was a combination of both. "You could have a concussion."

"Blame Sarge, he's the one who hit me. Drew was the driver, at least at first. Those two barely tolerate each other."

"Good to know," he murmured. He reached up to hold the compress and she stepped back. Hard to do in such a small space, but she managed to maximize the distance between them. "With your symptoms a concussion is likely, and we need to be careful with you to minimize damage." He rose to his feet. "You're lying down."

"We need to work on getting out of here."

Creaking came from overhead as someone moved around on the first floor. "I'll figure out a plan, because you're resting your brain."

"We'll both figure out a plan. I tried to keep track of our direction when we were in the van. Are we anywhere near your ranch?"

He nodded. "About three miles from here, as the crow flies."

"Do you know Sarge?"

"No."

"I don't think he or Drew expected you to become their captive. The plan was to use me as leverage to force you to free Frank Bannister and to make a decision on the side of gun rights on a

Second Amendment case. Mixed in with all the other nonsense, they also blame you for letting undocumented immigrants overrun the country."

Not for the first time, Sam wished he'd talked with Drew before his ideas had led him down the path he'd ultimately taken. Maybe Sam could have made him see the light. He gave a sigh of frustration as Ellie took the compress from his eye to run under cool water once again, then moved to stand between his knees.

He couldn't tell whether the compress was doing the job, or if it was simply that he was with Ellie. Regardless, the pain around his eye eased and he felt ready to take on every one of their captors. She stood close and he wanted more than anything to wrap her in his arms and simply hold her, but she kept her touch brief and impersonal.

He closed both eyes and allowed himself a moment to be grateful he'd found her. That she'd been hurt because of him only added to his anger. For now, he would hold on to the fact that she was alive, and once she was safe, he'd make sure every one of her captors, including his brother, paid.

"There's ibuprofen in the kitchen area. You should take some for the pain and swelling."

"I need to check for spy equipment, then I will." He rose to his feet, sighing in frustration when she moved to avoid him. "We'll get out of this, Ellie."

She looked away. "Sure we will."

\*\*\*

Ellie rested her head on the pillow and closed her eyes against the light. She wasn't sure how long she'd been asleep, but it felt like hours. Sam had insisted she lie down and her head hurt so badly she couldn't manage to argue with him. She had a vague recollection of Sam shaking her awake more than once. She pulled up the blanket under her chin as a shiver wracked her body. Even with her coat and under the comforter, she felt cold.

The events of the day played in her mind like a horror movie on endless loop. Her brothers and Bella had to have realized something had happened to her and Sam. The thought that even now they might be closing in on her captors gave her hope. She felt like she should be doing something, helping to search for hidden mics, formulating a plan of escape, fighting back, but her head was bad enough for her to know that she needed to conserve her energy. Add all her symptoms together and she was pretty sure Sam's concussion diagnosis was spot on.

Ellie heard him moving about and unscrewed her eyes enough to see what he was doing. He'd dragged a chair to stand on while looking up at the vent on the ceiling. Her vision blurred and she let her eyelids droop again.

She needed to put aside her personal feelings so they could act like a team to survive whatever lay ahead. She couldn't let the fact that he'd destroyed her heart get in the way. Sure, he probably cared for her in his own way, but that wasn't enough. She wasn't a woman who went to pieces when a man cast her aside or hurt her.

Not that Sam had cast her aside.

Technically, they hadn't even been together. Their entire relationship was built on a false premise, and if she'd lost sight of that, if she'd thought there was something more between them, then that was her mistake. Her heart would heal and she would move on without Sam Creed.

The mattress dipped and she opened her eyes to find Sam on the bed beside her.

"Sit up so you can take these. It's ibuprofen."

She propped herself with her elbow and he dropped the tablets onto her palm. She swallowed the pills with a mouthful of water from a paper cup he held out for her.

"Did you take some?"

"Yeah." He set the cup on the floor. "Look, I'm sorry about last night. I was way off base."

"I don't want to talk about it."

"I need to explain."

"No, you don't." She forced herself to stay alert when all she wanted was to burrow under the blanket and shut out the world. "Tell me how you were captured."

"I tried calling at lunch but you didn't pick up. Went home to see if you were there and not answering your phone because you're pissed at me."

"I wouldn't do that. It's not professional." It was easier to talk with her eyes closed.

"I was getting worried, so I had to check. The rest of your team was at the courthouse. I let them know I was heading home to find out what was going on." He glanced at her. "Then I made arrangements to get myself here."

She was drifting, so it took a minute for his words to sink in. "That doesn't make sense," she mumbled.

The bed dipped farther. "I'll explain later." There was a brief touch on her forehead that made her wonder why he would kiss her, then sleep claimed her.

\*\*\*

It seemed like only moments later that a hand on Ellie's shoulder was shaking her awake. She opened her eyes to find the room in darkness, only a faint light coming from the bathroom. "What's going on?"

"Shh. I'm making sure you're asleep, not unconscious."

Sam's voice, barely audible, came from immediately behind her, his breath warming the back of her head. She tried to sit up but found that she was cuddled next to him, his arm wrapped around her middle and his head next to hers on the pillow.

"How's the head?" he whispered.

"Not as bad." She matched her voice to his. "How's yours?"

"Swelling is down, so better."

"You're in bed with me."

"Observant, marshal. Feels right, don't you think?"

"God, how come you sound so chipper?"

"Not chipper, but at the moment, I'm right where I want to be."

She turned her head to try to look at him. "Held prisoner in a basement is where you want to be? I don't get you."

"That's because your brain is muddled. You'll figure it out. Until then, getting in bed with you keeps us both warm because it's damn cold down here. Plus, it seemed like the best option for keeping an eye on you, and there's only one bed."

"Oh." She figured she should object but couldn't gather the energy. Sam pulled her tighter against him, the warmth of his body sinking into her bones, and despite their current predicament, his outdoorsy scent and his strong arms wrapped around her made her feel safe.

When Ellie roused again, it was to Sam's low voice rumbling in her ear.

"Time to wake up, love."

Ellie blinked open her eyes and tried to clear the dream from her head, a dream that had included someone chasing her through a pounding rainstorm until she'd been captured, only her captor had turned out to be Sam, and they'd tumbled into wild, no-holds-barred sex. This was not the time to be having sex dreams about the man currently spooned snugly against her. "I'm not your love," she mumbled.

"Heard that, did you? Voices low, remember?"

"Right. What time is it?" She rolled over to face him. Considering the erection nudging her backside, it seemed prudent.

"According to the clock on the ancient VCR, almost five a.m."

"You didn't sleep?"

"No. I needed to wake you every two hours. That, and I had work to do."

Ellie tried to make sense of what Sam was saying. What had happened to the man who'd accused her of prostituting herself for the Marshals Service? His tone, his words, his care for her—none of those matched the cynicism with which he'd lobbed accusations the night before.

She'd like to blame her jumbled mental functioning on the possible concussion, though she suspected that might be better explained by Sam's proximity. It didn't seem to matter that he'd hurt her and she was still angry with him, or that they were in danger. All she could think about was how good it felt when he held her close. She spread her hands that had somehow become lodged against his chest, the steady beat of his heart reassuring.

"I didn't find any surveillance devices," he whispered. "Doesn't mean there aren't any, so we talk quietly. How do you feel about getting out of here?"

"Favorably."

"Good, because they plan to kill us."

A chill raced down her spine. She spoke so quietly she barely breathed the words. "Why would they kill us? It won't get them what they want."

"They screwed up, and they know it. Their original plan may have been to use you to pressure me, but now that they've kidnapped a federal judge they're adjusting. They think killing us will send a warning to others in the justice system, and potentially ignite their movement."

"I still don't get how you got caught."

"I'll tell you about that later."

His response made her wonder why he was stalling, but she let it go. "How do you know their plan?"

He moved his head on their shared pillow until they were nose to nose. "I overheard them. Remember how you said you heard me through the vent in your bedroom? There's a vent in the ceiling that must connect to the living room. I was searching it for a hidden camera and heard voices. They were having a nasty argument.

Couldn't make out every word, but I got enough to know they plan to shoot us and bury our bodies somewhere on this property. Drew argued against it, but the fucker was eventually brought around." His breath fanned her cheeks as he whispered. "Big Dog is in charge. He took off a couple hours ago, said he'd be back in the morning so they could deal with us."

She jerked her up to lean on an elbow. "Why'd you let me sleep? We need to do something. Now." She didn't know how, but there had to be a way out of the basement. Sitting and waiting for someone to come through the door with a gun wasn't an option.

He used a hand to her back to pull her against him. "I was waiting for Sarge and Drew to either leave or go to sleep."

"How would you know if they're asleep?"

"I can hear Sarge snoring. He must be on the couch or recliner. Drew doesn't snore so I know it's not him."

"So where's Drew?"

"That's the wild card because I don't know where he is. I heard a door being opened and shut, so maybe he left. His pickup was parked by the barn when Big Dog brought me in, so he could have gone to the ranch."

"And if he didn't, we'll deal with him."

"Exactly."

"Okay, I'll use the bathroom, then we'll have to figure a way out of here. We don't have much time."

"Use the bathroom, but don't flush. We don't want anyone upstairs to know we're awake." He turned on a lamp and when she returned, he'd stripped the pillowcase from the pillow and was filling it with water bottles and a couple of granola bars. He opened the box of Cheez-Its and stuffed a handful in his pocket, putting the rest of the box in the pillowcase.

"Hungry?" she whispered.

He shoved some in his mouth. "Yes, but these?" He indicated his pocket as he crunched. "They're for Fido up there."

"His name is Rex. What's your plan?"

He pointed to the door. "See that?"

Her brows flew up. The door was still firmly shut, but the pins had been pried out. She winced at the throbbing pain reminding her that the wound on her forehead was nowhere near healed. "How'd you get the pins out of the hinges?" she whispered.

He pulled the screwdriver from his waistband, tipping his head next to hers when he handed it to her. With their heads together they talked in low tones. "Here's your weapon back. Took time to work the pins out with that and not make a lot of noise, but the door's only recently been installed so the hinges are well oiled. They slipped out fairly easily, considering. We should be able to slide the door out, even with the deadbolt."

Ellie nodded, mind leaping ahead. "So our plan is to get out of the house as quickly and quietly as possible and not engage. If we have to overpower Sarge, we do it, but with Drew's location unknown, there's a risk of alerting him. Problem for us is Sarge likely has guns stashed around the house. I saw an AR in a corner of the living room, and two rifles on a rack over the fireplace. There were weapons in the van. He has at least two handguns, one of them mine. He could have guns under the couch, in drawers, under the cushions. He could sleep wearing his holster. There's no telling."

Sam nodded. "It'll help if the dog is outside. If he's inside, he could sound the alarm as soon as we go up those stairs. I hope he likes Cheez-Its."

"There's the front door and a sliding glass door by the table, plus the kitchen door. If Sarge is in the front room, the kitchen door will be the best option."

"Okay. Did you see where the barn is when you came in?" At her nod, he continued. "There's a big oak behind it. We get out and if we get separated, we meet there. From there, we're heading to Rock Creek Ranch."

"Can you get there from here in the dark?"

"It's a hike, but yeah, I can get us there. And dawn isn't far off."

He grasped the front of her coat and tugged her toward him.

"Sam, I can't—"

"Shh, I know. We need to talk, but later." He dipped his head and then his lips were on hers in a kiss that warmed her all the way through. They were both breathing more heavily when he stepped back. "We stick together and we'll get through this."

# Chapter Twenty

Ellie crept up the stairs, Sam behind her. The door to the basement now leaned against a wall. It had been surprisingly easy to remove, and since it was an internal, hollow-core door, it hadn't been all that heavy. The door at the top of the stairs was closed. The knob turned easily in her hand and she pushed the door open a half foot. The sound of snoring, much like a sputtering engine, filled the air. Sam's hand at her waist tightened and she turned her head as he reached the top step beside her.

"I'll go first." Even with his mouth close to her ear, the words were barely audible.

She shook her head. "I'm the marshal, I go first."

After a long pause, he gave a brief nod.

Pushing the door wider, she stepped into the room, standing frozen as she took in details. Dim light emanated from the kitchen, enough that she could see that Sarge lay in a fully extended recliner. From what she could tell, he didn't have a gun on his lap. That was something.

She didn't see Drew. Given the animosity between the two men, she didn't think he'd stayed the night in Sarge's home. A movement on the rug in front of Sarge's chair had her stomach sinking. Rex raised his head, dark eyes gleaming. He stood, head lowered, and padded toward her across the carpeted floor. Ellie took it as a win that he wasn't growling.

She reached out a hand to Sam. "Cheez-Its."

He filled her hand and she bent forward to hold one out. Rex's gaze moved from the Cheez-It to her face, then back.

Sam whispered in her ear. "We go for the kitchen door."

She nodded and tossed a couple Cheez-Its in front of the dog. He stared at them, seeming to weigh his options, then gobbled them up.

She angled herself so she was facing the dog, backed a few steps toward the kitchen, and threw down more crackers. Sam must have figured out her plan because he moved behind her, hand gripping the back of her coat as he guided her backward toward the kitchen. Every couple feet she tossed crackers. And so they went, the dog following them as they moved toward the kitchen and escape.

Grateful for the single low-wattage bulb over the stove that offered enough light to see where they were going, she stepped inside the kitchen. Though her nerves were stretched tight, she thought they might make it. Then the snoring stopped. They both froze.

Sarge gave a phlegmy cough, and his chair creaked. She controlled her breathing, willing back the panic that urged her to bolt for the door. From where she was, she couldn't see into the living room.

An electric whirr sounded overly loud and Sam's grip tightened on her coat. She knew that sound. The footrest of the recliner was being lowered as the back was brought up. Rex's gaze remained fixed on the crackers in her hand. The floor creaked and she straightened, waiting for the moment when Sarge would come around the corner and find them. But then another light came on, this one in the hall, followed by a shuffling of feet, and then the unmistakable sound of pee hitting water in the toilet. A minute later there was a flush and more shuffling footsteps. The chair creaked again, followed by the whirring sound. Giving a mental *ew* because Sarge hadn't washed his hands, Ellie reached back for more Cheez-Its. So quietly she could hardly make out the words, Sam whispered, "That's the last from my pocket."

Several agonizing minutes later while she was dropping crackers one at a time, the snoring restarted. Ellie was never so happy to hear someone snoring in her life. She and Sam continued their painstaking trek across the kitchen. After swallowing the last cracker, Rex turned his head, ears perked, with an expression that said *Where's the Cheez-Its?* his gaze shifting to Sam when he slid back the deadbolt and turned the knob. A cold breeze came through the opening as Sam stepped outside. He kept his hand on her coat and Ellie eased out after him. Sudden furious barking erupted as Rex launched himself against the door. Ellie reeled backward to be caught by strong arms. Rex had done them a favor by slamming shut the door so he couldn't come after them.

Sam released her and grabbed her hand, yanking her after him. "Run!"

They raced around the house. A door slammed and Rex's barking shot up in volume, and that told her he was outside.

"Go! I'm dumping the Cheez-Its from the bag to distract the dog." Sam must have detected her hesitation because he snapped out, "Run, I'll be right behind you."

She ran. It was near impossible to see more than shadows overlaying shadows, the only light coming from a fixture attached to one corner of the barn and the pale glow of a crescent moon.

The storm had cleared leaving a star-strewn sky. The grass underfoot was wet and the patches of bare ground muddy. Ellie moved as swiftly as she could. The front yard was an obstacle course that would be a challenge in daylight. In the dark it was a nightmare.

She hit mud and her feet slid from under her. She regained her footing only to trip over something half buried in the dirt. She bit back a howl of pain when what felt like a knife sliced through her jeans and into her knee. Forcing herself to block out the pain, she struggled to her feet. She couldn't hear Sam and could only trust that he was behind her. She pressed ahead, limping, her goal the tree on the far side of the barn. Even if the crackers slowed him down, if Rex wasn't leashed he'd be after them in seconds and the meetup spot wouldn't be safe.

Straining to hear over the thundering of her heart, she raced through the night, the pain in her knee excruciating. The barn lay up ahead. She'd circle the structure to the left to stay out of the light, hoping that as her eyes adjusted she'd be able to see well enough not to run into a fence or tractor or whatever else could be around.

In the pitch-black darkness at the side of the barn, she moved as quickly as she could, keeping her hands in front of her. She stumbled into a fence built against the corner. With a hand on the metal railing, she loped along as it turned back toward the barn and she realized it was some sort of corral. She paused, listening. A noise, like clothing rustling, had her reaching for the screwdriver. She patted her hip where it should have been, heart sinking when she realized she must have lost it when she'd tripped.

She kept still, waiting for Sam. She didn't dare call out to him. Then a distinctive sound had her blood turning to ice—the metal on metal clank of a round being chambered into the barrel of a gun.

"Well, well, isn't this a surprise. No sudden moves, now. I wouldn't want to shoot you before it's time."

Drew. Ellie swallowed. She thought she heard the faint thudding of someone running, maybe Sam trying to reach their rendezvous point. Rex continued barking, but nearer the house. She prayed Drew hadn't heard the running footfalls. Using the darkness, she shifted into the shadows.

"Hold it right there." A light flared and she blinked as Drew shined a flashlight in her eyes.

"Let me go. Don't make what you've done worse than it already is." Drew was a dark form in front of an outline of what must be a back door to the barn.

"You think you can talk your way out of this, sister? Not going to work. We'll take a little walk back up to the house so Sarge can see who takes care of things when he fucks up. The asshole thought there was no way anyone could break out of that room, but now it's up to me to catch the escaped prisoner."

Ellie's knee throbbed and she could feel blood soaking into her jeans. At least if Sam had escaped he'd be safe, and she'd only have to worry about getting herself free. The thought of Sam came with a strong yearning. When she was with him, she felt like somehow they'd come out of this mess alive. Without him beside her that optimism faded, but she refused to give in to the despair.

Drew's tone changed. "It'd be even better if I bring you back with Sam. Where's that brother of mine?"

"I don't know."

"Bullshit. Tell me where he is, sister. Do that and I'll try to get them to go easy on you." His attention caught on her leg and he lit it with the flashlight. "Fuck, you're bleeding pretty bad. Come on up to the house and we'll take care of it, but first tell me where Sam is."

"I really don't know. I tripped and we got separated."

He prodded her with the muzzle of his gun into walking in front of him. "Ha. He wouldn't leave you behind. Maybe Sarge caught him." The beam of his light shone on the ground in front of her.

"Who's the 'them' you mentioned? I only know Sarge."

"Asshole Sarge and Big Dog. Not going to lie, they're planning on killing you both. I don't much like that, but I get why they want it done. It'll send a message to the courts not to try to take our guns, plus show that we'll fight for our rights. We'll be heroes like Jesse and Frank James. Bet we'll have people falling over themselves to join our cause."

Ellie never got what made the robber and murderer Jesse James heroic but wasn't going to argue the point. "Murder is a lot more serious than simple kidnapping, Drew. You know all hell will break loose if you kill a federal judge or his girlfriend. Anything happens to us, this entire state will be crawling with law enforcement looking for you. And you will get caught. Things will be better for you if you let me go."

He shook his head. "You should never have gotten with my brother. He never heeded the warnings and pulled you into his mess, so this is on him. If he'd reversed his ruling and let Bannister out of jail, none of this would have happened. But fucking Judge Creed has no problem trampling all over folks' Constitutional rights."

They paused under the light at the barn. Drew's truck was in the shadows. Rex was still barking, but near the house. Sarge shouted something. Walking slower to stall, anything to give herself more time, she said, "He loves you, you know. Sam told me about you and your mom. He loved her, too."

"Don't you talk about my mother."

"I'm not talking about her, I'm talking about Sam. He believes in you, believes you can be the man your mother hoped you would be."

"Don't you fucking talk about my mother." His voice cracked and he shoved her forward.

"Sam said she made the ranch a home. That she loved you, and she even loved him. Would she be proud of you now, Drew?"

An explosion of barking and wild shouts erupted from behind the house, followed by the sharp crack of a gunshot splitting the air. Ellie slapped a hand over her mouth to stifle a scream.

Sam!

Blood drained from her head and her vision grayed. Had he been caught? She'd thought he'd run past the barn, but then what had Sarge shot at? Drew grabbed her arm and pulled her up the driveway to where light from the house illuminated the front yard. Rex bulleted from the back, racing past them at the same moment a repulsive, sulfurous odor assailed her nostrils.

"Goddamned dog!"

Drew clicked off the flashlight and pulled his coat over his nose. "He can't ever leave a skunk alone. You'd think he'd learn after he's been sprayed a couple times. Hope Sarge killed the damn thing."

Sarge charged around the side of the house, bringing the smell with him. Rex rolled on the ground, rubbing his face in the grass.

Drew took a hasty step back when Sarge stopped beside him, pistol in hand. "God, you reek as bad as the dog."

Sarge scowled. "Damned dog can't leave the fucking skunk alone. Thought he'd found our prisoners, but no, he had a skunk cornered by the woodpile. Sprayed him right between his eyes, then he tried to rub it off on me."

Seeing the men and dog occupied, Ellie again moved back a step to the edge of the light.

"You shoot the skunk?"

"Missed it. Damn thing got away, but now I've got a dog that stinks to high heaven and I'll have to burn these jeans. Damn dog can stay outside until he stops stinking. I can't be giving him a tomato juice bath every time he gets stupid."

The sound of a car engine coming up the road rumbled in the distance. She eased back one more step. Drew spotted her and she could have growled in frustration when he motioned her forward with a wave of the gun.

"I caught one of the prisoners you let escape. Good thing I stayed in the barn or she'd be gone. Guess your basement wasn't as secure as you made out it was."

"How was I to know they'd pry the door off its hinges? Now where's Creed, or did you let him get away, too?"

"Let him get away? You let him get away, asshole, not me. I got her, didn't I? You're the dumbass who let them escape."

"You think you're all that? Then go ahead and put a bullet through her head, dickwad. Those are our orders. Once she's dead, we'll go after Creed."

"You think I won't do it? You think you're the only one who can do the real business? After this, you'll give me some goddamn respect and call me Lobo."

"You'll always be dickwad."

Drew raised his arm, the barrel of the gun leveled at Ellie's head.

Ellie couldn't take her eyes off the dark hole in the muzzle of the pistol. She heard a vehicle roar around the bend and Drew lowered the gun. "We'll see what Big Dog says."

Ellie wheezed out a pent-up breath as a white truck with dual wheels in the back came to a hard stop under the circle of light by the barn. It struck her that the night wasn't quite as dark. A faint pink glow was lightening the eastern sky.

She breathed deep to slow her racing heart. Both men holstered their weapons, making her wonder who had arrived that elicited that kind of response.

There was a scuffle by the newcomer's truck.

"What the hell's going on over there?" Drew craned his head to see.

"It's got to be Creed," Sarge groused. "Big Dog will get him. We'll get our asses chewed that we let them escape."

"*You* let them get away, not me."

"All Big Dog will care about is that they escaped."

"Shit." Drew started shifting back and forth like he was nervous. "You think he needs help?"

Sarge gestured. "Does it look like he needs help?" Sam was walking toward them, a tall man behind him looming large.

As they neared the light, Ellie could see that the man following Sam wore an old-fashioned holster slung low on his thigh, the pearl grip of a revolver gleaming in the light from the house, a black cowboy hat tipped forward over his brow. He shoved Sam ahead of him.

Sam approached where she was standing, his gaze traveling over her, eyes blazing. He stopped in front of her. "You okay?"

At her nod, he mouthed the word "fight."

Fight? Against three men with guns? The odds weren't good, but they were worse if they did nothing. And taking the offensive would be unexpected and could catch their captors off guard. She gave an imperceptible nod.

Their adversaries clearly didn't expect the attack. Sam rotated on the balls of his feet, swinging up and landing a punch that caught Drew square in the face. He went down like a puppet with its strings cut.

The big man reached for his weapon, but Sam went in low, tackling him to the ground in a tangle of limbs that sent the cowboy hat flying. Ellie turned on Sarge, leading with a roundhouse kick as he went for his gun. The force of her kick spun him around, but when he came up, he had his gun in his hand. For the second time in only minutes, she found herself staring into the muzzle of a gun pointed at her head.

"Good choice," he said as she froze. "Creed," he barked, "give it up."

Sam gave no indication of having heard. Straddling the other man, he used an elbow to crack him across his cheekbone, ducked to avoid a swinging fist, and gave a short jab to the nose.

Sarge raised the gun and shot a bullet into the air, then brought it back down again to level on Ellie. Sam leapt to his feet, fists clenched.

"Time to decide if your girlfriend lives another ten seconds, Creed."

Sam's gaze whipped from Ellie to Sarge.

"Easy. No need to be any more stupid than you've already been." Sarge's voice was utterly cool as the other men breathed heavily. Drew rolled onto to all fours and slowly pushed himself to standing.

"You fucking assholes." The big man had gained his feet, wiping blood from his nose with his sleeve. He spoke with a deep voice rife with disdain. "Lower the gun, Sarge."

Sarge hesitated, then did as he was told. The man picked up his hat, swatting it against his leg. When he locked his gaze on hers, Ellie felt like a trapdoor had dropped from beneath her.

# Chapter Twenty-One

"You fucking assholes," Richard Jameson repeated. "You kidnapped a Deputy US Marshal."

"What the hell are you talking about?" Sarge snapped. "This is Creed's fiancée."

"I doubt that. This woman is a Deputy US Marshal."

"A marshal?"

Sarge turned to her but Ellie couldn't take her gaze off her father. Sam moved to her side.

She'd imagined this moment so many times. Would he know her? Would she recognize him? Would she feel anger? Betrayal? Love? Now she knew.

Resentment boiled over and her vision hazed red. She lunged forward, pulled back her fist, and rammed it into his belly. His breath wheezed as he doubled over. "That's for Mom, you bastard," she snarled. She pulled back a leg to kick him, but Sam grabbed her arms and yanked her back.

"What is she talking about?" Sarge's gaze tracked from Ellie to her father.

Jameson straightened. There was a stoop to his shoulders that reminded her he was close to seventy years old. "Sarge, meet my daughter, Deputy US Marshal Eleanor Jameson."

"Your daughter? What the hell is this about?"

"God damnit." Drew turned on Sarge. "I told you she was undercover, but you wouldn't listen."

Sarge ignored Drew. "How the fuck were we supposed to know your daughter is Creed's girlfriend, and that she's a US Marshal?"

Sarge's voice sounded tinny in her ears as Ellie wrapped her arms around her middle to quiet the sharp tremors shaking her body.

Memories of her mother's strength in the face of Richard Jameson's abandonment and betrayal had her bearing down on the emotional pain. This was not the time to sort out the destructive feelings her father elicited. Survival for her and Sam was paramount.

Jameson's gaze finally left Ellie as he replied to Sarge. "By using your fucking brains, that's how you know. And if she's here, you can bet her brothers aren't far off."

"Her brothers?"

"Both US Marshals."

"Shit. We're fucked. Do you think you could have shared this with us before we grabbed your kid?"

Jameson disregarded Sarge's irritation, flicking a glance at Sam, who had positioned himself beside her before Jameson returned his attention to Ellie. "Well, daughter, it's been a long time."

This man was not the father she remembered. She'd studied images of him taken by security cameras, but in those he'd been conscious of surveillance and had taken care to obscure his identity.

They'd never been clear enough for her to make out the details she observed now. A mane of white had replaced his once-dark hair, and his face held deep grooves on either side of his mouth. Despite the years that had aged him, he was still striking, though the warm blue eyes of her memory were no longer full of light. Instead, they looked glacially cold.

Nothing of the man of towering strength who would hold his daughter high above his head so she could pretend to fly was evident in the old man who stood before her now.

"A long time since you abandoned your family."

He shrugged. "Regrettable, but it had to be done." Time had changed his voice, making it gravelly and coarse. "Your mother would never have followed me in the life I wanted, and I didn't want to disrupt the lives of my children."

"You're a coward and a liar. You didn't care about Mom, and you didn't care about us kids. Let's get something straight, you're not my father. Archer Bollinger is my father."

"God, I can't believe Margaret married that asshole. He hounded me for years." Disdain laced his words. "But understand this, daughter, I was there when you were born and I raised you until you were nearly grown. It's my blood that's running through your veins. That makes me your father."

Ellie shook her head and let contempt ring from her voice. "That makes you a sperm donor who hung around too long."

Jameson's fists clenched, and Ellie thought he'd strike her. Then his face closed and he settled his hat on his head.

"Doesn't matter. These guys made a monumental screwup and now I've got to deal with it." He turned to Sarge. "You ready?"

"We're going through with it?" Sarge raised his brows.

"Why wouldn't we? We've got to take care of these two and get out of here. I told you she's a marshal. Her brothers are marshals. They won't be far behind her."

Any thought that her father would let her and Sam live evaporated. Richard Jameson had participated in courthouse bombings, but he'd never been involved in cold-blooded murder. But now he was ordering an execution. Hers and Sam's.

Sam wrapped an arm around her and pulled her back against his body, pressing a kiss against her temple. "I'll create a diversion. You run," he murmured the words against her skin.

"No, we stay together."

"No more chances, Creed," Sarge said. "You deserve this."

There was no time for any diversion. Sarge raised his pistol, and Sam shoved Ellie to the ground as a shot ripped through the air.

As she went down, Ellie caught a brief glimpse of Sarge reeling back, the top of his head a bloody mess. Sam landed on her, his hands covering her head. Another shot rang out. Ellie's only thought was to get Sam to safety. She pushed against his weight, pulling on his arm.

They scrambled to their feet, Ellie grasping his hand as she pulled him toward the back of the house. A rapid spate of gunfire erupted behind them. At any moment a bullet could cut either one of them down.

They rounded the corner of the building as a loud blast rent the air and the ground shook. She looked over her shoulder even as she ran. A huge orange fireball erupted into the early morning sky with a roar like thunder.

The gunfire stopped.

They ran past trees bordering the yard, Ellie refusing to let her injured knee slow her down. The next thing she knew she was being pulled behind a wide trunk. Sam backed her against the tree and wrapped his arms around her. With his face bent next to hers, he said, "I don't know what the hell happened other than the propane tank exploded."

She nodded and held on to him. They were alive. Beyond everything else that had happened, they'd survived. She tried to sort out the impressions of the past few minutes.

"Sarge is dead," she told Sam. "The first shot took him out."

"Who shot him?"

"I'm not sure. I think the team is here, so it could have been Bella as she's the trained sharpshooter." She paused. "I didn't see what happened to Drew, but with gunfire and an explosion, I don't think it's good."

She pushed against Sam and he loosened his hold. "The shooting's stopped. We wait here until the team comes for us when the scene is clear."

Sam frowned when Ellie stepped away from him, her arms crossed tightly in front of her.

*** 

She'd called it. Sam figured they waited no more than ten minutes before Seth came around the house. Ellie stepped from behind the tree and called his name. Her brother jogged toward them, not stopping until he'd scooped his sister up in a fierce hug.

"You're safe," he murmured as he held her, eyes closed. After a long minute he released her.

"We're good," Ellie assured him. "Linc, Bella?"

"Fine."

"Seth, Dad was there."

Seth nodded. "We'd gotten into position when he drove up and Sam allowed himself to get taken."

Ellie turned on Sam. "You let yourself get taken?"

"I couldn't protect you if I wasn't with you."

"It was *my* job to protect *you*. You should have stayed safe."

Sam kept his mouth shut.

Seth gave him a speculative look, then asked his sister, "He recognize you?"

She faced her brother. "He did. He knows we're all marshals, and that Mom and Arch are married." Her voice tightened. "He told Sarge to kill Sam and me."

"The fucker. He's beyond redemption, Ellie."

"I know. Any doubts I had are gone."

Seth put an arm across Ellie's shoulders like he still needed reassurance that she was in one piece. Sam wondered how Seth dealt with his sister being in danger on a regular basis. "You can hope he's better than he is, but he'll always disappoint you. He got away."

"What? How?"

"All hell broke loose and he slipped past us, that's how. First shot took out Petrie, the guy who owned this place."

"Sarge. The members of this militia give themselves code names. Dad's is Big Dog." To Sam's ears, Ellie sounded exhausted. He felt tapped out himself. His priority now was to get her checked at a hospital, then he'd be happy if they could go home and shut the door to the world for a week or so. That he saw her with him after her assignment was completed no longer surprised him.

Seth motioned them to follow him. "Let's go. That burning tank makes it too dangerous and too hot to go that way, so we'll go around." Seth led them in a wide circle, avoiding the house. They tramped along until they came to a fence and followed it to the barn. The propane tank continued to burn.

Through the trees Sam saw that fire had spread to a van parked next to the tank. He figured Seth was leading him away from the scene of carnage. He was pretty sure the fire would keep the team from getting to bodies. He asked the question that was at the front of his mind. "Is my brother dead?"

Seth turned to Sam, gaze steady. "I'm sorry, he is."

Sam waited for the wave of emotion. Nothing came except a feeling of numbness.

"Funny thing, though," Seth continued. "That first shot? Bella was sighting through her scope and saw what happened. Drew shot the guy you call Sarge before she could."

"Drew shot Sarge?"

Ellie grasped his hand. "He saved our lives, Sam."

"Or maybe he hated Sarge enough to kill him."

"He saved our lives," Ellie repeated. She turned to her brother. "How did Dad get away?"

"We think Drew was planning to shoot him, too, but Dad shot Drew first." He shook his head. "We were going to take Dad out if we had to, but you and Sam blocked our shot. Once you were out of the way, we waited to see how it played out. Dad started running, shooting at the propane tank. Damn thing went up like a fucking pyrotechnic show. He got to his truck and got away."

"We saw the fireball. There must have been a leak for it to explode like that. I thought I caught the skunky smell of propane when they first brought me here. Hard to know for sure, because Sarge was having trouble with skunks." She paused. "What happened to the dog?"

Seth shrugged. "Don't know. We'll keep an eye out for him."

They arrived at the barn. Richard Jameson's white truck was gone.

"How'd you know we were here?" Ellie's fingers were cold so Sam brought them to his mouth to blow warm air across them. His gaze stayed steady on Seth's when he saw the man give him a considering look.

"Got a call from Ben Montoya. Sam would know more about this than me. His father's the foreman of your ranch?"

Sam nodded. "That's Pete Montoya."

"When you two went missing, Ben went out to your ranch and he and Pete searched Drew's things. They came across evidence pointing to Drew's involvement in the SecAm militia movement and tying him to Petrie as well as to a plan to kidnap Ellie. Lucky for us you'd told Ben that Ellie is a marshal and that he'd met Linc. He contacted us." Seth spared Sam a glance. "You've got some explaining to do about how you ended up their captive as well."

Bella approached them, a rifle with a scope in her hand. She gave Ellie a one-armed hug. "Glad you and Sam are safe, friend."

"Me too," Ellie said.

Sam spoke quietly to Seth. "She's hurt. She's got a head wound, probable concussion, and her leg's bleeding."

Ellie shot him a look of exasperation.

"We've got aid coming," Seth assured him.

The deep wail of a fire truck in the distance and a whumping sound cutting through the air were welcome. In minutes a windstorm kicked up as a helicopter with an official insignia set down like an ungainly insect in a wide section of the driveway.

There was a flurry of activity as officers in law enforcement gear disembarked. Seth took a phone call, pressing a finger in one ear to hear. Sam saw a woman with a red cross stitched as part of her shoulder patch and waved her over. She introduced herself and followed him to where Ellie had hobbled to an upturned log to sit with her injured leg straight out in front of her.

"Ellie, this is Sue Delgado, she's a paramedic with the county."

He had to give Ellie credit because she didn't automatically claim to be fine, as was her usual response. "She has a head injury and possible concussion."

"We'll check that out," Delgado assured him, not taking her eyes off her patient.

"Her leg is bleeding."

Delgado nodded.

"She needs to go to the hospital."

"That's why she's being checked out." The paramedic grinned at Ellie. "Does he always hover like this?"

"Pretty much," Ellie grumbled.

"Aw. He cares."

Delgado opened her medical kit and took out a stethoscope. Linc came over to check on his sister, so when Seth beckoned, Sam figured Ellie was taken care of for the moment and went to see what Seth wanted.

The following hour passed in a blur. More official vehicles arrived. An APB was issued for Richard Jameson, though Seth said the effort would likely be fruitless because the fugitive was a ghost adept at disappearing.

Sam glanced in Ellie's direction and found that Delgado had cut off the leg of her jeans and was wrapping her knee. The propane fire finally burnt itself out, and the coroner took possession of the bodies, both charred beyond recognition. Sam watched as they were placed in black bags and thought of Drew's wasted life. His brother had made his choices, but that didn't make Sam feel any less guilty.

The goal that had been driving him for the past twenty-four hours of keeping Ellie alive had been achieved. Exhaustion was biting at his heels, but he needed to push through until he got Ellie home. Remembering the moment Sarge had raised his gun caused him to break out in a cold sweat.

He borrowed Bella's phone to call Pete and let him know about Drew, and that Pete should expect a team of US Marshals at the ranch later that afternoon to take possession of anything belonging to Drew they thought was relevant.

Sam stepped out of the house with Ellie's brothers. He'd shown the marshals the basement where he and Ellie had been held captive.

Seth studied Sam, brows pulled low over his eyes. "Want to explain how you found Richard Jameson and got him to bring you here? We've been after him for years."

"First, understand that I didn't know who he was. He introduced himself as Big Dog. Then I did what I thought I had to do to protect Ellie."

"Given that she's my sister, I appreciate that. But her job was to protect you, Judge, and what you did put your life in danger."

Sam responded, gaze steady on Seth's. "I won't have her sacrificed to keep me safe. Ever."

"Why don't you tell us what happened?" Bella asked. Sam figured she was trying to defuse the tension.

They were owed an explanation so he tried to organize what had happened in his head, wishing he had a quart-size mug of coffee.

"Okay. Yesterday morning I went home because I couldn't reach Ellie. I'd barely gotten in the house when a text came in of Ellie in cuffs." He remembered how a jagged hole had opened in his gut when he'd seen that image. "There was a warning not to call law enforcement if I wanted to keep her alive. I got a call from a different number belonging to a man calling himself Big Dog. He arranged a meeting, said if I didn't come alone, my fiancée was as good as dead. I met him in the parking lot of a closed business. He told me if their captive was going to survive—I don't think he knew her name—I had to reverse the ruling on Frank Bannister so he would be released, and make other statements from the bench that would help his cause. I refused."

Sam rolled his shoulders. "We, ah, ended up fighting. That made him mad enough that he decided to go for a bigger impact by killing a federal judge. I got the feeling he didn't really care about Bannister. I was counting on him bringing me to where they were holding Ellie. It was a risk, but it worked out."

Seth shook his head. "You should have called us. We could have done this without jeopardizing your life, or Ellie's."

"Your primary goal is to protect me, the federal judge. My primary goal was to protect Ellie any way I could. If I'd called you, you could have fucked it up and she'd have ended up hurt worse than she already was. Or dead. I wasn't willing to risk that."

"Your way almost ended up with both of you dead."

"Luckily, it didn't."

After a long, considering look, Seth finally nodded.

"What my brother means is thanks for helping keep our sister alive." Linc clamped a hand on Sam's shoulder.

"Yeah, that." Seth's expression didn't change. "Do we need to talk?"

Though he guessed what the Chief Deputy was getting at, Sam wouldn't make it easy on him. "About?"

"About you and my sister and your fake engagement."

Bella rolled her eyes. "If you value your life you won't do this. You know Ellie will be unhappy."

"I'm responsible for her."

Sam figured it was a good time to keep his mouth shut. Maybe Seth would forget about "the talk," but somehow Sam knew he'd come back to it. The rotors of the helicopter began spinning, picking up speed.

"As a marshal, maybe," Bella insisted, "but definitely not as a bossy big brother."

"You saw what kind of a dad we have, so it falls to me."

The noise from the helicopter increased until it took off with a roar of sound. Sam looked around and felt a clutch of panic.

"Where's Ellie?"

"On the chopper," Bella said. "That's what I came to tell you. The paramedic thinks Ellie has a concussion, and wants her knee stitched at the hospital."

"What the fuck? She can't go by herself. She needs me with her." Sam stared at the retreating helicopter and felt like half of him had gone with it.

Linc clamped a hand on his shoulder and grinned at the others. "See those little hearts circling his head? I think that's a definite yes to 'the talk.' This boy's got it bad."

# Chapter Twenty-Two

Ellie stirred, pain from her throbbing knee pulling her out of sleep. She blinked several times as awareness returned. She'd been flown to the hospital in Pendleton, lost the argument about being admitted overnight, and had finally been able to fall asleep sometime around midnight.

The muted glow of early morning shone around the blinds over the window, casting enough light to allow her to see the man sprawled in a chair beside her bed. Sam had arrived late in the evening and she had to admit that when she'd heard his voice, her anxiety dissipated. It was like she knew on a subconscious level that if Sam was there, she was safe.

Though she'd been ready to kick him out when he'd insisted that the doctor admit her after he'd diagnosed her concussion. The doctor had agreed with Sam's point that since the blow to her head wasn't the first incident affecting her brain in a matter of weeks, she needed observation.

Now, with long legs stretched in front of him and wrapped in a too-thin, too-short blanket, he hardly looked comfortable. Dark lashes resting against high cheekbones made her wonder why guys always scored long, thick eyelashes.

Tousled hair falling over his forehead would've given him a boyish look but for the bruising around his eye and the dark whiskers shadowing his jaw.

He had to be exhausted to be able to sleep in that position.

There were so many things about him she admired—his sharp intelligence, his sly humor, his basic decency—things that she would commend in many people, but in Sam they were on top of something more, something that had her feeling like she was dangling over a cliff by her fingertips. If she loosened that grip by even one finger, she'd free-fall into love with him, and that scared her as nothing in the past few days had.

Her feelings for him weren't exactly straightforward, because thrown into the mix was the knowledge that while he might care for her, caring was a long way from love. Their fake engagement had led to forced proximity, which by its nature amplified feelings that would wane as life got back to normal.

She wished Sam didn't feel responsible for her. And she wished even more that he respected her ability to do her job.

She shifted onto her back, trying to stifle a groan at the soreness in her knee. She wanted to use the toilet, brush her teeth, and, most importantly of all, take a shower and wash her hair.

Sam stirred and sat up. "Hey, you're awake. What time is it?"

She glanced at the clock on the wall. "Just after seven."

He tossed off the blanket and rose to his feet to stand at the side of the bed.

"How are you feeling?"

"Better. Headache is gone." She used a button to raise the head of the bed. "Would you help me get up?"

"I'll call the nurse."

"Fine, but while we're waiting, I want you to help me to the bathroom."

He pressed the call button as she pushed herself upright. "Hang on," he said. He lowered the side rail. "I'll carry you."

"No, you won't carry me. It's not like I have a joint injury and have to keep weight off my knee." He offered his hand and, holding on to him, she tested her weight on her leg. "See, I'm good. There's no additional pain."

"You're being stubborn. Let me carry you."

"No, I can make it." She walked with him to the bathroom, and when she got there, shut the door firmly lest he decide she needed even more help.

She returned to the room as Bella walked in carrying several bags.

"You found my purse? Thank you."

"And your phone, so you're welcome." Bella handed it to her, plus a plastic bag, before shrugging a daypack off her shoulder. She dug in her pocket to hand Sam his phone.

"Cool, thanks." Sam immediately began thumbing through messages.

"I brought a change of clothes and some toiletries you might need." Bella emptied rolled clothes from the daypack. "The pants and shirt are Seth's. They'll be too big but will fit better than mine or Linc's would."

"Whatever you brought is better than a hospital gown, so thank you again." Ellie opened the plastic bag to find a toothbrush and toothpaste, hair products in small bottles, and hand lotion. "This is wonderful. You're a lifesaver."

"How are you feeling?"

"Head's good, knee hurts." She picked up the bags. "I'll feel even better after a shower." Ignoring Sam's scowl, she made her way back to the bathroom.

When she got out, Bella had gone. Sam had pulled up the window blind to allow in the morning light, and stood with his back to the room, staring through the glass.

He turned when he heard her. "Bella said she'll be back later with your brothers and food."

"Okay." She studied Sam's expression, wondering if there was something going on with him.

"The nurse said he'd be back to change the bandages on your knee and forehead. He didn't sound happy that you were getting them wet."

She shrugged. "I hadn't had a shower in two days. Feeling clean will help me to get better."

She'd rolled the waistband on Seth's flannel pants, and the sweatshirt came well past her hips, but she felt infinitely better out of the hospital gown. She started to ease onto the bed when Sam strode over.

"Jesus, will you wait a minute? I'll help you."

"I'm fine, Sam. I'm not an invalid."

"Not unless being pigheaded makes you an invalid." He watched her with an eagle eye, clearly unhappy that he couldn't pick her up and arrange her on the bed himself. Once she was settled, he took her hand in both of his, rubbing his thumb over the engagement ring she still wore.

She stared at their joined hands. "Thanks for being here. You must have spent a miserable night on that chair."

"I couldn't leave you."

Her heart seemed to grow in her chest. "I'm glad you didn't."

He brushed a kiss over her knuckles. "Ellie, I want—"

Whatever Sam had been about to say was cut off when the door swished open. Ben came into the room, his white lab coat stitched with "Benjamin Montoya, MD." He grinned as Sam let go of her hand. "You're doing the engaged act really well."

Sam ignored the comment. "Thanks for coming."

"Glad you're both okay, brother." Ben stood at the foot of the bed, his dark gaze traveling over her. "How's the pain, Ellie?"

"The headache is better, but my knee hurts. A lot."

He consulted his iPad before saying, "Mind if I have a look?"

She shook her head, and he pulled back the sheet. "Didn't like the hospital duds, I see."

"Yup."

Sam stood on the other side of the bed. "She took a shower and got the bandages wet."

"Then we'll take those off." Ben pushed up her pant leg to reveal the damp bandage and peeled the tape from around her knee. "Someone got in their sewing practice, I see. Twelve stitches is impressive. It looks healthy."

"Is there permanent damage?" Sam asked.

Ben shook his head. "No. It should heal pretty quickly."

He followed the same process with the wound on her forehead and the old injuries on her back and behind her ear. "Everything looks good, you're healing well."

"Great, when will I be released?"

"Soon. You'll need to let the nurse replace the bandages and give you care instructions. Your chart says you're due for your pain meds. Once that's done, release will be dependent on what your convalescence arrangements are."

"She's coming home with me."

Ellie frowned at Sam. "Why? Sarge was sending the threats and he's dead. My assignment is done."

"Your assignment is done because that concussion has bought you a two-week off-work order, with full rest for at least one. That means no screen time, phone included," Ben warned. "We're not releasing you until we know you'll be looked after."

"She's coming home with me," Sam repeated. "I'll look after her."

"You don't need to do that. They'll make room for me at Marshal Central."

Sam was already shaking his head. "You're coming home with me."

Ben grinned at his friend. "You two work it out. Staff will check back to see what you decide." He turned to go, saying to Ellie, "I'll let your nurse know you're ready for the pain meds."

Sam walked out with Ben, returning minutes later with the nurse, who introduced himself as Kai. He reapplied the bandages and handed Ellie pain pills to swallow. Once he'd left, Sam dragged the chair he'd slept in closer to the bed and collapsed onto it. Dark circles shadowed his eyes.

"You should go home and get some sleep. You look exhausted."

"I am exhausted."

He picked up her hand through the bed rails, his thumb once again rubbing the engagement ring. "We need to talk, Ellie."

"That sounds ominous."

"Not ominous, but we need to talk."

It suddenly hit her, his restlessness, the way he kept touching the ring.

"Oh, right, the ring." She pulled her hand from his and began working it off her finger.

"What are you doing?"

"Giving you back your ring."

"Why? You don't need to do that."

"Of course I do. You must want it back. It was a prop. A beautiful prop, but not mine." She ignored the hollow feeling in the pit of her stomach and held the ring out to him.

His gaze locked on hers but she couldn't read his expression. With a scowl, he took the ring. "Right."

He tucked it into his pocket as the door swished open, this time admitting three US Marshals carrying Styrofoam take-out containers and a caddy with hot drinks. Sam stood and moved to lean against a wall, arms crossed over his chest. He took a coffee Bella handed him, closing his eyes as he took a sip. Linc commandeered chairs from somewhere, bringing them in to arrange around her bed as food was passed out.

The next time she looked, Sam was gone.

A shower, food, coffee, pain meds, Ellie should be feeling better, but instead her mood deflated like a popped balloon. So that was that. Her assignment was done, her ring finger bare. And somehow she'd ended up with a broken heart.

She thought she was hiding her feelings well enough until Bella raised a brow that Ellie read as *What's wrong?* She shook her head, swallowing against the lump in her throat, and forced herself to pay attention. She was a Deputy US Marshal, and she would do her job.

After answering the general questions about her welfare and eating most of her breakfast burrito, she asked Seth, "What happened? Did you get Dad?"

Seth dumped the container from his breakfast in the trash before answering, anger tightening his features. "No sign of him. Marshals from Portland are fanning out, visiting all known contacts in the area. If he's still here, they'll find him."

"Except he won't be anywhere around here."

Seth nodded. "Agreed. He'll be long gone."

"On the positive side, we've broken SecAm," Linc said. "We have possession of Sarge's computers and Drew's. If any members of the group are involved in the crimes Sarge committed, we'll have the evidence to prosecute them."

Linc shook his head. "Drew was using his last name as his password. We've already accessed his email account and have proof Sarge was sending the threats to Sam. Sarge was Freedom Defender. There were also details of the plan to target Sam while he was out running. Sarge wanted Drew to drive the truck, but when he refused, Sarge did it himself. Lucky for all of us, he failed."

Linc sipped his coffee. "Oh, one more thing. We found the dog. Smelled godawful, but we took him over to Rock Creek Ranch. The old guy, Pete Montoya, said they'd get him cleaned up and keep him."

"Oh, that's good." Ellie was glad the dog hadn't been left to fend for itself. "Thanks."

"We also discovered that problems at Rock Creek Ranch were Drew's doing," Seth added. "We found an email where Drew said ranches being harassed, particularly by environmentalists, would bring calls from the community for stronger protections of gun rights."

"And our father is part of all this, including being a member of SecAm." Ellie didn't pose it as a question.

Seth rubbed a hand over the scruff of his beard. "He is. From what we can see so far, he doesn't get his hands dirty. He posts ideological diatribes online that get their followers stirred up, then he leaves them to take illegal actions that might get them thrown in jail."

"We found C-four in Sarge's barn," Bella added. "Turns out he had explosives training in the military. It appears he's the one who planted it on Sam's car."

"To what degree was Drew involved?" Ellie asked. Whatever Drew had done, hopefully knowing that in the end he'd acted to protect his brother would soften Sam's feelings of betrayal.

"Only peripherally until he kidnapped you," Seth said.

"What about the flashbang thrown into Sam's house, and whoever drove through the backyard?"

"Linc's been working on that." Seth motioned to his brother. "Want to explain?"

"We're waiting on a warrant to search the vehicle and electronic equipment of nineteen-year-old Jeremy Finster."

"*Jeremy* Finster? Gordon's son?"

"Yeah. We've questioned both father and son. Gordon says his son doesn't belong to any militia groups because he knows it would jeopardize dad's job. But while he may not have joined any militia groups, we have evidence Jeremy participated in online forums advocating anti-government action to protect gun rights. We think he took it a step farther when he targeted you."

"How'd you figure out it was the son?"

"Gordon was having car trouble and borrowed his son's truck to drive to work. Same make, model, and color as in the video. We took it from there."

Kai opened the door, entering the room carrying a sheaf of papers. "I've got your discharge orders. We'll process them once I know where you'll go for convalescence." He raised his eyebrows in question.

Bella answered the Ellie. "She'll either be with us or with her fiancé, Sam. She will be looked after."

"Great. Here's a copy of her care instructions."

"Sam's not my fiancé," Ellie muttered after Kai left.

Linc was busy texting on his phone but looked up. "Tell him that. Are we ready to pack up?"

Feeling miserable, Ellie kept her unhappiness to herself as she took her seat in a wheelchair. Linc set her purse on her lap, slinging the other bags over his shoulder. "Seth and I will get the car."

The female attendant took the push handles with a sigh as the men walked out the door. "Those two? They're what my grandma would call a long, cool drink of water."

"Ha," Ellie said. "Don't let them hear you say that. It'll go to their heads."

Bella walked beside the wheelchair as they made their way through the maze of hallways. Once outside in the bright midday sunshine, Bella sat on a bench next to Ellie's wheelchair to wait for her brothers.

"I noticed you aren't wearing your engagement ring," her friend said. "Want to tell me about it?"

"It wasn't my engagement ring, and Sam broke up with me." Ellie knew that didn't make a lot of sense.

"He asked for the ring back?"

"Well, no. But he acted like he wanted it back. And we're not engaged, so of course he should have it back."

"Did you ask him? Never mind," Bella said. "I wish I'd taken a picture of that look on his face when you were flying off in the helicopter without him."

Ellie glanced at the attendant, then at Bella. "It was all fake, you know that."

"It may have started out that way, friend, but things changed for him."

The Land Cruiser pulled into the patient loading area and Sam stepped out.

"See what I mean? He's not done with you," Bella murmured with a grin.

The attendant fluttered a hand over her chest as Sam strode over. "Another one? You're one lucky lady, let me tell you."

# Chapter Twenty-Three

"Ready to go?" Sam's gaze traveled over her.

"Why'd you leave?"

"I had to get my car. Ready?" he repeated.

"My brothers are taking me to Marshal Central."

"Bella can come with us. I texted Linc that I was on my way to get you. Something came up they need to take care of, so this works out."

Bella was busy texting as Ellie settled in the front passenger seat and Sam put her bags in the back. Bella stepped away from the vehicle as Ellie waved good-bye to the attendant.

Ellie narrowed her gaze. "Aren't you getting in?"

Bella shook her head, smiling brightly. "Linc says they'll pick me up, so you two can go ahead."

"We've been set up," Ellie said as Sam drove away from the hospital.

"How so?"

"You're kidding, right?"

He gave her a quizzical look.

"Never mind." They drove through town, and Ellie thought Sam was steering more carefully than usual.

"What are you doing?"

His brow furrowed. "Driving."

"You're driving like a bump in the road will make me break."

He increased the speed by maybe five miles per hour.

"You missed the street to Marshal Central."

He turned onto his own street. "No, I didn't. It makes more sense for you to stay with me. There's plenty of room, and your things are there."

She crossed her arms in front of her. "But you no longer need marshal protection."

"True." He turned into his driveway.

Sam's house looked tidy and welcoming, the sun reflecting off the front window and chrysanthemum blooms waving in the breeze. This was what she'd been worried about. She loved Sam's home, and coming back made her yearn for something that couldn't be. The garage door rolled up, and Sam parked inside. Ellie slid from the vehicle with only a twinge from her knee while Sam retrieved her bags and purse from the back.

She walked through the yard littered with bright orange and brown leaves shed by the giant Oregon white oak. Her entire world had changed in the few weeks since she'd first come home with Sam.

The dogs were barking from inside. Sam opened the door and they scrambled out, tails wagging.

"Hey, beautiful babies." Her gaze rose to Sam's in alarm. "Are they starving? Have they been fed?"

"They're not starving. Before I went after you, I called Dalia. She took care of them and I swung by earlier this morning to feed them."

She looked at him sharply. "Before you went after me means you planned to get taken."

"We'll talk about it. Let's go in."

She followed Sam into the house, the dogs remaining outside. He took her bags up the back staircase and Ellie wandered around. The flowers she'd put in a vase on the window ledge had faded, the bananas in the fruit basket were now spotted. In the living room, Gumbie lay curled on the couch.

She scooped up the cat to hold on her lap as she sat. Gumbie began kneading her paws and purring. Water ran through the pipes upstairs and she guessed Sam was taking a shower. She should begin gathering her things together and pack her suitcase. As much as Sam said he wanted her to stay, she couldn't hang around. Two weeks of being off work was a long time. Maybe she'd fly to San Diego and spend that time with her mom and stepdad.

She'd gotten over Sam once before, she could do it again.

The other option was to simply talk to Sam and tell him how she felt. What if his feelings for her ran deeper than responsibility? The thought of opening herself, of being vulnerable, scared her like nothing else. But what did she have to lose? She could ditch her pride and lay herself open.

She closed her eyes and cuddled Gumbie, grateful for the cat's warm comfort.

\*\*\*

Feeling a little more human after his shower, Sam stepped into the living room, his gaze immediately drawn to the woman sitting on the couch with the cat on her lap. The pensive expression on her face pulled at his heart.

"You okay?"

He sat next to her, shoulders touching. Gumbie jumped to the floor with her tail swishing.

Ellie turned her head to face him, eyes sober. "Sure, I'm fine."

He didn't believe that. He reached out a finger to loop a lock of hair behind her ear. "I've got to be careful where I touch. You have so many injuries I could hurt you."

They killed him, every one of the cuts and bruises she'd received because of her assignment to protect him.

"The only one that still hurts is my knee." She plucked at a thread on the rolled cuff of the sweatshirt she still wore. Without looking at him, she said, "You let Richard Jameson kidnap you."

"Heard that, did you?"

"No, guessed it." She met his gaze. "You didn't trust me to get myself out of that situation."

"They sent me a photo of you in handcuffs. I had no idea what they were doing to you or how badly you were hurt. I felt you'd have a better chance if I was with you."

"I was supposed to be protecting *you,* that was my job."

He chose his words carefully. "You're good at your job, but you're not invincible."

"I was working on a plan." She tugged harder on the thread. "I think the problem is that I'm a woman. Since I started this assignment, you've been resistant to me doing my job. You think you have to protect women, so therefore a woman can't protect you. Maybe it has something to do with losing your mom and stepmom the way you did. You think women need saving."

He shook his head. "Interesting, but not accurate. You're more than capable, and you were doing a fine job on your assignment. I'm still in one piece, aren't I? But it's not women in general protecting me that I have a problem with, it's you."

"Wow. At least you're honest."

He grasped the hand worrying the thread. He used his thumb to stroke her palm, then raised it to press a kiss in its center. "Try this for honest: I'm in love with you."

She went perfectly still, so still that he didn't think she was breathing. Not a good reaction.

"What did you say?"

He turned to face her. "I'm in love with you, Eleanor." He brought her hand to cover his heart. "You grabbed me right here and I haven't been the same since. I don't want to be the same." He huffed out a breath. "There's a part of me that's you, Ellie. Maybe it's corny, but I was only half alive until you came into my life."

She didn't move. He was sure he'd misjudged, that he'd laid himself bare and she would politely tell him to fuck off.

But in the next moment she beamed a beautiful smile and launched herself into his arms to rain kisses over his face. "It's not corny, it's beautiful. You're beautiful."

His heart swelled until he thought it would explode. He gathered her close for a long moment where he felt everything inside him settle, then, hands framing her cheeks, he held her back so he could see her eyes. "No matter how good a marshal you are, and you're damn good, I'll always try to protect you. It's impossible for me not to."

Her arms went around his neck and she buried her face in his shoulder. He heard a telltale sniffle and his heart clutched. "Are those bad tears or good tears?"

She shook her head. "They're happy tears."

He tugged her back again. A tear slid down her cheek and he wiped it with his thumb. "Happy tears are good, right?"

"Yeah, they're good. Better than good."

She shifted so she was sitting on his lap. He closed his eyes as she ran a hand through his hair and pressed her lips to his like she couldn't keep from touching him. That was okay because he pretty much felt the same.

His eyes opened when she took his hand and mimicked his move, laying it over her heart. "I had a thing for you thirteen years ago. It never entirely went away. When I met you again it slammed back into me like a tidal wave, and it hasn't let up since." A brief flash of vulnerability crossed her face, then disappeared. "I love you, Sam Creed."

He felt the grin splitting his face. "We should say that a lot, make up for lost time." He leaned forward and their lips met. "I love you."

She kissed him. "I love you."

With a nip to her bottom lip he held her away from him, trying to reach the pocket of his jeans. "Move it, woman. I need something."

Her eyes danced as she rubbed against the bulge in his jeans. "Maybe I need something, too."

"Ha ha. Don't distract me."

He pulled the small box from his pocket. Her gaze locked on it like it was a magnet and she did the frozen thing again. He was beginning to suspect that it was her shocked speechless reaction. He opened the box and held the ring between them. He was probably moving too fast, but with his love so huge this was the only possible course.

"A young man gave my aunt this ring when he asked her to marry him. She cherished it for the rest of her life." He steadied himself with a deep breath. "Will you wear it, Eleanor? Will you marry me? Will you love me forever?"

The blue of her eyes looked deep enough to drown in. "Yes, Sam. I'll marry you. I'll love you forever."

He slid the ring back on her finger where it belonged. She held out her hand so the emerald-cut diamond caught the light. "I thought we were done when you took back the ring."

"You insisted I take it back. Worried the hell out of me because our fake engagement felt real to me. But I needed to propose properly."

She leaned forward and their mouths met as they clung to each other.

When she moved against the erection nudging her thigh, he shook his head. "It kills me, but we can't."

"We can, and we should."

"No."

"Why not?"

"Concussion, remember?" She wiggled again and he groaned, then set her away from him. "I asked Ben. He said you have to limit your physical activity for a couple of weeks, and that includes sexual activity."

"You're joking."

"I would not joke about that."

"It's going to be a long two weeks."

\*\*\*

Ellie and Bella sat next to each other at the small kitchen table while the men did the after-dinner cleanup. Ellie wasn't allowed to carry a dish or even fill the dishwasher, they said, for an entire week. For the moment, she was okay with that. Cleo and Tony lay on their bed, Cleo's soft eyes steady on Ellie. The little dog had remained close all afternoon.

Bella tapped Ellie with the toe of her suede boot. "I'm happy for you, El."

Ellie tipped her head on her friend's shoulder. "I'm happy for me, too." She held out her hand so the diamond caught the light. "See my ring? It's the most beautiful engagement ring ever."

"Agreed, it is the most beautiful engagement ring ever." Bella pulled out her phone and began scrolling. "I want to show you something." She tapped, then angled the screen.

Ellie peered at the image. Bella had caught the moment after Sam had first put the ring on Ellie's finger all those weeks ago. The emotion evident as they looked into each other's eyes jolted her. "It looks like we're already in love."

"It does. You were. I'm framing this photo as an engagement gift."

"Aw, thanks."

A knock sounded. Ellie stood and crossed to the front door to look through the peephole. A young man stood under the porch light, head bowed.

"Hold on." Sam came behind her and bent forward to look through the peephole. "I don't recognize him." Seth and Linc joined them. Sam draped his arm around Ellie's shoulder as he opened the door. The young man took a step back, his Adam's apple bobbing. He probably had a reason to be nervous, because two of the tall men looking at him were armed and wore badges.

The resemblance struck her, and Ellie guessed his identity.

"Jeremy Finster?"

A nervous gaze darted to her. "Yes, ma'am."

Linc stepped onto the porch. "Jeremy, I'm Deputy US Marshal Lincoln Jameson. I want you to turn around, spread your feet with your toes pointed outward, and lace your fingers behind your head."

He complied. Linc gripped his hands and did the pat down. "He's clean."

Linc allowed him to turn around and face them. "Why are you here?"

He cleared his throat. "I want to apologize to Judge Creed."

His hand still on Ellie's shoulder, Sam nodded to the others. "I've got this." After a long look, Linc returned to the house and closed the door.

Gaze direct, Sam said, "Well?"

Jeremy cleared his throat. "I'm sorry, sir. I screwed up. I should never have messed up your yard or thrown that flashbang."

"This is my fiancée, Ellie. If it had been only the yard, I wouldn't be so pissed. But Ellie's everything to me, and she got hurt with the flashbang. We're lucky the injuries weren't more serious."

Jeremy's Adam's apple bobbed again and he shifted his gaze to Ellie. "I'm sorry, ma'am." She couldn't see anything other than remorse on his face. "I was reading stuff online. It messed up my thinking. My dad talked to me, made me look at things different." He looked at Sam. "I know Dad has some other trouble at the courthouse, but he didn't know what I did until the cops came. I knew it was wrong when I did it, but I was dumb, and I know I'm still in trouble with the law. No matter what happens, I'm sorry."

Ellie nodded. "Apology accepted."

Sam extended his hand. "Apology accepted."

Jeremy looked relieved and shook Sam's hand. "Thanks."

They watched the young man walk up the driveway. Sam pulled Ellie into him, his chin resting on top of her head,

"That was hard for him," Ellie murmured.

"It should be hard. I'm glad he had the guts to do it."

"Me too."

Contentment seeped through her as they stood, arms around each other. Ellie tipped back her head. "I really like your house. Am I going to move in with you?"

"Is the house all you really like?"

"No. I really like you, too, Sam Creed."

"Hell yeah, you're moving in with me. Then we've got a wedding to plan."

He leaned forward and Ellie felt the promise of his kiss burst through her like a bright shining star.

# HIDDEN LOYALTY

# Chapter One

Bella was a pro at hiding her emotions, which was absolutely crucial given her current assignment. Her job this weekend? Be the knockout arm candy to the man sitting in the driver's seat of the car they were riding in. A man who wore sexy and remote as smoothly as James Bond.

Chief Deputy US Marshal Seth Jameson, her boss, her current partner, the man who equally intrigued and infuriated her, had his gaze focused on the road winding ahead of them. Which she knew was misleading. While he *appeared* to be thinking only of mastering the two-tone red and black Bugatti Chiron, she was one hundred percent positive his brain was reviewing and re-reviewing their plan to take into custody the elusive and dangerous fugitive they were after.

Keeping her emotions hidden from Seth was as essential as breathing. Her job depended on it. Her mental health depended on it. And actually, her life depended on it. That block that allowed nothing to show on her face? It formed the foundation of the solid wall she and Seth had erected between them.

Solid, impenetrable, bulletproof.

She allowed few people to get emotionally close to her, to *see* her. Seth Jameson wasn't one of them. She caught herself worrying her bottom lip and pressed her lips together and mentally recited a Russian children's poem. She'd learned the trick to distract herself when she felt the urge to fidget or do some other silly physical action that would give away her tension. Added bonus? The poems reinforced memories from her childhood. Good memories that sometimes she feared would fade to nothingness under the smothering weight of the horrible memories, which burned stronger in her mind.

Seth crossed into the opposing lane to pass two cars, one of them a Tesla Model X. The Bugatti roared as it ripped past the cars like they were the staid Soviet vehicles she remembered from her youth.

Expensive and exotic cars seemed to be the norm in this section of California's central coast, and the Bugatti had been chosen to add to the aura of wealth that would help make their ruse believable.

Bella stared out the window at the incredible view. Far below the highway, waves broke on the rocky coastline and sea lions lolled on the sand like giant slugs. Fascinated, she watched as a huge bull sparred with a smaller sea lion. She battled back the urge to share with Seth what she'd seen.

Keeping her thoughts and emotions to herself had become second nature. It seemed her entire life had been spent trying not to show what she was feeling. She'd learned that lesson as a young child—never let anyone know you wanted or cared about something. A doll you slept with when you were afraid, a bowl of porridge when you were hungry, a book of poetry given to you by your dead father. Caring about such things only made you vulnerable when they were taken away. Show happiness? Not a chance. That too could be stolen from you. Don't show surprise, feign interest if necessary, separate yourself from the present so as not to be affected.

All good training for the task that lay ahead of her.

She closed her eyes briefly, her face turned from Seth. A phone call that morning from her brother had brought unwelcome memories to the surface, and along with them, emotions she struggled to suppress. No one could destroy barriers and rip open the past like her brother.

She brought her attention back to her assignment. The mission was dangerous, maybe the most dangerous of her career, and she needed to emulate Seth's monumental focus to make sure she acted exactly as she'd been coached.

Their task was to gain access to and arrest the incredibly wealthy, eccentric, and heavily guarded fugitive Hugo Montenegro. The first step had been achieved. Seth had constructed a fictitious background as a fabulously wealthy antiquities trader, one who didn't mind skirting the boundaries of what was legal to commandeer items particularly desired by his clients.

Montenegro's interest was in instruments of death, especially those used in ceremonial deaths or notorious killings. Seth had learned of Montenegro's obsession with one item and had been able to use that as leverage to obtain an invitation to the fugitive's home.

Bella's job was to appear decorative. Normally when working, she maintained a professional demeanor as dictated by the policy directives of her employer. That meant wearing clothing that projected a positive image of the Marshals Service to the public and didn't draw attention to herself.

Conservative women's suits, minimal makeup, and her hair pulled back in a bun all served that function well. If sometimes the look felt uninspiring, she reminded herself it was an honor to serve in one of the finest law enforcement agencies in the United States, and there was no room for complaining about the dress code.

For this assignment, however, lowkey and staid had been thrown out the window. She'd prepared carefully, using the stipend allotted to her to purchase attire that would highlight her assets. She had the makeup and accessories to help create the look she'd wear for their overnight stay.

The kickoff was a formal dinner party, and she thought she'd hit the mark for that event. Her hair was pinned at the back of her head in a sophisticated upsweep that showed off her neck. She'd left a few stray curls artfully arranged for interest. She'd used copious amounts of mascara and eye shadow to accentuate the shape and the color of her eyes, making them appear more exotic and a deeper blue. She'd selected crimson red lipstick to draw attention to her mouth.

Her long dress gleamed an iridescent blue that reminded her of peacock feathers and showcased her curves, emphasizing the narrowness of her waist before flaring up, and with the help of an amazing bra, lifting her breasts like a sacrificial offering.

When she'd opened the door of her hotel room to Seth's knock, lust had zapped her with a white-hot jolt. He stood tall and impossibly handsome in black tie. The formal wear should've tamed him, made him look refined, polished, but somehow the smooth black jacket and the stiff white cuffs only served to provide a thin veneer of civilization.

There'd been a moment when she thought he'd been caught off guard. For mere seconds, his slate gray eyes had flashed generating a blistering heat as they'd swept her body from head to toe. By the time that gaze met hers, any reaction to her appearance had been walled off.

The ice man was back.

Looking out the passenger window, she clenched her fist when she realized she'd been rubbing her thumb across the platinum ring heavy with diamonds she wore on her left ring finger. A prop to strengthen their cover.

The car crested a hill and exposed a staggering view. Their destination lay ahead at the end of a long valley on a rise above a gleaming lake, the estate situated in a way that screamed dominance over man and nature.

The gleaming structure of stone and glass could only be described as a palace, but not in the often tacky way Americans had of trying to re-create the homes of European aristocracy. The beautiful façade appeared carved of granite, and glinted silver, its windows reflecting the sun setting beyond the ocean gleaming to the west.

Focusing on the imposing building wasn't enough to keep her thoughts off the man sitting beside her. He may have given her that once-over, but his appearance had hit her equally as hard.

Surreptitiously, she studied his profile which looked to've been carved of the same granite as the structure they were nearing. If she was a pro at hiding her emotions, Seth Jameson was a master. Which made her wonder if she was the only one to sense their strong emotions kept locked behind a fortress wall.

She gave an involuntary start when he reached out to grip her hand. He raised a cool brow. "You're messing with the ring. It looks like you're not used to it. Montenegro will notice that. He'll notice everything about you."

"That's the point, isn't it? He's a sexual predator, and we're counting on him noticing me. I can distract him, and he might say things to me that he wouldn't say to you."

"Right." He returned his hand to the steering wheel. A muscle worked his jaw. "You nervous?"

"A little, but you'll be there." His gaze flicked over her and she shrugged. "I'll do my job."

"No doubt."

They followed the curve of the driveway to the front of the house. Big men in dark blazers and sunglasses with mirrored lenses stood at strategic spots—an upstairs balcony, the front entrance, a walkway that rounded the corner of the house. Hugo Montenegro was taking no chances with his safety. He was a high-value fugitive shining a spotlight on himself this evening.

Seth pulled to a stop behind a Mercedes-Benz. A valet elbowed another to the side for the chance to drive the Bugatti. The young man stepped forward but Seth held him off with a raised hand. Instead of reaching for the door handle, he turned to face her. "We'll be sharing a bedroom."

"We've talked about this, sir. I know what to expect."

"Call me Stephen, even if you think we can't be overheard. You never know where there might be listening devices. We're Stephen Bullock and Anna Novak." Dark brows lowered over his stone-gray eyes. "It's more than the bedroom. We have to display a believable level of intimacy. As you said, Montenegro is a sexual predator and he'll be aware of a beautiful woman. You're supposed to distract him, but that's as far as it goes. The best way to keep him from attempting anything more is for you to stay close to me and make sure he knows you're mine. The story of our recent engagement will support that."

"I'll play my part, *Stephen*. You play yours. If you can convince him you have what he wants, we'll be able to complete this assignment and go home."

He glanced out the window. "The valet is watching. We start now." He leaned forward and pressed his mouth to hers. The shock kept her rigid, then heat flashed and her lips moved under his. The hair at the back of his head, the deliciously thick hair she'd had secret fantasies about, slid through her fingers.

He broke the kiss and moved back, a look crossing his face that was gone in a heartbeat. If she didn't know better, she'd say it was stark hunger. But, as he'd said, acting their parts was critical, and he'd already started.

She gathered her composure, nonchalantly rubbing her thumb across the skin at the corner of his mouth. "Can't have you going to a dinner party with lipstick smeared on your mouth, darling."

"Right. Let's go."

***

Seth rose from the car and took a carefully controlled breath. He hated feeling distracted. God knew Bella was distracting. That was a given and something he'd learned to deal with. Then there was the letter he'd received and had placed in his home safe the day before. A letter from his father designed to jerk his chain and make him feel like a loser. It wasn't going to work. The minute he let Richard Jameson undermine his confidence was when the fucker would win. Seth wouldn't let that happen, but it was still damn disruptive to receive a communication from the man for the first time in two decades.

He rounded the hood of the car and tossed the key to the valet. "The luggage in the back goes inside."

"Yes, sir."

Seth opened the passenger door for Bella. He forced himself to keep breathing as she took his outstretched hand and rose fluidly from the low-slung car. She was always beautiful, but the clothing she normally wore for work was, if anything, on the prim side.

She stood before him in the sharp heels that did amazing things to her legs. Prim was a memory he'd try to cling to. He cleared his throat when the dress all but shimmered over her. The slit up the side went nearly to her hip and had him biting back an oath. Her shoulders were bare, the smooth, flawless skin there another temptation.

The glitter of the diamond pendant nestled between her breasts was sinful, and brought to mind a recurring dream involving his lips being right where the pendant rested. That image always grew more erotic and too many mornings he woke hard, sweaty, and alone. He'd forced hiding his response to her to become routine, but he had the uneasy feeling that arresting the elusive Hugo Montenegro would be a piece of cake compared to controlling his hunger for Bella Nikolaev.

The Bugatti purred as the valet drove the vehicle past them. Bella draped a lacy wrap around her shoulders and took Seth's arm as they approached the wide stone steps to Montenegro's over-the-top trophy house.

A big bruiser stood at the base of the steps leading to an impressive entryway. The iPad he held looked like a toy in his massive hand. His coat gapped open and revealed a gun holstered under his shoulder. Seth would bet his next promotion that the pistol wasn't Bruiser's only weapon.

"Stephen Bullock, with my fiancée, Anna Novak."

Bruiser studied the iPad, then nodded. He raised his head and his gaze snagged on Bella's exposed cleavage. "I need to search you."

"Eyes over here, pal." Bruiser lifted his gaze as Seth growled, "Search me, but you're not touching her."

"I don't search her, she doesn't get in."

"You're not touching her. Call Montenegro. Make sure he knows you're blocking Stephen Bullock and his fiancée." Seth pulled up his sleeve to glance at his large black watch. "You've got two minutes."

Bruiser turned his back and pulled out his phone. In less than the allotted time, he turned back. "Welcome to Chateau Montenegro, Mr. Bullock." He nodded to Bella. "Ms. Novak. Please proceed through the entry doors to the reception room."

Bella's grip loosened on Seth's elbow and he escorted her to the impressive doors. Once inside, they stood in the foyer where guests milled about, looking at the artifacts Montenegro had staged for display. Seth scanned faces, then allowed Bella to lead him to a glass case where diffused light showcased what he recognized as a *tecpatl*, a ceremonial knife used by Aztec priests to cut open the chests of human sacrifices to extract the beating heart as an offering to feed the gods.

Another case displayed a club he knew for a fact had been looted from Mesa Verde: the ruins left by the Anasazi people a thousand years ago. A discreet card explained that the Anasazi had used the club to kill their enemies, some of whom were then cannibalized and their remains tossed off the cliffs where the Anasazi made their homes.

"I see that Montenegro is consistent in his interests," Bella murmured.

"He is that." The artifacts belonged in museums, not in the possession of an individual with twisted peccadillos who was willing to buy them on the black market.

They crossed the foyer to a wide room where other guests stood talking quietly in small groups. Montenegro wasn't one of them. Bella smiled but didn't engage in conversation. The room was overly decorated with European antiques, most French, which didn't look sturdy enough to sit on. He couldn't imagine relaxing on the gold-threaded couch with his feet up on the ornate coffee table watching a basketball game. Not that there was a TV in sight.

He guided Bella across the room with a hand at the small of her back. The material slid over her skin and enough heat radiated through to singe his fingers. Either she was running a fever, or he was the victim of some strange chemical reaction when he touched her. As much as it bothered him to admit it, the truth was probably the latter.

A small man with wire-rimmed glasses and a goatee spotted them and broke away from the couple he was talking with to approach them. "Mr. Bullock, welcome."

Seth nodded. "Mr. Needham, this is my fiancée, Anna." No doubt Needham knew exactly who she was, or at least who she appeared to be.

The little man bowed over Anna's hand. "Mademoiselle, it is a pleasure. Please call me Gerard." He straightened and waved over a server carrying a tray of drinks. "Dinner will be served shortly, but please, enjoy an aperitif and conversation with others, if you wish."

He shook a head at the server. Dulled senses could be dangerous when dealing with a snake like Montenegro. From the offered tray, Bella took a wide-rimmed glass that looked like lead crystal and sipped the bubbly drink, closing her eyes and giving a sexy little hum of pleasure as she swallowed. When those baby blues opened and she smiled up at him, the heat arrowing straight to his groin told him he was in deep shit.

With them playing a newly engaged couple deeply in love, the iron grip he'd managed to keep on his control felt like it had been slicked with oil. Damn. Another image he didn't need to conjure.

"That champagne? How is it?" Conversation might help focus his attention.

"It is champagne, and it's divine. Would you like a taste, darling?" Her eyes held a challenge as she stretched on those killer heels and put her mouth on his, parting her lips so the tip of her tongue slid against his.

His head exploded with the silky taste that he was convinced wasn't entirely alcohol. The effect ratcheted up what was fast becoming a craving to an almost unbearable point. Her hand tightened on his lapel as if she suddenly felt the need to hold on for balance, then she stepped back and gave him a sweet smile.

She was killing him one smile at a time. But if the second kiss in less than twenty minutes had affected her, she was hiding her reaction damned well.

"Do you like it?"

He felt buzzed, like he'd actually consumed a dozen glasses of bubbly, and he hoped to god his dinner jacket hid his response to her. "Yeah, I *like* it."

"Bullock. Wasn't sure you would make it."

Nothing like coming face-to-face with a wanted fugitive to pull Seth's head back in the game. Point for him he'd handled Montenegro well enough he hadn't taken Seth's attendance for granted. That was the idea—keep the guy guessing and on the edge.

Seth shrugged at the comment. "There's another party interested in the same artifact as you. He insisted I listen to his offer."

Something flashed in Montenegro's eyes but disappeared when Bella extended her hand and spoke. "Hello, Mr. Montenegro. I'm Anna Novak."

Seth studied his quarry as the man took Bella's hand as his gaze moved over her. He was a slick bastard with his three-hundred-dollar haircut and personally tailored tux that likely cost more than Seth made in a month.

If Bella found the way Montenegro's gaze lingered on her body distasteful, she hid her reaction well. He brought her hand to his mouth, where his lips lingered over her fingers before releasing her.

"How lovely. Welcome to my home. It's a pleasure to meet you, and you must call me Hugo."

"The pleasure is mine, Hugo."

"Anna is my fiancée." Seth kept his voice smooth as he caught Bella's hand in his, rubbing his thumb over the engagement ring. Montenegro caught the possessive movement, a hint of irritation crossing his face.

He gave a formal bow of acknowledgment. "Congratulations. Your good fortune is my loss." His gaze once again returned to Bella's cleavage. "I don't know how I'll be able to pay attention to my other guests with the delectable Ms. Novak in my home. Since you have accepted my invitation to stay the night, perhaps you'll join me for a nightcap before we retire."

"Oh, that would be lovely." Bella's lips curved in a seductive smile as she laid a hand on Montenegro's arm and leaned forward. A man would have to be a saint not to lock his gaze on the bountiful breasts before him, and Montenegro was no saint.

He cleared his throat and eyed Seth. "I don't suppose you want separate rooms?"

Seth flashed a humorless smile. "I don't suppose we do."

Montenegro turned back to Bella with a gusty sigh. "Tell me, Anna. May I call you Anna?" At her nod he continued. "Tell me, how does a man like Stephen Bullock propose marriage? Somehow, I can't see him down on his knee in front of you," he paused and his expression turned sly, "at least to propose."

Bella ignored the obvious innuendo, instead laughing delightedly, her blue eyes sparkling. "You're right, he didn't go down on one knee. That's too subservient for a man like Stephen, but he made up for it in other ways. He was romantic and sweet, and absolutely turned my heart to mush." She angled her face up to beam at Seth. "The romance was nice but telling me he loved me was all I needed. I said yes."

Seth felt her words wrap around his heart and squeeze, and he wrestled back the urge to loosen the bowtie at his throat.

A server stood in the doorway and nodded to Montenegro, who turned to the gathering and raised his hands to give a sharp double clap. "Dinner is served. Gerard is at the door. Follow him and he will lead you to your seats at the dining table."

Montenegro wasn't giving up pursuing Bella, and offered her his arm. It was what they wanted, but every instinct Seth possessed told him Montenegro was a threat, which made Seth want to keep Bella close to his side.

# Chapter Two

Bella cast a coy look over her shoulder as Seth followed her and Montenegro. Seth'd break the fucker's fingers if they slid any farther down her ass. It was a fine ass, and that shimmery material didn't leave much to the imagination. The desire to see the body under the dress was making him sweat. Seth knew what he'd do if he got his hands on her. He'd back her up against a wall, slide his hand through that sexy-as-hell slit in the skirt, then over the soft skin of her rounded buttock—there was no way she was wearing anything but a thong—and then around to the front where he'd—

His thoughts ground to a screeching halt.

*Fuck.* He buttoned his jacket and ordered himself to get a grip. No matter how much she might tempt him, Bella was his coworker, a subordinate, and his partner. No way in hell would he break the rules he'd sworn to uphold. If he couldn't control his thoughts in a room full of people, he was doomed.

They stepped into the dining room where the table was set with fancy dinnerware. Montenegro cocked his head to murmur in Bella's ear, and Seth caught the light sound of her laughter. They reached the end of the long table and Montenegro made an elaborate show of holding out a chair next to the host's seat. "Anna, I insist you sit next to me."

With another throaty chuckle, Bella smiled at him. "I'll sit here only if Stephen is on my other side."

Montenegro uttered an elaborate sigh. "As you wish, my darling, but promise me you'll understand if I monopolize you during the meal. I find you enchanting."

Seth didn't roll his eyes, but he wanted to.

Bella sat and Montenegro bent over as he helped push her chair forward, not bothering to hide that he was using his vantage point to ogle her breasts. His finger trailed along her shoulder and Seth clenched his jaw.

Montenegro's head dipped so his lips were against Bella's ear, but he didn't lower his voice, clearly intending to provoke Seth. "You are lovely in every way, Anna. Let us hope that we enjoy each other's company as much as I think we will." The bastard's smarmy voice lowered to murmur words Seth strained to hear. "I had feared that this evening would be dull, but now I find I am anticipating the coming hours quite keenly."

The inflection he gave his words made him sound vaguely European. This was an affectation. Seth knew Hugo Montenegro had been born and raised in a gritty neighborhood in East St. Louis, Illinois. He looked up and caught Seth's gaze on him, flashing a smile that reminded Seth of a ferret's: sly and cunning.

Montenegro took his seat and Seth leaned back and draped an arm across the back of Bella's chair, staking his claim.

Montenegro smirked. "Worried I'll steal your fiancée right from under your nose, Bullock?"

"Not a chance. Anna knows she's mine."

As Bella flirted with Montenegro, the waitstaff served the salad. The only ingredient Seth could identify in the pile of leafy greens in front of him was a sliver of radish. Bella's throaty laugh washed over him as she leaned toward Montenegro and chuckled at a comment he'd made. Seth would've never guessed his partner would be so good at undercover work. Playing up her assets and flattering their mark to the point where Montenegro appeared nearly blinded by lust seemed to be second nature to her.

Seth managed to pull his gaze off her when the man at his left made an attempt to engage him in conversation. As his team had compiled files on each person on the guest list, he knew the man owned a horse farm and olive orchards his current wife had acquired from her first husband in their divorce. Seth chatted easily as he studied the other guests. The men in black tie and the women in glittering jewels were exactly what they appeared—members of the local elite who'd be stunned to learn they were dining with a federal fugitive. Company CEOs, a winery owner, a county supervisor, all had no doubt been thrilled to receive an invitation from the wealthy Hugo Montenegro.

Seth cast an assessing gaze at Montenegro. Bella had him all but salivating, distracting their target, encouraging him to the point where he'd become preoccupied with her. But she kept enough distance to keep him challenged and in pursuit.

The goal was for Bella to bring the additional element of sex to the game. Not that the bastard was getting any closer to her than he already was. Seth's plan was to maneuver Montenegro into a meeting at a place of Seth's choosing, a location where the Marshals Service could detain him and keep the risk low. Two previous efforts to apprehend Montenegro had ended with one marshal wounded by hired guns. After that escape, Montenegro became even better at evading capture.

This time the setup was more elaborate, but it was justified. The Marshals wanted to get more than Montenegro. They wanted the antiquities he'd acquired on the black market. They had been able to procure a particular item, a rare object Montenegro coveted. If Bella managed to dangle the possibility of sex like a fishing lure, then Montenegro would be even more likely to take the bait and latch onto the hook.

Which was a good plan, an excellent plan, except that by doing her job, Bella was driving Seth insane. When she'd opened her door at the hotel, he felt like he'd taken a sucker punch to the face. She was fucking gorgeous, and he was the poor bastard with his tongue hanging out, panting after her.

For the year and a half since she'd been assigned to his office, he'd been fighting a losing battle against an over-the-top insane attraction. He'd thought that ignoring how he felt would cause it to wither and die.

The opposite happened.

They'd been circling around each other since they were first introduced, alternating between arguing and sniping, and being distantly polite. None of their evasive tactics worked because no matter what Bella did or said, he wanted her more than the day before. His problem, one he thought he'd had a handle on. But this weekend might prove him wrong.

Seth swallowed the excellent prime rib, then picked up his wineglass to sip sparingly of the Merlot. He spoke with the people around him at the table, all the while continuing to keep an eye on Montenegro.

At sixty-two, the man enjoyed the benefits of his wealth. The skin of his cheeks and forehead looked tight from a facelift or constant Botox. His teeth gleamed blindingly white, and his fingernails were buffed to a shine. His guests would never guess that until eighteen months ago, his address had been a low-security federal penitentiary. Low security being the problem. With the help of a helicopter and a couple of well-trained hired guns, he'd managed to escape a facility where he'd been serving his sentence for insider trading and securities fraud.

The international agents who'd helped him escape were someone else's headache. Seth's attention was focused solely on nabbing Montenegro.

Seth glanced around the ornately decorated room. He would add the fucking castle they were sitting in to his investigation. He wanted to know how the hell the house, with all its fancy furniture, had been hidden when Montenegro's assets were seized. The Marshals Service was in charge of asset forfeiture and he'd make goddamned sure the bastard forfeited these assets.

*** 

"Anna, are you enjoying the evening?" Hugo reclined at one end of the loveseat, turning to face Bella when she sat beside him. The rest of the guests had departed, leaving her and Seth with their host. Except her "fiancé" had excused himself and disappeared.

"I am, thank you. Dinner was delectable. You must compliment your chef for me." She let her gaze travel the room. "I love your home, Hugo. It makes me think of the wondrous estates of the country of my birth. This room especially has a definite European flair. It feels civilized. Quite a contrast to the objects you have displayed in the foyer."

He gave an easy laugh while toying with a lock of hair that had escaped from her updo. "I am a great admirer of unusual relics and feel compelled to own them. But tell me, beautiful Anna, from where do you come?"

"I am from Prague in the Czech Republic. Have you ever been to my lovely city?" Giving herself a hint of a Czech accent wasn't a stretch. Russian and Czech have similar grammar structures and vocabulary, and Bella had an ear for languages and accents.

When preparing for the assignment, she'd won the argument that Hugo would find her more interesting if she displayed a European panache.

"The Gothic cathedrals alone would demand my attention, but there is so much more to explore than what commonly lures tourists. I find European women particularly lovely." He leaned forward. His head was inclined so close to hers she was afraid he intended to kiss her. She ignored the instinct to back away from him. "In fact, I would like for you and me to become better friends. Would you join me later tonight? I would take pleasure in your company in the hot tub." He gave the word "pleasure" added emphasis.

His breath smelled of the whiskey he sipped from a crystal tumbler. "I'm sorry, Hugo, I'm afraid I've given you the wrong impression."

"Have you? No need to include Bullock, if that's what's concerning you. Three can be one too many."

Seth strolled in, his casual attitude doing nothing to tame his dangerous edge. She'd gone to their room alone to freshen up after dinner, using an elevator of all things. Of course, Montenegro would have an elevator in his home, the pompous twit. After she'd returned downstairs Seth had excused himself and disappeared. Most likely the move was intentional to give her time to work on their adversary, but that didn't make her any less relieved when he finally rejoined them.

A dark brow winged up and his gaze snagged hers when he caught sight of them on the couch. Raw heat was quickly banked.

Irritation flashed across Hugo's face. "Tell me, Bullock, do you make it a habit to leave your fiancée to fend for herself?"

"Does she need my protection in your home, Montenegro? I wouldn't have thought so. Regardless, Anna can take care of herself."

"I see. Bullock, have you experienced the wonderful culture of Anna's home country?"

Bella considered the mistrustful expression on Hugo's face as his tone shifted and became more aggressive. They couldn't afford to antagonize him.

"Stephen can't wait to meet my family and has promised that we'll visit Prague soon," Bella cut in smoothly. "Isn't that right, darling."

Seth leaned over her and she thought maybe he'd brush a kiss on her cheek before taking a seat of his own, but instead he pressed his mouth to hers. He murmured against her lips, "Whatever pleases you, my love."

She often wondered if her boss experienced the normal range of emotions. More than once she'd heard his brother Linc refer to Seth as a machine because he kept such tight control over what he was feeling. At the moment, his slate gray eyes burned with an inner fire that sparked an answering heat from deep inside her. She suppressed a shiver. She'd have to remember that his response to her was part of a well-acted drama.

He stepped back and his expression turned impassive. When she was sure her cheeks weren't flaming, she cast a quick glance at

Hugo. He leaned against the cushioned seatback, the speculative look back.

His smile turned cunning when he asked, "Are you willing to share, Bullock?"

Bella's stomach gave an uncomfortable jolt. Seth sat in a chair next to her side of the couch, crossing an ankle over his knee. "Share what, exactly?"

"Don't be coy. You know exactly what I'm referring to. Your fiancée, of course. Our bargain might be more advantageous to you if you were to allow me a night with the lovely Anna."

Seth's demeanor didn't change, but Bella wondered if Hugo was perceptive enough to notice what she did: the tightening of Seth's body, tensed like a panther before it pounced.

Hugo's gaze traveled over her again and she had the unsettling sensation of spiders crawling over her skin. "Don't worry, darling. I have unusual appetites, but I won't hurt you unless you want me to."

With his arm across the seatback behind her, he ran a thumb along the indentation in the column at the back of her neck. It took all her control not to move away from his touch, and she took comfort from the fact that with a minimum of moves she could have him on the ground and crying in pain. His attention made her wonder how many other women had been in a similar position with him but had no choice, and couldn't refuse his advances.

One at a time, Seth shot his cuffs forward and adjusted his sleeves before replying. "What do you mean by advantageous?"

Hugo sighed. "Americans have no subtlety, don't you agree, my beautiful Anna? They're all about the bottom line. Your fiancée is thinking 'how will this benefit me?' more than he's thinking of you. But I too can play that game." Bella breathed easier when he removed his arm to lean forward to address Seth.

"First, show me proof that you have what you say you have, the blade that sliced off the head of Marie Antoinette. I insist on seeing it. Show it to me with the appropriate provenance, of course, add a night with your delectable fiancée, and I will meet your exorbitantly high asking price. No uncivilized haggling or drawn-out negotiations." His mouth widened in a humorless smile that made Bella think of a coiled snake waiting to strike. "That is, unless I can convince your fiancée that her future is much more secure with me." He turned his black eyes on her. "What do you think, Anna? Can I entice you to leave your fiancé?" With a long, thin finger, he dipped between her breasts and lifted the pendant on its chain, rubbing the diamond with his thumb. His voice grew hoarse. "If you were with me, every secret fantasy you've ever held would be satisfied. You would have all the diamonds you could wish for, and your deepest, darkest desires met."

Bella felt a chill seeping into her bones and wished she hadn't left her wrap upstairs in the bedroom. She couldn't help but wonder what price a woman would pay if she agreed to his offer. What price other women had already paid. Bella leaned back against the cushions and Hugo dropped the pendant so it once again nestled between her breasts.

"I'm flattered you would ask me, but I value my engagement to Stephen and do not wish to break it."

"My loss then, but I think yours as well." He turned to Seth. "One night then, if that is all I can get. One night, and you will both be free to go on your merry way. I will get to experience the lusciousness that is Anna, and you will make a handsome profit on this relic I wish to possess. The blade that killed the French queen."

Seth's gaze remained steady on Hugo. "Done. You pay me my asking price and you'll get the blade as well as Anna for twelve hours. Anna is not to be bruised in any way. If she is, consider yourself a dead man."

The hollow pit in her stomach gave an unpleasant roll. Bella didn't know why she had anticipated a different response. She knew this was part of the mission, but she hadn't expected Seth to acquiesce to Hugo's soul-crushing demand. She felt insanely, intensely angry. Which was stupid. Seth was acting a part, she knew that, but that men had such power over women, and that in the past, no doubt women had been sold to Hugo Montenegro to fulfill his perverted sexual desires, filled her with a rage she struggled to control.

She'd sit next to the monster and pretend it didn't matter, focusing on the conversation that had continued after Seth's casual acceptance of a deal that included bartered sex.

"The guillotine blade, do you have it with you? I wish to see it." The buying sex portion of the negotiation over, Hugo was moving on to the next order of business.

Seth gave a snort of laughter. "You could hardly think I would bring it to your home, a home you have guarded by your own personal army? I have it secured in a safe place."

Hugo rose to his feet, his movements jerky. His suave façade had been replaced by the look of a little boy whose desire for a shiny object was being thwarted. "I want to see it now. It's rumored that there is still blood staining the blade. Is this true?"

"Perhaps, but that doesn't mean it's the blood of Marie Antoinette. Others were likely executed with the same blade after her death."

Hugo sloshed more whiskey into his glass, his knuckles white on the decanter. Bella wasn't sure if he was being ill-mannered not offering a drink to her and Seth because he was upset, or if the thought hadn't even occurred to him. He knocked back the amber liquid, then slammed the glass back onto the sideboard.

"Where are you keeping the blade? I told you before that I want to see it. If I can't see it now, I must see it tomorrow. I will not wait." Hugo's attention had shifted entirely. Where moments before he'd been focused on pursuing her, now he seemed completely absorbed in the grisly relic from the Reign of Terror.

"I'll call my people in the morning. We can set up a neutral location for you to examine what you're considering purchasing. If we can come to terms, I'd like to conclude the transaction at that time. I've already scanned and emailed you the documents to support its provenance."

"If the documents you sent me are accurate, how do you explain that a museum in London claims to have the same blade?"

"What they have is a fraud. They were duped, and refusing to acknowledge that fact is less embarrassing than the alternative. If you don't believe I have the true execution blade, the other party I mentioned is quite interested in purchasing it and has offered a price close to yours. If that's the case, let me know now and I'll be on my way. With my fiancée."

Hugo fixed a stare on Seth, then nodded curtly. "The deal goes forward. I'll expect to hear the location of our meeting first thing in the morning. Once I have procured the relic, I will bring it back here. With Anna. You'll be able to pick up your fiancée the following day."

# Chapter Three

Bella stood beside Seth and waited for the elevator door to open. She crossed her arms in front of her, breathing deeply through her nose to try to gain some level of calm. It wasn't working. She tried reciting poetry but couldn't remember the lines. She wanted to tap her foot against the stone floor because physical movement had always provided an outlet for her emotions, but she had to keep her reaction to what had happened buried or she risked blowing their cover. She clutched her arms tighter, every cell in her body vibrating with resentment. She was furious that there were men in the world like Hugo Montenegro. Men who, with impunity brought by wealth, got away with treating women as objects for their personal enjoyment. Her skin crawled at the memory of his touch.

On an intellectual level, she knew women were still exploited as they had been for all human history, and one of the reasons she'd joined the Marshals Service was to bring criminals like Hugo Montenegro to justice. If their mission was successful, he'd soon be back in prison in an eight by ten cell that held little resemblance to the country club prison he'd been housed in before. They'd get him, but dammit, the charges wouldn't include sex trafficking.

The exchange with Hugo brought memories to the surface that weren't easy to live with. There'd been rumors when some older girls had disappeared from the orphanage she and her brother had been sent to, rumors that the girls had been taken to a brothel in Moscow. Bella didn't allow herself to shy away from memories of that time. If she forgot her past, she couldn't honor those who had helped her and her brother survive, often at great sacrifice to themselves.

A big chunk of her simmering anger was directed at Seth. It didn't matter they were undercover. He'd perpetuated the idea that women were commodities to be traded or sold. Playing on Hugo's proclivities might help lure him out into the open where he could be arrested, but Seth hadn't needed to accept the prurient request. That he had infuriated her.

They'd left the room when Montenegro had received a call. It had been no surprise when his voice had turned low and sultry as he greeted the person on the other end of the line as *ma chérie*.

Seth leaned against the wall waiting for the elevator, his hands in his pockets, as relaxed as could be, looking at her with a slightly raised brow that struck her as infuriatingly arrogant.

She uttered a Russian expletive as she glared at him.

"I know what that means, you know." He straightened and raked his fingers through his hair, and she felt marginally better. He wasn't as unaffected by what had transpired as he might seem. The ice man never showed agitation, never made wasted movements that might indicate a lack of control. She liked thinking that he wasn't his usual restrained self. "I don't know what you're so upset about."

She spit out another, even cruder word.

His gaze narrowed and shifted to a spot over her shoulder.

"Take it easy," he muttered in a low voice.

The words were like a match to dry tinder. She drew in a breath to blast him, then heard footsteps as a member of the staff walked past them and down the hall. She felt like a wildfire was raging through her and she had to fight to contain the conflagration before it burned down the house. Imagining stabbing Seth in the eye with a fork helped get her through the interminable wait for the elevator.

The car finally arrived, the door opened, and they stepped inside. It slid shut, and Seth pressed the button to send the car to the third floor where their room was located.

She turned on him in the small space. "Easy? I'm supposed to take it easy? You bastard."

"Yeah, taking it easy is a good idea."

Something about his mildly amused expression, like he was humoring her while she had a snit, served as one last nudge to push her over the edge of her control. Her vision hazed red and she pulled back her arm, fist clenched. He must have read her mind. Before her intention was fully formed, he grabbed her elbows and tugged. Momentum had her sprawling forward into his embrace. He took her with him against the back wall of the car, his mouth clamped over hers. She bit down sharply on his lip. He grunted, swore ripely, then slanted his mouth. His tongue slid past her lips to glide silkily against hers as she tasted blood.

A white-hot flash had anger spiraling into desire, sweeping away the defenses she'd so carefully constructed. Over the past eighteen months, brick by brick, she'd vigilantly surrounded herself with a thick wall of protection against her feelings for him.

He was her partner and her boss, and was therefore way off limits. Not to mention, mostly he behaved like she was a pain in his ass. Except for those rare times when something she did or said made his slate gray eyes flash to silver, sending heat thrumming over her body.

She was a rule follower. With a few exceptions, that's how she'd survived her childhood. The Marshals Service rules said she couldn't have a relationship with her superior. But now her carefully constructed wall was in danger of crumbling around her.

Seth's hands shifted from her elbows, one moving to burn against the skin of her back, the other slipping through the naughty slit in her dress. He paused for a long, ripe moment, making her wonder if he'd pull back and she'd have no way to expel all the pent-up heat. She felt they both teetered on the edge of a monumental decision, then his hand moved, strong and sure under the silky material, smooth against her skin, and she felt her breath leave her body in a whoosh.

Bells warning her she was in the danger zone clanged in her head and were ignored as she groaned against his mouth. His rough, calloused palm caressed the back of her thigh before pulling her tighter against him. She was cradled in the spread of his long legs, and he made no effort to hide his huge arousal.

She shifted angles, pressing heat to heat, rubbing against the hard ridge of his erection. He deepened the kiss, his mouth ravenous on hers, and she had the feeling he'd broken all his self-imposed restraints. She tugged his shirt from his pants and ran her hands under the material, eager to touch his hot skin and hard muscle. Finally having this had her sighing with pleasure. "You feel so good," she murmured against his lips.

He pulled back, allowing a mere half inch between them. "You have no idea."

"I'm getting one."

She dipped a hand beneath his belt as the elevator came to a smooth stop. He grabbed her wrists. "Not here." His voice sounded ragged. "Inside the room."

The door opened and somehow they made it into the hall despite neither one of them letting go of the other. The moment was the cumulation of long months of denying herself her greatest desire. She'd had fantasies about his long, lean body, fantasies fueled by the sparks that raced through her whenever they accidentally brushed against each other, or she found his dark gaze on her.

His appeal went well beyond the physical. Just as sexy was the sharp intelligence that drove her to think through problems, to find solutions, to work harder. Then there was the wry sense of humor that meshed so well with hers.

Add his unshakable love for his family and she hadn't stood a chance against his gravitational pull. She'd come to terms with the fact that she'd fallen face first, head over heels, ovaries in a twist, in love with Seth.

Circumstance had forced her to bury those feelings to protect herself from the hurt that would invariably come from loving a man she could never have. There were times when she almost believed she'd succeeded. Then there were other times when she thought her feelings might be reciprocated, that Seth might feel something for her. He would grin at her and his eyes would warm, and sometimes he seemed to be watching her when he thought she wouldn't notice.

Eventually she'd been forced to admit to herself she was susceptible to wishful thinking. The ice man's control was legendary, and Seth letting his emotions show was like having an earthquake, an eclipse, and being struck by lightning all occurring on the eve of a blue moon.

But on this night, there'd been a cosmic shift and the world had tilted on its axis and she was going to let it ride.

He pushed open the bedroom door, stepped aside to let her precede him, and the minute the door shut and the lock clicked home, he backed her up against the wall. She thought he would dive in once more. She wanted him to dive in, but he took her face in his hands and held her still, studying her with a dark gaze that she felt could touch her soul.

"Seth." His name on her lips was a plea.

His fingers slid into her hair, combing through and scattering pins so it tumbled around her shoulders. "I love your hair loose like this."

He loved her hair loose? She was never again wearing it up.

He dipped his head and touched his lips to hers, softly at first, then more insistently. Need exploded through her like fireworks. Her lips fused with his as she undid the buttons of his shirt with shaky fingers. He pulled off his tie, and when his shirt opened, she ran her fingers over taut skin, loving the feel of his hard muscle and wiry chest hair.

His mouth moved, and he seemed as out of control as she felt. Once again, he sought the opening in her dress, his hard palms against her skin, her breath catching as his fingers slid perilously close to where she most ached to feel his touch.

She caught the lapels of his jacket and tugged him closer as his mouth moved from her jaw to her ear, the stubble of his beard abrading sensitive skin.

Their positions were reversed from how they'd been in the elevator, and he nudged her legs apart and moved between them, hitching up her dress, the material parting as she took his welcome weight. He pushed against her through layers of clothing, his erection rubbing with exquisite torture and sending her spiraling to the brink of control. When she leaned her head against the wall, he used his teeth to nip at her exposed neck, the brief pain causing her to gasp. He soothed the discomfort with a soft lick of his tongue.

"You taste so good," he murmured with his lips against her skin.

She reached for the button at his waistband.

He stopped, closing his eyes, his entire body going motionless. "Fuck. We can't do this." Then he pulled back and opened his eyes, and she saw what she'd never expected to see. No longer controlled, his eyes burned, sparks of silver flashing through slate gray.

"We are doing this."

He leaned back his head to take a shuddering breath, the muscles in his arms going rigid. He freed his hands from the folds of her dress and rested them on the wall on either side of her head. "There was a camera in the elevator. That's why I kissed you. I was afraid you were about to blow our cover."

Her stomach dropped and tugged her heart down with it. That was it? He'd acted like he couldn't stay away from her for another moment because there'd been a camera in the elevator? No. She wouldn't accept that. There'd been more to what had happened than an effort to preserve their cover. He'd wanted her too, and his attempt to explain away his reaction sharpened her tone. "Sacrificing yourself for the job? How noble."

His expression turned inscrutable.

With anger layering over being insanely aroused, she wasn't feeling exactly charitable. Seth's cheeks were flushed, his eyes sharp. She would never think of him as the ice man again. Whatever his motivation for kissing her, she could see he was hanging on to control by only the thinnest of threads.

"Like hell you kissed me like that for the job," she ground out. "There was more to that kiss and grope than a show for the camera."

"Okay, maybe."

"Don't be a coward. You may not like me, but at least you can admit you want me."

He opened his mouth, no doubt to tell her that any man would want her, that his was a normal male reaction. She heaved in a breath to fortify herself against his rejection, then his gaze swept down and she felt his quick intake of breath.

She looked down to what had snagged his attention. The bodice of her dress had pulled dangerously low and she felt the insane urge to giggle. Either that or die of embarrassment. She wasn't what one would call overly endowed, just a run-of-the-mill C-cup, but the dress and the magic bra managed to make her look voluptuous, and more than a little decadent with the diamond gleaming in the valley between her breasts.

But that wasn't where his attention was riveted. Her skin burned as his gaze fixated on the dusky areola of one nipple now visible above the shimmery material. He raised a hand and drew a fingertip along the edge of the cloth, tracing the exposed arc, then tugged at the material to uncover the entire nipple. He made a noise deep in his throat that sounded like a wild animal on the prowl.

As if in a trance, he tugged again, pulling down the material to bare her other breast. He brought up his hands to cup both breasts, kneading them, plumping them, then bent his head to take one in his mouth, the roll of his tongue over the tip nearly making her erupt in orgasm then and there.

His mouth was so hot she was surprised there weren't burn marks on her skin as he moved to give his attention to the other breast. While he feasted, she once more reached for the button at his waist, opening his trousers with quick movements.

Ah, there he was. Hard and silky, velvet over steel. She fondled and stroked and had him making that noise again, the vibration deep in his throat. She'd never experienced anything as erotic as the feel of him in her hand.

His mouth left her breasts and his gaze locked on hers. She saw a war raging in his eyes between control and wild abandon.

She'd die if he stepped back now.

"Do you want this?"

She gave a jerky nod.

"Say it, Bella. Do you want this with me right now?"

"I want this. With you. Right now."

He stared long and hard. "Then fuck it."

He picked her up and carried her to the bed and unhooked her bra as she kicked off her shoes. Then he gathered the material of her dress and drew it up and over her body in a silky glide, draping it over the foot of the bed.

He removed her bra and pressed his lips into the swell of her breasts as she pushed down his pants and reached for him once again. He raised his head, his eyes glittering in the shadowy light cast by a lamp in the corner. Something about seeing her naked, but for her turquoise thong, set him off. In seconds he was stripped naked and tumbling them both onto the bed.

In his arms, inhaling the clean scent of him, feeling the strength in his long, lean build stoked the need blazing within her. She loved his hands with those wide palms and blunt-shaped fingers, and he used them to wicked effect, stroking and sliding to bring her to the brink.

She gasped and he shifted to prop himself on his elbows, his thumb tracing the ridge of her cheekbone. Then he was pushing into her. He framed her face with his hands, took her lips with his, and thrust forward.

They both went wild as he plunged into her.

They moved in tandem, the tension, which had always been present between them, shifting and transforming into something new.

She met him, thrust for thrust, responding to his movements, her hands at his hips pulling him in deeper. Harboring a secret love for him explained why their coming together felt more exquisite, more perfect, than her most erotic fantasies. She held him tighter, hoping to lengthen the interlude. But as she was already primed and ready, the strong, sure drive of his body flung her to the top of the surging wave.

He was right there, riding the hard, bright crest along with her, stringing it out to prolong the moment until together they plummeted over the edge and dropped into oblivion.

Seth collapsed on top of her, his weight heavy and welcome. She nuzzled his hand where it cupped the side of her face, his thumb rubbing against the bridge of her nose.

She wondered if her heart might explode inside her chest. She wasn't sure what lay ahead for them, but in that moment she felt giddy they'd moved beyond their armed standoff.

Words she wanted to say were on the tip of her tongue. Maybe she wasn't ready to reveal that she'd been in love with him for well over a year, but perhaps she could work up to that. She could at least tell him that she *cared* for him, that her feelings went farther than simple attraction.

Then his thumb stopped moving and his body stiffened, and not in a good way. He pushed off her to lie on his back, not meeting her gaze, dropping his arm heavily over his forehead.

A moment before, she'd felt comfortably naked. Now she felt exposed.

It'd taken only a split second for the feeling between them to change from intimate to unbearably awkward.

She rolled off the bed, taking the top sheet with her. She yanked it from under his legs and wrapped it around herself. She could no longer bear to be uncovered.

She grabbed the smaller of her suitcases and retreated into the bathroom, carefully turning the lock with shaky fingers.

# Chapter Four

The bathroom door's decisive click resounded in the quiet bedroom. Seth pinched the bridge of his nose. He'd screwed up, probably the worst fuck-up in his adult life. He rubbed his fingers against his eyes, images from the past hour replaying in his mind. Yeah, he'd screwed up, but god, it had been amazing. He'd kept his crazy attraction for Bella bottled up so they could have a working relationship. He was her boss, for Chrissake. He'd even managed to keep his response to her in check after he'd kissed her in the car.

But they'd gotten on that elevator and she'd gone off like a rocket in his arms. She'd taken him under, and he'd felt like he was floundering, not even bothering to look for a life raft. He'd managed to gain a slippery grip on control in the bedroom when he'd had her up against the wall. Barely. Then he'd seen the edge of her nipple peeking from under the material and had felt something snap.

He was a drowning man and wasn't bothering to fight the force pulling him under. The control that had been second nature for him had broken clean through. He'd let go and led with his heart, allowing himself a few precious minutes where being with Bella, holding her in his arms and making love with her, was the center of his universe.

For that short span of time, he'd been free.

Denial and control dictated his interactions with Bella, and had done since day one. But from the moment he'd knocked on her hotel room door, this weekend had changed everything. He should've assigned a different marshal to act as his partner for this operation, but he'd wanted Bella.

He always wanted Bella.

They'd posed as an engaged couple and the plan blew up in his face. She'd be within her rights to ask for a transfer, and to lodge a harassment complaint against him. He pushed aside the thought it'd been worth it. Knowing how good it could be between them had shifted the paradigm and there was no going back.

What if they could work it through to the point where they could have a relationship? It would mean a change in their assignments. She could no longer be part of his team. That would be bad. He'd miss working with her. Watching her when she wasn't looking, and enjoying the view. But if it meant they could have a life together, he'd sacrifice almost anything for that. Who knew if she even wanted to be with him for a lifetime. Maybe she'd—

His brain shuddered to a halt. His hand lay motionless on his forehead as reality crashed around him like the proverbial ton of bricks. *Fuck.* He hadn't used a condom. God *damn* it.

For the first time in his life, he'd had sex without thinking about protection for himself or his partner. Which told him how badly he'd wanted Bella. How desire had pushed every rational thought out of his head.

Shit, shit, *shit.*

It felt like every interaction they'd had for the past year and a half had led to the moment when his brain had turned off and his instincts took over. Their sharp disagreements. Those sexy/snarky comments of hers that always got under his skin. The moments where he'd fought to block his reaction or keep from doing what he'd just done, nearly taking her against the wall with all the finesse of a raging bull.

All of it had sharpened the tension between them to the point of rupture, and the sane part of his mind, which considered protection, had been blown away.

He never allowed himself to lose control. Yet that's exactly what he'd done. What if she got pregnant? He scrubbed a hand across his face. Most likely she was taking a contraceptive, or had one of those IUDs. If she wasn't or didn't, and she conceived, they'd get married.

That's all there was to it. They'd get married and sort out the rest later.

The door of the bathroom flung open and Bella stormed out. She'd changed into a tank top and some sort of stretchy leggings that fit like a second skin. Her hair was pulled back in a ponytail, and her face was wiped clean of makeup. She looked so fresh-faced she'd be carded if she tried to buy a beer.

"What the hell, Jameson?"

And she was back. Her hands were balled and slammed into her hips. She leaned forward. Her expression screamed furious.

"What the hell what?"

"Don't be funny. It hit me when I was *cleaning up*. You didn't use condom."

Ah. Well. No getting around it. "No, I didn't."

"Why the hell not?"

"Because I wasn't exactly thinking rationally. It's no excuse, but I got caught up in the moment. I don't remember you saying anything."

"It is man's responsibility to use condom."

He couldn't have stopped the grin from splitting his face if she'd pointed a gun at his head. "'It ees man's responsibility'? Do you realize your accent gets stronger when you're angry? You drop your articles and pronounce 'i' like an 'e.'"

His brain was so out of whack he was saying shit he'd never say. He was in for it now.

Color suffused her face as she stalked to the bed. "I'll show you a dropped article, you bastard." She let loose a string of Russian expletives as she launched herself at him, fists swinging. He should've remembered she had a wicked temper when riled. The ripe curse she'd used earlier seemed to be a favorite because it came up a couple times. The rest was lost in the tussle when he grabbed her hands before she could make contact with his face, and then yanked her onto the bed. She pushed and heaved, bringing up a knee in a sharp movement that came entirely too close to emasculating him.

He flipped her under him and used his weight to keep her from trying the maneuver again. He reared back a moment before she could sink her teeth into his shoulder. Being buck naked was not an advantage in a fight with Bella Nikolaev.

"Shit, Bella. Stop trying to bloody me. I don't want to hurt you."

"Too bad, because I want to hurt you. Did I say that right? Did I use my article and pronounce the 'i' correctly?"

She worked a hand from his grasp and pinched the skin along his ribs, twisting hard. He swore, scrabbled again for her hand, all the while conscious that certain parts of him liked their situation just fine.

She struggled, squirming to work a leg from beneath him, drawing in a sharp breath when the movement brought his groin against the sweet vee between her legs.

She went still, and shutters dropped over her eyes.

The insane thought crossed his mind that since they'd already done it once, what would it matter if they did it again? Her chest heaved against his and he felt the hard nubs of her nipples through the material of her top. Shit. She wasn't wearing a bra. Once again, his control was slipping from his grasp.

"No. Not again. I don't want you."

He pushed back, his breath sawing out of his lungs. He took in the flushed rise of her breasts and when her thighs spread wider and he settled more firmly between her legs, he was even closer to heaven.

"I think we could argue that point." When he touched her cheek, she turned her head, teeth bared. "Don't you dare."

"I dare as I please."

"Not with me you don't. I don't know if you've had your shots."

"You're a bastard." The color in her cheeks hadn't abated, and she was breathing in shallow gasps. Her blue eyes darkened, edging toward violet, which meant she was as aroused as he was.

"So you keep saying. My mother might disagree. Regardless, you're the one trying the vampire routine."

"Get off me."

"I will, if that's what you want. But surely you've heard of the horse and the barn door."

"That's an American idiom that means it's too late to do the thing that would stop something bad from happening."

"Pretty much. You must've done well in school. In our case it means that we've already done the deed without protection."

"So we might as well do it again? Is that how your tiny brain works?"

"Can't deny that's where it went," he looked down at their position, "given current evidence." The insistent urge to peel off those leggings and let nature take its course had him grappling for control he barely held on to by a thread.

Her chest heaved and his mouth watered at the memory of the tight bud of her nipple against his tongue, which only made him ache for another sample. He closed his eyes to block the image. It didn't work.

*Fuck, fuck, fuck.*

This relentless craving for her was damned inconvenient and starting to piss him off.

He opened his eyes. "I'm going to let you go. Don't bite me." He saw the calculation on her face. "Or kick me."

He eased his weight off her and flopped onto his back, pulling a sheet over himself since certain parts hadn't yet gotten the memo the lady had said *no*.

"Too bad about your *evidence*, because I don't want you."

"So you said. Might be true intellectually, but physically? You want me bad."

"I hate you."

"Which isn't a denial." He propped himself on an elbow. He could've dealt with the stubborn chin and the defiance in her eyes, but the single tear tracking into the hair at her temple hollowed him out like she'd connected with that knee.

He'd screwed things up between them in the worst possible way. He was the boss. He was in charge. It was his responsibility to fix things. As much as he didn't feel like doing it, he did what he'd done countless time before: he reined in his treacherous emotions and made an effort to lock them into a seldom-used compartment in his head. A technique he'd found vital to keep functioning at his job.

"Are you on the pill?"

She shook her head.

"Using any contraceptives?"

Another head shake.

Shit. "Okay." He didn't think bringing up marriage would go over well at the moment. "We'll deal with a pregnancy if it becomes an issue."

He rolled out of bed, yanking on his briefs. He got clothes from his suitcase and pulled on gym shorts and a t-shirt, then quickly checked his phone. A text from his mom said she was looking forward to him being home, and that she was planning a family get-together.

Family time was good, but at the moment he had a mountain of other shit that needed dealing with. He slipped the phone into his pocket as Bella rose from the bed. He caught the surreptitious swipe of her hand across her eyes as she crossed the room to sit in an upholstered chair that looked too fancy to be comfortable. With her arms wrapped around her knees, those beautiful eyes big and sad, and her luscious hair coming loose from her ponytail, she looked fragile, making his heart twist. He battled back the impulse to scoop her up and hold her close.

Then her brows lowered and she jabbed a finger in his direction. "You didn't *have* to kiss me in the elevator."

Back to that, were they?

"How should I've stopped you from blowing our cover? Montenegro is paranoid and we should expect cameras anywhere in his house. I'd spotted the one in the elevator earlier. There's no audio, but his security would've picked up on you being pissed. For sure they'd have noticed you taking a swing at me. I grabbed hold of you to make it look like we were hot for each other. I had to do something. If this goes sideways, we're in danger, and we risk losing Montenegro and his assets for good."

"That's bullshit. You make it sound so reasonable when it's not. You agreed to sell me for sex. I'd think anyone watching would have understood perfectly why I punched you in the face, then found a rusty knife and cut off your balls."

"I didn't agree to sell you for sex. Jesus Christ." He hissed out the words, frustrated she was succeeding in needling him. "We're on an undercover op. I agreed my *fake* fiancée could be used for sex to benefit the deal."

"Exactly. Which is why you're a bastard. Any woman would've been angry if her fiancé sold her to that monster for sex. I was legitimately angry, but I was still in character."

He stared at the ceiling, hoping for calm. He chose his words and tone carefully. "There's no chance Montenegro will get his hands on you."

"In case you hadn't noticed, he had his hands all over me. You're not much of a fiancé to let that happen."

She scored a point with that one. When he'd walked into the room and saw Montenegro pawing Bella, he'd had to rein in the impulse to break every one of that POS's fingers. "Okay. Stephen Bullock is an asshole. You're pissed. I get that. But you were doing your job like I was doing mine."

"Is there a bug in here as well? That would explain why you had sex with me. How self-sacrificing to stay in character even behind closed doors. Hugo's security is probably picking up this interesting conversation as we speak."

"I scanned this room for devices earlier, and installed audio jammers. The suite is clean. But don't kid yourself. You weren't telling me to stop, sweetheart, so I'm guessing you got something out of it too."

She rose from her seat, nose in the air. "I'm going to bed. You can find yourself somewhere else to sleep."

"Fuck that. That bed is king size and large enough that you'll have nothing to worry about. If you can keep your hands off me, I can keep mine off you."

There was a moment where she looked ready to fight him over it, but instead, she lifted the corner of the comforter and slipped under the covers.

She curled onto her side with her back to him, so close to the edge he thought she might tumble off in the middle of the night.

Seth sighed and turned out the light, grateful he wasn't bloodied or suffering from internal injuries.

# Chapter Five

Seth steered the Bugatti around a curve in the road while Bella monitored the GPS on her phone. Working with marshals from the San Francisco office, they'd set up the sting operation to nab their fugitive. They were on their way to a park where Montenegro had agreed to meet them. Morning clouds had cleared to reveal a perfect early summer day and as they topped a hill, the graceful curves of the Golden Gate Bridge gleamed in the distance.

The passing streets held an eclectic mix of architectural styles typical of the Bay Area, but Bella's mind was stuck in the same rut it had been running in for the past few days. The tension between her and Seth, the *awkwardness,* had magnified since Friday night. She was doing her level best to pretend their hot sex never happened, but the effort was fraying her nerves. It didn't help she was still furious with him. She was angry with herself even more. Stupidly, she'd felt their relationship had taken a giant leap forward, and hoped they'd finally admit there was more between them than two people scratching an itch. Talk about being dead wrong.

They'd left Hugo Montenegro's home on Saturday and checked into a hotel near Fisherman's Wharf. Hugo wanted the relic and he wanted Bella, and it appeared that his too-short time in prison had only amplified his need for immediate gratification. They'd decided forcing Montenegro to wait would make him more impulsive and likely to make a mistake in their favor, so Seth ignored the other man's blustering and stalled when Hugo had wanted the deal to be finalized that weekend. Instead, they'd agreed to meet Tuesday morning, so here they were.

Seth had insisted they continue the engaged couple ruse. She got it, and was grateful to leave, though the ruse ended at the hotel room door. They were sharing a suite, not a bed. Yet, even that limited proximity did nothing to lessen her hyperawareness of him. She was starting to resent she noticed every little thing about him. His loose-hipped walk, the way his hair fell across his forehead, the stubble on his jaw in the mornings that made her fingers itch to rub the bristles. Before this assignment, there was palpable tension between them, but they'd become experts at burying their attraction. With the cat out of the bag, they were tiptoeing around each other and that they'd had unprotected sex. On a loop in her brain, she replayed "We'll deal with a pregnancy if it becomes an issue." Deal with a pregnancy? There were a dozen things he could've meant, but as far as she was concerned, if she was pregnant, any decisions were hers alone to make.

Reestablishing their earlier working relationship was crucial. Not easy, but crucial. Before this assignment the constant state of friction between them had made their relationship tense at best, but at least they'd been able to function. Since losing her mind and giving in to her desire, these past few days she worked to keep her emotions in check, tried to stay busy, and made sure any conversations were work related.

But every now and then, the idea she might be pregnant wormed its way to the front of her mind. It was stupid to even think about it. She wasn't due to start her period for another few days, so there was no point worrying. Which, of course, didn't stop the thought from hijacking her brain.

*What if she was pregnant?* Her world would change, for sure. Being a single mom would be difficult, but having both parents didn't necessarily make children any better off. Her own family was the perfect example. With any other man, the question would be met with more trepidation, but that Seth would be the father made her traitorous heart yearn.

He'd gone along with her assiduously avoiding personal conversations. They talked about their plan to capture Montenegro and the hunt for Seth's father, the domestic terrorist fugitive Richard

Jameson. RJ had dropped off the map months before and their team was following leads.

On conference calls with the team, invariably conversations veered toward the personal. Linc and Ellie, Seth's siblings and the other marshals on the team, were also Bella's friends. Bella, Ellie, and Mikayla, Linc's wife, had become increasingly close in the past year, which led to their lives becoming more intertwined. Too often, she and Seth were thrown together socially, something she found stretched her nerves so tight she feared they'd snap.

Three weeks before she'd served as maid of honor, and Seth stood as a groomsman at Ellie's small, beautiful wedding to Judge Sam Creed.

Negotiating all *that* and keeping her distance from Seth was nerve wracking. Especially since she'd catch him watching her, those slate gray eyes giving away not a damned thing. Now the tension between them had ratcheted up by a factor of a thousand. One dose too many of the hotness that was Seth Jameson and she hadn't had the willpower to say *no* when she damn well should have.

"This it?"

Bella yanked her attention back into the game. "Yeah. We take this street through the park and it's on the right."

She refocused to conjure her persona as Anna Novak. Once again she'd dressed the part of a rich man's fiancée. She'd paired loose-fitting pants of a filmy material with suede ankle boots and a knit jacket over a sleeveless linen top. Add in the sapphire and diamond earrings and gold chain to complement the engagement ring, and she thought she pulled it off.

The meeting was to take place at a stone bench outside the Conservatory of Flowers in Golden Gate Park. Montenegro expected to conclude the exchange for the relic and walk off with Stephen Bullock's woman. He was going to be sadly disappointed.

"There's the parking area."

Seth parked the car three spots down from a white van with the advertising logo "Catering by Maria" plastered on its side. The three marshals in the van—equipped with surveillance devices—along with half a dozen officers from the task force who were already in the park dressed as tourists, comprised their backup.

Hugo had insisted on a public location, probably assuming that an open, outdoor setting early in the day would offer him some protection. They'd chosen this time since there were fewer people in the park at this hour, but there was always the possibility someone could inadvertently crash their party. The marshals were ready to deal with any problems, as well as Hugo's hired security.

Seth turned in his seat.

"You ready?"

"Yes, sir."

His gaze went dark, and he nodded. They stepped out of the car and Seth opened the trunk and retrieved the reinforced locking case. Carrying it by the heavy-duty handle, he reached for her with his other hand, lacing their fingers and bringing her to his side.

"Acting like you're in love with me doesn't really make sense, you know," she muttered, deliberately keeping her voice low.

He raised a brow. "How so?"

"Because you've made me part of the bargain. What man allows another man to have sex with the woman he loves?" They walked along the path bordering gorgeous flowerbeds in front of the Victorian greenhouse that looked like a relic of a previous age.

"Back to that, are we?" He caught her sharp look. "Okay, point taken, but we keep going the way we started. As I said, Stephen Bullock is an asshole."

"Yes, he is," she agreed primly.

They spotted Montenegro, flanked by two bodyguards, approaching from the opposite direction. They met at the designated bench and exchanged greetings, Hugo's gaze lingering on Bella before switching to the case Seth held.

Bella didn't know if the avaricious gaze was from desire for her or what was in the case. Seth set it on the bench, went through the steps to unlock it, and lifted the lid.

There, nestled in the foam padding, was the ugly guillotine blade that had beheaded too many French citizens during the Reign of Terror, among them the complicated figure of Marie Antoinette. The diagonal blade was attached with heavy bolts to what Bella thought must be a weight. Hugo examined it meticulously, bending over and holding a jeweler's loupe to his eye, muttering to himself.

"Yes, yes. This dark stain? That must be the blood. It's good that the blade wasn't cleaned." He ran a finger roughly along the edge, then held it up. A smear of blood showed where he'd nicked it. "My blood has mixed on this notorious blade with that of Marie Antoinette." He looked inordinately pleased. "What must she have been thinking, lying there with her head resting in the lunette, waiting for this very blade to drop? One wonders how long consciousness remained with her head severed from her body."

He turned abruptly to Seth. "I don't suppose you also have the blade that killed Robespierre?"

Bella stifled the insane desire to laugh at his hopeful expression. In his home, Hugo Montenegro had seemed dangerous. Now he appeared ridiculous. A glance at his guards sobered her. Both wore mirrored sunglasses and stood watchful on the grass several yards away. In no way were they ridiculous.

If Seth was surprised by Hugo's query, he didn't let it show. "No, but I can keep an eye out. I believe that one has been lost to history."

"That's a shame. I'm pursuing the glass Rasputin drank the poisoned wine from, but that, too, has proven elusive. I'm also interested in the bullet that killed Robert Kennedy. Let me know if you come across either of those items. Acquiring such relics would be exquisite additions to my collection." Bella caught Seth tensing when Hugo reached into his pocket, but he only pulled out his phone. "As agreed, I will transfer the money to the account number you sent me."

Bella didn't let her anticipation show. This was an important step because the marshals wanted to know the source of his money. He might have it shielded, but the money trail could lead them to hidden assets. If they were able to get their hands on Montenegro's assets, the money could be used to pay restitution to some of the victims of his crimes. This was exactly why she'd signed up to do this work. People with money and power shouldn't be free to victimize whomever they chose.

Hugo's gaze rested on Bella and the look in his eyes made her stomach roll. "Once the transfer is complete, I'll take possession of the relic, as I will take possession of the beautiful Anna."

Seth brought out his phone, listened, and said, "It's a go." He reached under his jacket and smoothly withdrew his gun from its shoulder harness. "Hugo Montenegro, I'm Chief Deputy US Marshal Seth Jameson. You're under arrest."

Hugo spun around to find both his guards with their hands in the air as officers surrounded them, weapons drawn. They'd suspected that Montenegro would be armed, and when he reached down to where he likely had a gun in a leg holster, Bella moved quickly. In seconds, she had him face down on the pavement. She wrenched his hands behind his back as he sputtered with rage.

He squirmed, trying to dislodge her, but with her knee in his back he wasn't going anywhere. One of the officers tossed her handcuffs and she snapped them around each wrist. She couldn't help the grim satisfaction. There was sweet justice in being the woman taking down a man who preyed on too many women who didn't have the power to get away or say no.

Hugo Montenegro had been a fugitive from justice and a predator in so many different ways, and once again he'd be locked up, but this time in a cage from which he wouldn't be able to escape.

Seth holstered his weapon. He bent down and took one of Montenegro's arms, she took the other and they pulled the struggling bastard to his feet.

"Motherfuckers! I trusted you. I'll fucking kill you." His voice rose as he fought against his restraints. "I'll disembowel you. I'll eviscerate you. I'll cut you into tiny pieces and feed you to the sharks. You'll both die in pain." He twisted against their hold, screaming the words, spittle spraying from his mouth.

Ignoring the tirade, Seth searched him and, in addition to the gun in a holster strapped to his shin, Seth retrieved an antique folding knife from Hugo's pocket. Two other marshals took custody of Montenegro and frog marched him to the van.

"Good takedown, Bella."

"Thank you, sir."

"Cut it out," he muttered the words so only she could hear.

"I'm a marshal doing my job, sir."

The look he sent her promised retribution.

She suppressed a shiver.

The situation between them had gotten as personal as it gets, but it didn't seem like her efforts to reestablish distance were taking hold. They walked toward the parking area where she tried to hitch a ride in one of the other vehicles but, no surprise, Seth overruled the maneuver and she ended up in the Bugatti with him.

They drove through the busy streets toward the Phillip Burton Federal Building where the Marshals office was located. Her phone vibrated in her jacket pocket. She tapped on the screen, staring at the message as her heart clutched in her chest. She tapped out a response, then turned her head away from Seth, briefly closing her eyes.

"You okay?"

Trust him to notice every damn thing. "Sure. I'm fine."

He probably didn't believe her, but he let it drop.

The rest of the day was spent dealing with the paperwork. Even electronically, the multitude of forms, processes, and procedures was daunting. The diamond engagement ring and other jewelry Bella had worn were returned to the property room, as were the keys to the Bugatti. A steady stream of marshals filed through the office to check out the guillotine in its padded case before it was shipped back to the museum that had loaned it to them.

Seth came into the small conference room where Bella had set up a laptop to work, carrying his jacket under his arm. He still wore his gun and she told herself to get a grip when the shoulder straps of his holster struck her as unabashedly sexy. Even with her current preoccupation, she couldn't turn off her response to him.

She bent her head and busily resumed typing.

"Hey, workday's over. The task force is meeting at a pub a couple blocks away to celebrate Montenegro's arrest. You mind if we walk there?"

"Go ahead. I'll finish this report and then I'm going back to the hotel." She sipped from her now-cold mug of tea and wished for a couple of pain pills for the headache brewing behind her temples. The screen on her phone lit, and with a quick glance she saw only a calendar notification. No text.

The door of the conference room closed and she looked up in surprise when Seth pulled out the chair next to her. "Find someone else to play with, Seth. I'm busy."

"You remember my name."

"Of course, I remember your name."

"Since Saturday, you've been back to calling me *sir*. You know I hate it when you do that, right? Maybe that's why you do it."

"You're my boss, I'm supposed to call you sir."

"Fuck that."

"Okay." She tapped the pad to check the final box on her document.

He grabbed the arm of her chair and swiveled the seat to turn her to him, holding firm when she would have swiveled back.

Deciding she'd only lose the tussle, she went for cool and remote. "I take it you want my attention?"

"Since throttling you is against Marshals Service protocols, we'll talk instead. Tell me what's going on with you, and don't tell me it's nothing."

"Me? I'm typing a report. One you asked for. You, however, are having a snit." So much for cool and remote.

"Dudes don't have snits. The report can wait until tomorrow." His brows lowered. "You haven't answered the question."

"I don't recall there being a question."

"Okay, I'll restate. What's going on with you?"

"Are you asking as my boss about work-related issues?"

"No, I'm asking as your friend about Bella-related issues."

"Then I can't answer you. We're not friends."

He let go of her chair and leaned back. He scrubbed a hand along his jaw, his whiskers making a rasping sound, a rare indication of frustration. "What the hell, Bella?"

The flash of what looked suspiciously like vulnerability hit her like a gut-punch, but she forced herself not to give in to any softening of feelings toward him. Remembering his "that should never have happened" statement after what had been for her a life-altering experience helped. She crossed her arms over her chest and kept her mouth firmly shut.

"Look," he shook his head, "come to the pub with the team. Relax. Enjoy yourself. You can tolerate me for that long."

"You seem to be operating under the misguided notion this is about you."

"So there's a *this*. Something's going on. Tell me."

He stretched out his long legs in front of him like he was settling in for a long chat. She swiveled her seat and clicked a couple of icons to save her work, and closed the file. She'd do better talking to him if she didn't have to look at him.

"I've put in for personal leave. I'm taking the rest of the week off. I finished the report you asked for and I'll email it to you. I've got a flight to Los Angeles booked for this evening."

He sat forward so quickly his chair rocked. She chanced a quick look and found him wearing his *I'm digging in* expression. Damn.

"We made arrangements to fly together tomorrow. Why the change in plans?"

"I'm not obligated to tell my supervisor the reason for personal leave."

"There's fucking more to our relationship than work, Bella."

There it was again, his implication that they were friends. Another low blow. No matter how much she'd like it if Seth truly was her friend, there were some things experience had taught her were better not shared with anyone.

"It's personal."

He grabbed the arms of her chair again and turned her to face him, this time keeping her locked in. His eyes sparked silver as a muscle worked in his jaw. "Are you pregnant?"

"What? No. I mean, I don't know. But it's unlikely. It's too early to tell." Shortly after *the event,* as she'd taken to referring to it in her mind, she'd considered getting a Plan B pill, but had chosen not to for reasons she didn't want to examine too closely.

"You're not taking time off to have an abortion?"

"What makes you think that's what I'm doing? Besides, I'd have to be pregnant to get an abortion."

"Answer the question, Bella."

She was startled to see his control slipping. His knuckles were white where his hands gripped the arms of the chair, and a storm of emotion crossed his face. She was working to reconstruct the wall around her heart and he was battering it down with a sledgehammer without even trying.

"No, Seth. I'm not getting an abortion. Is that clear enough?"

He released the chair. "Okay. Then why are you leaving tonight?"

She pushed back and he released the chair. She shut down the laptop and closed the lid, standing to move around the table and unplug it. "I have to deal with some personal matters. It has nothing to do with you."

He wasn't happy, that was clear from the scowl pulling his mouth down in a frown. But when he rose to his feet, all he said in a gruff voice was, "I'll give you a ride to the airport."

God, he was a good man. Even when he was angry and frustrated with her, and she was leaving without explanation, he still offered to take her to the airport. Keeping him at a distance was vital for her mental well-being, but at every turn, he challenged her resolve.

He'd never admit it, even under the threat of a court order, but Seth was a nurturer. He took care of people. His family, the marshals under his supervision, her. Now he felt responsible for her because of what had happened over the weekend. Her days off would have the added benefit of giving them some much needed distance.

# Chapter Six

Seth got off the elevator, glancing in the direction of Bella's desk as he made his way to his office. She wasn't in yet but was due back today. He hadn't heard a peep from her since Tuesday evening in San Francisco. He could admit to himself that it bugged the hell out of him he didn't know what was going on with her. He couldn't help it. They'd been intimate, and for him that intimacy reached beyond sexual. Plus, he plain missed her. With her absent from the office, he'd come to realize how much he counted on her, how often he used her as a sounding board when working out a case, how he subconsciously kept track of her when they were at work. After what they'd shared, their relationship had taken a sharp turn and he was ready to figure out exactly where that turn was taking them.

Leaving his door open so he could see when she came in, he started the coffee, sat at his desk, and turned on his computer. His phone buzzed and he saw his brother's name on caller ID.

"Linc," he said, by way of greeting.

"I've got something."

Without asking, his brother's tone broadcast he was referring to news about their father's case.

"Tell me."

"Three more federal judges have received emailed threats. Two are district court judges in Idaho, the third is in Nevada."

"What do you know?"

"We know the Freedom Defenders have been expanding their recruitment efforts. There's the online presence, but they like their in-person book burnings and rallies, which have stepped up since the spring. They're using those as part of their propaganda machine to engage potential new recruits across the western states. We broke their organization in Oregon, but now others have popped up in Arizona and Idaho, and the one in Nevada has grown. They're bringing in other anti-government groups to affiliate with FD. It's like we're playing whack-a-mole with these guys. The threats against the judge in Reno are the most specific and credible."

"Why target this judge?"

"The situation is similar to what happened with Sam." Federal Judge Sam Creed, now their brother-in-law, had been targeted by the Freedom Defenders. The right-wing extremist group were intent on intimidating judges, going so far as to try to physically prevent those deemed *unfriendly* from sitting on the bench during Second Amendment trials, or any cases dealing with what the group considered challenges to their personal liberties. Seth figured what this group really wanted was to destroy any level of government that got in the way of them living their lives however the hell they wanted. They didn't understand or embrace the concept of the common good. They bullied their neighbors, tore up the land, and brandished weapons at whoever challenged them. The marshals had evidence they funded their efforts through the illegal gun trade, and there'd been rumors of sex trafficking. As far as he was concerned, they were an armed, anti-government domestic terrorist cult minus the religion.

Seth clicked open his email as Linc talked. "The judge's name is Carlos Rebollar and he sits on the bench at the federal district court in Reno. He has an upcoming case dealing, in part, with cattle grazing on public lands. For a couple of generations, a family by the name of MacDonald has been grazing their cattle on property belonging to the American people, and they've been paying pennies for the rights. In the past half dozen years, they haven't bothered paying the pennies. Recently, they were told to pay their past-due bill or their property would be auctioned to pay the tax debt. That seems to have set them off. They're challenging the fees in court, but there's also a lot of bluster on social media about government overreach. To make the issue even more complicated, environmentalists are also interested. A group has brought a suit naming both the government and the MacDonalds. The environmental group is trying to get the federal government to do its job and step up land management to deal with erosion and water issues. They also claim to have evidence that the MacDonald clan has been killing protected animals like mountain lions and bighorn sheep."

"They kill big horn sheep?"

"They've been accused of it. Guess they compete with cattle for resources. The environmental group is arguing that public lands weren't intended to be a free giveaway to ranchers. The ranchers claim a lot of shit, including that it's their god-given right to graze their cattle wherever the fuck they want. Their lawyers are throwing whatever they think will stick into the case.

"The MacDonald clan is part of an organization that has recently changed its handle to FDN, or Freedom Defenders of Nevada. They argue that they're sovereign citizens, that states' rights supersede federal, and that the government is violating their Second Amendment rights."

"Well, shit. How do they figure it's a Second Amendment case?"

"The local sheriff had been pretty lenient but was finally moved to take action when FDN set up roadblocks armed with AKs. The sheriff took exception to his deputies being shot at, and after a standoff, arrested the motherfuckers and confiscated their weapons."

Seth clicked on an email from his boss. "Montrose sent me the rundown. I'll read it later. Where does RJ fit in?" Since everything Linc had described matched what they knew of their father's ideology, he wouldn't be surprised to find Richard Jameson in the thick of it.

"Yesterday, ATF arrested two men at a remote Mexican border crossing driving a semi loaded with bales of alfalfa. Their destination was a town in Sinaloa known to be cartel controlled."

"I'm guessing they were hauling more than hay to feed their horses." Seth put Linc on speaker and walked to the sideboard where the coffeemaker stood. He filled his mug emblazoned with a marshal's star and returned to his desk.

"You'd guess right. Pressed inside those hay bales were enough weapons and ammo to help the cartel do their business for a good long time. We suspect the equipment was stolen from the military. The men were interrogated. Of course, they said they had no idea they were hauling anything but hay bales. Said they picked up the job in Reno and that the bales were already loaded on the flatbed tractor trailer. They also claimed not to have the name of the guy who'd given them the load and the instructions on where to deliver it, other than that he went by Big Dog." Linc paused. "Description matches RJ."

Seth sipped his coffee and let that sink in. As a teenager, he'd been insanely angry when his father had abandoned their family. But next to that anger, somehow he'd held on to a tiny flicker of hope that his dad would come through in the end. That there'd be an explanation for his behavior that Seth could understand. He hadn't wanted to lose all faith in the man he'd once loved and trusted. Seth had wanted his family back, and to have everything right again so his mom wouldn't be sad, his sister and brother wouldn't look like the walking wounded, and Seth wouldn't have to make a too-soon leap into adulthood.

But he'd gotten over all that, and now nothing surprised him about Richard Jameson, who went by the handle Big Dog. Certainly not that he'd turned up the previous year as mastermind of the FD plot to kidnap Sam Creed and Ellie, undercover as his fiancée.

"RJ hasn't joined a church choir. Anything else?"

"Not about that."

"Then what?"

Linc's tone changed. "I talked to Mom last night. She wants you to invite Bella for the Fourth of July weekend."

"To the family thing? Why?" Spending more personal time with Bella? Hell yeah. Spending that time under his family's watchful eye? Not nearly as fun.

"Because it's the Fourth of July. You know Mom and Arch put on a deal. Plus, Mom's all but ready to adopt Bella."

"What the fuck's that supposed to mean?"

"Easy, bro. Bella was at my wedding. Hell, she was maid of honor at Ellie's wedding. Both of you turned up at those weddings without a plus one. Neither of you danced much, but when you did, it was with each other." Seth remembered those dances, especially the slow ones, and the guilty pleasure of having Bella in his arms. Linc rattled on, and Seth could hear the humor in his voice. "Fair warning. Mom thinks you're an adorable couple."

"We aren't a couple, and we damn well aren't *adorable.*"

"I don't know, you seem pretty adorable to me."

"Fuck you."

A movement caught his attention and he spotted Bella dropping her purse into a drawer and sitting at her desk. The thing that'd been wound tight inside him eased.

She was dressed in a conservatively tailored women's dark brown suit, and had her hair pinned at the back of her neck in a schoolmarm bun. Hard to believe he was looking at the same woman who a little over a week ago had worn a dress that had showcased her incredible breasts and was so fucking hot he'd lost his head.

She was still fucking hot, but in a more restrained way. Restrained fucking hot.

"Seth, you still there?"

"Yeah, I'm here."

"You going to ask her? Because if you don't, Mom will."

Seth scrubbed a hand over his face. No one bucked his mom. "I'll ask her. She probably won't come, though."

"Ask her. If she says no, Mom'll call her and convince her to come. Mom said you're both to bring overnight bags so you don't have to drive back from San Diego. She wanted to know if I thought you'd be sharing a room."

Of course that comment made Seth's mind jump immediately to what had happened when they had shared a room. "Jesus Christ. No, we won't be sharing a room. She's not likely to come, so it's a non-issue. Are we done here?"

"Mikayla says hi."

"Tell your wife hi back, and that I'll pay her five hundred bucks if she'll smother you in your sleep."

"She won't do it. She loves me."

"God knows why. Later, Linc."

He tossed the phone on his desk. He hadn't realized the Fourth, his mom and stepdad's annual Independence Day celebration, was coming up so fast. If his mom was scheming to throw him and Bella together, it would make attending the family gathering complicated.

He tipped back in his chair, watching Bella at her desk. She may look prim and proper in the plain suit and restrained hair, but he'd bet the bank there was something going on with her that had nothing to do with work.

After nearly a week off, she should look rested, but she didn't. Her eyes were shadowed and her shoulders slumped. He picked up his cell again.

She picked up hers, glanced at him, then rolled her eyes. "Yes?"

"How come you're tired?"

She swiveled her chair so her back was to him. "You can't call me on my personal phone when I'm at work."

"Why not?"

"Because people working in this office will know, and I don't want to be talked about."

"How would anyone know you and I are talking? Besides, I'm your boss. Talking to you is what I do."

"You're on your personal phone and I'm on my personal phone, not on our official government-issued phones. People will know. And you're looking at me."

"Your back is turned. How do you know I'm looking at you?"

"I can feel it. How do you know my back is turned if you aren't looking at me?"

Another marshal crossed near her desk and she lowered her voice. "These people are my coworkers. They know I don't take personal calls at work, plus they're trained investigators. They'll figure it out."

"Then let's go out for coffee. We need to talk."

"You already have coffee."

"How would you know that if you weren't looking at me?"

He heard her sigh over the line and smothered a grin. "I may've glanced at you when I first came in. For a brief moment."

"Like I said, we need to talk. We'll be back in half an hour."

"I don't want to talk to you."

"Bella, I need—"

A call came through on his office line, caller ID said it was from US Marshal headquarters in Virginia. "Shit. I need to take this. We'll talk later."

The call from headquarters led to a conference call, which led to Seth being swamped all day. They all were. By the time he came up for air it was almost six, and the office was quiet with only a few deputies working late. Bella wasn't one of them. She'd clocked out at five sharp.

He leaned back in his seat, considering his options. He needed to pass on the invitation from his mom. Bella had looked tired. Weren't pregnant women tired all the time? Something was going on that was upsetting her, and not knowing was making him a little crazy. He had a compulsion to make sure she was okay.

Not examining his motives too closely, he loosened his tie, grabbed his coat, and headed for the elevator.

\*\*\*

In all the time he'd known Bella, Seth never been to her home. A few months ago, he'd been in the area. Curiosity had gotten the better of him and he'd looked up her address and driven by. Now he stopped his car in front of her building, putting it into reverse to parallel park between a Volkswagen and a Prius. The two-story apartment building appeared to have been built in the fifties and looked mid-century cool. Her unit was on the second floor. He went upstairs, found the door to 2D, and knocked.

The last thing he expected when the door opened was to be confronted by a shirtless man who looked like a goddamned Viking warrior. The guy was taller than Seth, at least six-five or six-six. His hair was a shaggy dark blond, with his beard a shade lighter. He had a rough, watchful look that made Seth think he'd had his share of fights. The scar through his left eyebrow and slightly crooked nose weren't trophies from beauty contests. One of those fights had been recent. His right eye was swollen nearly shut and bruises covered his face in varying shades of purple and green. He gripped the doorframe with fierce concentration, like he had to think about staying upright, and his skin gleamed with sweat.

"Who the fuck are you?" the Viking growled.

"I could ask the same of you, pal. This Bella Nikolaev's apartment?"

"Who's asking?"

"I'm asking." Seth pulled out his wallet and thrust his marshal's star and ID in front of the wide, square-jawed face. "Seth Jameson, US Marshal. Where is she?"

The hard glare from the eye that wasn't swollen shut shifted from Seth's credentials to his face. "Why do you want her?"

"Alexei, who is it?" Bella's sharp tone came from behind the guy who stood like a brick wall blocking the door.

The Viking turned, the movement revealing a tattoo of an eagle on his shoulder and a white bandage with a blossoming stain of red taped to the skin low on his back. "It's no one. He's leaving."

"I'm not leaving." The muscle in Seth's jaw twitched.

Bella put a hand to the man's hip as she peered around his back. "Seth? What are you doing here?"

"Looking for you."

"This guy bothering you, *lyubov moya*?"

"Go sit down, Alexei. You shouldn't be up."

Instead of following her order, Viking Alexei pulled her under his arm and pressed a kiss to her hair. Keeping his good eye on Seth, he murmured to Bella, his voice loud enough for Seth to hear. "Have I told you I love you?"

Seth thought his molars could be reduced to powder if he didn't stop grinding them together.

"All the time. Now go." She gave him a push. "Seth is my boss. Stop acting like a possessive idiot trying to make him jealous."

Alexei glared at Seth, then one corner of his mouth turned up. "I succeeded. He thinks he is more than boss." He sent Seth another warning look before releasing Bella. He swayed, then stepped away from the door. "I won't be far."

Seth narrowed his eyes when the big man retreated across the room to lower himself carefully into a deeply padded recliner lined with a blue and white pad, his groan as he sank into the seat audible from the door.

"He's Russian."

"What, did he drop an article? Mispronounce the letter 'i'?" She held up a hand. "Never mind. I don't want to argue with you. He's in pain. I think we all revert when we're in pain." She eyed Seth. "Or are angry."

She'd lost the prissy bun and her dark hair now tumbled in waves around her shoulders. Her colorful top and black leggings looked comfortable and casually sexy. The contrast with her office attire was intriguing.

He kept his expression neutral despite the compulsion to do whatever it took to make what was wrong with her all better. The effort to lock his feelings for her into a corner of his brain no longer worked, and he was starting to question whether he should continue trying.

Since the night at Montenegro's estate, he'd started to question why he should continue to hold himself back. He wanted to see how their relationship evolved. He wanted more.

"You want to tell me what that guy's doing here with you?"

"Alexei is my brother. He was messing with you, trying to make you jealous."

Brother? He remembered her personnel file had listed a brother. The ache in his jaw eased. He could deal with a brother. "He was doing a damn good job of it. Can I come in?"

Her eyes widened at his comment, then she backed up a step and held open the door. He stepped in and looked around. This was where Bella was most herself, and the space felt like her. The furnishings looked warm and comfortable. The walls were painted a pale gold, and cushions decorated the couch with vivid floral patterns he thought might be Russian. The scent of something cooking hung in the air.

She led him to a small kitchen, where she picked up a spoon to stir whatever was in a pot bubbling on the stove.

"What happened to your brother?"

"He was hurt."

"That's obvious." He studied her. "How?"

She didn't look up, instead lifting her shoulder in a shrug as she continued stirring.

He frowned. "Okay, we'll come back to that. First thing, he needs a doctor."

"He does, but he refuses to go. He's stubborn." She raised hooded eyes. "I'm worried about him. I think the wound is infected, but he won't let me take him to urgent care."

"Let me help."

"How?" She turned back to the bubbling pot. "You're not a doctor. I told him if he loses consciousness, I'm calling an ambulance and sending him to the hospital. So of course, he's been fighting to *stay* conscious because he's nothing if not stubborn."

"No hospital." Alexei stood in the doorway to the kitchen gripping the blue and white pad. He held it out to show a wide spot of blood. "I'm bleeding again."

Bella walked to her brother, speaking rapidly in Russian. Seth didn't have to understand the words to recognize the tone, since it was one he'd used with both his siblings—frustration borne from love and concern.

Alexei grumbled and retreated, and Bella turned back to Seth, lines etched between her eyebrows. "You should go. I don't want you to get in trouble."

"For what? Not following the rules and bringing him in if he's involved in something illegal?" Bella froze, only for a fraction of a second, but long enough to let him know he was on the right track. "Sometimes life is messy, Bella. I can deal with it. My question is, can you? You're the rule follower."

"It's safer to be a rule follower. Except when it's my brother, apparently rules don't matter so much to me." Indecision warred on her face, but then she set her chin. "I told him to lie on my bed so I can look at the wound. Will you come?"

Seth couldn't have resisted the plea in her eyes if she'd asked him to sever an artery.

"Of course."

# Chapter Seven

Seth followed Bella down a short hall to the bedroom. Her bed had a wrought-iron headboard, which matched the twisted-metal pulls on the dresser drawers. A framed photo of Bella, her brother, and a smiling older couple sat on a bookshelf crammed with hardback books. Alexei lay face down across the bed, the bedcovers pulled back with the blue and white waterproof pads beneath him. The bandage on his back was completely saturated with blood. Seth peered closer at the tattoo on the man's shoulder, an insignia gripped in the talons of the eagle.

Bella knelt on the bed and began peeling off the bandage. She caught her lower lip between her teeth as she removed the bloody pad and exposed an ugly wound. Butterfly sutures held the edges together, and they, too, were soaked with blood. The skin surrounding the wound was red and inflamed.

"Does the skin feel hot to the touch?"

Bella pressed her hand to the area and nodded.

"He's got an infection. I'm making a call." Seth drew his phone from his pocket.

"No hospital. No police," Alexei growled, the words slurred.

Seth eyed the patient. "For the moment, no law enforcement not in this room will know. I'm calling a friend. Markel's a doctor and he'll check you out. If he says you're to go to the hospital, you're going."

"No hospital."

"Hospital is better than dead, man."

Seth went back to the living room to make his call. Markel picked up on the second ring. Seth described Alexei's condition, listened to the response, then relayed Bella's address.

He was pushing the phone back in his pocket when Bella came in. "Will he come? Will your friend come help my brother?"

"He'll be here in a half hour or so, depending on traffic."

"Thank you." She took a shaky breath, her eyes brimming. In all their time together, he'd never seen her close to tears. "Thank you. I've been so worried about him. He wouldn't let me get help."

"You should've called me. You know I'd help, no matter what." Something had changed in their relationship, something he couldn't define, but what he'd said was god's truth. He had her back, no matter what.

"I guess I do know." She gestured to the kitchen. "I made borscht for dinner. It's high in iron and Alexei lost a lot of blood so I thought it would be good for him. I'll save some for him for when he wakes up. Will you eat borscht?"

"Sure, sounds good." Even though she rarely betrayed her origins with her speech, every now and then a turn of phrase or the hint of an accent reminded Seth that she'd been born in Russia and English wasn't her first language. They returned to the kitchen where she ladled beet soup into bowls, opening a foil packet from the oven and placing warm rolls on plates with little pats of butter. When she went to pick up the bowls, he stepped forward. "I'll take them to the table."

They sat at the small table in a corner of the kitchen next to a windowsill lined with potted succulents. Her eyes were on his as he swallowed a spoonful of the savory soup. "Do you like it? Americans often don't like beets."

He nodded. "Yeah, I like it. Did I tell you that my step-grandmother was Russian? The first time we visited her in Chicago, she had a big pot of borscht on the stove. Like your soup, it had carrots and cabbage and potatoes with the beets. It's a favorite." He thought she was relaxing for the first time since he'd come in the apartment.

"That's good." She glanced up at him as she ate her own soup. "You're trying to distract me from worrying about my brother."

He shrugged. "Maybe."

"You don't have to. But I appreciate you'd think of it." After another spoonful of soup, she asked, "How'd you get a Russian step-grandmother?"

He may have wanted to distract Bella, but he found he also wanted her to know something about him. "You met my stepdad, Archer Bollinger, at the weddings."

She nodded. "He's very handsome."

"Mom thinks so. But don't tell him or we'll never hear the end of it. Anyway, he married Mom when I was a teenager. His mom's family immigrated from Russia after World War I, fleeing the revolution and civil war. They'd lost family members to the Bolsheviks and decided to get out."

Bella nodded. "The Bolsheviks were brutal. Conditions only got worse when Stalin came to power." She stirred the soup in her bowl slowly and he wondered where her thoughts had gone.

"What happened to your family in Russia?" Bella had been adopted by an American couple, that much had been in her personnel file. He wanted to know more.

She shrugged. "Our parents were dissidents. They opposed the Soviet government during the eighties. Before they had children, they were involved in protests and had been arrested. My father several times."

Seth smeared butter on a roll while he considered her response. She'd never spoken of her family. She'd always kept that part of her life separate. Those lines were erased when he'd knocked on her apartment door. He was never going back to the way they were before. "What about after they had children?" She shrugged and he pushed harder. "Something must've happened for you to end up adopted by an American couple."

"Yes. Something happened. My dad continued his political work. He would spend months in jail, he would suffer through brutal treatment, then be released, but always with the warning that things could be worse for him if he continued his unlawful behavior.

During this time there was a lot of disruption and chaos in Russia. Then he disappeared. My mother thought he would be returned to us after the Soviet Union collapsed in ninety-one, but we never saw him again."

"Do you know what happened to him?"

"All we knew was that he'd been arrested. My mother got word that he'd been sent to a prison in the Ural Mountains, and she decided to try to find him. She took Alexei and me to our grandmother's. Mama planned to be gone only a few weeks, but she never returned. I've done some digging, and I'm certain that they were both killed. My father for his political views, my mother because she wouldn't accept the government's official explanation of his disappearance."

"Jesus. You and Alexei were with your grandmother. She cared for you?"

Bella spooned up soup, swallowing before answering. "If you can call it that. She was poor, was fond of cheap vodka. Mostly, she left us to fend for ourselves. Alexei was only three and I tried to take care of him. She put us in the orphanage when she decided we'd become too much of a burden."

Which would have made Bella only six or seven herself when she was caring for her younger brother. Seth shook his head. While he'd been playing baseball and trying to master algebra, she'd been fighting for her and her brother's survival. Seth had dozens of questions about her past, but was stopped by a rapping on the front door. He rose to his feet. "Let me get it."

He opened the door to a tall Black man, a classic doctor's bag in his hand. His teeth flashed in a wide grin as Seth clapped him on the shoulder and ushered him inside.

"Glad you could make it. I owe you."

"Friends don't owe friends. Especially since you've saved my ass more than once."

Bella joined Seth and he did the introductions. "Bella, this is Doctor Markel Dupont. We did our undergrad together at UCSD and were roommates there for three years. He's the smartest man I know."

Markel turned to Bella. "Don't let this guy fool you. He's the only person I know who reads history books for fun."

"Make that two people. I like reading history too." Bella extended her hand. "Nice to meet you, Dr. Dupont. I'm Bella Nikolaev, I'm also a marshal. Thank you for coming."

"Nice to meet a friend of Seth's, and it's Markel. No thanks necessary. Where can I wash before seeing the patient?"

After Markel had scrubbed his hands, Bella led the way to the bedroom where Alexei had shifted to lie on his side. Bella turned on the overhead light, then Markel did what Markel did best. He soothed his patient and after donning gloves, he got to work.

Bella answered questions and tried to calm Alexei when he growled his displeasure. After several minutes, Markel dug into his bag. "His face will heal well enough, and the bruising should fade in the next week. You did a good job with the butterfly sutures on that stab wound, though the scar won't be pretty. He'd have been better off with a drain, but it's too late for that. I'll replace the butterflies. We're lucky it wasn't any deeper. First, though, he gets a tetanus shot, then a jab of the good juice in his butt, because he's got a nasty infection going."

"Hell no." Alexei's eyes looked glassy, but his vision was apparently good enough to see the syringe Markel was prepping.

Bella said something sharp in Russian, which made Alexei glower at her. "I'm not a baby."

"Show us a butt cheek, my man. After the antibiotics, you'll get the double good juice."

"You said this was the good juice."

"It is, but the *double* good juice is the pain meds. You'll be feeling better and will be out like a light before you know it." After quickly and efficiently administering the injections, Markel took a marker and drew a line around the redness bordering the wound, delineating the extent of the infection.

Ten minutes later, after Bella had coaxed her brother into a more comfortable position on the bed, she walked out with Seth and Markel to the front room.

Bella gripped her hands together, strain evident in the shadows under her eyes. "How bad is my brother? Please tell me the truth."

Seth dropped an arm across her shoulders. He knew how worried she was when she leaned into him.

"The infection is bad, and if you hadn't called me today, he could have gotten much worse and gone into septic shock. He should've been taken to the hospital right away." Seth caught the miserably guilty look on Bella's face.

"The marshal here explained that wasn't your call." Markel shrugged. "If the meds work like I think they should, Alexei should be showing signs of improvement soon, for sure within a day. If they don't and he gets any worse, don't mess around. Call an ambulance and get his ass to the hospital. I'll come back tomorrow evening, and same deal. If the redness has spread past the line I marked or he's not feeling significantly better, he's going to the hospital. That's nonnegotiable. I don't let my patients die from stubbornness." Bella nodded and Seth tightened his hold.

Markel handed her a bottle of pills and a slip of paper. "Here are enough pills to get Alexei through to tomorrow when you can get this script filled. Directions are on the bottle. He can't skip doses."

"Thank you. My brother owes you his life." She took a deep breath, then released it slowly and Seth felt the tension in her shoulders ease. "I have borscht and dinner rolls. Would you like some dinner, Markel?"

"I'll have to take a raincheck on that, sweetheart. I've got a date with my fiancée tonight." Markel picked up his bag. He gave Bella a hug because he was that kind of guy, and Seth walked him outside to his car.

"I like your girl, Seth. About time you got serious."

He was about to deny that he was serious about Bella, but he could still feel her seeking contact with his body as she braced for news about Alexei. "Bella and I are something, but I'm not sure what. At the moment it's undefined."

"Yeah? Don't forget I know you. I saw how you are with her, and you've got it bad. I'd say you both do."

Seth watched his friend drive off in the Porsche he'd put a down payment on with his first paycheck as a doctor, and then climbed the stairs back to Bella's apartment, thinking about what Markel said. He was right, Seth did have it bad.

He shut the door and Bella came from the hallway. "Alexei okay?"

"He seems to be sleeping easier. The ibuprofen I'd been giving him didn't ease the pain enough for him to rest. What Markel gave him is much better."

He'd never thought of Bella as fragile before, but tonight she looked about done in. "Sit. I'll clean up from dinner."

She ignored him and walked into the kitchen. "I have to put the soup in a container and wash the dishes."

She pulled a glass storage bowl from a cupboard and set it on the counter. When she reached for the pot on the stove, he took her hands, holding on when she would have tugged them away.

"You have wine?"

She nodded slowly. "In the refrigerator."

He got the wine, opened a cabinet, and found a wineglass. He poured it half full and handed it to her.

"Go sit down, drink the wine, relax. I'll take care of the cleanup." He tried to make it sound less like an order and more like a request.

Their gazes locked and awareness of the mind-blowing, life-changing sex they'd shared was there between them like something he could touch. It took every ounce of restraint he possessed not to pull her closer and take her mouth with his.

They'd been together only one time, and all he could think was that it wasn't enough. They could be together every night for a lifetime and it wouldn't be enough.

Her cheeks flushed and he knew he wasn't the only one remembering how it had been. What had happened between them had shifted the dynamics of their relationship, and he didn't think either of them was sure where they stood.

But he didn't say anything. "I'll take care of the soup," he repeated.

She nodded slowly. "I'm racking up debts to you."

"You don't owe me anything. Didn't you hear Markel? Friends don't owe friends."

"You called Markel. Doing that might've saved my brother's life. I'm not exactly sure that we're friends, but I owe you."

"That's bullshit. I've got your back, Bella. Always."

Expression solemn, she turned away to walk down the hall. A moment later, he heard a door close.

He rolled up his sleeves and got to work. Since Bella was an organized soul, finding where things were in her kitchen was relatively easy. He stored the soup and bread. Since the 1950s apartment didn't come equipped with a dishwasher, he squirted dish soap in the sink and washed the dishes, leaving them to air dry on a bamboo rack.

He returned to the front room to find Bella curled on the couch, staring out the window into the darkness beyond, her mostly empty wineglass on the coffee table. The sun had set and the sky held a purplish haze.

Seth turned on a lamp and sat beside her. "You flew back to LA last Tuesday, but Alexei's injury isn't that old. What brought you back?"

She hesitated, rubbing her thumb back and forth over the material of her leggings. When she stopped worrying the fabric, she seemed to come to a decision. "Do you want the long story or the short story?"

"I want the full story."

"I thought you'd say that." She stretched, then settled back into the couch. "There was a boy at the orphanage in Russia, his name was Alexander. We called him Sasha. He was older than me and had been at the orphanage a long time. We were friends of a sort, and he helped me some with Alexei."

"What was going on with Alexei?"

She continued to look out the window, but he thought she must've been seeing images from her childhood. "He was so young, and he had trouble settling into life in the orphanage. He missed our mother. He would be so fierce during the day, trying to be strong, but then at night, he'd be sad. He was a little boy. He'd cry for our mother and wouldn't sleep. I was afraid he'd disappear, that we'd be separated, so I always tried to stay close to him."

Well shit. Hard to imagine Bella's experience as a child, fighting to keep her brother close so he wouldn't disappear like the other people who'd loved her. A telling clue as to part of the reason she wouldn't acknowledge a relationship between them. He wondered if deep down she feared that at some point he'd also disappear. "That was a lot of responsibility for a little girl. Go on."

"The younger boys and girls slept on the same floor, but in separate rooms. At night I could hear Alexei crying from across the hall. I'd sneak into the boys' room and lie with him on his cot until he fell asleep, then go back to my bed.

"Sometimes Sasha would bring Alexei to me. Even if I fell asleep, I'd wake up early or Sasha would wake me up. We always managed to be in our own rooms before the morning bell sounded. One time I overslept and was discovered in the boys' room."

"Were you punished?" Even though his father had been difficult, and at times harsh, until the day he had abandoned his family, Seth's childhood had been secure.

Thinking of Bella as a scared child in an orphanage made him wish he could go back in time and somehow fix things for her. He put an arm along the back of the sofa, threading her hair between his fingers.

She shifted away from him but didn't pull her hair free. "No. I was sure we would be, but the matron in charge of our floor decided to arrange a room for siblings. Other brothers and sisters got to move in there too. Alexei and I put our cots next to each other. The matron was a kind woman and truly cared for the children."

"So things were better?" He picked up another lock of hair, twirling it around his finger.

"Somewhat. There never seemed to be enough to eat, and I don't think I ever felt warm enough, but we survived. I kept Alexei with me all the time so he'd be safe, and Sasha helped protect us from older boys who bullied the younger children. He found my book of poetry my father had given me that one of the mean boys had stolen."

"That's a miserable way to grow up." Her fingers knotted together, and Seth reached for her hand. He brought it to his lap, brushing a thumb across her palm.

"Like I said, we survived. Eventually, we were adopted together and brought to the States to live in Boston. My American parents are the kindest, most loving people in the world. Alexei and I are fortunate they chose us." She sighed. "Anyway, it was Sasha who called me last week."

"He's here in the US?"

She nodded. "He was adopted by a family in Iowa. They're farmers and I think they wanted boys who could work on their farm." She shrugged, her gaze on their joined hands. "Even so, it had to be better than staying at the orphanage. They took him and another boy. Sasha found me on social media a few months ago, and contacted me when we were in San Francisco."

"Why did he contact you?"

"He said Alexei was in trouble and I needed to come back to LA."

Seth wasn't sure if she was aware that as she talked, she'd moved closer, their shoulders again touching.

"He'd been in contact with Alexei?"

"Yes. Sasha wanted to meet with me. He said it was important."

"That doesn't explain the three days off." Seth couldn't help being suspicious that Sasha's interest might be more than friendship.

"I took the days off because I was worried about Alexei and I wanted time to figure out what was going on. We always check in with each other, but I hadn't heard anything for several days. Then when you and I were in the car Tuesday, I got a text, which made me think something was wrong. I'd texted back and tried to call him throughout the day, but he didn't respond. Then Sasha texted me that afternoon. He said he was concerned about Alexei, but wouldn't tell me anything over the phone."

She realized how close they were sitting and shifted away, pulling her hand free and regarding him with a serious expression, lines between her brows deepening as she frowned. "I want to tell you something as a mostly friend, not as my boss."

He drummed his fingers on the cushion behind her head. "Despite what I said earlier, you know I have to do something if what you tell me is actionable. So do you, Bella."

"I know. That's why this has been so hard. I'm caught in the middle of things I have no control over." She stared out the window, and he figured she was thinking through the angles. "Okay, let me say it this way. I met with someone who might have connections to the *bratva*."

"Russian mafia. Shit."

"Shit is right. This person says the *bratva* is pressuring Alexei to join." Which, if Seth was reading it right, meant that Sasha was in with the *bratva* and had information he'd passed on to Bella.

Her gaze turned grim, reminding him that while she may have had the wind knocked out of her, Bella would come back strong. "Later I learned the *bratva* had hurt Alexei and will try again. They told him he could die, or he could join. They said they'd kill him if he went to the authorities."

"He was an Army Ranger?" .

"You saw his tattoo."

"Yeah. Was he?"

"He was. He got out of the army about three years ago and joined the Los Angeles Police Department. I've had no reason to question what he was doing." She sighed.

"It's odd that the *bratva* would want him if he'd been a Ranger. They must know it's hard to break the loyalty of that type of soldier."

She shrugged. "They count on Russian ex-pats having greater loyalty to Mother Russia and they can be manipulative and brutal. I was approached when I was going through Marshal training at Glynco." She glanced at Seth. "That's in my file. I reported it immediately. One thing Alexei and I have going for us is that we don't have family in Russia who could be threatened if we don't cooperate. Our grandmother died years ago, and there's no one else."

She breathed deep, held, then breathed out for a long count. He'd noticed her doing that before and wondered if she was practicing a relaxation technique.

"Alexei called me Friday night. He said he was hurt and was in an alley in West Hollywood. Did you know there's a Russian community in West Hollywood?" At Seth's nod, she continued. "He wouldn't let me call the police. I found him and got him into my car. His face was battered and he was bleeding so badly." She closed her eyes for a long moment, then reopened them. "He couldn't even hold his phone, could barely talk. He told me to make a call for him."

"Who'd you talk to?"

"I don't know. Alexei said to tell the man who answered that the plan was working but that he'd be out of commission for a few days. Then he told me to forget the number."

"But you didn't."

She sat up and pulled open a drawer in the coffee table and retrieved a pen and a small pad of paper. She wrote a phone number and held it out. "I'm trusting you, Seth."

"You know you can."

Alexei called from the bedroom and Bella leaned forward with her hands on her knees.

Seth tucked the paper in his pocket. "Sit, Bella. I'll see what he needs."

He understood it as a testament to how tired she was that she collapsed back against the cushion and let him take care of her brother.

Seth helped Alexei to the bathroom, waited to make sure he got back in bed without walking into a wall, then returned to find Bella with her feet tucked under her and her eyes closed. He tugged a blanket from the back of the couch and draped it around her.

For the next two hours, he sat at the little table in the kitchen and, using his phone, did some digging. After calling in a few favors and making a half dozen calls, he had answers to his questions. He returned to the couch, unlaced his shoes, and kicked them off.

With his feet on the coffee table, he leaned back and slung his arm around Bella, nudging her until she lay with her head against his chest.

He set the alarm on his phone and turned off the lamp.

He lay for a long time with Bella tucked against him, staring into the dark.

# Chapter Eight

Bella stretched, groaning from the crick in her neck. The arm draped around her tightened, bringing her more snugly into the warm body she was cuddled against. Her eyes popped open and she pushed up.

"Hey there. Slow it down. It's too early." The words were murmured in a sleepy, sexy voice.

"Seth, what are you doing here?" She nudged him in the ribs.

"Trying to sleep." He grabbed her hand and brought it to his lips. The whiskers on his chin rasped against her fingers.

They were lying lengthwise on the couch, which had to have been uncomfortably short for him. She wasn't sure how she'd ended up plastered against him, but she felt like they fit together perfectly. Her arm rested on his chest, her head lay on his shoulder, and one leg nestled intimately between his. The throw barely covered them but she felt plenty warm.

She rubbed her fingers against his bristly beard and he took her hand to bite lightly at her wrist. "You smell good." He licked where he'd used his teeth. "Taste good too."

The temptation to rub against the growing hardness in his pants had her wishing they were alone in the apartment. "We can't do this."

"We can. We've proven that."

He tipped up her chin and then he kissed her, a long, slow, sumptuous kiss that spread through her like light. She hated that one meeting of the lips was all it took to crumble her resistance. Even when she knew he would pull away like he had after they'd made love—no, *had sex*—like every other person she'd ever loved besides her brother, she couldn't prevent herself from responding to him.

He shifted her so she lay fully on top of him. Supporting herself against his chest, she stared into his depthless gray eyes before lowering her lids to hide the vulnerability she feared he might pick up on. Revealing too much was risky. If he thought what was between them was simple sexual attraction, she could deal with it. But if he guessed what was in her heart and then discarded her, she'd shatter into a million pieces. She knew that kind of hurt, and didn't think she'd survive it coming from Seth.

He wrapped his arms around her and pulled her more intimately against him. With a groan, she kissed him, her tongue tangling with his, then bit lightly at his bottom lip, all while moving back and forth slowly over his rigid erection. He slid a hand under the waistband of her yoga pants, cupping her rear and pulling her more tightly against him.

With emotions threatening to push her into an abyss she didn't know if she'd ever be able to climb out of, she broke the kiss and rested her forehead against his chest. "Wait,. Please wait. I can't think."

Her body rose and fell with his as he breathed. "I like it when neither of us think, but okay." His hands rested on her hips.

She jerked up, horror-struck. "My god, I didn't wake up for Alexei. He needs his medicine."

He tightened his grip before she could fly off the couch. "He's fine. I got up a couple hours ago and gave him the pills."

"Is he better? I need to check on him."

His chest expanded beneath her, this time with a sigh. "Go ahead and check on him. You'll feel better when you do."

The pale morning light from the window illuminated his short hair standing on end. She felt the inevitable pull on her heartstrings. Placing her hands on either side of his face, she pressed her lips to his. "You're a good man, Seth Jameson." She rose from the couch and went to check on her brother.

\*\*\*

Bella tipped back her head, hot water sluicing over her as she rinsed shampoo from her hair. Alexei was sleeping more comfortably. She'd peeked and saw the redness within the border Markel had drawn had receded. Only a tiny bit, but that slight improvement made her almost giddy with relief.

Given the circumstances, she'd slept well, and after waking in Seth's arms, she knew why. Since childhood, she'd always slept lightly, forever alert for any sign of danger. With Seth she felt safe and protected.

He'd done what she hadn't been able to do: gotten medical treatment for Alexei. She and Alexei were as close as siblings could be; their traumatic background created a tight emotional bond. Even when she knew what was best for him, she hadn't been able to override his wishes when he'd refused to be taken to the hospital.

Seth's arrival had come at a critical moment, and he'd gotten Alexei treatment, which probably saved her brother's life. As much as she loved her brother, she hadn't been able to do that for him.

On top of loving Seth and keeping those feelings closely guarded, now she was indebted to him in the most profound way. The only other person in the world she loved was Alexei.

She closed her eyes against a wave of emotion. Loving Seth wasn't something she could act on or expect him to reciprocate. Physically, there was hard evidence—she winced at the pun —he desired her. As her boss, he assumed responsibility for her. Adding in they'd had unprotected sex, his sense of duty would grow exponentially. He said he would always be there for her, but that wasn't the same as having a real relationship.

Not that she wanted one. She closed her eyes, frustrated with her internal conflict. When, after stupendous, mind-blowing sex, Seth had pulled back, she'd been hurt. Deeply. What she should've felt was relief.

She worked conditioner through her hair as she examined her rationale. Certain facts were immutable. Seth being her supervisor was a huge reason they couldn't be together. The other? The reason she should have been thanking him for saving her from revealing her feelings and taking a deep dive into an impossible relationship? She was living proof love was transitory and it was better to protect herself than being crushed under the weight of a kind of disappointment no person should experience.

At some point, Seth would move on. If she wanted to remain safe, it was up to her to make that happen. Never having a serious boyfriend had been intentional. She was careful never to be vulnerable and in a position to be easily discarded. Her parents' political activities had taken precedence over the safety of their children. Her grandmother had turned Bella and Alexei over to an orphanage. What grandparent did that to children who'd lost their parents? Institutionalized, abandoned, and bereft, Bella had lived by her wits to keep her and her brother safe and protected. She'd had no choice since the people she'd counted on to love and keep her safe had let her down.

There'd be no reliving that anguish.

Yet, something critical overshadowed everything about her feelings for Seth. The chance she had conceived. The possibility spun in her mind like a pinwheel, staggering in its implications. The only thing she could be certain of was no child of hers would ever feel unwanted. Her child would never for a moment feel unloved or unlovable.

If she hadn't conceived, any lingering strings attaching her to Seth would dissolve as he moved on with his life, and she hers. For her mental health, never mind her emotional one, it'd be a good idea to ask for a transfer.

Leaving the team and the friends she'd made would be like cutting off a limb, but continuing to work beside the man she loved who didn't love her back would slowly destroy her. Bella understood self-preservation better than most. No way was she going to stay in a situation where she'd wind up more battered and bruised than she felt already.

Going it alone would take its toll since it was possible she was pregnant. While she knew Seth would be responsible—he couldn't help but be responsible—he'd pay child support, start a college fund, send birthday cards and gifts, she had no idea what to expect from him otherwise. She massaged her scalp as she considered what he'd do.

Through work she'd come across plenty of men who'd had no emotional connection to their children. She couldn't see Seth being that guy. She had a feeling that if she and Seth had a baby together, he'd be involved, and they'd have contact through their child for the rest of their lives. She'd have to deal with her feelings for him, but geez, all that contact would hurt.

After a final rinse of conditioner, she turned off the taps and squeezed the excess water from her hair, all the while giving herself a mental finger shaking. She was getting ahead of herself and borrowing trouble.

Wrapped in a towel, she brushed out her tangles, moisturized, then finally gave in to temptation and pulled open the bottom drawer, rummaging behind tampons and pads to the back where she'd stashed a box after a run to the drugstore.

She studied the printed information like it held nuclear launch codes. The manufacturer claimed the test was *ninety-nine percent accurate* and could give her results *six days sooner*. Sooner than what, she had no idea, but she was late for her period by only a few days, which wasn't all that unusual for her. She chewed her bottom lip as she opened the box and studied what looked like a digital thermometer. A slip of paper said that for best results, do the test (pee on a stick) first thing in the morning when urine was most concentrated. She returned the inserts to the box and shoved it back in the drawer. Too late to get the first pee of the day, so she'd wait. Her period could start any time during the day, and that would be that.

She knew she was rationalizing her delay. The reality was she didn't want to take the test because she'd need time to mentally process the results. Doing that this morning wasn't going to happen.

Her brother needed her care, and she had work today. But the big no, *I'm not going to deal with this now*? The potential baby daddy was in the other room.

She wasn't ready to talk to him if the results came back positive, and he was too perceptive not to know something *more* was going on with her.

Delaying the pregnancy test seemed the best plan for the time being.

Calling herself a coward, she dried her hair, put it in a bun for work, and got dressed. She checked on her brother. He still slept, so she left the bedroom door ajar and walked down the hall.

She'd dressed in her usual demure and professional work attire, which Seth had goaded her about on more than one occasion.

He turned from where he'd been standing in front of an open cupboard. His gaze traveled over her and heat simmered in that all-encompassing look. She looked down to make sure she hadn't accidentally left her blouse unbuttoned to reveal the lacy edge of her bra.

Nothing was amiss. "What?"

His grin shot an arrow of heat to her belly. "After seeing Anna Novak in that hot blue dress, knowing what you're hiding under those straitlaced clothes is downright sexy."

"This outfit is *not* sexy. It exceeds the professional dress standards laid out by the Marshals Service."

His grin widened. How had she ever thought of him as the ice man? "I'm the one looking, and I say it's sexy because you're purposely trying not to be sexy. The flip-flops make the outfit."

"You make no sense. And I change into heels before I leave the apartment."

"Heels are definitely sexy."

"You're such a guy." She smothered a smile and gestured to the open cabinet. "What are you looking for?"

"You don't own a coffeemaker."

"True." She reached past him into the cupboard to pluck a carton from among the canisters of tea. "This is the best I can do." She tore open the box and handed him a packet from inside, then lifted the lid on a jar on the counter to get a teabag.

Seth took the carton from her and frowned as he read the label. "Freeze-dried coffee? Does anyone drink this anymore?" He'd taken off the button-down shirt he'd slept in and wore a white t-shirt untucked. With his hair sticking up and his morning beard shadowing his jaw, he looked adorably rumpled.

"It's either that or find the closest coffee shop. Alexei likes one that's down the street about five blocks."

Seth continued scrutinizing the label on the packet. "This contains caffeine. It'll do."

Bella busied herself filling the kettle and putting it over the flame, then opening a bag of bagels. She plunked two bagels on a cutting board and handed Seth a serrated knife. "Slice and toast."

"What's going on here?" Alexei's rough voice came from the doorway and had her turning to study her brother.

Despite the surly tone, which wasn't unusual for him any time before nine a.m., he looked clear-eyed. Relief flooded through her. He no longer looked deathly pale beneath the bruises that still colored his face, and he wasn't holding on to the doorframe for support. He'd pulled on an old college t-shirt she kept in her dresser. Paired with plaid boxer shorts, he didn't quite hit his normal level of intimidating, though the narrowed gaze he aimed at Seth showed he was trying.

Seth leaned back against the counter, long legs in front of him and arms crossed over his chest.

"Breakfast is going on here. How are you feeling?" she asked Alexei.

"Like I might not die." He nodded toward Seth. "What's he doing here?"

"Seth stayed last night." Her raised brow dared her brother to make an issue of the situation. "Good thing he came. It's because of him Doctor Dupont came by. You could have died."

The teakettle whistled and Seth turned to pour steaming water into mugs. Alexei scowled, but jerked his head toward Seth. "Okay. Thanks, dude."

Seth turned back to face him, gaze direct. "Your sister and I have a thing going. That a problem for you?"

"We do *not* have a thing going."

The hot look Seth shot her had her reassessing the validity of that statement. "You seeing anyone else?"

"No, not that it matters."

"Good. We'll see where this goes."

"Oh, we will, will we?" A spike of anger had her stalking toward him. "First off, I don't date arrogant men, and second, we don't know if I'm pregnant, so you're getting ahead of yourself."

"This isn't about you being pregnant."

"Pregnant? You got my sister pregnant?"

"I am *not* pregnant," Bella said between her teeth. At least she didn't think she was. How had this conversation gotten so off track? "I choose who I date, Seth Jameson, and I don't follow orders in my personal life."

With the bagels in the toaster oven, Seth returned to his spot leaning against the counter, looking relaxed and like nothing was bothering him while Alexei glowered, fists clenched like he was ready to take a swing.

"Alexei, *back off,*" she hissed.

Seth sipped from his mug, not even grimacing as he drank the instant coffee. He ignored her brother and addressed Bella. "Like I said, this isn't about you being pregnant."

She didn't know why his mild tone irritated her so much and made her want to kick him in the shin.

She opened her mouth to respond when Alexei cut in. "You got my sister pregnant. You marry her."

"Agreed."

"What?" She gaped at them, gaze flying from one to the other. "Are you idiots? Newsflash, we're not in the Dark Ages. *If* I'm pregnant, I can and will take care of myself and my baby. I don't need to get married, and I don't need you buffoons interfering."

"Guess we'll figure that out when we know." She thought Seth was being diplomatic until he added, "But here's another newsflash. *If* you're pregnant, I take care of you, and I take care of our child. That's nonnegotiable."

Alexei nodded like it was the most reasonable thing in the world.

"You want this freeze-dried shit that identifies itself as coffee?" Seth held up a packet for Alexei.

"If that's all there is," he grunted. "I'll have a bagel, since you're toasting them."

"What, now you're pals? How about we have coffee and a bagel and pretend we're modern men who respect women? I can't keep up." She wished her hair wasn't in a bun, because then she could tear it out by the roots. She needed something to shock her system back to reality, because somehow this crazy train she'd been riding for the last week had come off the rails.

"I respect women," Alexei muttered. "But married is better for you and the child if the man is good."

Seth was wise to keep his mouth shut.

Shaking her head, she got plates and set them on the table while Alexei leaned heavily against the doorjamb and Seth put another bagel in the toaster oven.

The smell of toasting bread permeated the air to combine with the aroma of fresh peaches as she finished slicing them into a bowl. Alexei laid his hand on her shoulder, then dipped his head to drop a kiss to her temple. He murmured in Russian, and she nodded.

Of course she'd forgive him. It was too much work to stay angry. The likelihood she was pregnant after that one time was low, so, she decided, she didn't have anything to worry about.

Probably.

Making breakfast and enjoying her brother's recovery nudged her toward an unexpected feeling of contentment.

Seth thought he was right about every damn thing and assumed too much; her brother was bossy and tended to be high-handed. But for the moment, Alexei was on the mend and she was oddly happy to be preparing breakfast with the two most important men in her life.

She reached out and plucked up the hem of Alexei's shirt. "I want to see how it looks." She knew she was looking for reassurance that he was recovering, but she liked tangible evidence. Occupational hazard.

The white bandage was unstained. The redness around the bandage continued to look healthier than it had the night before. "It looks good, Alexei."

"I'm getting better, *sestra*." He turned to lay an arm across her shoulders in a half hug.

"Sister, right?" Seth asked. "I've been learning Russian."

"*Da*," Alexei replied with a grin as he released Bella.

"You are not learning Russian." Bella stared at Seth.

"I am. Conversational, with slang and swear words. There's an app for it." Seth hitched a shoulder. "I practice in the car when I'm driving to work. This way when you swear at me in Russian, I'll be able to understand what you're saying."

Bella felt her heart give a slow, lazy roll in her chest. He couldn't keep doing that. Adding more little things to make her love grow even brighter, testing the fortifications she'd erected to keep those feelings safely walled off.

# Chapter Nine

Bella set the peaches on the small table, then brought over the cream cheese and plum jam. Seth poured hot water into a coffee mug for Alexei, and they sat at the table nearly knee to knee.

Licking plum jam from his thumb, Seth leaned back in his seat, stretching his legs to the side of the table. He nodded at Alexei. "You're working with the FBI."

Alexei sipped his coffee, then bit into his bagel, his expression carefully neutral as he chewed.

Bella paused, her loaded knife hovering over her bagel. "How do you know this?" If Seth said Alexei worked with the FBI, then Alexei worked with the FBI.

"I suspected, then did some digging. I have a couple contacts and gave them a call. Word is the *bratva* has been laundering money through nightclubs in West Hollywood, and using them as fronts for prostitution rings. The FBI has created a task force with a special LAPD unit. They're intent on crippling the *bratva*. Part of the plan is to infiltrate the organization." He looked at Alexei as he said the last part.

"But Alexei was beat up because he refused to join, he—"

Realization dawned and Bella turned to her brother. "You're playing hard to get."

He shrugged, slouching in his chair and rubbing a hand over his face, an indication that his energy was beginning to flag. "Let's hear what the marshal says. He seems to have all the answers."

"I have some. My guess is you allowed yourself to be set up. You were attacked by a seemingly random individual who demanded money to make you think you were being mugged. Am I right?"

At Alexei's nod, he continued. "Things got ugly and you got knifed. But it's a shallow wound. Your bad luck is it got infected. A member of the *bratva* would've rushed to your aid to help fight off the aggressor. He'd act like he's saved your life. Now you're indebted to them."

Alexei nodded again.

"Did you know the person who knifed you?"

Alexei shook his head at Bella's question. "The marshal is right. It was probably someone with the *bratva*. The guy who came to my rescue was for sure."

"It's a classic manipulation. Now you'll let them convince you. Once they think you're a convert, you'll be the inside guy keeping tabs on the *bratva* for the LAPD."

"Basically, yes."

Bella brought the kettle to the table, along with the instant coffee packets. "Sounds dangerous." Worry made her throat tight.

Alexei shook his head at the offer of more coffee. "What I'm doing is dangerous? What about what you do? You should be an accountant or a dentist. Not working at an agency where you could be hurt."

"You're the one who was knifed, who called me when he was bleeding and couldn't risk going to the hospital."

Her brother ran a hand down her arm. "Don't be mad at me. I couldn't tell you. If this operation is successful, we could save many women who are being exploited by the *bratva*." Alexei rose to take his plate and mug to the sink. "I'm applying to the FBI. This task force gives weight to my application. Go to work, Bella. I'll be fine today. I'm going back to bed."

Bella returned to the table when Alexei left the kitchen. The understanding in Seth's expression had her swallowing a lump in her throat.

"He's smart, Bella. He'll be careful."

"He's part of me. He's my only blood relative."

"Some of the people I care the most about are marshals, so I get it." The way he said it made Bella think that maybe he was including her in that group. "Most of the time it's not dangerous. But sometimes it is."

She pushed back her plate and picked up her mug. "Why'd you come here last night? You never said."

His gaze locked on hers, and her pulse quickened. At one time, she'd thought his impenetrable expression meant he didn't feel emotions, but now she knew that was his way of hiding them. She was beginning to suspect he kept a mountain of feelings strapped down tight, and that she was one of the few people he let see them.

"Several things. Most important? I was worried about you."

She had to tell herself worried wasn't the same as caring, and that as her boss, he'd see worrying about her as part of his job.

"Now you know why I came home early and took the days off, so you don't have to be concerned about me. I'm fine, and I think Alexei will be, thanks to you."

"You should've told me what was going on." His head tilt said *Am I clear?* "Another reason I came by was to deliver an invitation from my mom. She wants you to come to the Fourth of July thing in San Diego."

Bella set down her bagel. "How would you define a 'thing'?"

"The usual for Fourth of July. Arch will barbecue a mountain of burgers. Mom will make her potato salad, which by itself is worth going for. There'll be watermelon and corn on the cob. Linc, Ellie, and their spouses will be there, along with friends and family, and whoever else Mom invites.

"Arch organizes ping-pong tournaments and pool games for the kids. From the backyard, their house has a great view of the valley, so after dark we sit on the deck and watch the city fireworks show. It's a good time."

"That sounds more like a family thing. It's nice of her to invite me, but I don't think so."

"She wants you to be there, and, if it helps persuade you, I want you to be there."

Bella sipped her tea. "That's kind of you, and I'm sorry if this puts you in an awkward position. Send her my regrets and you'll be off the hook."

Seth was shaking his head. "You don't know Margaret Bollinger. My mom will hound you until you say yes. She's got a thing about having all her ducks together, and she considers you one of her ducks. Since the fireworks won't start until after dark, she told me you're to pack a bag and stay the night." He chewed the last of his bagel. "Ask Alexei if he wants to come. He'd be welcome. Mom would love to have him."

"How can that be? She doesn't know him. She doesn't really know me. We met at the weddings, and she was welcoming and kind. I thought you and your siblings are lucky to have her and your stepdad, but she and I had only a few conversations."

"Apparently, it was enough for her to decide you'd do for her eldest son."

She fumbled her fork, dropping it with a clatter against the bowl of peaches. "What do you mean, 'I'd do'?"

He held her gaze. "According to Linc, Mom noticed you and I went to the weddings with no plus one, and we only danced only with each other."

Panic clutched at her throat. Had she somehow given away her feelings? She'd need to be much more careful. "That's not true." She tried not to let anxiety seep into her tone.

"What part?"

"The dancing part. I danced with other people."

His gaze narrowed. "Who else did you dance with?"

"That little boy wearing the cute blue tuxedo and bow tie asked me. I think he's your cousin's son."

"That would be Christian. He's nine. He doesn't count."

"He's a charmer, but okay. Then there was that other cousin of yours at Ellie and Sam's wedding. He has gorgeous green eyes and he's close to my age."

"Gorgeous green eyes? Who the hell has—are you talking about Micah? Did he hit on you? He's only what, twenty-two or twenty-three? I didn't see him dancing with you or I'd have told him to get lost."

"Why would you do that? He was sweet, and obviously looks up to you. He's interested in joining the Marshals Service. We talked about that, and he plans to give you a call for advice."

"He's not sweet. The kid was a terror growing up." She smothered a smile when he scowled. "Whatever. You're officially invited."

That wiped the smile off her face, because while she was friends with Seth's siblings, and enjoyed spending time socially with them and their spouses, it sounded too much like she and Seth would again be thrown together as they'd been at the weddings. Those events had given her a painful glimpse into a life she could never have. No way would she torture herself more at a family barbecue.

She looked at the clock on the wall. "Oh, wow. Look at the time. We need to get to work. You'll want to get home to shave and change clothes."

"Good evasion, Deputy Nikolaev, but Mom will pin you down." His expression shifted. "I want you to come too, so think about it."

She sighed. "Okay, I promise to think about it."

"Good enough. Before I go, I need to bring you up to speed on Richard Jameson." She nodded. "I talked with Linc yesterday after you left the office." He relayed information about the threats to federal judges, and how the description of the man who'd organized the shipment of weapons into Mexico had matched RJ. "We knew the Freedom Defenders in Oregon were smuggling weapons into Canada, so it's not a surprise to find their affiliates are supplying arms to the cartels in Mexico. Regardless, this gives us a good idea what he's up to."

Bella ran water to fill the dish basin and Seth came to stand beside her. His expression didn't give much away, but he exuded a certain tension, which prompted her to ask him something she'd often wondered about. She knew the details of Richard Jameson's case, but she didn't know how Seth felt about it. "Are you angry with him? I'd be angry if he was my father."

He put the cream cheese and jam back in the fridge. When he turned toward her, his expression was guarded.

"He's just another fugitive."

"No, he's not. He's your father. He abandoned your family. That must hurt."

"That's not the issue. Here's the plan for this week. Ellie has developed a contact inside a militia group in Washington, so she's working that angle, learning what she can from him. Linc is in Nevada delving into the threats to the judge in Reno. Since it appears RJ was involved in shipping the load of weapons hidden in the hay bales to Mexico, and because that load originated in Reno, that's where we're focusing our attention. Today, you and I are combing through bank records to see if we can find financial links between Freedom Defenders and the Mexican cartel. If there have been other gun sales, I want to know about it. It'd be nice to pin international gun smuggling on their asses."

Not really surprised he'd deflected her question about his dad, Bella rinsed the plates and set them on the drainer.

"I need to go. You're dressed for work," he eyed her outfit, "but you can work from home today if you want to stay close to Alexei."

"No, but thanks. I want to make sure Alexei has everything he needs here, but I'll be in."

He gave a brief nod. "Okay, then I'll head out. I'm stopping at my apartment, then I'll be at the office."

He sat on a chair to put on his shoes and button his shirt.

"Thank you. For everything."

He stood and surprised her by dropping a swift kiss on her cheek before heading for the door, a gesture that made her heart yearn.

\*\*\*

Seth sat at his desk, staring at the paper in his hand. After leaving Bella, he'd swung by his apartment for a shower and a change of clothes, and to pick up his mail before fighting LA traffic to get to the courthouse, where the US Marshals office was located. One letter stood out from the usual junk mail. It bore no return address and was postmarked Modesto, California. He reread the handwritten message, holding it carefully by the edges when instinct told him he'd be better off jamming it through the shredder.

*Give up, Seth. You're not man enough to find me and never will be. Maybe that's my fault. If I'd stayed, your mother would never have married that asshole Bollinger and he would never have brainwashed my offspring and pushed them to join the feds. You think I don't know I'm the reason you're a marshal, and your brother and sister are marshals? I was sorely disappointed to learn you kids chose to follow Bollinger. What made you think you could ever find me? Instead of being adults I can be proud of, you betrayed me. I had important work to do, work that couldn't wait, and I had to leave to do it. Asshole Bollinger could never find me and neither will you. Be warned, if you keep trying, all hell will break loose. I have created an empire, which is destined to retake our land for the true Americans. If you keep after me, you will bring the wrath of God upon you and everyone you care about. You are my blood and your loyalty should be to me. Join me in my fight to rid this country of the scourge of unrestricted immigration and a government that has strayed from the Constitution. I don't want to hurt you, but if you try to thwart me, I will do what I must to see the fruition of my plan. If you don't stop harassing me, the deaths of many people, including your brother and sister, will be on your head. Heed my words. Richard Jameson*

Seth stared at the printing, the same slanted scrawl his father always used. The signature struck him as odd. He didn't know why he expected the letter to be signed *Dad*. Not that Seth had thought of him as that for years. Seth and his siblings had settled on RJ years ago. The man had abandoned his family, leaving home for work one morning, and never returned. In and of itself that would've been reason enough to spur seventeen-year-old Seth to hate his father, but they soon learned his crimes were more egregious than abandoning his family,

Three days after RJ's disappearance, US Marshal Archer Bollinger had appeared on the doorstep of their suburban San Diego home. A home his mom told him and his siblings they could no longer afford without their father's income.

Seth still remembered the sensation of being gut-punched while standing at his mother's side as she listened to Arch explain why the US Marshals were hunting the fugitive from justice, Richard Jameson.

Before his disappearance, RJ had been charged with federal crimes, accused of systematically embezzling money from the government agency where he'd held a managerial position. The sick feeling in Seth's stomach had worsened at the devastated look on his mother's face. They'd had no idea that his father had been in trouble, much less that charges had been filed against him.

One upside—there weren't any flashy cars or jewelry bought with his father's ill-gotten gains to be confiscated. Rather, it appeared the stolen money had been diverted to help fund an anti-government militia group.

Learning what his father had done was a bone-deep betrayal of everything Seth had been raised to believe in, and what he thought his father believed in: honesty, integrity, and loyalty. Seth had been brought up on those values, and his father had violated every one of them.

No matter how hard Seth worked to obliterate it, there was always that insidious voice in the back of his head telling him that he was no better than his father. Someday Seth would fuck up and show the world that blood was stronger than ideals, and he too could be corrupted.

For years, he'd been quietly feeding the burning rage he kept hidden deep inside him. Spewing it out wouldn't help and wouldn't change anything. He was the eldest, and it'd been his responsibility to pick up the pieces.

His baseball coach had been disappointed when he'd lost his starting first baseman, but the money Seth earned flipping burgers had been more important than playing varsity baseball. His mother had objected, but the reality was, they'd needed the money.

He'd corralled an equally enraged Linc, helping his brother channel his anger into football, and Seth made sure he was there for Ellie when his sister had been lost in the miasma of betrayal.

There'd been many late nights when he'd felt helpless as he lay in bed hearing the muffled sobs coming from his mother's bedroom.

It'd taken only a few weeks for her to square her shoulders and set about rebuilding her family. She'd arranged for every one of them to see therapists. God, Seth had hated those sessions. He'd endured them, and maybe they'd helped some. He'd come to realize that there'd been signs his father had been dealing with issues Seth hadn't understood, and from which his mom had likely been shielding her children.

Regardless, he'd been glad when the sessions were done. They'd moved into a smaller house and learned to economize. He'd been offered a scholarship to Stanford, but that dream had no longer seemed relevant. He'd wanted to take classes at the local community college so he could continue to work and be close to home to support his family, but his mother had been adamant he attend a four-year university. They'd compromised, and he'd gone to UC San Diego.

Through it all, Deputy Marshal Bollinger had been a constant, unflappable presence in all their lives.

While Arch had been looking for RJ, he'd fallen flat on his face in love with Margaret Jameson. When they'd eventually married, Arch had brought a steadiness to the family and had helped guide the

Jameson kids into adulthood. It was from him Seth had learned the true meaning of honor, and how to be a man.

Seth's chair creaked as he leaned back. RJ had betrayed his family and his country, and Seth was determined to prove he was a better man. Sometimes, it didn't seem to matter he and his siblings had made something of themselves, something that counted. He stared at the words his father had written and felt those old emotions churning, waiting for a weak moment to tear Seth down and make him feel like he was nothing.

He let the letter drop onto the desk and stared at it, fighting an internal battle. There was that voice in the back of his head that said he could make the letter with those hateful words disappear. He rose from his seat, took out his phone and snapped a picture of the letter, then, after scanning it at the copy machine, he went to the supply room to retrieve an evidence envelope.

Back at his desk, he put the letter inside the envelope, sealed it with evidence tape, and used a Sharpie to fill out the required information. He walked it to the evidence tech and watched as it was logged in, aware of the ache in his jaw where his muscles, rigid with anger, clenched his molars together.

Back in his office, he pulled his phone from his pocket. His sister picked up on the first ring.

"Hello, big brother."

"El, how soon can you get a flight south?"

Ellie dropped the lighthearted tone. "Soon. I'm in Portland, and there's a flight to LA that leaves in an hour."

"Good. Be on it. I need you and Linc here today."

# Chapter Ten

Bella sat at the large conference table in the Marshals' office, her laptop in front of her, the late afternoon sun slanting through the blinds. Ellie sat next to her busily texting as they waited for Seth to join the team.

Before leaving Alexei, she'd gotten a text from Linc's wife, Mikayla, urging her to come to the Fourth of July party at the Bollinger home. Then, while walking out of the corner café with an iced hibiscus tea, her phone buzzed. Answering it, since she knew she'd be hounded if she didn't, she'd talked to Margaret Bollinger for twenty-minutes.

Seth's mother was sweet, friendly, and unwavering. They'd chatted about this and that, and before she knew it, Bella found herself agreeing to attend the family Fourth of July celebration.

Once again, she and Seth would be thrown together socially. It didn't help that their relationship was in this strange place. They'd been lovers, but they weren't lovers. They were friendly, but they weren't exactly friends. She was in love with him, but he wasn't in love with her.

Her shoulders slumped as she traced a finger through the condensation on the outside of her cup.

"You gave in, didn't you? You're coming to the barbecue." Linc leaned back in his seat, a takeout coffee cup in his hand and a grin on his craggy face.

She gave him a wry look. "What do you think? Is anyone ever able to say no to your mother?"

"Not that I know of. She can be kind of scary when she wants something."

"Mom's not scary, she's determined," Ellie commented, not looking up from her phone.

"Your point, El. Hey, you texting Sam?" Linc asked his sister. "Tell him I've been breaking in my hiking boots and got a cool backpacking stove. It's lightweight and heats food super-fast."

"Tell him yourself. Then he can tell you about the new water treatment gizmo that he absolutely had to have. You guys have geeked out about this trip."

"Seth said he's figured out the best tents to get. I need to order mine. September will be here in no time and we'll be heading for the backcountry."

Ellie set down her phone, rolling her eyes. "Hiking to the top of Mount Whitney is not that big a deal. Lots of people do it. Some even do it in a day. It's not Everest."

"You're only saying that because this is a guys' trip and you're not a guy. Anyway, we're doing more than Whitney. We're hiking at least forty miles of the John Muir Trail."

"I don't want to go tramping through the woods for forty miles. Trust me."

Linc sent her a shrewd look. "No, you probably don't. But it bugs you that it's a guys' trip."

Ellie inclined her head regally toward Bella. "Let's plan something for the same week the he-men are *mountain climbing*." She used air quotes around the words.

"Hey, it is mountain climbing," Linc protested.

She ignored her brother and said to Bella, "Let's organize a girls' week. I've got my eye on a cabin in Mammoth in the eastern Sierras. It's got a deck and an awesome view of the Minarets. It'll be me, you, Mikayla, and Mom, Arch is going with the must-have-a-penis group." Ellie grinned at Linc's scowl. "Mammoth is awesome. There are a bunch of lakes connected by a network of bike trails. We can rent electric bikes, or hike, or spend all day lazing on the deck breathing in the mountain air and reading if we want. When we're done doing the fun stuff, we can hang out at the cabin and drink wine, eat tacos, and play Scrabble. You in?"

"I'm absolutely in. That sounds great."

"Hey, I want tacos."

"You'll be eating freeze-dried spaghetti and granola bars, so enjoy that," Ellie told her brother with a smirk.

Seth strode in with a stack of papers in his hand. He'd shed his suit jacket and turned up the sleeves of a blue shirt past his elbows. With a maroon tie knotted at his throat, and his gun in its holster at his shoulder, he looked like what he was: a solid, reliable chief deputy.

Okay, a hot, sexy, solid, and reliable chief deputy.

Was it only last night they'd cuddled together on her couch?

He passed a sheet of paper to each team member. Bella scanned the photocopied letter. It was addressed to Seth, and the signature at the bottom identified the sender as Richard Jameson.

"This arrived at my home address in yesterday's mail. The envelope was postmarked Modesto and dated three days ago. Take a minute to read it."

Bella read through to the end before glancing at Seth, whose face held his usual closed expression. He'd resisted talking about his feelings about his father, and he wasn't giving much away now.

"The fucker," Linc muttered. "He's trying to mess with your head. I want to know how he got your address."

"Our father is an asshole, and it's not too hard to find a home address, even a US Marshal's," Ellie added.

"There's a lot in this letter." The quiet command in Seth's voice refocused the conversation. "RJ rambles, but main points are that all of us, but mostly me, are a huge disappointment to him, and if we don't back off, people, including Linc and Ellie, will die and blame for that will be on my head."

"He's got an agenda and the team is interfering with it." Bella studied the letter. "How I read it is that we've been successful in disrupting his organization in Oregon and he's angry."

"I think Bella's right," Ellie said. "I'll repeat what Linc said. He's trying to mess with your head, big brother. He's pulling the disappointed dad card to get you to back off."

"He can't think I will."

"He doesn't know us anymore, Seth. His memory of you is as a teenage boy." Ellie's blue eyes were clouded. "I saw him for only a few minutes when we came face-to-face in Oregon, and my takeaway was that he is emotionally closed off from us. He doesn't care about his children at all. He had no problem ordering me killed."

"I think this letter gives us a clue on how we can bring him down," Linc said.

"Go on." Seth leveled a stare at his brother.

"What if you contact him, act like you're going rogue? Tell him you want to meet with him."

"He'll never go for it. He's a federal fugitive. I can't see him willingly meeting with a US Marshal, even if it is his son," Seth argued.

"He might." With all eyes turning to her, Bella went on. "I agree with Linc. For one thing, RJ expects that ultimately you'll have the same lack of integrity he had. We play to his ego, and while I'm not arguing with Ellie's assessment that he's distanced from you, I think there's a different way of looking at it."

"Go on."

"Ellie says he's closed off from you, his children. I agree. He no longer loves you as a father should."

"If he ever did," Ellie muttered.

"I believe he is still emotionally invested in you, or he would've never written the letter. He's vulnerable because of his ego. It bugs him you three became US Marshals like his nemesis, Archer Bollinger.

"Arch may not have been able to nab RJ, but he arrested his close associates, and he made it more difficult for RJ to operate, and forced him to go underground for a number of years. RJ sees him as more than a rival. Arch is the enemy who married your mom. That makes the dynamic even more volatile.

"He sees you following Arch's footsteps as a personal betrayal. If he could get you to join him and turn your back on the marshals, Arch, and your own family, then he's won a huge psychological victory. That may be too enticing a prospect for him to ignore.

"Add to that, it bugs him you don't respect his cause. He wants you to join him to fight for what he believes in, and if he can convince you, he's scored another victory."

She took a breath. "I think Linc is right. We figure out how to contact him and then convince him you're genuinely interested in his cause. The temptation of meeting you face-to-face might be too great for him to resist."

Seth frowned, staring at the copy of the letter in his hand, then gave a curt nod. "Okay. We'll explore that avenue."

***

Bella sat at her desk staring at the computer screen, worrying her bottom lip, scanning through images on the screen. Her brother was healing, which was a relief. No, she hadn't taken the pregnancy test. She wasn't avoiding knowing. Well, not really. She was avoiding knowing and not telling Seth. She wasn't ready to face him, especially after the caveman conversation he'd had with her brother. As she'd always done, she was being careful to protect herself. Yet, even with all the changes a pregnancy would bring to her life, deep in her heart she wanted Seth's baby.

Calling herself a coward, she pushed those thoughts aside so she could focus on her job. Since the team met to discuss the letter, she'd spent the past two days searching for clues where RJ was hiding out. If the guy wanted Seth to join the dark side, why hadn't he included something handy like an email address?

After an afternoon spent reviewing surveillance footage from a post office parking lot in Modesto, all she had was stiff shoulders and no leads. The office had quieted as most of the other deputies and staff had quit for the day. Ellie had flown back to Oregon to work on her contacts there. Linc, who was bunking at Seth's apartment, had been in the office most of the day and had taken off an hour ago.

Bella planned to leave soon and pick up takeout from her favorite Chinese restaurant for her and her brother. Alexei had started spending a lot of time on his phone, and wanted to get back to work.

He had a job to do, and his time holed up in her apartment where she knew he was safe would come to an end. She sighed. She wanted him to stay with her a little longer. She knew he wouldn't. He'd accuse her of being overprotective, but his injury had shaken her.

The night before, they'd talked about his role to infiltrate the *bratva*, and while she understood why he was doing it, nothing was going to stop her from worrying over his safety.

He was set on the mission and ultimately joining the FBI, and she'd learned long ago that getting her brother to change his mind once he'd settled on a course of action was like trying to stop the Santa Ana winds from blowing. It wasn't going to happen. Relief at his recovery felt like a giant weight had lifted from her shoulders. She would still worry about his mission, but at least he was no longer bleeding and nearly septic.

Bella clicked the mouse, scrolling through more feed from the date they estimated the letter had been sent. If they could identify the vehicle of the person who'd mailed the letter and trace its registration, they might have an avenue for tracking down Richard Jameson.

She knew the letter could've been mailed from anywhere in Modesto, and the sender never had to set foot in the post office. But tracking down every possible avenue meant scanning image upon image.

In Oregon, RJ had been driving a white truck with dual rear tires. He'd likely ditched that vehicle, but she still prioritized checking for any similar trucks that came into the post office parking lot, as well as vehicles registered in Nevada. The person mailing the letter might've driven over the Sierras to get the letter postmarked in a location designed to throw them off the search. She studied every white man who matched RJ's age and body type. So far, she hadn't come up with any matches.

A sound had her looking over her shoulder. Seth walked toward her desk. "Got anything?

She shook her head. "There are plenty of men who match RJ's general description, but so far not one of them is driving a vehicle with out-of-state plates. If we assume he drove to Modesto so the letter would be postmarked from there to throw law enforcement off the trail, then we're looking for a car that's not registered to an address in the vicinity of Modesto."

"Someone else could have mailed the letter for him." Seth came to stand behind her.

"Which is why I'm looking at all the vehicles, but focusing on those I think are most likely."

"Did you check the camera footage from the evening before? He could have dropped the letter in a mailbox after the last pickup for the day."

"True." Bella tapped on the field to call up footage from the previous day.

"You can do this tomorrow, Bella. It's time to go home."

"I'll leave in a few minutes."

"Bella."

She glanced up at him. He leaned against her desk, the look on his face making her catch her breath. His expression didn't give much away, but enough that she understood there was no going back to where they had been before.

No matter how hard she tried, the walls between them were crumbling. She didn't know how she'd exist if she ever let him fully in, and he left her. There was too much risk she'd end up like she had as a child, orphaned and struggling to survive. But she was a fighter, not a whiner. She answered him in the same tone he'd used. "Seth."

The corner of his mouth curled up. "You're using my name. That's an improvement. Let's go. I'll walk out with you. Tell me what you want, and Linc and I can pick up takeout and bring it to your place. Markel said he'd come by and give Alexei one last checkup. I'll call him to see if he wants to eat with us." His fathomless slate gray eyes studied her and she had the feeling if they weren't in the office, he wouldn't be so restrained. "What do you say? You want to spend the evening together?"

She found herself nodding while chiding herself for giving into the temptation of spending more time with him. "I want to go through this next file. I'll leave in half an hour. I promise."

\*\*\*

Seth stood with Linc on Bella's doorstep as she eyed all the bags hanging from their hands before stepping back and holding the door wide open. They walked past her, Seth leading the way to the kitchen, where he and Linc piled the bags on the table and started unpacking them.

Bella looked at the array of containers, brows raised. "That smells amazing, but did you order everything on the menu? That's an incredible amount of food."

"You know Linc eats like an underfed teenager, and we wanted to make sure there was enough for leftovers."

"Even Linc can't eat this much food."

"Hey, I'm a big guy. I need a lot of fuel."

Alexei wandered in. "That dinner? I'm starved."

"Speaking of someone who eats like an underfed teenager."

Seth caught Bella's expression. She looked so damn relieved her brother was feeling better, which reinforced how frightened she'd been. She made the introductions while Seth opened a cupboard to take down plates.

A knock sounded at the door and Seth followed Bella when she went to open it. Markel stood with his black bag in one hand and a grocery bag in the other. "Hey, lady, and my man, Seth."

Bella smiled and backed up so Markel could come in. "You're in time to join us for dinner."

He set his doctor bag on a side table and gave Bella a one-armed hug. "Thanks for the invite." He held up the grocery bag. "I've got beer, already chilled."

Markel checked out Alexei's wound and declared him on the road to recovery. Seth had watched Bella as the diagnosis lightened her eyes at the news that her brother was truly better.

They were all in Bella's living room. Alexei had taken the easy chair, and Linc and Markel brought in chairs from the kitchen table. They held their plates as they ate, beer bottles on the floor beside them. Seth sat elbow to elbow with Bella on the couch, the coffee table pulled close. She picked up his beer to set it on a coaster.

Across the room, Linc gestured with his chopsticks, as he tried in earnest to convince Markel and Alexei to join the guy backpacking trip.

Bella wound lo mein noodles around her chopsticks, swallowing a bite before saying to Seth, "I think I found the person who mailed the letter for RJ."

His gaze traveled over her. Her hair tumbled around her shoulders and the purple top she wore outlined her breasts. "Tell me."

"A woman with Nevada plates dropped an envelope in the outside collection box fifteen minutes after the last collection the evening. She drove a silver Honda Civic with plates registered to a Vivian Cochran with an address in Reno. She owns a duplex at the same address, but she doesn't appear to reside there."

"Did you come up with a photo?"

Bella picked up her phone from where it rested on the table and tapped the screen. Seth leaned toward her and she turned the phone so he could see. It struck him if their relationship were strictly professional, they wouldn't be sitting so close that he could smell the soap on her skin.

Vivian Cochran's driver's license had the usual stats: fifty-four years old, five foot four, one hundred and thirty-five pounds. She had hazel eyes, and while her hair was noted as brown, the photo showed Vivian with her hair bleached blonde.

Seth set down his beer. "What makes you think she's the one who mailed the letter?"

"A couple things. Her husband was the leader of a local chapter of a white nationalist group. Donald Cochran killed himself three years ago after a gunfight with the feds. He was facing charges in gun trafficking and was suspected of assaulting a Sikh man whom Cochran had accused of being an Islamic jihadist."

"The fucker thought the Sikh man was Muslim."

"Apparently he wasn't only racist, he was ignorant."

Seth shook his head. "What else you got?"

"Before Vivian married Cochran, she'd been married to a member of a similarly affiliated motorcycle club. That marriage ended in divorce."

"She has a type, and she's been part of the same world RJ belongs to."

"Exactly. There's more. Her car has popped up several times on automated license plate readers in locations around Lake Tahoe."

"Which means she, or someone using her car, is spending a lot of time there. It could be where RJ's staying. Forward this photo to me and the rest of the team. First thing tomorrow, write up what you have and send it to me. I'll assign Linc to track her down and pay her a visit, see what she knows." He paused. "Good work, Bella."

Her gaze met his and held. Seth felt like he was being drawn in, drowning in a sea of deep blue. He didn't like they hadn't nailed down the status of their relationship. As far as he was concerned, they were together. But Bella was holding herself just out of reach, keeping a distance between them that had the potential to become a chasm if he couldn't find a way to close it.

It'd been nearly two weeks since the night they'd spent at Montenegro's castle. He'd known he wanted to be with Bella for a long time. After that night, he was certain. With their work relationship it would be difficult, but he wanted a chance to work it out.

"Hey, Seth." His brother forced Seth to tune in to the conversation across the room. "Tell these two that backpacking food isn't so bad."

"Backpacking food sucks." Seth leaned back against the cushions. "But the mountains, the stars at night, and the fresh air will make the experience worth it."

Linc rolled his eyes. "Way to back me up, man." He turned to the other men. "Okay, maybe the food isn't great, but we'll bring fishing gear and we can have fresh trout cooked over the open fire, and what Seth said about the outdoors experience is spot on."

"I like sleeping in a bed with a soft mattress and no bugs crawling on me," Alexei commented, shaking his head.

"I'd rather rent a place at the beach," Markel added. "Spending a week soaking up the rays sounds a lot more fun than getting chased by bears."

Linc sighed in apparent disgust. "Where's your sense of adventure? You're a couple of babies."

Alexei casually gave Linc the middle finger. "Call me when you have a civilized vacation planned."

Seth glanced at Bella. She gave him the smile he was becoming addicted to, and then spoke in an aside. "Alexei embraced the conveniences of life in America from the first moment we got here. He has a special appreciation for American bathrooms. I don't think you'll get him to sleep outdoors, or do anything outdoors that can be done indoors."

Her phone chimed, and Seth saw the name Sasha on the screen with the first words of a message written in Russian. She grabbed her phone and leaned back against the cushions, reading for a moment, then busily texting.

Seth bit back on the irritation that made him want to grab the phone and text the guy to fuck off. Bella having connections to someone in the *bratva* could bring a shitload of trouble down on her. As a deputy US marshal, associating with a member of a known criminal organization was verboten. It was more than enough of a reason for her to avoid him, but Seth couldn't deny on a more personal level, it annoyed the shit out of him that she was getting texts from someone she had a history with, and who had made a point of reconnecting with her.

He raised his brow in question when Bella put down her phone, but she ignored him, and stood to take their empty plates to the kitchen.

# Chapter Eleven

Bella woke to a sharp knocking on her front door. She glanced at her phone to check the time and saw she'd missed several texts from Seth. She knew who was pounding on her door bright and early on a Sunday morning.

She stumbled to the door, peeked through the peephole, then pulled the door open. "Why are you here?" She crossed her arms in front of her and couldn't help the scowl she knew was on her face. Seth in jeans, a deep red cotton shirt with the sleeves rolled to his elbows, and scuffed leather boots was too much gorgeousness for her system to handle this early in the morning.

"If you checked your texts, you'd know."

"I was asleep. I don't check texts when I'm asleep."

"Let me in, Bella." He never used to let emotion show in his eyes, but this morning instead of flat gray, they glinted with humor, and when his gaze traveled over her, appreciation. Which made her remember that she was wearing an oversize t-shirt, which hung off one shoulder and barely covered her butt.

He held two lidded to-go cups, one dangling the tag of the tea she liked. She reached for it but he pulled it back.

"Damn it," she muttered, giving up on any thought that she'd get him to leave. "Fine. Give me my tea and you can come in."

He handed her the tea, and she turned around to shuffle into the kitchen. He followed, setting down his cup and snagging the bag of bagels from the counter. She watched as he got a cutting board and serrated knife from a drawer.

"Can I get you anything else, maybe your slippers or the Sunday paper?"

He shot her a grin that made her toes curl. "You know you're kind of grumpy in the morning?" She ignored him, instead sipping from her hot tea. He placed the bagels in the toaster oven and turned to lean back against the counter.

"Your brother here?"

"No, he insisted he was well enough to go back to his place. He—"

That was as far as she got. Seth snagged her tea and set it on the counter, then grabbed her hand to tug her forward.

In less time than it took to form a coherent thought, she was leaning against six foot plus of warm male who smelled of coffee and the outdoors.

He placed his mouth on hers and she melted like warm chocolate. This was a bad idea, there were reasons they couldn't be involved, but that didn't stop her from slipping her hand under the collar of his shirt to feel the warm skin of his neck while opening her mouth to his kiss.

He reached under the hem of her t-shirt to run his hands down her backside, pulling her into the cradle of his legs against the heat of him. The kiss was teetering on the brink of something more when he pulled back, drawing in a deep breath as he rested his jaw against her temple to whisper in her ear, "Good morning, Bella."

She dropped her head into the crook of his neck and breathed him in. "Why do you do this to me?"

"Do what?" He spoke in a low murmur.

"Make me want you. I'm not supposed to want you like this."

"Right back at you, darlin'."

Searching for a measure of calm, she said, "I should get the cream cheese from the fridge."

"Yeah." Instead of loosening his hold, he pulled her more snugly against him, his arms like a security blanket wrapped around her, keeping her safe.

Being held by him made her yearn for something she'd told herself was impossible, and made what was becoming a difficult situation even more complicated. She still hadn't started her period, and her plan had been to do the pregnancy test first thing that morning. That wasn't going to happen. Seth's being here put her plan on hold. If she was pregnant, she needed time to think through all the implications before talking to him. From what he'd said to Alexei, she was afraid he'd insist on getting married. Seth had a forceful personality, and she wasn't about to let herself be swept along with what he wanted until she was sure of her own wants and needs.

The toaster oven dinged and he loosened his hold. They went about getting breakfast on the table, and Bella was painfully aware her efforts to act like there was nothing between them were for naught. Their relationship may have been hard to define, but it was something, and at some point they'd have to deal with it, pregnant or not.

They sat across from each other at the little table, and it felt so normal to be sharing the first meal of the day with him. He spread cream cheese on his bagel, then handed her the knife. "We're heading to Reno today. Our flight leaves in two hours."

"Something's happened."

"Yeah, something's happened. Judge Rebollar's teenage son has gone missing."

Bella's brain was starting to wake up. "What do we know?"

"Parents say the boy, Anthony, has been testing boundaries lately. Took the mom's car without permission, missed curfew a few times, that kind of thing. But he's still tight with his family. Dad wasn't taking any chances after getting those threats and had security installed around their house. The system was on all night but didn't catch anything."

Bella sipped her tea, setting it down slowly as she considered the situation. "Inside job?"

Seth shook his head. "Linc thinks Anthony knew enough about computers to get around the system. Turns out he's got a girlfriend, and as both kids are fifteen, their parents don't let them date. Best guess is the kid had a meetup planned with the girl but it went sideways."

"Has Linc talked to the girl?"

Seth nodded. "She's denied meeting with Anthony, but Linc's read is she's scared. Her parents have threatened to send her to live with relatives in Mexico if she doesn't obey their rules, and they won't let her be interviewed unless they're present. She's clammed up and he won't get anything from her with her folks there. Linc's confident she knows something. He's working on getting the parents to ease up so the girl will talk."

"Could be Anthony and the girl had a fight and he's staying with a friend until he cools off. Kids do stuff like that. Why are you thinking this is more than star-crossed lovers, albeit young ones?"

"According to the judge, Anthony's never been gone all night, and he's not with the girl. Since he's the son of a federal judge who's had threats made against him, and who has a controversial case coming before his bench in three days, we're assuming the worst unless told otherwise."

Bella nodded. "Give me thirty minutes and I'll be ready."

***

Early in the afternoon, Bella and Seth walked into the hotel in Reno where Linc had booked a suite. On the hour-and-a-half flight, they'd worked from their laptops, purposefully sitting in the last row of the plane so no one could look over their shoulders. Seth's demeanor changed when they got to the airport. The man who'd shown up at her door that morning with a quick grin and her favorite tea, the man who'd kissed her like it was full-on sex, had been replaced by the no-nonsense seasoned marshal intent only on doing his job. For so long, she'd viewed him only in his role. It was the only part of himself he'd allowed her to see. It gave her a glow inside to know when they were alone, he was letting her see the more human side of him. For the time being, whatever was personal between them had been locked away and he was focused on the job.

The suite had only two bedrooms, and since she had no intention of taking the pullout sofa bed in the common area, she rolled her suitcase past the bedroom that had Linc's bag on the bed to claim the other room. When she came out, Linc turned an iPad on the coffee table so they could see Ellie on the screen.

Bella pulled a chair from the small table while Linc sat on the couch. Seth paced the room, still in the jeans and cotton shirt he'd been wearing when he'd shown up at her door, but now armed with his gun in its shoulder harness.

"Linc, you're up first. Update us on Anthony."

"No news on the boy's whereabouts. I've had more luck with the girlfriend, Serena. It took convincing her parents not to send her to Mexico to get her to cooperate and tell me what she knows. She finally confessed she and Anthony had plans to meet up last night around midnight. Dad wasn't happy to learn they'd done this before. Anthony texts her when he's outside her house, she comes out, and they go to a park a couple blocks away. Serena fell asleep waiting for him to text, and when she woke up this morning there was nothing from him. Poor kid's in tears and worried sick about her boyfriend."

"How does he get to her house?" Bella asked.

"Rides his bike, and then they ride double to the park. The judge confirmed his son's bike, a top-of-the-line mountain bike, is missing, as is Anthony's cell phone. The cell is either turned off or destroyed because it's not sending out a signal."

"His parents must be frantic," Ellie said.

"That's an understatement, but they're holding it together." Linc rose from his seat and crossed the room to the kitchenette where he opened an undercounter mini fridge. He returned with chilled bottles of mineral water and an apple. He passed the bottles to Bella and Seth and took a big bite out of the apple.

"Anything from FD, or any other group claiming they have Anthony?" Seth unscrewed the cap on his water, taking a deep swallow.

Linc shook his head. "Nada. The judge is watching his email, we're monitoring social media platforms where these types like to hang out, but there's been nothing. Local cops are doing their thing, checking with Anthony's friends, getting access to any security cameras that might've caught a kid on a bike."

"Okay. What about Vivian Cochran?" Seth's phone vibrated and he looked at the screen, brows dropping in a frown.

Linc chewed and swallowed before responding. "I went by the duplex at the address Bella found. All the tenants know is Vivian Cochran is their landlord and is hands off about it. She has a local handyman do the maintenance, and a lawn service keeps up the outside. They had nothing of note to offer. That said, the next-door neighbor had a lot more to say. Turns out the neighbor, Netty Pierce, who's African American, has had a few run-ins with Cochran."

Linc bit into the apple, talking out of the side of his mouth while he chewed. "Miss Netty's a hoot. She's has a pack of little yappy dogs, sings in her church choir, and has twenty-six grandchildren, seven great-grandchildren, and it sounds like every last one of them dotes on her."

Linc held up his hand at Seth's expression. "I know, get to the point. I may have spent an hour talking to her, but it got us some information. Turns out one of the duplex units became available for rent and one of her granddaughters submitted a rental application. She wanted to live close to her grandmother because Miss Netty's turning ninety in a couple months, though you wouldn't know it from the size of the garden she's got behind her house."

"Still haven't got to the point," Seth growled.

"Point is Vivian Cochran didn't accept the application, and didn't accept Miss Netty's son's application last year."

"What race are the current tenants?" Ellie asked from the iPad.

"White. Miss Netty isn't one to take racism without fighting back. One of her grandsons is a lawyer and the family has filed a housing discrimination lawsuit against Vivian Cochran. Discrimination against blacks in housing jives with her affiliation with known white supremacists. That's what I got," Linc concluded as he took another bite of his apple, then sent the core sailing into the trashcan, raising a fist in triumph when he made the shot.

Seth gave a curt nod. "We need to track down Vivian Cochran. She's got a history of hitching her wagon to men with racist affiliations. Could be that she and RJ are together." He shrugged. "If not, they move in the same circles and she may know where he's hiding." Linc nodded. "Moving on to RJ, an email came in from him a minute ago." He tapped on his phone, waited a second, then tapped a few more times. "Check your texts. The email is encrypted, but I took a screenshot of the message and sent that to each of you."

Bella found the text and began scrolling down.

"Blah, blah, blah, more of the same," Ellie muttered from the iPad. "He's still trying to manipulate you. Tell me you're not falling for all that 'my eldest son is a disappointment to me' crap."

"I'm not." Seth took another swallow from his water bottle. "Do you see this line he wrote? 'Good people have taken measures to protect our country from the mongrel hordes who have infiltrated the judicial system and are corrupting the government.'"

"That's the same kind of shit he always says," Linc muttered.

"But what if this time he's referring to something specific? What if his followers are the so-called good people and Judge Rebollar is one of those who RJ believes had 'infiltrated the judicial system and are corrupting the government'?" Seth asked.

"Rebollar is an immigrant."

Seth's gaze lasered in on Bella. "What do you know?"

She scrolled through the page on a website she was reading. "I found his bio on a professional organization for lawyers. His family came from El Salvador in the seventies, and he gained citizenship under Reagan's amnesty law that was passed in eighty-six."

"Then it's an even better fit. We're going to focus on whether RJ or other Freedom Defenders kidnapped Anthony Rebollar. We're also looking for a connection between the MacDonald clan and FD. If RJ's involved, we'll nail his ass."

Linc leaned forward in his seat. "RJ says he wants to meet with you." He looked up from his phone screen to zero in on his brother. "Set up the meeting, we arrest him, and get him to tell us where they're holding the boy."

"Now that we have a way of contacting him, yeah, we'll set up a meeting, but not to arrest him. RJ hasn't shown any inclination to cooperate. We arrest him and we could be writing that boy's execution warrant. It's better I make him think I'm interested in meeting with him, but with another goal in mind. Bella and I will work out an email to send him and make sure we leave enough crumbs for him to think I'm disgruntled and open to discussing his fucked-up ideas with him. I think he'll go for it."

Ellie said, "Okay, but one more thing. My contact has a buddy who was in with the Oregon branch of Freedom Defenders before we dismantled that organization. The buddy says Big Dog, aka RJ, has moved somewhere near Tahoe, on the California side. Since Reno's not far from Tahoe, arranging an in-person meetup is feasible. This also puts him and our friend Vivian in the same general area."

Seth nodded. "Good. They run in the same circles. I'll see if the IP address on the email will tell me where it was sent from. If it's from around Tahoe, we'll know we're on the right track."

"If RJ agrees to meet with you, that'll be further evidence," Ellie commented.

"Yeah," Seth said, "The more we know about RJ, the more—"

"Got something." Linc was staring at his phone. "Local PD says they've recovered Anthony's bike. A local homeless guy riding a high-end mountain bike caught their attention. The bike is registered and it belongs to Anthony."

"Homeless guy say where he got the bike?"

"Yeah. Says he found it behind a gas station that's on the likely route Anthony would've taken to get to Serena's house. PD is getting a warrant for surveillance footage from the gas station and the Chinese restaurant next to it."

"Shit," Seth muttered. "Any chance the homeless guy has Anthony?"

"Local LEOs don't think so. The guy is known to them. He has mental illness and claims the bike was left behind the gas station because God wanted him to have it. They've had only minor problems with him in the past. To verify, they checked where he's camping and other than having over a dozen Bibles in his tent, there's nothing there. There's more about the bike, though. Cops say scratches on the frame and scraped rubber on the handle grips indicate it hit the pavement hard." Linc sighed. "Working theory is that Anthony was forced off the bike, possibly being sideswiped by a car, and someone grabbed him."

Bella's stomach gave a slow, queasy roll. Vulnerable children always hit her hard. She could relate. Thinking about the terror a fifteen-year-old would experience being kidnapped off the street in the middle of the night, her fear over what he might be going through brought back too many memories. She sipped from her water bottle to ease her stomach.

A notification popped up on her laptop screen showing results for a search she'd initiated. "I've got something too." Seth inclined his head and she went on. "I searched property holdings in and around Reno, Lake Tahoe, and, since we got a hit from an automated plate reader there, from Truckee, a town that's roughly twenty miles north of the lake. I also searched for Donald Cochran. Cochran was Vivian's second husband and the white nationalist who assaulted a Sikh man," Bella reminded the group.

"And killed himself rather than be arrested," Linc added.

"That's him." She scanned through the search results. "There's a property owned by Donald Edward Cochran listed as being delinquent on property tax payments. Could be she's keeping a low profile by not informing the county her husband is dead." She tapped on her keyboard to bring up another screen. "I've got a map up. The Cochran property is about halfway between Truckee and Lake Tahoe, there's five acres with one dwelling and several other structures. It backs up to the Truckee River."

"You see a property history?" Ellie asked.

"Yes. It appears the property belonged to Donald prior to marrying Vivian. She was never added to the title."

"Do we know if Donald died with a will?" Linc tore open a small bag of peanut M&Ms and popped a couple in his mouth.

"I haven't dug that far." Bella shook her head when Linc held out the M&Ms. "But minus something like a prenup or children from a previous marriage, the property likely went to Vivian when he died."

"Could be," Linc went on, dumping candy into Seth's outstretched hand, "this is where she's been living."

"Can you pull up a satellite image?" Seth asked.

Bella waited until a picture popped up. "Here it is." The area was hilly with lots of tall trees and the Truckee River flowing along one border like a silver ribbon. "It's a big piece of property. The satellite image shows the closest neighbor is across the river, downstream about a hundred yards. Nearest neighbors on their side of the river are over a half mile away. That kind of setup might be interesting to someone like RJ looking for a place where he doesn't have anyone close by who might notice what he's doing."

"Can you magnify the structures?"

Seth dropped a hand on her shoulder as he bent forward, his head close to hers. Telling herself to ignore the tingles, Bella zoomed in.

Seth studied the screen before straightening. "There were a lot of vehicles on this property at the time the photo was taken. This image could be months or years old, but it's likely more recent than Cochran's death three years ago."

"It gives us a place to start. Why don't we knock on the front door, see who answers and how they react to a bunch of marshals on their doorstep?" Linc suggested.

Ellie fluttered her hand and made a sound like *pfft*. "Yeah, let's do that because we want to tip our hand and let Vivian and possibly RJ know we're on to them."

"Okay, then we play dumb. We go in dressed like a couple of hikers, pretend we're lost and ask for directions. We see what pops."

"Excellent plan," Bella picked up an eye roll from Ellie as she spoke to her brother, "until RJ happens to be there and guess who's at his door, the sons he abandoned twenty years ago."

Linc sighed. "Damn. Shot down again. Since I'm the idea guy right now, here's another one. How about we send up a drone and use modern technology to have a look-see?"

"We'd need a warrant, and at this point, I don't think we have enough to get one." Seth stood with his hands on his narrow hips, his brow furrowed. "Here's what we'll do. Top priority is finding the boy. The Reno Marshals' office is helping us coordinate with local LEOs. Linc, you're focusing solely on tracking down anything that comes up related to Anthony Rebollar. Bella and I will finesse our response to RJ. Once that's sent, we'll pursue finding Vivian Cochran, looking for anything to tell us if she's connected to RJ. Ellie, I want you to dive deeper into both the plaintiffs and defendants in the environmental case coming before Judge Rebollar. Look for any chatter that might be linked to a kidnapped boy. It's a long shot, but we need to pursue it.

"If this is what we think it is, Anthony was taken by the Freedom Defenders, my bet is they'll contact the judge today. They've let the parents worry and get anxious. When they think the judge is primed, they'll make their move. Their goal is to sabotage the case coming before the judge, and they can't do that if they don't make their demands known. Meanwhile, we tighten security around others involved in the case and bring in more marshals to protect the courthouse."

Ten minutes later, Ellie signed off, and Linc had left for a meeting with detectives from the Reno PD. Bella and Seth sat at opposite ends of the small table, both with laptops open in front of them. Seth had snagged a couple tangerines from the supply of groceries Linc had stocked in the kitchenette and began peeling them. He set a small pile of tangerine segments on a napkin at her elbow, then sat at his computer, eating tangerine.

Bella sighed. That was one of the reasons she loved the entire Jameson family. They were innately generous and so casually caring of one another. Somehow she was lucky enough they'd widened their circle to include her.

She read the shared document on her screen, studying the changes as Seth worked on his reply to the message from RJ.

"Since the kidnapping, I'm reconsidering my position on whether he'll meet with you or set you up. You're a US Marshal, he's a federal fugitive. He's too smart to put himself in a position where you could arrest him. I don't trust he's not doing this to hurt you."

"I think he'll meet with me. He's the one who brought up that I should come over to his side. But, like we discussed, we write this carefully, play to his ego, make him think there's the possibility I could go over to the dark side.

"The other part of this is that he thinks he's smarter than me, and everyone else. He'll figure he can stay one step ahead." Seth shrugged. "If he goes for it, we're winners; if he doesn't, we've lost nothing but a little time."

"Unless he says yes, but has something else planned for you."

# Chapter Twelve

Seth steered the rented SUV through morning traffic, such as it was. Compared to LA, they were cruising along. The sun was bright in a cloudless blue sky, reflecting off the windows of the tall hotels in the casino district as they headed away from downtown toward the suburbs. It'd been warm when he and Bella had stepped outside, and temperatures were likely to hit well into the nineties by noon. Linc had left early, then had called to report, as he'd predicted, Judge Rebollar had received an email making demands in exchange for Anthony's return.

They were on the way to the Rebollar home to meet with the judge and his wife, and the Reno PD detective assigned to the taskforce.

Which was exactly where Seth's attention should be focused. But, as was becoming the norm over the past few weeks, the woman riding beside him was playing havoc with his concentration.

He could smell her scent, which reminded him of his mother's flower garden in the spring. The urge to pull over and haul her into his arms was difficult to resist. Compartmentalizing his feelings was a necessity to do his job. Since the weekend at Montenegro's palace, he couldn't help thinking of her as *his*. As a permanent part of his life. As someone he wanted to be with every damn day.

They'd made love that one time, and it had been, hands down, the most incredible encounter of his life. From that moment their relationship had taken a monumental turn. His need for her was as essential for life as oxygen, and it meant he was no longer able to push his desire for her into a corner of his brain.

He'd been pretty successful doing that for the past year.

While his obsession with Bella was always there on the periphery, at least he'd been able to function. One lapse. One hot and satisfying lapse, and thoughts of her permeated his every waking moment, and most of his sleeping ones. His frustration was stoked on a near daily basis when he woke from erotic and explicit dreams featuring the woman sitting beside him wearing the blue dress that had driven him fucking crazy. He spent nearly every day aroused and aching.

Take Sunday morning. Showing up at her door hadn't been necessary. When she hadn't responded to his texts, he could've called her. She would've answered her work phone. But no, he'd seized on the excuse and shown up at her apartment.

He was blending the personal with the professional.

He steered the car to the off-ramp, pulling to a stop at a signal. He caught Bella clenching her fists, her face in profile as she gazed out the window.

"You okay?"

She turned, and per the norm, he felt a charge when her blue gaze settled on him. "Of course. Why wouldn't I be?"

"Cases involving kids bother you."

He caught her shrug before returning his attention to the traffic beginning to move through the intersection. "Cases involving kids hit everyone hard."

"Sure, but you always seem to be more affected." He accelerated around a slow-moving box truck. After what she'd told him of her childhood, he had better insight as to why. He drummed his fingers on the steering wheel, then finally asked the question that was never far from the surface.

"It's been a couple weeks since we were together."

"So?"

"So, have you started your period?"

He could feel her glare. "You can't ask me that. *If* I were pregnant, I would follow official protocols in informing my superior at the appropriate time." She crossed her arms in front of her, a classic defensive gesture.

"Damn it, Bella." He slowed and veered to the left to give a group of bicyclists more space. "Don't shut me out. I'm not asking as your boss, I'm asking as your boyfriend." Which was the wrong thing to say. He knew it the moment the words left his mouth. Just because he thought of himself that way didn't mean she was on board with the idea.

Her gaze turned lethal. "Did you skip a step or ten, Seth? How did we get from having sex a couple weeks ago to you being my boyfriend?"

He'd already blown it, so he figured he might as well play his hand. "You haven't been paying attention if you haven't noticed the steps. They may not have been conventional, but they've been there."

"Oh, you mean the step when you told Alexei that we have 'a thing'?" She used her fingers as air quotes. "Are you talking about that romantic moment? Or maybe you're imagining all those dates, you know, with walks on the beach and candlelit dinners, those dates we've never gone on."

He turned into a subdivision with well-kept two-story homes, many with what looked like native-plant landscaping. Arriving at their destination, he parked on the street, turned off the engine, and shifted in his seat to face her.

"Maybe we haven't done those things, but how about what happens every time we kiss? What about when you slept in my arms and how it was when we woke up together? How about every time I look at you I'm pulled in a little deeper until all I can see is you?" He wanted her to understand, and worked to keep his frustration under wraps. "Look, I know our relationship has been anything but typical, but we have a relationship beyond our professional one. What we need is to have an honest conversation, unfortunately, that'll have to wait. But, Bella, while we're waiting remember this. When I look into the future, I see you with me. That's what I want. You're going to have to decide if it's what you want too." He sighed. "Will you spend the day with me? The next free day we have. Will you spend it with me?"

She nodded slowly. "I'd like that."

Tension released the hold it had on his heart and he gave her a half smile. "Good. Let's go meet the Rebollars." As they walked up the sidewalk to the entrance of the stone-fronted home, it hit him that she hadn't answered his question.

A diminutive woman with a lined face opened the door and, after Bella and Seth presented their badges, she introduced herself in careful English as Carmen, Anthony's grandmother.

They entered a wide foyer of a warmly decorated home. Pottery and paintings displayed what Bella recognized as vibrantly colorful indigenous art from Central America. They were led into a dining area adjacent to a spacious kitchen with wide granite counters. The grandmother left them to climb the stairs to the upper floor.

A couple sat at the table and Bella recognized Judge Carlos Rebollar from his photos. His hair was grayer, and his face was more haggard. He sat erect with squared shoulders, and struck Bella as dignified. She thought he looked remote until she caught the haunted look in his eyes. This man was terrified and holding it together the best he could. Expression grim, he clasped hands with the woman sitting beside him, her face reflecting the anguish of a mother with a missing child.

Linc stood near the sliding glass door, which opened to a deck and pool. He was talking with a woman with hair spiraling in black curls to her shoulders and a badge hanging from a lanyard around her neck. Linc stepped forward and made the introductions. The woman with the badge was Lieutenant Keisha Browne, a detective from the Reno PD who'd been assigned as the department's lead on the taskforce.

Maria Rebollar let go of her husband's hand and stood. Her dark eyes were shadowed, and Bella wondered if the woman had gotten any sleep in the past thirty-six hours. She clenched her hands tightly in front of her. "Welcome to my home. I appreciate you are all here to help find my son. Let me get you some coffee." She indicated a corner of the counter where a coffeemaker stood next to mugs arranged on a tray. "Or, if you'd prefer, I can put water on for tea."

Bella stepped forward. "If you'll tell me where your kettle is, I'll put the water on, Mrs. Rebollar."

She shook her head and led the way into the kitchen. "Call me Maria. Being busy keeps my mind from dwelling on how scared my Anthony must be."

"Tell me about your son."

The woman busied herself filling the kettle and set it on the stove where she adjusted the flame. When done, she leaned against the counter, folding her arms tightly in front of her.

"You asked about my son. That's good, because knowing him might help you to find him. Anthony is my baby. He has two older sisters. They're both in El Salvador visiting their grandparents for the summer. We haven't told them their brother is missing. It is better to tell them when he's been returned safely to us." She spoke precisely in accented English. "Even though his father and I tried to be strict with him, I am afraid we spoiled him." She swiped her hand under her eyes. "He's always been a sweet boy, so good-natured. He gets his way through charm. He uses it on his sisters and his teachers, and he has such a way about him. He is a good boy."

"Have you met Anthony's girlfriend, Serena?"

Maria wiped under her eyes again, and when she spoke, her voice reflected the strain of holding back her tears. "No, we haven't met her. Her family moved to Reno a year or so ago, so she wasn't one of the kids Anthony went through grade school with. We thought he was too young to date. We wanted him to focus on school."

She took a deep breath and let it out slowly. "I understand her parents feel the same. Anthony made the varsity soccer team last year, the only freshman on the team, and he was excited about it. We thought being in honors classes and with sports, he had enough on his plate. Then he met Serena and was infatuated. First love hits you so hard. We knew he spent time with her when they were at school, and that was okay. We were glad when it was summer. We thought being apart would cool the romance some."

She sighed. "With cell phones these days, it's so easy to be in constant contact. It turns out Anthony was being dishonest and sneaking out at night to meet with her." She shook her head. "Hindsight is always twenty-twenty. We would have been better parents if we'd let him invite her over where we could keep an eye on them. If we'd done that, he wouldn't have been out at night where he was in danger."

"You were trying to be good parents and do what you thought was right."

"My job is to protect my son, and I failed."

"You aren't to blame. Anthony made a poor decision, yes, but the people who took your son are to blame."

The water in the kettle began to boil and Maria turned off the burner. Bella chose a tea bag from a small basket and poured the hot water. She didn't think she'd convinced Maria, but she hoped the mother would eventually forgive herself.

If Bella's mother or grandmother had been even half as concerned about Bella and Alexei's safety, her life might have turned out differently. She was happy to be where she was, and with her career. She wouldn't trade knowing Seth for anything, but she wished getting to this point hadn't been such a painful process.

The group gathered around the table where Judge Rebollar passed around papers from a stack in his hand. "This is the message that was emailed to me early this morning." He nodded toward Linc. "At Marshal Jameson's direction, I requested proof of life." His voice cracked at the words. "We haven't heard anything since then."

Seth spoke. "Judge, I'd like permission to look at your computer. I want to see if we can retrieve the IP address this email was sent from."

"Please, call me Carlos. And yes, of course, you have my permission."

Bella thought he'd gladly sacrifice his own life if that's what it took to get Anthony returned home safely.

Linc nodded at the look from Seth. "I'm on it."

"I'll take you to the office where the computer is." Maria led Linc out of the room.

Bella took the paper Carlos handed to her and read through the email he'd received, not surprised at the virulent racist language.

In the space of three paragraphs, Judge Rebollar was referred to as an illegal, a wetback, and a border hopper. The message included a rant about the Fourteenth Amendment and the need to revoke birth citizenship because mongrel hordes were defiling the country. The author claimed his organization had kidnapped Anthony to get the judge's attention. Previous warnings had been ignored and taking the boy had been a matter of necessity.

The author didn't identify him or herself by name or group, other than broadly as one of many "true American citizens fighting tyranny." Their goal was to stop what they claimed was government overreach by whatever means necessary. They condemned the actions of the environmental group, threatening to blow Judge Rebollar, the "tree huggers," and Anthony to "hell and back again" if their demands weren't met.

"Our assumption that this had to do with the MacDonald case was correct," Seth said.

"The case the environmental group brought named the federal government and the MacDonald clan. They want Judge Rebollar to dismiss the case with prejudice so they can't bring that case back to court again. Ever," Bella said.

"Linc told me who you all think is behind the kidnapping of young Anthony. You got anything more specific?" Keisha asked. "Whoever wrote this sounds like they're on the nutty side of the loaf."

Seth gave a short laugh. "That's apt."

"There are similarities with emails from RJ." Bella's gaze was on Seth, who was still scrutinizing the email as she spoke. "There's the use of the word 'mongrel,' which RJ has also used. He's targeting a federal judge, and there's the references to explosives, which we know is a preferred weapon. Freedom Defenders, and RJ specifically, have used explosives against federal courts. The group also blew up Sam's car," she said. She turned to Keisha and shared, "Sam Creed is a federal judge in Oregon. I think this situation has a lot of similarities with that case and with emails to other federal judges that have been turned over to us."

"RJ is Richard Jameson, Seth and Linc's dad, right?" Keisha asked. At Bella's nod, Keisha muttered, "That's got to suck. There was a buzz about that in the department when we heard what marshals were assigned to this case."

"It does indeed suck," Bella agreed.

Maria rushed into the room, a paper clutched in her hand she brought to her husband. "It's Anthony. They've sent a picture of Anthony." The couple stood close together, examining the image of their son. Maria's hand shook as she held the paper. "He's been hurt. Oh Carlos, they hurt him."

"But he's alive, and these are injuries he can recover from. Look at him, he looks strong. Our boy looks strong."

Linc came in. "This is the kidnapper's proof of life." He gave everyone a copy of the email containing the photo. There was no text, only the image of Anthony Rebollar, hair tousled, gaze defiant, holding a newspaper in front of him so the front page could be seen. What looked like a nasty scrape was evident on his forehead above his left eyebrow, and the cheekbone under his right eye looked swollen and bruised.

"This is the front page of today's newspaper."

Seth stared at the image. "Anthony looks like he's resisted, fought back. That's good from a mental standpoint. But we don't want him to do something that gets him hurt any more than he has been."

"Our son's never one to accept injustice," Carlos said, his eyes still on the image of his son. "When a student was suspended from his school for fighting a young man who was bullying another boy, Anthony rallied other students in protest. He wrote an article for the school newspaper and got many students and even a few teachers to sign a petition."

Seth's phone buzzed and he took it from his pocket to glance at the screen before responding. "That kind of temperament would make him more likely to fight against his captors. He could have gotten the scrape on his forehead when he came off the bike, but the bruising around his eye? Someone hit him."

"This email and the previous one have the same IP address," Linc stated, his gaze steady on his brother. "They also match the IP address of the email sent by RJ."

Seth stood stoically, absorbing Linc's statement before giving his brother an almost imperceptible nod. Bella thought he'd needed a moment to accept their father had reached another, deeper level of depravity.

"What does that mean?" Maria asked.

"It means we have a clear idea who took Anthony, and we have a direction to pursue to get him back."

The team left the Rebollar home and stood for a moment on the driveway. Seth gave orders for the next few hours. "Judge Rebollar will inform us immediately if more emails come in. Lieutenant Browne, I'd like you to take another run at the girlfriend. Anthony was snatched by someone who knew he was leaving the house at night. Find out if he talked about meeting anyone new, or if he'd mentioned anything he'd noticed that was out of the norm, like someone following him. I'd also like an update on the bike. It was dusted for fingerprints, so find out if that turned up anything."

"Sure thing. I'll get back to you with whatever I find." Keisha gave a good-bye wave and crossed the street to her car.

After her departure, Seth turned to his brother. "You work with the local marshals at whoever's in the judge's circle. Talk to the family, the grandmother, the sisters, any close friends. We want to learn if anyone noticed anything, no matter how small the detail. So far Freedom Defenders has been direct in their approach, but we want to cover all bases."

"What will you and Bella be doing?" Linc asked.

"We're still working the RJ angle. If he's got the boy, we've got to figure out where the bastard is. We've established a link between RJ and the kidnappers. RJ's connection to Vivian is inconclusive, but I'm going to find who I need to talk in the Reno office to get a warrant to send up a drone over the Cochran property."

# Chapter Thirteen

Bella sat at the table in the hotel suite, elbow to elbow with Seth. He always managed the team the same way. He'd give orders, sometimes pairing Linc and Ellie together, other times having them work independently, while she and Seth were almost always partnered up. She'd thought that was common procedure when she'd first been hired and was on probation. The chief deputy would naturally partner with the least experienced marshal on his team.

Once she was past her probationary period, the arrangement hadn't changed. Looking back, she wondered if there were more instances than she was aware of where Seth might've been revealing feelings for her, but she hadn't been reading him correctly. Those times when she thought he didn't trust her, she wondered if he'd wanted to be with her. The thought warmed her and gave her something to think about.

Their laptops were humming on the table in front of them, but at the moment, they were both staring at the screen of Seth's laptop. The image they'd received that morning of Anthony's battered face had added a renewed sense of urgency to finding him, and the county sheriff in California had been more than willing to help them obtain the warrant. Now that sheriff's department was using their drone to look at the Cochran property. Seth was on the phone to the operator as the drone images came through to his laptop. There was always a risk that the hovering machine would be spotted from the ground, but so far, no one had appeared on the screen.

The house was a rambling structure with a covered patio that looked out over a yard that sloped to the river. Tall trees grew around the house, which limited what they could see.

The operator panned over other structures. There was a small shed, which might hold tools, a carport provided shelter for a backhoe, and a large metal structure big enough to store heavy equipment or several automobiles. Behind the shed was an area that looked like it was being used as a firing range with an old, rusted truck riddled with bullet holes. The ground shimmered with reflecting sunlight, likely from shattered glass bottles used for target practice.

"Can you circle the big metal garage-like building so we can see all entrances?" Seth asked the drone operator.

The drone revealed a smaller door on side of the building, plus two side-by-side wide rollup doors. As they were watching, a car approached on a dirt road and the image widened as the drone gained altitude. The drone operator spoke through Seth's phone on speaker. "Sorry to have to pan out, folks. This drone is quiet, but not so quiet that if someone got out of that car they couldn't hear it and realize they're under surveillance."

Bella's knee bounced, and she moved forward in her chair. "That car is silver and could be a Civic. It might be Vivian Cochran's."

The car disappeared under a tree behind the house where the back end of a white truck was visible. A minute later a woman appeared carrying bags, possibly groceries, in the gap between the tree and the back of the house.

"Get as close a shot of her as possible," Seth directed.

Seth took a series of screenshots before the woman disappeared through a door next to the covered patio. While the drone continued its examination of the property, Seth sent the screenshots to Bella's computer. She clicked to pull them up and zoomed in as far as she could without distorting the images. The woman was shorter than average, looked to be medium weight, and had light hair. Bella wondered if it was bleached blonde. Seth leaned closer to study the images and Bella caught a whiff of him. So distracting.

"She seems to match the description of Vivian Cochran, and the car looks like the Civic at the post office in Modesto," Bella said. "If those are groceries, we've found where she's living."

Seth's brows dropped down. "Yes, but we still don't know anything more about whether Anthony's being held there, and if RJ is there."

As he spoke, the drone returned to the back of the house where the woman had stepped outside once again. She disappeared under the tree, then reappeared carrying more bags. For the next five minutes, the drone flew over the property, until the operator said, "I've got three minutes before I need to bring the drone back or run the risk of running down the battery."

"Copy that," Seth replied. "Is that the only drone you have? How long does it take to recharge?"

"Our other unit was recently damaged. This is the only one that's currently usable. It takes over an hour to recharge."

"Okay, I think we're—" Seth held up a hand. "No, wait, there she is again. Can you watch her for a couple more minutes? I want to see what she's up to."

"The drone is yours for two more minutes."

They watched her walk across an open area on the north side of the house, carrying a box. When she got to the big garage, she pulled keys from her jacket pocket. Even with the distance they could see the bright red puffball key fob. She unlocked the door and disappeared inside.

"I think that could be Vivian," Bella said. "It looked like something covered in foil in that box. Maybe food. If Anthony is in that building, she might be bringing him something to eat."

"Or that could have been a totally innocent woman walking to her garage with a box of whatever. We don't have enough for a warrant to enter the property."

Bella didn't know she was chewing on her lip until she noticed that Seth's gaze was locked there instead of on his computer screen. Her belly hitched. "Focus, Seth."

They might be neck deep in an investigation, their concern for Anthony's safety dictating that finding him was their primary focus, but despite all that, the magnetism between them was ever present, waiting for a break in concentration for it to rear its head.

"Easier said than done," he muttered, but returned his attention to the laptop. The woman stepped outside the garage, the box now empty, and crossed the open area to return to the house.

"You're clear to bring back your drone," he told the officer on the other end of the line. "Let me know when it's charged in case we want to have another go." He thanked the other officer and signed off.

\*\*\*

Bella felt as if she'd had a double hit of espresso with an extra shot of caffeine. Seth and Linc were in a huddle, discussing how Seth would handle the meeting with RJ. She and Seth had worked to get the tone just right in the email, and must have succeeded. RJ's response had been almost eager. Another exchange of emails and they'd solidified arrangements for a meeting. Which was why Seth was standing in the small living room of their hotel, dressed in jeans and a bomber-style jacket unzipped over a black t-shirt.

"I think I should go with you," Linc insisted. "RJ is working some angle, and I don't like you going in without backup. He agreed to this meeting too easily."

Seth was shaking his head. "Having both sons show up might set him off. He contacted me, and if he's working an angle, I'll figure it out."

"Not if you're ambushed," Linc stated.

Seth kept talking as if what Linc said didn't matter. "I think he's eager because we dangled the hook he feeds off. I'm unhappy with my job, and I'm open to hearing what he has to say. He knows it would be a major coup for him with his *followers*, and a personal victory if he could entice me to join his side. He took the bait. I don't want to spook him before I can find out about Anthony."

"Who cares if having both his sons show up spooks him? He could have his own backup with AKs. You don't know what you're walking into."

"I'll deal with whatever it is. I'm not going to jeopardize what we might get out of him by deviating from our agreement." Seth put a hand on his brother's shoulder. "You want to put a fist in his face and take my back. Got it. But not this time."

"I could be the backup." Bella was on the receiving end of a double dose of intensity as both the Jameson brothers lasered their attention on her.

"RJ doesn't know who I am. I could pose as Seth's girlfriend who wanted to tag along to the bar."

Seth scowled. "A US Marshal doesn't go to a meeting with his girlfriend. RJ won't buy it. I'm going in alone. That's the only way this will work."

"You're being stubborn," she said calmly, but felt anything but. "There's got to be a way to mitigate the danger."

Seth gave her his *I've made my decision* look. Linc asked, "You got both your phones, personal and official?"

"Yeah, I got 'em."

"Good. If RJ decides a Chief Deputy US Marshal is too big a prize to resist, at least if you have your phones, we should be able to find where they dump your body."

"Nice," Seth muttered.

"Here's another idea," Bella offered.

She wouldn't be so jittery if she was doing something productive, something that would help to ensure Seth came back alive and in one piece. "I'll go to the bar early. You know, just another girl at the Easy Rider on a Monday evening. I've seen enough photos of RJ. I'll recognize him. Once I identify where he's sitting, I'll find a seat where I can observe. That way if there's an issue, Seth isn't on his own."

"Easy Rider is a biker bar and you're too classy for anyone to believe you're a biker babe. You'd stick out like a sore thumb." The scowl on his face told her she was on the losing side of the argument.

She had to try anyway. "Give me an hour and I can be a biker babe."

Linc elbowed his brother. "I bet she could. Get her a short leather skirt. You know, black with silver studs, and a lacy thing under a leather jacket. She'd look hot."

"Fuck no." Seth turned to Bella, eyes blazing. "You go into that bar alone, you'll be pegged as looking for a hookup. Every unattached male will be hitting on you. Hell, even the attached ones will be hitting on you. You'll draw too much attention, which is exactly what we don't want."

Bella sighed in exasperation. Seth wasn't going to budge. "Then Linc and I will hang out somewhere nearby. I looked at a street view. Easy Rider is at the edge of a warehouse district in South Lake Tahoe. There's not much around there, but I did find an all-night diner where Linc and I can hang out. It's not a great solution, but at least you can call us and we'd be nearby if you get into trouble. I think that's the best plan."

He studied her, then gave a curt nod. "Okay."

Linc's phone chimed, and he pulled it from the pocket of his jeans, collapsing onto the small sofa as he texted.

Bella moved to stand in front of the window. Their room was on the twelfth floor and the granite slopes of the Sierra Nevada mountains to the west glimmered in the late afternoon sun. Despite the early summer heat, there was still snow on the peaks. She turned her back to the view when Linc spoke.

"That was Dave Fuller. He's the lead marshal from the Reno office. A witness has come forward who claims they saw Anthony the night he was taken. They're bringing him in and I want to be there. I'll be back in a couple hours."

Bella turned back to her perusal of the mountains, not surprised when Seth came up behind her. He slipped his arms around her and pulled her against him. He bent his head to rest his cheek against her hair, his chest expanding against her back as he breathed.

"You okay?"

She shrugged. "I'm worried about your meeting with RJ."

"I have to do it. I'll be fine."

"I know, but I can still worry."

He lowered his head farther and nuzzled the curve of her neck. She closed her eyes and leaned her head against his. It didn't seem to matter there were unresolved issues between them. In that moment, it felt like all the uncertainties were stripped away and they were simply Seth and Bella. Two people whose insatiable need for each other was laid bare.

She tilted her head to give him better access and as he moved his mouth to the underside of her jaw, she was acutely aware of the growing hardness pressed against her backside. She turned in his arms and then his lips were on hers in unrestrained hunger.

The heat that raced through her shouldn't have been surprising. It seemed they only needed to touch and she went up like a match to dry tinder. His hands swept down her waist, cupped her ass, and pulled her closer. Bella moved against the hard ridge of his erection, eliciting a groan.

He pulled back slightly and tipped her head up with his thumbs. "Do you want this? I sure as hell do."

She stared into his eyes stormy with emotion. Into his face, which she trusted in all matters except those of the heart. Being with him again could put her mental well-being in grave danger. It would leave her vulnerable, and she knew she couldn't take losing him.

But there was also the voice in the back of her mind saying maybe it would be worth it. Maybe being with him, for however long whatever was between them lasted, would be worth the heartache when he left her. Then she remembered that moment of devastation when she realized her mother was never coming back, and only months later, holding Alexei's hand as their grandmother drove away. She'd never be able to move past the love she felt for him if they continued to be intimate. Eventually, he too would leave her, and her heart would shatter.

"I think you better stop."

He stopped stroking her rib cage. "That doesn't sound like a hard no."

"It is. I'm sorry. I can't risk it."

"Risk what?"

She closed her eyes. She might as well say it. If he understood, then he would leave her alone. At this point, what did it matter if she bared her heart? Opening her eyes, she said, "Loving you."

She didn't think she could have shocked him more if she'd told him she was joining a traveling circus as the painted lady.

"You love me?" The disbelief in his voice would have been comical if he wasn't slowly breaking her heart.

She opened her mouth to reply when the hotel door swung open and Linc strode into the room. "The car has a flat, and can you believe it doesn't have a spare? The rental company is sending out a—" He stopped abruptly, his gaze traveling from his brother to Bella who were now standing three feet apart. "Am I interrupting something?"

"No, of course not," Bella replied, forcing a smile that threatened to splinter her face.

"You know, I'm interested in what that witness has to say," Seth growled. "I'll go with you."

Linc glanced at his brother, then back to Bella. "Okay, sure. Whatever you want."

# Chapter Fourteen

Seth paused inside the door of Easy Rider and took a slow look around. Motorcycle exhaust pipes served as handrails, a sign on the wall read "Hawg Heaven Highway," and a couple of flaming skull posters hung on the wall. He guessed biker bar interior decorating was SOP since all the dives looked the same. The big guy behind the bar seemed more likely to plant a fist in your face than pour you a drink, and made Seth wonder if the man's choice of defense under the bar was a baseball bat or a shotgun. In the dim light, he skimmed his gaze over the people sitting hunched on barstools, most of them staring into the glasses in from of them. The clientele was mostly male and gray-haired. Booths lined the walls where a few couples sat nursing their drinks. People came to a place like this for serious drinking, not for the ambience.

Seth glanced into a room to the left of the door. Two men were playing pool and looked like they'd come straight from central casting with leather vests over bulging beer guts, wallet chains hanging from their pockets, and stained beards. The taller of the two chalked his grimy pool cue while the other set up the table. An old-fashioned jukebox belted out a Creedence song, and John Fogerty's wailing competed with the cue ball clack making the break shot.

Seth had deliberately arrived early. He wanted the advantage of picking his seat and observing if RJ arrived with anyone. Seth headed for an empty booth in a back corner where he wouldn't have to watch his back. He caught the attention of the only waitress, who gave him a once-over as he ordered a beer and took a seat. That his seat also afforded him a view of the TV over the bar wasn't a hardship. He watched as the Dodgers' third baseman tagged out a player on a forced run, then winged the ball to first for the double play, retiring the side. He wondered if Bella liked baseball.

The station went to commercial, and he slouched back in his seat. He couldn't get Bella's voice out of his head. She was at risk of loving him? She'd dropped that bombshell, and before he could recover enough to form a coherent thought over the thundering in his ears, Linc had barreled in with all the finesse of a camel at a tea party.

Why was loving him a risk? He didn't know the answer, but he knew those few words changed everything. Now he had a starting point to work from, and there wasn't a chance in hell he was going back to where they'd been. He and Bella were going to see this thing through. As far as he was concerned, they belonged together.

And he'd better get his head back in the game before he blew this operation.

Dudes wearing leather over beer guts seemed to be the preference at Easy Rider as a few more came in and ordered their drinks at the bar before joining the players in the pool room.

Seth was sipping from a longneck when the door opened and two men entered. Neither of them was RJ, but their attire and demeanor instantly snagged Seth's interest. Both had shaved heads, full beards, and wore black leather jackets with heavy boots. Tattoos of swastikas and other symbols denoting white supremacy covered most of their exposed skin.

The shorter of the two, a stocky man with a thick neck, sported iron crosses inked across each eye. But what caught Seth's attention was the stylized "F" inscribed on his right cheek, with a "D" on the left. Freedom Defenders for sure.

FD guy scanned the room. His gaze latched on Seth and after a hard stare, he turned to the other man, a giant who had to top out at over three hundred muscle-bound pounds, and said something before they started across the room.

The bartender saw them coming and took a baseball bat from beneath the counter and set it on top of the bar in clear warning. The stocky man waved Godzilla to the bar, where a patron hastily vacated a stool to put distance between himself and the skinhead.

FD guy approached Seth. He placed a hand on his hip, pulling back his jacket in a move no doubt calculated to reveal the holstered pistol on his belt. Nevada was an open carry state, but California was not. The bar was barely a mile over the state line in California. Seth had spotted a couple other armed patrons, and guessed the guy behind the bar wasn't bothered by the violation of state law.

Seth studied the man coming toward him. The skinheads probably thought the tats made them look intimidating, but Seth thought that much ink looked a little OCD, like once they got started, they didn't know how to stop.

"You Jameson?"

"Who's asking?"

"Answer the fucking question."

Seth considered him. "Yeah, I'm Seth Jameson. Who are you?"

"Hell no, I'm not telling an asshole US Marshal my name. You can call me Dub."

"Okay, Dub, why are you and Godzilla here? The deal was I would meet with Richard Jameson. Only him."

"You'll meet with him, but not here. Think he would risk you having a team ready to grab him? Big Dog hasn't stayed ahead of the marshals all this time by being a dumbass."

"What about you, Dub? You a fugitive too? Though I guess that would make you the dumbass if you agreed to meet with me." Dub hesitated and Seth figured he'd hit the truth dead on. "Guess Big Dog didn't mind risking you meeting the marshal."

"Go fuck yourself. You don't know shit about me other than that Big Dog trusts me to fetch you." He jerked a thumb toward the backdoor. "Let's go."

Seth raised the bottle to his lips and took a slow sip, then set it down carefully. "I haven't finished my beer." He gestured to the bar. "By the looks of it, your pal Godzilla is just getting started." Seth couldn't have timed the comment better. Dub looked over as the bartender placed a lowball glass half full of amber liquid in front of the big man. "Looks like he's settling in. Have a seat so we can talk over our options."

Dub muttered an expletive and strode to the bar where he growled something at Godzilla who gave a defensive shrug and a scowl. Seth took the opportunity to tap out a quick message to Bella and Linc.

*RJ a no-show. Sent two skinheads to bring me to his location. Wait for update.* He hit send and slid his phone back in his coat pocket before Dub returned to the table.

"Let's go, asshole. I've got orders to take you to Big Dog."

"I told you, that's not what I agreed to. You don't really exude trustworthiness with those freaky crosses over your eyes, you know?" He took another sip of his beer.

Dub slid into the opposite seat, and then leaned forward with his elbows on the table. "Listen up, asshole. Big Dog said you might be reluctant. Said I should persuade you however I see best." He cracked his knuckles making a sound like popcorn popping. This asshole watched too many mafia movies. "I'll start by explaining the setup, and I'll say it real slow so you can understand. I'm in charge, and you'll do what I say. Me and Pete are here to transport you to a secure location. Before you can speak to Big Dog, you'll be searched for weapons and electronic devices. Once he's done with you, we'll bring you back here." The ink over his eyes stretched as he raised his brows. "You follow all that, pretty boy?"

Seth shook his head once. "No fucking way. I said I'd meet with my dad. I'm not going anywhere with a couple of dipshits decorated like pathetic clowns. No deal."

Dub grinned, showing stained teeth. "I'll say it a different way so you get the full meaning. Big Dog wants to meet with you, so that's what's going to happen. He sets the conditions, not you. You can leave here under your own steam, or Pete and I can carry you out of here. Either way, you're going. That's what Big Dog wants, and he's the boss." Dub's grin widened. "He said to get you there, but he didn't say what kind of condition you needed to be in."

Seth leaned forward, studying the other man's face. "Man, did that hurt when they inked around your eyes? I arrested this guy once who had the whites of his eyes tattooed. Can you believe it? The whites of his eyes were tattooed red. That had to hurt like shit. Where else you got ink?"

"What the fuck, man. You understand English? I gave you two options. Pick one, or I'll pick for you."

"Sure, I'm taking option three." Seth snaked out a hand to grab Dub by the front of his shirt and yanked him forward.

Seth kept his tone reasonable. "Don't even think of drawing your weapon, you fucker, because under this table I've got a forty caliber Glock pointed right at your dick. You make a move I don't like and I'll blow that tiny dick off and there won't be enough of it left for you to jack off with."

With his peripheral vision he could see the big man at the bar give a startled jerk when he figured out something was going on at the booth. He paused with his glass halfway to his mouth and appeared to need a minute to process what he was seeing.

"Wave off Godzilla, because the minute he starts over here, I shoot you, then I shoot him. Got it?" To make his point, Seth jammed the muzzle of the gun into Dub's crotch. Dub uttered a muffled scream and his face blanched. The big guy pushed up from his stool.

"Stay back before he shoots me," Dub wheezed.

Only one other patron in the bar seemed to notice what was going down. He hastily threw a couple bills on the bar and scuttled for the door.

Seth shoved Dub back in his seat. He sat back himself, resting the Glock on his thigh. "Your dick's still in firing range, so no sudden moves, *asshole*. Keep your hands on the table where I can see them."

"Big Dog's not going to like this."

"He'll have to deal. Tell me where he wants you to take me, then I'll decide if that's where I'm going."

Dub leaned forward. "I told Big Dog he couldn't trust you. You may be his kid, but you're a marshal and you'll double-cross him. He thinks he can bring you over to our side, but I know you'd arrest his ass the second you had a chance. At least he listened and agreed we wouldn't take you to the compound."

Seth kept his face expressionless at the mention of a compound. That was exactly where he wanted to go. He used the gun under the table to nudge Dub. "Get to the point."

"*Fuck.* He'll meet us at a turn out on the highway on the other side of the lake."

"Why there?"

"It's someplace no one's going to bother us," Dub sneered. "It's also where there's a five-hundred-foot drop-off to the river. I could kick your body over the side of the mountain and no one would know where to look for you."

"Way to sell it, shithead. I'm not meeting my old man there."

Seth's mind raced to figure out a way to salvage the situation. It was obvious Dub didn't support RJ meeting with Seth. Could be that Dub was RJ's top lieutenant and felt his position would be threatened if Seth were brought into the organization. He needed to believe he'd get positive intel if he were going to risk a meeting. He eyed the man sitting across the narrow table and gauged how he could get more information out of him.

He brought up his phone and, one-handed, snapped a photo of Dub. "Should've smiled, man, I could've sent you a copy to include with your Christmas cards." Seth shot him a mock-quizzical look. "Do skinhead punks like you even do the holidays? You know, that time of year when good people share love and joy? What do skinheads do, send their moms wishes of hate and dystopia?" He hit send. "Thanks for that pic, by the way. I'll check to see if you're in the system."

"You think you're a fucking genius, don't you?" Color rushed back into Dub's face under the ink. "You think because you're a big-shot marshal, you hold all the cards? We've got a card you want, asshole. Keep up with the attitude and you'll never get that card back."

That caught Seth's attention. "What are you talking about?"

"Guess you don't have all the answers after all. I'll lay it out for you. We've got something that you want. If you want any chance of getting it back, you'll cooperate."

"You're bullshitting me. You've got nothing I want."

Dub reached for a pocket and Seth made sure the man felt the muzzle of the gun pressed against his kneecap.

"I'm getting my phone. You think I'm bullshitting you? I got proof."

Dub pulled his phone from his pocket. He tapped a few times, then turned it so Seth could see. Anthony Rebollar stared at him from the small screen, expression defiant, eyes scared, and blood smeared under his nose.

"Got your attention, didn't I, asshole?"

Seth nodded slowly.

"Guess we got the attention of that fucking judge too. We're going to make things right in this country. You want this kid to stay alive, then you're coming with us. Got it?"

There wasn't any choice. "Yeah, I got it."

Seth put a ten under his empty bottle. They filed out the backdoor of the bar, Dub in front of Seth, and Godzilla behind him. They crossed the parking lot to the farthest corner where an older model, dark-colored Suburban sat parked in the shadows next to a Dumpster.

Confirmation that RJ and the Freedom Defenders had kidnapped Anthony changed the game. Seth had to figure out where they were holding the boy. His gut told him RJ was linked with Vivian Cochran. There'd been a white truck parked under the tree behind her house, and the last time they'd seen him, RJ had been driving a white pickup.

Weak evidence, but it was a start. When the drone had caught Vivian crossing the yard to the big metal garage, Bella had said Vivian had been bringing food to Anthony. Seth needed to do more than talk to RJ; he needed to get to the compound and gain access to that garage. A plan was formulating in his brain. It would be painful, but there was a possibility it could work.

Dub turned to Seth when they stopped beside the Suburban. "Give me your phone."

"No."

Godzilla opened his mouth in what was likely supposed to be a smile, silver-capped front teeth gleaming faintly in the light above the backdoor of the bar. He looked like he chewed nails for breakfast.

Dub shook his arms like he was loosening up before a boxing round. "Give me your fucking phone."

Seth braced himself. He should probably turn over his phone, but it didn't sit right. "No."

"Asshole has more guts than smarts." Dub lashed out with a fist, lightning fast. Seth ducked that one, but not the sharp jab thrown by Godzilla that snapped his head back. A hand to his back slammed Seth face first against the Suburban.

"Sweet, I get to frisk the cop," Dub gloated.

Godzilla kept a heavy hand on Seth's neck as Dub searched him.

Seth's phone was snatched from his pocket and his stomach sank when his Glock was taken from the holster at his shoulder. Shit. There was nothing good about this. Dub continued his search. Seth held his breath, then let it out in a hiss of frustration when his marshals-issued phone was discovered in the inside pocket of his jacket.

Dub chortled with glee. "A gun and *two* phones. Must mean you're a special kind of asshole. Not going to help you though."

Godzilla loosened his hold and Seth shrugged him off. A barking dog ringtone sounded from Dub's phone. Eyes on Seth, he put the phone to his ear.

"We got him, boss." He listened, nodding like the person on the other end of the line could see him. "Will do."

Dub disconnected and, in a casual move, tossed both of Seth's phones into the Dumpster. "Now we're ready to go. Dear old dad is waiting."

\*\*\*

The big Suburban took a turn at a dark intersection, driving straight into what looked like a black hole, headlights providing twin cones of light in front of them. Despite the wide swath of stars, the moonless sky didn't offer much light. They'd left the developed area around Lake Tahoe, skirting the lake on its western side before taking a winding road heading north. Seth had spotted a sign. They were taking the road linking Tahoe to Truckee. Trying to think past the ache to the side of his face, he brought up a mental map of the area and figured they were in the general vicinity of the Cochran property.

Seth wished he had a bag of ice. He couldn't see shit from his right eye because of swelling where Godzilla's huge fist had hit with the force of a freight train. The big guy sat on the driver's side of the backseat, but angled toward Seth, a forty-five resting across his lap. Dub drove, whistling under his breath as he sped into the darkness.

"How'd you guys get involved in this skinhead bullshit?" Seth asked conversationally.

"Shut up, asshole," Dub growled.

"No, really. I want to know. I'm always curious how the criminal mind works."

"We're not criminals."

"Don't talk to him, Pete." The glow from the dashboard caught Dub glancing in the rearview mirror.

"Come on, give me a break. I want to understand. Were you bullied in school and becoming a skinhead made you feel powerful? It'd explain those impressive tattoos. It's like wearing a blinking neon sign saying *I'm a badass, don't mess with me.* That's a powerful thing. I bet those bullies would give you respect if they could see you now."

"I wasn't bullied."

"I told you not to talk, dumbass."

Seth shifted so he could see Pete more clearly in the shadowy interior of the vehicle. "Seems like you're still hanging with bullies." Seth nodded toward Dub.

"I said I wasn't bullied. Kids at school left me alone 'cause I could kick their asses."

"So maybe you were bullied at home. Your dad beat up on you?"

"My dad didn't stick around. Mom beat the shit out of me pretty regular, though."

"Shut it, both of you," Dub snarled.

Seth ignored him. "Man, that sucks. Guess we have that in common. Not the mom part, but being abandoned by our dads."

"Yeah, it sucks. I played football in high school and my dad never came to one of my games."

"I get it. I played varsity baseball and my dad stopped coming to my games, too."

"You played baseball? That game's too slow. I like football better."

"That's fucking it." Dub slammed on the brakes and the Suburban fishtailed before sliding to a stop at the side of the road. He spun around in his seat. "No more, you hear me? Get a clue, Pete. Asshole here is trying to do what they call building a rapport." He gave the words extra emphasis. "He's not your friend, he's not your therapist. He's a fucking Deputy US Marshal, and he's Big Dog's kid. That should be enough to keep you from spilling your goddamn guts. And you," he swiveled to point a finger at Seth, "lay off, or *I'll* beat the shit out of *you* and tell your dad that you tripped over my fists. Got it, asshole?"

"That's Chief Deputy."

"What?"

"I'm a Chief Deputy US Marshal, not a Deputy US Marshal. Bit more of a mouthful, isn't it? Comes with a nice pay raise, though."

Dub lunged over the seat. This was the part where things could go sideways, and Seth had to hope for the best. He evaded the flailing fists, but he couldn't evade Godzilla and his forty-five. He caught Seth across the temple with the butt of his gun.

Seth felt his head explode, and with blackness closing in, hoped his plan worked.

# Chapter Fifteen

Bella stared out the window of the diner. Lake Tahoe glimmered between the buildings across the road, reflecting lights from the marina. She'd like to visit the area during the day when she was free to enjoy the mountain scenery she'd gotten a glimpse of from their hotel window. Despite the warm summer days, nighttime temperatures in the Sierras were regularly in the forties and, as the diner's door swung open to admit a gray-haired couple, both using canes, she was glad she'd packed her heavy zippered jacket.

She sipped from the mug she held in both hands. The green tea had cooled and wasn't working to settle her stomach. Seth had sent them a text, and then the photo, which had eased her worry somewhat, but she couldn't get rid of the feeling something could go wrong and Seth would be in danger. There were too many uncontrollable variables, which could sabotage the success of the operation.

RJ was notoriously unreliable, and the emotional dynamics between Seth and his father made the situation all the more volatile. She and Linc were too far away to provide backup, and the thought brought on a bout of nausea, which had been eating at her stomach for the past hour. Coming to a decision, she set down her mug.

"We should go to the bar."

Linc looked up from his phone. "Explain."

"Seth might need us. We already know that RJ isn't there so we don't have to worry about you being recognized. We go in as a couple looking for a drink, and we're there as backup if necessary."

Linc considered her suggestion. "He'll kick our asses if we mess up the operation."

"How are we going to mess it up?"

"For one, there's a chance RJ could still show up, though I think if that had been his plan, he wouldn't have sent the skinheads. I can pass as a dude who goes to a biker bar, but you, sweetheart? My brother called it. You're too classy for a joint like that. You'd stick out and people would notice you. Seth doesn't need that kind of a distraction."

She narrowed her eyes. "Give me a minute." She grabbed her purse, rose from her seat, and disappeared into the bathroom. She returned five minutes later and was gratified to see Linc's jaw go slack.

He recovered quickly. "How the hell'd you do that?"

"A little lipstick, hairspray, and I stowed the jacket in my bag. It's not a little leather skirt with silver studs, but I think I'll do."

After their conversation in the hotel room, she'd put a couple of things in her big purse, just in case. Bright red lipstick and hairspray to tease her hair worked to give her what she thought of as a sexy, vampish look. She was already wearing slim black boots with skintight jeans, and while she'd miss the added warmth, removing the jacket and half unbuttoning the bright plaid shirt underneath revealed her lacy camisole.

"Hell yeah, you'll do. Seth will swallow his tongue." At her startled look, he closed his eyes. "Shit, sorry. I shouldn't have said that, but sometimes I wish you two would get out of your own way."

"What's that supposed to mean?"

"It means I care about both of you and want to see you happy." He raised a hand when she opened her mouth. "That's all I'm going to say about it. Let's go."

Linc held open the door and they stepped out into the chilly night. In minutes they were in the car with Linc behind the wheel as Bella engaged the app on her phone to locate Seth's devices.

"His phones show him still at the bar."

"Good."

They arrived at the half-full parking lot and Bella was somewhat reassured to see Seth's rental parked near the backdoor. Linc put the car in park. "Let's go, sexy girlfriend."

She raised her brows in mock horror. "'Sexy girlfriend'? That's all you've got? I'll have to ask Mikayla what in the world made her think you were the one and only for her."

"Hey, I was on my game with her. Nothing like beating off an attacker and rescuing the girl to get her to fall for you. Just ask her. Now she loves me best." Linc's smile was as goofy as it was endearing.

They walked to the front of the bar. Linc laced his fingers through hers as they approached the door.

They stepped into the sounds of a bar at its evening peak. There was the clack of pool balls interspersed with the thud of darts hitting a target. A big-screen TV over the bar showed a guy in a blue uniform hitting a baseball that was caught by a guy in a red uniform. Linc tugged her into the room. Scanning the booths and tables, she rubbed a hand over her stomach when she realized, unless he was in the bathroom, Seth was gone.

The waitress motioned them to a table as she cleared off empties. They sat, Linc flashing a smile at the woman whose name tag identified her as Deb. Her face showed lines that might put her in her forties, but Bella guessed she might actually be younger. Deb gave Linc a tired smile back before lugging the bus tub behind the bar.

Linc leaned forward. "I'll check for the signal from Seth's phone. You talk to the bartender, see if you can learn anything."

Bella approached the bartender, and minutes later returned to the table. Her voice was clipped in frustration. "The bartender says he hasn't seen anyone matching Seth's description. Same response when I asked him about the skinheads. He says he runs a clean place and no skinheads come in here."

"He's lying."

"Yeah, he is. My guess is he keeps his clientele happy by minding his own business."

"The locator app says both Seth's phones are still in the area. We didn't check his car when we came in, so I'm heading back to the parking lot to do that."

Bella spotted Deb disappearing through the swinging door of the women's bathroom. "Okay, I'll meet you there."

Bella pushed through the door to the small restroom. Deb stood smoking a cigarette, blowing smoke through the small window opened to the outside. Bella bent over the sink to wash her hands, catching Deb's eye in the mirror.

"Could you help me out? I'm looking for someone I think was here earlier this evening." Deb lifted a brow as she took a drag on the cigarette. "He's late thirties, about six two, dark brown hair that falls over his forehead, intense gray eyes. He would have been here in the last hour."

Deb gave an incredulous laugh. "You mean tall, dark, and hotter than sex on a stick? That guy?"

Bella couldn't help laughing. "Yeah, that's him."

"What, are you collecting all the good ones? The hot guy you're with not enough for you?"

"I guess it's my lucky night, at least if I find the guy I'm looking for. Have you seen him?"

"Yeah, I saw him." Deb blew another steam of smoke toward the window. "Looked all cool and steely-eyed like Gary Cooper in *High Noon*."

"I don't know it."

Deb hitched a shoulder. "I watch old movies with my dad. He likes the westerns."

Bella made a mental note to check out the movie. She was always trying to fill the holes in her knowledge of American pop culture. "Did you see when the man left?"

"Yeah, I saw when he left. I saw who he left with, too. Those two were bad business. Had tattoos all over their faces and heads like a couple of freaks."

"When was that?"

"About twenty minutes ago. The three of them left out the backdoor. The one you're asking about paid for his beer, though, and left a decent tip."

Bella thanked Deb and left the bar to find Linc climbing out of the Dumpster in the corner of the parking lot. His tone was grim when he held up two objects in his hand. "He's not in his car, and his phones were tossed in the trash."

She swallowed hard as her nausea ratcheted up her throat.

*** 

Seth woke feeling like his head was a pressure cooker ready to explode at any moment.

He opened his eyes, or rather, his eye, to dappled sunlight. He was lying back on a bed. At least he was on a bed, and a cursory glance suggested he was in a bedroom. Memory of the night before had him pushing up, then regretting that movement as pain spiked.

"Bottle of Tylenol is on the table next to you."

The voice came from the man sitting in a chair next to a window. His hair was white and he had a face craggier than it had once been, with deep grooves bracketing either side of his mouth. His long, lean build was the same as Seth remembered. It was a shock to see what he might look like in thirty years. His father had lived hard and showed it. Seth hoped fate would be kinder to him.

His father stared at him with blue eyes Seth remembered from childhood. As a kid he felt like that stare could look right through him. A memory slammed into him. He'd been only six or seven, and was violently ill throughout a long night. He woke in the morning to find his father had stayed in a chair beside his side all night.

"Dad." Emotions he didn't want grabbed him by the throat and threatened to choke him. Seth thought he'd effectively cauterized any leftover feelings he might've had for his father, but they'd slipped under his guard, ready to undermine his control.

His father rose to his feet. "Take the meds, son. We'll talk when you don't feel like shit."

That rough, deep voice was another unexpected wrench back into the past. Yelling at him from the stands to slide into third, telling him that strong men didn't cry, explaining how it was Seth's responsibility to watch after his siblings. The last memory came with a jolt. It had never occurred to him his father had telegraphed abandoning his family.

Fast approaching seventy and with a slight rounding to his shoulders, Richard Jameson still exuded an aura of strength. Take him back a hundred and fifty years, and he'd fit right in with the gunslingers of the old west. He wasn't wearing the black hat, but he had a holster slung low on his hip, the pearl-handled grip of a revolver gleaming dully in the light coming through the window.

He left the room, closing the door behind him. Muffled voices came from the other side of the door, but Seth couldn't make out what was said. He boosted himself onto one elbow and reached for the Tylenol, gritting his teeth against the motion. Even that much movement made the world spin like he was on a carnival ride.

He didn't recall getting hit in the ribs, but they ached like a son of a bitch. He downed the pills with a half bottle of water and lay back against the pillow, closing his eyes to slow down the spinning. He'd give himself a minute, then he'd get up and deal with whatever came next.

The next time he opened his eyes the light had changed and he realized he'd slept for hours. *Shit.*

Swinging his feet over the side of the bed, he was glad his vision had settled. He took a quick survey. He likely had a concussion and should rest his brain, but that would have to wait. He was missing the bomber jacket, but still wore his clothes and shoes from the night before and his empty holster was draped over the footboard. It looked like they'd carried him in, tossed him on the bed, and called it good. He crossed the room to peer out a window, taking a moment to push it open.

His team had called it. A white pickup and silver Civic were parked under a pair of tall pines, and across the yard were the storage shed and long metal garage with its twin rollup doors. Beyond the garage the property sloped to the river. He could see water gleaming through the trees. He'd been taken to Vivian Cochran's property.

From the sun's position, he guessed it was late afternoon. He had to think the Cochran property would be the first place Bella and Linc would think to look for him. Locating Anthony was Seth's top priority, but once the boy was safe, Seth was going after Richard Jameson and the Freedom Defenders were going down with him.

Seth used the john attached to the bedroom, wincing when he caught his reflection in the mirror. His right eye was swollen shut, and the skin had split over a lump that was raised below the hairline on his forehead. Godzilla'd had a heavy hand with that forty-five.

Seth splashed water on his face, rubbing to remove the blood that had dried into his hairline. When the water ran clear, he dabbed his face with the towel. He left the bedroom, and saw a woman sitting in an easy chair with a laptop resting on a tray.

She glanced up, and then gave him a once-over. "You look like him. I'm Viv." Like in her driver's license photo, Vivian Cochran's hair was dyed blonde. She looked short, a bit overweight, and had painted fingernails that clicked as she tapped on the keyboard of the computer.

"I'm Seth." He was trying to figure out his status. Was he a prisoner? A guest?

"Rick gave those two boys hell for the condition you were in last night."

He didn't say anything. Calling Dub and Godzilla boys was like calling his Glock a squirt gun. Seth took note of the layout of the house.

The bedroom he'd been in was to the left of the living room, and a hall to the right suggested more bedrooms in that direction. He guessed wide openings to either side of the back wall of the living room would be to a kitchen in the rear. The floral patterns on the couch upholstery and the wallpaper reminded him of the décor in his grandparents' home when he was a kid. Dated but clean. Not that he'd expected Nazi flags or a copy of *Mein Kampf* on the coffee table, but there was nothing about the place that would lead someone to guess that it served as headquarters for a white nationalist terrorist organization.

"Guess you'll want something to eat."

"Where's RJ?"

"RJ? That's what you're calling your dad?"

"Got to call him something, and Dad doesn't fit anymore. Where is he?"

She shrugged, then powered down her laptop and shut the lid. A door opened and closed somewhere in the house. "There he is now. Follow me. There's hot coffee, and you can make yourself a sandwich if you're hungry."

"Thanks. Does RJ live here?"

"He does. We're not married, but we've been together for a year or so. Rick helped me through a hard time when my husband died."

Seth followed her into the kitchen.

RJ settled himself at a kitchen table, dropped heavily into a ladderback chair, and rubbed his knee. His gaze was on Seth. "He doesn't need to know any of that."

Vivian poured coffee into a heavy mug and set it in front of RJ. "I'll get your pills and some water." She returned a moment later with a vial of pills and an uncapped water bottle.

RJ gave Seth a look that seemed almost sheepish. "For arthritis. Got it in my knees. Doc says I need knee replacement surgery. At night I add pills for high blood pressure and cholesterol. Can you believe your old man's getting old?"

Seth shook his head, struck by a feeling of unreality. If his life hadn't taken a hard turn when he was eighteen, it might have been his mom bringing the pills, and he might have been sitting down with his dad. Instead, the man at the table was a stranger whom Seth had gotten half his DNA from. Weird thought.

RJ lifted his mug to sip. "You drink coffee?"

"Yeah."

"Then get yourself a cup and sit down, boy. We need to talk."

# Chapter Sixteen

Seth opened a cupboard, looking for a mug, and made a quick study of the kitchen. Most interesting was a row of hooks by the door containing sets of keys, one of them on a bright red puffball key fob. A plastic zip bag with what looked like a peanut butter and jelly sandwich cut into neat squares, a banana, and a bag of Famous Amos chocolate chip cookies sat on the counter. Vivian hastily stuffed the lunch into a paper sack and took a can of Coke from the refrigerator. "This is for one of the guys we have working here. He forgot his lunch." She quickly disappeared out the kitchen door.

Maybe there was a worker who hadn't brought his lunch, but it could also be for a boy being held captive. From the window, Seth watched Vivian until she disappeared from view.

Seth poured coffee, and since the fixings were out, put together a pb&j. RJ came into the kitchen to refill his cup, limping slightly.

Throughout Seth's childhood, this man had been a giant, and it was a shock to see he now stood inches taller than his dad. Big and strong, Richard Jameson had a scathing tongue that could cut through a boy's confidence with laser precision, leaving it in tatters.

Even as a child, Seth had been aware his mother had tried to shield him from the worst of his father's criticisms, and that his father had singled out his eldest child for harsher discipline than his siblings.

Seth had been held to impossibly high standards, which were ever-changing and unattainable. He had a moment of insight, and realized much of what he'd achieved had likely been driven by a desire to prove he was better than his father: more honest, hard-working, decent, and dedicated.

Whatever flaws RJ possessed, Seth had compensated by working harder to prove that those weren't his flaws, that he was a better man.

RJ stopped in front of Seth. "Got taller, didn't you?"

"Yeah, I got taller."

"What about Lincoln? That boy was born long."

"This why you wanted to meet, to catch up with news about the family?" Seth made an effort to even out his tone, but accumulated anger from the past twenty years was hard to rein back.

RJ returned to the table and Seth took a chair across from him.

"It's natural for a man to want to know how his sons turned out, don't you think?"

"Not when you abandoned them without a backwards look, no, I don't think your interest is natural. You haven't asked about your daughter. The daughter you ordered killed."

"She tell you I ordered her killed? She always had a quick temper, that kid. But you always knew where you stood with her. You, on the other hand, kept shit bottled up. When you finally lost your temper, you went off like a rocket. That time when you were twelve or thirteen and I'd told you to wash and wax the car. You did a shitty job and I made you do it again. You were so pissed, you backtalked me. Had to take a strap to you to teach you a lesson."

Seth noticed RJ didn't deny having ordered his followers to kill Ellie. Whatever this meeting was about, it wasn't about family. "You were an asshole who beat his kids."

"Watch your tongue, boy. You needed to be taught discipline. You should thank me for it. You got me in trouble with your mother that time, though. Said she'd kick me out if I laid a hand on any one of you ever again." He shrugged. "She'd have done it, too. I wasn't ready to leave at that point, so I found other ways to keep you in line."

Memories flooded in, dark and painful. Seth needed every ounce of that discipline to control the temper that rose up fast and fierce, wrapping around his throat and squeezing until it hurt to breathe.

His father had taught him that leading with his emotions led to pain, and that pain didn't have to be physical. He'd learned it was better to keep what you were thinking or feeling inside, safe and walled off. He supposed RJ was right and Seth could thank the old man for that.

He sipped his coffee, considering how he was going to finesse the conversation. He needed to find a way to gain credibility, gain the possibility of acceptance. He needed to find an opportunity to get that key and gain access to the garage. If Anthony was being held there, Seth would free him. Then he was going to bring down the hammer on RJ and every traitor working for him.

RJ leaned back in his chair. "I named you boys after Americans I admired. You're named for Seth Bullock, who brought law and order to Deadwood. Your mother decided to name Ellie after Eleanor Roosevelt, which, in retrospect, was a poor choice as she was part of the New Deal that led our country on the road to socialism."

"Your point?"

"My point is that Seth Bullock was no saint, but he stood for something important and lived by a code. You're sacrificing your life working for the feds, upholding laws passed by corrupt politicians. It's not too late to make your life mean something."

"By doing what, joining you in your noble crusade?"

"It is a noble crusade. I've sacrificed a lot for it, including my relationship with my family."

Seth was now able to see out of his right eye, but he was having trouble thinking past the pain in his head that had started throbbing like a sore tooth.

"You said in the email you wanted to meet with me. Why?"

RJ took a moment to sip his coffee. "I'm a fugitive, you're a fucking US Marshal. Better question is why you agreed to meet with me."

"To bring you in, of course."

"You think you're going to arrest me? I've got your gun, boy. My guys would beat the shit out of you again if I told them to. How are you going to arrest me?"

"It might not be now, but I will. That's a promise."

"That doesn't answer my question, does it? What's your real motivation? Why meet with your fugitive dad when you know you're not bringing me in? I'll tell you what I think. The reason is because you want answers from me." He leaned back in his chair, gaze steady. "You want to know how I could have abandoned my family, left my kids, and left my wife." His expression turned sly. "Some say I stole from the government, planted a couple bombs. How is it that your dear old dad could have done those things you think are so reprehensible? That's what you really want to know, isn't it?"

Seth took a bite of sandwich, taking his time while chewing and swallowing before responding. "I figured all that out a long time ago. Your family never meant shit to you, and you're a racist bigot who doesn't possess an ounce of integrity." He shrugged. "Those answers are easy."

"Just because I don't want our country overrun by foreigners doesn't make me racist."

Seth had to choose his words carefully and searched for a nuanced response. RJ would never buy it if Seth suddenly embraced the white nationalist ideology. He needed to give him enough crumbs for RJ to warm to the idea that Seth would consider joining his side.

"I don't want my country overrun by foreigners, either, but I don't plant bombs in courthouses."

"Sometimes there has to be sacrifice. Think about the men who signed the Declaration of Independence. John Hancock signed his name big enough that the king didn't have to use his eyeglasses to read it. If the Revolutionary War had gone differently and the British had won, every one of the men who signed that document would have been hanged for leading a rebellion. At some point, history will look back on my people as the founding fathers of a new revolution. You can be a part of it."

"There's no way you can succeed."

"Not as long as I have the US Marshals on my ass. You could get them to back off."

"I can't trust you."

"That's where you're wrong. You can trust me. I did what I did because I have integrity. I believe in the fundamental ideals of our country, in the principles of freedom and liberty that are enshrined in the Constitution. I committed myself to stop those who want to hijack the government and create a socialist nightmare where the races are mixed and our freedoms are trampled under the heels of Marxist revolutionaries." He eyed his son. "You should want that, too. You should want to protect our country from hordes of immigrants who are leeches, sucking the life out of the hard-working people who create jobs."

There were landmines all through RJ's diatribe and Seth had to step carefully to navigate through them. He needed to say the right words, and if Seth could finesse it, find the opportunity to search for Anthony. "The question is how far is too far? What actions are too reprehensible? And since when is it up to you to decide who gets to be in our country?"

"Not me, the Constitution."

"I'm not saying you don't have a point, and maybe I agree with some of it. I'm worried about the direction the country is going, and that American culture is being appropriated by outsiders." He sipped his coffee and lifted his shoulder in a shrug. The words soured in his mouth when he thought of Bella and Alexei, and Anthony's parents, immigrants to the United States, and all they and others had brought to it. "There's not much I can do about it."

RJ's expression turned calculating. "You can do something about it. Being a marshal, you have more influence than a lot of people. I have some literature for you to read. You should talk to some of our people."

Seth gave a disbelieving snort. "You mean like Dub and Pete? If they're the best you've got, you're scraping the bottom of the barrel."

"Dub and Pete are useful as foot soldiers. No, you need to talk to other leaders of our organization. They're the ones who can provide the intellectual foundation that you're looking for. The foot soldiers are good at repeating the slogans, spreading the word. They're your racists and they're thugs, but they're useful to me. It's the generals you need to talk to."

Seth leaned sat back in the chair, his legs stretched out in front of him. "I'll listen to what they have to say." He narrowed his gaze. "But tell me, am I a prisoner here, or can I leave when I want?"

"You're not a prisoner. If you'd cooperated last night, we'd have had our meeting and you wouldn't have ended up here and in the condition you're in." RJ sighed heavily, sounding like a man with a lot of trouble on his mind. "We're holding a general meeting this weekend. Those men I want you to talk with are gathering here, some coming from out of state. I want you to meet them."

Seth nodded slowly. "Okay. Out of curiosity, where exactly am I?"

"Don't worry about where you are. We'll blindfold you when you leave here and you'll be taken back to the bar where your car is. When you join us this weekend, we'll pick you up." RJ paused. "I want you to stay for a bit. Give us a chance to talk."

The kitchen door opened and Vivian entered, Dub following her into the house. Daylight enhanced the impact of the tattoos over his face and head.

Vivian poured herself coffee and brought it to the table to sit next to RJ. She was a wild card, an unknown dynamic. Seth watched her carefully, trying to gauge what part she played in the operation. Dub, on the other hand, was a known entity.

"Everything good?" RJ asked.

Vivian gave a nod. "Got something to talk to you about, though." Her gaze moved from Seth back to RJ. "Later."

Dub opened the refrigerator and took out a chilled can of Coke. "Everything's as good as it can be with this outsider here. I can take care of him for you, Big Dog." Dub kicked the leg of Seth's chair. "How's the face, asshole? Looks painful. Can't say I'm sorry, though."

"You belong in a freakshow, dude. Scare any little kids today with that face?"

Dub leaned against the wall, his arms crossed over his chest. His mouth turned up in a smirk that Seth wouldn't have minded removing for him.

"Shut up, both of you." RJ pointed a long finger at Dub. "My son might be an asset. He and I are having a conversation. He's interested in our fight."

Vivian's brows lowered, and suspicion laced her tone. "He's a marshal. He's interested in arresting you."

"Yeah, he's a marshal, but he's also my son. That means something."

"He threatened to blow my dick off." Dub reached out a foot to push at Seth's chair again.

Vivian stared hard at Seth and he stared right back until she looked away, shaking her head. "He's playing you," she told RJ. "I don't trust him, either."

"Mom's right, we can't trust him. He's an outsider and could bring a shitload of trouble down on us." Seth kept his expression carefully neutral, not letting his surprise show. Dub was Vivian's son? That was a twist he hadn't expected.

Dub rattled on. "Let me and Pete take care of this guy. That's the only way to make sure he's not a threat to our movement. We don't want any chance he could come after us. We'll do the job, then take his body into the backcountry where it'll never be found and where it can't be traced back to us." Dub cracked his knuckles and Seth again had the image of a low-level mobster.

In a practiced move, RJ pulled the pearl-handled pistol from his holster and laid it on the table. He leaned forward as he glared at

Dub from under bushy eyebrows, his voice as deadly as the implied threat from the unholstered six-shooter. "You lay a finger on my son and you won't survive the day. I'll plug a couple bullets through that simple brain of yours and watch you bleed out. Leave Seth to me. If he becomes an issue, I'll take care of him myself. Until then, you're to keep your hands off him, and everyone else, for that matter." The last words were said with pointed emphasis.

They may have been talking about his potential murder, but it was RJ's final comment that had Seth's interest piqued. He was certain RJ was referring to Anthony, and his words gave Seth an uneasy feeling.

Dub raised his hands as if in surrender, but his gaze shifted to his mother. That silent communication made Seth think they were up to something, something RJ was unaware of. There were undercurrents upon undercurrents, and Seth wished his head and ribs didn't hurt like a bitch so he could think more clearly.

RJ gestured toward Seth. "Viv put a clean shirt in your room earlier. Go ahead and take a shower if you want. We'll talk again later."

It was a clear dismissal, and he guessed RJ wanted to hear what Vivian had to say. Not seeing much option, Seth went to the room he'd passed the night in. A gray t-shirt and heavy flannel overshirt were folded on a chair by the door. He pulled off his boots and started the shower running in the miniscule bathroom. Then he opened the bedroom door a crack, listened carefully, and slipped into the living room.

Vivian's voice carried from the kitchen. "Rick, a buyer is interested in the military weapons we have, including the grenade launchers. They want to come tomorrow."

"Tomorrow's not good."

Her voice firmed. "It'll have to be. We need the money, and I don't want to put them off. Another letter came from the county saying they're going to seize this property if I don't pay the back taxes."

"The fucking government is always messing with people's rights." This came from Dub. Footsteps had Seth tensing, ready to retreat back to the bedroom. He heard water running in the sink and listened warily.

"Who are the buyers?" RJ asked.

"The guy who sent the email says his name is Zeb Petrov, though there's no way that's not an alias. Only an idiot would use his real name. They contacted me through a dark web connection," Vivian said. "I'm contacting a couple other people I know who'll be able to tell me if this guy's organization is legit. So far, he is. The word I'm getting back is that he's from the *bratva*."

Seth felt his insides freeze. The *bratva*? What did that mean? RJ made a garbled comment that ended with "fucking Russians," then spoke louder. "Do they have cash?"

"They say they do," Vivian responded. "They want the weapons quick. They say they have some of their people in Reno. I've heard the *bratva*'s involved in the casino business. Anyway, since that's close, they said they could send their buyers here around midmorning."

"I don't know. Sounds rushed to me. Could be a setup." RJ's voice sounded strained, and Seth remembered his father rubbing his knee.

"I'll vet them," Vivian said. "The *bratva* are a good connection. We've got that shipment coming from Washington next month, and if this works out, maybe we could do more business with them. Selling to them is easier for us than trying to smuggle weapons across the border to Mexico."

"I bet we could sell them a shitload of military equipment." Dub sounded eager. "Russians are white. I bet they'd agree with our beliefs, too."

"Let me get my laptop." There was the scraping sound of a chair sliding on the floor. "I'll check if they've gotten back to me."

Seth slipped back into the bedroom. He carefully closed the door, his mind racing as he considered the ramifications of what he'd heard. His team's working assumption had been that RJ was in control of the Freedom Defenders movement, but Seth wondered if RJ's control might be tenuous.

Seth stripped down and stepped into the shower, gritting his teeth when hot water streamed across the injuries on his face, though the water eased the ache in his ribs. A wide, purple bruise, about the width of the sole of a boot, was clearly visible on his right side. The cowards must have kicked him while he was unconscious.

Trying to focus beyond the pain, he processed the new information. The purported contact from the *bratva* added a new twist. If his hunch was right, the *bratva* popping up suddenly as part of the equation had to have something to do with his team. He couldn't be positive, but the coincidence glared at him as too unlikely.

If Bella, Linc, and Ellie had devised a plan to gain access to the compound, then he had to work it from the inside. Most urgently, he had to figure out where Anthony was and come up with a plan to keep the boy safe in case events turned violent.

He thought ahead to when Anthony was free and RJ was behind bars. Seth wanted this done and behind him. Only then could he have an honest conversation with Bella.

Being bashed in the head and taken captive weren't the best circumstances for clear introspection, but he knew some things for certain. He wanted a future with her. If she was pregnant, they'd get married as fast as he could arrange it. Regardless, he was going to do it right with a ring and a proposal, the whole deal. The thought of baring his heart to her scared the shit out of him, but that's what he'd have to do to have Bella with him the rest of his life.

Bare-chested and buttoning his jeans, he stepped out of the bathroom, coming to an abrupt halt when he heard low voices in tense conversation. He stepped closer to the open window and recognized Vivian and Dub.

"Rick says if the judge does what we tell him and dismisses the case, we have to release the little brat. We can't do that." Vivian's voice was low and urgent. "The kid has seen the weapons. He knows what we look like. If he goes free, he can identify us. We'd be in deep shit."

"What are we going to do about it?"

"My contact with the *bratva* says he's sending three of his people tomorrow in the late morning to check out the merchandise. I want to be ready."

Dub said something Seth couldn't completely make out, then Vivian responded, "I'll check them out before telling them where we are. No way am I letting people on my property until I'm sure they are who they say they are. They want to see the weapons before handing over a hundred thousand in cash. If they're satisfied with what we've got, they said they'd come back with a box van to transport the merchandise."

Seth eased closer to the open window, staying out of view.

Vivian continued, "Rick's going to be sleeping heavy tonight. I've got some sedatives, and he takes whatever pills I give him. I'll give them to him with his blood pressure meds before he goes to bed around eleven. That'll keep him out of the way and he'll never know. Once he's asleep, that's when you're going to get the boy. Take him to that quarry behind Little Mountain. The water is deep there. Do what needs to be done and put weights on him so his body stays at the bottom."

"I'll get Pete. We'll take care of it."

"Not Pete, Dub. Only you. You've got to do this yourself. You and I can trust only each other, like always. Understood?"

"Shit. Okay." There was a shuffling of feet. Seth didn't dare move. He didn't want them to realize the window was open.

Dub spoke, resentment lacing his tone. "What about Big Dog's asshole son? Big Dog acts like his shit don't stink, that his kid is going to help the cause. What about me? I've been working my ass off all along, doing the dirty work. I don't get respect for what I've done."

"Rick's blind when it comes to his kid."

"Then what are we going to do about him? He could really mess up the deal with the *bratva*. He's playing the old man. I swear it."

"Yeah, he's playing him, telling him what he wants to hear. No way in hell a guy who is a chief deputy is going to be our inside man with the marshals. I need to think about it. Maybe I can slip sedatives in a Coke or his coffee at dinner. If we could knock him out, you could take him to the quarry, too. Throw him in with a few weights and he'd drown."

"What do we tell Big Dog when the kid and his son disappear?"

"Leave that to me. If he doesn't like the answer, we can take care of him, too. He's about used up his usefulness."

Seth heard the rustling of footsteps. He chanced a quick peek out the window. Both had their backs to him and Dub was pulling keys from his pocket. "Pete and I are heading to town in a bit."

"Dammit, Dub, I need your help here. What's so urgent that it can't wait a couple days?"

"I want to hang out with my bros."

"You're going to buy weed."

"So? It ain't illegal anymore. My stash ran out, and I still want to hang with my bros."

She shook her head. "Be back soon. As soon as Pete's asleep, I'm counting on you to follow through with our plan. We need to move fast."

# Chapter Seventeen

Seth pushed out the screen, then climbed through the window. He'd feigned nausea and skipped the chicken strips and instant potatoes Vivian had prepared. Her fake concern turned his stomach. She'd brought him a pill she claimed was for nausea, and then watched with her beady eyes as he drank from a can of Coke. The chime of an incoming text had sounded and Seth had used the moment of distraction when both RJ and Vivian had been looking for their cellphones to drop the pill into her glass of wine.

The situation had gotten weirder. RJ was treating him like his long-lost son, but when he'd mentioned that he wanted to take a walk after dinner, both RJ and Vivian had said it wasn't a good idea. Vivian went so far as to mention that there'd been a mountain lion spotted a few days before and it wasn't safe. He'd claimed exhaustion and retreated to his room. Earlier, he'd noticed the door could be locked from the outside, and wasn't entirely surprised to hear the quiet click as the lock was engaged sometime later.

Now he stood outside the window in the shadow of the tall pine, the key to the garage safely tucked in his pocket, the red puffball key fob he'd separated the key from still on its hook so it wouldn't be missed. He'd also swiped the keys with the Honda insignia and a small flashlight he'd seen on a desk. Before dinner, Dub and Godzilla had sped off in the Suburban and, despite "the plan," had yet to return.

Vivian and RJ had retreated to a room on the other side of the living room. The sound of canned laughter from a TV program carried through the house.

A steady breeze had picked up, and it blew through the pines with a sound that reminded Seth of the ocean. The arc of the Milky

Way spanned across the sky, and Seth had the sudden memory of his parents taking the family camping when he was a kid, and sitting around the campfire with his head tilted back, staring at the stars while his father pointed out constellations. His dad hadn't always been a jerk.

He found the bomber jacket under the bed and zipped it up against the falling temperature. He didn't dare use the flashlight until he was inside the garage. Making a quick assessment, he figured the most risk of being seen would be at the garage where a light shone over the door. That was an exposed position, one visible from any window on this side of the house or anyone driving into the compound. He set off at a trot, staying under trees until he got to the garage, then circled around the back, keeping to the shadows. At the corner, he glanced back at the house, and seeing no one, fished the key out of his pocket. In seconds he'd reached the door, unlocked it, and slipped inside.

The interior was black as pitch. He turned on the flashlight, casting its beam over the interior. There were no windows, so he wasn't worried about the light being seen from outside. There was an assortment of vehicles: a small tractor, a utility trailer, a couple snowmobiles, and an old pickup truck without its rear wheels supported by jack stands. There was a rollaway tool chest next to wire racks that held an assortment of tools that Seth envied.

He walked to the back where building supplies and lumber were leaned against a wall. A table saw was set up and sawdust littered the floor. He couldn't smell freshly cut wood, and guessed the saw hadn't been used for a few days.

Darkness kept him from speeding up his search, despite the fact that he could be discovered missing from his room at any moment or Dub could return to carry out Anthony's murder.

Seth pressed on, scanning with the beam of the flashlight, moving hurriedly through the space. Anthony was likely being held in some sort of cage, maybe framed with the lumber that had been cut by the table saw.

But there was nothing. No place a boy could be stashed. Seth swore under his breath as his frustration grew. He'd been certain that Anthony was being held in the garage. Standing at the back of the garage, he cast the beam of the flashlight around the interior once again. He paused, frowning as he followed the light. Something was off. He studied the room for a minute more before realization struck.

The dimensions of the inside of the garage didn't match the outside. He cast the light up and saw what had been invisible in the dark. The back wall wasn't an exterior wall. It didn't meet the roof the same way the other walls did, which meant that it was a false wall. Knowing he was on to something, he began searching for a door. Equipment and free-standing metal storage shelves lined the wall, some on wheels.

Now that he knew what he was looking for, he noticed marks on the concrete floor indicating where one set of racks had been repeatedly moved. Its shelves were lined with bundles of insulation, making them lightweight. He grabbed the rack and pulled, moving it easily to reveal a door framed into the wall, which had been hidden behind the insulation.

The door was locked, and Seth held his breath as he slipped the same key into the lock. The tumblers moved easily and he opened the door.

The space created behind the partial wall was perhaps fifteen feet deep and ran the width of the garage. The beam picked up more heavy-duty metal shelving, these loaded with an array of weapons. Serious weapons: carbines, sniper rifles, machine guns, plus communications equipment and tactical gear, all military issue.

Pushing back the urge to hurry to find Anthony, he did another careful scan. The various rifles were piled together on three different racks, in no order, and an open crate was piled with empty magazines. One set of racks held three forty-millimeter, shoulder-held grenade launchers. Another rack held materials that could be used for making bombs. Not surprising since RJ was responsible for at least two bombings. Seth whistled through his teeth when he saw bricks stacked on a rack, the wrappers clearly labeled C4 in block letters.

This was what Vivian wanted to sell to the *bratva*. Seth's team had learned that Freedom Defenders had been stealing from military bases in the Pacific Northwest. He thought they'd shut that down, but apparently they were still active. Anyone with access to this kind of weaponry could cause a hell of a lot of damage.

A rustling sound came from his left. Seth moved the flashlight farther along the wall, then came to an abrupt halt. The cage was about the size of a jail cell, maybe six by eight. A chemical toilet sat in a corner at one end, while a cot with a sleeping bag occupied the other end. Anthony sat on the cot with his back to the wall, his arms wrapped tightly around his upraised knees. His gaze held the same spark of defiance Seth had seen in the photos.

"Get out of here, you fucking pervert."

Shit. Seth shined the flashlight in his own face so Anthony could see him. "Anthony, I'm Seth Jameson, and I'm a US marshal."

The boy leapt off the bed. "What are you doing here? Your face is a mess. Did you come to get me out?"

"Yeah, I came to get you out." Seth shined the light over the enclosure. It was framed with two by fours with heavy gauge chicken wire stapled to the wood. The makeshift door was secured with a heavy-duty padlock.

"You have the key?" Anthony stood on the other side of the door.

"Ah, no."

"Then how you going to get me out?"

"I'm working on it."

"I got some of the wire lifted up."

Seth eyed him. "Yeah? Where?"

Anthony pointed to the corner of the structure next to the door. "See? I worked the wire back and forth until the staple lifted up, then I used that staple to work some others out. I got four out. I don't want them to see what I'm doing, so I push the staples back in the holes, but loose, you know? It doesn't look obvious that the wire is loose."

Anthony pulled back the wire and Seth examined the small opening.

"I thought if I could make the opening big enough, I could get out and get one of those machine guns over there and I'd break out of this place."

"Good idea, if you could find one with ammunition. The magazines I saw weren't loaded and I didn't see any ammo crates. Machine gun's not going to be any help without ammo." Anthony's shoulders slumped. Seth had to ask. "Has someone bothered you? Physically assaulted you?"

"You mean the pervert?"

"Yeah. Who's the pervert?"

"Dub. He keeps looking at me. He's a weirdo with all those tattoos on his face. He came in here the first night and I screamed my head off because I knew he was going to try something. Big Dog came in and made him leave, and told him he'd put a bullet in his head if he touched me. But Dub told me when he brought me food the next day he was coming back, and if I didn't let him do what he wanted, if I told Big Dog, Dub knows where my girlfriend lives and he'd take care of her. I don't think he meant *take care of her* in a good way."

"But he didn't come back."

"No."

Seth felt grim relief Anthony hadn't been forced to endure the additional trauma of sexual assault. "Listen up. I have to cut this lock. There are dozens of tools out there. I'm going back in the garage to see if I can find bolt cutters or something to cut it."

"You'll come back? Promise?" The boy was putting up a good front, but panic edged his plea.

"Yeah, I'm coming back."

There were no handy bolt cutters, but Seth found a cordless grinder, which, thankfully, still had a charge. At the cage again, he had Anthony step back.

"This will make a hellacious noise and kick out a bunch of sparks. If anyone's outside, they'll hear it."

"What do we do?"

"Pray like hell no one's outside."

Anthony moved back and Seth started the grinder. Ten seconds was all he needed. He didn't think the noise would carry into the house, but if someone was outside, they'd hear it. They were the longest ten seconds of his life. When the lock dropped to the floor, he threw down the grinder and pushed open the door, his gut urging him to get the hell out of there, fast. "Come on, kid. Give me your hand so we don't get separated."

He pulled Anthony to the door in the false wall. Seth didn't waste time wishing Dub had also stored ammunition so he could grab a weapon from the rack and even the odds a bit. He paused, listened, then stepped into the cavernous space. He kept the flashlight beam on the floor so they didn't trip and fall on their faces. They were making their way to the front when the outside door swung open and the lights flooded on. He pulled Anthony with him as he dove for cover behind the truck.

"Come on, Dub, leave the kid alone." Godzilla Pete's voice held a whine. "I'm flying high, I got a bag of Cheetos, I got a six-pack of beer. Let's go back to the house."

"Shut up, dumbshit. I heard something. We need to check it out."

"Stop calling me dumbshit. I hate when you call me names. That marshal was right. You're a bully."

"Goddam it, Pete. We got bigger problems than me calling you a dumbshit if that asshole marshal is in here. I wouldn't call you dumbshit if you didn't act like a dumbshit."

Crouched low, Seth glanced at Anthony, whose eyes were wide and scared. The voices were moving to the back of the garage. Seth had closed the door to the back, but that would only buy them seconds. Seth put a forefinger to his lips and jerked his head toward the now open outer door. His kept his voice barely above a whisper. "We're making a break for the door. Once we get out, we're running for the silver Civic parked under the tree. I snagged the keys." Anthony nodded his understanding. Voice low and urgent, Seth added, "If anything happens to me, you take off through the forest. There's another house a half mile up the river. Run as fast as you can, go there and ask for help. Got it?" Anthony nodded again. Seth took a careful look around, then, crouching low, moved past the utility trailer and the snowmobiles.

"God dammit, fucking son of a bitch." There was crashing that sounded like the door being slammed, then a clattering as metallic objects hit the concrete floor. "That asshole has the kid."

Seth was already streaking for the door, Anthony sticking to him like glue. A glance to the back showed Pete rampaging toward them like Godzilla through Tokyo, Dub right behind him. Seth took a split second to yank down a wire rack stacked with boxes, sending it crashing to the floor in hopes of slowing their pursuit. He and Anthony broke through the open doorway at the same time the crack of gunfire split the night. Bullets pierced the outer wall inches above their heads.

They raced to the Civic, visible from light streaming through the windows of the house. All Seth could think was he'd miscalculated and made a mistake that would cost both of them their lives. Keys in hand, he yanked open the door and grabbed Anthony, pushing him across the driver's seat as Seth fell in behind him. "Stay down!"

"Hold it right there," Vivian's sharp command was followed by another spate of gunfire. Windows on the Civic shattered and he felt a punch in the shoulder as he took precious seconds to find the ignition. He turned the key, and the engine came to life. He blinked furiously, trying to clear a sudden haze across his vision. Where was the gear selector?

"Holy shit, you're shot."

Anthony's voice echoed in his brain as Seth fought to clear his head. If he could find the gear selector, he'd get them out of there but his brain seemed to have slowed down to a crawl. The driver's door wrenched open and rough hands grabbed him. He was yanked out of the car and thrown to the ground. He heaved himself to his feet, squaring off with Dub, blinking desperately to clear his vision.

Dub was grinning, his inked face straight from a nightmare. His mouth was moving but Seth's ears were ringing and he couldn't make out the words. Pete came around the car and dropped Anthony in the dirt, shaking a bloody hand. Seth's vision was narrowing, but not so much that he didn't see RJ joining the circle, pearl-handled pistol in his grip. Eyes on his father, Seth braced himself for the kill shot, and never saw the sucker punch coming that dropped him into blackness.

\*\*\*

"Don't die, mister. Please, don't die." The words were whispered like a prayer.

Seth fought through what felt like layers of gauze wrapping his brain to reach consciousness, then wished he hadn't. A burning hot poker was stabbing him in his left shoulder, every breath he took hurt like a son of a bitch, and he was lying on his back on top of that hot poker. He blinked open his eyes to darkness. Someone groaned, and it took several seconds before he realized the sound came from him.

"Hey, are you going to die?"

Since dying was a very real possibility, he thought it better not to answer. "That you, kid?"

"Yeah. You got shot."

"Feels that way." Seth forced himself to breathe despite the pain. There was a temptation to abandon the fight and simply float away to a place where he wouldn't hurt. He'd fucked up, but he still had a kid to save. He licked his lips and wished desperately for water.

"You hit?" Seth was surprised he could articulate anything approaching speech. His tongue felt twice its normal size and his body felt like he'd been put through an industrial meat grinder.

"I'm okay, I guess. I wish we'd gotten away."

"Me too. What happened?"

"You got shot, and they got us. Dub came up with his gun pointed right at you and pulled you out of the car. I tried to run like you said but Pete grabbed me. I bit him. Then the old man came out and Dub hit you and when you were on the ground he pointed his gun right at your head and I thought he was going to shoot you. The old man stopped him and said for them to put us back in the cage."

"Shit."

"Is the old man really your dad? Someone said that. I thought you said you were a marshal. My dad says marshals protect judges. I thought that's why you were here, because my dad's a judge."

"I am a marshal." Seth coughed and tasted blood in his mouth. He heaved in a labored breath against the fresh wave of pain that lanced through him. It was a minute before he could talk again. "The old man is Richard Jameson. He's my dad, and he's a fugitive." Another labored breath. "I came for you, but to arrest him, too."

"That sucks."

"Yeah."

A muffled sound reached them from outside that Seth thought might be a vehicle door being slammed shut.

Anthony dropped his tone. "We have to stay quiet."

"Why?"

"Cruella said she'd kill both of us if we made a sound, no matter what the old man said. I think someone is coming, someone they don't want knowing that we're here."

Fogginess was creeping around the edges of Seth's brain again. "Cruella?"

"Yeah. I don't know her name. She's Dub's mom."

"Why Cruella?"

"Don't you watch movies?" Anthony leaned forward to whisper. *"One Hundred and One Dalmatians.* She captured the puppies to kill them for their fur. She's evil."

"Got it. Dub's mom is Vivian, but I like Cruella better." Seth tried to work some spit into his mouth. "You got any water?"

There was a rustling sound. "Here. Can you lift your head?"

He could, barely. Anthony held the bottle while Seth gulped.

"Thanks. We're in the cage?"

"Yeah. You passed out and been asleep for hours. When the old guy wouldn't let them shoot you, they grabbed us and put us back in here. They didn't have a lock, though, 'cause you cut the other one, so they used some wire and twisted it. I can't reach it, but I worked more staples out. I got the flashlight from your pocket. I got your pocketknife, too. That's how I was able to get a bunch of staples out more easily. I think I can pull the wire back enough now that I can get out. I was working on that when you started making moany noises a minute ago."

"I don't make moany noises."

"Yeah, you do. That's why I thought you were dying. But then you woke up."

"Where's the flashlight?"

The light came on, illuminating Anthony's face. He had dark circles under his eyes and looked exhausted. The bruises on his face weren't as vivid as they'd been on the photo.

"I've been saving the battery. It's dark in here, but I think it's morning."

Seth rolled to his side and pushed himself to a sitting position, the pain threatening to take him back under. He closed his eyes, not opening them until he thought the world would stop spinning and stay in one place.

"You gotta stay lying down. I folded the pillowcase and bunched the sleeping bag behind your shoulder, kind of like a pressure bandage, to stop the bleeding." A glance showed the sleeping bag stained dark with blood. "You might bleed to death if you get up."

"You've got a lot of words, kid."

"Dad says words are my superpower. He says everyone has a superpower. You have to listen to yourself to figure out what yours is." The earnestness in his voice reminded Seth Anthony was young. Too young to be in this fucked-up mess.

"They put a big-ass tarp over the cage. They're trying to hide us."

"You're fifteen. You shouldn't be swearing." Seth found focusing on Anthony's voice helped to distract him from the pain radiating from his shoulder. That he could mostly move his left arm gave him hope that he wasn't too badly injured.

"Give me a break. I'm in high school. Besides, I use swear words in situationally appropriate ways."

"Your mom buy that?"

"Since I'm situationally appropriate, she doesn't know I swear. I'm not a dumbass like Pete."

"Bet your mom knows more than you think."

"You met my mom?"

"Yeah, and your dad. They're working with my team."

"Will your team rescue us? Do they know where we are?"

"I hope so," he said to both questions.

Metal rattled. Seth recognized it as one of the garage doors rolling up. With a click and a buzz, overhead lights blazed on, casting the cage beneath the tarp in a bluish light.

"They're coming back," Anthony whispered furiously. He clicked off the flashlight and shoved it in a pocket. "I bet they're coming for more guns. Before they put up the tarp, Dub and Pete took some of the guns from back here. They were arguing about which ones the *bratva* would want, whoever that is."

"Russian mobsters."

The highs and lows of people talking carried from the garage, far enough away that he couldn't understand their meaning.

Pitching his voice low, Seth spoke. "Right now they're distracted. That opening in the wire you made, is it big enough for me to get through?"

Anthony shrugged. "I don't know. Maybe if you weren't shot and almost dead. You're moving kind of slow. Oh." His eyes lit up. "I found something on the floor when we were hiding behind that truck." He dug in his pocket.

Seth stared at what Anthony held in his hand. "Kid, you may have just given us the break we need. Let's move, but quietly."

Suddenly, a clear voice spoke, only feet away.

*"We require the ammunition. What is the use of weapons without ammunition?"* The speaker must have been on the other side of the wall. Made of corrugated metal and with no insulation, the words were clear.

Clear enough for Seth to recognize the voice.

*Alexei.*

# Chapter Eighteen

Alexei's Russian accent was exaggerated way past his normal speech. Seth frowned, fighting to block out the pain and keep his focus, to clear his head enough to think through the implications of Alexei's presence. Seth's team could have brought Alexei in and they were executing a plan to rescue him and Anthony. He hoped to god that was the case. The other possibility, one that Seth thought stretched credibility a bit too thin, was that Alexei was executing his undercover mission with the LAPD and had infiltrated the *bratva* and his appearance was a coincidence. What if Alexei had been playing Seth, had been playing his sister, and had, in fact, joined the Russian mob?

"Damn straight you want ammunition, and you'll get it. We're expecting another shipment and will be able to supply all the ammunition you could want, for any of the weapons we have. I can let you know as soon as it comes in." Dub spoke in a rush, sounding anxious and eager to please.

Moving carefully, Seth pulled himself to his feet, jaw clenched, a hand fisted into the wire cage to keep himself upright. He was making up his plan on the fly and prayed it would work. He pulled back the section of chicken wire Anthony had loosened, motioning him through.

Another Russian voice spoke, not a deep as Alexei's. Who the hell was that? Alexei responded, the volume of their exchange rising to a near shout. Seth's language lessons didn't help much.

"Doesn't he speak English?" Dub asked. "What's he saying?"

"My friend isn't impressed with what you've shown us so far. Your communication indicated more weapons than you have shown us. He thinks you've made us drive this distance for nothing."

Alexei's words were clipped with impatience. "You haven't met our requirements. There is another seller who wishes to do business with us. You are closer so we came here, but you must have what we want to buy."

More was said in Russian by the unknown speaker.

"What did he say?" Dub demanded.

"He says he wants to see more."

Alexei was being diplomatic because what the other person had said was the Russian equivalent of *fuck you*.

"We've shown you only a portion of our inventory. We've got more, believe me." With FD's desperate need for cash, Dub's ingratiating tone made it clear they didn't want to lose their chance to build a business relationship with the *bratva*.

"We require automatic weapons, specifically the M4. Ammunition is available on black market. The grenade launcher you showed us is M203. We prefer M320. It is more accurate. The ammo is the 40mm grenade. We require the grenades."

"What the fuck, man? You trying to start a war?"

Dead silence followed that comment.

"Shut up, Dub," Vivian snapped.

"Sorry, sorry. It's a joke, a bad joke." Dub stuttered through his apology. "But no worries, man, we got a couple M320s, and I can see if I can get more. They're in the backroom. Pete and I will bring them out for you."

"We will go in backroom with you," Alexei stated flatly. "We wish to see all you have."

"Ah, it's better if we bring them out."

"Why don't you folks come outside and I'll bring you all coffee and something to eat." Vivian probably thought her tone sounded cajoling, but it was obvious she was steering the Russians away from the backroom.

"We do not come to drink coffee. We come to see weapons. We will go in backroom."

Relief flooded through Seth with a wave of dizziness. That was the voice he most wanted to hear, and it told him this *bratva* was with his team. Whoever the unknown Russian was must be working with the task force. This was good, but there was still a wild card, and that was RJ.

As quickly and quietly as possible, he moved into position. Back pressed against the wall, he closed his eyes for a brief moment. This might work if he could manage to stay conscious and not fall flat on his face.

\*\*\*

Bella moved with the others through the door and took a moment to survey the storage room. Evidence of the Freedom Defenders' theft of military hardware was fully displayed on the racks in front of her. Besides weapons, body armor and communications equipment were haphazardly stored on various racks. A blue tarp in the far-right corner obscured a large, rectangular-shaped structure, which set her instincts humming. It could be hiding anything, but the top prospect was an enclosure designed for a kidnapped boy.

She breathed through her mouth and resisted the urge to lay a hand on her stomach. Her constant worry over Seth and Anthony had her in a persistent state of nausea-producing anxiety. At some point in the past week, she felt her objectivity as a US Marshal had been lost, and her personal and professional lives were on a collision course. She was probably developing an ulcer. The other possibility she couldn't ignore, but for now she had to push aside the personal in order to do her job.

That morning at first light, the local LEOs had sent up a drone, and with no one in sight, had been able to hover it low enough to get a visual on the white truck. It had dual rear tires, consistent with what RJ had been driving, and they'd gotten a shot of the license plate. Which led to verification it was registered to Richard Jameson.

Bella thought it reflected RJ's arrogance that despite being a fugitive, he hadn't used an alias or registered the vehicle to someone else. The team had taken the truck's presence as an indication that RJ was most likely at the compound. The image that had gutted her was Vivian's Civic with its windows blown out and bullet holes piercing the driver's side.

Bella had felt the floor drop from beneath her as she thought through the possibilities of how the car had come to be riddled with bullet holes. All those scenarios involved Seth being shot at. When she saw the images, it had been Linc's firm hold on her arm that had kept her upright. With a last look around the room, she pushed aside the turbulent emotions before they paralyzed her.

The bullet holes in Vivian's car had led to a sharp debate within the team as to whether evidence warranted immediately storming the compound. Ellie and Linc had overruled Bella and the decision was made to stay with the plan, which, if it worked, would get them inside the compound where they hoped to locate Seth and Anthony while minimizing the risk to all involved.

She returned her attention to Dub, who was shifting nervously from side to side, his gaze flitting between her and the two men she'd come in with. With the photo Seth had sent from the bar, she'd been able to identify Dub as Warren Robert Jacobs, age thirty-two, with an arrest record stretching back to his teenage years. He'd lived most of his life in the Reno area, and had served time for two convictions, one for misdemeanor assault, and the other for a third DUI conviction for which he'd been charged with a felony and had his driver's license revoked. There was currently a bench warrant for his arrest in Nevada for failure to appear.

"These are all the weapons you have?" Bella asked Dub.

"Like I said, you pay in cash and I'll get you whatever the hell you want. I got a guy on the inside who can get me anything I ask for."

Alexei took what she thought might be a grenade launcher from a shelf, turning it over in his hands, putting it to his shoulder. She felt like telling her brother to put the toy down and stop playing.

Frustration and disappointment intensified the queasiness in her stomach. She'd been sure Dub had balked at taking them into the backroom because that's where they were keeping Seth and Anthony hidden. But unless the two were under the tarp and unable to speak, she and the team were no closer to finding them.

Alexei returned the grenade launcher to the shelf. His military experience gave him all sorts of useful knowledge on weaponry he used to pepper Dub with questions. Bella used the cover of them talking to more carefully examine her surroundings.

The huge man they called Pete stood to one side, busily chewing on a fingernail with his silver-capped teeth, while Vivian Cochran watched from the doorway. The team's communication with FD had been with Vivian, who'd identified herself by her initials VC. Of those present, Bella thought Vivian the most unpredictable, and the biggest unknown. Like every other person in the room, she wore a gun holstered at her side.

Then there was the missing piece of the puzzle, Richard Jameson. They'd seen no sign of him since their arrival. The last thing they needed was RJ storming in, guns blazing. In all the years the Marshals had pursued him, he'd been hands-on in the Freedom Defenders organization, and she was surprised and worried about what his absence from the welcome party might mean.

Everything about the situation was wrong. Too many people in a small, enclosed space, with too many chances of getting caught in a crossfire.

If Anthony and Seth were under that tarp and somehow unable to communicate, they'd be in danger if there was any exchange of gunfire. In what she hoped was a casual move, she walked around the room, examining the weapons on the shelves, but also moving closer to where the edge of the tarp met the wall, looking for an opportunity to casually take a peek underneath.

A dark spot on the smooth concrete floor snagged her attention. She rubbed the tip of her boot over it and it left a dry, dark red smudge. Blood.

Holding her breath, she looked around. More spots were scattered on the floor near the blue tarp. Vivian stepped into the room to stand beside Dub. She too noticed the blood on the floor. Her gaze rose to lock on Bella's. Her hand moved to her side.

The half-open door swung closed. "Don't even think about drawing that gun."

Bella's heart catapulted into her throat as every person in the room turned toward the rough voice.

Seth stood behind the door, leaning back against the wall while holding a big military gun, his face pale and bruised, and his jaw clenched. The left side of his shirt was dark with dried blood, and he looked like he was staying upright through sheer force of will. Only Bella's training kept her from dropping to her knees.

"What the fuck?" Dub's hand hovered over the gun holstered at his waist. Gaze riveted on Seth, he said, "Don't worry, I'll take care of this guy."

"What's going on?" Bella moved forward, brow furrowed, trying to look the part of a buyer of illegal guns upset by the turn in events. "Who is this man?"

A sneer distorted the tattooed patterns on Dub's cheeks. He ignored her, instead speaking to Seth. "That gun's one of mine, asshole. There was a reason we moved any ammo stored back here. That magazine is empty. You're bluffing."

"Want me to test that theory?" The strain in Seth's voice worried her.

She spoke, exaggerating her accent, "What is this about? Perhaps we take our business elsewhere."

"This better not be a double cross," Alexei added.

"Don't worry, we'll take care of him," Vivian snapped. "Dub, you sure his rifle isn't loaded?"

"There was no ammo stored back here for any of the guns. The fucker's holding an M4 carbine, and like a dumbass, Pete used the last of the M-four ammo on target practice."

Seth aimed the muzzle to the ceiling, squeezed off a shot, the loud, sharp report echoing in the small room, and then he leveled the gun on Dub. That got their attention. With the Freedom Defenders all focused on Seth, Bella caught Alexei's gaze. He gave a slight nod, then moving like they'd practiced choreographing it, they drew their weapons. Alexei aimed at Pete, and Bella leveled her Glock on Vivian. Sasha did as previously instructed, and stayed out of the way.

"US Marshals," Bella identified herself. "You are all under arrest. Hands behind your heads and get down on your knees."

For one long moment, no one moved, then Pete dropped to his knees with a heavy grunt, his hands already laced behind his head. With quick efficiency, Alexei pulled zip cuffs from a pocket and restrained the big man.

"You fucking coward," Dub snarled at Pete. He pivoted and lunged toward Seth, who moved to the side, swinging the butt of the M4 and catching Dub square on the side of the head.

Dub crumpled to the floor while Bella, holding her aim steady, repeated, "On your knees, Vivian. I can assure you that my weapon is loaded, and it's aimed at your head." Indecision warred on Vivian's face. Nudging her to make the right choice, Bella said, "There's no way out of this. You're done. Put your hands behind your head and get down on your knees."

The fight seemed to seep out of Vivian, and she did as directed. Only when she and Dub were both cuffed did Bella turn back to Seth. He was gone. "Where'd he go? Where's Seth?"

"He left a minute ago."

The voice came from the corner of the room. The blue tarp had been pushed aside and Anthony Rebollar stood outside a cage made of twisted wire. Relief at seeing Anthony warred with fear for Seth. Bella crossed the room.

She couldn't help her smile as she examined the kid's pinched face. "Anthony, it's really good to see you. I'm US Marshal Bella Nikolaev." She extended her hand to shake, but Anthony launched himself at her, his arms going around her in a hug. She held him tight, savoring the moment. She dipped her head to whisper, "Your mom and dad will be so happy you're safe. Serena, too."

He stepped back, wiping his eyes on a grimy sleeve. "Thank you for coming for me. But you have to find Seth, he was shot and he's hurt bad. I thought he was going to die."

Bella nodded. "You stay here." She turned to her brother. "You and Sasha stay with the prisoners and keep Anthony safe. I'm going after Seth." She took a quick second to text Linc and Ellie. They were standing by with the rest of the task force, close enough to arrive in minutes. She wished the ambulance that was standing by could be brought in, but it was still too dangerous.

Drawing her weapon, she headed for the door.

\*\*\*

Bella stepped into the cavernous garage, bright sunlight streaming through the rolled-up door. The side door was also open, and as she crossed the floor, she spotted what she'd missed before. More drops of dried blood spotted the floor. Worry was a greasy knot sitting heavily in her stomach. Dub and the others must have brought in Seth wounded, probably during the night.

Seth needed to get to a hospital, but she was certain he was going after RJ. As cool and rational as he could be, over the past weeks she'd learned that not revealing his emotions didn't mean he didn't feel them. They were locked down tight, but sometimes locks failed. She was afraid of what would happen when he confronted his father.

Above the door, the metal siding had holes pushed out from the inside. Someone had fired shots from inside the garage. Bella cautiously peered through the doorway to survey the scene.

A hot summer sun in a sky of deep blue warmed her skin, and she breathed in the earthy aroma of sunbaked grass. Sharp male voices drew her attention to the front of the house where the huge pine tree cast its shade. Weapon drawn, she trotted across the open area, using the big white truck for cover. The bullet-riddled Civic sat like a wounded warrior a few feet away. An older Suburban was parked beside it.

Crouching behind the truck, she heard a voice she identified as RJ's.

"You going to shoot your old man, boy?"

"Not sure yet. You going to pull the trigger on your son?"

Seth's speech was slow and deliberate. That more than anything had the greasy ball in her stomach swelling. Swallowing hard, she peered through the windows of the cab.

Seth's back was to her, his shirt darkened with blood. He had to be suffering from blood loss, and every minute he wasn't being cared for increased the chance of infection. Nothing mattered to her as much as getting him medical treatment.

As bad as Seth's condition was, the standoff in front of her was equally alarming. Seth stood with legs braced and his rifle aimed squarely at RJ's chest. RJ gripped a pistol pointed at Seth's heart. One twitch of a finger by either one of them could result in death.

The roar of an approaching vehicle eased Bella's fear a fraction. She dropped behind the front tire, her phone in her hand. Linc picked up at the first ring. "Seth and RJ are in front of the house, under the tree, weapons drawn. Park by the garage, prisoners are detained inside. Anthony is safe. I'm currently taking cover behind the white truck."

Bella raised her head to look through the side windows of the cab of the truck in time to see RJ slide his thumb and release the safety on his pistol, extending his arm like he was preparing to fire, the gun wavering slightly.

Bracing her arms on the hood of the truck, she took aim at RJ. "Richard Jameson, drop your weapon."

He ignored her, his gaze never wavering from his son. "Walk away, Seth. I don't want to shoot you, but I will if I have to. I haven't survived this long to give up without a fight."

Bella glanced over her shoulder when a big SUV pulled up the driveway, coming to a stop by the garage. Members of the task force exited the vehicle, most of them filing into the garage.

Linc and Ellie raced across the exposed space to join her, both wearing black polo shirts with the US Marshals star insignia.

"Got a plan?" Crouched next to her, Linc peered over the hood, Ellie on his other side.

"Not yet." They kept their voices barely above a whisper.

"Seth's not looking so good," Linc muttered. "He's not doing this alone."

"I'm with you on that," Ellie agreed.

"Then we'll all go," Bella said.

Together they stepped around the truck and moved to flank Seth, Linc on his left, Ellie on his right, Bella next to Ellie. All had their weapons drawn but pointed down. US Marshal protocols had been thrown out the window.

A layer of RJ's belligerence withered as he surveyed his adult children, united to confront him. He made no move to lower his gun.

"We're not going to shoot you." Seth sounded like he was speaking through clenched teeth. Bella didn't know how much longer his iron will could keep him from collapsing. "Richard Jameson, you're under arrest. We're taking you into custody to face justice for the crimes you have committed."

RJ's expression was grim, his face haggard. Despite that, it was jarring to realize how much Seth resembled his father.

"No way in hell you're arresting me. What I did, I did for our country, for what's right."

"It'll be up to a jury to decide if that's a credible defense. That's how it works, Dad." RJ flinched and Seth continued, enunciating each word carefully, his voice raw in a rare display of emotion. "We are a nation of laws. Individuals don't get to decide which laws they choose to follow. There are consequences for the ones you break, and it's time you faced those consequences."

Linc and Ellie stood with Seth in a unified wall, supporting each other as Bella knew they had since their father had abandoned them. She didn't discount her role but understood the importance in having the Jameson siblings confront their father together. Tension whipped between them and she wouldn't have been surprised to see sparks flying.

Then Seth crouched and laid his gun on the ground at his feet. Linc grabbed his arm when he swayed. After a slight hesitation, Linc and Ellie followed their brother's lead and set down their weapons. Putting her faith in Seth, Bella knelt to place her Glock in the dirt.

"If you shoot Seth, you'll have to shoot all of us," Linc said.

"Are you going to kill all three of your children?" Ellie asked. "Because that's your only way out. Would you do that to us? Would you do that to Mom?"

Something like panic flashed across RJ's face. "Let me go." Fear edged his voice. "You kids don't know what you're doing. Let me go," he repeated. "Let me go and walk away like nothing happened." RJ's gaze traveled over his children, his expression turning to regret and resignation.

"We're not letting you go. You're under arrest," Linc said.

"Put the gun down and put your hands behind your head," Ellie ordered.

The Jameson siblings were forcing their father to choose between their survival and his, and were counting on some remnant of love for his children to lead him to make the right choice. Bella didn't believe RJ had it in him to do that.

He blinked slowly, then nodded. He took a deep breath, released it, and bent his arm, arcing the gun toward his head.

"No!" Ellie lunged forward, but Linc beat her to him, taking their father down in a flying tackle. Linc's weight held him down and Ellie grabbed the hand holding the gun, forcing it into the dirt, and then disarming her father.

His children bringing Richard Jameson down and putting him under arrest would set them well on the way to the justice they were searching for.

"You should have let me do it. It would have been better for everyone." All RJ's vitality had leached out, and he looked like what he was, a defeated old man lying in the dirt.

"Shoot yourself in the head?" Linc spat out. "We're not letting you take the easy way out. Seth's right, you need to be held accountable for what you've done."

Linc rolled RJ over and searched him while Ellie pulled handcuffs from her back pocket and secured them around her father's wrists.

Seth coughed and swayed. Bella rushed to his side in time to catch him before he went down like a felled tree. She staggered under his weight, lowering herself until she sat with his head in her lap.

"Get that ambulance here now," Ellie snapped into her phone.

Bella leaned over, one hand fisted in Seth's hair, the other against his cheek, her face bent close to his. Tears blurred her vision. "Don't you dare die, Seth Jameson. I love you. You have to hang on for us." She murmured the words without thought, willing him to fight to stay alive.

He closed his eyes and she pressed her lips to his forehead, realizing every hope she had for the future was wrapped up with this man.

The wail of the ambulance echoed through the trees. Minutes later two big SUVs followed by an ambulance raced into the parking area, lights circling. Linc waved the EMTs over. The paramedics weren't able to rouse Seth.

She told them he'd been shot probably the night before. They worked swiftly and efficiently and in minutes had him on the gurney and were pushing him into the back of the ambulance.

Bella rushed forward. "I'm going with him." The paramedic nodded, and she climbed into the back of the ambulance, holding on tight to hope as the ambulance rocked and swayed on their way to the highway.

# Chapter Nineteen

Bella shifted in the vinyl seat, trying to find a comfortable position. Exhausted as she was, she couldn't sleep sitting up. Ellie had brought her a thick cardigan, and she pulled it closer around her. Linc and Ellie had both wanted to stay with Seth, but work demanded their attention, so once they were confident he was through the worst of it, they'd left the hospital.

The team was still combing through the compound for evidence and processing the individuals they'd arrested. An hour before, she'd texted them an update on Seth, telling them he was resting and they should go back to the hotel and get some sleep.

Bella sighed. She could admit her restlessness was partly due to feeling overwhelmed, which she hated, and knowing major developments in her life were outside of her control.

She felt overwhelmed with love for Seth, with fear over his medical condition, and with the growing certainty she was pregnant. Becoming a mother would have a huge impact on her life, and she needed to prepare. But as important as all that was, the most urgent issue was Seth's recovery.

The lights had been dimmed for night. The nurses who came in and out of the room hardly made any noise with their soft-soled shoes. The antiseptic smell reminded Bella of the strong disinfectant used at the orphanage. It'd permeated her clothes. Funny how smells could evoke such strong memories.

The monitors attached to Seth by a myriad of wires and tubes hummed quietly.

She stood to see him better. His face was a pale shadow in the darkness. She'd listened with Linc and Ellie as the doctor had explained that Seth's blood loss was his most critical issue, and they'd treat the problem with fluids and medications. Linc had offered an artery if Seth needed blood. The doctor had said he'd keep that in mind, and the local blood bank would appreciate any donations.

Bella took the blanket from the chair and arranged it over Seth's legs. He was so strong, and had such a forceful personality, it frightened her to her core to see him lying in a hospital bed. She tucked the blanket around him, stopping when she glanced up and saw his eyes open, his dark gaze fixed on her.

She gripped his hand. "How are you feeling? Are you in pain?"

He tried to speak, cleared his throat, then tried again. "Not sure. Kind of floating."

"You will be for a while. They gave you some of what Markel called the double good juice after your surgery." She swallowed against the tightness in her throat.

Seth's thumb rubbed over the back of her hand. "Surgery?"

"Yes. To take out the bullet and repair the damage it caused. You're probably going to need some physical therapy. You also had a partially collapsed lung." Sitting in the ambulance, she'd watched the paramedics roll Seth on his side and cut away his shirt, revealing the ugly bullet wound under his shoulder blade that had scared her like nothing ever had.

"Anthony?"

"He's fine, and ecstatic to be back with his family. He wants to come see you in the morning."

Seth nodded and she thought he was struggling to stay awake. Eyes closed, he said, "Coming in as the *bratva* was genius," he mumbled. "Tell me how that happened."

"I talked it over with Alexei, and he called Sasha. Sasha got us onto the dark web where Vivian had advertised the stolen weapons. I'm hoping to convince him to leave the *bratva*." Seth's thumb had stopped rubbing over her hand and his breathing was deeper. She leaned over and pressed her lips to his forehead.

***

Seth woke to his sister and brother talking nearby in low voices. He looked for Bella but didn't see her.

"Hey, you're awake. Let's get some light in here." Ellie pulled open the curtains and had Seth blinking at the wash of sunlight. She moved to the side of the bed. "Hey, big brother." Her words sounded light, but Seth could read his sister. She was worried about him.

Seth pressed the button to bring up the head of the bed. He had an IV in one arm being fed by a bag on a pole and his other arm hooked up to some other monitor. Tamping down on frustration over being virtually tied down, he growled, "When can I get out of here?"

Linc joined Ellie. "Not until you're a hundred percent out of the woods. You lost a lot of blood, in addition to having a bullet go through your lung."

"It went through a bit of your lung," Ellie corrected. "The doctor said it could have been worse. He also said you need to increase your fluids. We talked to Mom and Arch. Once you're released, they want you to recuperate at their house."

Seth understood his mom enough to know she wouldn't rest easy until she could see for herself that he was going to live. "I'll talk to her." Ellie held up a plastic cup with a straw and he drank the water gratefully. "Where's Bella?"

The door opened, and his question was left unanswered. Anthony Rebollar came in, followed by his parents. A grin split Anthony's face as he caught sight of Seth. Maria carried a pink bakery box, and Carlos an insulated bag in one hand and a stack of cups in the other.

"Hey, Seth, guess what? I was on the news."

Ellie and Linc stepped back to give the family room around the bed.

Maria placed a hand on her son's shoulder like she didn't want to be too far away from him. Seth guessed it would be a while before she allowed Anthony out of her sight. "We brought coffee and pastries. Would you like coffee, Seth?"

"God, yes."

She pulled a coffee dispenser from the bag and twisted off the spout. She poured the hot liquid into a cup and the rich aroma filled the room. He declined sugar or cream, and Maria topped the cup with a lid and handed it to him.

"Thank you." Seth gratefully took the to-go cup from her. He eyed Anthony. "The news, huh? Did they make you look good?"

"Serena said I looked hot, so yeah they did. The reporter asked about you. I didn't tell them your name or anything, but I told them you were a badass."

"Anthony," his mother exclaimed.

Seth felt the corner of his mouth turn up. Anthony's good nature was contagious. "This is situationally appropriate?"

Anthony gave his mom a sidelong look. "Maybe not." He reached into a pocket, then held out his hand with Seth's pocketknife in the palm. "Here's your knife back. It's good you had it."

"It's good you thought to use it to get out of that cage. That took brains, and that took courage. You did good, kid. Keep the knife, it's yours now."

Anthony's eyes lit up. "Really, I can keep it? That's awesome. Thanks." Anthony looked down, turning the knife over in his hand. When he spoke again, his tone was subdued. "I'm glad Dub and Cruella, and all them were arrested, but I'm sorry your dad was one of them."

"Yeah, me too." Seth motioned to Linc and Ellie. "These marshals are my sister and brother. You met Bella, she's on our team too. Richard Jameson is our father, but he made bad choices and broke the law. We did our job and arrested him before he caused any more harm."

"Like kidnapping me."

"Yes, like kidnapping you."

Anthony nodded, and Judge Rebollar spoke quietly. "We want to thank you," he nodded to include Ellie and Linc in his statement, "to thank all of you and the rest of your team for rescuing our son. We are in your debt."

Seth shook his head. "We may have helped, but I couldn't have done it without your son's help." He looked at Anthony. "You tell your parents about the stripper clip?"

"The bullets? I told them I found the bullets on the floor near that truck when we were trying to get away. I didn't know it was called a stripper clip."

"He found it in our failed escape attempt," Seth told Carlos and Maria. "There were three bullets still in the clip that I loaded into an M4 carbine. Luckily, I only needed to use one. Anthony picking up those bullets and prying loose the staples so we could get out of the cage were crucial to both of us getting out of there alive."

"It's good to know my son uses his head when it's important he do so." Carlos brought Anthony close to his side. "We don't mean to tire you, Marshal, but wanted to express our gratitude. If there is ever anything that I can do for you, do not hesitate to ask."

The door closed behind the Rebollar family, and Seth thought they took all the energy from the room with them. He suddenly felt exhausted.

Ellie smiled at Seth. "Nice gesture. Anthony is going to treasure that knife forever."

"It's one Arch gave me. Seemed appropriate." He paused, then repeated, "Where's Bella?"

"She was here until after midnight, then left first thing this morning." Linc opened the lid on the bakery box, picking out a glazed donut.

Seth scowled. "What for?"

"Montrose called her back. That guy her and Alexei knew in Russia, the one she calls Sasha? He helped us convince Vivian and Dub they were part of the *bratva*." That explained the third Russian speaker in the garage.

Linc held the open bakery box in front of Seth. He selected a maple bar and took a bite, chewing thoughtfully. "Okay, so?"

"Sasha wants out of the *bratva* and is willing to talk. Looks like the marshals could be setting up witness protection for him, at least for the short term."

"Why does that mean Bella has to go back to LA?" Damn it, he had things he wanted to say to her.

"Couple reasons. RJ will be questioned in LA, and, reasonably, Montrose didn't want RJ's kids escorting him, so that fell to Bella. Since she knows Sasha, Montrose said they're assigning her as part of his protection, at least for the time being."

Linc's words fell like lead weights.

"She's being pulled from our team." Seth knew it was more than that. Richard Jameson had been arrested and the Freedom Defenders dealt a devastating blow. The team had accomplished its goal and would be disbanded. He'd known the time would come, but that didn't mean he had to like it. "Guess they're breaking up the band," he muttered.

Linc nodded. "Feels like. But I'll be glad to stay close to home for a while. I miss my wife."

"I'm missing Sam, too. But don't worry, big brother. Our summer plans are coming together. Mikayla and I talked last night. We've decided to invite you guys to our cabin, so after you're done climbing mountains and getting all stinky and mosquito bitten, you can join us at the cabin for an extra week."

"I'm in if Bella's there."

There was a moment of silence, then Linc said, "Well, finally, bro. I thought you'd never make a move."

"How the mighty have fallen." Ellie smirked. "I'm glad, Seth. But if Bella takes the assignment to provide witness protection for the Russian guy, she may not be able to come."

Seth frowned. They'd see about that.

"Isn't she coming to the family Fourth of July get-together?" Ellie asked. "Mom will be thrilled you two are finally together."

"Nothing's for sure. I need to talk to her."

Ellie gave him a peck on the cheek. "My money's on you, big brother."

"Thanks."

The need to see Bella was a bone-deep craving. If Seth could get out of the hospital, he'd have a chance to make the move he wanted, a move that would bind his future with Bella's.

He prayed to god that she wanted that future with him.

# Chapter Twenty

Seth spotted a gap between two cars and pulled a U-turn, maneuvering into the tight fit. He stepped out of the vehicle into heat in the high eighties at only eight o'clock in the morning. He pulled at his shirt where sweat had it stuck to his back. His injured shoulder meant he'd forgone his preferred shoulder holster in favor of wearing his gun on his hip, a gun Linc had recovered from Vivian's house and made sure was returned to him.

He climbed the stairs to the second story, figuring being only partially winded was a good sign after having been shot all of three days before. He rapped on the door to 2D and was seriously pissed when it was opened by another Viking. He recognized him as being part of the *bratva* group at the Freedom Defender compound.

Sasha wasn't Thor-big like Alexei, but still had a look about him that said he'd seen trouble and could deal with it in whatever form it took.

"You're the marshal." His accent was thicker than Bella's or Alexei's.

"One of them. Seth Jameson. Bella here?"

The Viking gave him an assessing look, then stepped back. "Come in. I'm Sasha."

"Figured as much." Seth stepped into Bella's apartment to find Alexei sitting on the couch, an open laptop on the coffee table in front of him. He rose to his feet and grasped Seth's hand in a firm shake, running his gaze over him in an assessing look.

"You look like hell, man. Surprised they let you out of the hospital."

"I talked the doc into releasing me a little ahead of schedule." Seth did his own assessment. "Your face isn't as messed up as it was."

"I'm recovered. Your face is still messed up. You want coffee? It's Bella's freeze-dried shit, but better than nothing."

Seth banked his impatience. "Sure. Where is she?"

"Hey, did you hear I passed my background check and got an interview with the FBI?"

Seth ground his teeth. "Congratulations. Now where is she?"

"I'll put the water on."

Realizing Alexei would take whatever time he wanted, Seth followed him into the kitchen. Alexei filled the kettle with water and set the flame on the stove. He faced Seth, leaning back against the counter. The fucker was enjoying making Seth wait. Sasha took a seat at the table, arms crossed in front of him. He made a comment in Russian. Whatever Alexei said in response brought a scowl to the other man's face.

Alexei raised a brow and locked his gaze on Seth. "Now we talk. My sister is the most important to me. I won't let her be with a man who is not good."

"She won't thank you for interfering."

"Too bad. You will treat Bella well."

Since he also had a sister, Seth answered, "Yes, I'll treat her well."

"You will marry my sister?"

"Is she pregnant?"

A movement at the door caught his attention. In denim shorts that showed off long, toned legs and a bright yellow t-shirt, her hair a damp curling mass, Bella looked like a ray of sunshine. But hurt flashed across her face before shutters closed off her expression. *Shit.*

"I need to talk with Bella," he told Alexei. "Alone."

Not meeting his gaze, she turned to the other men. "He's right. Seth and I need to talk. You two go."

Sasha spoke in Russian, and Bella shook her head. Alexei took the opportunity to utter a low growl, "You hurt her, I'll kick your ass."

Seth nodded. "I won't stop you."

Alexei gave a curt nod, then motioned to Sasha. "Come on. There's a good coffee shop not far from here where they sell beignets. That's what I want this morning."

Bella followed them to the door, shutting it behind them and turning the lock. She faced Seth and crossed her arms in front of her. "I'm guessing you want to know how the questioning of your father and the others went. I filed my preliminary report yesterday, but we're not done. Vivian and her son are using the same lawyer, and he's not letting them say anything. The defendant Peter Hoyer is seeking a plea deal. He has a lot of information that will be useful building a case against the others so I think the prosecutor will accept the plea."

Bella's attention was focused someplace over his right shoulder. When Seth stepped forward, she retreated into the kitchen.

"That's not why I'm here. I want to talk about you and me." The last twenty-four hours had seen one frustration piled on top of another.

Feeling well enough, he'd gotten the doctor to agree to release him from the hospital at midday on Friday. Linc and Ellie had been busy analyzing preliminary data from Vivian Cochran's laptop, and since Seth's phone was being considered evidence and he couldn't use it, he hadn't been able to call either of them or Bella.

When he'd finally tracked down his sister and got Bella's number—he didn't have it memorized—the call had gone straight to voicemail. He'd decided what he had to say to her should be said in person, but he'd needed to hear her voice and felt unsettled when he hadn't.

The kettle whistled and Bella turned off the burner. She opened the cupboard and reached for a mug, her hand shaking.

"Bella, look at me."

"It's better I don't. I…um…" She paused, taking a deep breath before pressing on. "I'm pregnant." She retrieved the carton with the packets of freeze-dried coffee, busily opening it. "I took a pregnancy test this morning, but I've been so nauseous lately, I already knew. We'll probably need a lawyer to, you know, work out a custody arrangement."

He let her words sink in and warmth fill him. He was going to be a father, a dad. He'd do a damned sight better job than RJ had done. Seth had kept his emotions locked away for so long it was hard to bare his soul. Harder than staring into the muzzle of a gun pointed at his head. But he was all in. He wanted a future with her and his child, and that meant he'd offer her his heart on a platter if that's what it took.

"Bella, look at me," he repeated.

She fumbled the carton and the packets spilled across the floor. She backed away from him, shaking her head, hands clenched at her side. "My brother is being protective, but I don't need you to marry me. Your obligation is to our child, not to me. I don't need you." The words were like an arrow to his heart. "You should go now. We've got months before we have to worry about the custody arrangements. I think it would be best for the baby if he or she stays with me for the first several months."

He grabbed her hands when she would have knelt to gather the packets. "You may not need me, but I need you." He used his thumb to open her fingers and pressed her palms flat against his chest. She tipped her face forward, but not before he saw her blinking back tears.

"Jesus, Bella. Don't cry." Taking a leap of faith, he said quietly, "Do you feel my heart beating? It beats for you. I'm in love with you."

She brought up her head and finally met his gaze. The storm of emotion in her eyes gave him hope he'd finally succeeded in breaking through the barriers they'd used to protect themselves.

She remained quiet, and he spoke again. "You said you loved me. You told me not to die and to hang on for us. I didn't die and I hung on. For us, Bella. For all three of us."

"I didn't think you heard me."

"I heard you. It gave me hope."

Suddenly she was in his arms. He pulled her to him, ignoring the dull pain from his injury, his eyes closed as he breathed her in like oxygen. Seth released a shaky breath as it sank in—what he wanted most in the world was within his grasp.

Holding her with one arm, he reached into his pocket and pulled out a small box. He watched her face as he thumbed open the lid. Her gaze was fixed on the diamond solitaire.

"Oh my god. It's beautiful."

"Will you marry me, Bella? Will you be mine forever?"

Her blue eyes were depthless when she lifted her head, her smile dazzling. She nodded her head vigorously. "Yes, Seth. I will marry you."

She held out her left hand steady as he slipped the ring on her finger. "It fits with a traditional Russian interlocking set. I thought maybe you'd like that, but we can change it if you want something different." He met her gaze. "What's important is that you said yes."

She threw her arms around him, her mouth against his neck as she spoke.

He cradled her head, brushing away her tears. "You want to say that again?"

"I love you. I love the ring, and I love you."

Every barrier between them was washed away as their lips met. He felt his heart finally breaking free of the chains that had held him back for so long and kept him from fully feeling. Her tongue tangled with his as the kiss deepened and turned hungry. He ran his hands over her hips then under her t-shirt.

"Mm," she hummed against his lips. "Are we going to get naked, Marshal Jameson?"

He pulled back enough to see her provocative grin. "You bet, Marshal Nikolaev. As often as we can."

He moved his hands from her back to her supple breasts, and she gasped when he brushed a thumb under the lacy edge of her bra to find her nipple already tight. Her fingers worked the buttons of his shirt, then eased it over his shoulders, letting it drop to the floor.

Her touch was feather light over the fading bruises on his ribs. "What happened here?"

He shrugged. "Not sure. I think it's a boot print. My guess is either Dub or Pete kicked me when I was unconscious."

"You were knocked unconscious when they hit you here." She brushed his hair back from his forehead.

"Yeah. Gave me a concussion. I need to take it easy for a few days, let my brain rest."

Nodding her head, she said, "I want to see your shoulder, turn around."

"All you can see is the bandage." She twirled her finger and he turned.

He felt her whisper-light touch as she traced the edge of the bandage and thought he could die a happy man if she just kept touching him.

"How's the pain?"

"Better. I'm not supposed to pick anything up or overexert myself for the next couple weeks, but all in all, I'm grateful it wasn't any worse." He turned to face her again.

"You have the most incredible body," she murmured as she ran her hands over his abs.

"If I wasn't shot in the shoulder, I'd lift you up onto the counter so I don't need to bend down to kiss you."

"If you Jameson boys weren't so tall you wouldn't have to bend down." Bella boosted herself onto the counter. He moved between her legs, cupping her face as he kissed her, rubbing his growing erection against the hot center of her. She splayed her hands over his chest, making a sound in her throat that he could only describe as purring.

Even with his lips busily moving over her neck, he fought for restraint, trying to slow down. She wasn't helping because she unbuttoned the fly of his Levi's and slipped her hand inside. He nearly lost his mind when she closed her fingers around his erection, which had been growing more insistent from the moment she'd walked into the living room. She stroked him with strong and silky movements that felt like heaven, and nearly undid him.

He caught her mouth in a fierce kiss and grabbed her hand before she sent him over the edge. "I want you in bed."

She scooted off the counter and took his hand to lead him out of the kitchen. By the time they got to her bedroom he was so hard and ready it took every ounce of control he possessed not to rip off their clothes and let madness guide him as he plunged in.

Their first time together he'd felt like a stallion racing to the finish line. This time he wanted to savor her, to make it a promise of what was to come.

He nudged her to sit on the edge of the bed, moving back when she would have reached again for the open fly of his jeans. "We're doing this my way, and my way is getting you naked first." He tugged her shirt over her head. Bending over her, he murmured, "There's no rush. Let's take it slow and easy so we don't miss any steps."

He knelt in front of her, unsnapping her shorts, and she stood so he could draw them down her legs. The tiny little scrap she wore for underwear followed. She sat and he reached behind her to unclip her bra and groaned in appreciation as her breasts spilled free.

Her breath hitched when he pressed kisses to her breasts, to her hip bone, to the dark triangle of hair.

"We won't miss steps," she breathed.

"No, we won't, because this time I'm taking care."

He began to show her exactly what he meant, and pulled down the bedcovers to lay her against the pillows. Mindful of his injury, he

690

braced himself with his right arm to brush the hair back from her face, then used the tip of his finger to trace her lips.

"Have I told you how incredibly beautiful you are? How every time I see you, I catch my breath?" She stared at him as if mesmerized, slowly shaking her head. He kissed her because he couldn't help himself, then murmured, "See? That's a step I missed, because you are so beautiful. Do you remember when we were first introduced?" He spoke quietly. "You were the rookie, the new team member, and I was your boss. You were so off limits." He kissed her temple, under her ear, moving over her collarbone to the swell of her breast, taking in the scent of her with each breath. "I couldn't stop thinking about you, couldn't stop wanting you." Then his gaze snared hers. "Did you think of me, Bella? Did you wonder then how it might be between us?"

***

Bella felt like her mind was moving slowly, mired down by the overwhelming onslaught of sensations Seth was raining down on her. Every place he touched responded with a surge of heat that spread across her body, igniting fires, arcing from one kiss or caress to the next until she thought she would combust and go up in flames.

"I did. I wondered how it would be between us."

"You know what was driving me insane? That we couldn't be within ten feet of one another without generating sparks." He nuzzled between her breasts, his tongue laving the tender skin and setting it tingling. He continued to speak in that low, rumbly voice, which set her close to orgasm. "Every time we argued, all I could think was it was foreplay. If we ever were together, our minds would be blown. Then we were together and it happened, you blew my mind."

She caught his face in her hands and waited until his gaze met hers. "I fell in love with you so hard and so fast, it scared me. Especially when you acted so irritated with me half the time. You treated me like I was a big pain in the ass, and I was so confused I didn't know how to act." She pressed a kiss to his lips. "I've been in love with you all that time. It's always been you."

He turned his head and kissed her palm. "I fought it hard, trying to do what I thought was right. But no more. You're mine."

She said the words back to him. "And you are mine."

His hands stroked across her hips, the backs of her thighs, smooth and sensual, until finally, finally he had her releasing a pent-up sigh when he reached the sensitive folds of her labia.

He kissed her long and deep, using his fingers to build her response, working her to a heightened state of arousal. He pushed off the bed to shuck his jeans, then paused, gaze locked on hers in the dim light coming through the curtained windows.

"I have a condom, but there's that horse and barn door situation again. I was tested before I met you and am disease free."

She frowned at his phrasing. "I am as well."

He returned to the bed, whispering in her ear, "I haven't been with anyone since I met you."

She closed her eyes. "God, Seth, what took us so long? I couldn't be with anyone else either. The only person I wanted to be with was you."

She felt him shaking his head, and instead of speaking, he returned his attention to building her up to the point where she was shaking.

He wouldn't let her touch him, instead focusing on bringing her ever closer to the brink of release. She felt she would lose her mind and was panting his name when he finally, finally pushed into her, thrusting forward, filling her. He held still for a long moment as they both savored the feeling.

Wanting more, she put her hands on his buttocks and tilted her hips to bring him in deeper. With a throaty groan he began moving in long, hard strokes. The sensation of finally being fully together, mentally and physically, intensified her arousal.

Together they found a rhythm that built in intensity, growing, swelling to a final crest. She came with a keening cry, and he thrust twice more before following her over the edge of oblivion.

Panting, he collapsed over her, his face in the crook of her neck until his breathing evened out. He rolled, pulling her into his right side.

"Is your shoulder sore?"

"It's fine." He stroked her side, long sweeps of his hand from her shoulders to her rear. He stilled for a moment, and her mind flitted to the last time they had been like this and how her heart had been soaring before crashing with those fateful words, *That should never have happened.*

"Seth?" She hated the quaver in her voice. She propped herself on an elbow to see his face.

He reached up and ran his thumb between her brows. "Do you know you get a V here when you're worried? What are you worried about?"

She shook her head. "Nothing."

"It's not nothing if it worries you." He paused, then his own brows furrowed. "Are you thinking about the last time we were together?"

"It doesn't matter."

"It does matter. I hurt you, and I'm sorry." He lifted his head from the pillow to kiss her. "It might take time for you to completely trust me, but know this, Bella, I'm committed. I want you. I want our baby." He took her hand, lacing their fingers together, rubbing his thumb over her engagement ring.

She let the last of the walls she'd carefully erected around her heart fall away, and pulled his words around her like a security blanket.

"I trust you, Seth, and I love you."

# Epilogue

Seth relaxed with Bella's head tilted on his shoulder, their fingers laced together as they sat on a cushioned wicker loveseat on his parents' deck. They'd eaten until they were stuffed, and then eaten even more when Arch had proclaimed the homemade ice cream was done, so they'd polished off the Fourth of July barbecue with fresh berries and ice cream. Then Seth had asked for everyone's attention, and he and Bella had announced their engagement. They endured some ribbing with a lot of *what took you so long?* and *we knew you two were hot for each other* comments. Alexei had slapped Seth on his non-injured shoulder in congratulations. Margaret had kissed both him and Bella, tears shining in her eyes, while Arch had engulfed them all in a group hug.

"This will be so exciting." Margaret had taken Bella's hand to examine the ring. "We'll need to get your mother on a conference call so we can start planning this wedding."

"I already have an officiant."

Bella had looked at Seth with raised brows.

"Carlos Rebollar said he'd be happy to do the honors."

Bella's smile told him he'd made the right move by asking the judge. "There's more, Mom."

Her brows lowered. Margaret had been vocally displeased her eldest son had been shot, especially after Linc had been shot the previous year. "Tell me."

He'd glanced at Bella and, at her nod, shared the rest of their news. "We're pregnant. Only a few weeks along, and we're pretty damned pleased about it. You and Arch are going to be grandparents."

Margaret's hands went to her mouth and tears trailed down her cheeks. There were more hugs and kisses, then she put her hands on either side of her son's face and looked into his eyes. "You're going to be such a good daddy."

Her reassurance and confidence settled something in him that he hadn't realized needed settling. He glanced from her to Arch. "Thanks, Mom. I had a good example."

Word spread, and there were more congratulations. Now with the long twilight fading in the west, everyone had found a spot to watch the fireworks.

Linc and Mikayla were on another loveseat, while Ellie and Sam lay on a blanket spread on the grass. Some of the younger crowd were floating on inflatable loungers and inner tubes in the pool.

The first stars were showing themselves when across the valley the sky exploded with sprays of red, white, and blue light.

Bella nestled closer.

"You doing okay?" he asked in a quiet voice.

"Better than okay."

"How's the nausea?"

"Not so bad today." She rubbed her thumb over the back of his hand. "Don't worry so much."

"Not going to happen. You're the center of my world, and I intend to worry accordingly."

Volley after volley of mortars echoed off the hills and exploded into wild plumes of light.

"Independence Day is my favorite holiday," Bella murmured.

He pressed a kiss to the top of her head. "Why is it your favorite?"

She gave a slight shrug. "Even with its problems, America stands for something good. I will always be grateful to my American parents and to this country for taking a chance on a couple of orphans from Russia. I would never have met you in Russia."

He tightened his grip on her hand, and for the first time in his life, he believed some things were fated to be.

# ABOUT THE AUTHOR

USA TODAY Bestselling Author, Diane Benefiel has been an avid reader all her life. She enjoys a wide range of genres, from westerns to fantasy to mysteries, but romance is her favorite. She writes what she loves best to read—emotional, heart-gripping romantic suspense novels. In her stories, she puts the heroes and heroines in all sorts of predicaments that they have to work together to overcome. Her novel, *Solitary Man* was a National Readers' Choice Award winner.

A native Southern Californian, Diane enjoys nothing better than summer. For a high school history teacher, summer means a break from students, and time immersed in her current writing project. With both kids grown and gone, she enjoys her leisure time camping, especially in the Sierras, and gardening, both with her husband.

**Diane loves hearing from her readers**.
Website: dianebenefiel.com
Twitter: twitter.com/dianebenefiel
Instagram: @diane_benefiel
TikTok: @diane_benefiel_romance
Pinterest: diane_benefiel
Facebook: /DianeBenefielRomance
BookBub: /authors/diane-benefiel
Goodreads: /author/show/8075321.Diane_Benefiel
Newsletter: https://landing.mailerlite.com/webforms/landing/n1i2u8

Sign up for Diane's newsletter for sneak peeks and inside info on her new series.

www.BOROUGHSPUBLISHINGGROUP.com

If you enjoyed this book, please write a review. Our authors appreciate the feedback, and it helps future readers find books they love. We welcome your comments and invite you to send them to info@boroughspublishinggroup.com.

Follow us on TicTok and Instagram, and be sure to sign up for our newsletter for surprises and new releases from your favorite authors.

Are you an aspiring writer? Check out www.boroughspublishinggroup.com/submit and see if we can help you make your dreams come true.

Love podcasts? Enjoy ours at www.boroughspublishinggroup.com/podcast